DESPARDS—
WHERE WINNER TAKES ALL!

London, New York, Paris, Hong Kong. Wherever priceless art is at auction, even a father's legacy of love goes to the highest bidder.

This is the world of art, where flawless works—paintings, jewels, antiques—fetch staggering prices in an ambience of grandeur and greed. It is a world that sees fortunes made at the flick of the wrist, and passion disarmed at the crack of the gavel. This is Despards, a great auction empire, where two rival sisters, Kate and Dominique, are battling for control . . . and where treachery and revenge has been raised to the finest art of all. . . .

FORTUNES

"Lust, power, amorous intrigue . . . glitzy . . . opulent."

—*Publishers Weekly*

FORTUNES

Vera Cowie

AN ONYX BOOK

NEW AMERICAN LIBRARY

NAL BOOKS ARE AVAILABLE AT QUANTITY DISCOUNTS WHEN USED TO PROMOTE PRODUCTS OR SERVICES. FOR INFORMATION PLEASE WRITE TO PREMIUM MARKETING DIVISION, NEW AMERICAN LIBRARY, 1633 BROADWAY, NEW YORK, NEW YORK 10019.

Published by arrangement with E.P. Dutton. A hardcover edition was simultaneously published in Canada by Fitzhenry & Whiteside, Limited, Toronto.

Originally published in Great Britain in somewhat different form under the same title.

 Onyx is a trademark of New American Library.

SIGNET, SIGNET CLASSIC, MENTOR, ONYX, PLUME, MERIDIAN and NAL BOOKS are published by NAL PENGUIN INC., 1633 Broadway, New York, New York 10019

First Onyx Printing, September, 1988

1 2 3 4 5 6 7 8 9

PRINTED IN THE UNITED STATES OF AMERICA

PLUS ONE

September

1

The opening was on the late side; dusk was deepening to night as the last limousine turned off the park to join the line stretching down East 76th Street, ending at the red-and-white striped awning that hung above the red carpet dignifying the pavement in front of the newly restored town house.

A small crowd had collected, drawn by the mounted policemen, the photographers, the Famous Faces emerging from their glossy limos. It oohed and aahed like waves on a shore as each arrival was recognized. It was the opening of Despard's in New York. An auction house like Sotheby's and Christie's, Despard's was number three and bucking to be number one.

The auction was of Oriental porcelain, the collection left by Willard Dexter, who had died the previous year, and was expected to bring a minimum of five million dollars.

Once across the red carpet, up the shallow entrance steps, and inside the white and gold magnificence of the rejuvenated hall—one of Stanford White's most resplendent—the Famous Face handed over its engraved and numbered invitation to a uniformed flunkey, who grandly passed it on to an armed guard who checked it against a list. At the same time, a closed circuit television camera homed in on the Face to check that it matched its mug shot. Once confirmed as *bona fide,* it was then allowed to proceed in the direction of the superb staircase and join the line ascending it to where a pair of cathedral-sized double doors, ornately carved and gilded, had been thrown back to reveal a vast, mirrored, glittering room beyond. Receiving the throng was a tiny, exquisitely beautiful woman in a starkly plain black satin gown, her smile and her handshake commensurate with the amount of money each guest could be expected to spend.

The auction—New York had been talking about it for weeks now—was being held in what formerly had been the ballroom. Its specially sprung floor had been retained, along with the raised orchestra dais. One wall was lined with floor-to-ceiling windows overlooking the street and opened slightly to the mellow fall night; the other was mirrored and reflected and multiplied an already massed throng, all lit by two enormous wedding-cake chandeliers of Waterford crystal, multi-points of dazzling, splintering, glittering light.

The women, in Norell, Halston, Oscar de la Renta, Dior, Yves Saint Laurent, and Karl Lagerfeld, had all been to Kenneth for their hair and the bank for their jewels. The men patted inside pockets to make sure of checkbooks at the ready, and the air was redolent with the heady fragrance of five-hundred-dollar-an-ounce perfume and expensive cigars.

People circulated, eddied, swirled into groups, then split to drift for a while before forming yet another one. The women eyed the competition and those who had Old Money wrinkled noses at those whose money was very new. Others, whose thing was Famous Names, played at connecting them to Famous Faces. There was a large collection present. Blasé women squealed at the sight of the latest TV sex symbol on the arm of his current leading lady, and goggled at the Living Legend who had been at the top of the Hollywood ladder since—my God, would you believe it—1940! There were politicians, financiers, Wall Street tycoons, an Indian maharajah and two Hong Kong millionaires, as well as Prince Dimitri Poliakov and Count Alexei Onedin, once White Russian emigrés but now American billionaires and deadly rivals in the field of Oriental porcelain. There was big money here tonight: every dealer of note on the Eastern seaboard, not a few from the Western, and a goodly sprinkling of Europeans, all come to see how Despard's, that most conservative of auction houses, would fare in the glitzy, publicity-crazy madhouse of New York.

Two men stood on the sidelines watching the woman in the black dress; men always watched Dominique du Vivier.

"Did you get a load of what's not under that black dress?"

"Did I! That's one *entente cordiale* I'd love to establish."

"Too late. Blaise Chandler beat you to it—and you know why. He may be one-eighth Shoshone, but his Indian blood pales beside the fact that he will one day inherit one quarter of the national income."

"I don't see him here."

"He will be. This is his wife's opening New York auction, after all."

"Is it true what they are saying—that she was the one who persuaded old man Despard to open up here?"

"Absolutely. She wants to rule a big roost and London was his. Paris is small fry—you know how it is at the Galeries Drouot—and while Hong Kong and Monte Carlo are prestigious, they are small. This"—a nod to the magnificence around them—"is the big time. And to have gotten the Willard Dexter collection for openers is a real smack in the eye for the big boys."

"How did she manage that?"

The other man chuckled. "You've got eyes. You've seen what she's got and what she does with it. What Dominique du Vivier wants she gets, and what she'll do to get it is what most of us dream about nights."

His companion looked across to where a very tall, very dark man was bending from his great height to brush the magnolia cheek his wife was proffering.

"Yes, that's him. That's Blaise Chandler."

Dominique accepted her husband's greeting complacently, aware of the looks she was getting: lust from the men, envy from the women.

"So?" Blaise said, slanting a smile down at her. "Tonight's the night. The culmination of two long hard years' work. The top of the mountain." He turned to survey the throng. "What do you think of the view?"

His wife widened her extraordinary eyes at him. "But, I am the view," she murmured in her native French, and as she knew he would, he laughed, white teeth flashing in his Indian-dark face. Her *sauvage indien*. Undoubtedly her greatest *coup* so far—until tonight.

Tonight would see her crowned. The King was dead. Long Live the Queen. And it was not the culmination of two years' work, but twelve: since the day Charles Despard had married her mother. Then, she had been an eighteen-year-old daughter of the Faubourg with nothing but her looks and brains—and of course her name. Now, she was not only the art world's shining light, a respected expert in her own right and her stepfather's field—Oriental porcelain—but she was also a shrewd businesswoman bent and determined to change

Despard's image—the one created by her stepfather—into one more in keeping with the new world. She had sniffed the wind of change. London was losing its grip on the center of the art world and New York was increasing its domination. Why else were Sotheby's and Christie's here in strength? They knew it, too. That was why, tonight, she had instituted the black-tie, vintage champagne auction, provided an orchestra, a catalogue that was as much a work of art as the porcelain to be auctioned, and food that was ambrosial. She had also culled a representative dream of an invited audience, and made of those invitations a matter of life and death. She had planted stories in the press, whispered in certain ears, hinted in other quarters, and generally created a fever of speculative curiosity that had gathered momentum like a cyclone. But the final—unplanned—event that had made it even more of an Occasion had been, two days before, the sudden death from a massive heart attack of her stepfather, Charles Despard. She had striven for what she thought the art world needed now—glamour; she had not sought sensationalism, but once it came her way she used it ruthlessly.

"You're holding the auction as planned!" Blaise had frowned, not approving.

"Of course I will."

"How? You have no auctioneer."

"I shall take Papa's place."

"You don't have the experience. This is not Hong Kong or Monte Carlo. This is New York. This is my town. They expect nothing but the best here, and show no mercy to those who fail to provide it."

"Who was it who agitated for almost five years to get Despard's established here? I was the one who cajoled and persuaded, drew up plans, made detailed budgets, canvassed prospective sellers. I know what it takes and I would not be here if I did not also know that I have it in large measure. I was the one who drew up the invitation list; I know all the people who are likely to bid—I mean really bid; I have invited Poliakov *and* Onedin and I can handle them both. They are men, after all . . ."

Blaise had gazed at his wife's exquisite face, his own closed and impassive, as it always was when he was angry. Damn! he thought. Now that Charles had died—so suddenly and inconveniently—there would be no holding Dominique.

She would gallop headlong to where she had always believed she belonged. In the winner's circle. She had—for the most part anyway—been able to wind her stepfather several times around her finger, and Blaise had no doubt that he would confirm this by leaving her what had been the most important thing in his life—his auction house.

Now, with her own biggest auction only five minutes away, he expected to be able to confirm within twenty-four hours that Despard et Cie now belonged to Dominique du Vivier. Despite being Charles Despard's stepdaughter and Blaise Chandler's wife, she had never been known by any other name but the one she had been born to. The name under which she had become notorious. And a law unto herself. Only she would have the nerve to attend the opening auction of Despard's New York, held two days after her stepfather's death, wearing a dress that, although it was black, was no more than a slip of satin held up by two very thin rouleau straps and worn over nothing but her naked body, clinging to every curve and crevice, outlining the thrust of her pert, uptilting breasts and the cleft of her high, rounded buttocks, knowing it was obvious she was all but naked, but sublimely above and beyond it. Dominique made no bones about her attitude: it was part of her legend, like her beauty.

She was tiny, exactly sixty inches tall: an exquisite, hand-made doll of a woman. Her hair was glossy, blue-black, cut in the manner of a Japanese child, with fringe and slanting curve from eye to jaw, framing an oval face that took away the breath. Small, perfect features carved from a skin as fine and translucent as the porcelain she sold, eyes as large and vividly blue as the sapphires in her ears, and fringed with lashes as a lagoon is fringed with palm trees. Her body was small but flawless, and her pervasive sexuality hit men like a slow burn. Once seen, the mind henceforth writhed with erotic images. She could smile at you over her shoulder and steam fogged the eyes; or she could look at you from under the silken fringe of her lashes and your tongue all of a sudden filled your mouth. Her nickname was the Venus Flytrap, because the only way a man escaped from her honeyed, fatally sticky clutches, was when he had been sucked dry.

She had been married to Blaise Chandler for two years. They had met at a cocktail party at which she had been bored; he had been instantly aroused. Their eyes had met across the proverbially crowded room, held for a slow-burning twenty seconds, and then Dominique had gone to bid her hostess goodnight. When Blaise followed, two minutes later, she was already in the back of his car, waiting.

He felt he had been taken over: sexually skewered, hoisted, left dangling. Like Cleopatra, the more he had the more he wanted. But there were times when he knew, quite dispassionately, that he did not *like* his wife.

Now, she smiled up into his copper-skinned face, wrinkled her nose at him, and laughed in her gurgling way. "You will never understand, will you? The obsessiveness of the art world is quite lost on you."

"I don't covet things—except you, of course," he added gallantly.

"You pay great sums of money for horses."

"That's different. A horse has its uses. What can you do with a piece of porcelain except look at it?"

He reached out a long arm to lift a glass of champagne from the tray of a passing waiter, whose own uplifted arm cut through the throng like the dorsal fin of a cruising shark. One glass only; Dominique never drank when she was working.

She watched him sip the champagne and nod approvingly, then she shrugged, dismissing him as a lost cause.

She nodded to the flunkeys on either side of the door. "You may close up now."

"You are sure there is nobody else to come?" Blaise asked.

"If they do, they will not be admitted. The auction begins precisely at eight-thirty and I have to get to my rostrum." Her eyes laughed at him.

As she turned to go, Blaise called after her, "What *is* the lesson for today?"

She stopped, turned, looked at him under her lashes for a moment, a smile flickering across her luscious mouth, one he recognized at once.

"To him that hath, shall be given," she said finally, before turning on her heel. The crowd gave way before her. Like Queen Victoria, Dominique always moved with supreme confidence, knowing she would meet no opposition.

Behind her, the great doors slowly and ceremoniously closed.

Dominique made unhesitatingly for her rostrum, set on its

raised platform, a lovingly tended piece of burr walnut brought from London for the occasion; Charles Despard's own rostrum, made for his great-grandfather in 1835, the name *Despard et Fils* written in elegant copperplate across its front. Even as she reached it, a bell rang. There was an instant, undignified rush for the twenty rows of spindly gilt chairs, thirty in each, separated by a single aisle. Glasses were hastily replaced on trays, and the waiters silently and swiftly gathered up those left elsewhere before leaving the room. Dominique waited until every seat had been taken, and then the chandeliers dimmed and the room was left in semidarkness; only Dominique was brilliantly bathed in a single spotlight falling directly on her, highlighting the white shoulders, the black hair, the sapphires in her ears. She stood silently, and the room ceased its rustle once programs were opened, bottoms made comfortable, trousers hitched, throats cleared. Standing at the back—he was not staying long because he was leaving for London at midnight—Blaise had to admire the way she had set it up. Talk about the dramatic! Dominique was tiny, yet she dominated the room. Behind her, black velvet curtains parted silently, revealing a circular table, also draped in black velvet, lit as Dominique was by a single, powerful spot. Below her, and to the side, were two banks of telephones where transatlantic bids would be received and relayed to her; on her left was her clerk, John Deakin, who had been Charles Despard's clerk for thirty years. Invisible behind the scenes were the porters who would place the exhibits on the stands.

Still Dominique waited, letting the tension gather, feeling it as a spider feels the vibrations on the strands of its web, allowing the victim to blunder ever nearer to its doom. Only when she was sure she had hers beyond rescue did she say, in her enchantingly accented but idiomatically flawless English, "My lords, ladies and gentlemen, good evening and welcome to Despard's New York."

There were two lords in the audience; one was an English earl, long on lineage but short of money. Married to a rich American wife, he scouted for Despard's, reporting who had what to sell, and when. His counterpart was an Italian prince who did the same thing in Europe. Both were here tonight as come-ons. Dominique knew how Americans loved a title, and both these two were genuine.

"Tonight," Dominique continued, sounding calmly confident, "we reach the culmination of two years of preparation and planning. The establishment of Despard et Cie alongside its peers in New York. From now on there are no longer only two great auction houses in America. There are three. Despard's is finally where it has always belonged."

Somebody—as previously arranged with Dominique—began to applaud, and soon the entire audience had responded. Dominique inclined her head in gracious response and waited until the applause died down before continuing.

"It is therefore only right and proper that before we proceed to the auction, we remember the man who brought it to New York; that same man who, only two days ago, was taken from us in sudden and tragic circumstances. I refer to the late, great Charles Despard."

Once again, as arranged, the applause broke like a wave.

"Not only was he my stepfather," Dominique went on, "he was my mentor, my teacher, my best friend. I shall miss him sorely. We shall all miss him. I dedicate this, the opening auction of his newest, and what will undoubtedly become his greatest branch, to his memory."

Without warning, every light was extinguished, and remained so for fifteen seconds. When they came on again there was a concerted gasp of awe and appreciation. Occupying the center of the black velvet table was a thing of such transcendent beauty that even Blaise had to shake his head in admiration.

"Lot one, ladies and gentlemen." Dominique's voice had changed; it came out as a breath of barely controlled yet reverential excitement, pricking skin and raising neck hairs. This, she was saying, is something very, very special that even I, an acknowledged expert, find nothing less than amazing. There was an almost collective lean forward. Even Blaise found himself taking a step nearer.

"A superb and extremely rare dish in underglaze copper, red and white, the copper being rich and dark at the border and less strong at the center, with a translucent milky-white overglaze which has formed irregular pools and left small areas of unglazed biscuit, especially on the upper rim. Such perfection of glazing is unique, as you know, since early examples rarely fired the correct color. This one did. It is in flawless condition, not a chip, a scratch, or even a mark. It comes with its own fitted box, in which it has long been treasured. It is mid-late fourteenth century. I myself would date it as Yuan, around 1350. I know of only one other such dish and it is in the Hermitage at Leningrad. I will open the bidding at one hundred thousand dollars . . ."

From where he stood Blaise could not see the bidding, but he could hear Dominique conducting it. Her voice did not betray any excitement as the bidding rose in leaps and bounds. People began to murmur, to exclaim, even to applaud as the price mounted toward half a million dollars. Dominique's voice was calm, controlled, as she moved only her eyes from one bidder to another, right at the front and on either side of the central aisle. Where the really big gamblers had been seated. Probably, Blaise remembered now what Dominique had told him earlier with confident certainty, Prince Dimitri Poliakov and Count Alexei Onedin, deadly rivals in their pursuit for the title of "The World's Finest Collection."

". . . five hundred thousand dollars . . . five hundred and fifty . . . at five hundred and fifty thousand dollars, the bid is at the front—six hundred thousand—six hundred thousand dollars is now bid . . . against you, Prince Poliakov . . . six hundred and fifty thousand dollars. Six hundred and fifty thousand dollars at the front . . . six hundred and fifty thousand dollars . . ." Dominique paused fractionally and then, as if she knew the Prince would go no further, her gavel cracked down with the finality of doom. "At six hundred and fifty thousand dollars, then, to Count Onedin."

The room broke into a storm of applause.

Blaise found himself letting out a shaky breath. His heart was pounding. Jesus! he thought. Almost three quarters of a million dollars for a piece of china!

Dominique waited until the buzz had died, and then the lights lowered again. This time when they went up, they revealed six blue and white stem cups, each one perfectly balanced and of a singing shape which had the fingers longing to touch and trace it.

"Six Ming blue and white stem cups," Dominique announced, "each bearing the four-character mark of Hsuan Te and of the period, each four and three-eighths of an inch high, and with their own individual box. They are in perfect condition and quite unmarked in any way. As you all know, the late Willard Dexter was obsessive about the quality of his pieces; there is not one that is not quite perfect. I will begin the bidding at six hundred thousand dollars . . . seven hundred thousand, thank you, Count Onedin . . ."

By God, she was right—as usual!—Blaise thought, as excitement rippled through the room like adrenaline. They are going to cut each other's throats and bleed millions . . .

". . . one million dollars I am bid . . . the bid is at the front . . . one million and a quarter. A million and a quarter is bid from an overseas buyer . . ." One of the girls on a telephone had handed a slip to a youth who instantly handed it to Dominique. "One million and a half dollars is bid, then . . . and three-quarters . . . one million seven hundred and fifty thousand dollars . . . two million dollars . . ."

A further, almost sick ripple of excitement. Two million dollars! Jesus! Blaise thought again. This is incredible.

". . . two million five hundred thousand dollars, then . . . at two million five hundred thousand dollars . . ." The gavel cracked again. "To Prince Poliakov . . ."

As if Dominique knew that the excitement had to be cooled, the lights rose a little and the waiters reappeared with freshly loaded trays of champagne.

Blaise fixed his eyes on his wife. As he knew she would, she felt their weight, and lifted her head to look at him. He raised his clasped hands in a boxer's victory salute. She smiled slightly.

He ought to have known, he mused. When Dominique said she would do a thing she inevitably did it. And she had worked long and hard for this; pushed, heaved, and shoved Charles Despard toward New York and the opening of this horrendously expensive branch; taking a gamble because there were already two world-class auction houses firmly established here. Charles liked London. Despard's had been there for centuries, possessed of clients for whom they had acted as auctioneers as other men acted as family solicitors. He had distrusted the glamorous, Hollywood-gloss type of auction house that Dominique wanted. He was not an auctioneer trying to be a gentleman; he was a gentleman who happened to be an auctioneer, and a damned good one at that. When it came to Oriental porcelain his was the name that automatically came to mind; he had long ago cornered the field and invariably obtained the highest prices. His eye was infallible, his knowledge vast, his taste impeccable, his love for his craft bottomless. And that, Blaise reflected, was where he and his stepdaughter parted company. Charles had been in it because he loved auctioneering. Dominique was in it because she loved money.

It was Dominique who had brought in titled scouts. Charles had always preferred academic expertise to the Almanach de Gotha. Dominique had brought in the use of the numbered paddle for bidding against Charles' better judgment and the disapproval of the snootier dealers; she had insisted on opening on weekends, had established a subscriptions department, and had instituted a dozen new ways to make greater profits. She had even suggested employing an upmarket advertising agency, but here Charles had dug in his heels and absolutely refused to countenance such a thing. "Despard's is its own advertising" was his unshakable conviction. Nor would he do away with Despard's Downtown, tucked away in a Kensington side street, where low-priced objects only were sold, much to Dominique's distaste.

It had been Dominique who had made the regular appearances on television—Charles hating even the thought— because she had one idea: to increase Despard's share of the market, at present running some four percent behind Christie's, but still a long way behind Sotheby's. Last year's turnover had been three hundred million, twenty-five million up on the previous year. Dominique anticipated a seventeen percent increase this year, and if this auction was anything to go by, she would get it. Then, if and when she decided to go public—and as yet she had no more than voiced the thought, which still meant that she was considering it carefully—she would have a very juicy sprat to offer to the mackerel.

Yes, Blaise thought, as the lights dimmed once more, Dominique had prepared for this moment for years. She had the flair, the instinct, the ambition. And she had learned well. But then, in Charles Despard she had had the perfect teacher.

Look at the way she was conducting this, her most crucial auction yet, and at such short notice. Blaise recognized many faces he knew, either personally or through his grandmother, who knew them all. That so many had come in person, instead of instructing their dealer, was proof of the power Dominique held. The catalogue—for which she had, some people thought, the bare-faced gall to charge—had sold out long ago, further proof that this was the Auction of the Year. When the Super Rich gathered to put a price tag on the priceless, it was a matter of avid curiosity to those who could afford to do no more than look. No wonder they had oohed and aahed. There was more money and celebrity here tonight than at any Inaugural Ball; rumor had it that one famous courtesan had actually hocked a necklace or two so as to be able to boast, later, that she had bought a piece of the Willard Dexter collection at Despard's opening auction.

Like the one coming up now . . . This time, as the lights lifted slowly and dramatically, drawing the maximum amount of suspense from the presentation, there was a collective sigh that verged on a moan, as a bowl of exotic shape and beauty emerged from the darkness.

She had them right in the palm of her hand, Blaise thought. That she had managed it after just two lots was incredible enough; that she could reduce a sophisticated, worldly-wise, contemptuously secure-in-their-money audience to abject worshippers at her particular altar was proof that she belonged where she had always intended to be. At the top of the heap.

"Lot three, ladies and gentlemen, this superb early Ming wine jar, decorated with flying dragons and figures of the Immortals. Note that the cobalt exhibits the distinctive heaping and piling. It bears the reign mark of the Emperor Ch'eng Hua." Here two attendant porters reverently uptilted the vase to reveal its base and the Chinese characters incised there. "It also bears his personal cipher. Its perfection is unblemished by so much as a scratch."

She allowed them a moment to gaze and gloat before bringing them back to reality with a confident "I will open the bidding at two hundred and fifty thousand dollars . . ." Dominique was cool, the bidding fevered.

A few minutes later, "one million and a quarter dollars against you, Mr. Alexander—and a half, one million and a half dollars—thank you, Mr. Alexander—and three quarters—two million; two million dollars is now bid . . ."

Never had more than one million dollars been paid at auction for any single piece of Chinese porcelain. Despard's was not only breaking new ground; it was breaking records. Charles would have been proud, Blaise thought with regret. Dominique had learned from him the art of auctioneering, a delicate and precise one. She was leading—to the slaughter—but leading nevertheless, and, like the sheep they were, they followed blindly. But then, he thought, what man didn't, where Dominique du Vivier was concerned?

Blaise checked his watch. He really ought to be going. He had promised to collect his mother-in-law from Frank E.

Campbell's, where she had been all day receiving condolence visits. He would then fly to London for his appointment with Messrs. Finch, Frencham, and Finch on the subject of Charles Despard's will. But he found it hard to tear himself away. Normally auctions left him cold. He had no acquisitive streak; the only time he had wanted something to a degree that hurt was when he had first set eyes on his wife. He was an outdoors man; he rode, hunted, fished, skied, and flew his own plane. Dominique loathed all forms of sport, viewed the great outdoors with a shudder. She had never once visited the ranch, where his grandmother now spent most of her time. The very thought of Colorado and the Rocky Mountains made her recoil. He decided he would stay for one more lot. He could still make it to Campbell's, take Catherine back to the house, see her settled comfortably, and then make it to the Chandler building and the helicopter that would fly him to Kennedy. He settled back to watch.

"Lot four, ladies and gentlemen, a very fine late Ming figure of Shou Lao, the God of Longevity. Chinese legend has it that whoever owns such a statue will live to a very old age. Mr. Willard Dexter, as you know, was eighty-seven when he died." There was a ripple of amusement. "The figure is in porcelain rather than the usual pottery, probably executed for some dignitary or priest. Note the richness of the deep blue glazing and the warm color of the deer—another symbol of longevity—on which the god sits. I will open the bidding at fifty thousand dollars . . . sixty—seventy . . . and eighty . . . ninety—one hundred thousand dollars is now bid . . . two hundred thousand . . . three hundred thousand . . . at three hundred thousand dollars, then . . ." Dominique waited, gavel poised, eyebrows raised. She had brought them along gently, a smile at one opponent, a lift of an eyebrow at another, a calm, soothing voice for them both. Now, she knew they were reluctant, that she could prod them no more. Quickly and efficiently, she finished them off. The crack of the gavel made some women gasp, so caught up were they in the drama. "Three hundred thousand dollars. Count Onedin."

She would make her ten million all right, Blaise thought, torn between admiration and anger. He had—what, hoped?— that this time Dominique had overreached herself, been overconfident. He should have known better. Dominique did not make mistakes. She took too much time preparing her case. He helped himself to the fresh champagne that came around once again. He had winced when she showed him the cost of this night's opening. Now he knew she would recoup it ten times over and more. Despard's New York would also reap a fortune in publicity. This opening would be the talk of the town tomorrow.

Lots five, six, and seven were a collection of porcelain animals from the K'ang Hsi period; a "peach-bloom" circular cosmetic box; and a Ming blue and white fishbowl. All three were bitterly contested by the two growling Russian bears and a visiting South American millionaire with a Nazi past.

Blaise consulted his watch. He should really leave . . . but there was a sudden increase in the excitement. He had no catalogue and for once regretted it, but as the lights came up and he saw what was on the stand he knew he had to stay for this. It was what Dominique had described as the heart of the collection. A superb, early Ming blue and white ewer *(zhi hu)* painted with the traditional flowers: peony, camellia, gardenia, lotus, chrysanthemum, hibiscus, and other flowers and buds. It stood thirty-three centimeters high and was prized because of the extensive "heaping and piling" of the glaze, so typical of Hsuan Te wares; the cobalt had oxidized through the glaze where the pigment had been too heavily loaded onto the brushes. Dominique started the bidding at a quarter of a million dollars. At once, the two Russians began rapid fire. Both were known to prize early Ming above all other Chinese porcelain. And there were known to be only four other such ewers in existence.

Within a minute the bid was over a million dollars; another thirty seconds it was over two, the bidding now in quarters of a million. The room was vibrant with tension as the two men, by a flicker of an eye, the quality of a stare, indicated their bids. Both men sat, ostensibly impassively, heads crossed on top of their catalogues. Only the way they were clasped, too tightly, betrayed their inner perturbation.

". . . three million dollars, then, at three million dollars, Prince Poliakov . . ."

The room waited to see if the Prince's rival would do the unprecedented thing—bid *more than three million dollars* for a piece of Chinese porcelain. Dominique's hand, clasped around the gavel, lifted. She was warning that time was slipping away.

"At three million dollars, then," she repeated, in a way that made it clear it was for the last time unless . . .

The Count's face was impassive, but he was glazed with sweat and his knuckles were white, his breathing deep and uneven. The Prince stared straight in front, but he was aware with every pore what his rival was doing. The room waited, hardly daring to breathe. The seconds seemed to creep forward on hands and knees.

Crack! The gavel made the audience start convulsively, women put their hands to their throats. It was like seeing an execution—which, in a way, it had been.

"Three million dollars, then, to Prince Poliakov . . ."

People rose to their feet to applaud, to cheer, to slap the Prince on the back. The Count, hardly able to see for the sweat pouring from his brow into his eyes, waited until he could still the trembling of his hands before taking out a snowy white handkerchief and mopping his brow.

"Jesus Christ! Three million dollars! Did you ever in your life ever hear of *anybody* paying three million dollars for some itty bitty vase?"

No, thought Blaise, feeling his own tension snap, as if a big marlin had just dived deep and broken line, I never did, but there is a first time for everything, and as usual, it is because of Dominique . . .

And to think, he thought, as he went slowly down the magnificent staircase, that he had wanted Dominique to delay the opening. And *I'm* supposed to be the business-man, he reflected wryly. But his reaction had been instinctive, out of respect and affection for Charles. Dominique, ruthlessly and practically French as always, had put business first, sentiment second. They were the times when she made Blaise feel very parochial, very American.

Charles, equally French, never had. He had been ruthless in business, but he had been that rare thing in a Frenchman, sentimental. He had also been an emotional man. Dominique was passionate, but not emotional. She was cool, even calculating, never putting her head at the mercy of her heart. Charles, when he loved, did so without reservation, as he did everything else. He had been a man of enthusiasms, of passions and strong feelings. Whatever Dominique felt— and sometimes Blaise wondered if she ever felt at all—she never wholly revealed those feelings to anyone. Not like Charles. Nor her mother, come to that. Blaise had come to the conclusion that Dominique must take after her long-dead father, whom he had never known. Not as he had known Charles.

Blaise would miss him, still could not quite take in his death. He had been in Chicago when the call came from New York. Charles Despard had been felled by a massive coronary and all efforts at resuscitation had failed. Madame Despard was hysterical. Her daughter could not be reached anywhere. The only other name they could get from her was his, and would he come at once.

On the flight to New York he had had the airplane radio the places where he thought his wife might be. They finally ran her to earth in Hong Kong, where she spent a lot of time, since she had sole charge of the Despard's branch there. By the time she finally arrived in New York, Charles' postmortem had revealed the extent of his fatal heart attack, but what had been preoccupying Dominique, even then, was the auction.

"The finest mark of respect I can pay Papa is to hold the opening as planned," she had insisted. "He planned it for so long; he was planning it when he died; it was the most important thing in his life. I intend to see his dream become a reality."

"*His* dream?"

"All right, so I persuaded him, but once committed he was every bit as keen as I was."

"So you say."

"Allow me to tell you that I knew Papa a great deal better than you."

"Sometimes I think you didn't know him at all."

"I know he would want me to go ahead. Whatever else he was, Papa was a Frenchman. He faced reality. And reality is holding the auction as planned."

What else? Blaise thought now, as he waited for his car. Always that ruthless practicality. Very French. It made his own American pragmatism look like a feeble attempt at equality. The only other person who had it was his grandmother.

She had been silent for a long time after he had told her the news. "I shall miss him," she had said finally, in her Feodor Chaliapin bass. "He was an old and a good friend."

Then the sadness gave way to plain, old-fashioned loathing."
"And that bitch, your wife. How is she taking it? With both hands, I presume. I never thought to see the day, Boy, when I'd see you lying down under a woman's feet, her heel marks all over you."

"Stow it, Duchess. You know we will never agree on that."

"Just so long as you realize that she'll be all to hell and gone once she gets her hands on Despard's."

"Since, according to you, that's where she comes from, what else is new?"

His grandmother's laugh had bellowed across the long distance line. She loved their verbal standoffs. "You know my opinion of your so-called marriage," she countered enjoyably. "I told you that the day you said you were marrying her and I haven't seen any reason to change my mind since. She'll ruin you, Boy. Around that kind of woman men always carry their brains between their legs."

"Are you trying to tell me, in your own tactful way, that you don't like her?"

His grandmother's laugh bellowed again, astonishingly strong and vital for a woman who was coming up to her eighty-fifth birthday. "I'm just telling you that when she finally does, I'll still be here."

"Such confidence is on a par with the arrogance you always complain of in Dominique."

"My doctors tell me I'm good for another five years if I take care of myself, and that's a sight longer than I expect your marriage to last. It's only lasted this long because in two years you haven't spent above three months together." He heard her familiar snort. "What the hell sort of marriage is that? And why did you have to marry her in the first place? Don't tell me you couldn't go on getting what you had already without going that far."

"No, I won't," Blaise said, and that was when Agatha knew, by the sound of his voice, that she had gone far enough. Blaise allowed her, and only her, a great deal of license because he loved her, but even she knew when to stop.

'I worry for you, Boy. She's not what I want for you and that's a fact. However, it's another that she's got you so I must make the best of it. But I warn you—once she gets her hands on Despard's you'll find things changed. Don't be fooled."

"Hornswoggled or not, I am not entirely under the influence," Blaise pointed out gently.

There was another silence. "Well, keep in touch," his grandmother commanded gruffly. "I won't go over to the funeral. My five years are conditional on good behavior and right now, my doctors tell me, France is too far to go. You can tell me all about it." Then, casually, but not enough to fool her grandson who knew her insatiable curiosity only too well, she added, "I suppose he left a will?"

She's fishing, he thought. But for what? "I suppose," he answered, just as casually.

"You don't know?" Sharpness cut deep.

"No. Catherine may, except she's not with it—or anything—right now. She's taken it hard."

"What else? He was her life. As big a mistake as the one you made. Leaves too big a hole when you lose it. You bleed to death."

Blaise ignored the dig. "I have no doubt that Maître Flambard, Charles' lawyer, will be in touch."

But the old lady persisted. "Charles never gave you any hint as to how he intended to dispose of Despard's?"

"To Dominique, of course. Who else is there?"

There was a silence that had Blaise frowning. "Do you know something I don't?" he demanded.

"I should damned well hope so!" was the round answer and, as usual, she hung up on him.

Getting into his car Blaise took out the letter he had that morning received from Maître Flambard. He wrote that he had Charles' will disposing of his French property. That the disposing of his property domiciled in England would no doubt be in the capable hands of Messrs. Finch, Frencham, and Finch, Despard's—and Charles'—English lawyers. But the French will appointed his stepson-in-law, Blaise Chandler, as his executor.

It made sense, he thought now. Two wills. The laws of the two countries were different, and the English branch of Despard's had been financed, created, and incorporated according to English law. Every branch was a separate entity, registered in the country of domicile and according to its laws, but administered by a holding company set up in Geneva. As a corporation lawyer, Blaise approved of the way Charles had set up Despard et Cie (he had changed the name from Despard et Fils once it became apparent he would never have a son). New York had been set up as wholly independent in operation (but accountable financially to Despard's International), and Dominique had been designated its executive vice president, but now she would no doubt become president. Her mother, Charles' wife, would also have been very well provided for. Charles had adored *ma belle*, as he called her. It was for her sake he had taken her daughter to his heart also.

The car drew up outside the Madison Avenue entrance to Frank E. Campbell's. Crowded all day with people come to pay their respects, the funeral home was now deserted. Only the widow sat forlornly in a chair far too big for her, gazing desolately at the big French-type coffin. Catherine had been firm in her instructions and the lid was screwed down—even in death she was not prepared to share him. She had kissed him good-bye, placed between his clasped hands his first gift to her—a now faded and dried Malmaison rose—and then stood back to watch them hide him from her forever. Now, a tiny figure in unrelieved black, she sat and stared at the coffin and its attendant banks of flowers and candles. Her rosary was in her hands and her lips were moving, but Blaise knew she was not praying. She was talking to the dead man because, to Catherine Despard, her husband was not dead. She had nourished him as a dream during the nightmare of her first marriage; that she eventually did become his wife was, to her, all part of that same dream, and everyone knows that dreams never die.

As Blaise bent over her she trustingly raised her face to his. Like her daughter she was tiny, but as blonde as Dominique was dark. Catherine Despard had guinea-gold hair now carefully lightened and invariably exquisitely coiffed, cut short to flatteringly frame a face that had once been ravishingly pretty and was still worth a second glance. Her eyes were delphiniums, her skin the pink and white of a porcelain doll. She also had an air of vague helplessness that made men regard her with indulgence, and a trick of tilting her head to one side to eye them trustingly in a "you will take care of me, won't you?" attitude which either enslaved or enraged. Usually the former with men, the latter with women.

Now she smiled as Blaise kissed her tiny hand, bare of all jewelry but her plain gold wedding ring.

"I am sorry to be so late," he apologized. "The auction was an eye-opener."

Catherine's smile lost its spontaneity and became mechanical. Despard's, to her, was a rival; one that had tried to usurp her husband's affections all her married life. She had never once attended an auction and had played no part in the life of the business. Even Charles, when he came home at the end of the day, knew better than to bring Despard's with him.

"I am sure Dominique is handling everything . . ." Her breathy, little-girl voice trailed off in its usual vague, where-am-I manner, her French—she refused to speak English—pure but somehow erotic.

"You must be tired. You have been here so long."

"Tired . . ." Her voice drifted away again. She rarely completed a sentence.

"Let me take you home."

She was staying at his grandmother's town house on 84th Street. Agatha had little use for Catherine, who for her part was terrified of an old woman she regarded as an Indian squaw, but Agatha had ordered Blaise to do all that was necessary for Charles' widow.

Catherine murmured now. "So kind . . ."

And so comfortable. Catherine had an enormous, luxurious room and the attention of a houseful of servants with nothing to do except look after her. Dominique and Blaise had a penthouse in Chandler Towers, where there was plenty of room, but Dominique had been the one to suggest that her mother would be more comfortable in surroundings less . . .modern. What she meant was farther away. Dominique treated her mother, in the opinion of her husband, with a barely concealed tolerant contempt. He himself was fond of her in the way one is fond of a pretty child. He had often wondered what it was that Charles saw in his wife. She never seemed to have anything to say. Perhaps it was because she was restful. And she had featherbedded her husband to an extent that was ridiculous. His every raised eyebrow had been a command, and her pleasure—her happiness—had been in the fact of his own happiness. On the other hand, she had not hesitated to draw the boundaries of her own displeasure, and that he was willing to allow Despard's to remain beyond them was a measure of his husbandly devotion.

Looking down at her surprisingly tranquil face now, Blaise heard his grandmother's words echoing in his memory: "He was her life. Leaves too big a hole when you lose it. You bleed to death . . ." What *would* Catherine do now? What other interests had she ever had, apart from her husband? Only the embroidery she was never without. It was lying there now, half in, half out of the petit point bag in which she carried it wherever she went. He had never seen her read a book, though she devoured fashion and beauty magazines, and she had no interest in the theatre, though she did love watching the afternoon soaps on TV when she was in America. At dinner parties she was a gracious hostess, exquisitely dressed and jeweled, but with little to say, making her presence felt by her luminous smile. She was the kind of woman who sank her own life and personality into those of her husband, becoming the moon to his sun. What would she shine on now?

Catherine bent to pick up her embroidery bag. Seeing Blaise glance at it, she said with a moue that reminded him of Dominique, "Habit . . . and it is soothing. Always helped soothe me when things were bad, so that I kept it up when times, at last, were good . . ." She seemed to droop. "I was embroidering a new pair of slippers for Charles . . ." She stood with a funny, bereft look on her face. "He was gone from me so quickly. He sat up suddenly and with such a sound . . ." Her shudder made her body jerk. "He could not speak though he tried. I could see it in his eyes—such urgency—I saw his lips move but I had to put my ear to them to hear. Cat, he said, trying to say my name, my little Cat. And then he was gone . . ."

Blaise had heard it before, several times. It was the first thing she had told him when he arrived at the hospital, the last when he had gone to say good night, hours later. Twice since she had repeated the story, proud that even at the last, her husband's thoughts had been of her. Blaise nodded, smiled, made soothing noises, patted the hand tucked into the crook of his arm. There was that about Catherine that made you protective, if you were male. But he had seen Dominique looking at her mother with almost derisive contempt at times. Her own, all-pervasive attraction to men had nothing to do with helplessness. Rather the reverse . . .

He took his mother-in-law back to 84th Street and delivered her into the hands of her maid, an elderly, sour-faced Frenchwoman. Then, instead of ordering the car to take him downtown to the Chandler Building, on impulse he told it to take him back to Despard's. He would fly the Concorde to London instead of the 737, that way he would not have to leave until tomorrow morning. He had only intended to use the 737 so as to have talks on board with the group of company executives also making the trip. He could talk to them any time. Tonight was something else again.

They were at the tail end of the auction as he slipped back into the now euphoric gallery. Dominique was still at her rostrum, but the atmosphere had lost its tension—the last important lot had just been disposed of and, from what he heard as he made his way toward his wife, for another astronomical price to the Russian, Poliakov.

"What a night, Blaise!" a woman he knew exclaimed, seizing him by the arm. "Dominique was truly amazing! I had no idea she was so smart!"

As he pushed his way forward, Dominique saw him, flashing him a smile that burned like an Olympic flame. She had done it; she had shoved Despard's into the limelight and herself with it. The event would be on every newscast next day, and after that Dominique would be on every talk show. The audience was in a ferment; he was swept on the crest of its wave to the front, where Dominique was in danger of drowning in her success. He used his height and bulk to force his way to her side. She greeted him with glittering triumph. Well? her remarkable eyes blazed at him. Have I not proved how right I was? Am I not more than fit to be the new chairman of Despard's?

"Well done," he congratulated her. "Very well done."

As she took his arm, people formed an aisle down which he led her to where the two Russians awaited her. Both bent over her hand, while Dominique murmured something that had them both regarding her indulgently. Then the prince turned. As he made his way up the aisle—he never attended après-auction parties—he was followed by applause. As was his rival when he lumbered his way to the small table set up especially for him. On it were a dozen Chesapeake oysters, a whole, freshly roasted canvasback, and a bottle of Krug Blanc de Blancs, Clos du Mesnil. He always ate and drank the lot after a successful auction. Those who came up to congratulate him were never offered anything. He took the view that there was plenty of food and drink provided by the house. After porcelain, food was his passion.

For the audience, trolleys were now pushed in, laden with delicacies: small, piping hot vol-au-vents; stuffed mushrooms; tiny, bite-sized sandwiches of smoked salmon; heartier beef-stuffed ones; quail eggs, oysters, cold canvasback, and more champagne.

For a while, Dominique was kept busy dealing with congratulations, being interviewed for TV, even autographing programs. Finally, they wanted Blaise in on the pictures, and he got his own share of the questions.

"How do you feel about your wife's incredible success tonight, Mr. Chandler?"

"Proud and pleased."

"Did you expect prices to soar so high?"

"I never doubted for a moment that my wife would obtain them."

"Do you expect your wife to take over now that Charles Despard is dead?"

"There is no one better fitted."

"Did you think the total sale would reach 11.8 million dollars?"

"No. I am no expert, unlike my wife, but I had thought—perhaps—ten million tops."

Blaise lied smoothly. He had privately thought she would be hard pushed to reach five. Just as well he had never said so publicly.

Fortunately, he had never had anything to do with the running of Despard's. He had enough on his hands as executive vice president of Chandler Corporation, one of the world's largest multinationals, now that his grandmother, the president, could no longer travel as much as she had done. He had given Charles free legal advice many times; he was a corporation lawyer after all, but that was the extent of his involvement. The art world was a closed book to him—one written in ancient Greek. When interviewed before, he had always laughingly disclaimed either knowledge or interest; now, his instinct told him that it was time to play a different tune. What Dominique wanted from him right now—and it was the very first time, he realized with a shock, that she had wanted anything from him except his body—was wholehearted support. Well, he acknowledged, God knew she deserved it.

When he could, he got her to himself.

"Was it really 11.8 million?" he asked.

"Almost 11.9, but I rounded it down. One must not appear to be too greedy."

"You were magnificent. Surely the fact that I felt constrained to return for the end is proof of that."

"Oh, I saw you come in, and no, I was not surprised. This was a night to remember, in more ways than one." She moved closer. "And there is more to come. Must you go tonight?"

"I thought you were eager to know your fate."

"Not to *know* it—I have no doubts as to what that might be—who else is there, after all? No, what I wanted was confirmation, and tonight has publicly confirmed my right to Despard's. What I had in mind was a private confirmation of my right to you . . ."

Blaise could feel her like a fire. "I'll take the Concorde in the morning," he said.

She took his hand, put one of its long, beautifully kept fingers in her mouth and sucked it lasciviously. "Good," she murmured. "Now let us go and enjoy the party . . ."

". . . yesterday's auction of the decade brought Despard's of London to New York in a night to remember, culminating in the incredible sum of 11.8 million for a collection that had been estimated at between five and seven million dollars. Prices reached unheard of heights, as the world's connoisseurs fought bitterly to acquire some of the most precious items of Oriental porcelain from the collection acquired by the late Willard Dexter, of Dexter's Drugstores, over a period of fifty years.

"It gave warning to Sotheby's and Christie's, already well established here in New York, that they have a rival to watch. For more than two hundred years a force to be reckoned with in the London market, Despard's, in the future to be run by last night's auctioneer, Dominique du Vivier, who stepped in to take her stepfather's place after his sudden death last Tuesday, has announced that it intends to do the same thing here. In this reporter's opinion, it ought to be a battle well worth watching. Certainly, Despard's stunning new president is."

Blaise, who had been awakened by the sound of the television, sat up at that. "A bit premature, aren't you?" he asked, raking back tousled hair.

"You know I never say anything unless I am pretty sure I can back it up."

"My Indian blood says that's tempting fate."

"My French blood says it is only common sense."

Dominique was sitting, naked and cross-legged, at the bottom of their king-sized bed, dipping a morning-fresh croissant into a large cup of milky coffee. Celebrating, obviously. Normally she avoided anything with a high fat content. Blaise stretched, muscles creaking, and felt a twinge. After the workout she'd put them through last night, he thought gingerly, she could afford to eat half a dozen. He leaned forward to run his mouth down the length of her spine. Her skin was incredibly silky, and still smelled of sex and her own, special perfume, created for her by her Parisian couturier. She made a sound like a purr, moved her shoulders in a circular motion, but never took her eyes from the TV set facing the bed.

"Plenty of publicity?" Blaise asked, reaching for the coffeepot.

"A positive plethora—and all favorable. I have recorded it all on tape. And the papers are full of it, too. Look." She handed him a sheaf; the art pages were nothing but Despard's opening auction. "Blow by blow accounts; they make it sound like an Art Olympics."

"I thought it was."

"Well, I knew that if I put those ancient enemies together they would force prices skyward. They know their porcelain, but if one were not present the other would never bid so high. It is what keeps them alive, in my opinion." Dominique licked her fingers. "All they live for is their rivalry; to them it is the spice of their lives. They have all the money they need, and they are too old for women—besides which Poliakov has only ever liked boys. I did them a favor, really. I saw to it that they had a double dose, last night."

"And allowed them to spend eight million dollars between them?"

"What is that to them? They are each worth a hundred times that and more."

Blaise checked his watch. "And time I got going to see what you are going to be worth. I am due to see Mr. Finch at 4 P.M. London time and it is already 7 A.M. Thank God for the Concorde."

He swallowed coffee before leaping from the bed and loping into the bathroom. When he came out twelve minutes later and began to dress, Dominique, switching from channel to channel in search of every last scrap of news about the auction, ordered, "You will call me as soon as you know, eh? No matter where I am I will leave word that you are to reach me. Call me at Despard's and I will leave instructions there."

"What are your plans for today?"

"Future auctions, of course. We are set up for the next six months, but that is nowhere near enough. I have fired off our opening salvo; now I have to stockpile all the ammunition I can find."

"You'll have your work cut out. They know you're here—in spades."

"As I intended them to. I am lunching with Gervase Penworthy; rumor has it that he is disposing of his paintings. He has a Duccio that should bring five million dollars at least."

"And has probably arranged with one or another of your rivals to do so."

"Not so. He had a row with Sotheby's years ago when a picture of his failed to reach its reserve and he said they had not tried hard enough. And he once lost a Raphael at a Christie's old masters sale so he is not entirely happy with them either. He is a very difficult man but I have always been able to handle him."

"Show me the man you can't," Blaise murmured, bending to kiss her good-bye.

She held him by his lapels as he made to straighten, fixing him with an intense, sapphire gaze. "You will call me as soon as you know," she repeated.

"I promise."

She relaxed. Blaise never broke promises.

He hovered in the doorway, briefcase in his hand, feeling strangely loath to go. It was not unusual for them to meet at intervals of weeks or months; she had her work and he had his and it usually had them at opposite ends of the world. But, he thought now, remembering the explosion of physical passion that had left them both drained and limp last night, it made their reunions something to look forward to . . . So why was he loath to leave this time? Maybe because it meant having to confirm, finally and irrevocably, that his wife would now immerse herself even more deeply in Despard et Cie, taking from him what little time he spent with her. The plain and simple truth was, he realized, that he did not want his wife to inherit Despard's, because he did not want to share Dominique with anyone, not even an auction house. . .

Feeling the concentration of his gaze, she looked up with a query on her face and he smiled. She returned it. "Have a good trip," she said, blowing him a kiss. "And on your return then we will indeed have something to celebrate."

Will we? he thought, as he shook his head to murmur, "I'd better delay it, then. After last night I don't think I'll be up to it for some time."

He heard the slipper she threw thud harmlessly against the closed bedroom door.

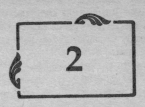

2

Blaise Chandler stood on the north side of the lower, unfashionable end of the King's Road and examined the small shop opposite. What a comedown from Despard's, he thought, disgusted. Just as well she doesn't trade under her own name. The fascia bore the elegantly italicized legend: *Kate Mallory—Fine Porcelains*. Whatever the reason she had rejected her father's name as well as the man himself, it still came as a shock to see that rejection writ large, even if the shop itself was so small. Yet her field was porcelain. Whether it was emulation or rivalry, it still led straight to further rivalry with Dominique . . .

He had called her, as promised, and her reaction had been, to say the least, unpromising.

"He has *what?*" she hissed.

"Split Despard's between you and his own daughter. She—"

"I know who she is," Dominique brushed him aside.

Blaise was thunderstruck. "You knew!"

"Of course, from the beginning. It was her mother Papa left in order to marry mine. How would I not know?"

"Then why the hell was it never mentioned? Why wasn't I ever told?"

"Why should you be?" Dominique was infuriatingly calm. "It was something Papa did not care to talk about and Mama—naturally—would not allow to be mentioned."

No wonder Catherine could not stand the thought of her husband's former life. Blaise now knew it included a daughter who was not hers. He felt that a blindfold had been taken from his eyes. "Then why the hell did you automatically assume that he would leave you as his sole heiress?" he demanded furiously. "You let me walk into this unprepared—"

"Because he had not seen her since the day he left her

34

mother, that is why. Because she has returned unread every letter he ever wrote her during the past twelve years. Because she always made it as plain as her own pitiably plain face that she already considered her father dead. It will be no news to her, I assure you."

Shit! Blaise thought furiously. What the hell are you playing at here, Charles? You dumped me right in the middle of a war. What am I supposed to do—act as umpire? "You could at least have warned me that she so much as existed."

"I should have thought Papa would have explained, seeing as he made you his executor," Dominique needled.

Well, yes, he had, Blaise thought furiously, scowling at the telephone, but in such a way as to give the impression that nobody else knew. Now it turned out that not only was his wife fully aware she had a stepsister, she had been so from the start, and so had his mother-in-law. Blaise felt distinctly discomfited and not a little put out. He had always believed that his father-in-law trusted him, that he was one of the few people who had his ear, but in spite of Charles repeating this in the letter he had left for Blaise, along with his will, he still felt as if he had been played for a sucker. God knows he had read the letter enough times. He knew it almost by heart . . .

My dear Blaise,

By now you will know that I have appointed you executor of my wills, the French one and the English one, and this letter is by way of explanation.

Briefly, what I want you to do, my dear Blaise, is to do your best to convince my own daughter to accept the legacy I am leaving her—Despard's of London.

I can almost feel your surprise. Her name is Catriona Susan Despard, and she is twenty-six years old. She lives in London, in the King's Road, above a little shop in which she sells—what else—porcelain, under the name Kate Mallory, her mother's maiden name. My daughter has not used my name since the day I left her and her mother to go to my Catherine. My reasons are set forth in the enclosed letters which I have, over the past twelve years, repeatedly written to my daughter in the hope that she would read them and, now that she is old enough, understand why I took that irrevocable step. Alas, she has never so much as opened any one of them. The first one came back torn to confetti inside another envelope; the others are simply marked in large red letters, as you will see: Not known at this address. Return to Sender.

I want you to get her to read these letters, Blaise. I want her to understand the reasons behind what she regards as my desertion of her, for which she has adamantly refused to forgive me since. I know and have never ceased to grieve about the pain and grief I caused her, which is why I have tried so hard for a reconciliation. The tragedy—and my failure—is that she will not forgive. I want my little Cat—that was always my name for her—to carry on the Despard tradition. She *is* a Despard; she has the eye, the feel, the instinct, as all true Despards have. When she was a little girl I made her a solemn promise: that one day Despard's would be hers. I am keeping that promise, because I want her own to be fulfilled.

But I must be fair to my stepdaughter, and so I have given her Paris, Geneva, Monte Carlo, and Hong Kong, which latter branch she has run single-handed anyway for some time now. I also give each of them one year's grace in which to prove themselves. Whichever one makes the greatest turnover in that one financial year and, after taxes, the highest profits, will then take over Despard's International. I also give Catriona time to learn, which she will need. Talent is no substitute for experience, which Dominique has in large measure. Catriona must have an apprenticeship. If I should die right at the beginning or end of our financial year, which commences April lst, then she must have the next year in which to learn: it is only fair. If my death should occur well into a financial year, then the remainder of that year will be her apprenticeship and the actual Year on Trial will commence on the following April lst. After one whole year's trading, when the audit is completed, whichever of them has done the best for Despard's in the way of financial profit shall assume my place as chairman and managing director of Despard's International.

This is the fairest way I can devise. Catriona is a natural whereas Dominique has applied herself. But the other side of the coin is Dominique's vast wealth of experience in a major auction house. Catriona has none. I think my scheme balances things out, but in case it should not, I give you, my dear Blaise, full power to deal as you think fairest with this situation. Hold a watching brief for me. I do not impugn her when I say we both know Dominique: you will know what I mean.

The means are yours to choose, my dear Blaise. All I ask is that you do your best to bring about the end I seek.

Thank you,
Charles

What a hell of a bloody job, Blaise thought now, still feeling he had been played for a sucker. He had not set eyes on Charles' daughter—the picture left with the letters had been one taken in the street and was not particularly helpful—but already he knew he did not like her one little bit. She was responsible for this wild goose chase. If she had kept up a vendetta for twelve years she was hardly likely to grant a deathbed forgiveness. Maybe—an idea struck him—if he could get her to next Monday's funeral. No way! his next thought followed. She is obviously an unforgiving bitch who nourishes grudges as other women nourish children. And yet Charles went on trying to heal the breach . . . why the hell didn't she ever read one of those heartbreaking letters he wrote her? Or isn't she capable of seeing anything but black and white? Well, if she tells me what to do with Despard's, that leaves me free to tell her what she can do with her black heart.

He crossed the road deep in the grip of his bad mood, causing an irate cabby to brake dangerously and hurl a volley of abuse that Blaise did not even hear as he glared into the tastefully decorated window of the small shop. Beige carpeting, café curtains in matching velvet, an intricately carved table—Chinese?—bearing a prancing horse in terra cotta bronze with a patina of green. No doubt also Chinese. He could not see into the shop because of the curtains.

He had debated about coming in person, finally decided that a woman who was capable of keeping a grudge honed and polished for twelve long years would obey no summons but her own. He would have to take her by surprise: a full frontal confrontation. If he could catch her on the hop he might get her to listen to him. As he pushed open the shop door, it was with such violence that the bell clanged like a fire alarm, causing the taller of two women, who both swung around at the frantic pealing, to say frostily, "If you will wait a moment, sir. I am with a customer," before returning to

her. Blaise eyed the eloquent back. It belonged to Kate
Mallory, he was sure, because it was wearing a denim jacket
that was a twin to the one she had been wearing in the street
picture. And similar jeans and matching cowboy boots. The
news was that the thick bush of untidy hair was a red that
made you wince; he had caught a glimpse of more freckles
than were good for any woman's looks and eyes like those
that had once stared out at him from dense brush in the
Brazilian jungle. But her voice had been as crisp as lettuce
and wholly English. He had somehow expected a French
accent, like Charles' . . .

Just then, Blaise felt the weight of a measuring stare and
looked in its direction. A tall, elegant man was standing just
to one side of the superb Coromandel screen that cut off the
rear of the shop from the showroom. Catching Blaise's eye,
his cynical Somerset Maugham face essayed a smile, the bad
smell sneer warming into a computation of Blaise's Savile
Row suit, the handmade shoes, the alligator briefcase, and
the general air of money that was his particular aftershave.
The answer proving eminently satisfactory, he glided forward and asked, in a gravelly, Hermione Gingold voice,
"Good afternoon, sir? May I help you?" The look, the
appraisal, said quite plainly what he would love to help
himself to.

"I should like to see Miss—Mallory?" The brief but deliberate hesitation had the effect of erasing the smile, chilling the
eyes already lacking minimal warmth.

"Miss Mallory is with a customer." His glance flicked in
the direction of the redhead who was still talking to her
customer.

"I will wait."

The uncompromising tone had the cynical mouth pursing,
and for a moment the grey eyes—almost colorless—held
Blaise's onyx ones, and then Rollo Bellamy eased himself
over to where the two women were haggling—if politely—
over the bowl Kate Mallory was holding. A brief murmur
and the bowl exchanged hands, the customer was moved
from one to the other without so much as a missed heart-
beat, and Kate Mallory, looking anything but pleased, came
toward Blaise, who was now standing by the shop window.
He noted that she was almost as tall as he was, colt slender
and plain as the proverbial pikestaff. Her voice, her eyes,
her whole demeanor were cool as she took the card he

handed her, glanced at it before asking, politely, "How can I help you, Mr. Chandler?"

The card was his Chandler Corporation one. He surmised that she had heard of the Corporation—most people had—but was at a loss as to what it wanted with her. He noted that her voice was as lovely as her face was plain. He was taken aback by such uncompromising plainness, and the fact that she did nothing to minimize it, but on second thoughts decided she was right. There could be no gilding the lily with this one. Her face was all bones, her mouth a slash. And that hair! So violently red it was an insult. No way was she a Despard to look at; Charles' hair had been brown, with eyes to match. This girl had obviously taken her looks as well as her name from her mother.

Kate, on the other hand, whose first impression had been of looming height and threatening presence, now found herself looking at the best-looking man she had ever seen. He was exactly as she had imagined Edward Rochester, her girlhood hero, except that as this man was American, the Rochester connection would be that of the New York town of the same name. He was that rarity, a man she had to look up to, into eyes so black they were like liquid pools of pitch, fringed by lashes any woman would have died for: long and thick and curling, oddly feminine in so masculine a face. He was as dark as a Red Indian, she thought bemusedly, which was no doubt why she was receiving a distinct impression of savagery. As well as an almost palpable wall of contempt.

"You are Catriona Susan Mallory Despard?"

Blaise saw the freckled face, already prominently boned, draw back as though the skin had tightened. He felt as though a door had been slammed—hard—right in his face.

"I am Kate Mallory," she corrected emphatically.

"But your father was the late Charles Despard?"

Blaise could feel as well as see the drawbridge being raised, the defenses manned, the alarm sounded.

"He was." It was short and it would have shaved ice.

"I am here in my capacity as executor of his will."

"I have no interest in anything to do with Charles Despard." She thrust his card back at him. "Good afternoon, Mr. Chandler."

But he did not move, just stood there in such a way as to make it necessary for her to go around him to jerk open the shop door, ringing another peal. The customer turned and

Rollo glared. Finally, in a voice that had somehow lost its heat, Blaise Chandler said calmly, "Rejecting your father's name is quite some way to go, even for a dedicated grudge bearer like you."

Kate's skin—fine, pale, almost translucent except for the freckles—flooded with color. "That is none of your business," she rasped, in a voice that warned.

"I must correct you; it *is* my business. Did you not hear what I just now told you? I am your father's executor, and it is because his will includes a specific bequest to you that I am here."

"I want no bequests from Charles Despard."

"Nevertheless my instructions are to acquaint you with his."

"I ceased to take instructions from him twelve years ago."

She jerked the door, making the bell dance frantically. "Good afternoon, Mr. Chandler."

But he still just stood there, looking at her in a way that made her want to hit him. As she got more and more heatedly upset, he grew colder and harder.

"Will you not be told!" Kate hissed at him venomously. "I have no wish to receive anything from Charles Despard. He gave me more than enough twelve years ago."

"Including those chips on your shoulders?"

He saw the golden eyes turn to stones. "Handmade by that same Charles Despard!"

Neither noticed as Rollo maneuvered the fascinated customer out of the shop before materializing between them.

"I think," he intoned in his best Gingold, "that we had better adjourn to where a public brawl may be conducted without spectators." To Kate he said, "You have already lost me one customer." To Blaise, "I must ask you to forgive my partner, Mr. Chandler, but I am afraid you do not understand that around here, the name Despard carries connotations not spoken of in polite society." He held out a well-manicured hand. "I am Rollo Bellamy."

Kate, who had done a double take at Rollo's smooth description of himself as her partner, now did her best to turn him to stone, failing as usual because he was already made of asbestos. She was shaking, inside and outside, feeling nauseated, near to uncontrollable tears, her inevitable reaction to any mention of her father. Superior shit! she raged at Blaise Chandler. Who the hell does he think he is?

Neurotic as hell, Blaise was deciding contemptuously. As highly strung as the mustangs they rounded up back home at the ranch every year; dangerous if you got too near and capable of breaking a limb if you did. Come to that, he thought, I would dearly love to tame this one myself . . .

"I think you owe Mr. Chandler the courtesy of listening to what he has to say," Rollo was lecturing Kate.

"You know very well that anything to do with Charles Despard is bad news where I am concerned," Kate retorted hotly. "He gave me more than I wanted when he abandoned me and my mother. I did not ask for anything then, either!"

"I was not aware you were an actress," she heard Blaise Chandler murmur silkily, but with such contempt that it was not only her face that flamed. She knew she was going over the top but, as always, she could not stop herself. She was programmed, she supposed. The trigger was the name Charles Despard, and it always catapulted her into the same boiling cauldron of rage, pain, grief, and despair.

"What I am or am not is nothing to do with you," she managed, in a voice strangled with loathing. "How dare you come in here and act like you know everything! Where were you twelve years ago? I have no doubt Charles Despard spun you some technicolored sob story about why he deserted me and my mother and about how *I* am the one who hurt *him*. Like everything else he ever said, that is a lie! He abandoned his wife and daughter for some strumpet, leaving us both behind without so much as a qualm. He lied and he cheated then and I see no reason to change my opinion of what he did or what he was." She was working herself up into a fine rage. "You can take whatever 'bequest' he has made to me and shove it right where it hurts! He has been dead to me these twelve years and his memory along with him—"

"But not your own? You are remarkably touchy about a man you profess to have forgotten."

Kate's face was anguished, her voice choked, her eyes sick. Why was it she could never control this same, volcanic eruption of feelings whenever her father was mentioned? She knew she was going too far, but her emotional brakes were not working.

"You are not prepared, then, to give what your father has to say a hearing? To listen to his explanation of why he did what he did?"

"There are no explanations for abandoning your wife and daughter. For betrayal and lies and cheating, for saying one thing, and doing another, for breaking a trust and your word. My father died when he abandoned me twelve years ago. I have had his legacy, thank you very much—pain and grief and much unhappiness watching my mother die of a broken heart. That is more than enough for one lifetime."

She turned on her heel and stalked to the door again, yanked it open, stood waiting once more, obviously over-wrought, obviously adamant, obviously and obsessively hung up, screwed up, and as twisted as hell. What she needed, Blaise thought grimly, was not a father but a psychiatrist.

"I shall require you to sign a statement formally relinquishing all claim to your father's estate," he told her, his unruffled calm concealing a strong desire to box her ears.

"In that I *shall* take pleasure!"

He swept her from head to foot with a look that reduced her to six inches high, made a flawlessly polite bow that hit her like a slap in the face, and walked out of the shop with the air of a man who had done his most unpleasant duty and was now, thank God, free at last.

This time the glass all but cracked. Kate's hand groped, seeking to find something to throw, her quick temper threatening to explode and shatter the immediate vicinity to smithereens. Rollo swifty removed the magnificent Meissen showpiece of Neptune in his chariot drawn by dolphins, a singing masterpiece in cream and gold, scarlet and green, and, holding it to his chest protectively, watched Blaise Chandler stride across the street and around the corner.

"You have made a bad mistake, dear heart," he pronounced, à la Judge Roy Bean. He raised a traffic-stopping hand. "I know, I know. Your father has a nerve after what he did to you and your mother, but Blaise Chandler probably knows only Charles Despard's side of the story. If you had kept a tighter rein on that quick temper—"

"I don't give a damn what Blaise Chandler thinks!" Kate tossed at him furiously. "And I will not accept anything from a man who obviously wanted to ease his conscience and buy off the devil!"

Rollo winced and murmured, "Too much, dear heart. I should change your writer if I were you, but even he could not change the fact that your father did write to you—many times."

"Guilt!" Kate rejected scornfully. "Trying to salve that same conscience. If he felt so guilty, why did he stay with his French widow? Why didn't he come back to us, where he belonged?" Her voice clogged again and she had to throttle back the nausea that threatened to make the room spin.

Rollo sighed. "You are just like your father. Before he took himself in hand, he swung on his own pendulum, with the same hair-trigger reaction. And stubborn as hell! If he could control himself, I suggest you learn to emulate him in that respect, too." He would have raised his hands helplessly except he was still cradling the Meissen. Now he carefully placed it back on its stand.

"Will you stop comparing me to my father!" Kate seethed. "You take too much on yourself. Like introducing yourself as my partner, for instance. Since when?"

"Since it sounds better," Rollo returned, unmoved. "I'm hardly going to tell a man like Blaise Chandler that I'm an unemployed actor who helps you out whenever I'm 'resting.' You still don't know who he was, do you?"

"No, and I don't care. Arrogant bastard!"

Rollo sighed. "Wasn't he though . . ."

"And straight!" withered Kate.

"Married to Dominique du Vivier, what else could one expect?" Rollo looked suddenly struck, like a clock. "Which makes him some sort of relation—stepbrother-in-law? At that you could do with some relatives, what with your mother an only child and your father's brothers being killed in the war—"

"Who needs relatives when I've got you?" Kate jibed, but there was affection in her eyes and voice. "I'm sorry if I got on my high horse, Rollo, but you know how I feel about—about what happened."

"Yes, far too strongly. After twelve years you should have put it behind you. Only you would take out your hate every day and polish it, as if it were some badge of honor."

"I only have to think of my mother to remember everything," Kate said quietly.

Rollo flicked her a glance and for a moment seemed about to say something, then changed his mind. But the way his eyes saw yet did not see her meant, had she noticed, that his mind was clicking away.

Rollo Bellamy prided himself on being Kate Mallory's Grey Eminence, and went to some pains to dress the part.

He had always bought the very best: in the end, his philosophy was, it was the cheapest. His grey suit was one of Huntsman's best superfine; his shirt came from Turnbull and Asser, white but with a broad red stripe and plain white collar; his tie was a Christian Dior, silver grey to match his pewter-colored eyes, heavy lidded and sunk in lizardlike folds of skin that, his surgeon had told him firmly, were beyond any further lifting. His face, therefore, always bore a look of consummate weariness, not helped by the downward curve to his mouth, which added an air of cynical contempt. He was just short of sixty-four, and having been born with a jaundiced outlook on life, all had always looked yellow to Rollo's eye. Expecting the worst he was rarely disappointed. By profession an actor—though these days he rarely trod the boards—his true vocation was that of salesman, but being the snob he was he never acknowledged that fact. He could depress with a lift of the eyebrow, encourage with a gleam of the eye, praise with a nod. It was due to his efforts that the little shop was kept—marginally—in the black. That and Kate's nose for a fine piece. She was, as he was fond of saying, a natural, adding (out of Kate's hearing), "Just like her father."

Now he said pensively, "You do realize you have probably just turned away a very great deal of money?"

"Contrary to your frequently expressed opinion, it is *not* everything."

"That is a vile calumny spread by those who have not got any. Like us, for instance. We are not exactly making our fortunes here, are we?"

"That takes time," Kate said defensively.

"You have been laboring almost five years. I would not call that overnight."

"I'll get there. Just give me time."

"I can't," Rollo said gently.

Instantly Kate's eyes were filled with fright. "Don't say that, Rollo! You are not sixty-four yet! You've got years ahead of you . . ."

"I hope so, but one can never be sure, except when one is as young as you are." He paused. "But it does concern me that you may have just turned away a shortcut."

Kate drew herself up. "Are you suggesting that I let my father buy my forgiveness?"

"I am not suggesting anything but that you listen to what

it is he has asked his executor to do. Does it not mean anything to you that even after his death he is *still* trying? That after all these years he was as obsessive about you as you are about him?"

Kate did not answer, but the look on her face spoke volumes, all of it slanderous. "I have nothing more to say on the subject," she told him shortly. "Let's drop it, shall we? I'm going to see Howell and Roberts about that Limoges *poudreuse.*"

"Stick to your price. They can well afford it."

"Don't worry. I know Brian Howell by now."

Rollo watched her walk off down the street with her long-legged, free-flowing stride, head up, shoulders back. Perhaps because of her complex about her lack of looks, Kate always walked as though she didn't give a damn about her appearance. And dressed accordingly, Rollo thought gloomily. Then, turning the OPEN sign to CLOSED, he went behind the screen to the back of the shop where Kate's big, untidy desk was. There he sat down, drew the telephone toward him and dialed a number he knew by heart.

"Despard's? Oh, good afternoon." He made his voice that of a snooty, impossible-to-put-down aristocrat, a part he had played to perfection in many a Wilde revival (which was why he did not work so much, of late). "I understand Mr. Blaise Chandler is in town. Would you be so good as to give me his whereabouts? It has to do with the estate of the late Charles Despard. My name is Rollo Bellamy. I spoke to Mr. Chandler earlier this afternoon . . . Thank you . . ." He waited, running through his mental card index. Rollo had a flypaper memory. Once stuck there, a fact was held forever.

Blaise Chandler. Chandler Corporation, Agatha Chandler's grandson. And heir. Charles Despard's son-in-law. Most salient fact of all . . . Dominique du Vivier's husband. Close to the seat of power and obviously a trusted confidant in the light of his appointment as executor of Charles Despard's will. And as gorgeous a hunk as ever I saw, Rollo thought. Could I sink my teeth into *that*—except that if he is married to a woman known as the Venus Flytrap it is probably all but bitten off already . . .

"What? Yes, it is urgent. Very urgent." He listened. "If it is within the next hour, then yes. I shall not be here after that," he lied, because he knew Kate probably would. He repeated the telephone number of the shop and then his warning: "Within the next hour, please. Very well. Thank you. Goodbye." He hung up. Despard's being cagey as always and refusing to give out telephone numbers. Still, as long as Blaise Chandler did ring back . . . Rollo was not about to allow Kate's emotional astigmatism to ruin her future. If Blaise Chandler bothered to call on someone in person, then he had big news to impart. Whatever Charles Despard had left his daughter it was worth a great deal. Shares? An interest, maybe? Everything else would probably go to that cunning stepdaughter of his. That little vixen would have worked on him for years, so if he had still left something to his own daughter, then it must be something vital. Which Kate had stupidly thrown back at him.

No way! Rollo thought vigorously. That Kate's virulent portrait of her father owed not a little to his own generous hand with the brush he now had cause to regret. But then, who would have thought . . . Well, he decided, I will just have to do some cleaning and restoring. It is time my fortunes changed. Wilde revivals and drawing room comedies were scarcer than hen's teeth, and neither the kitchen sink type drama nor the neorealistic school were his forte; he never used a sink except to wash dishes and he had carefully avoided the neo-real all his life. Just as Kate had carefully avoided the reality about her father. He sighed. His fault again. He had let his own dislike color his judgment. And that was another thing that would have to change: Kate's protective coloration. No way was he going to let her toss her head and stride off into the sunset in those God-awful cowboy boots she would insist on wearing. She would have to take off her camouflage of the unadorned, homely woman and stand up and be counted as the woman she really was, but which, since her father's rejection, she had been afraid to be.

She would have to be handled like high explosives, of course. An intense, sensitive creature, Kate's feelings rose and fell like the tide, and whereas for the first fourteen years of her life it had swept her along with her father, his desertion had left her beached on an emotional desert island. She was no militant feminist, but her father's betrayal had turned all men into The Enemy. Blaise Chandler—that sexy animal, Rollo thought hungrily—would have sent her straight to the trenches. Well, I've got to get into character and give the performance of my life, he decided. Trouble was, Kate was now adept at spotting where Rollo ended and The Character began. In which case, he would have to crate an entirely new one, and he was good at that . . .

Blaise walked back to Despard's at a fast clip, burning up energy and a white-hot rage. What a plain-faced harpy she had turned out to be. That spiteful, grudge-bearing bitch was Charles Despard's daughter! Why in God's name had he hankered after that for twelve years? He should have been well rid of her. She nourished spite like a baby. And was obviously a man hater. But with her disastrous lack of any sort of attraction was it any wonder? All bones and a spiny tongue. And then it hit him whom she had reminded him of. The young Katharine Hepburn. Same high cheekbones, same slash of a mouth. But behind this face was a corkscrew personality.

She had come at him all claws and teeth. Why? That was not the reaction of a woman who did not care, rather that of a woman who cared too much. As his initial anger cooled, he remembered the raw pain in her voice, her eyes, her whole body, when she had accused her father of deserting her. But then, she had not read a single one of Charles' many letters. And she had been only fourteen. The worst possible age. Neither child nor woman but smack in the middle of that fearsome no-man's-land between the two. And, he argued with himself uneasily, Charles *had* left his daughter behind when he had gone to his Catherine . . . but that was all explained in the letters. Maybe if she knew that explanation she would change her mind. Which was what he was supposed to do, right? He chewed it over in his mind until it was almost rags by the time he got back to Arlington Street. Charles had asked him to do his very best; he had warned that his daughter was difficult; he had explained how she undoubtedly still felt. But she had flown off her handle so violently it had had the effect of knocking him off his Oh, shit! he scowled, as he pushed through Despard's swinging doors. I suppose I owe Charles another try . . .

So that when he walked into what had been Charles' office, which he was using temporarily during his stay in London, to be told that a Mr. Rollo Bellamy urgently wanted to talk to him, his first feeling was one of relief that he would not have to make the approaches, and his second was that of suspicion. He knew all about Rollo Bellamy. He'd had a dossier prepared on that gentleman.

So he was cool when he called the shop.

"Thank you for being so prompt," Rollo told him courteously. "And let me apologize for Kate's behavior this afternoon. I can only ask you to remember that she feels she had a very raw deal from her father. Her hatred is so virulent because it is, as I am sure you must have realized by now, the other side of a coin that once bore a love equally as powerful. She feels she was rejected in favor of someone else."

"If she had bothered to read even one of his letters she would understand why."

"With your agreement, I intend to *make* her understand." Rollo paused to let that sink in and then said candidly, "I am the one person in the world who wields any sort of influence over Kate, Mr. Chandler. I took over where her father left off. In fact, I have stood *in loco parentis* since his—departure. She trusts me, and since her father's betrayal she trusts no one else. I have known her all her life. I held her at her christening, as her godfather." Another pause. "I was her mother's closest friend, you see."

"I know," Blaise replied.

"Ah . . ." Charles, Rollo thought. He probably told him the full story. "Then would you be prepared to wait while I try to persuade Kate that she should see you and listen to whatever it is you have to tell her—after you have first told me, of course? I cannot persuade her unless I know what it is you want her to accept."

"Strictly speaking," Blaise answered after a pause, "I am not supposed to tell anyone but the beneficiary, but circumstances alter cases, and in this one I don't really have any choice if I am to achieve my objective."

Rollo could barely conceal his utter astonishment when Blaise had told him, but he said only, "A legacy indeed, and one, I now see, Kate must accept."

"Are you sure she can be persuaded to accept it?"

"Kate is not immovable, Mr. Chandler. It is just that her views are—strong—where her father is concerned. I undertake to run you up a custom-made Kate Mallory," Rollo promised gravely, "but I cannot do it overnight. And I must do it in my own way. Today is Friday. Can you give me the weekend? I will call you on Monday morning."

"I shall be in France on Monday. That is the day of the funeral. But I shall be back in London on Tuesday. Call me in the afternoon—shall we say four o'clock—no," he corrected himself, remembering that Dominique would be in London, "I shall call you at the shop."

"Agreed," Rollo closed promptly. "Tuesday afternoon at four. Thank you, Mr. Chandler. You won't regret it."

"I shall know who to blame if I do," Blaise returned dryly, before ringing off.

Dominique paced back and forth, back and forth, like a caged animal, across the Persian carpet of her office on the top floor of Despard's New York. All the time her fingers worked, playing with her rings, hands unconsciously clenching and unclenching, betraying the turbulence of her thoughts.

How had she gone wrong? Where had she gone wrong? How had it been possible for her stepfather to do this—this *bêtise?* For twelve long years she had worked on him, fought to establish once and for all her ascendancy over his own daughter, to replace her in his affections. Now, she had to share—to *share*—what was rightfully hers. It was unthinkable. Despard's was *hers*. She was the one who had worked, planned, manipulated—biding her time, waiting, waiting . . . She had been supremely sure, especially every time a letter came back and she saw the look on her stepfather's face, that she was winning. That stupid bitch was using her pride to cut her own throat, and Dominique was quite willing to let her, careful to stand well to one side so as not to get blood on her clothes. How, then—*how*—had it come about that Charles Despard had left the jewel in Despard's crown to the daughter he had abandoned twelve years before? Why? What stubborn hard core of affection—love?—had remained, immune to his stepdaughter's blandishments, her persuasion, her subtle but constant undermining, resulting in this—this aberration? She smacked one fist into the other palm. It would not do. It had to be stopped. Now. Before it got any further. The very idea of that—that gawk of a girl so much as thinking she could take what rightfully belonged to Dominique du Vivier was insupportable. Nobody ever took anything from her. *Nobody.*

For a moment she had almost raged at Blaise, until she remembered that it was not his fault and anyway the less he knew the better. She had chilled into the arctic calm she

used to control her bouts of incandescent rage. Her own
father had taught her lessons indelibly learned about self-
control.

"You are quite sure of the legality of what Papa has
done?" she had wanted to know, when Blaise called her
from London.

"There is no doubt. The will is made under English law
and Despard's is incorporated in England, but the Swiss
holding company—Despard's International—maintains overall control. In the meantime, you each get to run your own
branches except for New York. That remains neutral territory, to be used by you both when and as the occasion
arises, and until such time as the contest is decided."

"Tell me again how the branches are split."

"Repeating it won't change things," Blaise said madden-
ingly.

"I get Paris, Monte Carlo, Geneva and Hong Kong, which
was mine anyway—"

"And she gets London, the English provincial branches,
and Dublin. Charles saw New York as untried as yet and
therefore to be fought for. You both have one whole year to
win it."

"She won't dare use New York!" Dominique had told him
confidently. "It is mine and she knows it!"

Blaise sighed. "It is *not* yours . . . you opened it, that's
all."

"But—"

"It is no use staking claims. Charles' will makes it quite
clear as to who gets what. I shall make that equally clear
when I see Kate Despard this afternoon."

"She has agreed to see you?" Dominique's voice was
sharp. She had been sure he would never get that far. Her
reading of her stepsister had convinced her that any emissary
from Charles Despard would be shot before he could parley.
Her husband's reply had reassured her.

"I intend to surprise her. From what Charles has told me
it is the only way."

Dominique sighed with relief. That was more like it. But
she still had one more suspicious question.

"Why you, anyway?"

"Because that's the way Charles wanted it," was his enig-
matic answer.

Dominique's face had hardened as they talked, become

set and ruthless, but there had been no hint of it in her voice when she said composedly, "I do not think there is any fear of my losing Despard's. Papa felt he had to make the gesture, that's all. After all, she is just not up to it, is she? What does she know? Who does she know? What experience has she had?" Her laughter had been a trill of amusement. "Running Despard's would be like flying the Concorde after only ever having piloted a Tiger Moth! No, my dear Blaise, I have no fears. Run along and do your best for Papa, but do not be surprised if she sends you off with a flea in your ear, as the English say."

"How do you know what experience she has had?" Blaise demanded.

Enjoyably she countered, "I knew what Papa knew. He had her watched all through those twelve years."

The silence on the other end of the line indicated Blaise's shock.

"I always thought he was wasting his time," she finished triumphantly.

Now, going over what had been said, an unaccustomed sense of doubt wreathed around Dominique like smog. Hitherto she had never so much as considered the fact that Kate Mallory, or whatever she called herself, would accept what Dominique automatically assumed would one day be hers. No, it had to be a wholly sentimental and emotional gesture on the part of her father, a last plea. He had been living in the nebulous never-never land of unfulfilled hopes and dreams when he had made that will, believing that wishing would make it so. Except he was not a man to subsist merely on hopes and dreams . . . No, she assured herself. Common sense and Kate Mallory's consistent, spite-filled response over the years made it impossible that she would accept her legacy.

But her pacing slowed, came to a stop. If there was even the slightest chance—she could not allow that. She would have to see that that eventuality could never come to pass. She would have to force the right response from Kate Mallory. And there was one certain way she could do that . . .

Unhesitatingly she turned and walked back to the telephone.

3

Blaise's intention had been to call his wife at once, as promised, to acquaint her with the situation vis-à-vis Kate Mallory, but no sooner had he put the telephone down on Rollo Bellamy than he had a whole raft of incoming calls which meant that, by the time he finally got around to placing his own, his wife had instituted one of her lightning changes of plans and brought forward the departure of herself, her mother, and the body of Charles Despard by twenty-four hours. A plane was no problem; there was always one or another of the ChanCorp fleet ready at Kennedy, and this time Dominique found a waiting 737. She then issued crisp instructions to Frank E. Campbell's before calling her mother's maid.

By the time Blaise's call had chased Dominique from one part of Manhattan to another the cortege was on its way to the airport, and by the time he had traced her there the coffin had been loaded into the hold, Catherine, in deepest mourning, was ensconced in the cabin, fitted out like a Park Avenue drawing room, and Dominique was issuing instructions to her French personal assistant, who would accompany Madame and the late Monsieur Despard to Paris, where the body would be transferred to a small airplane for the flight to Marseilles. There, a hearse would meet it for its final transfer to the small church in the village of Vent just above the ruined *mas* Charles had bought and restored as a country retreat. Two hundred years ago his great, great, great-grandfather, Gaston Despard, had left his native Provence for Paris and become a pawnbroker, thus founding the fortunes of the family. Now, Charles would return there, to be buried in the site he had chosen underneath an ancient, now wild bush of white Malmaison roses, his favorite flower.

When Dominique was told that her husband was on the telephone, she did not take the call. She did not want to have to make explanations at this stage. Blaise would think she was interfering if he knew her plans and there would be another argument, and she was in no mood for that right now. So she gave instructions that she was resting and not to be disturbed for or by anyone, even her husband. Time enough, she thought, as she returned to the business at hand, to explain her actions once they had resulted in the *dénouement* she desired.

Kate was in the shop alone. Rollo always spent an hour or two at Saturday lunchtime in a favorite pub with cronies from both the theatre and the homosexual worlds. Kate never did more than snatch a sandwich and a cup of coffee, because Saturday was generally their best day of the week. Only an hour or so earlier she had made a good sale. A nondescript man had paid eight hundred pounds in notes for a rare Masonic Staffordshire jug, which she had picked out from a motley assortment of odds and ends piled in a laundry basket on a stall in a country market. She had bought the lot for a fiver and, from under the grime of centuries, the prime piece of Staffordshire had emerged, miraculously unscathed. Lucky finds like that were rare, but her keen eye and inborn instinct as a "divvy"—a natural who knew by feel and shape and "look" whether a thing was genuine or not—had often served her well. Now, she went about the shop dusting and polishing, the violence of her movements in keeping with the turbulence of her thoughts. Her equilibrium was still not restored to the cheerfulness she usually displayed when her emotions were not involved. Blaise Chandler had taken a long spoon and stirred madly, and inside, she was still going around in circles.

The nerve of him! she seethed. The nerve of both of them. Trying to buy me! And my father thinking to buy absolution. No way! If he felt so badly about me, why didn't he come back to us and leave that fancy French piece of his behind? Cheat! Liar! Deceiver! I will never forgive him, never! My mother died of a broken heart because of him.

It was infuriating, she reflected in frustration, how the very mention of her father always brought on a hurricane. She had thought that by now she had the past safely put behind her, yet ever since Blaise Chandler's visit she had thought of virtually nothing else. Like her mother trying to persuade her to read just one of her father's early letters.

". . . he has not forgotten you, darling. See how thick the letter is?"

"Full of self-pitying justifications, no doubt. What he did can never be justified. He dumped us both for another woman and *her* daughter? How can that ever be justified?"

"There are complications about which you do not know."

"How can there be complications? He did not want us anymore, that's all. You've seen her picture, you know how beautiful she is—both of them are. We were not good enough for him, that's all. Papa always had this thing about beauty. . ."

Her mother sighed. "You are so young . . . perhaps, in a year or two, when the hurt is not so raw, you will let me explain." But she had been dead before then, during which time Kate's passionate love for her father had corroded under the acid of her bitterness.

When her mother entered the final stage of her long illness, bedridden for the last year, Kate had convinced herself that she was dying of a broken heart, no matter that the doctor explained it was congestive heart failure, or that was what the death certificate would read.

After the funeral, it was Rollo who made all the arrangements to sell the big house in Holland Park and took Kate to live with him. One of her mother's last requests had been to Rollo to look after her daughter.

Then Kate finished her education before going to the Courtauld, where she studied for a year before going to Florence for another year to do her doctorate in fine art. On coming home she had no difficulty finding a job with Sotheby's, in the Oriental porcelain department, where she stayed until she felt she had acquired enough knowledge and expertise to set up on her own in the King's Road, living in the little flat above the shop.

And all the time the letters had continued to come, every one of which she returned unopened.

And now, she thought, as she polished furiously, here I am, twenty-six years old and still going to pieces at the very mention of the name Charles Despard. It's ridiculous, that's what it is. He has been out of my life for twelve years; he died, for me, the day he left me and my mother, not last week. Then why had it hurt when Rollo had silently laid *The Times* in front of her, folded at the "Salerooms" column, detailing the triumphant opening of Despard's New York by Dominique du Vivier? It should have been me was the thought that instantly leapt to mind. So why had she sent her father's emissary off with a flea in his ear?

Oh, I don't know anything anymore, she thought angrily, rubbing hard at a small table as if to produce a reflection that would give her a rational explanation. My mind feels like the wash in a clothes dryer, all tangled up and almost impossible to sort out. Talk about "confusion is come again"!

Straightening up she surveyed her little shop. Everything shone or glowed or sparkled. "Well, at least I can do something right," she said out loud, with satisfaction. She would make herself a cup of coffee and go over the books. She had inherited her love of figures from her mother; there was nothing so soothing as a neat column of them adding up to the right total. Arithmetically, two and two *always* made four . . . When the shop bell rang she put down her pen with alacrity. Another customer and, with luck, another sale . . . Just what I need! she thought happily. But the smile on her face faded to stony rigidity when she saw who was standing waiting for her.

She had seen her picture in the trades and the glossies often enough. But seeing her in the flesh brought an instant wrench of helpless, hopeless envy, followed by its crony, self-hatred. Dominique du Vivier looked as all women dream of looking. She was in black: a velvet suit pasted to every singing curve, tight at the tiny waist, narrow as an arrow through the straight skirt, and with a high upstanding collar of black fox. Her flawless legs gleamed with the sheen of invisible nylons, her tiny feet in the highest of stiletto heels. On the black lacquered helmet of her hair sat a tiny pillbox, its drift of sheerest veiling misting her exquisite face. Sapphires gleamed in her ears and she smelled of something heady and sinful. Worst of all, her sensuality made the air hum.

Her smile was slow and, when it came, made Kate flinch. "But of course," she said in French. "You could only be her. So tall"—it consigned Kate to the category of freaks and misfits—"so *roquine.*" This last with the slightest wince, as if her hair was an insult in the worst possible taste. Then, crushing what was left of Kate's self-esteem, "You know who I am, of course."

"Yes. I know who you are." Kate answered in the same

language and the fine black brows lifted fractionally at the French of the French.

"But of course. Papa would naturally see that you spoke his beloved language." Turning to the Louis XVI armchair kept for customers: "I may sit?"

"If you must," Kate said rudely. She was acting badly again, because she had once more been thrown on the defensive.

"Thank you." Dominique sank into her seat like a drifting feather, aware of the hostility, bristling like porcupine quills, but having counted on it, wholly prepared.

"I thought it best we speak, face to face, in view of this impossible situation Papa has unwittingly created."

Situation? thought Kate. What situation? But she said nothing. She stood stiffly, chin jutting, painfully, humiliatingly aware of her gaucherie, her jeans, her boots, her untidy clump of hair. She felt overrun, overwhelmed, and overlooked. And about as feminine as a Sherman tank.

Dominique crossed her legs in a swish of silk, the sound erotic and enticing. "It will not do, of course, you must realize that. Papa was a sentimental man—but perhaps you do not remember? It has been so long, after all . . ." It was a direct slap in the face. "Twelve years is almost as long as the time you did spend with him. And you were so young. No, there can be no doubt that this unfortunate decision was made under the influence of sentimental regret."

Kate was beginning to smolder. How dare she speak about Papa that way—and call him Papa come to that. He was not *her* father. He was mine, she thought. Mine! "I remember very well," she said frigidly. "My father was not a man given to making decisions out of sentimentality. He was too French for that. He always knew exactly what he was doing."

"Ah . . ." the silky voice caressed, like delicate fingers. "Does that mean you have revised your long-held opinion of him?"

Stiffly, aware she had a very crafty adversary here, "I state facts as I remember them, not my present opinion."

"Then your hostility remains—unrelenting?" The sapphire eyes took another deadly measure, and the small smile pulled at the barbs already sunk deep into Kate's self-esteem. "Or is it that the very great deal of money—not to mention power—involved has served to paint a very different picture?"

Kate had thought of neither; her rejection had been an

instinctive reaction to a familiar pain. With her own contempt, one that had Dominique's face hardening she said, "If I did decide to accept my father's legacy, it would be because I am a Despard, and that being so, I have every right." To whatever it is, she thought, kicking herself now for not having found out.

"But you rejected the name Despard," Dominique said with silken spite, "when your father rejected you."

Kate almost blurted, *You mean, when you and your mother enticed him away,* but managed to curb her tongue. This beautiful bitch was obviously bent on stirring things up, provoking Kate into saying things she would regret. Careful, she warned herself. She's as clever as they come.

"I am the last Despard," she returned, in a way that had Dominique raising her eyebrows at the unconsciously arrogant pride. "No doubt my father had that in mind."

That Kate was executing a complete about-face never occurred to her; she only knew that Dominique du Vivier's casual dismissal of her father as a sentimental old fool had cut her deeply. What *she* said and thought about her father she had the right to say; he was her father, by blood and sinew, thought and deed. This woman had no such rights.

"In my opinion," Dominique was saying, "he had become anglicized by his many years in England. A true Frenchman would have known better. You did not read so much as one of the endless letters he wrote you." With a sympathy that was patently false, "Of course, to be rejected must be—difficult. One's father is, after all, the very first man in one's life; according to one school of thought the man on whom a woman bases her choice of men . . ." Her smile said snidely, *And you are still single, aren't you?* "You do not look like him at all," she went on, and this time the *alas* hung heavily on the crackling air.

"People who knew him and now know me all tell me I have inherited his character," Kate countered, creating Rollo into a multitude.

"Then you must realize, with his bracing common sense," Dominique said sarcastically, "that what he has done simply will not do. Consider, what do you know of Despard's?"

Another clue. "I was learning about Despard's from the age of five," Kate answered proudly.

"Things have changed since then."

"Not Despard's," Kate retorted confidently. "My father

was never a man to change for change's sake. He never altered things unless there were very good reasons for doing so." She made her own deadly pause. "But you would know all about them."

Again Kate felt the measuring insult of Dominique's stare. "So you think that what you learned as a child will stand you in good stead as an adult? I do not think so. By reason of hard work and promises given, Despard's is mine."

Kate felt faint, because what her stepsister was telling her was that it wasn't. It had not been given to her. It had been given to Kate . . .

She steadied her voice. "If my father had promised it to you he would have honored that promise. That he has not is proof that he made no such promise in the first place."

"It is mine by right!" Dominique was losing her patience— and her ground.

"But mine by blood."

That struck, but Dominique reared to spit back: "Isn't it rather late in the day to remember that—or are you a hypocrite like all your countrymen?"

"Better late than never, and hypocrisy has nothing to do with it."

It hasn't, she though dazedly. I have always believed this—just wouldn't ever admit it. In some way she could not as yet understand, she realized that she had been waiting for this for the last twelve years.

It was as though a great weight fell away from her. Unconsciously she flexed her shoulders, lifted her chin, and seeing it, realizing what it meant, Dominique jumped furiously to her feet. "Only you would have the gall to accept what long since ceased to be yours—morally, legally, any which way."

"My father obviously did not think so." Her smile bloomed. "He always told me I was the most important thing in his life."

"So he left you for my mother?" Dominique's laugh stripped skin.

But Kate was not to be moved now. Every insult only increased her determination. "The other love of my father's life was Despard's—and I am a Despard."

"Oh, but you are so much more English than French; only the English would display such shameless duplicity."

"At least I am honest in my reasons for wanting Despard's."

"*You* are accusing *me* of dishonesty?"

"Oh, you have Despard's interests at heart, I will allow that—but only because they are where your heart should be."

Dominique spat out a whole string of French obscenities such as Kate had never heard in her life, even from her father. Too late Dominique saw the mistake she had made; that Kate, only too like her father, also rose to any challenge, also took boundless pride in her ancestry. She should not have come; she should have left this girl in happy ignorance, let the long moldering and festering ideas retain their grip on her life, but no, she had had to come and shake them all loose. Fool! Dominique screamed at herself. Idiot! Imbecile!

Kate did not move, though she wanted to. A fiend looked at her out of Dominique du Vivier's eyes. In elevating her and her mother to the status of personal demons, it would seem she had not been wrong. She had never seen anything like the one now staring at her from the face of an angel.

"You will regret this," the fiend was saying.

"I don't think so. Whatever was between my father and myself—and that is none of your business either—the fact remains that I am his flesh and blood; you, who are wholly French, should appreciate what that means. He had continued, in spite of everything, to think of me as his daughter, and it is as Catriona Despard that he has remembered me. I don't give a damn about what you think is right. I don't give a damn about anything you might care to say or do. Had my father not cared about me he would not have left me so much as a fare-thee-well. You had your twelve years in which to persuade him to favor you, but in the end I was the one he was thinking of." Now Kate smiled; it was as cruel as anything Dominique was capable of. "I will accept what my father is offering, and gratefully. Kate Despard rules, okay?"

"Not for long!" Dominique hissed. The door slammed behind her, making the bell panic and the window rattle.

"A hell of a sight longer than you expect!" Kate shouted after her. Adrenaline was coursing through her veins, but she still had to sit down. When she lifted her hand it was trembling. Could it be true? Was she guessing right? Had her father actually left her Despard's? It couldn't be . . . but it had to be. What else would bring that bitch to hotfoot it to try and stop her from accepting? It had to be Despard's London, the flagship of Despard et Cie. "It has to be," Kate said aloud, getting up to walk to the lacquer screen, turning around to pace agitatedly the other way. "Oh, why didn't I listen to what that man had to say? Why didn't I let him tell me for sure. I've got to get hold of him—tell him I've changed my mind . . ." His card! Where did I throw his card? She went on her hands and knees and scrabbled in the wastepaper basket. It was gone! Oh, God, she thought— what was his name? Blaise . . . yes, that was it. Blaise what? Her father's executor. Despard's would know. Yes, call Despard's . . . She got to her feet again, felt calmer. Despard's, she thought. *My father has left me Despard's.* Oh, Papa, Papa . . . all this time you tried to make it up to me and I wouldn't let you but you still left me your very heart . . . She caught her breath with a sob, smeared tears away with the heels of her hands. She sobbed, sniffed again. I'll make it up to you. I'll show you I am worthy of your name, that I am the Despard I refused to be: the continuation of a line that began more than two hundred years ago. I haven't forgotten anything, not really. I only locked it away. I tried to forget but I couldn't, not Despard's, not you—ever.

And then she realized that the horrible feeling of nausea that had always overcome her at the mere mention of her father's name had gone, had not been present from the moment Dominique dismissed him as a sentimental old fool. From then on she was no longer battling against the head-winds of prejudice and injured pride, but had changed tack and found herself running before the breeze of confidence and restored self-esteem.

Now, as she stood at the window of her little shop, staring out unseeingly at the busy King's Road, she felt she had accomplished something infinitely more satisfying than any-thing else she had done in the past twelve years, except perhaps coming first in her class at the Courtauld. Then, as now, she had thought the same thing: *Papa would have been so proud of me . . .*

What *has* happened to me? she marveled, utterly at a loss to account for her radical about-face in her attitude toward her father. Perhaps it had to do with her self-created de-mons; in her mind they had been one thing, in the flesh they were something else again. The arrogance of the bitch! The condescending, patronizing—Kate found she was still seeth-ing. How dare she condemn Papa as sentimental! Loving yes, deeply loving. But not a man given to making sentimental gestures. No, Dominique would never be able to explain away Papa's action that way. She had just assumed too much, that was all. She had already been given so much—beauty, elegance, physical attraction—perhaps it was only natural she should assume her stepfather would give her Despard's, too. Yes, Kate thought. That is a woman who thinks she has a right to whatever she wants. Well, she won't get Despard's. I may not have her experience, but thank God for those endless Saturdays. Papa taught me so much, all of it remembered. She had repressed the memories, but still had almost total recall of what had been learned, if not sitting on her father's knee, then leaning against it. Thank God I also inherited Papa's flypaper memory, Kate thought thankfully. And so much else! Oh, Papa, forgive me, please forgive me. I have played the spoiled child far too long. Today I have finally grown up . . .

Rollo took one look at her and demanded, "*Now* what?"

"I had a visitor." Kate told him all "She was so damned superior! She looked at me so—so pityingly, as though I was some sort of circus freak. And she was so condescending toward Papa. If you had heard her dismissing him as a sentimental old fool! It got my goat, Rollo. She came to tell me that, of course, his bequest was no more than a gesture, and if I knew what was good for me I would realize that and leave the field free for her." Kate snorted. "The hell I will!"

Rollo said nothing, just looked at her in a way that had her pale face turning a hot, humiliated red. "I know . . ." she mumbled. "I seem to have done a U-turn. But it's not too late, is it?" she asked anxiously. "I mean—to tell Mr. Chandler?"

Rollo pursed his lips in such a way that Kate's flush ebbed away.

"Oh, God, it's not too late, is it? He said I would have to sign a revocation . . ."

"Blaise Chandler left London last night," Rollo said. "He has gone to France to attend your father's funeral."

Kate was quenched. She turned and walked to the window where she stood staring out at nothing, her back stiff. Reading it, Rollo walked across, laid one hand on her shoulder. "No, love. It would not do. For one thing, the present Madame Despard would not welcome your presence. Later on, well, you can visit his grave at your leisure."

"Isn't it odd?" Kate said in a wobbly voice. "I really did think he was dead to me. I was so sure he was—" Her voice broke. "Why does it hurt then, Rollo? Why do I grieve?"

"Because hatred was your means of handling the grief you've been toting with you these past twelve years. You never ceased to love your father, Kate. It's messed up your life—physically and emotionally—but maybe now you can stop marking time and start moving forward again."

"I loved him so much," Kate said in a stifled voice.

"That," Rollo pronounced trenchantly, "is the understatement of this or any year, but as it is in the right direction I will forbear to say more. However, I do have things to say in another direction, Blaise Chandler having, so to speak, shown me the way." To Kate's sudden nervousness he turned an imperious face, and in his best Edith Evans delivery, intoned, "I am empowered to inform you that your father's legacy consists of his most precious possession, Despard's of London."

Although only confirming Kate's suspicions, it still came as a stunning shock to her.

"Your sister is rightly incensed because she has been fobbed off with the minor branches—Paris, Geneva, Monte Carlo, and Hong Kong—you both get to use New York and have one full year's trading to prove who is best fitted to take overall control of Despard's International. We are to meet Blaise Chandler next week when he will explain all the fine print. In the meantime, now that not only your eyes but also your ears are open, it is time you heard the truth about your parents' so-called fairytale marriage."

"You blew it!" was Blaise's laconic greeting to his wife when he met her at Marseilles.

She eyed him surmisingly, a little frown knitting her perfect eyebrows into a stitch.

"Oh, Rollo Bellamy could not wait to get word to me," Blaise assured her.

"So I made a mistake," Dominique shrugged. "But it will be the last where she is concerned."

That she had made this one entirely suited Blaise's plans, but as always he knew better than to let her see so.

"What on earth made you do it?" he asked instead, curiously and, now that things were going his way, sympathetically. "It was the proverbial red rag to a bull. One look at you and she quite naturally came out fighting."

"I underestimated her," Dominique answered calmly. "I had forgotten that she is half English and therefore quite capable of saying one thing and doing another. The English always were supreme exponents of the art of declining a share whilst busy taking it all."

"Is that what you think she wants?"

"What she wants and what she will get—"

"Are two different things. I know the lyrics," Blaise interrupted. "All the same, don't discount her talents. By all accounts, they are considerable."

Dominique waved a very dismissive hand. "Talent is no substitute for experience."

"Wrong. It is experience that is no substitute for talent. I asked a few pertinent questions around fine art circles when I was in London and the general opinion is that she has inherited all her father's gifts. The word used—and I quote—was a 'natural.' "

Dominique laughed, the enchanting gurgle that took hold of men by the ear and held them suspended. "Yes, she is that, all right."

"Which you should have remembered," Blaise pointed out, fielding the ball. "Plain women like her do not appreciate having that fact rubbed in by beautiful women like you. You do tend to dim what light other women try to shed; that was why a face-to-face confrontation was wrong. You are everything she is not; you are also the nearest thing to a daughter her father had for the past twelve years. What *were* you thinking of?"

That I had it all, Dominique was thinking. How could I not have? New York had confirmed it. I was so sure that my plans had worked—well, so they are delayed. Be assured, Kate Despard. I will win in the end. I always do . . .

"So tell me," Kate said that night. They had had supper, the dishes had been washed and put away, and Rollo was sitting comfortably with his Courvoisier and his coffee, Kate on the floor at his feet in front of the gas fire with its simulated coal. "That truth you mentioned before. What did you mean?"

Rollo sipped at his brandy. "If your mother had had any sense she would have sat you down and made you listen all those years ago, but she never could face her own emotions, never mind anyone else's; she was a neat soul and in her opinion emotions were untidy things. Many's the time I longed to box your ears, except you always had your hands over them in stubborn refusal to give your father the benefit of the slightest doubt, hell-bent on his damnation. Your mother never had the heart to disillusion you, you see. She always knew that you were your father's daughter; that you were also a spite-nourisher and a sulky, spoiled brat she refused to see."

"Who wrote that?" Kate jibed, not a little angry and hurt at Rollo's catalogue of her faults. "Beaumont and Fletcher? You've been resting too long."

"Only on my laurels."

Still trying to make a joke of it, she retorted, "Is that why you are so bent on crowning me? You never had any love for my father that I knew of."

"It is your love we are going to talk about, dear heart."

"Then get to the point—if you have not already broken it."

"I have been sharpening it for years, ready to write the salient facts, like, for instance, that your father married your mother because he got her pregnant."

Time went by on tiptoe as the silence held its breath, broken only by the ticking of the clock and the faint hiss of the gas. Kate's eyes were wide and fixed as she stared into Rollo's unblinking ones.

"He got drunk one night, as a result of meeting his long lost love again—the woman he later left your mother for—and so smashed that he crashed his car and got arrested. Your mother bailed him out, took him home and offered him succor. He took it . . . and her to bed. He was so drunk he didn't even know who he was with; he kept calling her Catherine . . . And all that he felt for her he poured into your mother. Who duly conceived."

"How do you know this?" Kate asked when she could.

"Your mother told me."

Kate turned her head away, sat staring rigidly into the flames of the fire.

"Like all stories this one begins a long time ago, in 1946. That was the year your father, having returned to France not long before to pick up what was left of Despard's, went into the Ile de France to visit the Marquis de Villefort. Despard's had done no business during the Occupation;

Charles' father had prudently sent his son to London with everything that was worth anything in the summer of 1939. Despard's put up the shutters and, when the Germans came, Charles' father was able to say quite truthfully that he had nothing. For that bit of fast work he got sent to Frennes, where he vanished. When Charles returned to Paris after the war it was to tidy up his father's estate; it was then that de Villefort approached him about his collection of Sèvres, which had been hidden in sacks at the bottom of their moat. Charles went down to the chateau to look at it. That was where he first saw his *belle Catherine;* eighteen years old and ravishingly beautiful. It was, as his countrymen have it, a veritable *coup de foudre.*" Rollo paused. "She was, indeed, exquisite. Your mother showed me the picture your father always carried."

Kate turned her head to look at him; shock had her speechless.

"You didn't know that, did you? That all his married life—to your mother I mean—he carried a picture of another woman around with him."

Kate silently turned her head to gaze again into the flames.

"Unfortunately, Catherine was engaged to Guy du Vivier; the sale of the Sèvres was her dowry, and her parents had no time for her adolescent mooning about a nobody who kept a shop. When she said she wanted to break off her engagement and marry this same nobody they made her a virtual prisoner. Charles was banished—after they had come to a profitable arrangement about the Sèvres, of course, so very French—and Catherine safely married off. Your father had made plans for them to elope, but Catherine was too well guarded. He was in London when he read, in a copy of one of the French magazines his mother used to send him, all about Catherine's grand wedding."

When Rollo paused to sip at his brandy, Kate asked in a funny little voice, "Could I have some, please?"

Rollo obliged, watched her sip it, and when he thought she was ready, resumed his story. "Your mother was never the love of your father's life; he never loved her at all. Catherine de Villefort—du Vivier as she became—was the one woman he ever really wanted—for life, I mean. He had lots of *petites amours,* to which your mother turned two blind eyes, but they were never more than willing bodies to satisfy his physical needs. He was highly sexed, another aspect of his *mésalliance* with your mother—she was about as sexy as a wet weekend in Wigan. Her libido was stillborn. Anyway, your father's emotions had been taken over by Catherine de Villefort from the very first moment he set eyes on her, and he never got them back. I have all this from your mother—Charles told her and she told me. But to return to my tale . . . At the time of Catherine's marriage your mother came to work at Despard's; she kept their books. When your father acquired the St. James's site in 1948, she went with him and set up the new accounting department. He came to depend on her in many ways, and when she asked him if he could slot me in somewhere at a time when I needed somewhere to bestow myself, he readily agreed because it was for her. I had met her during the war, when we worked together and we became good friends; I was as fond of Susan Mallory as I was fond of anybody. Everybody liked your mother. That was her tragedy. Everybody liked her but nobody ever loved her."

"I did," Kate said, in a voice that bled.

"I know, but you also idealized her."

"She never asked for much—" Kate's voice cracked.

"Which is why she never got anything. People take you at your face value; something I have told you before. Susan never expected anything so she got nothing. Anyway, she and Charles became good friends. She was a good listener; she never had anything to tell but she could always listen. And it was Susan to whom your father told his sad tale of woe about his abortive love for Catherine; he used her quite selfishly and shamelessly as his wailing wall, pouring out his troubles, his feelings, his love, while she, good-natured to the last, sat tenderly and sympathetically by, soothing and comforting him."

Rollo sighed. "Just like Susan. Your father maudlin about his lost love and your mother providing soothing comfort while other women provided the sex; this is how things went on until 1951. That was the year of the Festival of Britain." Rollo shuddered. "Thank God you are too young to know anything about that, though it was indirectly the cause of your conception, because who should come over to take a look-see but the Vicomte and Vicomtesse du Vivier. Now the Vicomte was a nasty piece of work, handsome as all get out but a real son of a bitch. He liked to see people suffer. He knew all about his rival because he'd more or less tortured it out of Catherine, so what does he do but turn up at Despard's, her on his arm, with every intention of inflicting a little more of the same. Your father and Catherine du Vivier took one look at each other and it was as though the last five years had never been; nothing had changed. Each was still the love of the other's life. Guy du Vivier made a great fuss about them being old friends and proceeded to crucify them both on his particular cross of Lorraine. By the time he bore his wife away Charles was bleeding from the soul, and in his agony did what many a man has done before him; he got roaringly, blindingly, legless drunk and drove his car into a lamppost!

"Naturally, it was Susan he asked for when he was able to ask for anything. And she duly came down to the station and spun them a story about him having received the worst possible news, et cetera, et cetera. So they let him off with a fine and she toted him back to her flat in Belsize Park, where he sobbed out his troubles. She soothed him, patted him, made him black coffee, but he was in such drunken confusion that his gonads got the better of him and he took Susan's comfort for invitation and, as they say, forced his attentions on her, lost in fantasies about his beloved Catherine. Next morning, like all drunks, he remembered not one single thing except getting drunk. Your mother refrained from telling him he had all but raped her, and saw him off to work with commendable calm. Your mother, you see, was a virgin."

He heard the little sound that escaped Kate's compressed lips, knew he was turning her fairytale into a nightmare, but she had asked him to tell her the truth and he was doing exactly that.

"A couple of months later she came to me and said she was sure she was pregnant. She was absolutely radiant, and when I suggested a good man I knew she was primly horrified; she intended to have this baby. She had never expected to be so fortunate. And who, I asked, was going to provide the necessary wherewithal? Normally one would assume the child's father, but knowing her and her attitude to sex she had to have been visited by the Holy Ghost. When she told me it was Charles Despard I was, as they say, floored by the proverbial feather. She was sure, she said, sounding apologetic, that he would accept his responsibilities. She was actually anxious that he might suspect her of gold-digging! I pointed out that he could well afford it; Despard's was burgeoning even as she was. I offered to go with her—I wanted to see his face—but she wouldn't have it. It was between the two of them, she said.

"Next thing I know, she invites me to Caxton Hall. It seems that when she told Charles he had at first been appalled and then, as the idea grew on him, convinced that it was fate. You know the French and their fortune-tellers. He had been coming round to the idea that he had to marry to provide an heir; his two younger brothers had died in the war, both unmarried. He was the last Despard unless he provided a son. Here was his answer. He would marry Susan and have that son. They did not love each other but they liked each other; they got on extremely well and he knew she would make a superb mother. The child must be born in wedlock if it was to inherit under French law—he was still thinking in terms of France at that time—so it had to be marriage. For the sake of the child they would make a go of it. Many marriages had been made on far less. There was no hope where Catherine was concerned but—and this was Susan and her bloody sense of honor again—she insisted on a stipulation; if, at some future date, there was any chance of Charles having his Catherine then he was to feel free to have her. The one thing she asked was that the child remain with her if it was a girl. If it was a son, well . . ." Rollo sniffed again. "Bloody fool. Her and her Elsie Dinsmore ethics."

Once again Kate made that small sound, a cross between a moan and a sob.

"It was a marriage of convenience in every sense of the word—suitable, advantageous, comfortable, useful. Love never came into it at all. For both of them, the overriding matter of importance was the child—the son he wanted, the child she wanted, male or female. It was for the sake of the child that they got married at all."

"Me," Kate said.

"You. A quiet ceremony at Caxton Hall with me as a witness, and seven months later you were born. The fact that you were a girl was initially a disappointment to your father, but from the first you were Daddy's girl. He had wanted a replica of self—ego can go no further—but on you he lavished all the thwarted love he could not give to Catherine. And when, as you grew older, you began to display your heritage—that was it! He was bent and determined that you would take over from him. He would teach you all he knew, make you the greatest expert ever in Oriental porcelain; he had your future all mapped out and you just went along with him. Whatever he wanted was fine by you. The fact that you had inherited not only his talent but his love meant more to him than anything because he knew that love can never be taught—or learned. The Saturdays you spent with him at Despard's were the high spot of his week. He would come back and tell your mother every single word you had said; everything you had done, each and every question you had asked. In every respect except gender you were the replica he had wanted, so close a knife would not have slid between you."

"How come I ended up with one in my back, then?" Kate's voice was thick.

"He would never have gone to Catherine had he not been sure you would come round in time. Your mother told him he had unrestricted access; she knew you were your father's daughter much more than hers. My own opinion is that the second Mrs. Despard wanted no rivals. She had waited years to have Charles Despard and she wanted him unencumbered. I gather she is more than a mite possessive."

"And already had a daughter of her own."

"Even so. Your mother paved the way for your father to leave and eased his conscience out with him. What he had not even begun to consider was your reaction; that you would be so devastated, so mortally hurt that from the moment he walked out on you he was as good as dead. You told him so, remember? When you locked yourself in your bedroom and would not come out to him, plead though he might."

Kate needed no reminder; she could still feel the pain, could still hear her father's desperate voice. She had replayed that last day over in her memory ten thousand times, relived the words she had screamed at him: "If you leave this house and me then you are dead! Dead, do you hear? And I hope you burn in hell for it!"

Reading, as always, her expressive face, Rollo said quietly, "It was your mother he was married to but his daughter who acted like the jealous wife."

"He betrayed me. You just told me how I was Daddy's

girl. I believed that. I believed him. He lied." Kate was weeping.

"Like a great many men, he said a great many things which he never expected would come back to haunt him."

"Or prevent him from throwing me over for another woman."

There was a short, electric silence until, even as Kate's head came up to reveal her wet face and anguished eyes, Rollo asked softly, "Threw *you* over for another woman?"

"Go on, say it!" she screamed at him. "I was in love with my own father!"

"So?" Rollo was unshaken. "Isn't that how women are supposed to learn about love and men? Your trouble is that in your case, the fact that your father left you to go to another woman did you in emotionally. Where most women turn to or look for a man who reminds them of their father, you run a mile if any man so much as looks at you. You dress the way you do to make sure they don't. Those God-awful jeans, the sweat shirts, that hideous bomber jacket. I may not be a practicing heterosexual, but in my day, sweat was not a word one associated with a woman."

"I don't give a damn what or who you associate with. My life is mine to run. I've always given you a great deal of leeway, Rollo. Don't push your luck!"

Staring her down with his cold-water eyes, "You asked me for the truth, dear heart. It does not come out sanitized for your protection when *I* tell it."

For a moment they locked eyes, then Rollo, smiling to take the sting away, said, "Your father left you, Kate, because much as he loved you there was one thing you could not—incest being our last remaining taboo—give him. Your father needed sex regularly and often. That is what made him so attractive to women; he was a sexual animal. With your mother he had no sexual life; she did not attract him that way—more important, she had no interest in sex. It was Catherine de Villefort who had everything he wanted in a woman. From what I have since heard she has not one whit of your mother's compassion, her kindness, quickness or depth of mind, but Charles was not looking for those qualities. He wanted somebody who would be good in bed; somebody who would be an ornament and an adornment to him and to Despard's, and who would never have a headache when he wanted sex."

Kate had a funny, lost look on her face, so sad that for a moment he felt an unaccustomed pang in the region of his own heart. He had wanted to tell her all this for so long; now he found himself sharing her misery and pain. Love, he thought furiously, it will fuck you up every time.

So, with a sigh, he said, "Men are physical creatures, as I have good cause to know. They don't particularly care how clever, compassionate or understanding you are; what turns them on is a beautiful face, the soft curve of a breast, the promise of sex. We are biologically chained, all of us." Now his voice was bitter. "Ruled by our cocks—if you will forgive the graffiti. Your father left a good wife and a loving daughter because neither of them could provide what he really needed. In your obsession with your own needs, did you ever give a thought to what his might be?"

Kate burst into wracking sobs.

"That's better. Cry it away. All part of the healing process. I never thought to be thankful to the Venus Flytrap but God knows I am. She has made you grow up, accept that nobody is perfect. People do terrible things to each other in the name of love; they are weak, vain, selfish, greedy, but in the end, all we have."

Kate raised her blotched face to him. "Are you now telling me that people *are* worth the effort?"

"I am telling you that your father is. He did you a wrong which he righted in the only way he could. He has left you his most precious possession. Not his wife, not his step-daughter—you, the daughter he adored. Take it and prove to him you are that daughter and a Despard. If he could understand the strength of your hatred, the least you can do is forgive the weakness of his will."

"Not just a sop to conscience?"

"Surely the fact that he has turned out to have one is in his favor!" The gravelly voice became a shower of stones. "Has nothing I have said penetrated that stubborn prejudice of yours?"

"You have disabused my fond belief that I was the product of a happy marriage. Will that do for now?"

"Whatever the marriage, you cannot deny you had a very happy childhood." He thrust his handkerchief into her hands. "Here, wipe your eyes and blow your nose. I'll go and make some tea."

When he came back she was quiet, subdued, her eyes dry if red.

She gave him a watery smile. "How have you ever put up with me all these years?"

"By the time you took a turn for the worse I was in too deep. Besides, your mother asked me to look out for you."

Kate's face and eyes were as mournful as those of a bloodhound. "You should have looked out for yourself. I must have been the most tiresome child . . ."

"Well, you've grown up at last, haven't you?"

Kate was silent for a moment, then said in a low voice, "I feel so ashamed."

"That's the adult talking, thank God."

"I suppose," Kate went on slowly, "that I only ever saw him through those same child's eyes because I stubbornly refused to grow up. If I had, then I would have had to see him in a different light and—and, just as obviously, I could not bear to . . ." Remembering, for no good reason that she could think of, Blaise Chandler, she said in a wistful little voice, "I don't blame him, you know, Rollo. Now that I know, I don't blame him at all . . ." The wistfulness now tinged with bitterness, "Because I understand, at last, I suppose."

Kate finished her tea, laying down her cup. "So much to think over, so much to sort out . . . This has been the most traumatic couple of days in my life."

"Thankfully tomorrow is Sunday. You can sleep late and think long."

"I do feel like I could sleep for a week."

"Emotional exhaustion and that long walk you took, as well as the Mickey Finn I just gave you. That's enough for any one person to handle in a lifetime, but you've got a lot more coming your way."

Sounding fearful, Kate asked in a small voice, "You'll help me, won't you, Rollo? I need you more than ever now . . ."

"Try and stop me!" He put down his own cup. "Now bed," he ordered authoritatively. "We have work to do and I want you rested when you do it. There is no time to be lost if you have declared war on your stepsister. Tomorrow we shall begin our studies."

Kate's look was full of questions.

"You are forgetting," he reminded her imperturbably. "I too worked for Despard's and, unlike you, I have kept in touch. I still know what is going on, Kate, and the sooner I acquaint you with it the better."

To Kate, everything suddenly seemed to have assumed the surrealist qualities of the Mad Hatter's tea party; now she understood why he had made them all shift around the table, to see things from a different angle. She was chair-hopping herself now, only to be confounded and dumb-founded by so much, long hidden from her, which at last she saw plain. What Rollo had told her, with brutal bluntness, had had the cumulative effect of several hard slaps across the face, shocking her out of her hysterical fixation and bringing her back to the cold light of reality. *Cinema verité* indeed.

She lay wide-eyed that night, unable to sleep, unable to get her mind out of high gear. By 6 A.M. she was up, in her jogging suit and on her way through the empty backstreets of Chelsea, heading toward Hyde Park. She jogged regularly; she liked the exercise. At school she had always been good at games, had played hockey and netball and been the school's swimming champion. She had also had a passionate love affair with horses in her early teens, been torn for a while between a career as a show jumper and the one she had long been bound to, in fine arts. The arts had won, but she still rode as often as she could. When she wanted to think, though, she either walked or jogged.

Now, as she jogged, her unfettered memory roamed through the corridors of her life, mostly following her father. She could see him plainly: stocky—her own height came from her mother and her raw-boned Scottish forebears—dark-haired but for the white wings at his temples, his *oloroso* sherry eyes smiling at her, crinkling at the sides into a fan of tiny lines. For the first time in years she allowed herself to remember her life with him, to think of things once too painful to permit of recall. One by one she brought them up from the basement and examined them, slowly and with forgotten pleasure, but no longer with the eyes of a child. She had grown up; almost overnight she had ceased to think and act as the fourteen year old who had been emotionally frozen in time by a particular event and unable to move beyond it.

Now, from the vantage point of her twenty-six years she looked back and understood so much, not least her parents' marriage, revealed for what it really was in the fierce light of truth that Rollo had shone upon it. She had, she realized now, woven a fantasy about it because her instincts sensed that something was not right, that her parents' marriage was not as others were. She had been fiercely protective not only of herself, but of them. Her severely pragmatic, common-sensical mother, and her romantic, passionate, artistic father. Chalk and cheese, she saw now.

How her father's spirit must have beaten against the bars of his cage! Susan Mallory was kind, a born mother, a superb housekeeper, a faithful friend, but she had no imagination and her world was one devoid of anything but practicalities. Not for Susan the impulsive purchase, the high-on-excitement, stab-in-the-dark decision. Everything was thought out, planned for, gone over a thousand times. Even her clothes were robustly plain: tweeds that would wear forever, sensible woolens—she would never buy cashmere as she said it was "not worth the money." A good lambswool from Marks and Spencer would be much more sensible. Yes, thought Kate, that was my mother's mantra word: sensible. Yet she had buried even that small criticism; when she had longed for pretty undies instead of the "sensible" ones her mother bought she had stifled any rebellious thoughts. Her mother knew best, didn't she? And she loved her. It was disloyal to criticize.

Yet, when her father had brought her some wildly impractical gift from a trip abroad, something with no use but capable of giving hours of pleasure from just being looked at, she had been overjoyed. She still had every gift he had ever bought her, locked away in a trunk she had put in storage when the house had been sold. She had treasured them because she had known her father understood. She well remembered how, after bringing back exquisite jewelry for her mother which she never wore—"I'm not one for fripperies, Charles, as you know"—her father had eventually ceased to do so, bringing instead things like a "sensible" leather handbag, or half a dozen crystal wine glasses, or an embroidered tablecloth, which her mother had approved of wholeheartedly. Kate had been careful—or so she had believed—not to hurt her mother by emphasizing the fact that two corners of the triangle were bound together in a way that could never include the third. Now, she saw that far from being hurt, her mother had not really given it any thought. "Catriona is her Daddy's girl," she used to say with stolid practicality and contented acceptance. Or, "Och, I don't understand all this artistic nonsense. I used to do the accounts, if you remember, and to my eye there's nothing so satisfying as a lovely column of figures that adds up to the correct total."

Yes, Kate thought now, Mother was concerned with the nuts and bolts of life, Papa saw only the grand design. When he came back from a trip, while Kate had hurled herself into his arms, hugging and kissing and being whirled around, laughing and all but crying with joy, her mother had merely said placidly, "Well, Charles? And did you have a good trip?" She would want to know what he had acquired, and from whom, and how—the nuts and bolts—while, to Kate, he would describe the pieces themselves, making her see them in her mind's eye in all their beauty. And later they would go to their separate rooms, making no attempt to find excuses to be alone, to celebrate being together again after an absence of sometimes a month or more. Now Kate knew that with his second wife, the moment Charles returned from a trip he would have found her waiting for him, bathed and perfumed and wearing something that had his eyes lighting and his body responding, and within minutes they would be in the bedroom they shared, in the big double bed, inside and in love with each other.

Yes, she thought now, jogging effortlessly, Dominique would have called you Papa; you were that kind of man. And in her way she must have admired you because she made porcelain her field, too. I hope you were happy—I know you were happy, when I saw pictures of you in the trades, you always looked it—which is probably why I made myself believe that mother died of a broken heart.

It had not been Tristan and Iseult, more Ruskin and Effie, with the roles reversed, Susan the prude to her husband's vigorous sexuality. As Rollo had said, Kate had been so obsessed with her own feelings she had not given so much as a thought to her father's loneliness and longing. She had never been able to visualize life without her father; her worst moments of terror had been on the infrequent occasions when he was ill—she had spent hours in church pleading to God not to let him die. During her mother's last illness she had accepted that it was only a matter of time, had nursed her devotedly but not raged, as she would have

done had it been her father, against the dying of that particular light.

She stopped her jogging, bent, hands on hips, to let her
lungs gulp in great drafts of air. What she had been doing
during the past twelve years, she realized, was mourning. It
was to channel her grief where she could handle it that she
transmuted it into hatred.

She walked to the nearest park bench and sat down, arms
spread along the back. She sat there for a long time, thinking, thinking. Then, slowly, she got to her feet and began
the long trek back. She was not surprised, when she came
out of her abstraction some time later, to find herself outside
the Ritz. There, on the opposite side of the road, was
Despard's.

She had not been here since the day her father left. For
years she had avoided this part of town if she could. Now,
her subconscious had brought her back. Now, she stood and
looked her fill. She did not realize that the passersby were
staring askance at the tall, flame-haired girl in the green
tracksuit, standing outside the Ritz, tears streaming . . .
Rollo had been right—as usual. It *was* in her blood; she *was*
a Despard. All this was hers. And by right. It had been her
father's heartbeart. Now, it was hers. She could feel it,
pulsing through her, on her lips, in her throat, at her fingertips.

When at last she turned to leave, there was a spring in her
step and her face was dry. She felt she had been set free
after years of solitary confinement.

Rollo, too, had passed an uneasy night, had also got up
early, and was around at the shop by ten. When he went
upstairs the small flat was empty, her tracksuit gone.

His sigh was relieved. At least he knew what she was
doing. But as the day passed, slowly, he began to worry. By
four o'clock he was standing at the window debating whether
or not to call the police. And then he saw her coming: no
mistaking that height, that hair. He examined her carefully.
She walked normally, with her loping stride, and she looked
cheerful. Thank God.

When she entered the flat he was stretched out on the
shabby old blue velvet *veilleuse*, *The Sunday Times* spread
over his face, but in keeping with his reputation as the light-
est of sleepers he stirred at once, taking away the newspaper
to ask with a yawn, "Oh, it's you. What time is it?"

"Just on four o'clock."

He sat up in astonishment. "Is it? I've been dozing . . ."

"Did you come round for lunch? Sorry I wasn't here. I went out early this morning. I wanted to think."

"I saw your jogging suit had gone."

"Have you had anything to eat? You must be awfully hungry."

He had made himself coffee and sandwiches earlier but he said, "I am rather. You?"

"Starving!"

"How far did you go?"

"God knows . . . I jogged all the way to Bayswater and then I sat for a while and then I jogged right round the park and then sat and thought a while longer . . ." She went into the bathroom but continued to talk from behind the half-open door. "Honestly never intended to end up at Despard's. I suppose my subconscious had taken over. It was the strangest feeling . . . But you know something? I feel enormously better for it. Like I'd finally managed to face something I'd avoided for years and found it was only a paper tiger."

He heard the shower go on and went to put the pork chops obviously intended for lunch under the grill, got out a packet of frozen broccoli and some lyonnaise potatoes that only needed heating. Kate had been taught how to cook by her mother, and she was a good one, but her interest in food was not great enough to make her spend valuable time in the kitchen.

Ten minutes later, wrapped in her old terry robe, her damp hair brushed and combed, she sat down to her beautifully grilled chop and cleaned her plate. Another good sign. Kate lost her appetite when she was emotionally disturbed.

"So you wrestled with your demons and sent them packing?" Rollo asked.

"Well, I think I might have won on points this time."

"Never mind; that you won is all that matters. American influence has made itself felt over here to such an extent that losing is now a dirty word with connotations of shame."

"That's how I felt," Kate admitted candidly. "But I think I've got it all straight, now."

Rollo eyed her empty plate. "At that, you could do with some rounding off. And apropos your figure, you are going to have to get a whole new wardrobe. Despard's clientele are not the type to appreciate your particular taste in fashion."

"I know." For the first time, Kate did not bridle at his aspersion.

"My, but we have changed."

"I hope so." Kate's newly acquired confidence would not be shaken, even by him. She yawned.

"We were going to work today," Rollo reminded tartly. "As it is, we have accomplished nothing."

"Oh, I don't know," Kate said in a way that had him eyeing her keenly. But she needed no reminder to sleep well. She was asleep as soon as her head hit the pillow.

She slept for fourteen hours, and when she awoke she smelled coffee. Getting up she reached for her robe. Rollo's Christmas present a couple of years before, it was of heavy bottle-green slipper satin, severely cut and the perfect foil for her broad shoulders and flaming hair. Rollo had bought it, he said, because it was only when she wore a man's robe that she looked like a woman.

He looked up as she came in.

"Well rested?" he inquired. "I have not opened the shop. I do not think we need to do so again. Besides it is Monday, and what we laughingly call our trade is ever slow at the beginning of the week."

He poured her a cup of coffee and she sat down at the well-scrubbed pine table, cradling the cup in her hands and smiling at him over it. "What would I do without you?" she asked him lovingly. "You truly are my guardian angel."

"I have not played an angel since my one and only excursion into a nativity play but I appreciate the sentiment. Now, let us get down to the work we should have done yesterday—"

"Later," Kate said, making him look at her with some surprise. "I have to go out for a while first."

To Rollo's eloquently raised eyebrows, she told him simply, "I am going to church."

He made no protest. "As you wish."

Charles had been a Catholic, but Susan, good Scots Calvinist that she was, had balked at baptizing her child into that faith, and so it had been left to Kate to decide when she was old enough, and she had not been christened at all. Now, what Kate *wanted* to do was find a Catholic church where she could ask the priest to pray for her father's soul. It was a thing she felt she must do. The priest was young, obviously curious, but he accepted Kate's donation and on being assured that her father was, that very day, being buried according to the rites of his faith, said the necessary prayers for him in her presence.

She felt better as she left the church. She had sat there for a while afterward, her mind full of her father, thinking of him, as she was now able to, without rancor, without the sickening wrench of grief and pain, but with love, with tenderness and deep gratitude. She prayed for him, she wept a little, but she felt lighthearted as she walked back home. Somehow, she felt that she had been forgiven.

Rollo eyed her keenly on her return but said nothing. He had no use for organized religion himself; in his view it had been responsible for more misery than any other single force in history, but if it had helped Kate, in this instance, to go on into an unknown future, then good enough. She was quiet throughout lunch, bemused almost, and he let her be. She was obviously not conscious of what she ate, and she sat for long periods, chin on hand, staring at nothing. But gradually she came out of it, and when she said, finally, "So, are we going to work, then?" he forbore to tell her that they had little left of the day and wasted no time in getting down to it, beginning with his conviction that her main trouble in the times ahead would be her stepsister.

"She has good reason to hate you for what you are as well as what your father has made you. She has her own jealousies—of your inherited instinct and flair. She's good, by all accounts, but it is all hard work and application. Fortunately she had the same teacher as you, but whereas you started off knowing it instinctively, she has had to acquire it the hard way. Never forget, though, that in that direction you have the advantage and capitalize on it. *You* are the Despard."

Kate nodded, absorbing his every word.

"Now, as to the rest . . . I am glad to be able to report that you have allies—the old diehards who still remember you with affection—even though they haven't seen you since you took your fit of the sullens."

Again Kate's flush was guilty and self-reproachful, but her voice was incredulous when she asked, "Not old Mr. Smythe?"

"Still restoring pictures. He's only seventy-five, you know, and at Despard's that is comparatively young. Besides, he is irreplaceable. George Hackett is still pottering about his beloved clocks and Henry Brooke his glass. I see them regularly."

Kate stared. Of course, that was typical of Rollo. He never let go a contact once established—you never knew when it might come in handy again. And he had worked for Despard's, hadn't he? Known all the people she had known? Just because she had severed the tie was no reason to expect him to do the same. She stared at the cynical, worldly-wise face. No, not Rollo. He always allowed for all kinds of eventualities. What was it that had told him to prepare for this one? Did he know more than he was telling? With him, all you ever saw was the tip of the iceberg. Many a *Titanic* had gone down on what lay hidden underneath.

Had he known—did he know—something he was still not telling? Well, she defended stoutly, it would be for my own good. I don't give a damn what other people say; he has never been anything but good to me and for me, so just be grateful that he has kept in touch, does know so much. So what if he is grinding his own ax—he always has, hasn't he? What matters is that I know he won't sink it between my shoulders. If I can't trust Rollo then I'm done for because there isn't anybody else I can trust. So she smiled, shook her head resignedly. "I might have known . . ."

"The last thing I needed before this weekend; you might have had me court martialed for consorting with the enemy. As it is, your little group of allies would like nothing more than to see your stepsister booted out of Despard's, because they all know that once she gets control that is precisely what she will do to them. She is all for modernizing and rationalizing and computerizing and suchlike. Her sweeping changes will have them in the dustbin along with the rest of the rubbish."

"That would be stupid!"

"She does not have your loyalty to old friends—to anyone, come to that. Her only loyalty is to herself, and—"

"How are they?" Kate interrupted.

"Always interested to hear about you. Which is why I kept in touch." Rollo paused. "It also kept me in touch with current gossip."

"Which is?"

"Let them tell you themselves. They are dying to. Wednesday morning—early." Another pause. "We meet Blaise Chandler at twelve."

Kate's head jerked up, questions in her eyes.

"Yes, it is all arranged," confirmed Rollo. "He knows you have changed your mind."

"You've talked to him?"

"On the telephone. He asked to be kept informed."

Kate frowned. "Is he to be trusted, do you think? He is my arch enemy's husband . . ."

"But his own man. Alas."

"Fancy him, do we?" Kate asked sweetly.

"Chance would be a fine thing. He's straight, and the fact that he is married to the Venus Flytrap tells me where *his* sexual preferences lie."

"It's his prejudices I'm worried about," Kate said darkly.

"He's been appointed umpire, not judge."

"Why, is what I'd like to know."

"Your father knew his stepdaughter, too," Rollo said obliquely.

"You mean she'll cheat," Kate said bluntly but with distaste. Such behavior was anathema to her.

"Uphill and down dale."

"But how can he penalize his own wife? He's bound to favor her in one way or another."

"I disagree. Your father would not have made him umpire unless he felt he could be trusted to be impartial. Besides, he and his wife don't exactly live in each other's pockets. On the contrary, I think he's got his sewn up."

"Well, I'm reserving judgment," Kate declared, remembering that first, acrimonious, no-holds-barred confrontation.

They spent the rest of the day discussing tactics, Rollo making Kate privy to all he knew about Despard's present standing, information culled from the "Old Timers," as he called them.

"Fortunately, there are still people at the top who remember you; not all of them are new, though the Venus Flytrap has managed to insinuate a few of her supporters where it matters—which means we will have to contend with a pro-Dominique faction. Also, if I know her, she'll have a mole well dug in."

"How come you know so much about her?" Kate felt a rush of jealousy. Hitherto Rollo had been her property, inasmuch as he could belong to anyone. She was miffed that he should be interested enough to find out so much about someone else. And a beautiful woman to boot.

"We have met on the odd occasion," Rollo shrugged, forbearing to say that there had not been too many and that they had been quite deliberate on his part, in keeping with his need to know what went on at Despard's. His information had been that Dominique du Vivier's power there was as great as her physical attractions, but ever mindful of the letters that had kept coming to Kate, Rollo had realized that Charles was not wholly in thrall. Which meant a loose end somewhere, and one had to be vigilant for the opportunity to get hold of it and pull. After their first meeting he had known that he would like nothing better than to unravel that bitch's very carefully created pattern.

His rancor must have been in his voice, because Kate, ever sensitive to its slightest nuance, exclaimed delightedly, "You didn't get on?"

"It was a case of hate at first sight. She can't bend homosexuals to her will, you see, and men are her stock in trade." He gave Kate one of his wide-eyed looks. "Besides, the very first time we met, it turned out we both had our eye on the same prospect—"

Kate burst out laughing. For a moment, she had wondered . . . But of course they would not get on. Rollo, she supposed, was the one person who would see the real Dominique behind the façade. He always had been able to see the skull beneath the skin. Thank God, she thought with relief. The thought of Rollo and Dominique du Vivier getting together was unthinkable. Then why are you thinking it, she scolded herself.

That night, for the first time in many months, she got out her carefully and secretly amassed hoard of newspaper cuttings and photographs, culled from the dailies, the trades, the Sundays, and various glossy monthlies and pasted into a scrapbook. This time, she examined with greater care than usual those photographs containing Catherine Despard, noting, for the first time, the way she looked at her husband: worshipfully. Yes, she was lovely, if somewhat doll-like, the antithesis of raw-boned Susan Despard with her deflating common sense and solid lack of imagination. This woman obviously based her life on that of her husband—submissive, sexually serene, sophisticated. Susan Despard had, Kate realized now, lived her own life; she had only lived in the same house as her husband, though she had always taken a keen interest in Despard's. Catherine Despard was exquisitely dressed, lavishly bejeweled. She looked like the wife of a rich, successful man. Susan, Kate remembered now, had gone to Despard's dinners rarely, and when her father had entertained clients or associates it had usually been in a restaurant because his wife had been painfully shy, turning stiff as paint in the presence of strangers. Which was probably why, Kate also realized with a pang, her father had been at pains to see that Kate mixed easily, sending her to school to make friends and learn the social graces.

But no way as successfully as her stepsister. Once again gazing at that flowerlike face Kate felt her heart sink. How could she compete with that? Deeply insecure about her lack of looks, she had always hated her plainness since the day she had inadvertently overheard her Scots grandmother, as ruthlessly practical as her daughter, observe trenchantly, "She'll never be a beauty so it's to be hoped the good Lord gifted her with brains, because this one is going to have to fend for herself."

That still hurt, still had the power to propel her out of bed and across to the mirror on her dressing table. A death's head, she thought. Cheekbones like shelves and a mouth that had been slashed with a knife. And she had been either "Ginger" or "Carrots" all her life. She wished she could put on weight. She had not an ounce of surplus flesh, and what she had was stretched thin. She pinched her pale cheeks, winced yet again at the sight of her freckles. Her grandmother had been so right. Men had been conspicuous in her life so far by their absence. Of course, she thought justifyingly, I took good care to avoid them except where absolutely necessary. She had resolved, after her father's betrayal, never to trust a man again and had unconsciously adopted a bristlingly suspicious attitude toward them, with predictable results. But their avoiding her she unhesitatingly put down to her lack of looks. Everyone knew that men gravitated toward the pretty girls; hadn't she seen it happen often enough at school? She herself had been wallflower of this and every other year.

She went back to bed disconsolately. Dominique, now, had been created with hands in love with their work; she looked as if she was unpacked every day from a satin-lined jewelry case. But there was something else about her that thrust itself at you: an all-pervading sexuality. Something else, Kate thought with a pang, that she herself totally lacked. Shoving the book aside, she slid down in the bed and pulled the duvet over her head, a childhood habit when she was unhappy.

It was a case of brains versus beauty, that was all. Kate was as confident about her capabilities as she was lacking in confidence about her looks. She knew she was clever and had the prizes to prove it. She also had the beginnings of a reputation as an expert on Oriental porcelain, as well as one for probity and honest dealing. But was that enough to run a major auction house? She knew *how* Despard's was run; her father had explained it all to her, and he was the kind of man who, once he had a thing running perfectly, did not tinker with the works. So the past twelve years would not have changed its administration much. The art world itself she was familiar with. But running people? Her own little shop was something else compared to a business like Despard's. Rollo stood in for her when she went to sales, but it was a one-on-one situation. Despard's was many-layered. Her father as chairman and managing director at the top; his heads of department beneath, their managers beneath them, with the layer of administrative staff below them. Then there was the Accounts, and the Catalogue Department; there was Packing and Storage; Shipping and Export; and there was the department that dealt with the ramifications of the Department of Trade, with its tax and valuation experts. Despard's employed—or had when she knew it—close to a thousand people. She would have to control them, too. A rush of apprehension made her flesh crisp. A lot would have changed in twelve years; some people had gone, others had come. But she had her three oldest friends to look forward to, as much a part of Despard's as the bricks of which it was built. And there were others whom she remembered from her past, people who had been loyal to her father. Would they, though, be loyal to her as her father's daughter—or to the woman they knew?

Well, she thought, time will tell. And if I don't do it right, a hell of a sight sooner than I care to think about. But already, in the pit of her stomach, was a small tight ball of tension at the thought of Wednesday's meeting with Blaise Chandler, her father's emissary, on whose opinion Rollo seemed to think so much rested. Just exactly what powers did an executor have? All Kate knew was that they were somehow responsible for carrying out the instructions of a person's will. Had her father given such instructions to his son-in-law? It was that relationship which was most worrying, she decided. She just did not see how he could fail to be prejudiced against her. What were the odds against him being his wife's *agent provocateur?* He had to be loyal to her before all else. Husbands were—weren't they? Then she remembered her father leaving her mother and knew that for the fallacy it was. They were loyal so long as they loved them. But with a wife as exquisitely breathtaking as Dominique du Vivier, how could he fail to love her? Oh God, she thought, I'm getting myself into a state already. Calm down, she thought, drawing deep breaths as Rollo had taught her. Think soothing thoughts. She climbed out of bed, got down on the carpet, and assumed the lotus position, her long limbs folding themselves effortlessly into place. Kate had an athlete's coordination.

Hands lax, eyes closed, she breathed, counted, breathed, found herself eventually floating free of the grip of her tension; her heart rate slowed, her clenched muscles relaxed, and when finally she uncoiled herself and drifted back into bed, she fell asleep immediately.

4

When Catherine de Villefort married Charles-Edouard Guy du Vivier, her dowry, by that instant and obliterating transformation of which only the French are capable, at once became his as if it always had been. The de Villeforts had the money but the du Viviers had the lineage. They belonged to the *noblesse immemoriale,* being descended (in the female line) from the factions that had put Hughes Capet on the throne of France in 978, whereas the de Villeforts were merely *noblesse de robe.* But since the French nobility had always put money and power before quarterings, and Catherine de Villefort brought with her a considerable fortune, the marriage was celebrated with due pomp and circumstance.

Catherine came to her husband virginal and unbelievably innocent, as well as being hopelessly in love with another man. He came to her debauched, degenerate, and disillusioned, and although her flowerlike beauty and virginity held some slight appeal, once he had made her pregnant—which was on the third night of their honeymoon—he lost interest and returned to his whores, his boys, and his peculiar pleasures. Catherine was dispatched to the du Vivier chateau in Normandy to await the birth of her child, obedient and desperately unhappy.

She had known her marriage was, like most French aristocratic marriages, a trade, and that the prime mover had been her mother, who had been born Hortense Schmeisser in Alsace, the daughter of a millionaire foundry owner who was also a Jew. During the war, the RAF bombed the Schmeisser works to dust and smoke, and the reparations were a long time in coming. The Germans had looted the chateau of every work of art they could find, but the priceless collection of Sèvres had been hidden, wrapped in sacks, and lowered into the moat. It was this collection that Charles Despard came to inspect and, eventually, to take back to Paris, where he sold it for considerably more than even the Marquise had hoped for. Her daughter was safe. She would not suffer the snubs and slights that had been Hortense Schmeisser's portion. She would be *noblesse immemoriale*. Nobody would dare. All this was impressed on the silent Catherine, who had been brought up to do exactly as she was told. She did not love her parents, but she feared them. She had never loved anybody until she met Charles Despard, when it hit her with such force that it unbalanced her slightly, a balance that was to become even more precarious as the years went by.

When her husband casually started knocking her about, she knew it would be a waste of time to tell her parents, so she took to her bed, where she stayed until her daughter was born. Dominique was the image of her father, who was inordinately pleased even though he had wanted a son. When his wife's doctors told him that his daughter would be his only child he was at first furious, but as he had been told by his own that he was now entering the final stages of syphilis of the brain, he conceded that perhaps it was just as well. His daughter he spoiled to ruination; he called her *petite reine* and she grew up believing she was indeed someone very special, which was reinforced by her acknowledged extraordinary beauty. For her father she cherished an admiring adoration; he was—until his disease began to ravage him—the most handsome man she had ever seen; he was also dashing, commandingly arrogant, and wholly self-centered. What he wanted he took; he had neither time nor interest for the little people whose duty it was to give, which belief he inculcated in his daughter.

For her mother Dominique felt nothing but contempt. She was weak, timid, hopelessly vague, spending most of her time up in her tower room sewing and dreaming of her long lost prince. Guy du Vivier had told his daughter the whole story as an enormous joke as soon as she was old enough to understand. Nothing her father did to her mother produced any sign of spirit; even when he made her watch him disporting himself with women, or boys, or a mixture of both, she sat, hands folded, eyes open but not seeing, and remained like a ghost until he shouted at her to get out of his sight. When, in his now rapid descent into madness, her father invited her to watch, Dominique had done so coolly and critically, afterward offering comment with a dispassionate calm that, for once, made him shiver and look at his daughter uncertainly. For the first time he wondered what he had created here—what lay behind the flawless face and perfect body. He only knew it made his own depravity seem like the pranks of a spoiled child.

When at last he lapsed into drooling idiocy it was Dominique who had him shut up, under the care of a deaf and dumb keeper who was glad of a bed to sleep in and food to eat. For two years, the last three months of which he was a danger not only to himself but to other people, Guy du Vivier lived in his locked tower in the fastness of the chateau deep in the remote countryside of Normandy. When finally he died, it was Dominique again who had him brought down to lie in state in the great hall. Dead, all trace of his madness was gone; only his wasted body showed evidence of his illness, which she had told everybody was cancer.

He was buried with great pomp and circumstance, and followed to the family tomb by his wife and daughter, both heavily veiled. Catherine was glad of hers because she could not keep from smiling; Dominique was glad of hers because she was furious. Her father had died penniless and deep in debt. Dominique had plans, but they demanded money. And it was as she was wandering through the chateau, looking for something her father had perhaps overlooked when he sold everything that would bring a fair price, that she remembered Charles Despard.

He turned out to be a very pleasant surprise. Despard's was now a highly successful business; the past twenty years had wrought great changes in his life-style. He was rich, very rich. He also had a wife and daughter. No matter; they could be disposed of. The first thing to do was see if her mother's magic still worked.

When she wrote to him, he had no idea who she was. He knew his Catherine had married a du Vivier but they were a considerable clan, and this girl, when he saw her, had a lush, darkly sensual beauty quite unlike the spun gold of his lost love. When she asked him for a job he was astonished. Surely, the daughter of one of the noblest houses of France. . .

"My name is my only fortune," Dominique explained with a bitter shrug.

"Not with that face," Charles offered gallantly.

"Mama said you were *gallant.*" Adding, to his raised eyebrows, "You knew her as Catherine de Villefort."

She saw his face change. "How is Madame du Vivier?" he asked at last.

"In mourning for my father and with no idea that I have come to see you. My father left us nothing but debts. I need—I must—work. It occurred to me that I have *entrée* into the world wherein you do most of your business. I wondered if you would care to employ me in the capacity of a—scout, I believe you call them? A sort of pointer to who has what to sell. My salary would be a commission on your final selling price."

Charles was both impressed and bemused by the calm assurance of this young girl—she could not be more than eighteen—setting out what were obviously well thought-out terms, and he recognized at once the importance of her offer.

"I would, of course, not let it be known that I was in any way associated with Despard et Fils. That way I could move quite freely around the Faubourg . . ."

Charles nodded, his mind busy. "You have finished your education?"

"Yes. I came back from England for my father's funeral but I was in the last quarter of my final year."

Charles sat forward. "You interest me, M'selle. Let us discuss your proposition further . . ."

And so Dominique became a scout of Despard's. From the first she proved invaluable. She took her place in the social strata; she went to cocktails, dinners, receptions, balls, showings, first nights, ostensibly a butterfly exercising newly unfurled wings, but in reality making substantial commissions, which she put away in a numbered account in a Swiss bank. Her father she had declared bankrupt. There was no way she was going to waste her hard-earned money on his mountainous debts. She took her mother's jewels in to Charles Despard and asked him, sadly, it he thought they would fetch much. It would look better if she seemed to be sacrificing something. The du Vivier family jewels belonged to Guy only for his lifetime; but Catherine had received pearls from her father, and a very fine pair of sapphire solitaires as a wedding present from her grandmother. Charles Despard bought them himself for a very fair price—the pearls were first water and the sapphires without flaw—and presented them back to Dominique, as she had expected him to. It was then that she invited him to tea, to renew his acquaintance with her mother.

She literally dragged her mother to Paris and had her gone over. She was unwilling, being quite content, now that her dreaded husband was no longer around to torment her, to live in the country. She could work in the gardens now, do the things she wanted to do. But Dominique said she had a surprise for her, one which necessitated her mother looking her very best. She had her coiffed, maquillaged, manicured, and superbly dressed by Balmain, so that when, on the appointed day and at the appointed time, Charles entered the drawing room of the Hôtel du Vivier, he saw first the shimmering gold hair, then a face that to his stunned mind seemed unchanged. She had begun to smile, her polite, meeting-strangers smile, but when she saw who it was her hand went to her mouth and with a sob in her voice she breathed, "Charles?"

"Catherine! *Ma belle!* Catherine—!"

Dominique gave them ten minutes. If it was not done then it never would be done. After one look at their faces when she reentered the room she knew that it had been.

If, after Catherine and Charles were finally married, quietly in Provence by the mayor of the village from which old Gaspard had first left for Paris two hundred years before, Dominique ever gave any thought to her stepfather's first marriage, it was with indifference. If the family had wanted to keep him they would have fought. Indeed, she had expected to have to fight and had prepared a battle plan. That, once he had left them, there was no communication between him and his first family from that time on, suited her purpose, and she took care to avoid the sleeping dogs. She, for her part, was delighted to have the famous Charles Despard as a stepfather, and sought his permission to call him Papa almost immediately. She made herself indispensable to him from the start; it was to her that he told, many times, the story of how he lost his Catherine, to her he confided that, for him, Catherine de Villefort was Female Incarnate. He was now, as a middle-aged man, able to satisfy his sexual longings, found deliriously that Catherine worshipped him in such a way that had *he* commanded her to watch his sexual activities with women, boys, or even dogs, she would have done so happily, so glad was she to do whatever he asked.

As it was, late in life she too discovered sex, and her own sexuality—not dead even though it had been buried for so long and every bit as powerful as her husband's—came to bursting, glorious life. Catherine became all that Charles had fantasized she would be: richly erotic, voluptuously abandoned, passionately adoring. He was not to know that only now was she putting into practice what she had seen done when she had been forced to watch her husband playing out his sexual fantasies.

Charles was happier than he had ever been in his life, and only some months later did Dominique sense a diminishing of his pleasure. It was then that she discovered the letter he had written to his daughter had been returned, unopened. Sympathizing (ostensibly), Dominique sadly told him of her own mother's unhappiness in her first marriage, obliquely made it clear that should Charles ever leave her a second time, it would kill her. His daughter was a child, she murmured. When she was an adult, able to understand, then would be the time to approach her. Through Dominique, Charles perceived that his dream was a fragile one; that he had to tread carefully with his Catherine because he now knew that he was her whole life. He also knew that she could not bear to have his other life so much as mentioned; that if he suggested bringing his daughter over she would not be able to cope, would see it as evidence that she did not come first with him as she needed to—somewhat neurotically he thought uneasily. She tended to become hysterical when his attention strayed; she was even jealous of Despard's. Of course, considering the life she had led with that beast of a first husband . . . He was grateful to Dominique for explaining so much. He would know how to treasure his Catherine, how to keep her happy. She was so much more fragile than his little Cat, who would in time, as Dominique kindly said, come to understand. Fourteen was an awkward age. When she was sixteen, perhaps . . . And he would keep on writing. It would do no harm.

To her mother, Dominique explained how Charles had been withering away in a loveless marriage, made for one reason only: loneliness.

"It was providence, Mama. That Charles should come back into your life once you were free to let him. He was the last person in the world I would have expected to meet at a boring cocktail party. And I could tell at once that you were still the love of his life. If you could have seen his face when I told him I was your daughter . . ."

By the time Dominique had finished weaving her web, Charles was so hamstrung that he was helpless. Just as she had engineered her mother and stepfather's reunion, so did she now see that reports filtered back to London about Charles Despard's newfound lease on life. And when the letters he wrote to his daughter came back unopened, Dominique, contentedly satisfied, was able to commiserate and soothe, reinforced in her task of replacing Catriona Despard as Daughter of the House. When Charles' daughter was eighteen, it was Dominique who suggested he go to see her, having first planted in the press stories, accompanied by photographs, of the wildly successful Charles Despard and his beautiful wife, with yet another rehash of the long-lost love story. As she expected, Charles came back with his tail between his legs.

So the gulf widened as the years mounted, and Dominique became, she believed, the daughter Charles Despard loved. She in turn was astonished to find she was becoming fond of him. He was that rarity: a kind man. He hated to cause pain, which was why, no matter how she tried, she could not dislodge the stain of the loss of his daughter from his soul. As he got older, the worse it got. Dominique discovered that he had put an inquiry agent on to his daughter; this came to light when, after a visit to London, she at once made it her business to tell him that his daughter had opened her own shop under the name Kate Mallory.

"I know," Charles had said sadly, looking and sounding mortally hurt. "It was reported to me."

"I am so sorry," Dominique murmured disconsolately. "But it seems she is determined to erase you from her life."

Surely, she thought, he will give up now. She must hate him infinitely to go to the length of refusing his name. And for a while she saw no sign of returned letters.

She was therefore utterly dumbfounded when she discovered that he had left Despard's London to that same daughter. *Why* had Charles Despard done this thing? *Where* had she gone wrong? Had he secretly been in touch with his daughter behind her back? She had gone through each and every one of his desks; in New York, in London, in Paris, and had found nothing to cast doubt on her conviction that everything would be left to her. Only afterward, when she was pondering events, did she remember that she had not found the letters.

It was not until her husband told her that Charles had made him his executor, and asked him to accept a watching brief on behalf of his two beneficiaries, that she knew what Charles had done with them. But she did not ask. Blaise was sharp, and the less he knew the better. She let him see that she was disappointed, chagrined even, at this astonishing turn of events, but she also made no bones about her absolute confidence that at the end of the forthcoming financial year she would be the one in control. "Have I not had twelve years of study?" she asked her husband practically. "Papa taught me the business even as he taught me about porcelain. I suppose it was that conscience of his—oh, I know he had one. It was all those years he lived in England. You may laugh if you like but I tell you he became anglicized; he would never have done this so—unFrench—thing had he not been influenced by living across the Channel. Well, so be it. I think he knew the outcome. I have no worries. What is a year's delay? My plans for Despard's will have to wait a little longer, that's all."

But not too long, she was thinking, as she lay face down on the padded massage table, head pillowed on folded arms, eyes closed, while the masseur—six feet of solid muscle and bone—kneaded her nude body with skilled hands. Massage was one of her favorite erotic delights. She loved the feel of muscles being probed and loosened, of flesh being stroked, the little pangs as a thumb dug into a pad of muscle sending jagged rills of pain-pleasure almost too exquisite to be borne along her nerve endings. She drowsed in the oil he used, a compound of fresh flower essences and mountain herbs. Afterward, she felt all loose and pliable, as though made of brand-new elastic, and then went straight into the shower. First warm, then cooler until, for a bracing thirty seconds, the water became a blast of icy coldness leaving her glowing.

From this daily ritual she unfailingly emerged on a high, keenly aware of and ready for the day ahead and whatever tensions, problems, dramas, and conflicts it would bring. Like the funeral of Charles Despard the day before. It had been quiet, just his wife, his stepdaughter, his son-in-law, those ancient members of the Despard family still alive, and old friends who had worked with him at Despard's for many years. The service had been plain and simple, the interment in the sunny plot of land on the hillside above the small church. Later, Catherine would lie beside him. The Provençal *mas* he had bought twenty years before—as he had hoped, his eventual retirement hideaway—could be seen on the other side of the valley, perched on its own hill. From its terrace, the small cemetery could likewise be seen. Afterward, when they got back to the house, Catherine had had luncheon served, and when Dominique and Blaise left she had been sitting in her big, fan-backed cane chair, her ever present embroidery in her hands, facing the other side of the valley and her husband's grave. As funerals go it had been a pleasant one, quite unlike the solemn ritual that had accompanied the interment of the body of Dominique's own father, with its high mass, its cardinal, its acolytes and incense. Charles had not been a practicing Catholic, and his wife had never had any use for religion ever since the de Villefort family priest told her coldly that her duty was to her parents and what she wanted did not matter in their choice of a husband. Her duty was to produce children and obey her husband in all things. She had never ceased to regard her failure to produce the required son as some kind of revenge.

As soon as the funeral was over and the necessary customs observed, Dominique had made her own exit, driving her husband to the airport where he caught a plane for London while she flew to Geneva. He had his forthcoming meeting with Kate Despard. Dominique had her own plans.

Now, after drying herself and applying handfuls of fragrant body lotion, she walked naked into the mirror-lined room that housed her clothes, and sliding back a door brought out a specially built rack of flat half-moon shelves on which her lingerie was kept. She always wore natural fibers: pure silk, slipper satin heavily trimmed with lace, and invariably black—it looked so good against the translucent whiteness of her skin. A brief half-bra, semitransparent, a pair of matching French panties, a wisp of a garter belt with extra long garters to allow a flash of white thigh when she crossed her legs. She always wore sheer, pure silk stockings; panty hose were both unhygienic and the cause of at least twenty seconds' delay when sex was unexpectedly called for, as well as being decidedly off-putting when a man slid his hand between her thighs. She wore no girdle—her figure needed no constraint—nor did she wear underslips. All her dresses and skirts were lined, all fitted to perfection. She was very exacting when it came to the hang of a skirt, the set of a sleeve.

Today she chose white; she felt white, today. Virginal, in fact. It must be what she had in mind . . . So, the Saint-Laurent suit, the skirt as narrow as a Puritan's conscience but slit six inches at the back to allow ease of movement. It slid down her hips with a whisper of pure silk taffeta lining, and she closed her eyes at the sheer pleasure of it. Dominique had a strong tactile sense. Next the jacket: broad shoulders, puffed sleeves, nipped-in waist, small frilled peplum. Its broad revers were faced with silk moire and just stopped short of the gathering at the top of the sleeves. The jacket had a one-button fastening and was so cut that it hinted at, without quite revealing, a mouth-watering décolletage.

Finally, plain black satin pumps with four-inch heels. Only when she was fully dressed did she walk to her dressing table, lit by a bank of spotlights, to do her face. She wore little makeup. Her flawless skin needed no foundation, merely a moisturizer. Eye shadow—three colors skillfully blended, a touch of mascara on already black lashes, a glossy silk lipstick, and a matching blusher that gave a sheen to her exquisite cheekbones. A spraying of *Dominique*, the perfume made for her, rounded off her creation. The final touch—her signature—were the brilliant cut, ten-carat solitaire sapphires she screwed into her ears, matching the ring on her left hand. Rising from her dressing table she went to stand in the center of the room where she made a 360° slow turn, examining the reflection that came back at her from all sides, giving her a total picture. Satisfied that she was perfection itself, she would not glance at a mirror again.

Leaving her maid to tidy up behind her, she went through the house in the direction of the terrace.

Her villa was in the hills above Geneva, right on the edge of France, with Switzerland at the bottom of the hill. It was her own property, bought with her money and not the Chandler billions. Now, as she went out onto the terrace, she felt a *frisson* of pleasure as her eyes swept the panoramic view: the lake, the city, the sky, the trees, the distant mountains. The water sparkled like champagne, and the grass and trees seemed newly painted. The smell of fresh coffee—made on a signal from her maid just before she finished dressing—tantalized her nostrils, and the pure orange juice, freshly squeezed, exactly four ounces, refreshed her mouth. As she replaced her emptied glass, Jules, her butler, picked up the coffeepot with one white gloved hand, the silver milk jug with the other, and poured a perfectly judged mixture of both into a large white soup-type bowl, at the bottom of which was one large sugar lump. Smiling up at him her thanks, Dominique cradled the big cup in both hands and sipped, closing her eyes beatifically.

Satisfied that everything was as it should be, Jules withdrew, leaving Dominique to stretch out a hand toward the two unbuttered tartines, take one and dip it into the milky coffee before eating it slowly and rapturously. Breakfast was her favorite meal of the day, although she only ever ate sparingly. Her first action on rising was to go to the bathroom; if her weight differed by so much as half a pound from the perfect one hundred, she would drink her coffee black, no sugar, and eschew the tartines. But today her weight had not deviated. Her mood was calm, reflective. She had made her plans. Now it was time to set them in motion. She liked the pre-active time of day, when she could sit in tranquil calm and anticipate.

Not until she had finished her second cup of coffee, which she poured herself, did M'selle Desmoulines, her secretary, come on to the terrace with her notebook and the appointments diary, as well as the morning's mail.

"*Bonjour, Madame.*"

"*Bonjour,* Hortense. What have we today?"

First they dealt with the mail, Dominique deciding, with the aid of the thick, leather-bound diary that was handed her, whom she would see, and when. Then Hortense, who had an old maid's propensity for gossip, would report what she had heard.

"Monsieur Lebecq says that there is a rumor that the Marquis de Beausoleil is selling his Monet, and that he is in the middle of a double deal between the Druout and Sotheby's, though nothing is yet settled. Monsieur Lebecq is of the opinion that the Marquis is still open to approaches, and as Madame de Beausoleil is an old friend—"

"Where is she?"

"In Paris, Madame. At the house in the Avenue Foch."

"Call her." Dominique pursed her lips thoughtfully. "The Monet is, as I recall, an exceptionally fine one."

"Indeed, Madame. *Madame Marigny et sa fille,*" offered

Hortense. She was as knowledgeable as Dominique as to who owned what.

"Good. Make it your first task, Hortense. I will see if it is Solange who needs the money . . ." Dominique made a moue. "No doubt she has been running riot at Dior again."

Hortense consulted her notes. "The de Vries consignment has arrived at the shop for viewing."

"Good. I will be there at four."

"And you have M'sieu Lang for lunch."

"Ah, yes." Dominique set down her cup. "We will lunch here," she instructed. "Tell Toinette I will see her in ten minutes."

"*Bien sûr*, Madame."

Antoinette was the cook, a paragon from the Dordogne who created masterpieces with stolid practicality. She was also a shrewishly skillful manager, who shrewdly bargained—as though there was any need—with the shopkeepers and the market vendors, who had come to know better than to try and put one over on Madame Mollard. Dominique allowed her to keep whatever she made; it acted as a spur.

Now, she left the breakfast table to go back inside the villa to her study. Here she did her telephoning—she had a private line—wrote her letters, did her wheeling, dealing, and cajoling. When Antoinette came in, in her black dress and spotless apron, she wished her mistress a stolid good morning and stood, hands folded, in front of the desk.

"I have a luncheon guest, a man—an Englishman." Their eyes met, Dominique's with a resigned shrug as if to apologize that such a philistine was invited to partake of Antoinette's ambrosial delicacies. "He should lunch well, but not too well . . ."

Again a look was exchanged. Nothing in the broad peasant face betrayed the shared knowledge that the luncheon guest was to be set up for the kill. "The lamb is good. Perhaps *sauté d'agneau au citron* with *endives aux champignons* and *petits pois printaniers?*" she suggested.

Dominique nodded. "Good, good. With fruit to follow, I think, and cheese. Englishmen like cheese."

"And my sorrel soup to start?"

"Excellent."

Unlocking her desk drawer Dominique took out a cash box from which she extracted several notes, which she handed over to her cook, noting the amount in a small black book.

"Merci, Madame."

When Antoinette had gone, Dominique pressed the small bell, positioned on the floor where her foot could easily reach it. This time, the butler entered.

"Ah, Jules, a luncheon guest today, an Englishman. We are having lamb."

"Might I suggest the Mouton Cadet 1971, Madame? It is not too heavy for the time of day and young enough to complement the lamb."

"Excellent, and as an aperitif a bottle of the Krug '63."

Jules bowed. An important guest, then, if he merited the '63. Someone from whom Madame wanted a favor—or more. By the selection of the wine he knew exactly what was called for. "At what time, Madame?"

"He will arrive at one for one-thirty."

That done, Dominique went into her dressing room to touch up her makeup, always the last thing she did before leaving the house.

Her car, a Rolls-Royce Phantom IV, was waiting, Jean-Paul, her chauffeur, at the wheel. "The shop," Dominique ordered, as he opened the door for her.

It was exactly ten o'clock when the car slid down the long drive toward the gates, and out on the N-1 to Geneva.

The Honorable Piers Lang had been Charles Despard's personal assistant for three years, and he had gotten the job through Charles' loving stepdaughter, who had made it clear that in return, he was to keep her informed of everything that went on in the chairman's office. As he was both greedy and ambitious for the good things of life, which as a younger son he had no choice but to work for, he had taken it. In turn, he was useful to Dominique because through his parents—his father was a viscount and his mother the daughter of an earl—he was connected to half the English aristocracy and thus knew who had what heirlooms to dispose of. In that regard he had proved invaluable.

He had also lusted after his patroness from the start but had been careful never to do more than let her see it. And when she married that half-savage he had waited patiently for her to add him to the list of her lovers—for marriage had made no difference to her sexual activities, though it had made Piers extra careful because Blaise Chandler was not a man he would care to cross. Now, as he drove up the hill toward her villa, he wondered at this sudden summons to Geneva. Being who and what she was, it could only mean that his patience was at last to be rewarded. Things had changed, after all. She now had a rival to contend with. Who would have thought that the old man, who had seemed so taken with her, would have taken Despard's London and handed it to the daughter from whom he had been estranged these past twelve years? I'll bet the Venus Flytrap is plotting plans and scheming schemes, he thought, which hopefully will include me . . . in more ways than one. He knew—as did all of Despard's—of her prodigious sexual appetite; it was spoken of in awed whispers, and women as incredibly skilled as she in the sexual arts did not come a man's way that often. Having—or rather being had—by Dominique du Vivier was, by all accounts, something a man never forgot. He had heard things . . . He shifted in his seat. Just thinking about it had him hard and ready. He hoped she would not waste too much time . . .

The villa made his mouth water. Soft-footed servants, morning fresh flowers, sumptuous furnishings and paintings that were the real McCoy. That Renoir still life was a beauty, and would you look at that Meissen group—not to mention the Sèvres—and wasn't that a Fragonard?

"Madame will be with you directly," the deferential servant murmured.

The sooner the better, Piers thought, as he prowled around. God, but she was a lush piece—as lush as her villa. That face and that body had his cock springing to the salute instantly. He bowed over the hand she extended. "Madame . . . a pleasure to see you again."

"And you, Mr. Lang. How is London?"

"In a ferment, naturally. The news was—well, it knocked us for a loop."

"All of you?"

"Well, the old timers—the ancients as we call them—seem delighted, but they are past it, living in the past, which of course is just what we don't want. You are what we want—need, Madame. The twentieth century. You *are* Despard's, Madame, to those of us who know."

"My stepfather thought otherwise . . ."

Piers Lang shrugged. "His years in England changed him. Normally we are sentimental only about animals but"—

another shrug—"with all due respect, Madame, it will not do."

Dominique smiled. Greedy, she thought. Vain. Unscrupulous. With an eye to the main chance. And to a profitable fuck. Well . . . She let him say all the right things: what a loss her stepfather was; how unjust that Despard's had not gone to her; how everyone was on her side, et cetera, et cetera. His loyalty, Dominique thought contemptuously, was toward himself. He liked his job, wanted to keep it, was willing to pleasure her if it would do the necessary. Something to be used, she decided. Worth nothing more than that use. And to be discarded afterward. She smiled at him. His loyalty was much appreciated, she told him. She was touched by it all . . . He was hers, before she had so much as set a finger on him she knew.

Luncheon was perfect. The soup slid down, the lamb was ambrosia, the vegetables *al dente* and the cheese just right. He drank three glasses of the Mouton Cadet and accepted a *filtre* of Armagnac with his coffee. As Jules withdrew, Dominique said casually, "We are not to be disturbed . . ."

Piers felt his cock swell. It was not only the champagne, the wine, the Armagnac, and the sultry nearness of a woman who had him coming apart at the seams, it was also the visions in his head; what was the male equivalent of mistress— *maître?* Yes, *maître* of a woman like this—what could he not achieve? They would get this little nobody of a Despard out of the way and go on to glory together . . .

Dominique eyed his glazed face. Fool, she thought. She knew all about him—his debts, his greed, his weakness. He had long since ditched his scruples, took, on the side, small commissions from customers—a thing forbidden at Despard's. He was a *thing,* to be used and then cast aside. Using people gave her a deeply pleasurable thrill not attainable even in sex. It was some sort of revenge, she knew, but had never probed deeper than that. This one was ripe for the using. Look at him, she thought. Glazed with lust and cupidity. The way he kept crossing and recrossing his legs betrayed the difficulty he was having with his erection.

Judging the perfect moment, she leaned forward, first to pour a little more Armagnac into his glass, then to place a hand over his zipper, right over the bulge of his erection, burning through the fabric of his trousers. Her eyes met his hypnotized gaze, her own flat and inimical, though he neither knew nor saw it, being conscious only of the fingers gripping his cock. His breathing became harsh, the panting of a man in extremis. She unzipped him; her fingers were cool and he groaned deeply. She caressed the head, her fingertips brushing his taut scrotum. "Oh, Jesus . . ." he groaned. "Oh, Christ." He rose from the couch, thrusting into her hand. She gripped him and he subsided. His eyes were dazed, a combination of alcohol and sexual intensity. She leaned forward, and her lips enclosed the throbbing head. "Christ!" he shouted in an agony of pleasure. Her tongue flicked and another groan was wrenched from the depths of him. He was being sucked inside out . . . Oh, dear Christ . . . that tongue . . . He felt it probe, flick, then penetrate deeply, and he arched, gasping, "Oh, Christ do it, yes . . . do it please . . ."

Deliberately, with cool control, Dominique led him through pleasure into ecstasy beyond imagining. Her tongue laved his thick, throbbing penis, her hand cupped the heavy, pendulous balls. He moaned, he shouted, he groaned, his hips thrust. She was incredible. He had never felt like this before, never. He was about to die from pleasure . . . He came in a red haze of multiple sensation; every nerve end quivering with exquisite pain, spurting in uncontrollable jets which Dominique carefully avoided staining her clothing. Her face was without expression as she watched him, her eyes cold and empty. Fool, she thought with icy contempt. But she milked him deliberately, callously judging the moment when she knew he could take no more. Then she let him fall back, face red and sweating, mouth open like a gasping fish, chest heaving, penis wet and shriveled, hiding itself once more in his thick, coarse bush of pubic hair.

Leaving him there, already snoring, Dominique went back through the house to her suite where she stripped, handed her clothes to her maid to be cleaned, showered once more, then redressed in a suit that was a duplicate of the first. When she went back to him Piers was still in his sexually sated stupor. She sat down in the chair opposite, lit a cigarette, smoked it, and after stubbing it out, heard the small Sèvres clock strike the half hour. Then she leaned forward and shook him. He opened bleary eyes, saw her, brightened and sat up eagerly. He saw her smile, that smile that made his heart lurch, filled as it was with undreamed of promise, all tinged with skin-prickling threat. My God, she was incredible, every which way. He had never experienced such sexual fulfillment in his life! He had to hang on to this shooting star because she could take him to infinity—in more ways than one.

Dominique knew he was hooked. She recognized the greed in his eyes—greed for her, for what he could achieve through her. What a foolish man, she thought with contempt. So easily caught, just as easily disposed of if need be. Still smiling, she told him what she wanted him to do, saw the shock, the shuddering thrill of pleasure as she explained her plan; the spiteful glee, the barely concealed triumph at what he thought was his own cleverness in allying himself with the undoubted winner.

"You'll never get away with it," he breathed automatically, squirming with the delighted knowledge that of course she would—this was Dominique du Vivier. She shrugged. "It is no more than warning. A shot across the bows, so to speak." Her smile widened and she saw him shudder again. "The next one, of course, will be the torpedo . . ." Again the masochistic shiver.

"Oh, let me be there," he pleaded, "I'd love to be there."

"Do this one right, and you will be," she promised throatily, knowing that if he did not, he would never be anywhere with her again.

On the Tuesday morning when Rollo turned up at the shop, he was not alone. With him was a woman of indefinable age and superb elegance.

"Kate, I want you to meet a very old friend of mine, Charlotte Vale. I have asked her to come and give you the benefit of her vast experience and flawless taste in the matter of your remodeling."

Charlotte saw the tall girl stiffen, and the face she turned to them was, Charlotte saw with a pang, not only plain but defiantly so. No confidence, Charlotte knew at once. No self-esteem. Pretends not to mind, hence the jeans and sweatshirt, but minds agonizingly. "Rollo exaggerates," she said with a smile, "as usual. I told him I would help only if you asked me to."

"You do need refurbishing," Rollo said impatiently. "What you wear is fit only to be thrown away—I wouldn't insult anybody by giving it."

The pale face flamed in mortification.

"And Charlotte was the Best Dressed Actress of her day," Rollo finished triumphantly.

Charlotte laid a hand on his arm. "Rollo, do go away and sell something to someone. Miss Despard and I have no need of you here."

And to Kate's astonishment, he went. Charlotte turned to Kate. "I really did ask him to ask you first, but you must know—as I do to my cost—that Rollo is more given to telling than asking."

"Too right," Kate agreed, thawing somewhat.

"Rollo has explained your—circumstances to me, and as I no longer have the means to go out and spend, spend, spend as I used to, I get a vicarious pleasure out of assisting other women."

"I've never spent much on clothes," Kate said defensively. "My mother was of the opinion that the highly expensive kind were not worth the investment. Marks and Spencer provides everything I need."

"Not, I think, for the chairman and managing director of Despard's," Charlotte said gently.

Kate swallowed. "I suppose not."

Moving in for the kill like the experienced huntress she was, "Why don't I take you to some places where I am known? We do not have time to have things made but there is some superb *prêt-à-porter* around nowadays."

But not which you would wear, Kate thought. She knew instinctively that what the actress was wearing was *haute couture*, if a long way from being new. The dress was navy blue, the skirt of a length reminiscent of the Fifties, as was its style: fitted to the body like a glove, with a fan of pleats behind for ease of movement. It had an upstanding collar and flyaway turn-back cuffs of crisp white piqué. Her hat was also white, a tiny slanting beret of very fine straw, tilted over one eye with a rakish feather curving above the eyes and down one cheek, a mist of veiling giving perfect flattery to a skin that was no longer young but remarkable for a woman of—what? Kate thought. She'll never see fifty again, that's for sure . . .

"I am sixty," Charlotte Vale, disconcertingly reading her mind, told her without a qualm. "And this dress is twenty years old. I wore it in a production of *Separate Tables*—Victor Steibel designed my wardrobe—I always wore *couture* on stage. My unkind critics used to say that was why women came—to see what I would wear." Her shrug was amused. "Whatever the reason, they did come. But these days they do not put on the kind of plays Rollo and I appeared in. The times have left us behind . . ." A small sigh. "So nowadays I give the benefit of my experience and taste to those who can afford it. Like you." Candidly. "You are very much younger than my usual clients, but no matter. Just so long as you understand that I do not go for what is fashionable now, at this minute, but for what will always be worth wearing."

Kate was wide-eyed.

"I get a commission, you see, on what you spend at the various—shops—we shall patronize."

Kate was the one who was embarrassed. That, she thought, much impressed, was the greatest display of *sang-froid* she had ever seen. And as she tended to blunt-instrument honesty herself, it appealed to her.

But the thought of spending a small fortune—because that was what it would entail, she knew—on clothes appalled the thriftiness her mother had instilled in her. At the same time it brought to mind a picture of her father showing her mother a glossy ad in a magazine, a beautiful woman in a glorious dress with matching fabulous fur, and saying, "Would you not like something like this for a change, Susan?" and her mother, scandalized and with that scorn in her voice at what she saw as sheer, wanton, unnecessary extravagance, replying, "Och, Charles, what are you thinking of? I'd never sleep nights at the thought of all the expense just for something to cover my back." Sensible yes, but depressingly commonsensical. Never would her mother join her father in throwing a bonnet over a windmill. Bonnets cost money and had to last for years . . . It's not as though I can't afford it, Kate told herself roundly, realizing she must have said it aloud when Charlotte agreed tranquilly, "I would not be here otherwise."

She really was something, Kate thought enviously, quite without the daggers-drawn elegance of Dominique but nevertheless supremely elegant, in her person as well as her dress. Her hair was a soft, becoming gold, and as neat as wax; her skin was porcelain and expertly maquillaged; her nails were painted, not like the talons of Dominique, but a pretty pink that matched her mouth. There were pearls set in diamonds in her ears, and a plain gold watch on her wrist. She wore a wedding ring and a half-hoop of diamonds on her left hand, and the pin in her hat was small, discreet but also genuine. Her handbag and shoes were of supple, shiny calf, as were her gloves.

"I suppose it is important to look the part," Kate observed slowly.

"Vitally important. A man may not always remember what you said, my dear, but he will never forget how you look."

"Oh, but this is strictly business," Kate corrected in alarm. "He is already married to my stepsister."

The way Charlotte looked at her told her she had said something revealing, and she felt herself flushing again.

"There are more men than women in power at Despard's, are there not?"

"Yes," Kate admitted.

"Then they must be considered. You are young, my dear, and as I remember they are not."

"No."

"Then they must not feel too threatened. Once you are secure in your position, well, then you may do as you please, but for now you need them, do you not?"

Once again flabbergasted at this unnervingly calm woman's correct assumptions, Kate nodded.

"Then your clothes must be *right*."

Beginning to comprehend, Kate nodded again.

"Good. Then will you let me do what I can to help?"

"Yes, please," Kate said fervently, by now putty in Charlotte's hands. Then she looked in dismay at her jeans, plucked at her sweatshirt.

"Have you a dress or a skirt and blouse?" Charlotte asked briskly. "Perhaps you had better let me see what you do have . . ."

It was not much, and true to form, most of it from Marks and Spencer. A couple of skirts, a couple of shirts, matching jackets. Well, thought Charlotte, they will not be worn again so they will do for now. She picked out the heather tweed set and Kate changed as quickly as she could. Not enough weight, Charlotte thought clinically, but good bones. Small ones, fortunately, a wonderful long back, a superb throat—and just enough in the way of breasts to help rather than hinder the hang of her clothes. Good hands and feet, but that face . . . She sighed. Something would have to be done about the freckles, and the hair would have to be toned down several shades; well, Henry could do that. And makeup could work wonders in the right hands . . . Her own stage experience would stand her in good stead.

Several hours later, Kate sat at a table in the Ivy and counted, dazedly and with an inward wince, just how much she had spent that morning. Certainly all the profit from the past year's trading in her little shop. She smoothed the faultlessly tied stock of her heavy, cream silk shirt, fingered the solid gold pin keeping it tied. Then she admired the russet sheen of her new boots, of the same leather as her shoulder bag with its Hermés clasp. Her suit—or rather culottes and a matching jacket—was of a wonderful loden green velvet that went marvelously well with her now several-shades-darker hair: no longer carrot, it had the glossy sheen of a newly emerged horse chestnut.

Charlotte's hairdresser—"one of a dying breed, alas, so much more than a pair of scissors"—had taken Kate's hair from its pins and exclaimed as it fell down her back, thick and heavy, a positive mane.

"Badly in need of cutting," was his verdict. "And also badly out of condition. How do you wash it?"

"Why—with shampoo," Kate had faltered.

"What kind of shampoo?"

"Well, the kind my mother used to use . . ." She named a brand that had been on the market since the year one.

"Wrong for your kind of hair, which tends to dryness. That particular shampoo will have done nothing but make it drier. I shall have to cut off all these split ends—at least four inches."

"If you say so," murmured Kate obediently.

"It is also far too thick, it needs thinning and shaping, but it does have a natural curl. And it is manageable—or will be when I have finished with it."

"Something easy to deal with, please," she ventured. "I'm not much good at ornate hairstyles."

"Just as well, because I do not arrange them," was the crisp reply.

And when Henry had cut, shampooed, cut again, dried—by hand and with an old-fashioned bristle brush—Kate was astonished at her reflection. Her hair sprang from her forehead and waved over her head, cupped her chin and glowed like a fire. No longer scraped back and emphasizing the bones of her face, it softened them, so that instead of a death's head looking out at her from the mirror, there was a finely toned, arresting, double-take face.

"Wow!" she breathed, impressed unto awe.

"You will wash it no more than twice a week until the dryness is cured and you will use nothing else but the shampoo and conditioner I give you; you will also come to me once a week for a special oil conditioning."

Again Kate nodded meekly. She would do anything this particular magician ordered her to.

His bill had also taken her breath away but she had paid it gratefully. It had made a hole in her bank account, but she consoled herself with the thought that she would soon have more money than she had ever had by virtue of her new life. She had also quelled the guilty feeling that she was being extravagant, her mother having instilled into her the ever present necessity of thriftiness, of always having a supply of "rainy day" money but at the same time never going without an umbrella. You can afford it now, she told herself firmly, as she looked in wonder at the stranger in the mirror, and thought of the boxes and packages in the car. For the first time in her life she had pure silk and satin lingerie—sugar almond colors trimmed in real lace from Janet Reger; she had pure silk shirts and organza blouses; a real suede coat the color of a lion's pelt, cashmere sweaters, sensuous pure wool dresses in colors she had never before worn, such as plum, slate blue, pale grey, and chestnut; she had a trouser suit of velvet in a green so dark it was almost black, which did wonders for her skin and hair; she had half a dozen handbags, an equal number of pairs of shoes—she had far too much to be contained in the one wardrobe in her bedroom. But then, as Rollo had commented casually, "You'll be moving into the penthouse anyway."

Strangely enough, she had never thought of that. She knew her father had created the flat above Despard's once he had lost his London base—the house where he had lived with his wife and daughter. Kate had never been in it.

Still dazed by the enormity of it all, she ate mechanically, let the conversation float about her head, catching only a word now and then, as well as a drift of the new perfume she was wearing. "I think," Charlotte had said, after watching Kate sniff bottle after bottle, "that there is only one for you; it is young, crisp, very much of today and yet sophisticated enough to be worn day or night. This one." It had been

Yves Saint Laurent's Y. Now Kate felt it eddying around her, intoxicating her already bemused mind. She had not, she realized, really thought it all through: what it would mean, accepting her legacy. She had seen no more than herself running Despard's, in her simplicity had made of it a simple thing. Now she saw it was not; it was endlessly complicated. Like what Charlotte had said about not antagonizing the men . . . They all knew her! As a child she had considered them her honorary uncles. Why should they resent her—her father's daughter? What would they think she intended to do?

". . . early tomorrow morning." She realized Rollo was speaking to her.

"Sorry—what did you say?" she apologized.

"I said I have arranged for us to have a look-see early tomorrow morning. Eight o'clock at Despard's."

"Eight o'clock! But—"

And then as she met his eyes, and saw the look in them, she realized that Rollo was thinking as against her dreaming. Going back to Despard's would be an emotional thing; she would probably find it hard to handle, even more so in front of a sea of greedily curious faces. It did not open for business until nine-thirty; at eight o'clock the building would be empty, allow her to come to terms with her past in peace. So she smiled, nodded, reached across to press his hand.

"Yes, of course," she agreed simply. "You are right, as always."

"Charlotte shall advise you on what to wear. You've got to correct the bad impression you made on Blaise Chandler the other day. He sits high on the roost at Despard's so it behooves you to mend your fences. It is essential to get him on your side." He proceeded to lecture Kate on her behavior, her actions, what she should say, and in the middle of it all Kate caught Charlotte's eye, saw in it the droll resignation she felt, and as they exchanged a long look Kate knew she had found a friend, and fortunately for her one who would be more than able to counter the swamping influence Rollo had exerted on Kate since her mother died.

"How long have you known Rollo?" Kate asked, as Charlotte helped her unpack the pile of boxes later that afternoon.

"Oh, since before the war. I was a young ingenue and he was the second lead in a production of a Coward play at the Adelphi."

"Was he then as he is now?"

"He was turning into it. Rollo's outlook on life was curdled with his mother's milk, but he helped me through a bad time—the leading man was a matinee idol who thought he had *droit du seigneur* over the women in all his productions—and I foolishly fell in love with him. Rollo was a brick. He can be awfully trying and he does tend to take you over with his possessiveness, but he is the best of friends."

"Isn't he though," Kate agreed with enthusiasm, "except he is, as you say, a mite possessive—"

"A mite!" laughed Charlotte. "Rollo expects you to run to his timetable." She paused. "You will have to be careful, once you start at Despard's. Rollo would like nothing better than to pull your strings."

"Oh, I know they already call him my Grey Eminence," Kate admitted honestly.

"Yes, well, don't let him take too much unto himself," Charlotte warned gently. "Make your own decisions, Kate; accept your own responsibility. Then you can really face yourself in the mirror every morning.

"I can face myself in the mirror with pleasure!" Kate exclaimed. She had to go and peer at herself again. "Honestly, I didn't know it was possible to change a face so much just by powders and gels . . ."

"The face that can be seen without them is very rare. I saw but one in my life, and she was indeed legendary."

"Who was that?"

"Gladys Cooper. She was the most beautiful creature I ever saw." Here, Charlotte eyed Kate thoughtfully. "At that, you remind me of the young Hepburn—Katharine not Audrey, though you and Audrey share the same lack of weight. It's your facial structure and the red hair. They do say that everyone has a double somewhere and you could do a lot worse than look like one of my very favorite actresses."

Kate flushed with pleasure. "I am so glad Rollo brought you," she exclaimed impulsively. "And you will continue to help me, won't you? Rollo has all these ideas about dinners and receptions and cocktail parties and press conferences . . ."

"All very necessary in your new role," Charlotte reminded.

"Yes, I know. It's just that I had seen everything in much more simple terms. But it isn't, is it?"

"No. You have inherited the main branch of a world-famous auction house. There is already a great deal of gossip and, of course, an enormous amount of curiosity—about you and your stepsister.

"Who is no doubt the odds-on favorite?" Kate tried to make it light but it came out heavy.

"Yes," Charlotte replied, with her usual candor. "People are at a loss to understand what on earth your father was thinking of. Those who knew him well knew about you, though he never spoke of you to anyone. After such long silence—and estrangement—they were naturally more than surprised when he left to you what everyone had assumed he would leave to his stepdaughter. In certain quarters gossip had it that you were the disappointment of his life, that you more or less turned your back on him."

Kate's ever-ready flush rosied her face before ebbing to whiteness. "He was the one who left me."

"No," Charlotte said gently. "He left his wife."

Kate's face shrank on its bones. "That's what Rollo says," she whispered miserably. "That I was the one who acted like a jealous wife . . ."

"You loved him," Charlotte said simply.

"Yes, yes, I did, very much," Kate sighed, knowing that Charlotte understood it all.

"A woman scorned can do the most self-destroying things," she said. "Look at Medea . . ." She got up from the bed, turned to look for handbag and gloves. "But he also loved you and showed it by leaving you Despard's."

"I intend to live up to every one of his hopes," Kate vowed.

"Of course you will. You are a passionate young creature, Kate. So young—and so vulnerable. You have much to learn, and not all of it will be pleasant . . ." She came to stand by Kate, who was still sitting on the bed. "Whatever I can do, my dear, you only have to ask."

Kate wanted to hug her, but was afraid to disturb the bandbox perfection. Her innate perception sensing it, Charlotte bent to kiss her cheek. "You know where I live, and you have my telephone number. Use them both."

With a smile she was gone, and Kate heard her talking to Rollo, then the soft tinkle of the doorbell, then Rollo coming upstairs again.

"A very good day's work, if I may say so," he observed contentedly as he entered the bedroom. "Charlotte's invaluable at times like these—and she needs the money. She was a good actress, but unfortunately Coral Browne got all the parts so she never quite made it to the very top. Add to that a disastrous taste in men—they took all her money—and she was on her beam ends until she took to acting as Guide to the Right Behavior in Polite Society. Normally she advises the *nouveaux riches*, but when I explained your situation she agreed at once. I can assist you in most things, but there are certain areas where a woman is the only one who can really help."

Kate said nothing. Now was not the time. She had to gain experience, confidence, knowledge, and strength before she could begin to pry loose Rollo's grip on her life. She had been content, before, to let him *arrange* her; she had been happy to let him help in the shop when he was "resting," had paid him a small salary that she could ill afford, but Kate was loyal and Rollo had always been there in the wilderness of loneliness after her mother died. For that alone she would be hard put to repay him. But now she saw that it would not do to let him run Despard's through her. That was not what her father had intended. That was not what Blaise Chandler was expecting. He was not going to push his wife; her father would not have given Dominique such an edge. Therefore it was only fair that Kate should also remain uninfluenced. But now, she knew, was not the time to broach the subject. She had a little less than seven months in which to learn the ropes; once she knew how to tie the necessary knots, then she would tell Rollo that she intended to make her own way. But even at this long distance, she still felt her stomach turning over at the very thought . . .

"Anyway, tomorrow you have to be up bright and early, and you have had quite a day today what with one thing and another—"

"One thing!"

"Yes, well. It was worth it, wasn't it?"

"Was it not! Thank you for Charlotte. I like her enormously."

"I knew you would," Rollo allowed complacently. "Now, I shall be round tomorrow morning at a quarter to eight. Look your best." He put a finger to his nose. "And if you are a good girl you may find I have a surprise for you . . ."

5

Despard's occupied a whole corner block between Arlington Street and St. James's. Its main entrance was in Arlington Street: a classical façade, a portico with a shallow flight of stone steps—red carpeted for the big, important sales—and high, glossy double doors painted a deep, bottle green complete with brass knocker and matching, discreet nameplate proclaiming DESPARD ET CIE.

Throughout the year, along the sills of the ground-floor windows, flowers bloomed in well-tended window boxes: daffodils, hyacinths, tulips, and bluebells in the spring; small hybrid roses, carnations, marigolds, and shaggy-headed daisies in summer; shrubs in autumn, giving way to red-berried holly as Christmas approached. Inside, too, once you were through the small lobby with its large doormat and into the reception area itself, there were always morning fresh flowers, arranged French style: *en masse* in celadon bowls or silver epergne or even a Tiffany Fevrile glass vase.

There was always a fine display on the superb circular giltwood table, with its Italian marble top, which occupied the center of reception. Behind it rose the stately staircase, carpeted in plain red Wilton; at its foot, in the small section immediately in front of the carved wooden door marked STAFF ONLY, stood a Louis XV *bureau plat* with gilt brass foliate mounts and caryatids, on cabriole legs. Here sat the receptionist, for many years Miss Hindmarsh, now retired. She, too, always had flowers, in the same Vincennes bleu lapis two-handled tureen next to the Art Deco desk clock that, in Kate's memory, had also always been there. Her chair was one of a set of Louis XV beechwood *fauteuils,* upholstered in raw silk the color of vintage champagne, which matched the swagged curtains at the windows. On the wall to the left of the main entrance, in a small alcove, hung the portrait of Gaston Despard, the firm's founder. In a small glass vitrine set beneath the picture were his gavel, his wire-framed spectacles, and his first ledger.

There was a set, strained look on Kate's face as she stood there at eight on that first morning, and Rollo wisely left her alone with her memories for a while. She was staring at what old Gaston was holding in his hands: a rare Vincennes watering can, striped blue and gold and decorated with full blooming roses. Her father had told her its history. "Queen Marie Antoinette used such a watering can to sprinkle perfume onto the porcelain flowers at Versailles." The can itself she knew was upstairs in his office; when she used to come to Despard's he had let her hold it, rare as it was; a measure of his confidence in her. And to capture and fix the image for all time, he had presented her with a bottle of Roger & Gallet *Quelques Fleurs,* which he let her sprinkle over a Chelsea bocage group.

As Kate turned away Rollo saw that her eyes were bright with emotional tears. He had expected her to be badly undermined by memories; that was why they were here before the staff had arrived. And when Kate left the alcove and walked around the table, her fingertips trailing on the cool marble, she sniffed sentimentally before coming to an abrupt halt.

"Mr. Smythe! And Miss Hindmarsh—oh, and Mr. Hackett and Mr. Brooke!"

Mr. Smythe, small and white-haired, his face beaming and his sharp blue eyes alight with affection, came toward her, hand outstretched. "Welcome home, Miss Cat, welcome home."

Kate burst into tears.

"God, you must think me a watering pot," she sniffed feebly, some time later, sitting in Miss Hindmarsh's chair as she had occasionally been allowed to as a child.

Henry Brooke patted her hand. "It was a shock, seeing all of us at once. We should have prepared you, but Mr. Bellamy said it was to be a surprise.

"That it was," Kate said with feeling. "But a lovely one. To be welcomed back by my old friends means so much to me—and so early in the morning."

"Oh, we all come in for eight," Wilfred Smythe explained.

"We leave at four, you see. It avoids the worst of the rush hour. But Miss Hindmarsh came up from Reigate specially, she is retired now—has been for seven years."

Kate was suitably impressed. Miss Hindmarsh (Kate still had no idea of her Christian name) had been Despard's headmistress, with her iron-grey hair and matching discipline. She had begun with the firm as a clerk-typist when it was no more than a funnel for goods destined for Paris; she had known Charles Despard since he was a schoolboy, and had therefore been able—and had always taken the opportunity—to talk to him as if he still were one. Now, here she was (and she had to be well into her seventies because she had been of, if not past, retiring age when Kate had known her) as straight-backed and formidable as ever, her pince-nez (she was the only person Kate had ever met who wore one) fixed firmly over penetrating steel-blue eyes, her hair cut in the flapper style of fifty years before. Even her clothes were unchanged: the mid-calf length navy skirt of best barathea, one of her pure silk blouses with a frilled jabot, today in a soft French blue, and the little fob-watch of gold and enamel over guilloche, which had been her choice of a golden anniversary present from Despard's, pinned to her flat chest (Miss Hindmarsh had never had any breasts to speak of).

"It was the least we could do for you, Catriona," she said severely. "It is about time you returned to your rightful place. Your father wanted nothing more. As one of his oldest friends, the least I could do was to be present to see you take it."

"Indeed," nodded George Hackett. "We would not have missed it for the world."

"You all look exactly the same!" marveled Kate sentimentally.

"Not quite," Henry Brooke admitted with a sigh. "Older."

"I only hope everything else is as unchanged as you are."

They looked at each other. Henry Brooke, a gentle soul, coughed behind his hand. "Oh, a lot of the old faces are still here," he allowed, "but there have been some changes . . ."

"And not for the better," pronounced Miss Hindmarsh. "But now that you are back, Catriona, you will see that everything once more runs along the right lines. Despard's run by anyone but a Despard is unthinkable."

The three old men nodded in agreement, and Kate was aware that to her old friends, her advent was akin to the relief of Mafeking. None of them had wanted to be taken over (and booted out?) by Dominique du Vivier.

"That's why I'm here," she said.

They all nodded again. "We knew you would be," Wilfred Smythe said simply.

He had always been Kate's "special" friend at Despard's; she had loved visiting him in his eyrie at the top of the building, the room with its ceiling of glass where he spent his days restoring works of art deemed worthy of his talents. He was a polymath—an expert restorer of paintings, he could also repair porcelain, and it was this that Kate had loved to watch him do; his skillful fingers holding a pair of fine tweezers, picking up fragments of porcelain that he then placed in position so cleverly that the joins could not be seen with the naked eye. She loved the smells: linseed oil, glue, turpentine, and paint. Forever afterward, these smells would carry her back in time to those Saturday mornings at Despard's.

"Now then," Henry Brooke announced, "we are going to leave you to look around on your own. And after your meeting, we are all going to have lunch together."

Kate looked around for Rollo, who said blandly, "The Ritz is just across the street. And you have an expense account now . . ."

He took the four old people away in the lift, leaving Kate alone to wipe her eyes and put her shattered composure together again. When she felt able, she started on her slow pilgrimage into the past.

There, on the walls, were the paintings, each bearing a small round sticker with the date of the sale in which it would be offered and a small square one giving its lot number. There, against the far wall, was the George III giltwood sofa, upholstered in the same champagne silk of the curtains; there on the small console to its right were the catalogues of forthcoming sales as well as copies of *Despard's*, the in-house magazine issued four times a year, which gave a rundown of business during the previous quarter and the high spots thereof. There was the pile of explanatory leaflets, *Disposing at Despard's*, which detailed the many services offered to the prospective customer and the names, addresses, and telephone numbers of all branch offices, both home and overseas. They contained judiciously chosen full-color plates of choice items recently sold at auction, and the closing dates of others yet to be held. Kate leafed through them, noting that Despard's was still holding its own when it came to disposing of the cream of the world's art.

Then, fingertips lightly trailing the polished pine of the balustrade, she went up to the next floor. Here were the galleries: GLASS, PORCELAIN, CERAMICS, FURNITURE, PAINTINGS, CLOCKS, JEWELRY, ARMOR, a whole series of splendid rooms opening off a central corridor, where customers could browse. Even the carpets on the waxed parquet floors were for sale, each tagged for easy identification. At the center of the group of rooms was the square open office marked SETTLEMENTS; here customers paid up for purchases, unless their stature was such that they had an account. This was the floor on which sales were decided upon; on the floor above they were concluded in one of the three great salerooms. In each of these rooms were the walls thick with paintings, the middle packed with chairs and at the far end stood the auctioneer's rostrum on a raised dais, under the electronic indicator that would give details of the bids in U.S. dollars, French francs, German marks, Swiss francs, and Japanese yen, as well as pounds sterling. Each was also fitted with closed-circuit television.

This was the heart of Despard's: where the excitement lay. Kate could sense it; over the years the walls had absorbed it. Here she had seen her first auction, stood on a chair at the back to watch her father sell a Poussin for the then unheard of price of one million pounds. She had felt that excitement then; in the pit of her stomach, in her trembling legs, dry as dust in her mouth. Afterward, if there was a really big auction and she was home from school, she would always come to watch it. Now, standing in the main gallery she could once again smell the cigar smoke, the perfume of the women, the pungency of an atmosphere that was sweaty with excitement. When she looked down at her wrist, wonderingly, she saw that it was covered in gooseflesh.

She went up the next flight of stairs; they were wooden, not carpeted, and led to the specialist departments: untidy, jammed with books, papers and crates, cases and boxes stacked to the ceilings. The floor space had been subdivided so many times that it had become no more than cubbyholes, big enough for a desk and a chair, often without a window. Here toiled the students, working for their doctorates in art, learning their trades and their specialty, waiting to be summoned downstairs to give air to that knowledge under the eagle eye of their head of department, of which there were some thirty-odd; men and women who were supreme in their field, from dolls and toys to old masters, running through English silver, European porcelain, Oriental porcelain, English armor, Continental armor, French furniture, English furniture, and so on. Here it had been quiet but for the hum of voices; now Kate saw that the word processor had arrived, that Despard's now used a computer to store its knowledge.

Here, too, at the far end of the building, was the boardroom, where the monthly meetings—"inquests"—were held and questions were asked in the confident expectancy of the right answer: why a certain item had not reached its reserve; what to do about a certain dealer who had had the temerity to operate a "ring" during a particular sale; what course of action should be taken with respect to a client who, once a big spender, was now in serious financial trouble. Kate stood at the big table and looked around. The Memling Madonna still hung above the fireplace on paneling that had come to Despard's in the sale of a demolished Dominican priory, and been bought by Charles Despard himself. The chandelier was a Waterford, the carpet, a rare pictorial Chinese silk, depicted the lake and gardens of a royal palace, all faded rose, deep blue and clotted cream. She walked right around the table and out of the door again, wandering slowly and pleasurably in and out of offices, putting off the moment she was both longing for and dreading: her ascent to the top floor, where her father's office awaited. Clients were taken up in the lift; Kate used the stairs, still wooden, but meeting carpet when they reached the hall. Here all was quiet, the double doors closed. Rollo had been so right, she thought, as she laid a hand on the Lalique glass door handle; she needed this time alone to confront her ghosts and lay dusty memories to rest.

It was the smell that hit her first, rolling her, like a carpet, back into the past. Cigar smoke—her father's Romeo y Giuliettas—mingled with the special wax used to polish his large partner's desk, circa 1785, and the rose potpourri in the lovely little Chia Ching vase with its pierced cover, set at one corner of the marble mantel. A serenely omnipotent jade Buddha stood at the other end and, in the center, a celadon incense burner. Above it a painting that changed with the seasons, now it was a flower piece, a lovely Renoir: masses of white lilac in a large blue and white Ming vase.

Her father's desk stood in front of three tall windows hung with heavy velvet curtains of burgundy red that picked out the rich rubies and blues of the Bessarabian carpet; between them stood twin George III sofa tables, each under a fine giltwood mirror. In the center of the room was a superb example of Italian *pietra-dura,* a glory of fruit and flowers on black and gold. Taking its cue from the table, against the wall opposite the fireplace stood a Japanese black and gold lacquer cabinet on a George II ebonized stand. Kate knew it contained her father's stock of whisky, brandy, and fine old sherries, as well as glasses. Facing his desk were the seats for visitors, two large, comfortable George III mahogany dining chairs, with pierced gothic pattern splats; two more flanked the Japanese cabinet. There were no papers to be seen; they were kept by Charles Despard's secretary, whose office was through the door to the left of his desk. In Kate's time it had been a Mrs. Hennessy, plump, pouter-pigeon officious but prodigiously efficient, who, having married late in life, had discovered that she preferred her job.

Kate stood a long time in the doorway, assailed by the past as by a mugger, reeling as memories came pounding at her. Only when she felt able did she go into the room and close the door behind her. Then, taking a deep breath, she walked slowly around it, touching, stroking, lifting, caressing—and remembering, reenacting an old superstition formed when, as a child, she used to come here with her father and wait while he made important telephone calls. She had believed that if she did not go around touching everything on arriving, and then again on leaving, she would never get to come back again. Now her fingertips relearned the fine patina of old wood, the smooth warmth of soapstone, the satin of old ivory. She was lost, twelve years back in the past where her father loomed so large he obliterated everything else. Suddenly he was there with her, watching her, smiling at her, lovingly, indulgently tender as he had always been.

She approached his desk, finally, as she would an altar. It was exactly as she remembered. The expanse of green blotter, changed as soon as it showed use; the tray containing his pens, he never used ballpoints believing they made for sloppy writing; the Victorian inkstand containing the Indian ink he preferred; his leather-bound diary, always in green with his initials in the bottom righthand corner. There was the humidor carved from Chinese ivory; the Tiffany Wisteria leaded glass and bronze desk lamp, which when lit gave little light but which her father had loved for the way it looked. Three telephones: one external; one, with many buttons, internal; one, a white one, his private outside line. The little Lalique clock in the shape of a parasol still kept excellent time. She picked it up, as a child it had endlessly fascinated her. The center had pierced filigree hands. As she studied it, the other clock in the room struck the hour; it was nine already. That clock was one of George Hackett's beloved pieces, an early Georgian green lacquer longcase decorated with chinoiserie. But it, too, told of flying time. She went around behind the desk and, as she did so, saw that something new had been added: a picture, in a plain silver frame, of her father's second wife. Her own mother's had never stood there.

Kate felt a pang. Yes, Catherine Despard was as beautiful as Susan Despard had been plain. Spun-gold hair, cornflower eyes, pink and white skin. Her shoulders were bare, but around her neck was a triple row of pearls to match the drops in her ears. Kate had never known her mother to wear jewelry. The photograph was placed where her father could rest his eyes on it whenever he pleased. Kate drew out the chair, another comfortable Georgian carver, and sat down. As she pulled it forward, her foot touched the button placed by the right hand pedestal and almost at once Mrs. Hennessy's door flew open and she stood there, hand on heart.

"Goodness, but you gave me a shock. For a moment I thought—" She released a theatrically exaggerated breath. "I wasn't expecting you so early."

Too late, Kate remembered that, at Despard's, Mrs. Hennessy was known as the "Eyes and Ears of the World." She extracted gossip from the air, like ozone. Like Catriona Despard coming back at 8 A.M. of a Wednesday morning. Now there was both frank surprise and greedy curiosity on her high-colored face, the legacy of the tightly corsetted, but her eyes were hard and watchful. "This is a surprise and no mistake. It's been a long time."

"Yes."

"I suppose I must call you *Miss* Catriona now, seeing as you are no longer a child."

"Miss Despard will do," Kate said.

Sheelagh Hennessy's pink cheeks went plum color. She had never liked Kate, being of the opinion that Miss Catriona Despard was spoiled rotten by an overindulgent father, but it had been well known at the time that "the Hennessy" had designs on Charles Despard; that she wanted to be his office wife in the true sense of the word, and when she failed she justified her failure by blaming it on the detrimental influence of Charles Despard's daughter. Now, her slate-blue eyes were pebbles of dislike.

"I have a meeting at noon with Mr. Blaise Chandler," Kate went on, "during which we are not to be interrupted by anyone."

She saw the thin lips tighten almost to invisibility and went on with great enjoyment, twisting the knife.

"We'll have coffee when he arrives."

"I know Mr. Chandler," Sheelagh Hennessy said snottily. "He comes here all the time, with or without Madame." Then she overreached herself. "Which is more than I can say of you, these last twelve years."

Kate leveled her golden cats' eyes at her. "Then don't."

Sheelagh Hennessy's cheeks empurpled alarmingy. "Will you be in your office until Mr. Chandler comes?"

"No. But I will ring you when I need you. You will be in your office?" This last was said pointedly, as a warning.

"Of course."

"Good. Then you will always knock before you come into mine, won't you?"

The blue eyes bulged and the door slammed but Kate felt exhilarated. She had done it! She had shown her own authority. Old employee or not, Sheelagh Hennessy would have to go elsewhere in Despard's; Kate knew she could not work with her. She also knew that everything she did would go straight back to the du Vivier faction. How come Mrs. Hennessy was in so early this particular morning anyway? Was there already a leak? Something else to be investigated . . .

"Staff are beginning to arrive," Rollo announced, coming in without knocking. "I caught a glimpse of the Hennessy, by the way. Still the Eyes and Ears of the World. She'll have to go. She's virulently anti-you and pro-Dominique."

"I have already decided to move her," Kate replied crisply. Her tone was reasonable, matter-of-fact, but there was steel underlying the softness. Rollo's eyes narrowed. It was as though she had donned a new personality along with her clothes, yesterday's loden green outfit, which suited her so well, with its glossy knee-length boots. Her hair gleamed and she had gold lover's knots in her ears matching the pin in her stock. She was suddenly a woman, not the untidy, hot-tongued, chip-on-both-shoulders girl he was used to.

"I've had a most enlightening chat with the old pros," he told her. "Miss Hindmarsh still keeps in touch with a lot of Old Timers in the building and she is, as always, a mine of information." Rollo paused, an actor's trick. His timing had always been flawless. "The knives are out. The Old Guard is pro you because Dominique is anti them, thinks of them as old hat. The Young Turks are for her to a man—seeing as they are mostly men. Some of the women have taken her as their model. 'Rationalization and Reorganization' is the current slogan." Another pause. "I also found out that Blaise Chandler is generally regarded as an honest man. He had your father's ear. It seems he got Despard's out of what could have been a nasty lawsuit a couple of years ago—thanks to a devious bit of business that went wrong, initiated by his wife according to Miss Hindmarsh."

There was a knock on her door and Rollo saw Kate's face light into a smile as someone came in. He turned to see that it was Nigel Marsh, deputy chairman, who had been at Despard's for twenty-eight years and used to dandle Kate on his knee. As he saw Kate, his face broke into a smile that was both incredulous and delighted and she found herself moving toward him, holding out her hands.

"Catriona—or should I say Cat?"

"Nobody has called me either for years," Kate admitted tremulously.

"Perhaps I should call you Miss Despard, now that you are a young lady . . . And how good it is to see you here again, where you belong. The building is buzzing with the fact of your return. Why didn't you tell me?"

"I wanted to do it as quietly as possible, after so long . . ."

He pressed her hands understandingly. "Of course." His faded blue eyes went over her admiringly. "But how changed you are. How grown up."

"I am twelve years older."

"So am I."

And she saw that the hair she remembered as iron-grey was now silver, that the eyes were set amidst more wrinkles, that he seemed to stoop more.

"I want to meet all my old friends later," Kate said.

"And they you, I assure you. I know you've got Blaise Chandler coming in this morning, but perhaps—this afternoon?"

Kate hesitated and Rollo was just about to interrupt smoothly when he heard Kate say, "It's only nine-twenty and my meeting is not until noon. Shall we all get together at ten-thirty—have coffee together in the boardroom?"

"What a good idea," Nigel agreed. "Informal, what? Chance to see old friends, catch up on old times."

"Yes, quite informal," emphasized Kate. "I don't take over formally until next April."

Nigel nodded relievedly. "Of course." Again he pressed her hands. "It is good to know you are taking up where your father left off."

"I intend to carry on as though there had been no break," Kate told him.

"Good, good." He was obviously both approving and relieved. "You can rely on me to do whatever I can to help. There are—divisions, as I am sure you must know, but most of the board are behind you, my dear. Behind Despard's as we all know and love it."

"Thank you," Kate said warmly.

"At half-past ten, then. I'll make sure everyone knows." He nodded at Rollo whom he both disliked and distrusted, but one had to take the rough with the smooth, "Bellamy."

Rollo acknowledged the greeting with a stately inclination of the head. "Mr. Marsh . . . Pompous old windbag," he muttered as the door closed. "Your father only took him on because of his connections. Deputy Chairman is like vice president—all title and no responsibility. Anyway, he must be pushing sixty-five."

"Surely not," protested Kate.

"He's older than I am and I'm sixty-four next birthday! Your father was four months older than I was." Peevishly, "And I had arranged for you to spend more time with the old timers. I'd ordered champagne—"

"We can still have it, but at lunchtime, before we take them out to lunch," Kate soothed. "This is a heaven-sent opportunity, Rollo. I can get the feel of things that much sooner."

"Well, I suppose one must cut one's cloth," grumbled

Rollo. "But at least come up and see them now. They are waiting for you."

She spent almost an hour with the Old Timers, talking over old times and learning much of the new ones, what changes had taken place in the past twelve years and, more especially, what changes were feared, should Dominique du Vivier ever take over. That was also the theme when she got downstairs to the boardroom to find a dozen people there waiting for her, faces she had once known on a weekly basis, although there were some missing, presumably because they were in the opposite camp.

The first one to come across to her was Claudia Jamieson, Despard's Victorian art expert. "Catriona, it's about time you came back to us. That was a ridiculous feud and I told your father so more than once."

She would have that right, Kate thought. She knew now what she had not known when she was young; that Claudia Jamieson had been for a time her father's mistress, and that once the affair cooled they had remained friends. She was now fifty; she was fatter, her blonde hair brassier and her face more haggard, but she still smoked her cigarettes in a long jade holder, and wore enough gold to depress the market should she sell it.

"Why on earth did you cut yourself from *us?*" she wanted to know in her loud, carrying voice.

"It was an all or nothing situation," Kate explained wanly.

"For twelve whole years! Mind you—I was just as shocked myself when I heard." For a moment there was a darkening of the brown eyes and a rictus of something like pain on the painted mouth.

"She made him happy," Kate heard herself saying.

"True," Claudia agreed with a sigh. "He lost ten years after he married her. Not a brain in her head and absolutely no interest in Despard's, but"—an expressive shrug—"she was what he wanted." She drew fiercely on her cigarette. "It's her daughter who is not wanted—not around here, anyway."

"She won't be here," Kate said.

"Thank God for that! I always insisted your father was not taken in by her, in spite of their apparent closeness." And thank God I was right, Claudia was thinking. She could handle Kate, use her to strengthen her own position, already dangerously undermined by that bitch Dominique du Vivier who had seemed to lead her stepfather around by the nose. In fact, at one time, she had suspected he was being led around by something else, because sex was that French harlot's stock in trade. Kate was different. Nice child, totally inexperienced in the ways of a major auction house but surely that was to the better: she could be instructed . . .

Kate became aware, almost at once, that her return was being greeted with almost desperate relief. These people were frightened. And all by the same woman. Most of them were well over fifty, some over sixty; all had served Despard's for many years; all were aware that had Dominique du Vivier taken over they would have been thrown out with the garbage. So it was as a savior that they welcomed Kate. Of course they would need to see how she ran; they could advise her, show her, lead her, control her . . . She was their chance to make themselves indispensable.

Practically every one of them took her aside to murmur the same thing: "Just between ourselves, you know I don't usually tell tales, but . . ." before proceeding to regale her with an account of their particular grievance against her stepsister. The general consensus was that she wielded far too much power; that she was quite unscrupulous, using methods never before countenanced at Despards; that she was nakedly ambitious; that she was also untrustworthy—everything, in fact, Kate was not.

Kate listened, sympathized, said the right things, feeling sadder and sadder. These men and women had once been Olympians to her, bending down to her level to give her a pat on the head, a box of chocolates, the occasional half a crown, asking her jovially how she was getting on at school, murmuring approval as they watched her handle, without wincing, pieces of porcelain or crystal worth several fortunes, ceasing to worry as she grew older and they came to realize her potential.

"She's your daughter, Charles old man, no doubt at all . . . remarkable understanding for one so young, and the same love that you have . . ."

Now, with the benefit of an extra twelve years, Kate saw that they were also men and women who, having hollowed out a comfortable niche in life, were terrified of being turfed out of it. They were running scared. Claudia, for instance, always a scurrilous gossip, related to Kate within five minutes several libelous anecdotes, opened several cupboards marked with illustrious names out of which tumbled a whole assortment of skeletons, and muttered vengefully through clouds of smoke that she had plenty more where they came from.

"How on earth do you know all this?" Kate asked lightly, but realizing that Claudia could be a fountain of knowledge if used properly.

"People confide in me," she shrugged airily. "The things I could tell you . . ."

"I hope you will," murmured Kate conspiratorially. "I need all the help I can get, too, you know."

Claudia closed one eye in a knowing wink. "Fear not, darling. Claudia is here—to stay, in spite of what that French piece has in mind. You shall know all you need to. Knowledge is power."

"Absolutely," Kate agreed, vowing to learn as much as possible, then turning as Peter Markham, head of Rare Books, took her arm.

"If I might have a word, Catriona . . ." He was a fussy, pedantic man, who loathed the real world and preferred the rarified one of his books. He wanted to warn Kate about her stepsister's plans to amalgamate Rare Books with the Rare Prints Department. ". . . will not do, as I am sure you will see. They are two separate disciplines. Oh, I know other houses have them amalgamated but we never have, never. One cannot just lump them together for the sake of something called rationalization. Now you"—here he squeezed her arm—"know better than to destroy the harmony of decades—centuries even. You know our traditions because you were born to them. You are a Despard, my dear Catriona; *you* understand us . . ."

"Something else you have inherited," remarked a soft voice, and Kate turned to see a tall, thin woman smiling at her with hesitant shyness. Kate smiled in return but could not for the life of her remember who the woman was.

As if it was no more than she expected: "You don't remember me, do you?" the soft voice asked matter-of-factly

"It has been a long time . . ." Kate apologized tactfully.

"Twelve years. I remember when your father used to bring you here, every Saturday morning. You loved it then . . ."

"And still do."

"Yes, I can see that. I'm Venetia Townsend."

"Of course! Early Renaissance. My father told me you knew more about it than anyone. You were the one who stuck to your guns when the experts derided your labeling a particularly fine Raphael as a fake . . . You would not change your opinion though they howled you down, and eventually the world's leading expert proved you right."

"You have your father's memory," Venetia Townsend complimented, her pale face coloring with pleasure.

But it was not only the affair of the Raphael—Venetia Townsend's only claim to fame apart from her undoubted scholarship—that had sparked Kate's memory. It was her other name, the one by which she was familiarly known at Despard's. PoorVenetia, they called her, with condescending pity, no doubt, Kate thought now, because she so resembled the archetypal spinster. Forties, faded, probably frigid. Painfully shy and withdrawn, she had no interests outside her work, and was at ease with few people—always women. Men she avoided. Did she know of her nickname? Kate wondered. There was nothing memorable about her appearance. Her father had told Kate, "Miss Townsend does tend to fade into the woodwork, but she is a great scholar. Sotheby's and Christie's would love to take her away from me. I would not care to lose Venetia Townsend, so treat her with the respect she deserves, my little Cat."

So Kate's voice was warm when she asked, "How are you, Miss Townsend? It is so nice to see you again after so long. I hope you are still happy at Despard's."

"Just so long as Despard's is happy with me," was the shy reply.

"My father told me long ago that you were to be treasured," Kate said candidly.

"Did he?" Surprise flickered in the pale eyes.

"He warned me that Sotheby's and Christie's would love to steal you. I am so pleased and relieved to find you still immune to their blandishments."

"Oh, I would never leave Despard's," was the quiet reply. "Especially now . . ."

"Thank you," Kate said, with her own pleasure.

"It is obvious that your father treasured you," Venetia Townsend went on, and something in her voice gave Kate a pang. She knew instinctively that nobody had ever treasured this quiet, introverted woman.

"I wish you luck," Venetia added hastily, before moving off in the same manner. Kate knew why when Rollo's voice said: "Good God! I had forgotten all about Poor Venetia."

"That's her trouble," Kate said in a sad voice. "Every-body does."

"Come, now. It is not our fault if she decided the world was far too dangerous a place for her. It was her choice to retreat from it."

"That is cruel," Kate rebuked sternly, for she could not help but ponder that there, but for the grace of God and her father . . .

Returning to Despard's was like coming home, after years of traveling, in hope mingled with fearful trepidation that those awaiting her might not be glad to see her, only to find that they were delighted. Whatever she was not, she *was* a Despard; she was continuity, she was stability in the face of threatened change. Despard's, it seemed, was riven by rival factions: the people here this morning were on her side; the missing faces—and there were as many as those present— were in the opposite camp. Most of them, she realized, were younger; in favor of Dominique's modern methods, of her business efficiency, profits-are-all-that-matter outlook. Thank God Claudia had more or less told her not only who but why. She tucked away the information in her memory bank, along with everything else she managed to cull until, at eleven-twenty, she went back to her own office, where she sat down at the desk to collect her thoughts. It was quiet; Rollo had gone back upstairs, there was no sign of the Hennessy. The only sound was the ticking of the clock. Yet the very air she inhaled was full of her father. She closed her eyes, rested her chin on her hands and drifted.

Help me, Papa, she asked silently. Give me your strength, your wisdom. If I am indeed your true heir, help me to make people realize it. She let her mind empty, as she did when she meditated, retaining only one word in it. *Papa*, and sat as still as a graven image.

The receptionist told Blaise Chandler that Miss Despard was in the boardroom with some of the senior staff, so Blaise said he would wait in her office. But when he opened the door, quietly as always, because he invariably moved with an Indian lightness and grace, he saw that she was sitting behind the desk where he was so used to seeing her father;

her hands were clasped under her chin, her eyes closed; the air was so still and vibrant that he knew he was intruding on a moment of the most intense privacy. She looked different, he thought fleetingly, because it was only a matter of seconds before he retreated again, in both surprise and some confusion.

Mrs. Hennessy all but jumped from her desk. "Mr. Chandler! Why did nobody tell me you were here? I would have come down. Really, I don't know what has come over this place today. You would think it was the Second Coming . . ." That she did not was evident.

"I said I would come up unannounced," Blaise answered. "Perhaps you would tell Miss Despard I am here, though."

"But, of course . . ." The Hennessy hesitated, then went on, "Mr. Chandler, I want you to know that I think it should be Mrs. Chandler—Madame du Vivier as we call her—in that office. It is not right that—"

"It is what Mr. Despard thought right," Blaise interrupted, and in such a way as to make her flush. "Now, Miss Despard, if you please." The emphasis he put on the name made Mrs. Hennessy bridle, but she knocked on Kate's door and went in.

This time Kate was standing at the window, the light behind her, and for a moment it gave her the burning halo of a saint.

"Good God, all you need is your avenging sword," he said amusedly.

"At that, I think I am going to need one," Kate replied calmly, as she came toward him. Now he saw her plain and was astonished to find that she no longer was. The hair was no longer an insult; it glowed like wine through a candle; she was elegantly dressed and her face was delicately made up. She also smelled feminine.

Kate saw the open astonishment and thought vengefully, One in the eye for you, Mr. Chandler, as she shook hands. His hand was warm, firm, and large.

"May I congratulate you on changing your mind?" He began, with deceptive smoothness.

Kate indicated one of the Georgian carvers, went around behind her desk and sat down. "The credit for that belongs to your wife," she retorted coolly.

Hiding his astonishment at the full frontal attack, Blaise asked, "Is that so?"

"You know she came to see me?"

"Yes."

"To tell me that my father was a sentimental old fool who should have known better."

"I am not responsible, in law or out of it, for my wife's opinions," Blaise said pleasantly.

"I am not blaming you. I am telling you. She more or less told me that if I knew what was good for me I would let everything go to her. It had the opposite effect. I can be led to the water, Mr. Chandler, but I'll be damned if I'll drink if I'm not thirsty."

By God, so she has spirit after all, Blaise thought. I prefer that to spite any day.

"I am telling you this so that you know where I stand," she continued. Then with a sudden flash of a smile, "Or rather where I sit, because it places you in a somewhat awkward position. Your wife and I, Mr. Chandler, do not see eye to eye. What she wants and what I want are two different things. If you feel that this—enmity—prejudices your position then I shall quite understand if you decide that it makes it impossible for you to continue in your capacity as—mediator?"

"I wouldn't miss it for the world," Blaise assured her enjoyably. "And to save you the embarrassment of asking, I will tell you that no, I have no ax to grind where my wife's own career is concerned. I have never interfered and do not propose to do so now. Your father knew this and it influenced him when he appointed me his executor."

That Charles also knew he was the only one who could handle Dominique he kept to himself. Along with the knowledge, sudden, surprising, but quite positive, that he wanted to be a privileged bystander in the forthcoming battle. He had expected to have to work, along with Rollo Bellamy, to persuade Charles' sulky brat to change her mind. This composed, poised, even confident woman was another matter. Oh, Dominique, you did much, much more damage—to your cause—than you'll ever know, he thought. You are not going to find it so easy after all.

"I suppose I ought to be grateful to Dominique," Kate was saying dryly. "It was she who made me change my mind." Charm him, Charlotte had urged. Don't antagonize. Be honest—or seem to be so. Get him where you can use him, not the other way round. "She really should not have said that about my father."

"I see," Blaise said evenly. "That right belongs only to you, is that it?"

"He was *my* father," Kate reminded.

"And hers, even if only in law."

"Only in law," Kate repeated.

"Which suddenly made you accept the fact that he was yours by blood?"

"All right, so it was illogical. I know it and I've no explanation. I threw the legacy back in your face at our first meeting but—well—I did have cause."

"Divorce is a fact of life in this day and age. I myself had three stepfathers before I was nine."

"I only had the one until I was fourteen—a real father. I could not handle his—leaving me. It hurt me deeply and left—well, it led to our long estrangement, for which I accept most of the blame. But whatever you think, whether you approve or disapprove, be assured of one thing, Mr. Chandler. I will take my father's bequest and do my damndest to come out on top. I intend to do him proud."

"Better late than never."

Superior shit! Kate thought rancorously. "It is what he wanted," she said, "and he showed his faith in me. I know the art world. I know Despard's, and anything I don't know I will soon learn. This place is part of me, it is in my blood. Just how much, I have learned today. I am a Despard—"

"I am glad to hear it."

Kate looked at him steadily. He didn't like her, never would like her, so she had nothing to lose. Besides, whatever he said to the contrary, he could not be anything else but biased toward his wife. So she said, "If I can dispense with my prejudices, surely you can get rid of yours."

"I am a lawyer, Miss Despard, and in this particular case a sort of devil's advocate. Your father may have loved you, but it was not his intention that Despard's substance should be wasted."

"Nor will it be."

"That remains to be seen."

"And will be, once the year is up."

At the way he pursed his lips, she asked derisively, "What will you do if I have not been a good girl? Take it away from me?"

"Under the terms of your father's will that is what I must do. It is now September. You have till the end of the current financial year to learn the ropes. There are plenty of experienced people to help you. Beginning next April first, it is up to you to see that Despard's London makes the best financial showing in the following twelve months; sales volume, turnover, profits realized, all will be counted—and by me. I am appointed referee, if you like, to see that the contest is a fair one. Apart from that you have a free hand to run your end as you see fit."

"I know my trade," Kate told him warmly. "And I know procelain—"

"Perhaps, but fine art is big business nowadays. Gone are the old gentlemanly days. New people have the money and their standards are different. The competition is cutthroat because the world's works of art are becoming scarcer and scarcer, sold and resold, for prices that are ridiculous."

"You don't approve, do you?" Kate asked, strangely relieved to find the chink in his armor. "Because you don't understand."

"No, the obsessiveness of collecting is lost on me." He bent to pick up his briefcase. "Now, if we might go over some figures I have brought . . . it is necessary that you know exactly where you stand before you embark on your year of grace."

"And favor," Kate added swiftly.

"Let us hope that at the end of the next year, things stand in yours."

Kate's glance was fulminating, but she said nothing as he spread various documents in front of her. "This is a copy of the firm's accounts as they stood at the time of Charles Despard's death. There is no problem with cash flow; your father was ever strict with buyers and dealers, and he never had anything but the highest caliber of artifacts for sale. His standards were very high."

"You are telling *me?*" Kate inquired with poisonous sweetness.

"Twelve years is a long time," he countered, unmoved. Kate could have gnashed her teeth. He was stainless steel. All she got when she lashed out was a numb hand. "I am sure that hard work will bring you up to date."

"I am no stranger to that. Besides, I have a lot of old friends to tell me everything that has been going on."

The black eyes turned her way. "Indeed. I am glad they remembered you."

Kate seethed but, jaw clenched, she said, "Only too well, and are both delighted and relieved to see me. I am aware of how an auction house is run, Mr. Chandler. You forget, I worked in one for two years—the biggest of them all, the daddy, as I believe you would say. I know that auctioneering is more than selling what happens to be in fashion art-wise, as again I believe you would say."

"No," Blaise replied, "I wouldn't."

Oh, you smug son of a bitch! Kate seethed.

"I am also aware that my father has bequeathed me a flawless reputation." She held the black eyes and made her voice clear and ringing as she said, "That is why I decided I would accept his legacy, to make sure that reputation remained unsullied."

It was a direct challenge; she had flung the gauntlet at his feet. But he only said, "I should hope so."

They were still holding an inimical glance when the door opened and Mrs. Hennessy staggered in under the weight of the Georgian silver tray, the very best Sèvres, and not one but two platefuls of biscuits. Kate shot her a smoldering glance. The Georgian silver was used for only the most important clients; the Hennessy was making her loyalties plain.

"Shall I be mother?" she asked archly.

"No," Kate said clearly. "Thank you, Mrs. Hennessy."

Kate poured the coffee, burning with an anger that had her forcibly controlling a trembling hand, but while he drank his—two cups, and munched pleasurably on chocolate biscuits, taking all the best ones—she noticed sourly—she studied the figures once again. When she asked her first question he put down his coffee cup, rose, and came around behind the desk where he stood over her, using one long forefinger to point at various figures underlined in black. Kate could feel the warmth of him, smell his sharp clean fragrance, felt her gaze blur and had to concentrate fiercely on what he was saying, which was an enlightening exposition of how Despard's stood as regards future sales fixed, past sales and profits made, expenses, overheads, salaries, et cetera, along with a brief picture of what her father had hoped to achieve.

"And I get to use New York as and when I wish?" Kate asked.

He bent a sardonic eye. "Hadn't you better learn to run London first?"

"I do have a whole year," Kate reminded coldly.

"It could take that long to get the hang of this one branch. Concentrate on what you know, is my advice. Besides, nobody knows you in New York."

"That could soon be remedied."

"I wouldn't count on it," Blaise told her bluntly. "My wife made a considerable impression at the opening auction. Right now nobody would be prepared to give you a hearing in the face of her success. You will have to prove yourself first."

"I will," vowed Kate. "Don't worry."

"I'm not," Blaise said, surprising her and himself. It was obvious that she was bright. The questions she had asked were those he would have asked himself, and she had spotted the doubtful starters at once. And look at the way she had taken herself in hand. Who, he wondered, was responsible for that? Somebody with influence, obviously.

Was there—*could* there be—a man in her background? With an eye to the possibilities? "As I say," he went on, "you have the remaining six months of the current financial year to run yourself in"—with you running me down? thought Kate—"before you start the full year of trading. Probate will, I hope, be obtained before that begins. I shall certainly move things along as fast as I can."

"Oh, I am sure you could move mountains," Kate remarked dulcetly.

She was sure she saw the tough but well-shaped mouth twitch, but he said nothing, only thrust a hand into his jacket pocket and brought out a small bunch of keys. "You will need these." He held them out and dropped them into her outstretched hand.

"Thank you." The keys to her father's desk, his private files, the liquor cabinet, the safe.

Blaise Chandler nodded at the documents on the desk. "Your copies. Study them if you like. I'll be happy to answer any questions your accountants can't. You have my card?"

"Somewhere," Kate lied, having thrown it away. "Perhaps you had better give me another."

He did so, taking it from a silver card case.

She went with him to the door, as her father had always done with important visitors, and shook hands again.

"Good luck," he said.

As he walked away down the corridor toward the lift Kate called after him, "You didn't say—may the best woman win."

He turned. "That's because, in my experience, the best ones don't always turn out to be winners."

Kate slammed her door. "God," she said out loud, fuming. "He is the *most* infuriating man I ever met in my life!"

Rolo was there before she had reached her desk.

"Well?"

"He painted me a very pretty picture," Kate said flippantly.

"So? Are you going to buy it?"

"I'll wait until the actual bidding starts. I can't say I feel at ease with him, but by all accounts he is to be trusted—so I can't do anything but go along with that."

"Well, let's have our celebratory drink, instead. It's twelve-thirty. Let's go and collect the Old Timers."

They took them all to Victoria, where they caught their respective trains, just after four o'clock. Miss Hindmarsh was somewhat crumpled, her remarkable diction blurred by the quantity of champagne she had drunk, while the three men were in high spirits.

"Most enjoyable, dear Cat, most enjoyable," Wilfred Smythe told her happily. "Quite like old times . . ."

They had drunk innumerable toasts to each other, before Rollo gently but persistently drew them out about the state of affairs at Despard's. Now as they rode back to the King's Road, he said smugly, "That was a very profitable afternoon. It has shown us where the lines are drawn."

"Has it?"

"Well, apart from a few fence-sitters like Venetia Townsend, who has never declared any opinion that has not to do with art, I think we now know who is on whose side."

"Like Piers Lang, you mean?"

"Exactly. Nobody I spoke to had a good word for him, probably because there is nothing good to say. I learned that he was brought to Despard's by the Venus Flytrap herself, which tells me it was for no good reason except her own interests. Nor was he present today. My information is that he is in Europe. So, right now, is she. Need I say more?"

"No, but you probably will," Kate said.

"Come now, Miss Smarty Pants. You heard what was

said. That he runs after her with his tongue hanging out. Anything else and he'd be arrested for indecent exposure. I intend to keep both eyes on him in future. I have one of my feelings where the Dishonorable Piers is concerned."

"You've had them before and still been wrong."

"Not very often."

Impatient with Rollo's tendency to regard the slightest doubt as incontrovertible proof of the blackest villainy, and for some reason still oddly troubled about Venetia Townsend, about whom she resolved to do something nice, Kate said shortly, "I will accept that he *may* be her lover, but you have no proof except scurrilous gossip. And while he may not generally be liked, that does not prove he is a blackguard. If he is, then that means he successfully fooled my father for nigh onto three years, and that I will not believe." Proudly, "Nobody ever fooled Papa for long."

"For how many years did Sir Anthony Blunt fool the entire English establishment? When it comes to spotting fakes, I would advise you to stick to art. People are my province. The fact that it was your sister who introduced Piers Lang into Despard's points, to my suspicious mind, the unmistakable finger. She never does anything from the kindness of her heart, only the furtherance of her ambitions."

"To what end? Papa trusted her implicitly, didn't he? Why then, should she need to spy on him? You see plots everywhere, Rollo. Comes of appearing in too many bad melodramas. Piers Lang has brought in lots of fine sales to Despard's. He is invaluable as a contact man."

"The kind of contact we have to keep in mind is the one he has with Dominque du Vivier!"

"If he had been acting on her instructions all this time Papa would have known. And what instructions, might I ask?"

"Steering sales her way for her own branches to push up figures and show how invaluable she was." Rollo paused. "But in reality, being *in situ,* ready to use when the time came. What I believe is termed a 'sleeper.' "

Kate's laugh was scornful. "I can well believe it, because you have certainly dreamed this up. You sound like somebody out of MI-5."

In her indignation she missed the quick flicker in Rollo's eyes. "You have got a positive mania about plots and double dealing. I, on the other hand, was taught never to condemn without a fair hearing. I shall await proof that Piers Lang is not to be trusted."

"I am telling you he cannot and I thought you always trusted me."

"To get hold of the wrong end of the stick, and then use it to beat your suspect black and blue." Kate turned on him roundly. "Has it never occurred to you that people may be jealous? You of all people should know how success breeds envious hatred. And Piers Lang assisted my father to dispose of many a superb lot. All I hope is that he continues to do the same for me."

"Fat chance! From now on they will go to your stepsister, mark my words."

"In that case, we shall have the proof I need, won't we?"

Kate's curtness chopped off the discussion, but Rollo had no intention of letting it bleed to death. Let her continue to believe that everyone played her own honest game. He would continue to make sure nobody was using a marked deck.

But he had to have the last word. "What you fail to understand, dear heart, is the nature of your stepsister. She is totally alien to all you stand for. To her, plots and cabals are her way of life." As they are mine, he thought. "She suspects everybody, so naturally she believes everybody suspects her. She is a bad 'un, plain and simple." He sniffed. "She is a very shrewd businesswoman and a clever auctioneer, but when you think of her you don't think of those things. You think of the face and the body and the sexual promise. She uses sex to get what she wants from men." Another sniff. "I would advise you to cultivate your own, sadly neglected sex appeal . . ."

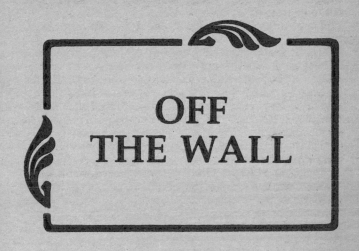

OFF
THE WALL

November

6

"Now," said David Holmes. "Start the bidding."

Kate, in the rostrum, checked her auctioneer's catalogue for the bids—the reserve in red, the blue for a commission bid from someone who could not be present in person or did not want his bid to be known beyond the rostrum. Quickly she rehearsed the increments in her mind, remembering David's instructions about setting a rhythm so that the figures came automatically, and that she should never take more than two bids; only if one dropped out should she look for a third.

She cleared her throat. "Lot five, a Georgian silver salver, circa 1730. I will commence the bidding at one thousand pounds—one thousand two hundred—one thousand four hundred—one thousand six—"

Her eyes darted around the half-dozen people, all Despard's employees, sitting in the chairs in front of her rostrum; each had his system of bidding and some had been instructed not to bid at all but to make movements designed to confuse. She saw a man, somebody from the accounts department, scratch his nose and said quickly, "One thousand eight—"

"No," David said exasperatedly. "That was not a bid, Kate. He didn't just touch his nose, he really was scratching it. You must learn to tell the difference; besides, nothing was arranged beforehand with him about how he would bid. You have to remember these details; they are vital. Now begin again."

"Never mind him," she heard her clerk, George Allen, whisper. "He's like that with all the learners and seeing as how you've got to be better than anybody his reputation is on the line."

George had been a godsend; he sat patiently while she

recited the increments at him—the classic, goddamned, all-important, soul-destroying increments that she found herself murmuring in her sleep. She lived auctioneering these days; of all she had to learn it was the most difficult. She had been a pupil now for two months and this was her first mock auction. Desperately she tried to remember David's advice, to put into practice the techniques of the senior auctioneer at Despard's who had been at it for thirty years.

"*You* are conducting the auction—look on the audience as your orchestra, but always remember that you cannot conduct them beyond their own pace; at the same time never lose control. You must always be in charge. Watch the way the bidding is working, where it is coming from . . ."

His training was vigorous; Kate received the same lessons as all Despard's hopefuls, of which, at best, only fifty percent succeeded in becoming auctioneers. Having so much else to do, she had to fit in her lessons whenever she could, and perhaps because of this David was more stringent. At best not a patient man, he sometimes had her on the edge of tears, though she never allowed them to break loose. She was damned if she was going to be beaten, was her attitude.

She had memorized his instructions by repeating them over and over again before she went to sleep.

One: Sense the atmosphere, it is an indication of what will happen.

Two: When you attend my auctions, watch how I relate to and control my audience.

Three: Remember that even if one lot fails, do not worry; go on to the next.

Kate had sat through dozens of auctions, watching, learning, saw that it was, as her father had told her, an art. He had been so skilled that you did not perceive the art; so was David Holmes. It was only when Kate watched those with less experience that she saw the seams, the gaps, the rough edges.

The mock auction was an ordeal to which Despard's, in the shape of David Holmes, subjected all its trainees. Kate was now trying to control the bidding in order to "land" on the reserve, and so far she had fluffed twice. This would be her third try.

"Now remember, Kate," David called from the front row, "the reserve is two thousand five hundred; that is the figure you must land on, or rather make your bidder land on."

Kate nodded, feverishly calculating in her mind, as though playing a counting game, where she must start so that, as the bidding bounced back and forth, it would end up at £2,500.

"Kate, you should know where to start," rapped David.

"I will open the bidding at one thousand pounds," Kate said loudly. "One thousand two hundred—one thousand five—one thousand eight hundred—two thousand"—this time she ignored the hand smoothing back a thick head of hair—"two thousand two hundred—two thousand five hundred . . ." There was no more movement. She had landed on the reserve, the girl in the third row back. Kate waited. "At two thousand five hundred then . . ." She held the gavel, tucked in her palm, poised. A catalogue was lifted at the last moment. Was it to be read or was it a bid? There had been no movement from that quarter so far. She gambled. "Two thousand eight hundred—three thousand pounds—three thousand pounds is the bid . . ." Again she waited, her eyes nervously darting everywhere. Nothing, she crashed the gavel down. "At three thousand pounds, then . . ."

Her palm was slippery with perspiration and the gavel slipped from it, fell to the floor.

David sprang from his chair to pick it up, place it on the rostrum. "Better," he said, but not particularly warmly. "You still need a lot more practice, Kate. If you are to learn auctioneering you must find more time to devote to it."

"David, I would if I could," she said tiredly, for the hundredth time. "And there is plenty of time. I've got another four months before my year begins."

"Then find more time during them to polish up your skills. You are nowhere near ready to take a real auction."

Kate went back to her office dispiritedly. It was now late November and she was well into her apprenticeship. Learning to conduct an auction was the hardest task she had had to learn. She had managed the administration, the meetings, the discussions, the monitoring of stock, the valuation of submissions, which she did for pleasure as well as experience, especially when it was Chinese porcelain. She had given a successful series of dinners, receptions, and cocktail parties at which she met all Despard's staff, their most valued clients, dealers, rivals, and the press. She had acquiesced agreeably to interviews, even on television, she had posed for pictures—but the first curiosity about her was now dying down.

Meanwhile, from across the Atlantic, came the news that Dominique du Vivier was going from strength to strength, conducting her own auctions—now an established part of New York social life—and reaching unheard of prices. A lot of stuff that had formerly come to Despard's London was now finding its way to New York. There had been a board meeting to discuss it.

"There's no doubt about it, New York is dazzling everyone right now," Nigel Marsh had said gloomily. "A lot of first-class items aren't even coming our way. They are going straight to her."

"Is it any wonder, when you look at the prices she gets?" asked Derek Morley, the head of Accounts. "The sooner Miss Despard is able to conduct her own auctions and receive commensurate publicity, the better it will be."

"I am doing my best," Kate said stiffly, "but I do have a great deal to do and I cannot spare any more time."

"Then we must see to it that you do," Nigel said soothingly. "Surely we cannot expect Kate to do everything," he reprimanded, looking around the table.

"The round of parties and such is over," the head of Accounts said, "and they must have taken up a considerable amount of time." And money, was the implication.

"They were necessary. People had to see that Despard's was unchanged, that it was merely a case of the torch being handed on," Nigel said floridly. "People had to know who and what she was and where she had come from. We gained a great deal of valuable publicity."

"Not much good when we have also lost valuable sales."

"It's Charles—because he is not here," Claudia Jamieson said. "He was an institution. He *was* Despard's."

Just as Dominique du Vivier is New York, flashed through Kate's mind.

"What we need, then, is to make London Kate Despard's," Nigel said firmly, as if the same thought had occurred to him.

"How?" asked somebody.

"Why, some notable sale—"

"Not if she has to conduct the auction," David Holmes said firmly. "She is a long way from ready yet."

"Can't you hurry things up?" asked Nigel wheedlingly.

"No, I can't. When I allow Kate to get up into the rostrum to conduct an important sale it will be when I think she is ready."

And she was nowhere near that. Dominique had already established a commanding lead. Something would have to be done once she started her year proper. She had to learn auctioneering. She had to. She would just have to cut back on other things. Claudia was right. A woman auctioneer was a rarity; one that Dominique had played to the hilt. Something of the same had to happen in London or it would find itself relegated, and when it came to the crunch, Kate would have not a hope in hell of making the best showing.

When she went in to her office an agitated figure who had been pacing back and forth across the carpet turned to her with relief, and burst out, "Thank God! I'd have interrupted you but David is so damned prickly about your not giving enough time to auctioneering—"

"What is it?" asked Kate.

James Grieve, head of Oriental Porcelain, was pale and trembling, obviously deeply upset.

"I've just had a violently abusive Rolf Hobart on the telephone from New York—it seems the T'ang horse we sold him is a fake."

Kate stared, feeling a cold hand take hold of her heart and squeeze. Every expert's nightmare. A second Van Meerhgren, the most brilliant forger of all time, was at work. "Impossible," she managed when she could.

"That's exactly what I said, but he's had it checked by thermoluminescence. You know how distrustful he is no matter what your reputation—he read me the lab report. The horse was made within the last five years . . ."

Kate sank into the nearest chair. "Oh, no." She closed her eyes, felt sick.

"Oh, yes. If this gets out we are in dire straits. Despard's being fooled by a fake and selling it for a quarter of a million pounds."

"It can't be a fake," Kate said hollowly. "It can't. If it is, then we are indeed in trouble because there is a genius of a forger at work . . ."

They stared at each other.

Then James said heavily, "I told him there was absolutely no doubt at all about the horse's provenance; that I had examined it and that you had also authenticated it as genuine, both of us acknowledged experts in our field. He told me that we were both stupid shits who ought to have known better and why the hell didn't we have it checked by thermoluminescence?"

Kate's flush had risen. "Because we had no reason to doubt that it was genuine," she said, and then added slowly, "What I would like to know is what or who made him doubt."

James now sank down into the facing chair.

"Oh, no," he said weakly. "You are not implying that the whole thing was a setup . . . *everything* fake?" Then, more strongly, "Surely not. That would impugn the probity not only of a Despard's employee but of a very upmarket firm of solicitors . . . No, it cannot be that. Even the thought is monstrous."

Is it? wondered Kate. What if Piers Lang is Dr. Frankenstein?

He had returned to Despard's a few days after she had begun her apprenticeship, and she had taken an instinctive dislike to him, uncomfortable at having to agree so soon with the general climate of opinion. He was too handsome, too smooth, too much of a "remittance man." There was something about the loose-lipped mouth and the bold eyes that rubbed her the wrong way. He had offered congratulations, assured her of the same support he had given her father, but Kate found his flattery too fulsome, his protestations too Uriah Heep. To her, he was the kind of man who would cheat at cards and brag about his female conquests. How could Papa have put up with him for three years? she had thought, only to answer herself: because he was good for Despard's. Well, I am prepared to do all I can for the company but I don't know if I am up to having this smarmy piece as my personal assistant. Rollo was right, after all . . . but then, isn't he always?

And to make it worse, about a week later Rollo had come to her, cock-a-hoop, triumphantly bearing proof of his indictment. "I told you that the Dishonourable Piers was in that bitch's pocket; well, now we know he is also in her bed. He was spotted leaving her house in Chester Square yesterday morning at the ungodly hour of 6:30 A.M."

"By whom?" Kate asked automatically. She had not even known her stepsister was in London. "Your private detective?"

"Better than that—a member of your own staff. One of those deliciously hefty young men who work in packing. He is a dedicated fitness enthusiast and jogs every morning before work. He lives in nearby Pimlico and as he was jogging through the square, just as he passed Dominique's house, who should stagger down the front steps but the Dishonorable Piers, looking—I use the young man's very words—like a rag that has been well and truly wrung. He was so bleary eyed he failed to recognize the young man who ran past him, if indeed he even knew him. The Dishonorable Piers is the type who does not notice anyone not from the Upper Echelons. The young man recognized him, though, and naturally, as soon as he got to work he related his tidbit to his colleagues, who passed it on to their friends in other departments. By noon it was round the entire building. This morning, the young man has been transferred to Despard's Downtown on the instructions of Mrs. Hennessy."

"She has *what!*" Kate's voice soared in outrage.

"Now, you know your father gave her a certain amount of leeway when it came to disciplining the junior members of staff. She has acted as headmistress since Miss Hindmarsh retired. But in this instance, I think we now have proof as to where *her* allegiance lies. But I wonder why she should act so swiftly . . . on instructions, perhaps? Everybody knows the Venus has more lovers than I've had hot dinners, so why the haste to play this one down?"

"Because he is an employee of a company she partly controls?"

"Bollocks! She's had affairs with two men here that I know of—thanks to the Old Timers. And she didn't care who knew. So why does she want to conceal her affair with Piers Lang?" A triumphant sniff. "Because he is also her spy, that's why."

So when, a couple of days later, Piers Lang had come to Kate, looking like the cat who had swallowed the canary, she had looked at the Greek god-type face and wondered: Are you?

"I am now in a position to tell you what it is I have been on the trail of, this past week or so," he told her confidentially. "Something rather special."

"Oh?" Kate said warily.

"A piece of first century T'ang."

Kate's interest was caught at once. "Oh?" she had repeated, but with more warmth.

"I got wind of this old recluse wishing to dispose of his

T'ang horse because his insurers have just trebled his insurance premiums." An indulgent chuckle. "I ask you . . . he owns a piece of first century T'ang and is too mean to keep it insured! Anyway, the firm of solicitors who have been asked to act for him in the sale also act for my father—Pothecary, Tillman and Tillman of Lincoln's Inn. Fine old firm, highest reputation. Julian Pothecary is by way of being a friend of mine—we went to school together—and of course, he thought of me at once . . . He knows a bit about Oriental antiquities and he says the horse is first-rate."

He might have been talking about a pretty girl; whatever his reasons for being at Despard's, it was not because he was a lover of fine art.

"Who is this 'recluse'?" Kate asked.

Now Piers Lang looked apologetic. "Julian told me he wishes to remain anonymous. Evidently he's terrified of the Inland Revenue getting wind of the sale as he fights a running battle with them and is terrified they'll come down on him for their share of the proceeds. Julian has been empowered to conduct all negotiations." Confidently, "Julian Pothecary has a flawless reputation in the legal profession, I assure you. All will be absolutely above board. It is not unknown, after all, for items to be set down as 'Property of a Gentleman.' "

"To the public," Kate agreed. "But we, as auctioneers, normally know the consignor."

"Then I think it best you discuss the whole thing with Julian and let him show you the horse."

"He has it?"

"Yes . . . locked away in the vaults. But I can set up an appointment for you to see it."

"Do you know anything of this anonymous gentleman?" Kate asked, not liking being kept in the dark.

"Only that he lived in China for many years—worked for one of the big banks in Shanghai, during which time I gather he acquired some choice bits and pieces. Julian will put you fully in the picture. All I wanted to know is, are you interested?"

"Very much so," Kate answered promptly, resolving to ask this Julian Pothecary several searching questions. "I think we had better call in James Grieve . . ."

And it was with him that Kate, along with Piers Lang, had gone to Lincoln's Inn to the offices of Pothecary, Tillman and Tillman, to be received by Julian Pothecary himself, another example of the Old School, elegant as a model out of *Tailor and Cutter* but sharp as a razor under the urbane surface. He offered them sherry and they chatted generalities for a while before he rose to ask, "And now, may I show you the horse?"

It had been placed on a small table in front of a casement window, so that it was bathed in thin October sunlight, and the moment Kate saw it she felt her skin prick. At first sight it was worth every penny of the quarter of a million pounds reserve the anonymous old gentleman had put on it—and Julian Pothecary's explanation as to that had been genuine, too. Now, a quick glimpse at James told her he was as excited as she was.

Slowly, they walked around the table, examining the horse from every angle. It vibrated with life, from its arched neck and flying mane, to the pawing hooves and flaring nostrils. The patina was right, too, worn as it should be for a bronze so old, a glorious melange of green and bronze and gold, with occasional streaks of ochre where the paint had worn. It was a variation of the famous T'ang flying horse; just as miraculously handled, just as singing in its lines and glorious living *being,* created by the hands of an unknown, unsung genius. Kate found her throat thick, her eyes pricking as they always did in the presence of something approaching perfection in art.

"May I?" she asked Julian Pothecary, who was watching her keenly.

"But of course. I trust you, Miss Despard, to be able to handle the finest and rarest pieces."

He was grave but Kate knew he was also mocking her. She didn't like him, either. She hefted the horse; it felt right, balanced properly. She examined it as closely as she could without a loupe; that would be done once they got it back to Despard's. The faking of T'ang was a time-honored art in itself, and there had been some remarkable ones, emanating from the "factories" in the New Territories. This one looked, on first acquaintance, all right; she could see no signs of modern molding, the marks of a file. Without comment she passed the horse to James, who gave it the same intense scrutiny. Then he gave her an almost imperceptible nod.

'We should be glad to dispose of the horse in a forthcoming sale," Kate said smoothly to the attentively waiting solicitor. "It is fortunate that there is just such a sale in six weeks' time; we will be able to have the horse photographed for inclusion in the catalogue."

"Fortunate indeed," Julian Pothecary agreed, beaming.

"Subject, of course, to further confirmation of the horse as genuine and the provision of any provenance you—or the vendor—may have," Kate went on.

"Indeed," agreed Julian Pothecary fervently. "My client has furnished me with the bill of sale for the horse which he bought in Shanghai in 1908. It had been in the possession of a noble family for some centuries until then. The documents are in Chinese, of course, but I can furnish you with a translation."

It was arranged that the horse would be delivered to Despard's the following day, but they could take away a copy of its provenance, the original being delivered with the horse.

"That was as smooth a customer as ever I saw," James Grieve said, when he and Kate—Piers Lang had other plans and did not accompany them—were in the taxi going back to Despard's.

"Do you think it's fishy?"

"He is—there are crooked solicitors no matter how upmarket—but the horse is genuine, in my opinion. And a rare specimen. T'ang like that does not come on the market often, but if the present owner has had it hidden for the past seventy years then it is no wonder."

"It was a wonder," mused Kate dreamily. "I've never seen anything like it outside a museum."

"It should reach its reserve easily; a piece of such quality always has willing buyers."

Kate sighed. "It is a lot of money, even for a T'ang bronze."

"Prices are ridiculous, I agree—look at the ones your stepsister obtained in New York; but then, she played off two famous enemies against each other. That was what made that auction so spectacular—greed and bitter enmity. Would that we could bring it off here but, alas, neither of those two Russians has ever showed much interest in bronzes. However, there is an American—a bit of a bounder but enormously rich—who's been advised by his financial people to get into collecting and he's decided on bronzes; we sold

him some very fine Benin heads earlier this year. He'd be on
to the T'ang like a shot."

"Yes, there are various names that come to mind," Kate
agreed pensively.

"Then we must see to it that they are informed."

And they had been; the horse reached its reserve in a matter
of seconds; it took exactly twenty-two of them to be sold to
Rolf Hobart for £275,000. And now he was screaming bloody
murder and threatening to sue them for as much as the
traffic would bear because it was a fake.

"He's talking lawsuits and plucking figures out of the air,"
James was saying apprehensively. "We've got to stop that,
somehow. If at all possible we've got to keep this quiet. I've
offered to go across but he won't see me." James paused.
"He'll talk to nobody but you." At Kate's expression, "You
have to go. If word of this gets out you are ruined before
you begin; you authenticated the horse along with me;
Despard's good name is muddied and that's before your
term of trial starts. Dear God, this could not have happened
at a worse time."

Kate was rigid. James eyed her worriedly. She was a
highly strung filly, but he admired the way she'd knuckled
down this past couple of months; worked like stink, she had,
at the office till all hours. Mind you, having only to go
upstairs to be home was a godsend. Charles had been so
right to convert the penthouse. But this was bad; this was
the worst possible disaster that could befall an auction house:
to be played for suckers and sell as genuine a fake that was
known as soon as the proper tests were applied. Which
would have been done had there been the merest *whisper* of
suspicion, he justified to himself. And there wasn't. The
provenance was genuine; we checked as far as is humanly
possible. My God, this bodes ill. How many of the damned
things are there? And who is the genius who made the fake
in the first place? He is going to ruin the market . . .

Which was what Kate was thinking. Is this whole thing a
frame? It all seemed to fall into a pattern that made her
uneasy. Piers Lang introduces the horse to Despard's. The
vendor is adamant about remaining anonymous. A well-
known and reputable firm of solicitors handles all the negotiations. All right, so perhaps James was right when he said
that there were crooks even among them. But the prove-

nance had been so detailed, so—authentic. So had the horse.
God, why didn't I have it double-checked by thermoluminescence, she thought wretchedly. Because you only use that
where there is doubt—and there was none here, absolutely
none. I'd have sworn that horse was real. Just like Venetia
Townsend did about her Raphael—except she was sure it
was a fake. Oh, God, Kate thought miserably. I don't even
have the expertise of one of my own heads of department.
But James authenticated it, too, and he's as knowledgeable
as anyone. Oh, dear God, she thought. Have I been set up?
Have they got me smack in the center of the vise so that
Rolf Hobart can clobber me?

Rollo's mouth had turned down when she had told him who
was showing interest in the horse.
    "Rolf Hobart? He's a nutcase, that one."
    "Is he?"
    "Got a bad reputation in the market. Scads of money but
no finesse. Uses it to clobber the opposition and woe betide
if he loses. Your father hated having him at a sale. You
could depend upon him complaining that his bids weren't
being recognized or some such codswallop. However, when
he wants something price is no object, so . . ."

A very clever fake and a "nutcase" has to go and buy it,
Kate thought, burying her head in her hands. Well, they
couldn't set that up. James told me about him . . .
    "James," she said suddenly, aloud, raising her head from
her hands. "What made you think of Rolf Hobart in connection with the horse?"
    "Well, he is already a customer—albeit an awkward one—
and I knew he was into bronzes and wanted some Chinese—"
    "Yes, but where did you hear that fact?"
    James frowned, recollecting. Then he brightened. "It was
Madame du Vivier. I remember now. At your father's funeral . . . we were talking about business in general and she
happened to mention that Hobart had bought several fine
pieces from her in Hong Kong last year."
    Bingo! Kate thought. She set me up, all right. It *has* to be
her. She plants the horse on Julian Pothecary, who handily
happens to be Piers Lang's family solicitor, and then sows
the seed of Rolf Hobart in James' receptive memory. Dear
God, she must have been working on this even then! But I

have no proof, she thought, tormented with frustration. And then another idea hit her. She rose to her feet.

"Will you excuse me for a moment, James? I shan't be long."

Quickly she ran down two flights and along the corridor to the small cubbyhole Piers Lang shared with the secretary whom he also shared with two other men. The secretary rose to her feet in some fluster at the sudden descent of Kate Despard from On High.

"Miss Despard . . ."

"Miss Sharp, isn't it?"

The girl went pink with pleasure at being known. "Yes. Can I help you?"

"I hope so. Could you check Mr. Lang's diary for me; see when it was he went to Geneva last. I believe it was the week I took over but I cannot remember the exact day . . ."

The girl was reaching for the diary. "Yes . . . it was Monday the seventeenth. Only it was Lausanne he was really going to, but as there is no airport there he had to go to Geneva and then get the special airport bus. He had a midday appointment at the Beau Rivage Palace so I got him on an early flight—"

"Thank you," Kate interrupted pleasantly. "Monday the seventeenth. That is exactly what I needed to know. Thank you, Miss Sharp." And if that rat fink gets to know that I know, so much the better, she thought, as she went back upstairs again. But a further thought stopped her cold. What if I was *meant* to know? What if all this is a little exercise in claw sharpening? Putting the frighteners on me so as to shake me up, rattle my confidence. Yes, it's her style . . . undermine the opposition first. *The little bits of clues have been too easy to find.* The connecting thread too exposed. And didn't she make it only too clear what she thought of my so-called capabilities first time we met? But she would know what Rollo's are . . . Just my luck that he is not here and I've got to work it out for myself. But I'm sure I'm right. It all fits too perfectly. And I've discovered it for myself. Me, Kate Despard, Girl Detective. Rollo smelled the rat but I'm sure I have tracked it to its lair . . .

The adrenaline of her self-confidence was in full spate when she went back into her office.

"I'll call Rolf Hobart," she told James crisply.

"Won't do, I'm afraid," James said, uncomfortable with

his own guilt. "You have to go. I suppose he wants you to grovel—he's that kind. By all accounts a really sadistic piece of work. That, as his compatriots say, is how he gets his kicks—from other people's degradation and humiliation. We'll have to reimburse him, of course, plus a sizable amount by way of compensation. That's no doubt why he wants to see you. You are the only one who can authorize how much."

Kate's face was tight on its bones. Humbling her pride hit her where it hurt. She, bucking to be the world's leading expert on Oriental works of art, had been fooled first time out. Inwardly she was already writhing with humiliation. Oh, how clever Dominique had been. She had read Kate like a book, knew the fierce pride and loyalty she took in her heritage. She'd spouted off about it at their meeting, hadn't she? Painted in foot-high letters that Despard's was what mattered in the long run. Now, she was being called upon to honor her IOU. To the tune, if she knew Rolf Hobart, of half a million pounds at least . . . Of which how much would go to her stepsister?

"Yes, of course I must go," she said finally, tonelessly.

"The Concorde is called for, I think. The sooner you get there, the better," James hinted.

"Yes, of course." Kate said.

"Should I—would you—will you be all right alone? He's got an appalling way of handling people, Hobart. His ex-wives all say he beat them up—"

"Then I could sue him," Kate returned sardonically. "No, from what I saw of Mr. Hobart at the sale he will give me a verbal beating." Her eyes, her voice, were bleak. "Which is no more than I deserve for not spotting the fake."

"No more did I," James said stoutly. "And in my opinion, I very much doubt if anybody else would have either. I've got almost thirty years' experience at Despard's and it's the damnedest fake I have ever seen; it brings into question the same standards that were disputed in the Vermeer forgeries—"

"For which we have no time now. I've got to get to New York before he calls the press."

"You are sure you can handle it alone?"

"If he insists that I go down on my hands and knees then I must," Kate answered.

For one fleeting moment she wished Rollo were here, but he was out of town, visiting an old lover who was selling several of his blue period Picassos, having lost a fortune on his latest musical which had done a belly flop.

"Leave it to me to pick the choicest," Rollo had told her, gleefully rubbing his hands. "He's a darling is dear old Martin, and he won't miss them. He was collecting modern art when you couldn't give it away. Besides, it will be a nice surprise when he sees me turn up."

So he had gone into deepest Worcestershire yesterday afternoon. His official position at Despard's was as Kate's personal assistant, Kate easing him in because she intended to ease Piers Lang out. Now, she decided, she would transfer that piece of slime to the boondocks, and now rather than later. Without absolute proof she could not fire him, but she could demote him. Australia, she thought vengefully, I'll banish him to Sydney. It's a fledgling branch, no glory there, just hard slog—and better still he will be of no use whatsoever to his mistress. Then I'll turn Rollo loose to sniff and poke to his heart's content. He'll soon turn up any more hidden moles. I should have known better than to doubt him in the first place. It will also, she thought cannily, keep him from meddling in other things and antagonizing those loyal to me; people I need more than ever now.

I could do with Rollo right now, she thought again. But, no. This has been served up on your plate; you have to handle it yourself. You are In Charge, aren't you? So act like it.

She buzzed for her assistant secretary. She had taken on a second, though Mrs. Hennessy had not liked it one bit, to deal with the social side of things that had preempted so much of her time, and it was her intention to ease Penny in as she eased Sheelagh Hennessy out. Penny Campion was Kate's age, bright, cheerful, efficient, and she had the further merit of being recommended by Miss Hindmarsh, who was an old friend of Penny's grandmother. Penny and Kate had "clicked" at once, and when she came in now, book and pencil at the ready, Kate said briskly, "Penny, I need to get on the first Concorde to New York. It's an emergency. I don't know how long I'll be gone but hopefully it will be out and back in a day—what time does it leave?"

"You're too late for the morning one but I'll see if I can get you on the six o'clock. But then you'd have to stay overnight because you wouldn't make the eight o'clock back to London. Perhaps tomorrow morning would be best—the ten-thirty flight?" Penny reeled off the flights with ease; in her last job her boss had been almost a Concorde commuter.

"No, it has to be as soon as possible. See if you can make the six o'clock, will you?"

That flight was fully booked, as were all the jumbos; it was not possible to get on a flight before the ten-thirty Concorde next morning; they had a cancellation.

Kate then put in a call to Rolf Hobart, who subjected her to a hail of hysterical abuse and vilification, ending with: "You had better get your ass over here little lady, because if you don't I'm releasing the story to the press. And you'd better be prepared to talk big bucks because if you aren't, then I'm suing you for five million dollars *minimum*."

"I will be in New York at nine-twenty your time—shall we say ten-thirty in your office?"

"I'll give you till eleven o'clock—after that I call a press conference."

He slammed down the phone, leaving Kate both seething and shaking. She hated bullies. Especially those who shouted.

She had a bad night; sleep eluded her. She had got out the copy of the provenance of the T'ang horse; in addition to the translation provided by the solicitors they had made one of their own. Their Chinese expert said the documents were genuine—the style, the kind of paper, the language. He had checked out the name of the family who had sold the vase to its present vendor; they had also turned out to be a genuine aristocratic Mandarin dynasty. She had studied the photographs that had been made of the horse from every angle, some of them closeups, a lot of them magnifications of various parts of it. She could see nothing wrong. But thermoluminescence was the ultimate arbiter. It was an expensive process, the equivalent of carbon dating, but it could prove the age of metals or painted bronzes to within ten years. And Rolf Hobart's lab report said the horse was less than five years old. How? Where? Who? Why? When? revolved round and round in her brain all night, so that she was in a febrile state when she took her seat on the Concorde the next morning. She had no eyes for the Mach meter, the indigo curve of the sky, or ears for the polite German who sat next to her. All she could think of was the forthcoming confrontation. She had a blank check in her handbag; a hurried meeting of the board had agreed that Rolf Hobart had to be placated, by as much as it took. What they were buying back was Despard's good name as well as a fake T'ang horse. She knew, as they left the boardroom, that they were both shocked and disappointed. To have failed them so soon . . . she and James Grieve both. It would not have happened in your father's time, was the unspoken reproach.

Blaise Chandler was also arriving in New York, and it was as he was getting into his waiting limousine that he caught a flash of red hair, an arm urgently raised for a taxi. He straightened, said, "Wait a moment, will you," and, dodging the traffic and the crowd, sprinted across the curve of the road outside the terminal.

"Miss Despard!"

Kate whirled, and he was taken aback at the relief in her face. "Oh, thank God! I was beginning to despair of a taxi and all the limousines are booked. I have to be in New York by eleven; it is literally a matter of life and death. Can you give me a lift?"

"Sure. That's why I came across. I've got a car. Come on . . ."

"Oh, you are an angel in disguise," Kate told him gratefully, as she sank back against the pale grey cushions. It was already quarter-past ten. She had waited endlessly in the passport line, fretting at the delay, checking her watch minute by minute.

"What's the urgency?" Blaise asked.

Kate hesitated, and as she did so saw the liquid softness of the black eyes harden to onyx.

"You still don't trust me, do you?"

Kate had to decide. She took a deep breath and told him all.

"You are tangling with a nasty customer," was his comment. "I don't know him as well as my grandmother, she knew his father, too. Evidently they are all more than slightly crazy, devoted to far-out right-wing causes and suspicious of everything and everybody. He'll want not only his pound of flesh but the commensurate amount of blood." He frowned. "Why you? Alone, I mean? I wouldn't let my wife near him and she's a good deal tougher than you are."

"I am not made of sugar," Kate snapped. It was all right for her to be nervous but not for him to suspect it.

"So I hear," he commented dryly.

"How?"

He turned his head, met her affronted stare. "How else?"

"My God!" Kate muttered fiercely. "Is nothing sacred?"

"I can't be there so I get reports," he said matter-of-factly. "Don't worry, they are good ones."

"But I haven't even started my year yet!" she said indignantly.

"Which is why I am getting reports now. Once you start officially then you are indeed on your own and I cannot interfere. I just wanted to know how you were doing, that's all."

Kate flushed guiltily, moved uneasily. She had not expected any interest on his part.

Blaise was tapping his fingers on his briefcase. "Where do you have to go?" he asked.

"The Hobart Enterprises Building on Fifth Avenue."

"I know it. I'll drop you off."

"Will we make it in time?"

Blaise glanced at his watch. "I don't see why not, but there's no harm in making sure."

He flicked a switch and spoke.

"Jim, we need to make the four hundred section on Fifth Avenue by eleven."

The chauffeur's voice came back confidently: "Will do, Mr. Chandler."

The car picked up speed.

"I thought they didn't like you exceeding fifty miles an hour," Kate observed nervously.

"They don't—if they catch you." After a silence, "How long are you in New York? Will you be going to Despard's?" he asked.

"I doubt it. I go back on the Concorde flight this afternoon."

There was another silence, then, "You say Piers Lang was instrumental in finding the horse?"

"Well, he was approached . . ."

She answered his probing questions for the rest of the journey into New York, and when they drew up outside the skyscraper that housed Hobart Enterprises, Blaise got out first. Instinctively Kate craned her neck. Her first skyscraper, her first visit to New York—and in such circumstances. No, she would *not* be visiting Despard's, not this trip. Nobody had to know she was here. She was not sure whether it was good or bad luck that Blaise Chandler's arrival had coincided with hers, but she felt oddly relieved that he knew. Suddenly she was confident that he would not talk.

"Thank you," she said gratefully. "I'm on time—and you made it possible."

"I'm on your side, if only you would believe it," he said, leaving her open-mouthed as he got back into his car and was driven away.

7

Rolf Hobart had an office only slightly smaller than Wembley Stadium, with his desk—a miniature skating rink—at its far end. Kate was announced by a toad-faced man, and as she walked the length of the room her eyes were magnetized by the horse that was standing smack in the middle of the desk.

"Well?" Rolf Hobart rasped. "There it is. The fake you tried to palm off on me." He was big, looming, threatening, with the hectoring voice of a bully and the arrogance of a man who thought his money entitled him to it.

"Fraud was not intended," Kate corrected, quietly but firmly.

"Don't tell me that you, the supposed expert, were taken in by it!"

Kate forbore to say that he had been, too, until he had had it tested, and admitted truthfully, "Yes, I was. In all my experience I have never seen a fake like this one. May I look at it again?"

"You can take the goddamn thing away with you—once you hand over your check for one million dollars."

One million dollars! It was blackmail, but she was buying back Despard's good name and that was worth many millions, not just one. She knew that if he had wanted he could have refused to accept even that and demanded ten times the amount; he could have refused to accept any unofficial reimbursement and sued them for the usual fantastic amount of zeros. She knew she was being shown who was boss; that it was a cat and mouse game, with her being spared this time, but come the next . . .

She examined the horse. Even now, knowing the results of the thermoluminescence test, she could still regard it as a

158

work of art; all right, it was not old, but it was every bit as beautiful as any made two thousand years ago. Now she understood how the experts must have felt when Van Meerhgren, before their very eyes, created a glorious Vermeer . . . Kate felt reduced to stupidity, her knowledge counting for nothing. First time out she had been caught by a fake, such a fake but, nevertheless, not the real thing. She laid the horse down, reached for her handbag, took out the blank check, made it out for the sum demanded, countersigned it, and held it out silently.

Rolf Hobart all but snatched it from her. And then, not able to leave well enough alone, he launched into a tirade of abuse; his voice rose, his eyes bulged, he came round the desk, stood over Kate and screamed, spittle flecking his lips and occasionally spraying her. She thought he had gone mad, cringed as he held a clenched fist above her head. The ravings became more and more the rantings of a lunatic, to the effect that she had deliberately tried to make him look a fool, that he would not forget this in a hurry, and that he would never set foot in Despard's London ever again; he had only gone there because they were supposed to be *the* house for Oriental fine art. In the future he would stick to his own country, where men were honest; he might have known the goddamn limeys would cheat; they always had and they always would . . .

Suddenly a telephone rang. Rolf Hobart stopped in mid-tirade, turned and snatched up a receiver. Kate could not hear the conversation; her heart was pounding in her ears and her legs had turned to jelly. She had never been so terrified in all her life. She had been sure that at any minute he would lose control of his precarious balance and begin to beat her with those enormous fists. Only his enormous money and power had kept his other beatings from becoming police matters. Leaving the check on the desk, she turned and began to totter to the door. Suddenly she heard Rolf Hobart say, "Wait!" in a totally different voice. She froze but did not turn, hand outstretched for the knob. When he spoke from just behind her she could not believe it was the same man.

"Why didn't you tell me you knew Agatha Chandler?" he said in a voice so conciliatory as to be anxious. "That makes things different . . ." But the blue eyes were still pebbles; he was making some sort of apology because of someone called

Agatha Chandler—*Agatha* Chandler?—but he was not happy about it.

"Let's forget this whole thing, huh? Before Kate's astounded eyes he tore her check into confetti. "All I wanted to do really was teach you a lesson. Nobody puts one over on Rolf Hobart, okay? Just give me back what I paid and we'll call it quits, huh? No hard feelings?"

To Kate's utter bewilderment he held out one of those steamshovel hands. She recoiled disbelievingly before turning to yank open the door and make her escape.

In the lift she leaned against the wall and shook. The man was mad! One minute about to beat her to a pulp, screaming abuse and physically shaking with rage; the next offering an apology because of somebody called Agatha Chandler. And then, as her befuddled brain began to come out of its state of paralyzed shock, she remembered Rollo saying " . . . Agatha Chandler's grandson, and she owns half the world. Old as Methuselah but incredibly powerful still . . ."

When the doors opened she was still leaning there, and not until a voice said, "Miss Despard?" did she come out of her trance to find a uniformed chauffeur, cap under his arm, regarding her somewhat concernedly.

"Yes?" Kate answered.

"Mrs. Chandler has sent a car for you."

"What? A car? Oh." Relief coursed through her. To get away from this place . . . "Thank you."

It stood at the curb, a block long and with darkened windows. The chauffeur eyed her white face, and as he shut the door on her said, "You'll find some restoratives in that console, Miss."

As Kate stretched out a hand to lift the burr walnut flap, she saw that it was shaking. But she managed to lift up one of the crystal decanters from the tantalus, pour herself a double brandy into the shot glass that was also used as a lid. It burned through her veins, jolted to her frozen brain and relaxed her like a poleaxe. She closed her eyes and heaved a tremulous sigh. What a morning! What a madman! What a devious, spiteful, cruel plot. Had she made an enemy or had she not made an enemy of her stepsister?

Dominique had made a declaration of war, and now she was putting in hand her first commando raid. You fool! Kate berated herself. On all sides you were told she was not to be trusted, yet what did you do—you sat back and did nothing.

Rollo was right. You expect everybody to have your own high standards. Shape up, girl, or ship out! This last had her opening her eyes to see that they were driving up a wide avenue with bushes in the middle. That was Park Avenue, wasn't it? And as the lights changed at a cross street she caught a glimpse of the street sign. East 80th Street. East 80th Street! She knew enough of New York to realize that they were going north. Queens, her destination to catch the Concorde that left at 1:45, lay to the east.

She leaned forward to tap on the glass. "You are going the wrong way!"

"No, Miss." He heard her though the glass was thick. "I am to take you back to Mrs. Chandler."

Kidnapped! thought Kate, half hysterically. What a day this was turning out to be!

Agatha Chandler was as bad as Rolf Hobart; what was it about enormous amounts of money that gave you an advanced case of megalomania?

She sank back again, saw the chauffeur pick up a telephone and murmur into it. They turned right into the next cross street. An expensive part of town if the houses were anything to go by, and the streets were clean and well kept. The car drew up outside a large double-fronted house with a pair of French-style entrance doors varnished to a mirror gloss. Just as the car stopped they opened and an elderly butler came down the steps, preceded by a footman who opened the car door. Wanting to pinch herself, Kate got out.

"Good morning, Miss Despard," the butler said gravely, and Kate smiled as she heard the English accent. "Mrs. Chandler is waiting for you."

He led the way up the steps, through the doors and into a high, wide and very handsome hall, with a chessboard floor and a soaring, curvilinear staircase under a magnificent chandelier. Sitting in a wheelchair in the middle of the hall was an old lady; beside her stood—Kate did a double take—an Indian squaw! The old lady touched the arm of her chair and it moved forward toward Kate, silently.

"So, you are Charles' daughter," she boomed, in a voice that could have been heard out in Long Island. "I'm Agatha Chandler. Your father was an old and valued friend of mine."

"How do you do," Kate said stupidly, taking hold of a

hand that was bent and twisted with arthritis, the joints swollen, the fingers out of alignment.

The old lady laughed; it was a guffaw. "Caught you on the hop, didn't I?" The relish in her voice said she loved that. "But when Blaise called me and put me wise to what that crazy Rolf Hobart was up to I decided to take a hand."

"Holding a whip?" Kate managed.

The old lady laughed again, delightedly. "That's the girl!" she enthused. Then more gently, "Was he bad?"

Kate shivered. "Is the world round?"

Agatha Chandler cackled again, slapped one knee as best she could with a crumpled hand. "I soon cooled his ire. Told him I'd cut off his supply of copper if he treated you badly, not to mention a few other things he gets from the Corporation. I've known both Hobarts, father and son. Both nutty as a fruitcake and with power complexes bigger than their egos, which are already oversized. Now come on in, child, away from this drafty hall. Soames!" she bawled at the ancient butler. "You sure the furnace is workin' properly?"

"Yes, Madam. And the thermostat is turned up high."

"Don't feel it," grumbled the old woman.

Kate was beginning to realize that the hall was a hothouse, and that in one corner—the flicker of the flames had caught her eye—was a vast marble fireplace in which there was a fire of the kind that must have burned down Chicago.

"Hate this cold city," Agatha Chandler grumbled. "Only come when I have to. Sooner I get back to my mountains the better. Turn me round, Minnie," she commanded the ancient crone standing silently by. "This is m'cousin Minnie Elkhorn," she said to Kate. Minnie nodded impassively. If anything she was even older than Agatha, which was confirmed when the latter said with relish, "I only keep her around because she's even older'n I am! She don't speak much English but she understands it. Now let's go where it's warm. Come on, Kate."

By now utterly fascinated, Kate followed the procession down the hall. The butler led the way, opened the door, then stood to one side and allowed the wheelchair, pushed by Minnie, to roll through. Kate brought up the rear.

"Now you can bring us some coffee," Agatha ordered. "Hot and black."

"Very good, Madam."

Minnie sited the wheelchair in front of an equally roaring

blaze, and the old lady fumbled among the Crown Jewels liberally bestowed about her person to bring up a lorgnette. "Let's have a good look at you then, Kate Despard. Did you know your father and I were friends?"

"No," Kate answered truthfully.

A grunt. "Not surprisin'. We only met a few years ago, but we hit it off straightaway. You don't look like him."

Nor was she as plain as Blaise had let on. "Straight F's in the looks department," he had said, "but straight A's in brains." She's no Dominique, the old lady thought, but she has commanding height and her legs go on forever. And her hair wasn't carrot at all. Somebody, somewhere, had taken her in hand. Good for her, Agatha thought.

"May I take off my coat?" Kate asked.

The old lady chuckled. "Heat gettin' to you? I have to have it; my blood's awful thin—that's why I come to New York, so the old sawbones can look me over and give me due warnin' of how much time I've got left. You make yourself comfortable."

Kate took off her fleece-lined car coat. Under it she was wearing a pair of cavalry twill trousers tucked into boots, with a chunky bottle-green sweater from Claude Montana over a honey-colored shirt.

"If it's too hot you don't have to come near the fire," Agatha cackled, so Kate bestowed herself on a sumptuously upholstered chesterfield far enough away to be warm without roasting.

There was a tap on the door and the butler came in, carrying a box.

"Now what?" asked the old lady.

"For Miss Despard, Madam. From Mr. Hobart."

"The horse!" exclaimed Kate, rising to her feet with alacrity. "I forgot the horse!" She took it from the butler and, lifting off the lid, confirmed that it was, indeed, the fake horse.

"Can I see it?" Agatha asked.

Kate took it over. The old lady could not hold it but she examined it interestedly. "Why, I think there's somethin' like that back at the ranch," she said finally. "One of my daddy's bits and pieces and he bought a mint o' them from all over the world."

"He collected?" Kate asked.

"Not in your sense of the word; he just bought what took his fancy, is all." Then she said directly, "Is it a good fake?"

"It's an incredible one. So good that never for one moment did I suspect it—nor did my Oriental porcelain expert. This," Kate said feelingly, "is the most dangerous piece I have ever seen in my life."

"Ruin the market, eh?"

"Disastrously."

"Hmm . . ." The old lady brought up her lorgnette again. "Well, put it away safely. I've no doubt you'll be holding some kind of investigation when you get back to London."

"Indeed we will," Kate promised grimly.

"Got any clues?"

"Only suspicions," she replied evasively.

The door opened yet again and in came the coffee, borne by the butler on a massive silver tray. Minnie brought forward a small table on which it was placed. Kate's eyes gleamed at the silver. It was not her province but she knew at once that it was of superb quality.

"Paul Revere," the old lady said, reading her glance.

"Your father?"

The old lady nodded, pleased.

Minnie poured the coffee. "I can't handle things anymore on account of this dratted arthritis," Agatha said roundly. "But it hasn't reached my brain yet." Her laughter boomed again.

She had a vitality that would have shamed anyone half her age, and a presence that stunned. Her face, copper-colored but not as deeply as Minnie's, was like an eagle's and it was incredibly unlined. Her hair—it had to be dyed—was as black as her grandson's, and straight as a ruler. It was dragged tightly back from her face and coiled behind her head in a heavy chignon that was decorated with an ornate Spanish comb of gold set with stones that Kate knew instinctively were emeralds and rubies. She wore what could only be described as a robe—it was far too grand to be called a caftan—made of some heavy brocade encrusted with rich gold embroidery, and around her neck was a collar the like of which Kate had only seen in illustrations of Inca kings: it was literally paved with the same emeralds and rubies. Barbaric eardrops, of the same stones set in gold, hung from her pierced ears, but the only ring she wore was a plain gold wedding band on her left hand. Minnie, on the other hand, wore what Kate recognized with delighted shock as traditional Indian dress, of skin that looked as soft as it no doubt felt, trimmed with beads and fringing and the color of unripened corn. Her hair was snow white and worn much like Agatha's, but without ornament. She gave the old lady her coffee in a special cup that had two handles, through which she threaded her twisted fingers.

"Want somethin' in that?" she asked, as Kate took her cup.

Feeling she had better keep her wits about her and still feeling the stiff slug of brandy she'd had in the car, Kate declined. One sip of the coffee confirmed the rightness of her choice. It was black as sin and hot as Hades.

The old lady's laugh resounded. "My daddy taught me how to make coffee; sometimes it was all he had if he hadn't managed to shoot anythin' to eat, so it had to keep body and soul together."

"I should think it would weld it," gulped Kate, and the old lady yelped with laughter again.

"My Boy said you had spirit. That's why he called me. 'Duchess,' he said, 'you've got to call off Rolf Hobart before he tears a defenseless girl to ribbons.' "

"I am not defenseless," denied Kate, affronted.

"No, I see you are not, but it's hard to get a word in edgewise with Rolf when he gets goin'. Anyway, Blaise seemed more'n a mite put out so I did like he said. He don't ask me for much so when he does I know it's serious."

Kate was silent, her tongue stilled by surprise. He was the strangest man, she thought confusedly. He had no time for her yet he had gone to the trouble of calling his grandmother to use her influence. Which had her asking involuntarily, "Is that what he calls you? 'Duchess'?"

"That's what I was when me and the Boy first set eyes on each other, my then husband bein' an Italian duke. I've had four," she said enjoyably. "Outlived them all. Anyway, the Boy always calls me that—he's the only one who does, but I'm known as Agatha Chandler. It's the name I was born with and it's still the best one I ever had."

"And you call him Boy?" Anyone less like a boy she had yet to meet, Kate thought.

"That's what he was first time we met; only nine years old."

Kate was by now seething with curiosity, and sensing it,

the old lady held out her cup for a refill and settled down for a cozy chat.

In short order, Kate learned that Agatha had, in spite of her four husbands, only one child: Blaise's mother Anne. That like her mother, Anne had had four husbands; that Blaise was the son of her third. She and her fourth had been killed when their car went over the edge of a road during a bad storm while they were driving from France to Italy; that Blaise had a half-sister, Consuelo, who was the daughter of his mother's first husband, an Argentinian, and a half-brother, Gerald, the son of her second husband, an English viscount. They were, according to Agatha, "not worth a light, either of them," but Blaise, whom she had adopted and given her own name, was the light of her life. "He's my heir and he gets the lot," she said vigorously, nodding her head. "Consuelo has had three rich husbands and her fourth isn't exactly piss-poor while Gerald got his father's title and estates. I only see them when they want something; they don't generally like it known that they've got a half-breed grandmother. Gerald's a fool but Consuelo's got brains, 'cept she puts 'em to the wrong use. Can't get 'round her jealousy of Blaise. He's the Chandler, y'see, while she takes after her father, that South American, and I never did trust him."

Under the contempt Kate heard the pain and her expressive face mirrored her feelings, which the old lady saw. "Enough about me," she said briskly, "tell me about yourself. How are you doin' at Despard's?"

"Not as well as I had thought, obviously." There was a shadow over Kate's face and voice.

"If your father hadn't thought you up to it he wouldn't have let you loose. He told me he thought you had the right stuff in you."

Kate's astonishment radiated delight. "He talked about me to you?"

"Many a time. He couldn't do it to his wife, seein' as she more or less rubbed out his life before her, and his step-daughter was in a peculiar position, if you see my meanin'. Besides, she's never been really interested in anyone but herself. The one thing your father wanted was to be reconciled with you. It grieved him sore when you sent his letters back, but I reckon you were doin' your own grievin'." The old lady's voice was plangent, so much softer when she said, "I set great store by my own daddy, so I reckon I understand more than most. If he'd gone off and left me—why, I guess I'd just have died of the hurt."

"I thought I would," Kate said, able to, to this astonishing old lady.

"What changed your mind?" Agatha asked.

Kate hesitated. Dominique du Vivier was this old lady's adored grandson's wife. "Somebody opened my eyes," she evaded. "I'd always seen things from my own point of view. It was seeing them from a different angle that showed me I had to come back out of the cul-de-sac I'd landed myself in."

The old lady nodded sagely. "I've been down one or two myself."

They smiled, perfectly in charity, already thoroughly at home with each other.

"Thank you for coming to my aid," Kate blurted impulsively.

"Only because Blaise asked me to. I reckon it was right lucky for him to be comin' back to New York at the same time as you." Here she sighed. "The Boy does a mint o' travelin' seein' as how I can't—not any more, leastways. This dratted arthritis has got me hog-tied like some steer."

"I shall thank him when I see him," Kate said politely.

Which turned out to be sooner than expected. She was glancing at her watch, astonished to find that an hour had gone by and about to make her farewells and leave, when the door opened again and in came the man himself.

He nodded at Kate, went across to bend over his grandmother, who put her hand up to his face with a look that had Kate glancing quickly away. When he straightened, Kate cleared her throat to say, "Thank you for—for coming to my aid, or rather, asking your grandmother to do so."

"It worked, then?"

"I never saw anybody change so quickly."

Blaise glanced down at his grandmother with affection. "Hobart Enterprises does a lot of business with the Corporation; we are their only suppliers of certain vital commodities, besides which, the Duchess always could beat a Hobart at arm-wrestling."

The old lady guffawed. " 'Twas my daddy who taught me" she allowed. "That's him," she said to Kate, nodding to the portrait above the mantel, at which Kate had wanted to stare for some time. "Black Jack Chandler was his name."

He was a man in his forties, with the spreading moustaches of the period—late eighteen hundreds—wearing ringed buckskins and carrying a rifle across his crossed knees. He had black hair and bright blue eyes and the weatherbeaten skin of a man who lived outdoors. Kate looked at it and then stood up to look closer. Finally, in a funny voice she said, "Correct me if I'm wrong, but—isn't that a Remington?"

The old lady was mightily pleased. "Well now, if that don't beat all. Not many people ever spot that."

"I know he didn't paint many portraits but there is no mistaking his style."

"You know Western art?"

"I'm learning. It's a hobby of mine. I had not realized there was so much of it or that it was of such superb quality."

"I reckon there's a whole slew of Remingtons back at the ranch," the old lady said. "My daddy and Frederic Remington were friends."

Kate felt lightheaded. Even one Remington was worth a fortune.

"We got all sorts come to that—paintings, sculptures, Indian work—why, there's a wooden Indian so real you'd check you still had your scalp."

Looking at the sparkling golden eyes, the vivid interest in the face, the obvious longing to see all this, Agatha made one of her lightning decisions. "Tell you what, Kate. It's Friday and I'm flyin' back to Colorado this afternoon. How'd you like to come with me and spend the weekend?"

Kate drew in an ecstatic breath. "Could I?" Then common sense asserted itself. "No, I should be getting back to London with the fake—"

"Why? What can you do over the weekend? Why don't you go and call London, tell them you won't be back till Monday mornin'. We've got Corporation planes goin' back and forth across the Atlantic all the time and we could put you on one from Denver Sunday night. You tell them you'll be back at your desk nine-thirty Monday morning. After all, aren't you the boss now?"

That she was still coming to terms with the fact, Kate forbore to mention, but it galvanized her to say, "I am, aren't I? And we've got the horse—"

"And you can take my word that Rolf Hobart won't say

so much as a syllable about it all," the old lady promised. "Boy, you take Kate to a phone so she can call London."

Kate looked at him. "With pleasure," he said, but in such a way that she could not tell whether it was or not. He *was* a puzzling man, she fretted. One minute going to the trouble of involving his grandmother to pull Kate's all but blackened chestnuts out of the fire, the next acting as though she ought to have taken them elsewhere to eat. Oh, I give up, she thought, as she followed him to a smaller sitting room, just as overfurnished and overheated as the drawing room next door. All in all, Kate thought, the decor was of an age with its owner. This room and the one she had left could have been transplanted into a museum without moving a thing; overstuffed furniture, heavily framed pictures, antimacassars, ferns in pots and all.

She spoke to James Grieve, whose relief almost melted the transatlantic line. "He is quite satisfied?" he inquired anxiously.

"Yes, quite. He wishes to regard the whole matter as closed. We have lost a client we can well do without, but we have kept Despard's good name unsullied."

"Kate, you are a marvel," James exulted. "You deserve your weekend. I think I shall go out tonight myself and get drunk. I've been wearing a hole in my carpet waiting for your call. Well done, *very* well done!"

"Thank you," Kate said. She had not told him of Agatha's intervention; she would explain the whole when she returned. "Do you know if Rollo is back yet?"

"Haven't seen him. Do you want me to find out?"

"No, it doesn't matter. But tell him if he does return and wants to know where I am."

"With pleasure," James agreed warmly. "Have a good weekend. I know I shall enjoy mine. Bless you again, Kate."

"Well?" the old lady wanted to know.

"I should love to come to Colorado," Kate said happily. "Whereabouts is the ranch?" she asked eagerly.

"Roaring Fork Valley," Blaise said. When that meant nothing: "You've heard of Aspen?"

"The ski resort? Oh, yes, who hasn't?"

"Aspen is at the head of the Roaring Fork Valley."

Kate's eyes shone.

"Do you ski?" asked the old lady.

"I never have, but there's always a first time."

"Well, we'll see what time we do have. Now then, don't you worry none about clothes. We've got plenty of stuff at the ranch as'll fit you fine. Do you ride?"

"Oh, yes!" The mobile face radiated joy.

"We've got three tennis courts and two pools, one inside and one out so you won't lack for exercise." The old lady turned to her grandson. "The Boy here, he's a demon for sport."

"I like it myself," Kate agreed happily.

Odd, Blaise mused. He had thought her beyond redemption, yet had he not known who she was, he would never have connected the sullen, chip-on-both-shoulders girl with her defiantly slovenly dress style and her truculent attitude with this bright, sparkling, vivid young woman whose thick glossy hair shone like a newly released chestnut and whose clothes showed both taste and knowledge of what was right for her.

"And you can have a good look at all the stuff back at the ranch," Agatha was saying enjoyably. "My daddy was a magpie; he never could see anything that took his fancy and not buy it." She looked up at the mantel, crammed with photographs, all of them sepia-colored and in original frames, and searched for the clock, almost hidden by them. "We'll have a light lunch and then we'll leave about three o'clock. You're stayin' to lunch, aren't you, Boy?"

"Don't you want me to, now that you've got a captive audience?"

The old lady cackled. "Go along with you."

It was obvious, thought Kate, that theirs was a deeply bonded relationship. There was a teasing quality to the dark voice when he called his grandmother "Duchess," but the bedrock was solid with love.

Lunch was at a table which would have held fifty, in a dining room again heavy with turn-of-the-century furniture; lustrous mahogany that Kate would have been delighted to include in any Despard's sale. The food was western style; first a delicately flavored, freshly caught trout—"from the Roaring Fork," the old lady informed Kate, "we brought it with us"—followed by a steak, "bred right on the ranch," of a size and tenderness such as Kate had never experienced. Accompanying it was a baked potato, also of a flavor and consistency that was new, piled with a dressing of sour cream and chives. There was a bowl of sweet corn, and the biscuits were hot from the oven. And when it came to the dessert, Kate was at once converted to American food, for it was pecan pie.

As she cleaned her plate of a second helping, Kate sighed, "If that is what you call a 'light lunch' I tremble to think what a heavy one might be."

"Nonsense! I like to see a good, healthy appetite. And it won't do you no harm to put a few more pounds on that frame of yours. I bet you wouldn't believe I was once like a willow myself—now I'm more like a whole grove of oaks." The old lady took her five-by-five size in her stride, as she took everything else.

When the time came to leave, it was Blaise who carefully wrapped his grandmother in a sable cape that had Kate's eyes popping, handed over to her a small, brass-bound leather box which she carried on her lap. Minnie, who waited impassively to one side, answered placidly when the old lady questioned her sharply in a language Kate did not understand and which sounded like grunts and clicks. Finally, Kate bringing up the rear, the chair was pushed down the ramp that had been laid over the front steps to where the enormous car waited. Now Kate realized why it had such a specially wide door. Blaise bent to put one arm under his grandmother's knees and another under her shoulders, then he swung her up and into the back seat. The wheelchair was folded and stowed away in the trunk, and as Minnie got in beside the chauffeur, Kate took her seat by the old woman, on her far side.

The old lady leaned forward to raise her face to her grandson. "Now you'll remember what I said about that Anaconda business?"

"Don't I always do as you say?" he asked.

"Ha! I could give you more than one instance where you did anything but!" snorted the old lady. "I know you tell me one thing and then go off and do another." But as he bent to her she put her arms around his neck and hugged him fiercely. "Take care," she commanded gruffly.

"I'll call you tonight."

"Mind you do, now."

As she sat back, he looked across at Kate. "Have a nice weekend," he said.

"Thank you, and—for everything—thank you," Kate said.

He smiled and she blinked. Then he stood back, shut the door, and the car moved off.

The luxurious interior of the car, all grey suede and burr walnut, was every bit as overheated as the house, but the Duchess—Kate was already beginning to think of her as that—huddled inside her sables.

When they were on their own for a few moments, Blaise had taken the time to explain to Kate the reason for the hothouse atmosphere. "My grandmother has a rare blood disease and she feels the cold intensely. Unless there is constant heat she tightens up. That's why she comes to New York to be gone over, not for the arthritis."

Kate had nodded, both touched by his concern and grateful for his explanation. "So bear with the heat if you can."

"No sweat," Kate had returned blithely, and felt oddly and elatedly rewarded by his grin.

Now, the old lady turned to wave, and Kate saw that in spite of the bitterly cold New York day, Blaise stood on the pavement until the car turned the corner. Agatha turned from the window to sigh contentedly. "That's my Boy," she said proudly.

They drove to a far part of JFK that was used by private planes, and there they boarded a Grumman Gulfstream painted a bright copper color, with the logo of the Chan-Corp—an entwined C—emblazed on its tail fin. The Duchess's chair was put onto a hoist, while Kate climbed the stairs, and found herself in a well-appointed lounge, all cream and beige, from the carpets on the floor to the curtains at the windows and the comfortably cushioned fauteuils placed in front of them. There were lamps on the tables and a pile of the latest magazines. A smiling stewardess greeted them.

"Last lap," the Duchess sighed gratefully, as she divested herself of her sables.

"Just three hours to Aspen and then thirty minutes to the ranch. We should be there by six o'clock—Mountain time," she explained to Kate, who looked surprised, seeing as it was already four P.M. That's two hours behind New York."

Of course, Kate reminded herself. This is a continent not a country . . .

"Did you have a good visit, Mrs. Chandler?" asked the stewardess.

"I've had better. How's things back home?"

"Just fine. Weather was perfect when we left Denver this morning, cold and bright."

"You had some snow, I hear."

"Never stopped over the weekend. Good news for Aspen and Snowmass, though."

"I reckon," the old lady agreed. "Kate, this is Gloria. She always looks after me when I come to New York. Gloria, this is Miss Despard. She's comin' for the weekend. Never been to Colorado before."

"Or America for that matter," Kate sighed ruefully. "But I'll be coming again."

"I'm glad you like it," Gloria smiled, with all the complacence of one who knew that nothing else was possible. "Can I get you anything?"

"No, thank you."

"We'll have a nice cup of tea once we're airborne," the Duchess said. "Minnie, did you bring my tea?"

Minnie, so silent that Kate had forgotten her, displayed a tin of what Kate recognized as the best Assam.

"You want anything, you just ring now," Gloria ordered. "Bell's right by your chair."

Kate had been born, if not to luxury, then to comfortable living. The house in Holland Park had been a large one, and well furnished; she had never gone short of money, but her mother's innate thriftiness had instilled in her an almost Calvinistic horror of ostentation. By her standards—by just about anybody's standards—the Chandlers were among the Super Rich; Rollo had told her that Croesus could not have mustered bigger assets and she had been conscious, since being picked up by the car outside Hobart Enterprises, that she was entering a world where millions were handled the way she handled hundreds. Was that why Dominique had married Blaise Chandler—aside from his obvious physical attractions, of course? The fortune was based on copper, Black Jack having found a fabulous strike in a place called Lucky Dollar Mine, but the Corporation was now multinational and in addition to copper it mined tin, tungsten, vanadium—whatever that was—and something else called molybdenum. It also produced lead and coal. It also owned oil wells. And the Chandler Bank, a chain of hotels, and an enormous amount of real estate. There was a shipping line . . . All this Kate had learned from a quick peek at a copy of *Forbes* which she had found in the sitting room where she had made her phone call. Now, surreptitiously glancing at the magazines on the table she saw another copy of the same magazine. She would be able to finish the article.

The jet's engines rumbled but as Kate waited for it to roll forward, the door at the far end of the cabin opened and a middle-aged man with iron-grey hair and a deep tan wearing a uniform of the same copper color as the plane stooped to come in from the cockpit, taking off his hat as he did so.

"Well now, Jake," Agatha hailed him. "Are we going to have a nice smooth flight?"

"Should do, ma'am. Nothin' between us and Denver 'cept clouds, and not too many of them."

"Good, good . . . This is Jake Larsen, my pilot for many a year," the old lady introduced.

The pilot smiled at Kate. "Welcome aboard, ma'am. Anything you want, you just ask. We'll be takin' off any minute but I always come and see how Miz Chandler wants things before we do."

"Just fly her straight and smooth, is all," Agatha said. "I'm feelin' a lot better goin' home than I was comin' away. Don't you worry about me none. You've been talking to that grandson of mine, haven't you? I always get the porcelain treatment once he's been around."

Jake grinned. "None of us has a hankerin' to be around Mr. Chandler if somethin' happens to you," he said.

Agatha grumbled on, but proudly. She gloried in the obvious fact of Blaise's care and protection, which was not, Kate knew with absolute conviction, given because he was her heir.

The pilot went back to his cockpit and almost at once the airplane began to roll forward. By the time they took off Minnie was sitting stitching away, while Agatha had her face buried in that morning's copy of the *Denver Post*. Only when the plane had leveled off, at what the altimeter above the cockpit door said was 38,000 feet, did Kate notice that Agatha's hand, when it set down the paper, trembled slightly. Noticing Kate's concern, "Never can get used to bein' off the ground," she said gruffly. "But I'm not supposed to spend days on a train and a car is out of the question, so when I have to come and be put under the microscope I have to fly. Blaise says to let the doctors come to me, but it don't seem right totin' all that equipment clear 'cross the country."

Once she had her tea she perked up noticeably, and Kate found the journey flew by under the influence of Agatha Chandler's unflagging tongue. She loved to gossip, leapfrogging from topic to topic without a break. Thus Kate learned that she neither liked nor approved of her grandson's marriage; that Kate's stepmother was a ravishingly pretty noodlehead with a jealous streak a mile wide; that there was no love lost between Blaise's wife and grandmother; that she, too, had idolized her father, her mother, a full-blooded Shoshone, having died in childbirth, along with her son, when Agatha was five; that she worried about what would happen to her grandson once she was gone, hooked as he was on a woman who had deliberately started him on the habit.

". . . women since he was old enough to go into long pants. He loved 'em and he left 'em and I didn't mind because that's the kind of women they were. For lovin' and leavin'. I knew he'd settle down in time, but I never expected he'd end up being dragged around by the only tail men have behind a woman who's likely to do him in unless he comes to his senses. That's all I hope for. That one day he'll kick the habit, see the light or whatever it takes to come back to himself . . ."

The old lady was more or less rambling out loud, but loud enough for Kate to hear. She sat, red-faced and embarrassed. Rollo would have told her to sit tight and memorize every word, but she had not his penchant for eavesdropping. Besides, Blaise Chandler would be steaming if he knew what his grandmother was doing. Now she knew why he had looked so unforthcoming when Agatha said she was taking Kate back to Colorado. But to do him justice he had not intervened. It had not been said, but Kate was strongly of the impression that Agatha Chandler had not much time left in which to be indulged by her favorite grandson.

". . . course, he works damned hard. Only time he relaxes—really relaxes—is when he comes home to the ranch. He loves the place, as I do. Took one look when he was a boy and fell in love with it. Sat a horse like a sissy Frenchman at first, but we soon had him in a western stock saddle and spending eight to ten hours in it every day. Got good enough to compete down at the Colorado Springs Rodeo. Sits a horse like he is growin' out of it. Just like my daddy. Now there was a horseman . . . But then, if you've got Indian blood you can ride. Comes natural."

"Your father was part-Indian, too?"

"His mother was a full-blooded Blackfoot; Shining Water was her name. She got taken by a war party of Crow and my daddy's father rescued her. He was a mountain man. My daddy was born in a gully while my granddaddy watched some Crows and Blackfoot fight it out. He told him she never made a sound . . ."

The old lady nodded, smiling to herself, and still smiling, fell asleep. Kate let loose a long sigh, and in doing so caught sight of Minnie, who was watching her. As they held eyes Kate saw the face lighten, the eyes match the smile that appeared on the mouth. She's old, it said, and she's lonely. Bear with her. She's worth it. Kate nodded, and Minnie's eyes went back to her beadwork while Kate first sat and stared out of the window seeing only her thoughts, before turning back to the magazine that was such a mine of information. She read the article, her mind boggling at the figures given for the net worth of Agatha Chandler; the kind of figures quoted when the House of Commons debated the chancellor's budget: billions rather than millions. And it had all begun when a poor prospector with a squaw wife found a mother lode of copper bearing ore.

Agatha woke up and continued talking as though she had just stopped momentarily to collect her thoughts, uncannily echoing what Kate had been reading. " . . . the Chandlers were mountain men way back when they first traded up the Snake River more'n a hundred and fifty years ago. We are Western through and through. The Old West, that is. The one I remember, and it had been put to an end even then by the railroad. My father, when he was young, he wouldn't see hide nor hair of a livin' soul for months at a time. You could lose yourself in the wild in those days, but then, you still can if you don't know your way about."

"How big is the ranch?"

"Not so big, now. Down to forty thousand acres. Once was a quarter of a million. Forty thousand is enough to keep an eye on nowadays, though. Ranching ain't dude ranchin'. The Lucky Dollar is a workin' ranch. 'Sides, we're ten thousand feet up. Gets cold of a night. Then there's the snow. That's why we fly in and out by helicopter. Time was, we used to be snowed in for the winter."

Gloria, ever alert to the needs of the old woman, came forward to ask if anything was required, and Agatha requested a bourbon and branch water. Kate settled for black coffee, desperate now to keep awake. The heat of the cabin, the wine at lunch, and the constant drone of the old lady's voice made her eyelids weigh as much as the plane but lose the struggle to stay up.

Agatha smiled as Kate's head dropped, and she signaled to Gloria to cover the sleeping girl with a light blanket. What a nice child, she thought. Yes, and at the opposite end of the pole from Dominique. She sighed as she always did at that name. She neither liked nor approved of her beloved grandson's wife. Hothouse orchid! she snorted inwardly. Never set foot on the ranch or come within a thousand miles of it, wrinkles her nose at the word cattle and only rides horses if she can be duded up in all those fancy tight pants and hard hats. And it ain't as though we don't have all the creature comforts she sets such store by, neither. Why, my daddy installed the first bathrooms west of the Rockies! She sighed again, heavily. I don't care what they say about modern marriage, she thought, disgusted. What my Boy's got ain't one at all.

They landed at Denver just before six-thirty, having encountered a headwind blowing a blizzard over the Rockies that had left everything a dazzling white. Kate was half asleep, but the cold and the thinner air to which she woke made her glad of the heavy suede coat she was wearing. They crunched across snow, even now being cleared by a snow plow, and bestowed themselves in a huge station wagon that drove them several hundred yards to a Sikorsky helicopter that awaited them. Inside, it was as comfortable as the Gulfstream, and every bit as hot. It was dark, so Kate could see nothing out of the windows except, in the distance, the shining snowcaps of mountains lit by the new moon.

"The Rockies?" she asked the Duchess, excitedly.

"The same," the old lady confirmed jovially.

They landed on a brightly lit helicopter pad, and Kate was surprised to see the enormous bulk of a three-storied house loom up not fifty yards away. She had expected a frame house, or at least one built of logs. This was brick and reminiscent of Versailles . . . They walked—or rather trotted because it was bone-piercingly cold—along a brick-paved path and then into the hot-oven heat of a conservatory, as green with plants as the Congo and moistly damp with humidity.

"Ahh . . . that's better," pronounced the Duchess, throwing off her sables. "Had some more snow, I see."

"Started just before noon, but forecast is for fine dry weather over the next couple of days," the man pushing her wheelchair said.

"Good, good . . . don't want our visitor to be snowed in first time round. Kate, this is Frank Kramer; he's my—what would you say you were, Frank?"

The middle-aged, craggy-faced man removed his Stetson and scratched his grizzled short-back-and-sides head. "Well, I guess you could say I do just about everything you ask me to," he allowed.

"Secretary-cum-general factotum?" smiled Kate as he shook her outstretched hand.

"This here's Kate Despard," the Duchess said. "All the way from England for the very first time. We have to show her some Western hospitality, Frank."

"It will be our pleasure, ma'am," he promised.

"Let me get settled in, and then come see me and tell me what's been happening while I've been havin' my goin' over," the old lady said. "Stay to dinner."

"I'll do that, ma'am," he promised, touched his Stetson and left through the vast, engraved glass doors, letting as little cold air in as possible.

"Right . . . now I can drive myself," the Duchess said. She led the way, Minnie following carrying the sables and the leather box, Kate bringing up the rear. The conservatory led into a large hall, hung with the heads of hunted and shot game; there was a staircase as ornately carved as a cuckoo clock up which a stagecoach could have been driven, but they took the small elevator next to it, which let them out on a gallery two floors up. The floor was tiled, Spanish style, and there were more animal heads hung on the walls along with several paintings. Kate longed to look closer, because she was sure she recognized some of them as famous and high-priced names, but she followed through the gallery to a big door which Minnie opened.

"This here's where you'll sleep," the old lady said.

The fourposter would have slept six and once again the furniture was turn-of-the-century, standing on a carpet that Kate was willing to swear was a rare pictorial Chinese silk.

The walls were crowded with pictures—all Western—and when Minnie flung open another door it was to reveal a magnificent Edwardian bathroom, all marble and mahogany.

"I'll have some clothes looked out for you," the old lady said, "but don't bother to change if you don't want to. We don't sit on ceremony around here. Dinner's at eight. Somebody'll come up to show you where." A chuckle. "This is an awful big house."

Left alone, Kate prowled around her part of it. The ceiling was an intricate mass of molding and cornices, the wallpaper flock, and the paintings—she caught her breath and felt dizzy—one was a Bierstadt, two were Catlins, and the fourth was a Remington. In the bathroom, on the plain white wall, hung a glorious Eastman of a buffalo hunt. It was, like all the paintings, behind glass. Thank God for that, Kate thought with a heartfelt pang of relief. It may not be the done thing but it has been the saving of these canvasses.

Back in her room she sat down on the bed, then looked closer at the bedspread. It was of patchwork, mainly blue and white, of a design that struck a chord in Kate's memory. It was also hand-stitched. The pillows were trimmed with real cotton lace, and when she looked at the bell pull hanging by the ornate bedhead, she discovered that it was made of Indian beadwork: the kind of thing Minnie had been doing on the plane.

"This is not a house," Kate said out loud. "It's a living museum!" Excitement was making her skin prick. What other glories lay around, only waiting to be identified?

The water was boiling, the toiletries modern: bath oil, talcum, soap. There was a shower but it was as old as the bath and Kate was not sure how to operate the knobs and levers, so she left it alone and soaked instead in water deep enough to swim in. The towels were sheet-sized and warm from the heated towel racks, and when she went back into her bedroom there on the bed were a pair of clean but faded Levis and a check shirt.

Well, she did say informal, Kate thought.

It was funny, she reflected later, as she eyed her fully dressed reflection. Shirt and jeans had been her uniform before, but with her hair cut and styled and a modicum of discreet makeup, they now looked completely different on her. She lifted her feet to examine the cowboy boots. They were astonishingly comfortable. Her own boots had disappeared.

She was wondering who would come to collect her, when somebody knocked before opening the door.

"Evenin', ma'am. You ready to go downstairs now?" She was young, black-haired, very pretty and a pure-blooded Indian.

"Yes, please."

"I'm Nula."

"How do you do," Kate said.

"I'll be lookin' after you so whatever you don't see you just ask me, okay?"

"Fine. Thank you."

The girl eyed her. "Those clothes fit pretty well. How's the boots?"

"Very comfortable. How did you know my size?"

"Took your own boots away. Miss Agatha, she likes to keep a stock of clothes for unexpected visitors. She likes company, and we don't get so much nowadays seein' she don't get around too well."

Nula led the way along Kate's side of the gallery to a door at its corner, where they found a staircase which ended at another door and a long corridor. Cabinets lined the walls, filled with chunks of various minerals, and the walls were hung with all kinds of guns. There were also more animal heads. Kate recognized a wolf and a bear, a buffalo, what looked like a lioness, and others with horns to which she could not put names. Nula saw her looking. "That's a pronghorn, and that one's an elk."

"Who shot them?"

"Miss Agatha's daddy. He was reckoned to be the best shot in Colorado." Chattily, "His mother was my own mama's great-grandmother's sister."

Remembering what the Duchess had told her, Kate said, "So you are a Blackfoot?"

"Yes, ma'am."

Wait till I tell Rollo, Kate thought. He was going to be absolutely *livid* at the thought of missing all this.

The Duchess was in the conservatory, a specially designed small table pulled over the wheelchair and her lap, on which were piles of papers. Sitting beside her was Frank Kramer, who rose to his feet as Kate approached.

"Well, now you look more the thing," the Duchess approved.

"Do you keep a shop here as well as everything else?" Kate joked.

"Don't need to," answered the old lady. "My daddy always used to keep a whole slew of outfits for folks as came unprepared and I guess I've continued the habit. Now then, how about a drink before dinner?"

"Could I have a whisky sour?" Kate asked tentatively.

The Duchess smiled. "Sounds like you want to try something you ain't had before."

"I haven't tasted one but I do like the sound of it."

The taste was even better; Kate sipped, licked away the froth which stood an inch deep at the top of her glass and said, "Mmm—it is delicious."

"That's the bourbon," the Duchess told her. "Which is what I drink. Though nowadays it's more branch water than sour mash whisky."

"What's branch water?" Kate asked, fascinated by this new language.

"Pure water from the branch of a river, in this case the Roaring Fork. You'll see it all tomorrow. I'll take you over the whole spread."

Dinner was in a cavernous dining room with a fireplace that would not have looked out of place in Brobdignag. Kate and Frank Kramer sat opposite the Duchess with Minnie on her other side, where, as she had done at lunch, she unobtrusively saw to it that anything the old lady needed was within easy reach; she also, Kate noticed, cut the thick slices which came from what looked like a side of beef into manageable bite-sized portions, easily picked up by the gnarled, arthritic hands. This room was paneled, and she made a note to examine it as and when she could because it looked to her like sixteenth-century linenfold, and knowing what she already did about Black Jack Chandler, it was bound to be the real thing.

Like the Tiffany lampshade that hung low above the dining table, and the vast sideboard that appeared to be a very fine example of Art Deco. It was only when she at last managed to give her attention to her food, and picked up her knife and fork, that she realized from the weight and the polish that the cutlery was solid silver. By the time she had worked her way through dinner, aided and abetted by two glasses of superb claret that slid down her throat like silk, she was beginning to feel the cumulative results of her

crammed-with-incident day; that and the altitude combined
to all but knock her off her feet.

She remembered apologizing, yawning profusely, and stum-
bling after Nula down corridors and up flights of stairs, back
to her bedroom, but she could not remember undressing or
climbing into the big fourposter. She woke up in the night
feeling terribly thirsty—unused to the claret she had drunk
and not one but two whisky sours before that—and, finding
her way to the bathroom, drained two tumblerfuls of the
most delicious, mountain-fresh, ice-cold water. Making her
way back to bed she felt hot, and feeling the old-fashioned
radiators beneath the window, found that they were full on.
Pulling aside the bobble-fringed velvet curtain she found a
heavy Nottingham lace one beneath that, but managed to
open and heave up a few inches the bottom casement window. Instantly, icy air had her bed-warm flesh sprouting
goose pimples and she retreated, but not before she caught a
glimpse, in the distance, of the Continental Divide riding the
sky like some glorious spaceship, the moon turning its snow-
cap to sparkling silver. And as she gazed, heedless now of
her chilling flesh, she heard a sound that stilled her breath: a
strange, coughing sound. In response, she heard the nervous
whinny of a horse, and then the cough again. She had to let
out her breath, but the lungful she drew in was so cold and
thin it made her cough and she scuttled back to her cooling
bed. Curling up into a ball, she sighed once, deeply and
luxuriously. She just knew she was going to love Colorado.

The smell of fresh coffee woke her, nose twitching like Brer
Rabbit's, and she emerged from under the bedclothes to see
Nula placing a tray on the marble night stand.

"Mornin', ma'am. I guess you slept well?"

Yawning and stretching, "That I did," admitted Kate
happily.

The clock on the night stand said ten o'clock. She had no
idea what time she came to bed; she had not been conscious
of time.

"I've brung you all the fixin's. The mountain air always
gives folk a powerful appetite."

"Do you know, I am hungry," Kate confessed amazedly.
Normally, food was a hit or miss affair with her; if she was
busy and pressed for time her lunch would be a Mars bar,
and breakfast was normally a big cup of black coffee. When

she removed the tray's silver cover she saw that the plate on the tray contained bacon strips, scrambled egg, mushrooms, tomatoes, hash browns, and a thick yellow square that Nula told her was cornbread. There was also a tall glass of orange juice so fresh and cold it made her teeth protest. And the coffee smelled ambrosial.

"I'm to take you down to Miss Agatha when you're ready," Nula smiled. "You just pull on that rope and I'll be with you straight off." She took away the clothes Kate had worn the night before and left her to enjoy her breakfast.

Munching away, Kate eyed the telephone by the bed. She longed to call Rollo, turn him green with envy and rabid with curiosity; she felt the need to tell *someone* of the marvel that had befallen her since providence took pity and arranged for Blaise Chandler to see her at Kennedy Airport. Finally she decided against it; let him stew in his curiosity. It was what he invariably did to her. Besides, this is your show, Kate. Rollo didn't even get to audition . . .

This morning, feeling like a shower, she investigated the knobs and dials and by dint of experimentation managed to get a perfectly judged mixture of hot and cold. She sang as she scrubbed, and bringing back fresh clothes, Nula heard her and smiled. The Lucky Dollar did seem to have that effect on folks . . .

Dressed not only in fresh jeans and a shirt but also fresh underwear, Kate once more followed Nula downstairs, but this time she hung out of open windows to see each section of the house. The exterior was of pink brick with a white trim, and from one window she caught the astonishing sight of a formal French-style parterre, with a Crystal Palace–sized conservatory beyond—that had to be the one she'd been in last night.

"Where is the ranch?" she asked naïvely, making Nula laugh as she answered, "This is the ranch, ma'am." Her laugh became an understanding chuckle. "I guess you were expecting a frame house like you see in the movies."

Kate had the grace to blush, as she realized that to the Chandlers the ranch was what San Simeon had been to William Randolph Hearst.

This morning, Agatha was wearing a divided skirt of heavy brown tweed over boots not unlike the ones on Kate's feet. Instead of a shirt she had a rollneck sweater and a thick matching tweed jacket with leather patches on the elbows and rimming the cuffs. On her head was a Stetson. She had divested herself of all her jewelry except the barbaric earrings. This time, the man with her was steeple-tall and sunbleached blond, wearing, Kate realized with a thrill, the uniform of a cowboy. Levis, chaps, shirt, and Levi jacket. Held in his hands was a sweat-stained Stetson.

"Mornin'," the old lady greeted. "You slept real well, Nula says."

"Like a log, except when I had to get up because I was thirsty. Oh, and I heard the strangest sound, some kind of an animal, well—coughing."

The tall blond man smiled. "That would be a mountain lion, ma'am—I guess you call them cougars?"

"This here's my foreman, Jed Stone. I've been askin' him to cut out a horse for you."

Kate's hand disappeared into a large, calloused one that was surprisingly gentle. "Welcome to the Lucky Dollar, ma'am."

"Jed was born on the ranch," the Duchess explained, "and hasn't ever been out of the state."

"Denver is as far as I ever got," the blond giant confessed amiably. "I don't have no hankerin' to explore, I guess. 'Sides, nobody in their right mind would want to leave Colorado."

From anyone else Kate would have winced at the homespun corniness, but from Jed it was no more than simple truth. There was something about Westerners, Kate was beginning to realize. There was something rugged, Mother Nature–like, simple but by no means stupid about them. They were indeed different. Kate had loved the West since she was a child; not for her heros like Robin Hood or King Arthur; she had reveled in Kit Carson and Wyatt Earp and General Custer dying gloriously at the battle of the Little Big Horn. Seeing, experiencing, feeling, *being here,* was so much more than she had ever dreamed of, yet still a dream come true.

"I've got just the horse for you, Miss Kate," Jed was saying. "Good as gold and used to strangers. It's like sittin' in an armchair."

Which, Kate thought, was what a Western saddle was.

"But that's for this afternoon," the Duchess interposed. "I thought, this mornin', maybe you'd like to see around the house?"

"Could I?" Kate's face lit up.

"Sure . . . Ain't nuthin' I like better than goin' round my daddy's bits and pieces."

The brick chateau-style mansion was not, as Kate had surmised, the original ranch house. That had indeed been built of logs. ". . . it's over to the river a-ways; you always sited a cabin near water if you'd any sense. I'll show it to you later on. This house he copied from one he saw when he was in France. Every bit of stone was brought from there, along with the wood and a lot of the marble." Which had been used to create a whole series of impressive staircases, as well as vast expanses of floor. There were also intricate stuccowork, various kinds of plasterwork of flamingo pink and azure blue, alcoves tiled with ceramics imported from Spain, Waterford crystal chandeliers, and furniture that Gargantua would have felt comfortable with. There was also a profusion of greenery that flourished in the humid atmosphere: tall fronds of palms and ferns, tubs of azaleas and rhododendrons, as well as the native alpine flowers of Colorado. As the heat was maintained at a constant high temperature, just short of hell in Kate's opinion, the plants flourished. Fireplaces were large enough to roast a steer, but never thank God, Kate thought again, lit. Not only because of the heat; she was thinking in terms of a fire, and not just because of the heavy velvet *portières,* the ornately figured glass, the handwoven carpets or the overstuffed furniture. She was concerned for what was carelessly distributed among the rooms like so many family pictures and mementoes: a collection of Western art such as she had never seen or heard of before.

Agatha had been right about the Remingtons. There were so many Kate lost count, and not only paintings but bronzes, even a couple of half completed carvings in wood, unmistakable in their leaping vitality. But not only Remington, every major American Western artist was there, as well as a profusion of Indian art. There were robes, painted buffalo hides, pipes, much bead, feather, and quill work (now she understood what it was Minnie occupied herself with), painted buckskins telling pictorial stories of historic events in a tribe's history; there was so much that Kate could not take it all in at once. And when the old lady proceeded to get out album after album of what Kate was sure were historic early photographs, Kate knew what had to be done.

"Mrs. Chandler—"

"Agatha to my friends, but you can call me Duchess, if you like."

Kate went pink with pleasure at the honor. "Duchess—do you know what you have here?"

" 'Course I do. My daddy's things, things he liked to have around him, part of his life, you might say."

"I would say they are much, much more than that."

"Well, now, that might be because you see things in a different light."

"But don't *you* see, that's what these things actually are— different. What to you is a collection of family treasures is—to me and to anyone with an eye to see—a collection that is not only remarkable but unique."

"Well, that's right nice of you to say so. I know my daddy shared your opinion but that's because he thought the West was God's own country. He only traveled around the rest of the world to prove his theory right. He didn't ever think of all this as a 'collection.' Nor do I."

Kate wet her lips. This was delicate. "But"—she took a deep breath and dived—"have you thought of what will happen to it when you are no longer here to look after it? It could be dispersed, which would be a tragedy. If only I could make you see the importance of this collection. I don't think there can be another like it in the world. There's a famous collection in Oklahoma, but this is unique. Even the photographs are priceless. It should be left to a museum somewhere—"

"Never!" The old lady was sharp. "My daddy didn't hold with museums; everything behind glass and notices not to touch. He liked to live with his things."

"Then you must make sure that it goes to somebody who thinks as he did."

"Ain't nobody," Agatha said shortly.

"What about your grandson?"

The old lady's face softened. "He would do it for me, but Blaise and art are a million miles apart. He's grown up with these things, but he still refers to this place as a mausoleum now and again. Mind you, if I was to ask him he'd see that everything went on as it has done these past eighty-odd years."

"Then you must do so," Kate said decidedly. "Please, Duchess. This is the most fabulous collection of Americana I have ever seen—Western Americana, I mean. It would be a tragedy if it were dispersed."

"Even if you was to have the sellin' of it?"

"That would be an even worse tragedy," Kate said vehemently, "Collections like this must be kept together. Too many of the great ones are being dispersed to the four corners of the world. Even if you don't want a museum, wouldn't you want people—your people—to see their heritage? Because that's what you've got here."

"You ain't talkin' like an auctioneer," the old lady said with a twinkle.

"I'm talking as an art lover. There is more to art than its value. All right, if I was to sell this lot at Despard's I could make you millions—but you don't need them, and the collection would become no more than a random scattering of paintings, bronzes, and suchlike; it would cease to *be* a collection. It belongs here, in this house!" Kate flung out a passionate hand. "It would be the most terrible kind of divorce to separate one from the other. They should go on into the future for as long as is humanly possible."

Agatha was smiling slightly. "You are your daddy's daughter, all right. Just like him . . . gettin' all fired up over bits of canvas and wood and such." Her nod changed to a headshake. "I'd swear they meant more to him than his own flesh and blood,'cept the fact that he left his heart's blood to you proves me wrong." She patted the hand resting on the arm of her chair. "What you've said I promise to think about. To tell the truth I've been wondering what would happen to it all once I'm gone. The ranch is okay because Blaise runs it anyway, but the house and everything else—well, that's a horse of a different color." Her gaze sharpened. "You say all this is valuable?"

"Immensely."

"Well now, there's a thing." Her laugh was robust. "If his wife knew that she'd be here so fast her skirts would shrivel."

Greatly daring, "Then don't tell her," Kate said, trying not to plead. "She'd urge you to sell, and I may be cutting my own throat but I urge you not to. Other people have no choice—they need money. You, if you will allow my bluntness, need it like a hole in the head. You can *afford* your collection. I haven't been back in the auction business long, but I knew at once how much it had changed. It's big business now. It's not the beauty of a work of art that counts; it is its appreciation value—" She stopped dead suddenly. "Did you say Dominique has not seen it?"

"Never set foot on the ranch since she married my grandson."

"So she has no idea . . ."

"Nor interest. She thinks we still wear six-guns and Stetsons and eat jerky and salt beef. Chicago is on the edge of civilization as far as she is concerned, and it doesn't begin again until San Francisco."

Kate's sigh was almost a sob of relief. "Thank God for that."

Agatha frowned. "It's that serious?"

"Once she saw all this she would move heaven and earth to sell it through New York—and it would be oh so easy. Once collectors knew . . ." Kate's fear showed. "Do they—know, I mean?"

"Who?"

"Well, knowledgeable people, art world people."

"The only one I knew was your pa and he never came here. Everybody hereabouts knows, and now and again I get an inquiry from Denver and once somebody came out from New York but that was a long time ago."

"Thank God for that," sighed Kate. "Once word of something like this gets out it's war to the death. Dominique would urge you to sell for two reasons—a fortune in commission and a leapfrog to the top of the financial table."

"But you don't?"

Kate shook her head again. "My head says I should but my heart—and my senses—say I must not. This sort of thing should belong to the world, not to a few dozen rich men."

Agatha nodded. "I knew you were a girl after my own heart."

"For God's sake don't tell anybody," Kate said wryly. "As it is, if I were to tell Rollo he'd probably try to have me committed."

"Rollo? Oh, your fairy friend." At the change in Kate's expression, "I take that back. Blaise told me you set great store by him."

"He's my best friend," Kate said truthfully.

"Then I'm doubly sorry. Good friends are hard to come by. Ain't no business of mine which way his particular wind blows."

Kate began to laugh. "I only hope that someday it blows him in your direction. You would positively meld!"

"Is that so? In that case, next time you come bring him with you.

"He'll expect me to!"

Relationship restored, as well as good humor, they made their way back to the conservatory where a light lunch waited for Agatha: a cup of soup, the inevitable steak—but a small one—and a salad.

"Doctors say I have to eat regularly," Agatha sighed, "but I don't enjoy any meal 'cept my dinner."

"If I can have a cup of coffee I'll keep you company," Kate offered, and by chatting lightly and easily, telling stories that made the old lady chuckle, she saw Agatha through her bouillon, most of the steak, and half the salad.

Then, while Agatha was taken upstairs for her afternoon nap, Kate went riding with Jed Stone.

The snow was deep but, as the carol said, crisp and even, and in the just above freezing temperatures it made a surface the horses were obviously used to. Kate's horse was a bay gelding called the Colonel, obviously an old campaigner, both sure-footed and unflappable. As she had known it would be, the Western saddle was like an armchair, and wrapped up in a fleece-lined windbreaker over her flannel shirt, with a Stetson on her bright head and warmly lined gloves on her hands, Kate was able to breathe deeply of the sparkling air, though at first she found she could not seem to get enough. What there was, though, was exhilarating, but not quite as much as riding a real cowpony beside a real cowboy, with the foothills of the Rockies no more than forty miles away.

Even the pines that crowded in on the meadows were laden with snow, but it did not seem to worry the cattle, which continued to eat, stolidly indifferent to the horses, from the big bundles of hay that had been distributed around.

"White-faced Herefords?" Kate hazarded a guess, knowing that bulls had been imported from England at the end of the nineteenth century to be interbred with the leaner, tougher native longhorn and produce beef cattle.

"Right," Jed confirmed, both surprised and pleased. "Most of them come from a bull Miss Agatha's father imported from England. He had some awful long name but on the

ranch he was known as Pa, because he sired more'n a
thousand calves before a blizzard got him. Old Black Jack,
he had him dug out of twenty feet of snow and buried, like
he was family. You can see his grave in the cemetery behind
the house.''

They rode most of the afternoon, allowing Jed to check on
far-flung groups of cattle.

"How do you know where they go?" Kate asked, fascinated.

"The 'copter spots for us. It's a godsend. Before, it meant
days and days ridin' to check on them, especially after a
spell of bad weather. Now, the 'copter goes out and radios
back and we know exactly where to go if necessary.''

"And what exactly is necessary?" asked Kate.

"Oh, steers in trouble, buried maybe, havin' difficulty in
deep snow, injured sometimes after bein' attacked by a
mountain lion.''

"What I heard last night?"

"We know he's there," Jed nodded. "But unless he starts
killin' cattle we leave him alone. Now that the snow's down I
reckon we'll keep a closer watch.''

Jed did not seem to guide his horse, rather he just sat on it
and let himself be taken. "Old Hank, he knows where to go.
He's been doin' it for years.''

Hank looked dispirited, plodding along, but on the way
back, when Jed touched him lightly with his spurs, he at
once perked up, head tossing, prancing like some Lippizaner,
and even the Colonel pricked up his ears and did a sideways
sidle. When they came over the brow of the hill and saw the
vast pink house plonked square in the middle of the expanse
of snow, Kate laughed and said, "They'll never believe this
back home," and in a sudden burst of high spirits urged the
Colonel on to a gallop.

For a horse with a reputation for being sedate the Colonel
turned out to be a fraud, and as they slowed to a trot, Kate
leaned forward to pat his arched neck. "You enjoyed that,
you old reprobate. But then, so did I . . .''

8

In the king-sized bed in their cathedral-sized bedroom in the Chandler Towers triplex, Dominique stretched out a languid arm to tap the ash from her cigarette into the Lalique ashtray.

"You smoke too much," her husband said drowsily, too sated to make the attempt to remonstrate and knowing it would do no good anyway.

"It does not impair the way I function, does it!"

He opened one eye. "You'll be the first to know if it does."

"You demonstrated your approval not once, but twice." Her hand drifted from the smoothness of his armor-plated chest over his flat belly to the thicket of tangled black curls at his groin, where, in spite of making love to her twice within the space of fifty minutes, she felt him stir under her hand, nuzzling blindly and greedily into her warm, damp palm. Truly, she thought, marveling as she felt him thicken and lengthen in her hand, he is, as they say, hung like a horse.

"My beautiful stud," she murmured, putting her mouth where her hand was, making him grunt and catch his breath. "You have truly missed me, I think."

"So what made *you* come to New York to find me?"

Dominique smiled. One of the things she really liked about Blaise Chandler was the way he invariably escaped from her net. As much as any man she had him well and truly skewered on the hook of her sensuality, yet she continued not only to wonder at but also to appreciate their ongoing sexual compatibility. She did not fool herself, any more than he did, that they shared anything more than that. It was her considered opinion, anyway, that two years was the maximum any sexual attraction could be expected to last, no matter how powerful. The one that had gone into spontaneous combustion the minute they had first set eyes on each other had been like nothing either of them had ever known. But everything, once it reached its apex, had nowhere else to go but down, and every time they came together was a bonus. Which was, she thought dispassionately, what kept the marriage going. It was more like a long-running affair; their meetings—in cities where they both happened to be at the same time—were like clandestine, snatched half hours with a jealous husband and a vicious wife waiting in the wings. Had they ever lived together for any length of time the flimsy fabric would not have held: both liked the atmosphere spiced with the illusion of risk. It was, Dominique mused, her hand around the shaft of his silky penis, her fingertips brushing the head, a kind of adulterous affair. In truth she was married to Despard's while he had a very demanding and jealous wife in the Chandler Corporation. Their meetings were times stolen from a legal partner, dense with intrigue and the danger of discovery.

"I should be in Honolulu sitting around a table right now . . ." Blaise would say, or "I am supposed to be en route to Geneva," Dominique would murmur. "You realize you are costing me money as well as time, *mon beau sauvage . . .*"

"I like playing hooky," Blaise would return, proving how much.

And they would leave each other refreshed, until such time as one or the other would pick up a telephone, institute a search, and eventually place a long distance call that would result in another meeting in another bed in another hotel. They had no permanent home; when in Paris they used the house on the Avenue Foch, and in London had always used either the penthouse, if Charles was away, or Dominique's house in Chester Square if he was not. In Hong Kong, they would repair to Dominique's highrise flat on The Peak, and in New York there was the Chandler Towers fortieth floor triplex. In just about every other city there was a ChanCorp suite.

They never went anywhere together. They were never seen in nightclubs or discos or international receptions or splashy first nights. When they met it was always to have sex; they had absolutely nothing else in common. But the sex was of such caliber and potency that it was enough to sustain a relationship that never even ventured beyond the physical.

Blaise had asked Dominique to marry him in the first flush of a delirious affair when even the thought of another man having her brought a red mist to his eyes; Dominique had accepted because of who and what he was: access to limitless sums of money and the international business world, which was as yet an unplundered field for the planting of art treasures. For a while back there, Blaise had fancied himself passionately, everlastingly in love; it was only when the lava cooled that he saw that only the passion was real. And such was Dominique's sensual prowess that, even now, a summons from her brought the familiar hollow of sick longing and a hard-on that stayed with him until he was able to lose it in her. In two years he had not looked at another woman; Dominique always drained him so completely that when he was ready again it was to her he turned, for more of the same. He was fully aware that his wife was a sexual animal; that what was to him a pleasure, with her was a need. She could not go long without it, and on those occasions when he denied her—a combination of true business needs and his own to retain at least some independence of her—he knew she would seek satisfaction elsewhere. But that she inevitably came back to him was proof, he thought, of his own success in that direction. He never let his thoughts stray in the opposite one. Besides, there was always the added kudos, catnip to any man, of other men's envy, of other women's hate. Dominique du Vivier was one-of-a-kind, and Blaise Chandler held the copyright.

Now, Dominique was purring like a sleek cat, nuzzling him, nipping at him with her small white teeth; she always called him her beautiful savage, and naked, that was what he was. The copper-colored body of an athlete at the peak of physical fitness. No matter where he was Blaise either jogged, ran, or worked out. He enjoyed stretching his body to the limits, while Dominique enjoyed the results. She slid over him, fitted him inside her and began to ride, her black hair swinging, now bending to let her breasts brush his chest, nipples meeting tantalizingly, now grinding into him with the circular motion of a pestle in a mortar, her hands busy behind her, her small but perfect breasts bouncing up and down. Dominique could make it last; she knew by the grip of his fingers on her tiny waist, or the way he sought her thimble-like nipples with his tongue how close he was to completion, and she could keep him hanging in ecstasy until exactly the right moment.

She loved the feeling of power it gave her, the control, the exultant sense of ascendancy, and when she finally let go, urging him on like a jockey on a thoroughbred, she gloried in the thundering finish, the shout as they crossed the line and the ultimate in nerve-shattering orgasm, which lifted her up to spasm stiffly and convulsively, jerking against him again and again, until she slid, boneless, off his shiny-with-sweat body and collapsed, arms and legs spread, on the stained and rumpled bed finally, for the third-time-of-not-bothering-to-ask, well and truly exhausted.

It was later that she asked, sounding drowsily replete and no more than indifferently interested, "And what news have you of the little Despard?"

"She could give you ten inches," Blaise retorted, at the same time knowing better than to let his wife either see or feel his instant alertness. In his two years with Dominique du Vivier he had come to know her much better than she either realized or would have liked; he knew for instance that when she gave the impression she was not interested it meant she was, and deeply. Her brain, like her body, was never satisfied.

"She was fine last time I saw her," he said with a yawn.

"And when was that?"

"Would you believe yesterday?"

Dominique sat bolt upright, small jutting breasts jouncing softly. "She is here, in New York?"

"She was."

"Doing what? Had she come to see Despard's? Why did I not know? Did she tell you why she was here? Where did you see her, anyway? Has she any clients here? What did you find out?"

"Nothing, because I didn't ask," lied Blaise blandly. "All I know is that she came to see a client."

"Who?"

"I don't know. And I don't care. I'm not concerned until your year begins properly, and that's some time away yet."

Dominique lay down again. "A client," she laughed. "I can imagine . . ."

Something in her voice, the velvety, satisfied purr to it, told Blaise that not only could she imagine, she knew. Beneath the controlled exterior, Blaise Chandler concealed a perception that worked like long-range radar, and it had long since found his wife's wavelength. He knew, for instance, that she was smugly complacent about her possession of him: his name, his body, his passion, his money. So sure that had he been unfaithful, she would not have worried because it would have meant nothing. Where it counted he was hers, and would be until she decided differently. Dominique had to control; yet at the same time she loved to flirt with danger, getting her kicks from balancing on the knife edge of disaster. This gave her the thrills her character demanded, whether sexual or emotional. He was sure she was playing a cat and mouse game with Kate Despard.

He also knew that she would not hesitate to involve him, as an added spice and to test his loyalty.

"Where did you run into her?" she was asking idly.

"Fifth Avenue," lied Blaise, giving a deliberate hint and waiting to see if she would follow it.

Dominique traced the broad planes of his chest. "I wonder who she saw . . ."

"You could always ask the Duchess," Blaise suggested, safe in the knowledge that she was the one person Dominique would never ask—anything.

Following his specification to the letter, "The Duchess?"

"I took her back there for lunch. She had time to spare and the Duchess had curiosity to satisfy." He saw that sink in by the way the sapphire eyes flashed, as if a warning light had gone on. "As a matter of fact," he closed in for the kill, "they both went back to Colorado for the weekend."

"*What?*"

"They hit it off right away," Blaise explained helpfully.

"Your grandmother would go to any lengths to hit out at me."

"Well, how many times has she invited you?"

"Only because she knows I will refuse." Dominique threw back the covers and slid from the rumpled silk sheets. "I am surprised that the Despard has time, but it proves I think that her trip was a prospecting one. By all accounts Despard's London is desperate for new clients."

"Whose accounts?" Blaise asked lazily.

Dominique laughed low in her throat. "Oh no, *mon sauvage*. You know better than to pump me."

"I thought I'd just done a pretty good job.

That delighted her. She leaned over him, black bell of hair swinging. "And so you did. About that I have no complaints."

She went into the bathroom and he heard the sound of the shower. But he knew she was not through yet. Dominique always went her own way, and it was a devious one.

And sure enough, when she came back again wrapped, sarong-wise, in a towel, she sat down at her dressing table and leaned forward to examine her face, before saying, "All the same, I should like to know who she came here to see. I do not trust her. Only a fool trusts the English. We are engaged in a fight to the death, she and I; I told her so when we met."

"I think she got the message," Blaise said.

Dominique reached for a jar of cream, began to massage her throat. "I heard that Rolf Hobart had bought a particularly fine T'ang horse from her recently."

"Really?" Blaise sounded bored.

Dominique sighed, shook her head at him. "If I said Hobart Enterprises you would know!"

"That's different. That's business."

"And mine is not? I happen to know that Rolf Hobart is in the market for Oriental wares."

"Is that so?"

Dominique looked at him through the mirror. He lay there, hands behind his head: a sated big cat, amiably meeting her gaze. Her shrug was irritable and he knew she had abandoned the game. "It is just as well I do not rely on you for information concerning *my* customers," she said tartly.

"If you don't know by now that the collecting of anything except just and due debts holds no interest for me then you never will." Blaise shrugged. "You should also know that I have no intention of acting as a fifth column in your war with Kate Despard. I hold a *watching* brief, remember?"

Dominique's sensual lips curled. "I do not need you to fight my battles."

"Thank God."

"But if it is a watching brief, then you will keep it at that, won't you?"

"You know I hate to get involved," Blaise answered equably.

"Then don't," Dominique said gently. "Just—watch."

"Charles meant watch out *for*," Blaise said helpfully.

"I will not allow his sentimentality to prejudice my chances." Her eyes were brilliantly sapphire. Warning him.

"I would very much like to know what prompted Papa to appoint you his executor," she said, watching him through the mirror. "You are my husband and your first loyalty in this, as in everything, is to me."

The way yours is to me? Blaise thought clinically.

"Nor can I understand why you accepted the appointment. It is not binding in law, is it? You can decline if you wish."

"You can, but it usually leads to endless complications, and in this case if the court had been appointed, or the bank, you would have found yourself on a tight rein."

"Is that why you accepted—to give me a free rein?"

"That, and because Charles made a particular point of asking me."

"Which brings us back to the beginning—why you?"

"He trusted me," he answered.

"To do what?"

Keep an eye on you, Blaise thought. He knew I didn't want you to have Despard's, and he made it plain to me that he did not want you to have it; but having made a mess with his own daughter, he did not want to make the same mistake again so he was trying to let you off lightly. And I'm the one who has to see you don't hit the ground too hard.

"Be impartial," he said now.

Dominique's eyes seemed to glow, like neon. "I have yet to detect any impartiality where I am concerned," she taunted.

Blaise said nothing, just lay there, an infuriatingly knowing expression on his face. Perhaps that was what kept her with him, she thought now; it was dangerously exciting to lead him on, to the point where those scruples of his, the old-fashioned ideas of probity and honesty and integrity his old squaw grandmother had instilled into him, would be called into question. So far somehow he had always been too strong to get right to the edge, but she never ceased trying. There was something about her that had to test everything to its breaking point; once broken she discarded it, whether it was a thing or a person, but until it did she could not let up on the pressure.

Now she knew she had found the ideal testing ground. His

vaunted impartiality. She did not believe for one minute that Charles had asked him to watch over his own daughter; it was to watch out for his stepdaughter. Dominique had always suspected, in spite of the openly expressed affection, the publicly pronounced pride, that her stepfather loved her not for what she was, but in spite of what she was. That was why Despard's had not been given to her. It was as if he was saying, "I am sorry, Dominique; you have worked hard and well and I am full of admiration, but I am also full of distrust. I love you but I am not blind to what you are and it is not what I want for Despard's unless you can do it honestly and well—and I trust Blaise to see to that."

Yes, she thought acrimoniously. Trust Blaise . . . Then she laughed. The odd thing was—she did, although trust was something she had learned from her own father to despise. In this world you trusted no one but yourself because everyone else was out for their own self. You made your own way—had she not made hers? After a childhood spent with a father prepared to be indulgent as long as it did not interfere with his own comfort, and a mother who regarded her as some kind of changeling, she had got—well, almost—what she wanted at no cost to herself. Only the stubborn intransigence of a man who did not like to lose had made her pause on her upward climb. But it was only a pause. That Charles Despard had, after all, managed to evade her snares only proved how untrustworthy the human race was. People were pawns in the game of life, as her father had taught her. Use them, manipulate them, but always remember they are dangerous. Never let them get inside you, because one day, sooner or later, they will blow you apart. Look, watch, find your opportunities, use them, but do not get involved. They are not worth it.

That the result was a conscienceless, incapable-of-love-except-of-self, egocentric monster she neither knew nor cared. She only knew she wanted power, to reach a place where nobody could ever reach her. Only then would she be safe.

"I see what you mean by God's own country," Kate said, as they rode slowly back to the house. "It's so clean and pure and oddly untouched." Everything was white but the tops of trees; the dark green of spruce and pine, as well as strands of delicately quivering aspens, showed through. "No smog, no fumes, no pollution."

"All that's got to Denver, though. People used to come there for lung diseases; not any more. Now they go to Arizona."

He is a nice man, Kate thought, and his curiosity about her own line of work had been a salutary shake. He was totally baffled as to why people would pay hundreds of thousands of dollars for a piece of china or a chair or a painting. A good horse, now; why a good horse was worth its weight in gold out here, especially when the snow came, like now, and a horse was an absolute necessity when working with cattle, in spite of the helicopter. Why, he had paid three hundred dollars for Hank, whom he had broken himself. But paying several fortunes for a plate or a vase and such was beyond his comprehension. Kate was nonplussed to find herself defensive at his tolerant dismissal of what was her life.

She found herself having to defend that world as she tried to explain to him just exactly what collecting meant. His dismissal was not like Blaise Chandler's disinterest. He understood the art world, even if his own interests lay elsewhere. Jed did not even begin to comprehend it: the fierce competition, the possessiveness, the acquisitiveness, the sheer greed. It all struck him as the height of foolishness, and its effect on Kate was that of opening a window, allowing in a blast of air as cold as that blowing from the Rockies. It replaced the hothouse atmosphere which, if you did not occasionally deliberately step outside it, became the only kind you could breathe, and it had a salutary effect on her because it exposed the real reason for her panic-stricken dash to New York. Despard's reputation was all-important, but even more important, she saw shamefacedly, was her own. She was the one she had wanted to protect; her own burgeoning reputation as an "expert"; only one small part of the total, overall Kate, the one Jed saw with eyes as clear and sharp as they needed to be out here. It reduced her to her proper size and put everything else into its true perspective. The world was an entity made up of countless smaller ones, and the people who inhabited those smaller worlds came to believe that theirs was the only one that mattered. Wrong, Kate now realized. There were worlds where hers held no importance at all; where T'ang horses, Ming vases, old masters, and Georgian silver meant nothing because they were not *necessary*. Jed came from a world like that.

Her trouble, she thought now, was that she had never known—never tried to know—any world beyond the one into which she had been born. All her life, her world had been bounded by fine art. After school, where she had always done well in the arts courses, she had gone to the Courtauld, where the work she did, the friends she made—those she allowed into the even smaller world she had created for herself—were from that art world; her year abroad had been spent in Florence, a city that was in itself an artwork. And now Despard's . . . She had all but forgotten that there was a larger world outside. Jed's tolerant indifference had shown her just how large that world was and exposed the minimal boundaries of her own. His attitude was, well, it was a good enough job for a woman . . . but for a man! Not for one who really was male, anyway.

All in all, she realized discomfitedly, this trip was turning out to be instructive in more ways than one. When she looked up at the mountains she felt reduced, and when she looked around her, so was everything else. She had, she saw now, worn her jeweler's loupe even when she was not examining for valuation, with the result that she could not see the wood for the trees and so got walloped and knocked to the ground by the first hanging branch. A fake T'ang horse was not going to change anybody's life except hers, maybe, and those who shared her enclosed world.

She had been becoming obsessed, she supposed: eating, drinking, sleeping, thinking Despard's. And once you lost touch with the real world you were done for. Why had she not remembered her father telling her that? He had been a gregarious man, had liked people, socializing. It was her mother, from whom Kate had inherited her own shyness, who dreaded large gatherings, hated the thought of entertaining. Kate had had to force herself to do her own share in recent months, but she preferred small, intimate dinners with friends of long standing with whom she could relax and talk. Except she realized now, with unflinching honesty, she had no friends. After her father's defection she had put up a guard, and you had to be special before you were allowed through it. Twice, she had allowed men into her private world; twice they had turned out to be figments of her imagination. The girls she had known at the Courtauld had been friends only while they studied together; afterward they had lost touch or, Kate realized guiltily, she had not made the effort to keep up with them. Rollo had been the only one and he had come to assume the stature of a giant in her personal world. Now, from ten thousand feet up in the Rockies, she looked at him and saw that he was, after all, as mortal as other men, as flawed. And certainly no bigger.

What was it about this air, she wondered bemusedly, that made you see so clearly? To whatever it was though, she was fervently, relievedly grateful. More than ever she was convinced that Fate had taken a hand in her particular Game of Life. The thing was to watch how that hand was played . . .

Blaise was not sure what made him decide to change his plans and, instead of catching a plane to Johannesburg, catch the first one to Denver. He only knew that the moment the door shut behind his wife and he went back into the bedroom, to survey the wreck of the bed, sniff the pungent reek of sex and Dominique's perfume, he realized that most of the ten hours that they just had together had been spent in the so-called act of love, except in their case love had nothing to do with it, and he was revolted. It had been sex: rutting, greedy, animal sex, and it both sickened and angered him. Suddenly he wanted fresh air and open spaces.

He called the transport division of the Corporation and found that there was a jet out of Newark that would get him to Denver at 6 A.M. He went into the shower, scrubbed himself almost violently, as if the miasma of Dominique's presence had somehow contaminated him. He scrubbed until every lingering trace of her was gone, and when he dressed it was in jeans, a flannel shirt, and the flying jacket he had held on to after Vietnam. Putting them on was like putting on a new persona. Every now and then the mood swept over him and everything else before it: the yearning for the West.

He did not call his grandmother; she liked surprises, provided they were pleasant.

They landed in Denver at 6:05, and from there he took a helicopter to Aspen, where it stopped to pick up the papers and other daily supplies for the ranch. It was as they were coming in, over the ski runs, fresh and unmarked from the night's snowfall, that he again made a spur-of-the-moment decision. The powder was perfect—nowhere did you get powder snow like the Rockies, that great barrier for storms blowing inland from the West Coast; he could see from the 'copter that, this morning, conditions were also perfect; that skis would cross that powdery snow with the minimum of resistance and yet support a skier through its deepest parts.

"What brought this on?" Walt Vernon wanted to know, watching Blaise change into the ski gear he had provided from his shop.

"I had a sudden hankering," he replied truthfully.

"I guess you must get kinda stifled in New York and all them places you keep visitin'."

"That's exactly how I felt."

"Well, we've been havin' heavy falls this past couple of weeks so you should find yourself a good run in any one of a dozen places."

"I thought I'd take Aspen Mountain."

Walt raised his eyebrows. "If you mean off-piste as usual, you ain't gettin' any younger."

No, Blaise thought, which was no doubt why he had the urge to pit his skill and strength against something other than a woman's body. He wanted speed and an edge of danger; he wanted exhilaration and that wiping-clean-of-everything sensation that skiing always gave him; he wanted to feel the wind on his face, the shush of snow under his skis as they whispered over the whiteness at sixty miles an hour. When he got off the ski lift, not the first because there were already several ski bums up there keen to have the mountain to themselves for a while, he drew in lungfuls of air and felt it invigorate his blood. I was getting stale, he thought, I should do this more often. He settled his goggles comfortably, gripped his ski poles so that they rested comfortably in the hollow of his palms, and eyed the drop, almost sheer for its long length, and then becoming more gradual as it broadened out between clumps of pines to the level of the valley.

"You wanna go first?" a nasal voice asked him. She was young, blonde, obviously could not understand what an old man like him was doing on a tough slope like this, all 2,500 feet of it and all vertical.

"Be my guest," Blaise said, moving aside.

She flicked him a glance, shrugged, and then with effortless ease moved off with her left ski; the right one came alongside it like the blades of a pair of scissors and he watched her slam straight down. He took a deep, excited breath and shoved himself off after her. She was good; she began wedeling at the perfect moment, making feather-stitch tracks in the snow which he followed, almost duplicating them. He felt body and mind meld; one part of his mind controlling his movements, the other appreciating the beauty of his surroundings, the wine of the air, the powder of the snow, the scent of the pines; while all the time hips and knees moved in perfect synchronization. The girl was in front of him still, and he saw her glance back fractionally, and then tuck her poles beneath her arms and bend at the waist and knees.

"Bloody little fool!" he thought, but she was effortless in her mastery, and once down the vertical she swept around in a flawless parallel and a contemptuous flick of snow and stood waiting on her poles. Shoving up her goggles she inspected him frankly. "Say, you really can ski," she said. "I should have guessed, seeing as you're out this early. You a professional?"

"Yes, but not at skiing," Blaise answered.

"You want we should do it again?"

"No time, sorry."

She shrugged again. "My tough luck," she admitted candidly. Then she turned toward the ski lifts.

It was eight-thirty when the helicopter approached the ranch, losing height and circling over the house as it came in to land. As it did so, Blaise sighed happily. He was back home . . .

He had been born in Paris, lived in France until he was nine years old when his mother and current stepfather died, but he had never thought of himself as anything other than American even though his own father had been French. It was to his grandmother that he owed what he was, who he was. She had eradicated the European influence, made him a Westerner, imbued him with pride in his inheritance. Even now the sight of the valley had the power to lift and calm him. He had traveled the world many times over; he had spent two years in Vietnam, but coming back to the Roaring Fork Valley was still the greatest sight in the world. In spite of not having slept, in spite of the familiar ache in his groin, the soreness of the nail gouges on his back, he still sent the helicopter soaring and swooping in a sudden aerial fit of the giggles, as he pictured his grandmother's face. She never pulled any punches, which was what he loved about her, always had, since first setting eyes on her as a lonely and frightened nine-year-old, his mother and his stepfather newly dead, his future unknown. He had looked up at the barbarically glittering old lady with the face like an eagle and thought she was a queen. Until he had discovered she was a Duchess.

"Do you know who I am, boy?" she had boomed.

"Bien sûr. You are my *grandmère Americaine."*

"Speak English when you speak to me, boy."

"Yes, Grandmother."

"I don't give a damn what your mother told you and I don't give a damn about your father bein' French. The Chandlers are American, you hear?" She had stumped around him, disgustedly eyeing the French clothes, the French haircut. "First thing we have to do is get you lookin' American. You ride?"

"Yes, Grandmother."

"But not like we do out West, I'll bet, on a real saddle, not some itty bit of leather like a saucer. We'll teach you to do it properly. Do you know what the West is?"

"Yes. It is where the cowboys and Indians live."

"Right. And Minnie here, is an Indian." She had fixed him with her fierce black eyes. "So am I. So—in part—are you. One eighth Indian."

His eyes had rounded in delight as he asked breathlessly, "Which tribe?"

"Shoshone."

He had repeated the name over and over to himself. He was part Indian! Shoshone!

Hitherto, he had believed—had been taught—that his American grandmother was a savage, had grown used to hearing his mother's voice shudder when she spoke of her. His mother, he now realized, had been ashamed of her Indian heritage. For the life of him he could not understand why. But then, he had not understood his mother. But he liked his grandmother. She was *une grande dame,* a real Duchess, and from then on he never thought of her as, or called her, anything else.

Now, his nine French years were buried so deep he rarely thought of them; rarely saw his half-sister, whom he considered a grasping, shallow bitch, or his half-brother, whom he knew to be a fool. Unfortunately, his grandmother was vulnerable where they were concerned, for in spite of what they were they were also of her blood—even if they never came near her except when they wanted money. None of his half-brother's Debrett connections had any idea that his grandmother was half-Indian; what he would call "a half-breed." His half-sister knew and turned it into the height of sophistication, for her father had been Argentinian and puritanically obsessed with the purity of his own Spanish blood, burying deep the strain that was as Indian as that of his wife's grandmother.

Blaise was proud to be Indian: a *real* American. One of the people who had, as Will Rogers put it, "met the boat" when the *Mayflower* arrived.

Now, as he swept across the river and the pink house came into view, incongruously set in its Italian-style severely formal gardens, he felt again that rush of exultant pride. They could mutter "execrable taste" as much as they liked: it was home to him. As he lost altitude, he saw a figure bent low over a horse galloping at full, glorious stretch toward the fence that marked the boundary of the gardens. The horse he recognized with a muttered, "What the hell?" surprised rather than angry, for the General had an uncertain temper and a disdain for strangers to which his lineage entitled him. He was a big, raking black, seventeen hands high, and once he got the bit between his teeth he took some stopping. Right now he was headed straight for the fence that separated lawns from pasture, and as Blaise watched he took it like a bird, tucking his hind legs under him and leaving inches to spare; as he landed, the rider's Stetson blew off and Blaise let out an explosive, "I knew it!" as Kate Despard's flaming red hair flaunted itself to his affronted eyes. He banked the 'copter—the General was used to them coming and going—and saw her rein the horse in, prancing delightedly as if to say "and aren't I the fine fellow?" and shading her eyes, look up at the helicopter. He lost more height, circling so low she could not fail to see him through the glass of the cockpit, saw her smile flash even as her hand waved; then she was left behind as he turned away to the pad behind the house, at the far side of the conservatory.

By the time he got into the baking heat, she was there before him, but from the face his grandmother turned toward him he realized that she had not spoiled his surprise. He nodded his thanks as he bent to his grandmother's upraised arms.

"Well now, Boy, here's a nice surprise, and you know how I like them."

"I suddenly had a yen for the wide open spaces, so I thought I'd come home, too."

His grandmother's face shone.

"I wish I had somewhere like this to go home to," Kate said enviously.

"You are enjoying your weekend, then?"

"Enjoying will do for now until I can find the perfect word."

"The General seemed to be having a good time, too."

"I told Kate to go ahead and take him out," Agatha said. "Jed said she was good enough to handle him else I wouldn't have let her, you know that. I guess she found the Colonel a mite slow."

"He is," Blaise said, "but he's safe. You ride very well," he said to Kate.

"I was horse mad when I was a teenager, torn between antiques and show jumping. Now, I ride when I can, which isn't all that often, alas."

"I've told Kate that whenever she has to come over here she is welcome to stay with us," Agatha said comfortably. "I expect she'll be comin' over quite regular once she gets New York goin'."

Blaise was aware of Kate's quick sideways look, but she said nothing.

"You're just in time for breakfast," Agatha went on.

"Which means you must have been up at the crack of dawn," Blaise said to Kate.

"Who could sleep on a morning like this?" She stood up. "I'll just go wash up, as you say over here."

In jeans that exhibited her length of leg and narrowness of waist, as well as a spry and limber athleticism, she went off with a walk that had her hair, tied back in a pony tail, bouncing perkily.

Gazing after her, "That girl's a natural," Agatha sighed fondly. "Jed says she's right at home on a horse. That's why I told her she could ride the General when she asked—"

"She asked?"

"Said he looked so reproachful-like at her when she was taking out the Colonel . . ."

"The General only ever has one expression and that's condescension," Blaise retorted.

"You're the one as paid all the money for him. You don't mind the girl ridin' him, do you?"

"Of course I don't—so long as she knows what she is riding."

"Oh, Jed set her right, and he went with her for a while. Come back to say the General knew she wouldn't stand no nonsense."

Blaise laughed. "I'm beginning to discover that for myself."

Agatha chuckled. "She does have a right brisk tongue in her head." Innocently she asked, "I don't suppose it's any use me asking if your bein' here has anythin' to do with escapin' from one?"

"No, it isn't," Blaise answered equably.

His grandmother grinned. "Didn't think it was." Adding contentedly, "So, how long can you stay?"

"As long as I can manage."

"Can't be too long for me."

"Riding gives you an appetite," Kate said blithely to Blaise's raised eyebrows when she came back to the table with another plateful of bacon strips, eggs, sausages, hotcakes and hash browns.

"You need feedin' up," Agatha pronounced. "You got the minimum of skin on those bones of yours and that's a fact."

"It's my metabolism," sighed Kate. "It won't let anything I eat turn to fat." She brightened. "But I got on the scales in the bathroom this morning and found I'd actually put on three whole pounds!"

"You need that times another three before it will show any good."

"What have you been doing with yourself?" Blaise interrupted, before his grandmother's spade-calling had Kate six feet under.

"Riding, mostly. And trying to find someone to give me a game of tennis."

"Oh, Blaise will," Agatha said. "He's why I had the courts laid in the first place."

Kate glanced uncomfortably at Blaise Chandler's uncommunicative face. She had the feeling that playing the Good Shepherd to Kate Despard's stray lamb was not what he had envisaged, but he said, "I'd be glad to give you a game. I need to knock off some of the sedentary flab I've put on."

Kate looked surprised. "I don't see any," she said without thinking, only to flush scarlet as he said blandly, "I wasn't aware you'd noticed."

"Don't tease," Agatha interrupted calmly. "It's just he likes to keep in shape," she explained. "Thought you played squash twice a week," she said to her grandson.

"I do if my schedule allows."

Which, thought Kate later, when he walked onto the indoor court, he obviously goes to some pains to ensure. In white knitted shirt with the little crocodile over the left nipple and white shorts, she was aware of a powerful breadth of chest and well-developed muscles, as well as narrow hips ending in long legs and, from the way he moved, perfect coordination. Like a cat, she thought, lightly and on the balls of his feet, walking easily from the hips with a long, fluid stride. She was going to have a hell of a job getting the ball past that endless reach, but she could try . . .

He hit the ball like a bullet, she discovered, once they had knocked up a bit and got the measure of each other. At first Kate's strokes were defensive, then as brain, hand, and eye began to meld, she started to return devious drop shots which fell just over the net, making him dive for them.

But she can play! Blaise thought to himself, surprised yet fatalistically accepting, before beginning to do so himself in earnest. When he slammed balls at her feet they came back with a speed and accuracy that had him on his mettle. She was fleet of foot; not surprising, he thought grimly, since two-thirds of her body was legs. He was also surprised to see, as the game got tougher and her cotton shirt began to cling, that she had breasts. Not very big, but firm and high and no sag as they moved. When once she raised an arm to wipe her forehead, they moved provocatively and he found himself stirring. Jesus! he thought. He had not expected any response there for some time considering the workout Dominique had put him through, and also considering Kate Despard was not exactly his idea of an attractive woman.

They changed sides, and she served him three lightning aces in quick succession. That did it. If he had made allowances for her sex before, he deliberately overlooked them now. He played her to the limit of her endurance and skill but the score ding-donged, and though he could see her flagging, she hung on, like a determined terrier. She had guts. After forty-five minutes, when she had squandered three match points and let a fourth die of weakness, her fast disappearing strength vanished and she sent a service wide. It was all over and he came out of his concentration to hear applause. Turning, he saw that most of the servants had come to watch, as well as a few of the hands, and there sat Agatha, clapping with the rest.

"Well done, Kate!" she called.

"Indeed," Blaise congratulated, as they met at the net. "You play tennis like you ride."

Kate flushed vividly. "Thank you."

"Now let's see how you swim."

She started out with a triple somersault from the high board and entered the water like a knife. The swimsuit Agatha had provided was black, and it fit her like a second skin. The trouble was, Blaise thought, as he watched her cleave through the water like a ship's prow, her first was far too tight. Right now, she was too skinny for her height. But put another ten-twelve pounds on those bones and it might be a different story. Whatever, he thought, as he dived in off the side, Dominique had no competition in that quarter.

At dinner that night Kate ate with good appetite, unaccustomedly sharpened by so much exercise in one day, and not now restricted by her nervous awareness of Blaise Chandler. The man who played and swam with her in no way resembled the cold, hostile lawyer with whom she had crossed swords, and she had never thought to get on so well or so easily with him. That this was in no small measure due to her athletic prowess she accepted as par for her particular course. She had known since she was old enough to, that sexually she was a dead duck. Blaise Chandler, like his wife, was one of the so-called Beautiful People, except that in his case it was the Gospel Truth. In brief black swimming trunks he had made her swallow hard. For the first time in her life she found it hard to look elsewhere than at what was bunched inside the thin black silk. She had been aware that he was powerfully built; she had had no idea it was also beautifully.

Kate's success with men had been marked by its complete absence. Her father's rejection, coming as it had when she was at her most vulnerable, had savaged both pride and self-confidence, leaving the one swearing vengeance and the other dead. If her father had left her for another woman then it had to be because she was, as her grandmother had so prosaically said, not worth staying for. This was proved, to her mind, beyond reasonable doubt, when she saw her first picture of the second Madame Despard. A dream of beauty. Men wanted pretty women, she realized; men wanted sexy women, women who turned them on. Her father's defection from his plain daughter to a very beautiful woman germinated in her the seed of prejudicial self-hatred, which sprouted from the chips on both shoulders and concealed her from the few men who were caught by her personality rather than her face. And when, in her first year at the Courtauld, the man who had shown interest in her for a while dropped her flat when he discovered that she was on the outs with her father, she scraped her ego up from the pavement and buried it deep within herself. During her year in Italy, she met a graduate student on a Fulbright scholarship, as unattractive and unwanted as she was. Their very loneliness drew them together, each seeking to assuage it. He had been clumsy with inexperience, she inept in her innocence; the "affair" was an abysmal failure. After that, they avoided each other as much as they could.

He had been Kate's last encounter with the second sex. Her dealings with them ever since had been wholly impersonal. Rollo, she realized with an inward sigh, had been right as usual. It was Charles Despard's daughter who had acted like a jealous wife. But that, Kate saw now with painful clarity, was because he had treated her like one. It had been to her he described his day, her with whom he shared his hopes and dreams, to her that he confided his troubles. His daughter was the one with whom he had shared his life, not his wife. Susan ran his home, saw he always had a clean shirt, was always happy to know about the financial success of his business but took no interest in what provided that success. That, too, had been Kate's job. It was *not* all her own fault, Kate saw belatedly with those same suddenly opened eyes. No wonder her father had felt so guilty: he had treated Kate as a wife every which way except sexually.

Kate felt as though a lightning bolt had hit her. She cut her food, brought it to her mouth, chewed it mechanically but tasted not a thing. Oh, Papa, she thought . . . it has taken me a long time to get here but now that I am I see it all, and it was indeed so much more complicated than I ever began to understand. Her hand, when she reached out for her wine glass, was trembling. She drank her heavy burgundy straight down, blinked and felt it spread, like tentacles, outwards through her body. Everything was illuminated by a light so white, so bright, so dazzling, that she could only sit and stare at the picture in her mind.

Later, when they sat having coffee, Kate shook her head at Blaise's offer of brandy or a liqueur, already intoxicated by her discovery, and suddenly realized the Duchess was talking to her.

" . . . Chandlersville tomorrow," she was saying.

"Chandlersville?"

"Where ChanCorp began," Blaise explained. "The original mine where Black Jack discovered his copper, and the boom town that grew up around it that died with the mine."

"Oh!" That penetrated Kate's absorption, made her sit up and take notice.

The Duchess chuckled. "I knew you'd be interested."

"Very much so."

"It's a whole day's trip getting up to Chandlersville and back," Blaise said with a frown to his grandmother. "Too much for you."

"Nonsense! The train takes us all the way up, doesn't it? And I've got my chair and you to get me over any rough spots. 'Sides, I've got a hankerin' to see the place again. Might be my last chance."

Kate's soft heart was immediately touched but Blaise only countered sardonically, "Cut the hearts and flowers, Duchess. Hail to the Chief is more in your line."

The old lady threw back her head and her earrings flashed as they danced. "I'm glad to see I still can't fool you none," she laughed. Then, to Kate, "You'd like to see a real ghost town, wouldn't you?"

"Would I!"

"Then we go tomorrow."

Blaise rose. "In which case I'd better go set things in motion. It takes the old girl quite a long time to get steam up nowadays."

"Old girl? Steam?" Kate queried, fascinated.

Blaise turned to her. "Chandlersville is almost eleven thousand feet up in the mountains and the only way there is by narrow gauge railway, so my great-grandfather built one."

Kate's face was a positive sun, and for a moment he felt uncomfortably churlish at giving the thumbs-down to a trip he knew would be tiring for an old lady, but his concern for his grandmother was such that he wanted to prevent even the slightest chance of something going wrong.

"It's slow," he warned, fighting a losing battle with himself. "The engine is old, the gradient steep, and the air thinner even than this."

"It's also right comfortable," Agatha Chandler protested roundly. "Why, the parlor car was the last word in luxury when my daddy had it built; those cushions are real French velvet. And who cares if it takes an age; the view's worth it."

Blaise gave up. "It will mean an early start, leaving at eight. Days are short this time of the year."

Unlike the previous night, Kate found it hard to sleep once she had climbed into her big fourposter. She tossed and turned, her mind full of the day's events, of her mind's discoveries, of the promised delights of the coming day. She felt inexplicably charged with energy, though her lungs had labored for quite a part of the day, endeavoring to gulp in as much of the thin yet champagnelike air as possible. Now, it was as though the bubbles were still in her bloodstream. She had to work it off somehow, and the only way to do that at this time of night was to swim. There would be nobody about, and swimming nude was inexplicably pleasurable anyway. Before she could reconsider she was out of bed, belting around her the quilted dressing gown with which she had been provided, slipping her feet into fur-lined moccasins. Lights burned in all the corridors in case the Duchess was taken ill during the night and the household was roused; they were dimmed but showed the way clearly as Kate made her soundless way downstairs.

The heat of the conservatory enfolded her like a hot towel, but the door to the pool let in a draft of cooler though still warm air—and the sound of splashing. Kate's heart sank. Somebody else had had the same idea! Oh, well, she thought, I hope it's a female.

Quietly she padded down the steps and from behind a vast Swiss cheese plant surveyed the water; somebody was doing a racing sprint down the length of the pool, and from the speed and power, a man. As she watched, a hand touched the pool's edge and then whoever it was turned, slid under the water like a seal, and then emerged much further down, still powerfully churning water. Twice more he did the length of the pool and then, reaching the far end, put his hands flat on the marble top and vaulted on to the side, legs dangling. Which was when she saw it was Blaise Chandler. Instinctively she recoiled and the leaves of the plant moved. He glanced up sharply and she froze, praying he would not come to investigate, to find a Peeping Thomasina in the person of Kate Despard. Her cheeks were hot, her heart thumping, but when he lost interest in the plant, put up his hands to run them through the black hair, squeezing out water, she did not move. She was rooted to the spot.

He was naked, as she was under her robe, his body streaming with rivulets of water. Kate became aware that she was clenching her hands, that her heart was bumping so hard she quivered with every beat, that her mouth was dry and her body damp. Unable to move she stood behind the sheltering plant and gazed at Blaise Chandler, moodily kicking his feet in the water, staring down at it with a slight frown on his face. Then, as if coming to a decision, with one, lithe movement he was on his feet. He raised his hands once more to squeeze the last drops of water from his hair and Kate's eyes widened as her breath stilled. He was like the nudes she had studied in Florence; Donatello had carved him many times. His body hair was as black as that of his head, and he was, she realized, what women meant when they said a man was well endowed. Her knowledge of male genitalia was that of the art student; she had only ever seen two real sets in her life, and even then had tried not to betray her ignorance and inexperience by staring. Now, her eyes went to his groin and stayed there, riveted, and as they did so she felt a treacherous tide of warmth begin between her own legs, and a jolt of electricity as powerful as that which had charged through her the first time she met the dark eyes. Her concentration on him was so intense she was almost incandescent; she had lost all awareness of her surroundings, the faint smell of chlorine, the lap of the water, the soft drone of the air-conditioning. He stood there only for seconds, but it seemed like forever, and it fixed his image on her retina for all time.

He turned and walked in his loping way to a chair where he picked up a towel and began to dry himself. He was like some beautiful animal, she thought, as for the first time she comprehended what women meant when they talked of male beauty; he was a great tawny cat, sleek-muscled, powerfully controlled, and he evoked something in her she could not explain. Inexperienced as she was, she had no idea that it was sexual hunger. Always before she had fled from the first flickering signs of interest on the part of any man. Now, she stood peering through the heavy leaves of the cheese plant and her whole being was on fire, aglow with fierce longing for this handsome, powerfully stirring male.

She had known from first setting eyes on Blaise Chandler that he was wholly beyond her aspiration; men like him did not even see women like her. Now, she looked at him as though it was the first and yet the last time she would ever see any man, as beautiful or as naked; she watched him dry himself, rubbing himself briskly, raising one leg to rest it on the chair and bending to dry his legs and feet, the action tautening the long sheaths of muscle running down his back into his right, firm buttock. She watched him towel his back, his arms, between his legs in an intimate action that made her sink her teeth into her lower lip. When he had dried his hair, he picked up a short thigh-length toweling robe and slipped it on, and whistling softly, picked up his damp towel, thrust it into a nearby wicker basket, and disappeared beyond a plant as luxurious as the one she was hiding behind. She heard a door close. She was alone.

The breath she released was ragged, her cheeks were hot, and she was trembling like the aspens for which the nearby town was named. There was a strange, liquid warmth deep in her belly, and she could feel the thick, pounding beat of her heart—on her lips, at her fingertips, and most disturbingly of all, between her legs. Instinctively she put her fingers there, felt, with disbelieving shock, that she was all wet . . . The muscles in her thighs were quivering convulsively, also dissolving in the liquid heat spreading through her, until she slid in a heap onto the ground. What was happening to her? She had never felt anything like this before, afire with strange longings and a heavy, dragging ache which for some reason had her on the verge of tears. Her breathing was deep and harsh, her palms were damp, and her entire body exuded heat like a furnace. All she could see, when she closed her eyes, was that beautiful, naked body, especially what nestled between the powerful thighs. With searing discovery she realized that what she wanted was to feel that body against hers; she wanted those strong hands on her breasts, his mouth on hers, his tongue—and his very self—invading her. Her mind was a jumble of confusion, blurred yet keenly *aware*. She had never known she could feel so—physical. Her body was responding independently of her mind, which was racing to catch up. She wanted Blaise Chandler, fiercely, hungrily and she moved restlessly, moaning again. The sound shocked her back to her surroundings, where she was, what she was doing, causing her to leap to her feet to plunge frantically into the pool as though to escape, needing the shock of the cold water to jolt her back to normality.

The water parted like oil, not the bracing shock she had hoped for but warm and caressing in a way that made her thrash through it as though escaping from a shark. She did as many lengths of the pool as she could until her muscles were screaming and then she dragged herself out to sit on the edge, physically exhausted but still emotionally keyed up to almost screaming pitch. When at last she dragged herself to her feet it was with the tired movements of an old woman, and when finally she closed her bedroom door behind her and got back into bed, it was to lie wide-eyed and staring, seeing nothing but that beautiful naked body. Just before dawn, she finally drifted off to sleep, only to experience a dream so erotic, so unbelievably real, that she awoke with his name on her lips.

Nula brought her breakfast at seven, but Kate could not face it. She was too churned up inside, filled with an inexplicable terror at the thought of facing him. She felt possessed of an intolerable secret that would burden her for the rest of her life, and wished with all her heart that she was anywhere but here, where she would have to spend the entire day in his company. Her dream was so vivid it was still with her when, as she got downstairs, she saw him, in the same sort of clothes as she was wearing, jeans, a flannel shirt, and a thick sweater, talking to his grandmother. As he turned to wish her good morning she felt her face flame, could not meet his eyes, and went instead to pour herself a cup of coffee she did not want, hearing the cup clink against her teeth her hand was trembling so.

"You all right, Kate?" the old lady asked, her sharp eyes missing nothing.

"I didn't sleep very well," Kate mumbled.

"Well, it's a couple of hours on the train so you can have a snooze if you like."

"I don't want to miss the scenery," Kate joked lightly.

"On the way back, then," the old lady maintained. "Now, did Nula give you the jacket I got out for you?"

"Yes, here . . ." It was leather, lined with sheepskin.

"Good, it's almighty cold up there this time of year." The old lady was wrapped up like an Eskimo in what looked like a silver fox full-length coat, with fur-lined boots and a muff-in which to place her crippled hands. Minnie, as ever in attendance, was similarly swathed in furs.

"Right, let's be off."

A van took them to where the train waited, hissing gently, steam wisping from its large, wine-strainer funnel. Its livery was the familiar copper color; there were two day coaches, a parlor car and a caboose. In spite of her inner perturbation, Kate could not resist running forward delightedly.

"Now there's a girl as still finds pleasure in ordinary things," the old lady approved.

"A bit naïve, don't you think?" Blaise asked with a shrug. "She's twenty-six, not sixteen."

But her delight was infectious; he found himself sitting beside her, she kneeling at the window like a wide-eyed child, while he told her the names of the peaks that soared above them.

"It's just like in the movies," she exclaimed gleefully. "Oh, how many times have I seen a parlor car just like this. . ." She ran her hand over the red, deeply buttoned plush, the bobble fringes of the curtains.

"It just might be it was this one you saw," Agatha told her. "It's been hired by movie companies a couple of times over the years."

"Can we go out onto that little platform at the back?" she asked Blaise eagerly. "We don't have such things in England."

"Why not?" Again he found himself answering her many questions. She had a knack of communicating her own pleasure in everything she was seeing; he found he was quite sorry when the train chugged into the station with its ticket office, telegraph office, and board that said CHANDLERSVILLE, ALT. 11,403 FT. POP. 462.

Kate peered in windows, admired the water tank, even had a word with the train driver, who let her up into the cabin and told her how things worked. By that time, the Duchess had been unloaded and the curator had come to welcome them, a tall, spare man accompanied by a large dog of unspecified ancestry.

"Take her around, Joe," the Duchess said. "Bring her back to the hotel for lunch about noon."

The curator was knowledgeable, a Western buff just as she was, had the answers to all her questions. He showed her the street with its livery stables, the few stores—including an undertaker—the barber shop with its red-and-white striped pole and chairs, still fully equipped down to the shaving mugs with the names of long-dead men on them. She inspected the jail, had to go inside a cell and have the door locked on her just to see how it felt; she went over the hotel, with its plush central banquette and its aspidistra, explored the bedrooms above, and saw her first bordello—*Madame Rose's House of Joy*. Finally, she had a drink at the bar, her foot propped up on the brass rail, staring up at the Rubens-type nude reclining on a cloud, strategically draped in gauze.

They went into the dining room, with its red-and-white-checked tablecloths, where a table had been laid for them, and the big potbellied stove lit for the occasion.

Lunch had been brought in large baskets and various pots and pans, which Minnie heated up: the ever present steak, with hash browns, fried eggs and beans, followed by apple pie à-la-mode, as served during the tourist season. Then, while the old lady and Minnie dozed by the potbellied stove, the curator took Blaise and Kate to the mine.

It was well-lit—"We have to be extremely conscious of the public's safety," the curator told her solemnly, but with a twinkle in his eye, "especially in this litigious country." The entrance was wide and high and opened out into a wide gallery, where there was a narrow railway on which tubs of ore had been pushed. This branched out, like the tentacles of an octopus into other narrower tunnels, deep into the heart of the mountain. The roof was supported by wooden struts—"In some cases, the original beams," the curator explained, "but we keep a careful eye on them at all times. We get thousands of people through here in the summer months."

"What provides your electricity?" Kate asked curiously. She had seen no signs of pylons.

"We have our own generator. Come summer I have a dozen people working here; it is only during the winters that I am alone."

"Don't you find it lonely?"

"No, I appreciate the solitude after the bustle of summer."

The air was fresh; obviously the generator also provided air-conditioning. Kate listened courteously to the curator explaining what had been mined and how, but she heard his voice rather than his words because consciousness of Blaise Chandler had tended, all day, to crowd everything else from her mind. He was standing a little apart, letting the curator—who obviously liked to talk—do all the explaining, but Kate could feel his eyes and was careful to keep her own face turned away; she had been told too many times how expressive and treacherously revealing it was to trust her command of it around him. Suddenly with a "that reminds me," the curator turned from Kate to ask Blaise something, and she took the opportunity to move casually away from the discussion about the smelter, as old as the town and in need of overhaul before being started up during the coming summer.

She was aware that her awkwardness with Blaise had been noted and, she surmised uncomfortably, not understood. She had felt his eyes on her more than once, which made her even more uneasy, and her tongue run away with her in an effort to cover her tracks. She could almost feel his exasperation—and no wonder. They had been getting along so well; she had believed the abrasive edge to their relationship had been smoothed away; now, all because she had felt like a midnight swim, it was gone, because every time she looked at him she saw him as he had been: a nude marble statue of such beauty and mouth-drying masculinity that it totally did in her composure. She wandered along one of the tunnels, so deep in thought that she did not notice when she turned a corner and became lost from view; nor did she realize that the lights here were fewer, that further down the tunnel there were none at all; all she was seeing was the copper Apollo in all his splendid nakedness, and feeling that same heat that had almost consumed her last night.

Only when she tripped on a stone, put out a hand to steady herself and touched something small and furry that squeaked, did she realize that she was in a no-man's-land of dim light with total darkness only a few yards away. Her common sense told her that what she had touched was a bat; they lived in caves and they liked darkness and they also hibernated in winter; but her skin crawled at the visualization of the bat itself; she had always regarded them with revulsion and, while she knew they were harmless, she could not prevent that revulsion from turning to terror if she got too near them. She let out a squawk and to her horror, heard a whole chorus of squeaks coming out of the blackness. She turned and ran, her hands over her ears, her eyes shut, cannoned into a wall and let out a howl of pain as her forehead met stone with a crack. When she again cannoned into something she was in such a state of panic that she screamed and struggled until a voice commanded sharply, "Kate! Be quiet! You are making enough noise to rouse the dead!"

She felt hands on her shoulders and threw herself against the body they belonged to, burying her face in a flannel shirt and managing to gasp, "Bats . . . there were bats . . ."

"You must have gone down one of the unused sections," the curator said, concerned. "The mine is a natural habitat for bats in the winter I'm afraid . . ."

"She's all right," Blaise Chandler said calmly, putting his arms around her shivering body. "Just startled, that's all."

"I don't like bats," Kate said weakly.

"Nobody does except a few naturalists," the curator sympathized.

Kate's heart was beating wildly, but it was as much being held against that same body she had seen in all its splendor the night before as her panic. He smelled of something sharp and yet musky, and his chest was like a wall. Tall as she was her head still fitted his shoulder perfectly, and her mouth was only inches away from the firm column of his neck; she could feel his warmth, inhale it, was suddenly overcome by an aching desire to press her mouth against his skin and even as the thought formed, jerked upright and jumped away from him, mumbling, "I'm sorry. I shouldn't have wandered away like that."

"Your mind must have been somewhere else at the time," Blaise commented dryly.

"I'm sorry," Kate apologized again, feeling both humiliated and foolish as well as an emotional rag, and looking fixedly at the ground like a penitent child.

She heard Blaise sigh and say impatiently, "We are not going to stand you in the corner, you know."

"Perhaps Miss Despard would prefer to go outside again," the curator suggested.

"Yes, please," Kate agreed with such alacrity that Blaise glanced at her sharply. The old lady waved away Kate's shamefaced explanation. "Can't stand the things myself. Always used to be scared they'd get into my hair."

"With the radar they've got?" Blaise inquired.

"I don't give a damn what they've got," his grandmother retorted. "I always feel they are goin' to get tangled in my hair and that's that. I expect Kate feels the same way."

It was almost three and time to go. Darkness came early in these winter months. Kate sat in silence most of the way back, ostensibly keenly studying the guide booklets the curator had pressed upon her, in reality not reading a word but cursing herself for being a stupid fool. Any advantage she might have gained with Blaise Chandler—and she now accepted as an irreversible truth that she wanted as much advantage as the traffic would bear—she had foolishly thrown away by revealing herself to be just another irrational female; the one thing, she had always fervently believed, she was not. He had been impatient with her; she had heard his sigh. No doubt he was also contemptuous, thought her a stupid idiot of a girl who knew no better than to wander off down unknown tunnels in a strange mine. Fool, fool, *fool*, Kate mourned, as the words of the booklet blurred before her eyes, the wheels of the train clacked rhythmically and the engine chuffed sturdily; while the old lady dozed, and Minnie quietly did her beadwork, and Blaise Chandler, when she surreptitiously risked a glance through her lashes, was deeply immersed in the latest copy of *Forbes*. He had already forgotten the incident. What to her was a milestone on her particular road in life had been no more than a passing stranger to him. Her heart felt heavy and her chest tight. She laid down her pamphlets and sat staring sightlessly out of the window, not realizing that her face was reflected, as in a mirror, by the gathering darkness outside and the bright lights inside, so that when he looked up from his magazine, Blaise Chandler was at a loss to account for her expression of bleak misery.

It was her last night, and it found her torn. On the one hand she hated to leave; on the other she could not get away fast enough from Blaise Chandler's disturbing presence and her even more disturbing reaction to it. But she put on a cheerful face, made herself eat food she did not want, because she also did not want anyone to notice anything wrong. Again she lay sleepless most of the night, falling asleep just before dawn.

She was up early, went to say her good-byes to Hank, the General, and Jed, who warmly bid her to visit again.

"I'd love to," she told him fervently. "Perhaps next year. . ."

To the Duchess, Kate said thickly, "Thank you for the most marvelous weekend I ever spent—I'll never forget it."

The old lady embraced her. "You come back whenever you want," she instructed. "You've got the phone number—use it."

"I will, oh, I will," promised Kate.

She turned to Blaise, standing by his grandmother. He was staying on another day. "I'm glad we met as we did," she said lightly, as she had rehearsed it over and over in front of her mirror. "Thank you for everything."

"My pleasure," he said, and his smile was friendly and his handshake firm. "I'll be in London shortly. I'll call in."

"Yes," Kate managed coolly. "Do that." Please, she prayed in fervent silence.

She kept her nose pressed to the window as the helicopter rose above the pink house, set like a decoration on a vast white cake, and headed for the distant mountains and Denver, where she would pick up a flight to Kennedy. She watched until the house dwindled and then, as the helicopter banked and turned, heading east, was lost from sight. Her sigh was heartfelt.

"Ain't it though," the pilot, thinking she was impressed by the view, said amiably.

"Yes," Kate agreed quietly. "It sure is . . ."

9

"I was beginning to think you were taking out American citizenship," was Rollo's greeting when he met her—unexpectedly—at Heathrow.

"Hardly," Kate denied firmly, sensing at once that he was in a snit. Probably because he was jealous that she had actually gone without him. "I went on Friday morning and I am back Tuesday night. I have also lived a whole lifetime's magical experience in those few days."

Rollo eyed her. "You do look somewhat—bewitched."

"I can't begin to tell you—"

"But you will. However, I have something to tell you first." His delivery of the line told her to stand by for a Revelation. "Guess who popped in on Saturday?"

Kate met the grey eyes, alight with malice. "What did she want?" she asked calmly.

"To see what she could find out, of course. She was fishing like mad."

"But caught nothing?"

Rollo chortled. "I tied her line in knots."

"Did you tell her where I was?"

"Seeing a client, I said, leaving her unenlightened as to whom and where." His sharp eyes investigated her luggage. "You've got the horse?"

"Yes."

"Well?" Rollo urged sharply. "What did he say? How did he react? Is he going to sue?"

"He said a great deal—all of it unpleasant. His reaction was all but violent and no, he is not going to sue."

Rollo's eyebrows almost merged with his silver hair. "You *have* worked wonders. I'd heard that he was ready to strangle you."

"At one time I thought he might," Kate admitted.

Rollo eyed her again. She looked at once lit up and yet curiously subdued, as if her light was not providing the right kind of illumination on something—or someone.

"So, what about your magical experience?" he asked with a curl of the lip that always went down well in Wilde revivals.

"I saw the most magnificent collection of Western art— not just one Remington but dozens of them! Paintings, sketches, and bronzes. And the others—Rollo, it was unbelievable . . ."

The silver eyes glittered as though newly polished. "A sale?"

"Oh, no! That would be desecration!"

Rollo stopped dead and dropped his hand from Kate's elbow. "Am I to understand," he asked, with that dangerous quietness that meant she had better have a good story or else, "that you came across a superb collection and did not acquire it for disposal at Despard's?"

Kate met his eyes head on. "That is exactly what I want you to understand," she agreed.

"Are you mad?" thundered Rollo, à la Mr. Barrett, one of his best parts.

"No, even if you are," Kate answered composedly.

"Spare me another of your Saint Catriona acts."

"You are the actor," Kate pointed out gently.

Rollo glared, but she did not look away or blush or fidget. "Whose collection?" he asked finally.

"It belongs to Blaise Chandler's grandmother."

Now Rollo was, for once, speechless. "Agatha Chandler!" he managed at last.

"Is there another one?"

Rollo drew in a breath that hissed like escaping steam. "You may have delicate qualms concerning the disposal of art for high prices, my dear Kate, but once that old lady— and she must be aged indeed by now—is dead, your stepsister will have no such compunction, and if that happens once your Year of Trial has started you are done for! What in God's name were you thinking of?"

"I told her that the collection should be bequeathed to the American people," Kate said.

Rollo closed his eyes. "I must sit down," he said. "I feel quite faint . . ."

But there were no seats nearby.

"I also told Blaise Chandler the same thing," Kate said helpfully.

Rollo moaned. "You *are* mad," he said hollowly. Then, "And what did *he* say?"

Kate remembered now how Blaise had looked at her oddly. "I don't get it," he'd said finally.

"Nor should anybody else," Kate had told him unflinchingly. "What you have here is a fabulous collection of Western art that should—must—be kept together and bequeathed to the nation, not split up and sold to the highest bidder. It's your country's past!"

"Americans tend to live in the present."

"Maybe, but they envy my country's heritage. Why, then, dispose of your own?"

"Something we do tend to do," Blaise agreed, surprising her yet again." 'But selling such heritage is how you earn your living. Aren't you cutting off your nose to spite your face by seeing to it that you won't ever sell this one?"

"No, I don't think so. A good auction house is not just a giant maw where goods go in at one end and money comes out the other. If this were England you wouldn't be able to sell the collection at all unless the government allowed you to."

Blaise laughed but his voice was velvet covering steel. "That is not likely ever to happen in *this* country."

"All the more reason to see that the house and its contents become the Agatha Chandler Museum of Western Art."

He had stared at her so long and so hard she thought he was X-raying her, until he asked finally, "And you have told my grandmother all this?"

"Yes."

"Then you must know that the final decision is hers. This house and its contents mean a very great deal to her; there is no way she would part with them while she is alive . . ." The dark eyes held an odd gleam. "But you think I would—or rather my wife would?"

"I know she would," Kate returned bluntly, tossing the flaming torch right in the middle of all her boats.

But his voice was without heat. "My wife has no idea what the house looks like or what it contains. She has never been here."

Kate forbore to tell him she already knew that, pointing

out instead, "Maybe, but once the Duchess is no longer around . . ." Again she stood her ground unflinchingly against the onslaught of those hard black eyes.

"What would you say the collection is worth?" he asked.

"Oh, God knows—at a rough guess, the paintings alone would raise about ten million dollars—but money is the least of *your* worries, surely?"

"Mine, yes, but not yours."

"I do not and never have believed in selling for selling's sake," Kate stated proudly. "Not when it comes to a great collection like this. Let it stand as the wonder it is. Let all Americans see it and take pride in their heritage. I shall get sales elsewhere; there are plenty of people wanting to sell, but don't split up something rare and remarkable."

Once more she withstood his probing gaze, as if he were trying to find out the vital ingredient in her makeup that made her do this thing. "I have no doubt my grandmother will think it all over very carefully," he said finally and dismissively. And that was all.

Now, she said to Rollo, "He said he and his grandmother will think about it."

"Think!" snorted Rollo. "Once his wife hears what is being thought about she will be there so fast the snows will melt. Art is big business, Kate. For God's sake don't let a word of this get out. You are finished if it does; everyone, instead of just me, will know you are still a sentimentally altruistic green girl, ready to make a meal for a whole marketful of worldly-wise sharks." From way up on his high horse, he looked down and pronounced, "This, dear heart, is not what your father had in mind when he bid you don his mantle. He left it to you in a condition to give you many years' wear. By the time you are through with it, it is going to be nothing more than a dish cloth!" While Kate was in America, Rollo had got down to his favorite occupation: propagating, disseminating, and then gathering information. Had there been an Olympic gold medal for gossip Rollo would have been an unbeatable champion. He could sniff out a skeleton no matter how long the body had been buried, and took a fiendish delight in digging up the bones. He had turned his attention to those that lay buried at Despard's, his nose questing the air for the slightest whiff of corruption, no matter how expensive the perfume or after-shave that tried to mask it.

He was perfectly placed to do so. Through his birth—on the wrong side of the blanket in a noble bed—he had access to the aristocracy; through his school—not Eton because, as his actual father observed brutally to his mother, "That's where my own boys go"—but Harrow, where his putative father had gone, he had access to the Old Boys network; through his acting to the world of theatre, cinema, and television; and because he had once written the occasional fine arts column for a national daily he also had entrée to the Third Estate. Finally, through Despard's, he knew and was well known in the art world, from the grand auction houses through the expensive dealers to the small, sometimes shady dealers on the side. All these worlds interlinked, much as the Olympic symbol did, and he thus moved easily from one to the other, dropping the right (or in his case, wrong) word before allowing the ripples to carry him on their current.

He took a leisurely stroll through his circles, Edith Sitwell-type nose a-twitch, his air of always knowing everything causing those who didn't to try and show they did, invariably revealing more than they realized and coming away with pretensions crushed when Rollo, in his gravelly Gingold voice, "dear-boy'd" them to futility. Nobody liked Rollo Bellamy, but everybody agreed that it did not do to get on the wrong side of him. His arm was known to be as long as his memory (which matched his nose, the more spiteful ones said) and his tongue was to be avoided at all costs. Besides, he knew absolutely *everybody* and you never knew when you might need an intro.

There was more than a hint of mystery about him; the stories about him were legion, but nobody was ever able to say for sure that they were true. Some said he had worked for MI-5, or was it MI-6, others said he was still an active agent for some impenetrable secret government agency, that his acting and everything else were only covers; that his sexual proclivities made him the ideal man to compromise people whom the government wanted to trap into blackmail. It was said that he had been involved in the Burgess-MacLean affair, that he was on intimate terms with more than one bigwig at the Foreign Office . . . They said all sorts of things about Rollo Bellamy, but never to his face. So the stories eventually came to be accepted as truth, and his reputation to precede him like an advance man, always the signal to scatter. The only person not to believe the stories was Kate. She scorned them as pure invention. He was Rollo, for heaven's sake! Her mother would never have made a confidant of a man who was supposed to have done all those things. He was the man who had wiped her nose and scolded her, told her marvelous stories and taken her to dress rehearsals, on the understanding that she utter not a sound. He was the man who had been there when she needed him, who had known and loved her mother, even as she had, and been a rock to them both. It was fear or envy that created the stories and she dismissed them. All right, so he knew a lot of people in all sorts of places: she for one was grateful for they had helped her when she started out. People feared and disliked him because of his acid tongue, his biting sarcasm. She refused to believe a word against him. She *knew* him, after all.

So it was that Rollo had dropped in on an art dealer of his acquaintance who had once tried to sell him a Khmer figure as absolutely unrestored, but which Rollo had unerringly spotted as having a recut mouth. They sparred and fenced lightly over a drink and a superb Benin head, Rollo indicating that he just happened to know an American—a very *nouveau riche* Texan not yet used to his petrodollars and advised by his accountant to invest in art—who was interested in acquiring just such a head. Everybody knew that Benin bronzes—especially with this argument going between Britain and Nigeria—were the "in thing," so as a trade the dealer let fall the fact that it was Piers Lang who had casually dropped the poisonous word into the ear of old Wilfrid Shelby, who had in turn told the other trustees of the Penhaligon Estate, that the untried and inexperienced daughter of Charles Despard was not really up to handling the sale of the Penhaligon old masters and that it was to her stepsister they should look if they wanted the best possible prices.

That little tidbit sent Rollo—after promising to send the American along—into the next circle where an Old Boy told him with pursed lips that young Lang was not the man his father was; in addition to being a gambler of the *folie de grandeur* type and hip-deep in debt, he was known to pass rubber checks. This eddy carried Rollo onwards to the circle where a BBC producer he knew who had done a documentary on London's gambling clubs confirmed the fact that Piers Lang was a high roller who lived way beyond his means in a much-admired and gossiped-about flat. Rollo then drifted into the orbit of a well-known interior designer with whom he had once had a fling and who he had heard was casting covetous eyes on Piers Lang's blond beauty. Under Rollo's delicate goading he revealed that Lang was a bisexual who was dabbling more than a toe in a pool of a deep copper color and bearing the logo CC with a pair of horns rampant.

By the time Kate returned, Rollo knew for sure not only who the stool pigeon was, but why, how, and who for. So, after picking her up from the airport, instead of going back to the penthouse, they went to Rollo's cozy basement flat in Royal Avenue, which he occupied rent-free thanks to the fact that his real father's family owned the freehold and a ninety-nine-year lease had been granted to his mistress, Rollo's mother, along with the income from invested capital which brought in what Rollo considered to be the measly sum of one thousand pounds a year. However, it paid his property taxes and his telephone bill and he knew he would always have a roof over his head.

Over the cassoulet he had left in the oven and the bottle of Gevry-Chambertin, instead of telling her what he had found out he sulked; in the past that had always led to her coaxing him out of his fit of the sullens and him eventually and graciously accepting her apology. But she did not do that this time; she ate in silence, almost abstractedly. Whatever she was thinking of it was obviously not him or their spat. With shock, he realized that she had dismissed it—and him—from her mind.

So he said spitefully, "You haven't asked me what's been happening while you were away."

She glanced up at him. "If there is anything, I have no doubt you will tell me in your own good time."

Again he was confounded. This was a different Kate. What *had* happened to her over this particular weekend?

He decided to tell her about his, but first he cast a lure.

"I think it is time we fired the Dishonorable Piers."

"You know we can't, not without proof." Kate was curt.

"About the fake, yes, but while you have been partaking of the fruits of wealth, *I* have been beavering away on your behalf, and for what I have discovered he has been up to, he *can* be fired."

"Like what?" Kate asked, still far too cool for his liking.

Baldly he gave her the facts, but her reaction was not what he expected. Instead of anger, Kate's response was a calm, "I have already decided how to dispose of him."

"Have you indeed! How, may I ask?"

"I am going to transfer him."

"Transfer him! Where to?"

Kate smiled and it made him scowl back. Really, she was far too much in command of herself for his liking. It hinted at an unexpected declaration of independence. It was obviously she had been consorting with Americans!

"Australia," Kate said.

Rollo's jaw dropped, then a look of grudging admiration appeared. But he could not let her get away with all of it. "Who put that idea into your head?"

"I did. He won't go, but that is what I am counting on. That way, all that is left is to resign."

"Positively Machiavellian," Rollo sniffed. Then his silver eyes gleamed. "At that, though, it is an inspired choice. He regards Australia as still being a penal colony."

"Exactly," said Kate.

"You *are* learning, dear heart," Rollo said menacingly.

"What interests me is what else you have learned," Kate answered crisply. "Like about the fake horse, for instance."

"Nothing—yet. I have investigated Thingummy Whatsit and Hoojah, but apart from acting for the biggest crook in the city—who has not as yet ever been convicted of anything—they are above reproach. It seems they never actually met the 'old man'; all dealings were done with a secretary—you know, à la Howard Hughes? The only people who know where that horse came from are your stepsister and her paramour."

Kate's eyes were unfocused, so deep was she in her thoughts. Finally, "She went to some lengths to show me what she can do, don't you think? And quite deliberately. Had she not wanted me to, the fake would have been of something outside her field—and mine; something we would never have connected to her. Yet she made it Chinese . . ." She frowned. "What I would like to know more than anything is who made that masterly fake. Whoever he is, he is dangerous."

"I have my nose to the wind," Rollo assured her.

"Well, in the meantime, I intend to subject that horse to every test known to science."

"As a matter of fact"—Rollo shrugged at her hard stare—"I have already handed the job to a friend who happens to be an expert in such things."

"Who?" demanded Kate indignantly.

"A dealer in Chinese antiquities. I will let you know if he comes up with anything."

"I should hope so," Kate snapped. "You had no right to make such arrangements without asking me first."

Hoity-toity, Rollo thought furiously. All that hobnobbing with the rich and mighty has made her think she can act like one. That and a smug sense of having solved the Crime of the Century. Well, let her, he thought grimly. It won't last. She has not made a move in the past nine years that did not involve me so she will soon find she needs me as much as ever. He fell to fantasizing how he would make her beg for his forgiveness . . .

But Kate was no longer thinking of the horse, or Rollo. She was thinking—as she did so much and so often in the last few days—about Blaise Chandler. How *could* Dominique? And with a spineless wimp like Piers Lang. But then, she reminded herself, it would not be for what he could do in bed, but how useful he could be that would matter. He had furnished the contact with the upmarket firm of solicitors; he had brought the horse to Kate's attention. He had been something she could use. When you compared the oily smoothness of Piers Lang to the rocklike strength of Blaise Chandler there was no contest. To her mind, only one of them was a man. And such a man . . . Once again her mind switched on the picture of Blaise standing by the pool, naked as a jaybird, raking his wet hair back, revealing himself to her in all his glory.

" . . . Martin to sell his Picassos," Rollo was saying. "That should provide a ripple or two through the market."

"How many?" Kate asked, switching points to follow Rollo's train of thought.

'Six—and all choice. Three blue period, three others variations on that 'demoiselle' thing of his. I can never tell one from another because they all look the same to me, but I am assured by Those Who Know that they are the master at the peak of his genius, and if that is what people are willing to pay fortunes for . . ." His smile threw barbs.

"I did what I thought was right for the Chandler Collection," Kate told him, with that same quiet firmness which was new. "As I have told you before, there are some things more important than money."

"Then for God's sake don't spread it around," Rollo snapped.

"I am as concerned for Despard's as you are—more so, since I am a Despard, which fact you seem to forget sometimes."

"*I* forget! I did not go so far as to change *my* name!"

Kate flushed. Satisfied that he had drawn blood, or the signs anyway, Rollo relented. "So tell me all about this ranch or whatever . . ."

Kate needed no prodding, and as she elaborated, Rollo was confirmed in his suspicion that Kate had undergone some kind of transformation in Colorado. Move over St. Paul, he thought sourly.

"And Chandler—was he a good host?" he asked casually.

"He was very kind," Kate replied stiltingly, but her cheeks flamed and she reached for her glass to bury her nose in it again. Rollo, who knew his Kate inside, outside, and upside down, felt jealousy knife him, until he told himself that where Blaise Chandler was concerned, Kate had not a hope in hell. Men like him did not even see women like her.

"What's the odds that he doesn't go straight to his wife and tell her what his grandmother is sitting on?" he observed snidely.

"He wouldn't!" Kate answered instantly. Then, her flush deepening, "I know he wouldn't. He's very attached to his grandmother. He said she would never ever sell anything while she was alive."

"But it's all his when she's dead."

He saw that cause a moment's flush, but she shook her head. "He wouldn't. I just know he wouldn't."

"What happened to the superior shit you couldn't stand?" Rollo marveled acidly.

"He is still in residence, but so is the man his grandmother loves and trusts."

"What a lot you accomplished in a few days."

Kate's face closed up and, for the first time, Rollo was left outside. Again, he felt a *frisson* of something like fear. Always before he had been the only one, since her mother, to have a key to Kate Despard. Now, all of a sudden, she'd had the locks changed. He tried a different tack.

"It's just that I don't want this dream weekend affecting your judgment," he explained with a negligent shrug.

"With you likely to appeal against it at every turn?"

That was better. "And don't think I won't."

He turned the talk to other things, told her of the sale that had taken place in her absence, where an Arab, who five years before had owned nothing more than two wives and four camels, had paid four million pounds for a lushly erotic Titian. ". . . didn't give a damn about the great art; all he wanted was to hang the picture in his tent and gaze at all those acres of sumptuous flesh." Rollo's disgust was all but palpable. "The Cézanne went, as you had surmised, to Lombardi; I gather he has a rich Californian all lined up." He paused to refill their glasses. "However . . ." Kate's head came up. That masterly pause meant a revelation to come. "The rumor that has everyone talking right now concerns Hong Kong. Nothing has been announced, but from various leaks it is believed that the Venus Flytrap is in the process of arranging what is being touted as the Sale of the Century—and I do not mean the TV quiz. Some Hong Kong millionaire, scenting the winds of Communist change, is about to dispose of what is rumored to be the finest collection of Chinese art yet seen. It is months away, of course, but if it is true, from the figures being quoted, the game is lost before it is begun."

"How much?" Kate asked.

Rollo's shrug indicated a lost cause. "Thirty—forty million dollars. U.S., not Hong Kong." At Kate's expression, "And you just threw away a chance to sell a unique collection of Western art . . . think on that!" he snapped, as he got up to clear away the dishes.

Kate sighed. Rollo was in a snit; with that devilish internal radar of his, he had detected that something had happened to her in Colorado. He had always been able to pick up her feelings at once. What she had not expected was that he would exhibit signs of jealousy, and yet, it was not to be wondered at. Rollo had wielded a great deal of influence in her life since she'd been on her own. She had turned to him at a time when she needed him, and when, after a while, he had not been disposed to relinquish his proprietary hold, she had good-naturedly let him. Besides, it had suited her. But not now.

He was already stirring madly at Despard's. Unofficially

she had appointed him her personal assistant, but in his lordly way he was taking it upon himself to act as her éminence grise, indicating that he was the final arbiter when it came to decisions and/or actions. More than once Kate had had to soothe ruffled feelings and calm lacerated sensibilities. Now, she sensed that he was anything but pleased that she seemed to have reached some sort of rapport with Blaise Chandler. Rollo had always been the only man in her life and he would regard any other male influence as a threat to this position. Which meant he would stop at nothing to maintain it. He would have to be deflected.

As she got up to dry the dishes she glanced at him. He was washing up with his usual scrupulousness, but the way he placed the plates in the drainer, handled the dish mop, and shook away suds showed his displeasure. So did the twin spots of color flying their flags on his usually parchment cheeks. Rollo, she realized with something akin to pity, was afraid.

Rescue was called for.

"There will be other sales," she said quietly. "I intend to do my damnedest. And haven't you already cornered six first-water Picassos? To be sold after my year has started, of course."

Slightly mollified, "Would you expect anything less?"

"Not of you," Kate told him seriously. "Never of you, Rollo."

The spots of color were fading. "Then do not, I beg of you, expect too much from Blaise Chandler."

"I expect nothing," Kate said quietly. "I know better than that."

Rollo slid her a glance. Yes, he thought. One good thing Susan left her daughter was a fund of common sense. And then, his own coming to the rescue: "At that," he conceded, "you might have done yourself a bit of good by not displaying the same greed his wife would undoubtedly have done. If, as you say, he is deeply attached to his grandmother."

"He is," Kate said. "Very much so."

Rollo nodded as he emptied the washing-up bowl. "Then you undoubtedly did the right thing. I'd heard myself that he is a veritable St. George where the old girl is concerned."

"She wields a mean sword herself," Kate told him wryly.

"Do tell," begged Rollo.

And by the time she had done so, making him laugh, eyes

sparkling with relish, he was exclaiming, "I insist upon meeting her; she sounds like a woman after my own heart."

"I don't think she would go that far," laughed Kate, "but yes, I think you would get on."

"And with a friend like her, who knows how such a friendship might enable *you* to get on."

As always he was spinning webs, finding ways to make use of whatever came his way—or Kate's.

"What would I do without you, Rollo?" she asked affectionately, knowing full well, now, but knowing it would not do to tell him so.

"Be eaten by the first wolf which came along."

Kate's eyes were veiled again, in that way that was new, but her voice was its normal self when she said, "Blaise Chandler is no wolf, Rollo. Not where I am concerned, anyway. Mind you"—her tone took on a more cheerful note—"I don't think he sees me as a tiresome charge on him anymore. He is not nearly so disapproving. We got on quite well, really. The disapproval has changed to . . . well, not quite unqualified approval, but a qualified one. And that, surely, can do us much more good than harm. As you so rightly pointed out, his grandmother is indeed a powerful old lady. Having her for a friend can definitely do us nothing but good."

Rollo nodded, adding with relish, "Especially since, as you say, she does not care for her grandson's wife."

Kate forbore to enlighten him of Agatha's trenchant remarks in that direction.

"And if you can get yourself involved with this, what do you call it . . . ?"

Kate knew that he knew—Rollo had a flypaper memory—but she went along with it just the same. "The Chandler Museum of Western Art."

"Yes. Whatever. Well, that, too, can bring nothing but good. I still believe it would have been even better if you had clinched the sale, but collections seem to be the thing in these conservationist days, and it might not be bad to have a few friends in that quarter." He nodded, considering this. "Yes, all in all, a shrewd move, dear heart. I congratulate you.

He was affability itself, good humor restored.

Kate smiled back, hiding her relief. She would have to tread carefully in future; Rollo's *amour propre* was, like that of all men, unbelievably fragile. A little sop would not come amiss. So she said warmly, "Praise from you is praise indeed, since it comes so rarely. You know you are the one constant thing in my rapidly changing world."

Rollo was touched, ego burgeoning. "Where else would I go? And don't say that place wherein I have been wished lo, these many times. I never could stand high temperatures!"

BOUGHT IN

December

10

Dominique turned the Citroën onto the brick drive Charles had laid over the rough, rutted track that led steeply up the hill where the *mas* lay behind its brick wall, nestled into a fold of the hillside above Vent. Its gardens were filled with fruit trees, olives, oleander, and jasmine and she could smell the old, familiar scent of the herbs Marthe grew mixed with the tangy citrus of the lemon trees placed in pots along the terrace, as well as the sweeter fragrance of apple, pear, and apricot trees. Rolling down her window, she reached out a hand to pull the old iron bell rope, heard it clang sonorously in the distance, and in a few moments old Jeannot slowly trundled back the big double doors, showing no surprise at the visitor, merely grunting good morning.

The full force and brilliance of the gardens on which her mother worked so lovingly hit her, especially the scent of the honeysuckle that swarmed all over the inside of the wall, and she drove the last fifty yards of the slope toward the brick-paved circle in front of the grey stone house, with its staggered red-tile roof and white painted shutters, unaccountably feeling a sense of coming home. As she shut off the engine she saw Marthe, her hands as always thrust deep into the wide front pocket of her blue-and-white-striped apron, standing at the front door.

"Bonjour, Madame." It was as though it had not been more than one week since her last visit, instead of her first since the funeral.

"Jour, Marthe. Comment ça va?"

"Well enough," Marthe replied.

"I've got a load of things in the back for you."

Before driving up, Dominique had gone into the big *Geant Casino* at Villeneuve-Loubat, the ultimate in supermarkets, and stocked up on the delicacies her mother loved. Marthe grunted as she saw them: *foie gras,* truffles, quails in aspic, *marrons glacés.*

"She won't eat them," she observed with a disapproving sniff. "She eats like a bird, these days, though she makes me cook for two, as always. The waste . . . And Jeannot is growing fat as a pig."

"For two?"

"Everything here is done for two. Madame, your mother, and M'sieu her husband." At Dominique's incredulity: "She talks to him all the time; I have to lay his place at table, lay out his pajamas and robe at night. She never watches television and the only music she plays are his favorites. And all the time embroidering something for him—a pair of slippers, a bookmark, a case for his glasses. She also reads aloud, as if to him."

Dominique asked bluntly of a servant who had been with her mother for years, "Are you trying to tell me she is mad?"

"No. I had Dr. Morel here to talk to her—without telling her why, of course—and he says she is not insane; she just prefers her fantasy world to the real one."

"That is nothing new." Dominique had long known that her mother had taken a look at reality years ago and decided it was not for her. Had she not, her first husband *would* have driven her insane.

"Where is she?" Dominique asked now.

"Where she always is at this time of the day. On the terrace."

She was sitting in her usual garden chair, the one with the footrest placed under the shade of a large, striped umbrella, facing the magnificent view down the slope of the mountain toward the distant sea and the town of Antibes. She was, as usual, simply but exquisitely dressed in citron-yellow cotton, her tanned legs bare, gleaming as though they had been polished, and her toenails were small squares of scarlet, matching her perfectly manicured nails. It was also obvious that she had been to the hairdresser—or more probably the hairdresser had been to her—and that she was devoting as much care to her appearance as she had ever done. And for the same man.

"*Maman.*" Dominique bent to kiss one smooth and fragrant cheek.

Catherine lifted her eyes, saw her daughter without surprise, and then asked approvingly of Dominique's suit, "Saint Laurent?"

"You still have the eye," complimented her daughter. "I had thought, perhaps, buried down here, you had lost interest."

"A woman should never lose interest in her appearance," reproved her mother. "If she does, so will her man."

Dominique sat down in the other recliner and poured herself a tall glass of well-iced *citron pressé*. It was, as always, nectar.

"So, how are you, *Maman?*"

"As you see, I am perfectly well." Catherine reached for her small, jeweled scissors, part of a sewing kit that, so its provenance said, had once belonged to Madame de Pompadour. As if *she* ever sewed, Dominique thought, amused.

"You are happy, then?"

Catherine raised surprised eyes, as large and as lustrous as those of her daughter, if of a different blue. "Why should I not be? This is my favorite place. I have always been happy here."

"You are not—lonely?"

"I am never lonely here."

True, reflected Dominique. Normandy and Gonville were, to her mother, the places where she had served her sentence as Madame la Vicomtesse du Vivier. Only here, at *La Galinière*, bought for her by her second husband, was she what she had only and ever wanted to be: Madame Charles Despard.

"Don't you get bored?" Antibes, though not Dominique's favorite spot on the Côte d'Azur, was one thing; this place miles up in the hills was another. There was a village about a mile away, but it consisted of nothing more than a café, a couple of shops, a church and a collection of old men who played *boules*, watched by a similar collection of old crones. The young always left as soon as they were able to, heading for the land of the living.

"Bored?" Catherine was again surprised. "I have my garden, my books, my music, my embroidery. And I have Charles. No, I am not bored."

"*Maman—*" Dominique stopped short, cut off by the sharp look her mother gave her. Like all malleable people, Catherine had her sticking point, except hers was an obsession: Charles Despard.

"I do not ask you what you do with your life. I have never interfered—"

Because you never cared, Dominique thought.

"—so I ask you not to interfere with me. I am happy; this place is my real—my only—home. I shall not leave it, ever again. Here, there is no Despard's, no pressures, no people to distract and detract. Here, I have all I want . . ."

And Papa to yourself, thought Dominique.

"I am quite content, I assure you. Do not concern yourself. Now, I shall give you lunch and afterwards you shall give me all the latest *on dits* . . ."

They had lunch on the terrace: red mullet done with lemons, succulent brown *poussin* stuffed with tarragon from Marthe's herb garden, ending with figs warm from the sun, golden apricots, nectarines, and great golden globes of peaches, along with the cheese of the region, *Brebis du Pays*.

"I shall have to do penance for this," Dominique sighed, as they sat over *café filtre* and brandy. "But it was worth it."

She eyed her mother. For lunch, the table had been laid for two only, and her mother's talk had, as usual, been boringly banal. Not once had she asked about Despard's or her husband's daughter. They had long ago been relegated to the back of her life, so far behind that they did not exist for her. Catherine Despard had always possessed a strange ruthlessness when it came to seeing only what she wished to see. Like the child she really was, Dominique thought now. Children invented imaginary friends; her mother had invented an imaginary life, shared with a husband who had held her cradled in the center of his adoration. She had always been vain, self-centered, and deeply insecure, needing constant proof of affection, and only one person had cared enough about her to provide it.

This house, Dominique thought, was his gift to her, and here his wife had brought from the big house on the Avenue Foch all those things that were a part of his life. His portrait—which should by rights have gone to London to be hung in the foyer—now hung above the fireplace in the large living room; to the left of the fireplace was his chair, with the footstool Catherine had embroidered placed before it. Ready for his feet were the velvet slippers that were also embroidered with his entwined initials, and the bookmark that kept his place in the book he was reading—*had* been reading, Dominique corrected herself irritably—was also his wife's work. Ready at hand on the table were his box of Giuliettas and the big brass lighter. And all around the room his favorite things: the *sang de boeuf* plates, the exquisite ivories, the small but glowing Cézanne, the Tabriz rugs, the lamp base of rock crystal. And always flowers everywhere; he had loved their color, their shape, their scent. Deep pink carnations were massed in the Sèvres soup tureen that was missing one handle; there was a bougainvillaea in a Vincennes cachepot. Nothing had been changed; nothing ever would be.

Later, when her mother was at her customary afternoon nap, Dominique prowled around the house; she had already seen, on accompanying her upstairs and taking down her mother's thin cotton wrapper from the hook behind the door, that Charles' toweling robe also hung in its accustomed place. And on the bathroom shelf his shaving gear waited, his big bottle of Eau Sauvage half empty. Strange, mused Dominique, that it was now, as a widow, that her mother was at last living the life of her own design. She knew the story of the *débacle* of her mother's first marriage, had heard how, on her wedding day, Catherine had been forced to leave her veil lowered because her face was so blotched with weeping. But since her remarriage the disaster had never again been referred to. It was as though her eventual triumph had erased it. Madame Charles Despard and Madame la Vicomtesse du Vivier were two different women. Her mother had blossomed in the radiance of her beloved Charles' adoration, had become a woman Dominique had never seen before.

Now, here was yet another Catherine, one who was confidently tranquil to a depth that shook Dominique, indicating as it did the ultimate in security. Because, Dominique thought with a sardonic smile, at last she has Papa where she always wanted him: safe from any other human being. At last Charles belonged only to his wife; there was nothing to threaten her hold on him—no Despard's, no flesh and blood daughter, no past, no future even. He lived in Catherine's mind, in the fantasy world she had created out of the depths of her misery without him. Now her dreams were her reality.

Talking to Marthe, this opinion was confirmed.

"Oh, yes, she is *tranquille,*" Marthe said, shrugging. "Here, she has nothing—and no one—to trouble her. Here the routine never varies. Even at night, there is the usual large glass of that Clos Vosges your father loved, and a cigar burning away in the ashtray, while she sits in her small chair beside his and chats away to him. I find myself looking for him, listening to him as though he were talking, he is so real through her. He is more alive now, when he is dead, than he ever was when he lived here."

"Does it frighten you?"

Another shrug. "No, it is not frightening. More . . . pathetic. But," she said unemotionally, "she is happy. Who can ask for more?"

Not I, thought Dominique. I need not concern myself further. She has all she wants; all she ever wanted. Now I am free to concentrate on what I want, what I should have had. Ah, Papa, she thought, you were the sly one . . . I should have realized. Behind your affability, your seeming control of all things at all times, you never could quite heal that bleeding conscience. You treated me as a daughter, yes, but you never thought of me as one except as part of your Catherine. Your daughter was the one who rejected you. Ah, she was clever. You never could stand being rejected, could you? Had *Maman* not done so, would you have clung so tenaciously to her memory, I wonder? Was it because you could not have her when you wanted her that you kept her memory untarnished?

Like Catriona. I should have realized, just because your wife was so jealously insecure she could not stand even to have your previous life mentioned, that you would not cease to think about it. You lulled me with your kindness—and I was not used to that. Perhaps it was gratitude. I was the one who brought you together, after all, even if it was for my own ends . . . Did you know, I wonder? You saw so much behind that smiling blandness.

For a moment she closed her eyes and felt, even as her mother did, the presence of her stepfather: a kind man, a patient man—when it suited him, a loving man. When she had asked, with wide-eyed and shy naïveté, if she could call him Papa, he had said at once, "But of course. What else?" with grave seriousness. I should have realized, Dominique thought again. I knew he was clever, knew he was subtle, knew he was, when the occasion called for it, doggedly

stubborn, just like his daughter. He let me think I had
replaced her in his life, even in his heart, but he had her
placed where I could never reach.

Suddenly she wished with all her heart that her own father
had loved her like that, but he had never really loved anyone but himself. He had been proud of her beauty, of her
ruthlessness, of her sexuality, but had she not been all these
things, he would have relegated her, as he had his wife, to
the backwaters of his life. Her mother she had expected
nothing from, and that is what she had got. Ah, love is a
luxury, she thought now, and one on which nobody, if they
have any sense, would waste their substance. Still, love had
left her mother very well provided for. Charles had indeed
been a generous man. She would want for nothing for the
rest of her life. Let Marthe wince at the waste of that
uneaten second place, the unsmoked cigars, the undrunk
wine—the last would be thriftily used for cooking anyway.

What mattered was, as Blaise would say, that her mother
was out of her hair. Why should she worry? *Chacun à son
goût* she smiled to herself, as she went to say her goodbyes.
Just as long as it is not mine . . .

ESTABLISHING CREDIT

May

11

As was her custom nowadays, before settling down to her day Kate came down the stairs into the main hall just after nine-thirty to find that business was already brisk, with members of the public standing at the public counters. She took a deep breath, inhaling the smell that was the very essence of Despard's. Here was where it all happened. Where people with something to sell first came into contact with Despard et Cie. Here they came to be told, they hoped, that their treasured family heirloom was worth a small fortune; that their picture or their clock or their sideboard was a long lost work of art. As Kate looked around she could see Julian Markham examining an ivory netsuke, his glass screwed into his eye as he turned the tiny figure in his long fingers; over there Andrew Clarke had a Chelsea harlequin in his hands, and not far away stood Alec Ross pleasurably turning the pages of an illuminated manuscript, while in his gentle, tactful way, Tom Herriot was explaining to an anxious lady why the small box she thought to be Fabergé was in reality a good copy.

Sitting at his desk in his cubbyhole was David Holmes, studiously familiarizing himself with the catalogue marked for his use for the first auction of the day, due to start at ten o'clock, of Victorian miniatures. Upstairs, at that same hour, Kate would meet the General Purposes Committee to discuss future plans, problems from the present, profits from the past. Now, her inner ear listened subconsciously to the hum of the place, her sensors searching for a missing beat, the slightest hint of sand in the engine. There was none. She nodded, said good morning to the cashier who was marshaling her receipt books, bill heads, and newly unlocked and stocked cash drawer for the day's business. Another day at Despard's.

Kate smilingly answered the various good mornings offered to her, satisfied that everything was functioning as normally as it ever had, and certainly since she had officially taken over a month ago.

She sat straighter in the chairman's chair nowadays. Without more than a small hiccup, the changeover had gone smoothly. Kate had proved her willingness to learn, to assimilate, to study, to accept responsibility and make the decisions only she could make. She had learned what advice to accept, and what to disregard. She had been honest and forthright as the occasion called for, had bluntly asked for help and patient understanding; she had laid on the table those cards she thought it politic to display, keeping up her sleeve the few aces she had been dealt.

She had instituted a new system for checking rare Oriental porcelains offered for sale. In the future, they would go through the most rigorous checking, not only the provenance and history books of such works, but also the vendor. Where there was even the slightest doubt, thermoluminescence would be used. The head of finance had raised his hands in horror at the cost, but Kate had insisted, compromising with him by agreeing that the cost of thermoluminescence would be borne by the client should he not be sufficiently well-known to Despard's.

She also notched up her first "acquisition." While running her little shop, she had once been offered a Korean blue and white dragon jar of the seventeenth century, which she recognized at once as being part of the Steyning Bequest: a fine collection of Eastern art formed by a former British ambassador to various Eastern countries. The man selling it, who seemed personable enough, gave himself away by asking for only a fraction of its worth. As Kate's bedtime reading was catalogues and brochures and histories, and she had an encyclopedic knowledge of what existed in which country house, she knew the vase at once. Telling the man she had a client who was keen on Korean ware but that he was unfortunately out of town, she asked him to return later that day, once she had managed to contact him. After some hemming and hawing the man agreed, and as soon as he had gone out the door Kate called the curator of the Steyning Bequest. The vase had indeed been stolen, more than five years before, since when there had been no trace. When the man called back the police were waiting. The trustees of the

Bequest had been deeply grateful and, when Kate refused a reward, had been instrumental in putting a fair bit of business her way. Now old Justin Steyning, the last family trustee, had died, and under the terms of Lord Steyning's will the Bequest was to be sold. Despard's was chosen to hold the auction.

"Mr. Justin never forgot the way you recovered the Korean vase—a particular favorite of his," Mr. Matheson, the senior trustee, told her.

Kate's stock soared. The Steyning Bequest, now some hundred years old, had appreciated greatly during that time, and contained some particularly fine pieces: not only porcelain, but also ivories, carpets, jades, robes, netsukes, lacquer work, and some very fine Japanese prints, most especially a rare pillow book, painted on vellum in indescribably delicate colors and vivid detail. When Kate was summoned to Steyning, the pillow book was in a locked case and the remaining trustees, not one of whom would see seventy again, coughed behind their hands and said that, of course, she would take its contents as unread, but she could examine the binding if she wished . . . Kate demurred and contented herself with handling the delicate ivories and the exquisitely carved jades. The reserve on the collection was five million pounds.

"Kate, you are a godsend!" John Steadman, her deputy managing director, chortled. "A capital sale, capital! The Steyning Bequest, by God!"

"I want a particularly fine catalogue for this one," Kate said to the head of that department. "If illustrated properly, these ivories and lacquers will have certain people drooling. The reserve is five million, but if what has been happening at comparable sales recently is anything to go by, we should exceed that quite easily."

"And make a very fine commission into the bargain," John said. He was not one of the Old Timers; he had been at Despard's only ten years and was more a figurehead than an active director, in that he was extremely well connected—his mother was a cousin of the Queen Mother—and had been responsible for bringing in some important sales. Nor was he part of the Dominique faction: his wife was a dragon, who kept him at heel at all times. But he made an excellent front man. The first page proofs of the Steyning catalogue had just arrived on Kate's desk and she would go through them later.

Kate felt that this success made up for the previous failure—
her first, which had brought her up short and given her a
nasty fright. To remind her not to make the same mistake
again, she had hung on her office wall the framed "Salerooms" article from *The Times* which had caused her so
much heartburn, and which she now knew by heart:

Porcelain dealers were left stunned yesterday when Christie's sold part of an early Worcester (c.1750) tea set,
decorated in the popular "boy on a buffalo" pattern in
pretty imitation of Chinese brushwork, for prices roughly
three times current levels.

A teapot went for £2,600, Christie's estimate £600-£800;
the cream jug was knocked down at £1,850, estimate
£400-£600; and a pair of slop bowls made £500, estimate
£150-£200 each.

At Despard's, on the other hand, a stone's throw away,
prices were light years distant.

A thin crowd refused to bid for Chinese blue and white
porcelain of the K'ang Hsi period (1662-1722) which had
been bitterly fought over only last autumn.

Even Kate Despard, whose curiosity value must have
been a godsend to Despard's of late, could not manage to
achieve anything but painfully low prices. Items that had
previously gone for upwards of £500 reached only £200,
and a great deal, an estimated 40%, was left unsold.

Miss Despard expressed disappointment at the poor
response, but remained confident that the downturn in
the market was only temporary. "You can't win them
all," she said. All the same, it would clearly be in the best
interests of both buyers and sellers if an auction house of
the caliber of Despard's kept a keener eye on the state of
the market, and advised clients to hold on to their collections until such time as it is willing to pay the prices asked
for.

Kate had never been so humiliated in her life. Especially
as she had been warned that the consignor was placing too
high a reserve on his collection.

She had never had to buy in before. It was a downer that
salesrooms hated, because it reflected badly on their ability
to obtain the best prices, which Kate, in her innocence and
newness, had thought would never happen to her. She knew

that every auctioneer experienced it but had never expected to undergo it herself—or so soon. She had thought the crest of the wave she was riding would never break, only to find herself drowning in shamefaced mortification.

What made her squirm was that she had been warned. James Grieve had told her, "Andrew Forrester is being unrealistic in the setting of his reserves, Kate. Prices have either been static or fallen over the past few months . . ."

"Andrew Forrester is an old and valued customer."

"True, but in my opinion he is also a greedy one."

"Have I failed yet?" Kate had asked, with all the cocky confidence of one who had yet to do so.

"You came to us at a time when the market was exceptionally buoyant. The peak has, in my judgment, passed."

"Well, *I* still have my curiosity value."

"That is not what our customers pay for," James rebuked.

And from the start, it had become obvious that they were not going to pay for that or the porcelain, even if Kate Despard was selling it. Normally, at an auction, lots went at a rate of about one hundred an hour or one every thirty-six seconds or so. Kate's stopwatch had told her that she was taking sixty. One whole minute to sell a single lot—and at a low price—during which she should have disposed of two at high prices. Sickening, she had realized her mistake, then foolishly compounded it by trying to speed things up.

"*You* set the pace," David Holmes instructed her when she was learning. "But you never crack the whip."

With the result that she was the one who had felt its lash. She had seen the "told you so" shrugs, the "perhaps now she will listen to her elders and betters" glances. Her first real auction and she had made a hash of it.

"Don't worry about it," David Holmes told her tersely. "Learn from it."

Kate had hung her head in red-faced, burning shame. But she had learned her lesson, and every time her glance encountered the framed clipping it was reinforced. Now, she felt she had recouped some of the ground—and her standing on it—that her reckless disregard of experienced advice had lost her. She had learned that the bread-and-butter sales, of which there were hundreds for every spectacular "biggie," were the ones that brought in Despard's steady income. And if clients demanded an unacceptably high reserve, she politely but firmly told them so.

With the Steyning Bequest there would be no such need, and it would go some way to salvaging her savaged pride.

As she made her way through the building, already bustling though still early, she was satisfied that everything was ticking over nicely. At present, the sales taking place or scheduled for the next three months were those that had been arranged either before or immediately after her father's death, when she was still on a dry run. Though she had acquired the Steyning Bequest and important sales of old masters, early English silver, and Persian and Chinese silk carpets, the estate she would dearly like to get for Despard's was Courtland Park, crammed to the ceiling with the magpie collection of the late John Randolph Courtland. He had been an American millionaire who left his native land in search of a more aristocratic life at the turn of the century. He had spent millions in his attempt to acquire a title, but it never came his way because, they said, of his espousal of "the Prince's cause," when the late Duke of Windsor had been trying to have his cake and eat it, by providing Courtland Park as a hideaway for him and Mrs. Simpson. From the time of the abdication he had become a hermit, sealing himself off from life but never ceasing to amass a collection of whatever took his fancy. He had lived to be ninety-eight and, after his death, it was announced by the trustees of his estate that the house and its contents were to be sold. Sotheby's and Christie's were known to be keenly interested.

Kate had an added spur to her own determination: the now almost suffocating smog of rumor concerning her stepsister's forthcoming sale in Hong Kong of an unparalleled hoard of Chinese treasures. It was also rumored that the forthcoming catalogue was in itself a work of art; full-color, every piece photographed and accompanied by a detailed provenance, from a simple bowl and tripod from the Shang Dynasty of 1,500 B.C. to the most exquisite K'ang Hsi vases made during the eighteenth century. The talk was that prices would reach unheard of heights. Kate had to get hold of Courtland Park or the battle was over before it had begun. Despard's had been invited to appraise and value—but so had Sotheby's and Christie's. It was a sale of massive proportions; there were thousands of lots including paintings and furniture that had not seen the light of day in fifty years, among them two Rembrandts, a Rubens, a whole plethora of French paintings—Boucher, Fragonard, Delacroix, and Ingres—and French furniture that had once stood in the halls and rooms of Versailles.

She was just about to go upstairs when she saw a familiar face at the public desk.

"Mrs. Swan?"

The old lady turned and her face lit up. "Miss Despard? Oh, how nice to see you again. I had hoped . . . I read all about you in the papers—such a surprise—but I was going to ask . . ."

"Have you brought something for us to sell?" Kate interrupted the disjointed flow gently.

Mrs. Swan had been a frequent visitor at the King's Road shop, always with some small piece of china to sell. Her husband had been a collector, nothing big, but always choice, most of it acquired from small country markets in either a filthy or neglected state but of a shape and line his expert eye—he had been a restorer by trade—had spotted. Kate had sold a fine Chelsea bocage set, a superb Meissen swan and a whole collection of Staffordshire figures for her over the years. Now, the old lady delved into her bag and brought out a lump of newspaper that she handed over to Kate.

"I had hoped never to have to sell this, but times are hard and things cost so much nowadays . . ."

Kate unwrapped the layers of newspaper to reveal a coffee-pot. Her eyes gleamed. It was early Worcester—circa 1705—white with sprays of rambler roses writhing their way around the body and up the spout. She lifted the lid to peer inside—not a crack. She inspected the base: there were the marks.

"But of course," she said with a smile of such positive assurance that the old lady relaxed at once. "This should go easily—it's Worcester."

"Tom's favorite . . . One of the first buys he ever made, got it in Keighley market long before the war. Half a crown he paid for it."

"Well, it will fetch much more than that," Kate assured her. "Very much more."

The old lady's face shone but her eyes were anguished. "Seems like parting with a bit of Tom each time I have to sell one of his treasures . . ."

"But one must live," Kate said gently. "There are very many people like you, Mrs. Swan, just as there are others more than willing to pay a good price for something as fine as this and treasure it, just as he did."

The old lady nodded, sighed with something like relief. "I knew you'd see me right," she said. "You always did in your own little shop. Always gave me a fair price . . ." She hesitated. "How long . . .?" she asked awkwardly.

"We've got a sale of eighteenth-century china coming up later this week," lied Kate. "Tell you what," she improvised. "I am so sure this will fetch a good price that I am willing to advance you some of it right now."

The old lady's cheeks warmed. "If that's how you do it . . . I've never sold anything at auction before, only to shops like yours. That's why I came here, because I knew you and trusted you. You were always very fair with me before . . ."

"Come with me," Kate said, and taking Mrs. Swan's arm led her to the accounts desk where she had a word with the cashier on duty. Out of earshot of anyone else, Kate pressed an envelope into the old lady's hands. "There's five hundred pounds in there," she said, "an advance on what the jug will make."

"How much . . .?" the old lady asked this time, and anxiously.

"Well, we sold a similar jug last month for five thousand," Kate said.

"Never!"

"Yes. It's Worcester and it is in perfect condition. I think a reserve of five thousand pounds is not too high."

"What's a reserve?" quavered the old lady.

"What you say is the lowest price you will accept."

"Well, if you say so . . . You are the expert."

"I do say so. You are still at the same address?"

"Oh, yes. I shall never leave there now . . . Five thousand pounds!" she repeated in awed tones. "He only paid half a crown for it . . ."

"More than forty years ago," Kate pointed out gently. "Prices have changed enormously since then—for the better—for people with things to sell."

"I've not got much left now," the old lady admitted. "But this will see me right for such a long time . . ."

"Have you a bank account?" Kate asked. Previously she had always paid the old lady cash, at her request.

"Tom didn't hold with banks."

"I think you ought to do something about opening one.

Tell you what, once I've got your money, I'll come and see you and we can decide how to keep it safe then."

"So kind," murmured the old lady disjointedly. "So kind." And then, "Five thousand pounds. I never thought, five thousand pounds . . ."

Kate made sure the envelope containing the five hundred pounds in notes was safely bestowed in the capacious leather purse, and placed at the bottom of her shopping bag, under the crumpled newspaper wrappings that had swathed the jug. She then persuaded the old lady that she could afford the price of a taxi back to Fulham and got George to get one.

As she went back into the hall, a tall elegant man who looked as if he had stepped from a page of *Tailor and Cutter* approached her, bowler hat and cane in one hand, his velvet collared coat superbly fitted across broad shoulders, his handsome face bearing a charming smile. "Miss Despard?"

Kate stopped. "Yes. May I help you?"

"I hope so. I am Nicholas Chevely."

The man responsible for deciding who sold Courtland Park and its contents. Kate was glad she had taken care with her clothes that day because she had a VIP client coming in at eleven; she wanted him to give Despard's the sale of his superb Velázquez. She knew she looked good in her russet tweed suit with a fleck of the same gold as her eyes; her hair was a burnished helmet and thanks to Charlotte she was now skilled at making up her face to best effect. She met the gleam of admiration in a pair of hazel eyes and said in her nicest way, "Of course. I had been hoping to meet you, Mr. Chevely, but this is an unexpected pleasure." They shook hands. His was firm and lingered.

"I hope you don't mind me dropping in unexpectedly like this. I wanted to get the general feel of Despard's, to see how it functions."

"Of course. I think that is an excellent idea. Would you like me to show you around?"

She managed a quick glance at the clock—9:50. She had time.

"I should like that very much." Another charming smile. "I have not had much to do with auction houses I'm afraid, or the art world come to that."

No, thought Kate. People like you have dealers. Nicholas Chevely was a stockbroker, and he had handled John Randolph Courtland's share portfolio, obviously so well that the old man had appointed him executor of his will.

As if he could read her mind, "Mr. Courtland was somewhat of an eccentric turn of mind. It is typical that he should choose someone completely apart from the art world to handle the sale of Courtland Park and its contents."

"And the choosing of the right auction house to dispose of them?" Kate asked.

"Indeed."

"So you came to look us over?" It was said nicely, but with the absolute in confidence.

"The death duties are such that the highest prices are a vital necessity," Nicholas Chevely admitted smoothly.

"From all accounts, Courtland Park is an Aladdin's cave," Kate remarked.

"Well, it is certainly stuffed with all sorts and kinds of objects."

"I am looking forward very much to seeing them."

"I also came to arrange a date when you could do so."

"Whenever it is convenient, we are ready and willing," Kate assured him. She looked around for George, who at once came across to relieve Nicholas Chevely of his hat, coat, and cane. He should have been a male model, Kate thought, dazzled. Never had she seen anyone so elegant. But she knew better than to accept the surface as the whole man.

By all accounts he was nobody's fool; in her methodical way she had made it her business to find out all she could about him. Like her father, Kate could be, when she chose, a fine salesperson, and she had also learned a great deal from Rollo, including what *not* to do. She knew that there was a great deal of psychology involved in selling, and to this man she had to sell not only Despard's but also, in a manner of speaking, herself.

"I must say," he said, as they began to mount the stairs, "it would be an occasion indeed to have such a sale conducted by a woman."

Kate repressed her inner start of squeezed-heart panic; she was by no means ready yet, even though, to quote her mentor David Holmes, she was "coming along nicely." But to conduct the Courtland Park sale! There and then she resolved that if she had to work twenty-four hours a day perfecting the art of auctioneering, she would do so, if it meant landing the sale for Despard's.

"One I would look forward to very much," she told him pleasantly.

She gave him the Grand Tour, explaining whatever he asked about, showing him everything, dealing with one or two small queries along the way, thankful that they were ones she could answer immediately and glad of the opportunity to show that she was very much In Charge. She introduced him to several heads of department, and then at half-past ten took him to her office.

"Most interesting," he said, as he took the chair she offered him. "I had not realized that an auction house was such a complex operation."

"It has been going for so long that we tend to take its smooth running for granted," Kate told him truthfully. "My father was not a man to change a thing once it showed that it would work—and perfectly."

"Quite right."

They then got down to discussing how Despard's would handle the sale. Kate had already devoted a great deal of time to thinking about it, so she had her spiel prepared. "We should have the catalogue ready some months in advance," she said. "From what I gather it will be a hefty one, there is so much to go into it. We should take full-color photographs, of course. This is the sort of thing I had in mind. . ." She brought out the catalogues that had been prepared for the Chantry House sale that had taken place the year before, a magnificent Palladian mansion filled with treasures of English art.

"Superb," murmured Nicholas Chevely, as he leafed through it. "I congratulate you on your photographer. Even the pictures make one's mouth water."

"That is the object of the exercise," Kate said with a smile.

"If the sale came to you, when would you envisage holding it?"

"In the autumn," Kate answered unhesitatingly. "When everyone is back in London and we have held a preview. It will take that long to catalogue the contents before the actual thing is printed, and it is a good thing to create as much interest as possible."

He nodded, but said with a moue, "I am afraid the house

is in no kind of order. Mr. Courtland had no—pattern—to his collection, nor had he a catalogue of his own, though he knew where everything was, down to the last silver teaspoon."

"As it should be," she said smoothly.

"When could you come down to take a look at it?"

"I think the sooner the better."

He nodded again. "Yes. Shall we say one day next week, then?"

Kate reached for her appointments book. "Would Wednesday suit you?"

He reached inside his jacket for a wafer-thin diary. "It would do very well. I could collect you here and drive you down. We could spend the day there—it will take that long, I am sure, to see everything. Shall we say ten o'clock?"

Kate wrote it down, crossing the entire day through with the words *Courtland Park* in red.

Coffee was brought in and they chatted of other things, but Kate was conscious all the time of Nicholas Chevely's awareness of her, not so much as the chairman of Despard's but as Miss Catriona Despard. It had never happened before; not with a man like this, and she found it both warming and exhilarating. Now she saw how it was Dominique du Vivier did so much successful business. Not, she told herself, that I intend to go as far as she does. But she was still astonished that the thought should have entered her mind in the first place. Times had indeed changed—even as she had. At five minutes to eleven she put her cup down with just the right show of reluctance—something she had learned from Charlotte who had it down to a fine art—and said with regret, "I am afraid I have a client coming in at eleven . . ."

He rose with alacrity but showing the same amount of regret. This time, his hand lingered even longer in hers.

"Until next Wednesday, then."

"I look forward to it," Kate smiled. She rang for her secretary to see him downstairs.

When they had gone she let out a deep breath. "Wow!" she said out loud. He had seemed impressed, had lingered at the back of the salesroom where the day's first auction was taking place, had murmured "fascinating" several times, and had shown the keenest interest in everything. But she had not been deceived. He was a businessman first and foremost: Chevely Brothers—he had a younger brother—was one of the city's foremost firms of stockbrokers, handling the share portfolios for some very important people. He was used to money, and to getting full value for it. Despard's would have to be on its toes. She still felt, though, that she had made a good impression, and this high carried her through her meeting with Lord Eversleigh, which ended in his signing the contract giving Despard's the sale of his Velázquez, with a reserve of five million pounds. It would be the high point of the forthcoming old masters sale.

When he had gone Kate was doing a little dance around the room when her door opened and she turned to see Blaise Chandler standing there. She blushed furiously, especially at the amusement on his face.

"Well, seems spring is here," he commented.

"I've just landed the sale of probably the finest Velázquez to come on the market since his *Juan de Pareja*," Kate told him jubilantly. "And on top of that I've got a good chance of landing Courtland Park!"

The black eyebrows lifted. "Congratulations—and my grandmother sends her love. She wants to know when you'll be visiting her again."

Kate let out a sigh. "Oh, how I wish I could, but we are so frightfully busy just now."

"That can only be good, surely."

"Oh, yes, I'm not complaining. Would you like some coffee? This is cold but I can ring for more—or would you prefer a drink?"

"A glass of your father's Amontillado would not come amiss."

"Have you come especially to see me or are you just passing through?" Kate asked as she went to the drinks cabinet.

He had come over for the official handing over, after which there had been a cocktail party, noticeable for the absence of her stepsister and a great deal of publicity in the art columns. Kate had found her picture in the papers, wearing a particularly fetching Bruce Oldfield crêpe dress, under the caption: BIDDING FOR FAME? For a while she was flavor of the month, interviewed both for the press and on television, a great deal being made of the rivalry between the two stepsisters, an issue on which Kate diplomatically refused to be drawn out. Instead, she had seized on the curiosity and interest generated to secure as many future sales as possible.

She had thanked God for Charlotte, who had been a tower of strength, advising her not only on what to wear and how, but what to say and when, and to whom. At first Kate had kept her close at hand, but as her confidence had grown and her personality emerged from the shadows, she had come into her own. Look at the way she had handled Nicholas Chevely. Yet the hand that gave Blaise Chandler his glass of sherry trembled.

"I am glad things are going so well," he said politely.

"How well?" Kate dared. "I don't suppose you can give me any idea of how I stand—just a hint?"

"No, I can't. It's four weeks to your first quarter; I'll be back then to tell you how things stand." At her downcast face, "But if you really want to know," he said harshly, "you are lagging behind."

That should hold her, he thought. He had been dismayed when he saw the latest figures—he had instituted a system whereby he was appraised of the totals not only month by month but also sale by sale, and every month it was the same: Dominique's lead was lengthening.

Of course, she had really pulled out all the stops. He saw less and less of her; she was always wining, dining (he shut his mind to the rest) somebody or other in pursuit of a sale, and she had her scouts working twenty-four hours a day. No whisper went unchecked, no loophole not slipped through, no introduction unused.

"How far lagging?" Kate asked in a subdued voice.

"If you don't narrow the lead then you haven't a hope of catching up with her. New York is running practically nonstop, and no doubt you've heard about this Sale of the Century in Hong Kong." His voice was curt. "From the figures being bandied about, you'll need something like the crown jewels to break even."

Kate was silent. He felt annoyed with her. He wanted her to win, but on the other hand he was loathe to interfere—or even seem to. When he'd found his grandmother was putting an oar in as many of Dominique's spokes as she could, he had been furious . . .

"For God's sake, Duchess, I can't be seen to favor either of them. Legally I have to stay out of it. Executors have to be strictly impartial—that's the law."

"Stuff! Ain't your wife in one corner? Don't tell me folks don't think you are givin' her the long count."

"I don't give a damn what they think—it is what I do that counts."

"I thought Charles was your friend as well as mine. You know damn well what will happen once that bitch gets her hands on Despard's."

"If you are so almighty disposed toward Kate Despard then you should know better than to underestimate her."

"I don't—but I don't underestimate your wife either, and she's the one to watch. We both know what she would have done with my daddy's bits and pieces if she'd bothered to come and see them. It's Kate's honesty and integrity that's doin' her in. Your wife would sell me if she thought I'd fetch a good price." She scowled at him. "I'm not sittin' still for no walkover, and that's a fact. I'm for Kate and I don't care who knows it. I ain't for your wife and I don't care who knows that either."

The irritant sand of her words now made him glower at Kate as if it were all her fault. He had, for the first time, parted from his grandmother with acrimony. "You may call me Boy," he had roared at her, "but I stopped being that a long time ago. You are so used to running everybody and everything that you forget they've got minds of their own. Leave it alone, Duchess. I mean that."

But he knew damn well she wouldn't. His feelings toward Kate were ambivalent. On the one hand he respected her integrity about his grandmother's collection; on the other he thought her a damned fool for not using every weapon at hand. Oh, shit, he thought. I wish I'd never got mixed up with this damned circus in the first place.

He forced himself to be polite. "Have you got anything good coming up?"

"I'm hopeful," she answered guardedly.

Jesus! he thought virulently. She doesn't think I'm capable of being dispassionate either.

"How is your grandmother?" Kate asked brightly.

"Embarked on the necessary wheeling and dealing to set up the Chandler Museum of Western Art. The ranch and its contents will be deeded by gift to the state of Colorado."

Kate's face lit up. He was taken aback. Why on earth did I think her plain? he thought.

"Oh, I'm so glad . . ."

"You realize that if you had the sale of that collection you'd probably be even-Steven," he said unpleasantly.

"Yes, but I'd still do what I did again."

"What is it with you and the sacredness of art?" he snapped in exasperation.

She regarded him in a way that made him flush angrily. "It's not something you can explain to non-art people," she said finally.

"Who the hell are they?"

"People like you."

Why you little bitch! he thought furiously.

"I mean people who neither know nor care; Jed was like that. He could not see the point. It's like me and big business. What is the point of that except to make more and more money? Art is forever. Art is human greatness. Great art is also the greatness of the human spirit. Art—illuminates, if you like. It tells you things about people, about the world. I sell it at auction because people ask me to, but if I had a choice I would rather it was permanently protected, like your grandmother's 'bits and pieces,' for future generations, so that they can look back and see how we were, and what we were—and why. And just for the sheer beauty and pleasure of it. Haven't you ever sat in front of a great painting and felt better for it?"

"No."

She shrugged. "You see . . ."

Again he felt as if she had relegated him. He set his glass down with a crack and rose to his feet. "I must be going. I have important things to do."

"That's what I mean. You don't think that what I do is important, do you?"

By now thoroughly exasperated, "No, I don't," he said. "I think people who pay thousands—millions—for a square of painted canvas or a piece of china are in it for profit, not love of your great art."

Her smile was faint. "You've just explained why I told your grandmother not to sell hers."

"Why you—" He bit it off. Then, unexpectedly, he laughed. "Which corner do I stand in?" he asked dryly.

Her own laugh once again transformed her. How *bad* he thought her plain.

"Let's agree to disagree," he said. "At least you hold to your opinions."

"Don't you?" she asked innocently.

He laughed again. "Touché." But his handshake was friendly and so was his smile as he bid her good-bye.

She stood by the window until she saw him cross the pavement to his big black car. Well, at least he has a sense of humor, she thought. Sighing, she turned back to her desk to find Rollo standing in front of it. "Must you creep up on me like some assassin?" she asked crossly.

"I came to see how you did with old Eversleigh."

"He signed the contract."

"Good for you."

"And I'm going down to Courtland Park next week. Nicholas Chevely came in earlier to ask if he could take me down to view."

The grey eyebrows lifted themselves ever so slowly. "You have had a good morning . . ." Then, greedily, "That's the big one, dear heart. The big boys are marshaling their batteries."

"Which is why I want it for Despard's."

"And need it, considering what your sister has got lined up. Did *he* say anything?"

"Only that he knows it is in the offing."

"Did he say what, though?"

"No."

"Didn't you pump him about *anything?*"

"Don't be a fool, Rollo, or take him for one. He'd have known at once."

"Which won't stop her extracting every last word about you from the same source?"

"I have told you and told you—I don't do things her way."

"More's the pity."

The door slammed behind him. Kate dropped into her chair with a sigh. Rollo was becoming increasingly difficult the more she asserted herself, feeling the slack in his hold on her. As if she did not have enough to cope with!

She had not realized that Despard's with its calm surface and seemingly measured pace was in reality a veritable anthill; that it combined the scholarship of a world-class museum with the skills of a merchant bank and the commercial acumen of a large department store. She got up from her chair and went into her private washroom to tidy herself for a working lunch with the Board. They would be discussing the forthcoming old masters sale, and she realized she would have to tell them that, should they land the Courtland Park sale, it would be on the understanding that she would conduct the auction . . .

Next morning she was talking to David Holmes about that very thing, and about her next tryout on the rostrum—a minor sale of Victorian oils—when her secretary rang through to say that a Señora de Barranca was downstairs insisting she see Miss Despard.

"Who is she?" Kate asked, knowing Penny would have found out.

"She's the wife of Jaime de Barranca, Argentinian, very rich—the polo player? But she's American."

"What does she want?"

"She won't say to anyone but you—and she's not the type to deal with underlings."

Kate was intrigued. It did not do to turn anyone away; you never knew when you might be offered a sale. "Sorry, David. Can we resume this later?"

"So long as you understand that we will have to work really hard if you are serious about Courtland Park, which in my opinion is foolhardy. To start at the top is not the way to do it—"

"I'll do as many small ones as I can, graduating to one or two larger and then a couple of biggies," Kate said for the umpteenth time. "If it is conditional on securing the sale then I must conduct the auction. You'll be there to keep me straight."

"It's not right," he muttered as he went out. "Not right at all . . ."

"Then I shall have to make it right," Kate muttered savagely. "I want that sale; I'm going to get that sale if I have to conduct a thousand auctions beforehand."

Señora de Barranca swept in on a cloud of Joy and Black-glama mink; fortyish, elegant in a hard-faced, inhuman sort of way, carrying a large alligator handbag and a flat, brown-paper parcel about eighteen inches square. So, a painting, Kate thought.

"How do you do, Señora," Kate said. "Welcome to Despard's. How can we help you?"

"I've got a painting to sell and as I am short of time—I leave for Paris this very afternoon—I thought it best to go to the top." She eyed Kate up and down critically. "You are younger than I thought, but they tell me you know about Western art.''

"I have studied it," Kate admitted cautiously, "but it is a personal hobby rather than an expertise."

"I've got a Remington here . . ." She was opening the package as she spoke, revealing a small oil on canvas.

Kate saw delightedly that it was a Western landscape, her delight changing to rigid shock once the painting was turned right side up and handed to her, because she recognized it at once. The last time she had seen it, it had been hanging on the wall of an upstairs corridor in the pink palazzo known as the Lucky Dollar Ranch.

"I am told this is a particularly fine Remington, rare because he did not usually do landscapes. This is Colorado . . . It has been in my family for many years. My grandfather knew Frederic Remington."

Which was when Kate realized who Señora de Barranca was: Consuelo, Blaise Chandler's half-sister, the granddaughter who never bothered with Agatha Chandler unless she wanted money. The painting she was offering for sale was, Kate was positive, not hers to sell. She had probably stolen it. She looked up at the cold, hard face and controlling the fire of her anger said evenly, "Yes, this is a very fine Remington.''

"Your branch in New York sold one a couple of months ago for half a million dollars. What is your estimate of this one's worth?"

"I should place a reserve of a quarter of a million pounds sterling on it without hesitation.''

The dark eyes gleamed. "How soon?"

"It will have to be placed in the first suitable sale."

"—as soon as possible. I can't afford to wait."

"And I shall need its provenance."

"It was a gift to my grandfather," Consuelo de Barranca said. "He was Black Jack Chandler. If you look on the back, there is an inscription.''

Kate turned the picture over. *To my old friend, Black Jack Chandler in memory of happy days. Frederic Remington. October 1899* was written in faded ink. "If you need more, check me out . . . here." She opened the magnificent alligator bag, extracted a card case of the same skin, and took out a card which she thrust at Kate. "However, I do not wish my name connected to the sale." A hard shrug. "If it were to be known that I am selling my art collection . . ."

Your collection? Kate thought.

"It is a temporary need only, but"—a frozen smile—"you know how it is . . ."

"Why did you come to me?" Kate asked.

Another smile, this time knowing. "I believe you know my half-brother—Blaise Chandler?"

Kate expressed the required surprise.

"Are those credentials good enough?"

"Mr. Chandler is known to me, of course, but in that case, why did you not offer the painting to his wife?"

"Dominique? I would have—once—but we don't see each other anymore. Besides, aren't you in some sort of competition with her?" The thin-lipped, scarlet mouth curved viciously. "Anything I can do to do that bitch in . . ." Without asking permission, the scarlet-tipped nails lit a cigarette. "How do you get on with Blaise?"

"I hardly know him," Kate replied stiffly.

"Hard case, isn't he? As wooden as those Indian carvings my grandmother has all over her house. He and his wife are well matched. You have met her?"

"Once."

A hard laugh. "And no love lost . . . no, once is all it takes." Then, getting back to what she hoped to take, "How soon—the sale, I mean?"

"We have a sale of Americana coming up in the next six weeks."

"Six weeks!"

"If you wish to sell the painting privately, at once—"

"But I'd get more at auction, wouldn't I?"

"There are plenty of collectors interested in acquiring American art; it is now highly fashionable."

"No. I want it to go to the highest bidder. Six weeks it is, then."

Kate had not said directly that she would sell the painting; Consuelo de Barranca arrogantly assumed she would. To her, the matter was settled.

"The address on my card will find me; if I'm not there any message will be sent on to wherever I am. Is that all, then?"

"Don't let me keep you," Kate said politely.

"But you'll keep the painting?"

"Yes," Kate said. "Leave it with me."

Consuelo let out a satisfied breath. "Excellent." Stubbing out her cigarette she rose to her feet. "I must rush. My plane . . . Nice meeting you, Miss Despard. Give my regards to Blaise. I have no doubt you will see him before I do."

She swept out, leaving behind a haze of Joy and black hatred in Kate's heart. That arrogant bitch had actually stolen a painting from her own grandmother. Which left her standing in what Rollo, in his pithy way, would have described as the shit.

No doubt Consuelo had believed one small painting among so many would never be missed. Obviously she does not know her grandmother, Kate thought. She knows where everything is and when it was placed there. Now I have to tell her where this one is. I can't possibly sell stolen property—because that is what this is, even if that hard-faced harridan is related to the owner. Why didn't I say I recognized it; that I knew where it had come from? Because you don't tangle with that sort of woman or accuse her of being a thief if you know what's good for you. And the Duchess would hate it if it should get out . . . Oh God, why does this have to happen to me now? All she had learned in recent months about Despard's sacred trust, the confidentiality, the unspoken yet precious probity, hammered at her. She studied the painting again. Perhaps it was a copy, or perhaps right now the copy was hanging where the original had been. She took the painting over to the window. No, she was sure it was genuine. What was Consuelo de Barranca thinking of? And as for that fib about being on the outs with Dominique . . . Dear God! The thought hit her like a brick. I'll bet she was the one who put de Barranca up to it! She's trying to do me in again! Then she remembered Dominique had never been to the ranch, had no idea what treasures it hid.

She looked at her watch. It was seven A.M. in Colorado. She would have to wait until the Duchess was up and about, which was never later than eight. Then she would call and explain.

But she worried just the same. Should she have refused to sell? Then it would only have gone to another auction house which would have no idea it was stolen property. No, she was sure that, once the Duchess knew, she would take the proper steps where her granddaughter was concerned, and if Dominique was involved then that would put a spoke in her

wheel, too. As for Consuelo de Barranca's future disposi-
tions at Despard's . . . she could go anywhere she liked as
long as she did not return to Despard's. And that, Kate
thought with a rueful sigh, is as likely to happen as hell
freezing. If she put it about that Despard's was unworthy—
but that was unlikely, too. Because they knew she had tried
to sell what did not belong to her. Stalemate. I hope, Kate
prayed fervently. Oh, I do hope . . . At least, thank God, a
contract had not been signed, because it was virtually impossible to withdraw a painting from sale once that had been
done. She scribbled a note on her reminder pad: talk to
Louis Bishop about revising standard conditions of contract. . .

Her internal phone buzzed. Dorothy Bainbridge, head of
Cataloguing, asked if she could come and see her. She
sounded angry. Now what? Kate thought long-sufferingly.
What a day this was turning out to be!

Dorothy Bainbridge was a woman in her mid-forties and
one of Despard's new—to Kate—additions. She was unmarried, except to her work, and very good at her job. She ran a
tight ship but her training was the best a young student could
get anywhere. Now she was breathing fire and smoke.

"Miss Despard, I am not one to make a fuss, as you
know," she began truthfully, "but I must complain most
strongly about the interference of Mr. Bellamy in my department. He is constantly making unwarranted suggestions to
my staff, derogatory remarks about the way we work, and
seeking to impose his own ideas." She inhaled a quivering
breath. "It has come to this, Miss Despard. Either he goes
or I do!"

Oh, hell thought Kate. Rollo, you will be the death of
me . . . "Please, do sit down," she suggested soothingly. "I
hate to see you upset and not for one moment will I countenance you leaving Despard's. If Mr. Bellamy has been interfering, rest assured I will speak to him about it."

"And not only my department," Dorothy steamed. "He
pokes his nose in everywhere, ostensibly on your authority."

"That," Kate said firmly, "has never been given by me."

"He would not agree with you. He seems to think that
personal assistant also means second in command."

"That is not true either."

Slightly mollified, "I did not think it could be. The late
Mr. Despard always made it quite clear that a head of
department was just that."

"It still is, as far as I am concerned."

Dorothy relaxed still further. "I know he is a good friend of yours, Miss Despard, but he seems to think he has some God-given right to issue orders to the rest of us."

"Not on my authority," Kate repeated. "Mr Bellamy's position is somewhat—elastic, I admit. But his primary role is to assist me where I require assistance, and that is all. Rest assured that I will speak to him about this in no uncertain terms. You will not be bothered again."

For the first time a smile appeared. "I thought it best to come to you. Mr. Despard always liked any complaints to be laid before him and you seem to be continuing the rest of his traditions."

"I know a good thing when I see one," Kate said quietly, "and I remember enough to know that it works."

Dorothy nodded vigorously. "It does indeed."

Kate got up and went to the liquor cabinet. "I am glad you came up," she said. "I am telling you this in confidence, but we have been approached by the executor of the late John Randolph Courtland about the sale of his house and its contents. It is going to require something rather special in the way of a catalogue—"

"Courtland Park! That would be a feather in our caps."

"Well, I haven't yet got my bird," Kate cautioned with a smile, "but I intend to give it my best shot." She placed a glass of sherry before the now calmer woman. "Tell me," she said, as she took her own sherry back to her chair. "How would you go about preparing something that would have mouths watering from here to Timbuctu? I know how scrupulous you are and the trouble you take." Her smile was warm. "I am also aware that Despard's catalogues set a high standard of bibliography that is a byword among works of reference."

"Well, I took over from John Carter, who did it for forty years and was a legend because he initiated so many things and set such high standards; all I have done is follow in his footsteps."

"I think you have made your own mark. Not just the accuracy but also the little pieces of information which give life to what might otherwise be nothing but a dull mass of facts."

Dorothy Bainbridge flushed with pleasure. It was not only the sherry that made her pink when she rose to go some fifteen minues later, having made, she thought, several eminently acceptable suggestions.

As soon as the door closed Kate rang through to her secretary. "Penny, will you find Mr. Bellamy, wherever he is, and tell him I wish to see him at once."

He strolled in ten minutes later. "Madame Chairman," he bowed ironically. "I hear and I obey."

"You will in the future, Rollo, or you will not be here *to* obey."

He reared like a cobra, looking at her down his long nose with the sneer that had hitherto always quelled any signs of rebellion. Now he saw that Kate was flaming—and not because of the color of her hair.

"I have just had to placate a very angry Dorothy Bainbridge who threatened to resign because of you and your nosy-parkering in her department."

"That old trout! Treats her staff like they were first formers."

"She is one of the best cataloguers in the business; her father was a dealer and her knowledge of art is encyclopedic! I warn you, Rollo, if it comes down to a choice between you and her, *she* stays!"

He had gone white with anger and disbelief.

"You are meant to be my personal assistant, Rollo, not my personal disaster! I have enough to do without trailing behind you with mop and pail!"

"There is more cleaning up to do here than Hercules ever faced in the Augean stables!"

"Only in your opinion!"

"I have made suggestion after suggestion—"

"—to change things to *your* satisfaction. Around here, Rollo, they run to mine."

His eyes were chips of ice and the red spots had appeared on his cheeks. "Well, hoity-toity indeed," he sneered. "Your elevation has gone to your head. You are chairman of Despard's London, my girl, not Margaret Thatcher!"

"Yes, I am," Kate said quietly. "That is what I am asking you to remember. I give the orders around here."

"I am nobody's hireling!"

"You never were *hired* as such," Kate flung at him. "You automatically assumed that you went where I went because you were my shadow."

"You were content that I should be for long enough."

"That was before," Kate said. "This is now. Things are different, I am different—"

"By God you are! And not for the better!"

"You told me to grow up, Rollo. Why can't you accept that I have?"

"You may be five feet ten, but to me that is no height at all. This is me, Rollo! I have known you since you were knee high to a grasshopper."

"And can't or won't accept that I ceased to be that a long time ago."

"A few short months is by no stretch of the imagination a long time!"

"I had to do it quickly; I had no choice. It was grow up or get out and I have no intention of doing that"

"But I must, is that it?"

"If you won't disabuse yourself of the idea that you are my right and left hand and the only one who can lead me where I should go—then yes."

They stared at each other.

"Why, you ungrateful little bitch!" Rollo spat, face livid with rage.

"No, I am not ungrateful. I owe you a great deal, but I have other debts to pay and I cannot allow you to bankrupt me."

"What I have done for you could never be repaid!"

Kate's laugh rang free. "Give over the East Lynne routine, Rollo. You are very well paid for what you do."

"That is where you have changed for the worst," Rollo declaimed dramatically. "You have become a money grubber."

"Ha! Since when did you cease to regard it as the be all and end all?" She tried again. "Look, all I am asking you to do is stop putting people's backs up. Let them get on with their work in their own way; they were doing it long before we came on the scene. I give you an enormous degree of license; I don't quibble about your two-hour lunches, I let you go where you please as you please—"

"And don't I bring back the goods?"

"Yes, you have more than proved your worth and I do need your eyes and ears, but I can't spend all my time staunching wounds and drying tears. You have a serrated tongue and you use it indiscriminately."

"You of all people should know that I cannot suffer fools gladly or any other way."

"Then give them a wide berth. Do what you are so good at; circulate where and how you like, bring me back all the gossip, tell me who is thinking of selling what and to whom; spend money like water—and you have, Rollo, you know you have—but don't antagonize other people I also happen to need. I can't be doing with it, especially right now."

Something in her face, some tautness in her voice had the effect of applying his brakes. "Trouble?"

Her smile shone. "You see. *That's* what I need from you. Yes, trouble . . ." She told him about Consuelo de Barranca and the Remington.

"It's the horse all over again, of course."

"Probably. All I know is I have to tell Mrs. Chandler."

"Of course you do. The truth and nothing but the truth."

"That is what I am going to do—right now." Her smile appealed to his better nature—what little there was of it. "Now do you see what I am getting at? Don't add to my burdens."

"Now who is milking her lines?" he withered. Then he sniffed. "Sniveling little creeps. As if I care a tuppenny damn about them or their drab little departments. I have better things to do." And with that he swept out.

Kate leaned her head on her hand. In spite of herself she had to laugh. Rollo was a buoy that floated back to the surface no matter how bad the storm. She checked her watch—eight-thirty Colorado time—and reached for the telephone.

Agatha heard out her terse telling in silence, then said, "So that's where she took it."

"You knew it was missing?"

"I was told the day after she left. We do take a duster over things, you know."

Relief flooding her voice, "I was sure it would be missed sooner or later," Kate said.

"Sooner in this case. She wanted money and I wouldn't give her any. I suppose she took the painting in a fit of pique. Now don't you worry none. I'll handle my grand-daughter. You keep the painting safe and I'll see that it's collected. You did the right thing and I'm obliged to you."

"There is nothing legally binding; I only agreed verbally to sell the painting."

"I knew you had more sense than that," the old lady said gruffly. "She placed you in a bad position, Kate, and I'm sorry it was so. Don't you worry anymore, you hear? How is the rest of it going?"

"Well, it's going," Kate admitted with a small laugh, "but as yet I don't know where it will end up."

"First at the finishing line, of course," Agatha told her promptly.

"Duchess, you are a shot in the arm."

"As long as it ain't heroin!" She heard the familiar cackle down the transatlantic line, then, "I'll be in touch," and the dial tone.

Kate replaced the receiver and let out a long sigh. "Bless you, Agatha Chandler," she said out loud.

Blaise Chandler was in bed with his wife when his grandmother's call came through. With his wife regarding him both impatiently and resentfully, he was wholly noncommittal in his response.

"Consuelo swiped a Remington because I wouldn't advance her a goodly portion of her inheritance; she took it to London and offered it for sale to Kate Despard. She recognized it and called me. I want you to get it back." Agatha was peremptory.

"Do I have to leave right this minute?" he inquired with exquisite sarcasm.

"No, but don't leave it too long. I told her someone would be by."

"And I am the inevitable someone?"

"This is a family matter. I don't want it getting out." The old lady could be equally sarcastic. "Consuelo is your sister."

Whom I never liked and who has always hated me, Blaise thought. This is probably just another way of getting at me because she knows I'm your favorite. "I'll get to it as soon as I can," he promised, resolving that it would be later rather than sooner.

"That's my Boy," he heard her say approvingly.

That's the trouble, Blaise thought gloomily, as he hung up. You still won't see me any other way . . .

"L 'Indienne?" Dominique inquired with sweet venom, as he turned back to her. "I am becoming convinced she has us bugged."

"She likes to know I can be reached at all times."

Dominique ran one long, scarlet-tipped finger around the smooth brown throat. "That leash must be awfully chafing," she remarked. "How is it you are willing to do for her what you would tell me to do for myself?"

"She is eighty-five years old."

"And very, very rich?" Dominique murmured silkily.

He merely looked at her, and as always with him—the only man who could do it—she looked away first.

Really, she thought, annoyed with herself; why do I allow this? What is it with him that has me running like a bitch in heat? He is good in bed but not the best I have ever had. But there was a single-minded intensity about him which, when focused on her, she felt to the last cell in her body, and it had come to be a pleasure she was not disposed to do without. It was not love. She had never loved anyone in her life. But he had become a habit, one she found she was unable to give up. It was probably because, she decided, he was not fooled by her one little bit. Other men could be flattered, cajoled, gently led; Blaise, once he took up a position, could not be moved. If she tried then he would look at her, as he had done just now, in such a way that she had to laugh in spite of herself and the chagrin she felt. Oh well, she thought, as she proceeded to reestablish the mood that the telephone had broken, I suppose it makes a pleasant change . . .

All the same, she bethought it politic to inquire lazily, "And what was it this time?" as she ran her expert hands over him lightly, applying pressure where it would give the most exquisite pleasure-pain, digging in her nails for just the right fraction of time until she felt him gasp, following her hands with her tongue, flicking it against the ardor-dampened skin, nipping the satin pelt with her small, sharp teeth.

"Nothing important," Blaise answered hazily, conscious only of what she was doing to him.

"To call you *now* is not important?"

"She knows where I am, not what I am doing," he murmured, breath catching.

"And what did she want you to do?"

"Clear up another mess, as usual."

"Ah, my poor *sauvage*. I don't know whether it is because she trusts you to handle no matter what she gives you, or whether she still sees you as the boy she took under her wing all those years ago . . ."

"Both," Blaise replied with a gasp.

She was about to probe further, when he said hoarsely,

"Don't stop . . ." She decided to leave it till later; a post-coital Blaise would be that much more inclined to tell her. She set to work to render him wholly malleable.

"So . . ." she said throatily later, her face on his chest, hearing the breath rasp under her cheek, "have you seen *La Despard* since you've been here?"

"Yesterday, as it happens."

"Did she say anything about how things are going?"

"Only that they were—and I quote—very well."

"I understand she has been approached to sell Courtland Park and its contents—which is as far as she will get. I know of the man who is to make the choice and she is not his style at all."

"But you are?"

Dominique's mouth curved in a smile at once tantalizing and demure. "Oh, yes. I most certainly am."

"Then why did he not approach you?"

"New York is not in the running this time, alas. But a few more years, and I assure you it will be the first place they think of."

"I wish I had your confidence," Blaise said dryly.

"Where would I be then?"

"Just as long as you are here now . . ." With one swift movement he reversed their positions; she under him, pinned but unprotesting. Her eyes gleamed. "So soon?" she murmured practically, her fingers touching, stroking. "Indeed. . ." She sighed, fitting herself around him. "But this must be the last. I am due in Paris first thing tomorrow morning."

12

Fate having decided to take a hand, Consuelo, not having seen her for months, ran into her former friend in Paris. They met at Saint Laurent, Consuelo on her way out, Dominique on her way in. They were both dressed to kill, Consuelo in swaths of honey-colored suede thickly edged with Emba champagne mink, a mink shako perched rakishly on her dyed blonde head, Dominique in a sable poncho over black velvet baggy trousers tucked into shiny black boots. For a moment they both stopped dead; then Consuelo, inwardly gloating at having done Dominique out of a nice little commission, gushed, "Darling! It's been an age . . ."

"Has it? I hadn't noticed," Dominique answered sweetly.

"Such a silly spat over nothing," Consuelo urged fulsomely.

"Oh, I wouldn't say that. He was quite something, believe me . . ."

Bitch! Consuelo seethed, but she smothered her hatred. "How are things with you, angel? Look, are you going to be long here, or have you got time for a drink and a chat?"

She wants something, Dominique thought. And badly enough to swallow her pride. "Why not," she decided. "I can come back later." Turning to the *vendeuse* hovering respectfully at a distance, "I'll be back in about forty minutes. I'll have my fitting then."

"So," Consuelo said, when they were settled at a table at Maxim's where they could see and be seen. "How are things with you? And how goes the fight?"

"Fight?" Dominique sounded amused. "There is no fight, I can assure you."

Consuelo brayed. "I must say, she does not look like much competition. More a giraffe!"

"You have seen her?" Dominique's suspicions had been right. Consuelo was after something.

"Just the other day, in London. I left her a painting to sell." At Dominique's stare, "Well, we were on the outs, darling. Besides, I was curious. I mean, your stepsister and my half-brother being, shall we say, involved?"

Dominique ignored that red herring. "What kind of painting?" she asked.

"Oh, a Remington."

"I didn't know you had any."

"Well, I don't actually—not yet, anyway. But my grandmother has dozens of the damn things, some of which will be mine eventually so I just anticipated a bit, that's all."

"Dozens?" Dominique repeated slowly.

"God, yes. That hideous pink palace is crammed full of all sorts of hideous Americana. Jaime nearly lost his eyesight the first time he saw it; he says the entire collection is worth millions." Then Consuelo revealed her hand. "But you've never been there have you, so you wouldn't know. You can't stand the West, can you—or my grandmother, come to that."

She smiled into Dominique's still, calm face, her eyes filled with unholy glee. Ah, thought Dominique, so that is it. You want to make me eat the dirt you wallow in, to know that I have not a hope in hell of selling so much as one piece of a fabulous collecion I have, through my own folly, ignored. Which, she told herself calmly, my husband has never so much as mentioned. Very well, so he has no interest in art. But I do. And he knows that. Just as he knows that I am engaged in the battle of my life, and that the selling of such a collection at auction, allied to my Hong Kong sale, would make victory over that Despard chit a foregone conclusion. Ah, yes, she thought, meeting Consuelo's hard, dark eyes with a tranquillity she did not feel, now I see why you have decided to make it up after all this time. To do what you like to do best: hurt, spite, trample, break . . . She allowed a small smile to appear, saw Consuelo's own become uncertain instead of triumphant. Dominique let her wait; such insolent presumption deserved the utmost in retaliation. Oh, and have I got one for you . . . Thank, God the little Despard paid that visit to Colorado. Really, she thought, it is at times like this that I almost believe there is a God above.

Lifting her glass with a steady hand, "What are you asking for your Remington?" she inquired negligently.

"Well, the Despard girl set a reserve of £250,000. My old squaw of a grandmother must be sitting on God knows how many millions." Consuelo sounded exasperated, but she was watching Dominique's face. Serve the stuck-up bitch right, she thought viciously. She won't get her hands on one of them. The old squaw will see to that. Go on, sit there calm as you like; I know you're on fire inside. You made a mistake, didn't you? The great Dominique du Vivier has actually gone and done herself out of the possible sale of more Western art under one roof than any American museum could dream of. "Such a pity," she purred, "that you and my grandmother have never—got on. You might have done yourself some good."

"I was just thinking that you have probably done yourself a great deal of harm," Dominique answered, that same, snottily amused tone in her voice and an actual smile on her lips. "Kate Despard must have recognized your Remington."

"Recognized? How recognized? It has never been shown anywhere that I know of."

"It had no need to be. Kate Despard paid a visit to your grandmother's ranch recently. Knowing her, I am sure she made a thorough inspection of the contents, especially if they include a collection of Western art. Blaise says she is very knowledgeable about it." This last was a lie but Consuelo was not to know, nor would she want to prove it, not if the painting she had asked Kate Despard to sell was one she had, to all intents and purposes, stolen.

Consuelo's face paled, her letterbox mouth standing out vividly scarlet. She swore, in Spanish, a language that contains more foul oaths than any other. "She never said a damned word. Cool as a cucumber, the dissembling, deceiving bitch!"

"Oh, that she is. I have no doubt she has her eye on the disposal of your Remington, my dear Consuelo, and in her eagerness to get in with the old lady will no doubt have gone to her immediately, crying a very loud wolf."

"Jesus Christ!" Consuelo's voice throbbed. "I'll kill the bitch!" People at other tables turned, stared. "Damn, damn and triple damn! I need that money. I've got debts a mile wide . . . Jaime will kill me if he finds out. Christ, that double-crossing bitch!"

"Did you sign a contract?"

"Contract?"

"Ah, she learns fast, that one. All items of value such as 'your' Remington are sold under contract; until one is signed there is no valid agreement under which you could sue—only her word against yours. Did she actually say, 'Yes, I will sell it for you'?"

It was like pulling teeth. "Not in so many words."

"What exactly did she say?"

Consuelo squirmed. "Well . . . I just automatically assumed. I mean she seemed really interested—and she said there was a sale of American art coming up in the next six weeks."

"But did she say your painting would be included in it?"

"No."

"So, in actual fact, she never did say she would sell the painting at all, did she?"

"But she never said she wouldn't either."

Dominique shook her head. "She played you beautifully. She recognized it at once, and no doubt as soon as you had gone called *l'Indienne* to tell her."

Consuelo met the sapphire eyes and felt their silent laughter.

"The little Despard took the right course legally. She informed the owner of the painting that it had been offered for sale by another person. This would not look good for you were it to get out."

"Then it mustn't," Consuelo said in quick fright. She swallowed hard, got down on her knees to the woman she had hoped to force onto hers. "You won't say anything will you? Especially not to Blaise—you know how he is with the old woman, and he's so stuffed-shirt holier than thou when it comes to being seen to do the right thing and that sort of crap. It will be bad enough once my grandmother finds out . . . God, if I had that bitch here I'd strangle her!" Glaring around for the waiter she ordered another drink. "By God, but she'll pay for this," she vowed viciously. I know lots of people who use Despard's, but they won't anymore, not if I have anything to do with it!"

"I would feel the need for revenge myself," Dominique sympathized, stoking madly. Consuelo de Barranca's vicious tongue at work on Kate Despard would be of great assistance, as would the fact that she and Dominique du Vivier were known to be on the outs because of a certain Brazilian

beach boy. And if she were to sweeten the poison . . .
"Come now, dear Consuelo," she soothed. "Do not upset
yourself over that chit. She will get her comeuppance. You
do not imagine I am going to allow her to do me in, do
you?"

"Anything I can do to help!" raged Consuelo.

"No, it is I who can help you. If you are temporarily short
of money let me help. After all, what are friends for . . .
Come back to Saint Laurent with me and then we will go to
my office and come to some amicable arrangement."

"God, Dominique, you are an angel!" swore Consuelo,
babbling with relief. "Just to tide me over . . ."

Oh, I know I will never get it back, Dominique thought
with tolerant contempt, but it will still have been worth it.
Consuelo made a vicious enemy. Kate Despard would probably lose a lot of sales because she had crossed her. Which
still does not gloss over the fact that I have made a bad
mistake in not cultivating Agatha Chandler. Why did Blaise
not so much as mention what was back at the ranch? All this
time he has known and never said, watching me dig my own
grave . . . Dozens of Remingtons, eh? Well, she thought
with a pleasurable spurt of vengeance, he will pay for this.
The next time we meet I will make him pay and pay and pay. . .

On Wednesday morning, Nicholas Chevely turned up promptly at ten o'clock. He was dressed for the country in flawless
tweeds, and a jacket with leather patches on the sleeves. He
only needed a shooting stick to be the perfect country squire.
Kate had consulted Charlotte.

"Nicholas Chevely!" she had murmured, raising her eyebrows. "In that case, something extra is called for. He is
never seen with any woman who is not perfection itself."

"You know him?" Kate asked naïvely.

Charlotte smiled. "Yes, I know him," she answered. "London society really is a very small world, you know, Kate. He
was a cousin of my first husband." And a lot else beside, but
that was another story . . . "Tweeds, I think," she decided,
after some pursed-lip thought. "I know just the place . . ."

So when Kate came down the main staircase she was very
conscious of looking her best in a fine dogtooth check suit
and culottes, the jacket slashed at the back like a man's
hacking jacket, with real bone buttons. Her boots, with sensible low heels, shone, and so did her shoulder bag, a capa-

cious pouch into which Charlotte had suggested slipping a pair of Gucci loafers with fringed tongues. "Just in case you have to walk on any precious carpets," she said, adding with a smile, "the preparation is all." Kate's sweater was of cashmere as russet as her hair, her silk scarf from Hermés, and Charlotte had suggested a discreet use of Alliage. "Perfect for where you are going and what you will be doing."

Kate saw Nicholas Chevely do a quick assessment and allow his approval to show in his eyes, though his greeting was courteous punctiliousness at its best.

"I thought we would dispense with the formalities," he said, as he ushered her into a Jaguar XJS the shade of a new penny and immensely flattering to Kate's coloring. "But they know of our arrival and I have arranged lunch . . ."

"Lovely," murmured Kate. Rollo had sniffed superciliously when he saw her. "Talk about a dog's dinner," was all he said, except for a parting, "Mind you don't get eaten, too."

She felt as eager as she was nervous: eager to see Courtland Park and its contents, nervous about Nicholas Chevely. During the preceding days it had been made plain that the staff knew what was riding on this day's outing. Claudia Jamieson had said cryptically, "Best foot forward, Kate, but keep an eye out for his, won't you?"

John Steadman had pontificated, as usual, giving her a whole list of do's and don'ts. David Holmes had shaken his head. "I would dearly love to see Courtland Park and its contents in a Despard's catalogue, Kate, but remember what it will entail if you manage to pull it off. Some *real* hard work . . ."

Charlotte had said sincerely, "You look lovely, my dear. But don't—oh, dear, I sound like an elderly aunt dispensing advice to a young virgin—don't take anything at face value, especially promises. Women are grist to his mill, and as always what matters will be who can deliver the goods, in this case not only the highest prices."

"I am selling Despard's," Kate had answered spiritedly. "Not myself."

Charlotte had smiled. "That is exactly what I meant. I see you are a fast learner . . ."

And on the journey into deepest Sussex, Kate learned a great deal about predatory men. In the most charming way, without ever so much as mentioning it directly, Nicholas

Chevely made it plain that he was open to the most persuasive arguments as to why Despard's should conduct this sale.

Later, when they had driven through an enormous park and sighted the vast edifice, a Jacobean extravaganza with mullioned windows and barley-sugar chimneys, Kate thought, "Would it be worth it? I've got to have this sale, but do I have to sell myself to get it?" And almost by return heard her father's voice, "One must do all one can when bidding for a sale, but never go so far as to compromise the integrity either of Despard's or oneself. Remember that, my little Cat; it will be most important when you are running Despard's."

I remember, Papa, she thought. I will do it the right way. *Your* way.

The house was an eclectic profusion of rubbish and the rare: nothing had any order. Rooms, large, ornate, and badly lit—the windows were heavily hung with faded, almost threadbare curtains—were crammed with furniture, ceramics, bronzes, marble, crystal, paintings, many of them unframed and simply stacked against walls. In some rooms there were several carpets laid one on top of the other; Kate bent to turn back a corner in one room and found six, the last of which, laid on a marble floor, she saw was a rare Kazak.

As they made their way slowly around the ground floor, her mind kept a running tally of what she saw; her estimates were rough and in cases where she was in doubt she always underestimated.

Upstairs, the bedrooms were used as storerooms; French furniture of extraordinary quality stood cheek by jowl with monstrosities of Victoriana and superlative examples of art nouveau; the paintings included several Rembrandts, a breathtaking Rubens nude, at least a dozen Dutch interiors, all of first importance, two Gainsboroughs, a Lawrence, and a Stubbs which Kate knew to be of prime importance. The late Mr. Courtland had not cared for modernists; the most modern painting was an Augustus John of 1910.

The china was breathtaking. Whole sets of Sèvres and Vincennes crammed into cupboards, exquisite Venetian glass, and a set of seventeenth-century Italian goblets set in silver gilt that made Kate's mouth water. There was a bed that Nicholas Chevely believed had belonged to Madame de Pompadour; its hangings of silk velvet were thick with dust.

"Ladies of her era used to receive in their bedrooms, did they not?" he asked with just the right hint of deprecatory amusement.

"Well, if you could watch the king rise, there would be nothing amiss in paying a call on a lady in her bedroom," Kate said with equal lightness. "Besides, there was really no privacy in those days."

"Not even when she was with the king?"

Kate turned her head to meet the gleam in the predatory hazel eyes. "She spent a great deal of her time seeing to it that other women met him in privacy. Then, while he amused himself she got on with running the country."

He laughed. "I take your point."

But over lunch he was still sparring skillfully, even while asking her how she would go about organizing, cataloguing, and readying such a hodgepodge for preview.

"I should heave out everything that was not saleworthy, sort the valuable stuff into period and classification, and then, after the house had been cleaned from top to bottom, I should have everything rearranged by a topflight decorator so that when people came to the preview they would walk through completely furnished rooms. I would have flowers everywhere, those hideous curtains replaced and hundred-and-fifty-watt bulbs instead of forties. I should wash every single piece of crystal and china, have every stick of furniture polished, every painting removed from its frame and cleaned—and I have the best restorer in the country at Despard's—and then I would hang them where they can be seen to best advantage. I would prepare a catalogue that would set mouths to water and tongues to wag; I would create a whole special kind of ambience for this sale which, of course, would be a black-tie occasion—"

"And how long would all this take?"

"A minimum of six months."

"Which would bring us to the end of October." He paused. "I should warn you that the government might decide to make an offer for the house and its contents." In the face of Kate's consternation, "Inheritance taxes," he told her succinctly. "More than seven million pounds."

Kate winced.

"If they decide to accept Courtland Park and everything in it in lieu, then I am afraid there would be no sale."

"Is it possible or probable?"

An expressive shrug. "Negotiations have been going on since Mr. Courtland's death, but as you know the wheels of bureaucracy grind exceeding slow. There is also a certain conservationist who is stirring madly on behalf of the country retaining those works of art which, in his opinion, are national treasures."

"He means the pictures—especially the English ones—and a lot of the furniture."

"Whatever—you are the expert, not I. But he has influence where it counts."

"Yet you still want Despard's to let you have a detailed exposition of how we would go about disposing of those same treasures should you decide to do so?"

"Yes. One cannot stand around and do nothing. I believe in being prepared for all eventualities."

Yes, thought Kate, I bet you've got a ready-packed bag in the boot, just in case I was willing to stop at the nearest quiet country hotel . . .

Strange, she thought, not only was she disinclined to do so because if it became known—and these things invariably did—that Kate Despard was willing to offer sex to clinch a sale, she and Despard's would both lose what reputation they had, but also, though he was an attractive man, he did not stir her in any way. It was pleasant to bask in the warmth of his appreciation, to use his flattery to polish up her self-esteem, but as a man he just did not turn her on. If it had been Blaise Chandler propositioning her with those eyes she would not have hesitated for one minute . . .

"It might be a good thing in the end, you know," she said slowly, her mind returning to what mattered.

"What would?" he asked hopefully.

"To have a public outcry over Courtland Park. In my opinion it can only do good to have the public realize just what it costs to keep treasures like this, how punitive taxation is, threatening the existence of so many houses containing not only treasures but history. When people pay their £1.50 I am sure they think it goes on a new car or a winter cruise."

"Well, whatever the rights and the wrongs of the case, the fact remains that the government is considering whether or not to make an offer, but don't let that stop you from making your presentation to the executors. And October will have to be the latest date for the sale; after that duty becomes payable not on probate value but the price raised at auction. I was most impressed by what you told me about the incredible increase in prices over the last few years alone; when one considers that a great deal of what is contained in this house has been here for half a century. . ."

"Indeed," Kate found herself echoing him gravely. She saw his mouth twitch. At least he had a sense of humor.

After lunch, which had been eaten on a corner of the tennis-court-sized dining table that had been cleared, and had obviously not been cooked on the premises (Kate had seen the kitchen and it was clearly not geared to cooking anything resembling food) but brought down from London, they went into a part of the house that had not been lived in for many years. Here the neglect was obvious and Kate said thankfully, "I'm glad this sale is coming off soon; it is going to recirculate so much that would just have rotted away, *such* a waste . . ."

"Oh, I am against waste myself," Nicholas Chevely agreed promptly, plainly hinting at the time they were wasting, which could be much better spent in an experience she would treasure. She had never met a man so consummately skilled at allusion, not once did he come out directly and say, "I find you very attractive. I would very much like to make love to you. May I have the pleasure?" while nevertheless making it clear that he felt a desire that grew keener by the moment, and at the same time conveying in the most subtle of ways that any reciprocation on her part would not go amiss when it came to considering Despard's bid.

Kate knew that her stepsister would not have hesitated; it was common knowledge in the art world that Dominique used her body to get what she wanted, but in some strange way that was part of her: she was a woman of such transcendent beauty that it was accepted that of course, she would do so. It was also understood by other women in the art world who had not the Venus Flytrap's physical beauty or sex appeal that, had they been so fortunately endowed, they *might* have done the same thing. Yet Kate knew that if she were to do it, it would not be the same; that it would be regarded with shock, horror, and outright condemnation. Because, she realized, she was accepted as an expert in her own right and also as a Despard—Charles Despard's daughter. Dominique was accepted because her stepfather had wanted it so, but she was not really *one of them;* how could she, then, be expected to know the right way to behave . . .

Dazzled by the sudden cold, white light that illuminated her brain, Kate was suddenly aware that Nicholas Chevely was speaking to her. "What? Oh, I'm sorry. I was miles away . . ."

"I know," he said ruefully. "You really do get carried away by all this, don't you? It means everything to you."

"Yes," Kate answered with simple, prideful truth, "it does."

He took her hand, raised it to his lips with that elegant gallantry that was so much a part of him. "It is obvious that you would do your damnedest for us—should the sale come to you."

"It would not occur to me to do anything else for any client," Kate reminded him gently. She removed her hand and moved away; then, as something caught her eye, she made an exclamation and darted away to the other end of the attic. "I don't believe it!" she moaned.

"What is it?"

Kate gestured at what seemed to be a wall piled with furniture. "French eighteenth-century furniture," she said hollowly. "A fortune of it . . . and look at the way it is stacked. It has got to be removed from that—that bonfire!"

One look at her face and Nicholas Chevely found himself obeying. He sent downstairs for the two men who lived on the premises, a caretaker and a watchman. Not only that, he also found himself helping to lift down superb marquetry commodes, boulle desks, thronelike chairs, and glorious silk-upholstered sofas.

"I don't believe it," Kate said helplessly. "He had all this squirreled away as if it was a store of firewood! Obviously I am the first of the triumvirate to see it. Nothing has been disturbed for years."

"Yes, you are the first," he admitted.

One up, Kate thought with a spurt of confidence. A forethought rather than an afterthought.

He watched her stroke the marquetry on a massive boulle desk, found himself imagining that long-fingered, sensitive hand on him, and felt his desire build. He had thought it would be child's play; his antennae had sensed her inexperience from the word go and he had thought to combine a little business with a lot of pleasure. Yet she had fended him off in a way that left his pride intact and her value as a conquest increased a thousandfold. Not only works of art appreciate with time, he thought. There was something so fresh and young about her, those lovely long legs, the fine bones, her coltish elegance. She was also excellent company. And so obviously in total command of her chosen field. She made him see things of which he had never been aware, and to appreciate why old man Courtland had been such an obsessive collector. There was no doubt that her ideas were also first class. His fellow executors—of which he was the senior—had shaken dubious heads when he suggested approaching Despard's as well as the two other big houses.

"If Charles Despard had still been running things," they demurred. "His daughter is as yet inexperienced, too new to the job; in a few years, perhaps . . ."

Not so, he thought now. She knows exactly what she has got here and what its possibilities are. Just as he was beginning to appreciate hers.

"How long would it take to sell all this?" he asked.

Without hesitation, "A maximum of ten days," she told him. "There are thousands of items." Her eyes were agleam, her whole being lit with some inner fire. "It could be televised . . . give people who have never been to such a sale a chance to see glories like this. Entrance by ticket only. Superb refreshments. I have on my staff a man who is a genius at staging such events." Rollo would be in his element, she thought. His unfailing sense of theatre would be a godsend at Courtland Park. And to Despard's, for he would be out of the way.

Nicholas felt her enthusiasm kindle his own. By God, he thought with rising excitement. She really has got the right ideas.

"You do realize that time is of the essence," she went on crisply, giving him the full benefit of her remarkable eyes.

"Indeed."

She frowned. "It's the government who is the fly in the ointment, of course."

"Well, I do have a good friend rather high up at the Department of the Environment," Nicholas murmured. "Perhaps a word in his car . . ." Why am I doing this? he asked himself bemusedly. She answered his question by the smile she gave him. Oh, well done, little Despard, he thought admiringly in spite of himself. You do learn quickly. And to think I regretted that it was not your stepsister. I doubt if even she could have given me so enjoyable an encounter."

When they got back to London it was after seven o'clock. "Dinner?" he suggested hopefully.

"Not tonight, I'm afraid."

Which gave him the right to ask, "When, then?"

"Call me," she invited, as she got out of the car.

"I will," he promised with more fervor than he had shown in an age. Sotheby's and Christie's could only be a letdown after this; their representatives were both men. He wondered if they had yet realized that Despard's now had a secret weapon.

Once inside the penthouse Kate threw down her bag, did a whirl and let out a "Whoopee!" She felt she had acquitted herself and Despard's one hundred percent. Charlotte, you are a godsend! she thought, and had to telephone her.

"It went well, then?"

"I don't want to boast, but I think he's hooked," Kate said gleefully.

"On you or Despard's?"

"Both. He's asked me to dinner. I shall need your advice again."

"Any time, my dear. You have no idea what vicarious pleasure I am obtaining from all this."

"I handled him exactly as you suggested."

"And was it fun?" Charlotte asked wickedly.

Kate giggled. "I haven't had such fun ever." And then added in a slow, wondering voice that was shaded with regret, "Now I know what I have been missing."

"You are young," Charlotte said, her sigh echoing her own regret, "you have all the time in the world."

"Well?" Rollo asked, as Charlotte returned from the telephone to resume their game of whist.

"She's as high as a kite on success."

Rollo's face showed what he thought of that.

"Come now, old friend," Charlotte chided. "As she grows up she also grows away. She has come on so well these past few months, don't begrudge her her late entrance into the adult world."

"One should crawl before one runs," he rasped waspishly.

"She has no time for that. One short year and a world-class opponent to beat." Very softly, "You do *want* her to win?'' she said and then added warningly, "Even if she loses she won't go back to what she was."

He did not answer. Instead he began to shuffle and deal the cards again. Picking up her hand, "You also taught her a great deal," Charlotte said matter-of-factly. "I recognize where she got her shrewdness from, and her clear-sightedness. She sees the skull beneath the flesh; don't keep showing her the worms too."

She left it at that. Rollo did not listen to many people but she knew he had always heard her. All she could hope was that he would also see.

Kate set to work at once. When she reported back to the Ways and Means Committee they were delighted, but cautious about spending money where there was no definite hope of return.

"To put such a catalogue in hand—even a mock-up—will cost a small fortune," her head of Finance warned.

"I am confident enough to take the gamble," Kate answered. "And don't forget there is the six-month deadline. Besides, you've seen the figures . . . a minimum of ten million pounds; surely a small sprat to catch such a fat mackerel is a worthwhile risk to take."

She argued so persuasively that she brought them around; estimates were put in hand; the outline she had prepared, set in stages over the ten days and covering everything from refreshments to car parking, was printed and circulated to the various heads of departments. Printers' dates were set; several deliberate leaks were engineered by the publicity department, designed to create an intrigued interest; a definite date for an interview by a woman's magazine for inclusion in a series on "Executive Women," which Kate had been unable to fit in for lack of time, was now agreed upon: it would take place at Despard's and be accompanied by a photo montage.

The major core of resistance she ran into concerned placing Rollo in charge of the entire "show." The publicity department took umbrage, until Kate persuaded Rollo to give them his own presentation, accompanied by full-color drawings she herself had made. She and Rollo spent two whole days and nights creating a multiscened drama out of the hoped-for sale, and Kate wisely let him have his head when it came to the meeting to consider it. He brought every historic art to bear, and there was a unanimous if, in some quarters, still grudging acceptance of his ideas, once it was put to the vote.

"My God, if it comes off *this* will be the Sale of the Century, never mind Hong Kong," she heard somebody say as the meeting broke up.

"Considering what it is going to cost it will have to be," someone else answered sourly.

"Once she gets the bit between her teeth there's no stopping her."

"Just like her father."

Oh, I hope so, Kate thought, as she went back to her office. Oh, I *hope* so . . . She could have no finer accolade.

She went back to her office high on adrenaline and the figure standing by the window turned as she entered. It was Blaise Chandler. He had not seen why he should change his schedule, so it was ten days since his grandmother had called him.

"Hello," Kate said with a smile that made him blink. She was giving off sparks, he thought.

"I've come to pick up the Remington," he said.

The sparks died, replaced by the steady glow of unshakable conviction. "I had no alternative. I recognized the painting at once, and Despard's does not sell stolen property." Even when offered by your half-sister, hung invisibly on the line stretched taut between them.

"You did right," he said without heat. "I hold no brief for thieves either, whether they are in the family or not. My grandmother conveys her apologies that you should be drawn into such a sordid little affair." They held eyes. "I'm sorry," he said, and something sizzled and crackled across the line.

Kate turned away feeling breathless. "I'll have the painting brought up." Her fingers trembled as they reached for the intercom.

"I hear you are up for the Courtland Park sale," Blaise observed easily, dispelling the unexpected tension.

"Yes. I've just come from a meeting discussing that very thing." She turned back to him.

"Good," he said, and she knew he meant it. "I'll be rooting for you."

"If it comes off it will prove a very effective counter against Dominique's Sale of the Century." Just then her phone rang. "Excuse me . . ." She picked up the receiver.

"Mr. Chevely on line one, Miss Despard."

"Put him through," Kate said eagerly. "Nicholas?"

"You said to call and I would have done so earlier but I had to go out of town and only got back this morning, so I am hastening to make amends."

"Consider them made," Kate assured him with a note in her voice that had Blaise Chandler eyeing her sharply.

"Then may I suggest this very night?"

"You may indeed."

"I'll call for you at seven-thirty."

"I shall be ready and waiting."

Nicholas Chevely could not believe his luck. His gambit at letting her stew had worked. "Do you have any preference in restaurants?"

"I place myself entirely in your hands."

"I shall remember that."

I'll bet you will, Kate thought, who had chosen her words quite deliberately because she was conscious of Blaise Chandler's looming presence.

Replacing the receiver, "Sorry," Kate lied smoothly, part of her standing back astonished at what she was doing. Never in her life had she played one man off against another—this is ridiculous, she thought. Get a grip, Kate Despard, before you make a complete fool of yourself. This is one man you can't fool.

"How is the Duchess?" she asked pleasantly.

"Shoving fingers into every pie and complaining if they don't taste just right."

Kate chuckled. "She is an amazing woman. I like her enormously."

"I am aware that you have formed a mutual admiration society." It was said dryly, but there was an underlying edge to his voice, which told Kate that he was fully aware of what his grandmother was doing: shoving her in his way at every opportunity. The Remington could have been picked up by any subordinate from ChanCorp, no questions asked, but the old lady had instructed her grandson to come. He loves her, Kate thought, that's why he does it.

There was a knock and the Remington was brought in, already in its special flat transportation package.

"Would you like to check it?" Kate asked.

"No need. I trust your judgment." But he asked abruptly,

"What did my sister say when she brought the painting to you?"

"That it belonged in her family, but that she was to remain anonymous."

"That figures. What was she asking?"

"I told her it was worth a quarter of a million pounds." At the raised eyebrows, "Great art, remember?" she said ironically, harking back to their last conversation.

"Let's not get into that again," he commanded brusquely.

"It was fortunate that I recognized it. Had I not gone to Colorado . . ."

"You'd have notched up another commission and done yourself a bit of good. Too bad," he said.

"Had I not seen it I would have sold it—and damned quick!"

He studied her. "But you don't regret the way things turned out?"

"No, I don't. There will be other Remingtons, but there is only one Agatha Chandler."

"Thank God," Blaise said, and Kate laughed.

"Go on," she rebuked. "You know you wouldn't have her any other way. I wouldn't."

Again that gleam in the tar-black eyes. "No . . . I know."

But I would have you this way as against that god-awful one I met last year, he thought. She was still the fast-tongued young amazon he had faced that memorable afternoon in the little shop in the King's Road, but something new had been added: pride in her appearance. There was a burnished gloss about her, the final polish that only confidence could bestow. Well, he thought, she no longer carries those chips on her shoulders, and she can attract men of the caliber of Nicholas Chevely. He had been both curt and disapproving when he heard that they were laying bets. Not on Kate Despard, he had thought, affronted. That's not her style. And as if he had pressed the right button, up popped the thought: But it is Dominique's.

Kate found he was scowling at her. God, she thought. Talk about being moody . . . She scowled back and he did another about-face. "Sorry, I was thinking."

"It looked like it hurt," she said tartly.

His grin became a laugh. "No wonder you get on so well with my grandmother. She doesn't mince words either."

Kate felt those words light a glow. To be compared to his grandmother was the ultimate in compliments.

"Give her my love, won't you?" she said warmly.

"She told me to tell you she'd rather do it in person."

"Oh, if only I could . . ."

"Well, whenever you can." He paused. "I am also instructed to tell you that Jed says 'hi.' "

"That was nice of him. Return the greeting."

"You made a hit there," Blaise observed. "Normally, Jed is scared stiff of the opposite sex—"

She went off like a rocket. "You think he didn't regard me as a member of it?"

Ah, he thought. Still not one hundred percent sure of herself. "No way," he said. "Not these days, anyway."

He saw the bright color flood her face at what he supposed was a backhanded compliment, and some perverse impulse made him say, "You are no longer a card-carrying member of the movement, are you?"

"I never was," she replied, stung.

"You could have fooled me."

She smiled and now she saw a dark flush rise under the copper skin. "How do you know I didn't?"

He felt as if she had put her tongue out at him. Oh, she is learning, he thought sourly, not sure whether he was pleased or put out. Angry with himself, not her, he turned away to pick up the painting. "I'll see this is returned safely," he said distantly.

"Which reminds me—is there any sort of alarm system at the ranch? If it was my grandmother I should be very worried if there wasn't, surrounded as she is by a fortune in art . . ."

"She has a bunkhouse full of ranchhands who would die for her," Blaise said flatly. He turned to face her. "But as it happens, once you had told me what she was sitting on I had a system installed—a photoelectric cell barrier which, once breached, sets off lights, screamers, and an alarm in the local sheriff's office. There are new locks on all windows and doors, and at night we let loose half a dozen rottweilers. Remember that for future visits in case you ever go wandering around in the night."

In amazement he saw her turn scarlet. What the hell . . . ? By God, was that why Jed had sent the message? Had she been wandering around at night—down to the bunkhouse, maybe? Nah, he thought, disgusted. Jed and Kate Despard! Two babes in the wood? Jesus, he thought, love is not only blind but it is deaf and dumb! He hefted the painting, reached for his briefcase, made his good-byes swiftly, and got away from there, vowing to tell his grandmother that she could find somebody else to do her goddamn errands in future—as far as Kate Despard was concerned anyway.

Kate put her hands to her hot face. She had caught the look in his eyes, first surprise, then—disgust? Then surmise . . . He thought she had been making midnight assignations with Jed. Jed! She wanted to laugh, found instead that if she did she would cry. It was you, you Superior Shit, she felt like shouting after him. You . . .

Rollo found her sitting there ten minutes later, staring heavily at nothing.

"Why did you not tell me," Dominique asked without preamble, "that your grandmother was possessed of a most formidable collection of Western art?"

Blaise looked across at his wife. "Since when has my grandmother been a topic of conversation between us?"

Dominique laid down her knife and fork. "I am talking about a collection which would be a considerable coup should Despard's New York dispose of it—through me of course."

"My grandmother has no intention of disposing of her collection. How come you all of a sudden know about it anyway?"

Dominique lifted her glass. "Come now. Do not pretend you don't know your sister lifted one of the paintings and tried to sell it through Despard's in London. She told me so."

"I thought you weren't on speaking terms."

A shrug. "Oh, she could not wait to tell me."

"Which was when you told her that Kate had been to the ranch?"

A slow smile. "But of course."

"You wasted your time. The Duchess spotted the painting was gone. She knows to the last square inch of canvas what she has. The painting is back where it belongs."

"So Despard's lost the sale."

"It was not about to be sold."

Dominique's perfectly kept eyebrows lifted. "She ratted?"

"She doesn't go in for selling stolen property." Blaise

looked steadily at his wife. "Whatever she is, Kate Despard is not dishonest. In that, she is indeed her father's daughter."

"As I am not?" Dominique asked, soft as a feather.

Blaise was unmoved. "Well, you aren't, are you? Except in law, and as a lawyer I know what that means."

"Indeed you are a lawyer!" Dominique said, with a toss of her head that was wholly French. "Sometimes I think legalities mean more to you than feelings."

"Do you?" asked Blaise, in a way which made her say crossly, "You know very well what I mean. Why did you not tell me about the collection at the ranch?"

"If you had availed yourself of even one of the many invitations extended to you, you would have seen for yourself."

"I would have gone had I known."

"I know," Blaise said.

Dominique looked at him from under the fringe of her lashes. He was in a funny mood, had been ever since he arrived, when he had diverged from the usual pattern and not taken her to bed. Instead he had spent more than an hour on the telephone, dealt with a pile of letters, and sent a whole raft of cables. By then, dinner—Dominique had planned a candlelit *tête-à-tête* to get him in the right frame of mind— was ready. She had planned to retrieve much of the ground she had lost, tell him she had been wrong in neglecting his grandmother, make a penitent confession of *mea culpa*. But his manner had been short and quite unsoftened; he answered when spoken to but that was all. Normally when they met he could not be restrained; this was the first time ever that he had not been more than ready to make up for lost time. A little alarm bell had rung immediately. If his fever for her was cooling then it had to be fanned. She had no intention of letting Blaise escape; not now, when she had discovered that he held the key to a sale which, following on her Hong Kong sensation, would put her so far ahead that there was no hope of Kate Despard catching up.

Now Dominique knew she would have to forego the punishment she had had in mind; she had intended to do the denying: let him wonder what *he* had done wrong. She had not expected the positions to be reversed. But she gave no sign of concern, chatting of this and that, and ignoring the dispassion of his gaze, the unhurried, unreachable note in his voice. She saw to it that his glass was always full, and set out to charm, to make him *aware* of her—when she got up to get him more wine, seeing to it that her breasts brushed his shoulder, that her hair swung against his face, that her perfume combined with the bouquet of the fine claret. And when they went into the living room, with its bank of floor-to-ceiling windows giving a superb panorama of New York at night, curling up next to him on the huge chesterfield.

But though he had eaten and drunk well, he did not immediately draw her close to him, cup her breast in his hand, his long fingers stroking the nipple, which would be followed by his mouth, which would eventually lead to the gradual shedding of clothes, and passionate, explosive sex. Instead he picked up *The New York Times,* began to read the "Business Day" section. The Dow, Dominique noted in passing, had risen 11.47 to a new peak. As if it matters to him, she fulminated. ChanCorp has more money than the Bank of France! And as for that priceless collection of Western art . . . She did not for one moment believe that his grandmother would refuse to sell once she knew the prices she could get. She was a shrewd old woman who probably still had the first dollar she ever made . . . except that it would now be hidden at the bottom of billions. God knows she wore enough of them. Like some garish Christmas tree, Dominique thought with distaste. But Blaise had been very definite when he said nothing would be sold during his grandmother's lifetime. Such a pity. It would have made an ideal sledgehammer with which to flatten Kate Despard's hopes. That *and* Hong Kong . . . Still, she was old, that one. It was only a matter of time. All she had to do was work on him subtly. Dominique had no doubt she could do it; Blaise Chandler was not a malleable man, but in one, particular direction he was like clay on a potter's table, to be molded in whatever shape she pleased. Sexually, she dominated him, held him spellbound, besottedly hooked on her body and what she could do to him, bring to him, by its expert use. He was not abnormally highly sexed—it had never been a case of any body will do; indeed, it was only because hers was the particular one that rang all his bells that she maintained her hold on him. She had never fooled herself that it was love, just as she was never fooled by sex.

"How is the little Despard doing?" she asked idly, curling up closer and allowing one bare leg to emerge from the long slit in her silver-tissue skirt.

"Not as well as you."

"But of course! Has she anything big in the offing?"

"You get the gossip long before I do; you tell me."

"Oh, I know she has landed a superb Velázquez which should bring in about five million, but what else has she?"

"I am only interested in what she has had; I look at sales figures, remember? I can't take into account what she either hopes to have or make, only what has been paid into the bank."

She pretended to be poutingly hurt. "I know Papa made you referee, but surely you can tell me, your wife!"

"It is because you are my wife that I can't." He turned to look at her. "As you well know."

She almost flung away from him in temper, but her self-control kept her soft against him. "No wonder Papa made you his executor . . . he always said that what he liked about you was your integrity."

Then she said reproachfully, "You are angry with me because I told your sister about Kate Despard recognizing the Remington."

Blaise flung down his newspaper. "Which I have no doubt you did because she had not brought it to you—who would have sold it without a qualm."

"Of course. *I* would not have been able to recognize it!"

"Which is what burns you up. You are kicking yourself black and blue because you've lost out on a monstrous sale—now and forever. I told you before and I'll tell you again. While my grandmother is alive, not one item from among the hundreds at the ranch will be sold, nor, for that matter, after her death. The house and its entire contents are to form the Chandler Museum of Western Art and be given to the state of Colorado."

Dominique stared and stiffened, the sapphire eyes turning to blue ice. "Ah . . . the little Despard has been at work, is that it?" She sprang away from him. "Knowing she cannot have it, she has made sure that I will not have it either!"

"That is not what happened. You never came into it." For some reason, his wife's constant reiteration of the "little" Despard irritated an already sore spot.

Obviously, it was more than her height that provided Dominique's own irritation. "Already she is making her influence felt on your grandmother. She saw her chance and she took it."

"You had yours," Blaise answered brutally. "Not once but many times."

"All right, so I made a mistake! It is not one I will make again."

"You won't get the chance. The Duchess is already in the process of setting up the foundation that will finance the museum once the state takes over. You've no hope of adding that particular scalp to your belt."

Dominique wanted to hit him. Instead, she swung on her heel and flung into her bedroom—not only slamming the door but kicking it.

Blaise exhaled a hefty breath. Shit! He had been in a bad mood since collecting the Remington and his subsequent meeting with his sister . . .

They did not meet often—there was nothing to meet for—but he had deliberately sought her out to give her a piece of his mind. She had been in her own ugly mood, and it had ended in a shouting match, with her accusing him of feathering his own nest to the exclusion of her and their half-brother.

"Don't think I don't know what you are up to," she screeched at him. "You want the whole damned shebang. Well you won't do it. I'll sue you through every court in the land!"

"Try it"—Blaise obviously relished the idea—"and I'll cut you to ribbons. You don't give a damn for her, you or that chinless wonder. You never see her from one year's end to the next unless you need money; if she hadn't any you wouldn't even give her a thought."

"Just as you give her all yours, sucking up to her, spoiling our chances and making sure you get all the money for yourself."

"You spoiled your own chances by just being your own rotten self. You made it only too clear that your father's family were more to your taste, and Gerald had a title to inherit. I had nobody but my grandmother."

"And since the day she took you in you've done nothing but your damnedest to do me and Gerald in."

"You hit rock bottom a long time ago."

Her hand cracked across his face. "That's for humiliating me, you selfish bastard, letting me take that painting to a girl who would recognize it!" As usual, she had rationalized the blame for her own shortcomings, placed it squarely elsewhere. Her exposure as a thief hurt her pride, and now, in the presence of the half-brother of whom she had always been insanely jealous, her feelings exploded in a torrent of abusive rage.

He walked out on her, left her hurling gutter language after him. Connie always had been a bad loser, and she had resented him from birth. Their mother had been madly in love with his father—the love of her life—and had devoted herself to her son by him in a way that made Consuelo, his elder by six years, both jealous and resentful. Gerald, their half-brother, a fat, slow-witted boy, had been four when Blaise was born, and as Consuelo was already the embryo of the snob she would eventually become, she fawned on him because he was the future Viscount Stanstead.

It was after Blaise's father was killed—and all he remembered about that was his mother darting about the great white villa at Cap Ferrat, screaming hysterically, tearing her clothes, trying to throw herself off the terrace on to the rocks below—that she turned against him. He had thought it was because he reminded her of his father; his nanny told him that sometimes happened, that it took time for the hurt to heal, but gradually he came to realize that it was because he did not; he could see it in her eyes, a revulsion, an accusation, a distaste. He did not understand it and his nanny could not explain it without making things worse; that it was because he did not resemble his father at all; that he was a throwback to Black Jack Chandler, Indian-dark and a pointer to the truth of his mother's antecedents. She had cut herself off from her mother years ago, died her black hair blonde, gone to enormous lengths to disassociate herself from the hideous fact that her grandmother had been a full-blooded Shoshone. And now she saw that her son by the man she had adored bore no resemblance to either of his parents, but to the half-Indian who had married that squaw.

That was when the bad days started. Consuelo, ever quick to scent a change in the wind, knew she had *carte blanche* to make his life hell, and proceeded to do so, balked only by his nanny, until Consuelo trumped up some charge against her that resulted in her dismissal and another, stricter nanny being hired. The divorce settlement allowed Anne Chandler to have her daughter for six months every year, and they were the months Blaise came to dread. From April to September. Gerald spent only summers with his mother, and was always accompanied by his own nanny, who was quite ready to gossip with her *confrère* and deplore the fact that they had to look after a boy who was obviously some kind of darkie. That was when Consuelo held sway, when life became one hellish day after another. She was a bully and she delighted in inflicting pain. Gerald, slow-witted yet shrewd enough to know on which side his bread was buttered, was her willing acolyte, and between them they gave Blaise no mercy. They broke things and blamed him; they stole things and blamed him; they made his food uneatable with salt; they put spiders and lizards and ants in his bed; they played games in which he was the Indian and they the cavalry come to torture him. They were the games Consuelo liked best. Bending his fingers back until he screamed, holding him with her cruel strength while Gerald tied him up and lit matches under the soles of his feet, losing her temper and lashing out at him with a branch or a piece of rope when he refused to cry.

"Cry, damn you! Cry!" she would scream at him. "You know you want to, go on, cry . . ." But he wouldn't. Indians didn't cry. Indian boys were expected to bear pain in silence. It was only at night, his head buried in the pillow, that he wept his heart out. To Consuelo, to his mother, to the nannies, he showed the impassive face and unrevealingy polite voice he carried with him into adult life.

It was not until Consuelo went too far: used too much brushwood in the fire she lit, the game being that Blaise was to be burned at the stake, that everything abruptly changed. A fierce old lady whom Blaise was sure was an Indian queen descended from the sky and proceeded to terrify his mother and turn Consuelo into a blubbering coward, while Gerald tried to squeeze his fat bulk under his bed.

After she went away again, Consuelo and Gerald no longer tortured him, no longer bothered with him at all, though Blaise knew that Consuelo's hate for him, rather than being squelched, had been increased by the way the Indian queen had fussed over him, told his mother to "look after the boy, or by God, don't expect me to look after you." From then on, he believed that the lady who had come had been his guardian angel. He did not see her again until he was nine, after his mother and her current husband had been burned to death when their car went over a precipice during a drunken argument as to who had lost the most at the casino in Monte Carlo. Once more she descended from the sky—

but by then he knew it was a helicopter—and this time she told him she was his grandmother.

When Consuelo learned that Blaise, and only Blaise, was to go back to America to live with their grandmother, she blubbered with terror. Her father had told her to win back all the ground she had lost with Agatha Chandler—or else; he had also told her what was at stake. Too late, Consuelo cursed her mother for not telling her that the "Indian squaw" whom she had taught her daughter to despise and feel shame for was probably the richest woman in the world apart from the queen of England. It had been her money that paid for the villa, bought her mother's divorces, paid the servants, even put the food in their mouths. And it was this same despised squaw's grandson, Blaise, who was the image of Black Jack Chandler, their great-grandfather. What Consuelo had tortured and tormented Blaise for turned out to be the one thing her grandmother would never forgive her for. Her father was so incensed he beat her black and blue and then shut her up in a convent run by a strict order of nuns in a quiet suburb of Buenos Aires, where she stayed until eloping at the age of seventeen with the first man she could induce—and seduce—to do so.

Her grandmother gave her an allowance—on condition that she spend it as far away from Colorado as possible. Gerald—"my brother, Lord Stanstead," as she liked to call him negligently—was strapped by the enormous upkeep of Stanstead Abbey, and she knew that his chances of partaking of those same billions were as negligible as hers. As her grandmother got older and relinquished more and more control of ChanCorp to her grandson, Consuelo knew that her days were numbered. Desperately she had tried to repair her relationship with Blaise, deliberately cultivated his wife, a woman she neither liked nor trusted, in an effort to get closer to him, but he had not forgotten and would never forgive the cruel treatment he had received at her spiteful, jealous hands. He had not liked her then, he did not like her now and saw no point in being hypocritical about it.

"But she is your sister," Dominique had pointed out, as Consuelo asked her to.

"Only because it now suits her to be. When she thought I had nothing and nobody she didn't want to know." He knew exactly what she was up to. Consuelo had always been as subtle as a bass drum.

Just as Blaise had known, as soon as he set eyes on his wife today, that she was on a softening-up mission, and it had given him great satisfaction to punish her by remaining obdurate. He had wanted her badly—he always wanted her badly—but he refused to let his body dominate his mind. Now, having done so, he felt deflated and frustrated, in spite of a good dinner and a '59 Chateau Latour. He grinned. He could always tell the seriousness of an occasion by the food and the wine Dominique laid before him. He could still read her like a book . . . except he had not thought she would turn out to be one he read and reread time and time again. Still, the fact that he still had the upper hand restored his good humor. Time to let up on the rawhide.

He followed her into the bedroom. She was in the shower; he could hear it hissing. Quickly he stripped off his clothes, slid aside the glass door of the enormous shower stall, and stepped in to join her. She was standing with her face up, eyes closed, the water from three strategically placed shower heads hitting her with punishing force, the water streaming down her perfect body in gleaming rivulets, her black hair plastered to her head like a swim cap. He did not know that the pose was deliberate; that she had been standing there waiting for him, only one shower head running so she would be able to hear when he came in, as she had known he eventually would. But her start, as he silently stepped behind her, pulled her against his gently pulsating erection, was flawless, as was the way she made a small sound in her throat, leaned back against him, lasciviously rubbing her firm, rounded buttocks against him, moaning softly as he cupped her breasts, bent to nip her throat with his strong white teeth. With one swift movement she turned to face him, arms going up and around his neck. Reading her signals he put his hands on her waist, lifted her up. Quickly she found him, squeezed him in promise and, when he let her down, was slowly and deliciously impaled on his thick, throbbing penis, locking her ankles behind his back, his hands under her buttocks, her head back, allowing him to suck greedily on her urgently stiff nipples, at the same time as she skillfully used her inner muscles to squeeze and caress. She felt him shudder, then go wild.

After that it was downhill all the way.

BEARS
SIGNATURE

June

13

Dominique sat at the desk in her office at Despard et Cie (Hong Kong) Limited, and checked through the list of names—in order of importance and wealth—of those who would be attending the three days of her Sale of the Century, due to open in five days' time. She was well satisfied, just about every big name and big spender was on it. Which was as it should be; she had spent a long time on this sale, as well as a great deal of money. She had carefully leaked the rumor that she had acquired, via some unknown Hong Kong millionaire now selling everytning—en route for pastures new and far away from the impending Communist takeover—a collection of T'ang and Han tomb figures the likes of which had not been seen for many a year. Which, Dominique thought with a small smile, was absolutely true. Figures like this most certainly had not been seen, much less offered for sale at auction, in most people's lifetimes. They were, she sighed happily, perfection.

The catalogue notes, which she herself had written, said that the collection had been acquired before the Second World War and brought to Hong Kong when the owner fled from Shanghai during the Sino-Japanese war. He was "a well-known Hong Kong millionaire who wishes to remain anonymous," and his identity was therefore a matter of intense speculation. He had, however, furnished flawless provenance for most—if not all—of his pieces, some of which, the catalogue stated candidly, had been acquired through channels other than "the usual ones," but inspection at the preview would confirm their quality. The two preview evenings had been sellouts. As would the auction itself be. She sighed again as she looked at her provisional figure. It was daring, it was incredible but, she was sure, it would be reached. Be bold, her own father used to tell her, and people will believe you. Hesitate and you are lost, because they will exploit your doubt. Tell them a thing is so often enough and they will come to believe it as a time-honored truth. Which was why she had prepared for this auction over long months, bringing it forward once she knew she was going to have to fight Kate Despard. She had run into some opposition on that, but had argued persuasively for advancing the date because of the publicity it would generate. "The feud is already a newspaper fact; all the columnists keep it in sight and alive. My stepsister and I are what the Americans call hot news, which can only benefit our forthcoming sale."

She had gone to great pains to ensure that her sale would generate the optimum in atmosphere as well as attendance and profit. She had employed a Chinese decorator to make of the enormous conference room where the auction would be held a hall in a Chinese palace; she had plundered Despard's storerooms for carpets, hangings, tables, incense burners, paintings, and exquisite examples of Chinese calligraphy. The predominant colors were red—the Chinese color of good luck—and yellow, also of fortunate aspect. She herself planned to wear a traditional Chinese robe, once worn by a mandarin, of red and gold silk, with a Good Luck Dragon breathing Fortunate Fire curving its way around the body, and bands of exquisite embroidery around the wide sleeves. The whole ambience was one of sumptuous grandeur, a fitting setting for the pieces themselves, which would be displayed on a lacquer table, itself unique and worth a fortune.

She had even gone so far as to consult a geomancer on the most propitious day to hold the auction, to establish the correct *feng shui,* when the eight elements of nature and the spirit of the *Yin* (female passive) and *Yang* (male active) would be balanced to perfection. She knew that even a whisper of bad *feng shui* would keep rich Chinese buyers away. The fact that it was good had been of incalculable assistance in creating the now near-panic to attend. Even the refreshments she would provide were classic Chinese, consisting of the five tastes: acid, hot, bitter, sweet, and salty. She would provide a Chinese wine—*mao tai*— as well as vintage champagne, Krug '59, for the Europeans, along with several kinds of tea, including *bo lay,* or black tea. She knew, after running the Hong Kong branch of Despard's for seven years, that presentation was everything to the Chinese. If her guests went away less than ecstatic, it would not be for want of trying. Her own ecstasy would derive from the prices reached.

Her feeling of sure success served to smooth away the irritation caused by her *faux pas* over the Chandler collection. She had also succeeded in resoldering her husband's chain, dropping entirely the matter of the collection once she saw it was absolutely beyond bounds. For now, anyway. Once the old lady was dead . . . that was another story, one she would have no hesitation in rewriting. It all served to confirm her view of Kate Despard as an inexperienced *ingénue* with no head for business, and only a bowl of mush where her heart should be. Even so, Dominique was in no way inclined to let the sale of Courtland Park and its treasures go her stepsister's way. That would be far too dangerous. From what she had learned, it was London's biggest auction of the year and a match to her own; it would give Kate Despard far too much of a lift up the ladder. That was why Dominique was flying to London later that night. Everything was in readiness here—she had time to spare; why not use it to make sure every rung on the ladder was sawed through . . .

She got up from her desk, stretched like some sleek cat, and then walked over to the windows; dusk was falling, the lights of Hong Kong beginning to glow. She loved this city, loved its bustle, its thrusting impatience with anything that stood in the way of a large, fast profit. Money was Hong Kong's *raison d'être*, and as it was also her own, she understood it. She had come to Hong Kong to learn, to keep London supplied with a steady stream of Chinese artifacts, and had gradually built up a thriving salesroom of her own. When Charles had seen how well she handled it, he had given her a free hand. It was *hers*, in a way that London had belonged to Charles, and New York would, if she had her way, eventually belong to her: she wanted it all, but most of all she did not want to lose Hong Kong.

Now, she thought contentedly, as she gazed out over the sparkling lights, I won't. Everything ready to go off here, and enough time to pay a quick visit to London to make sure Courtland Park is off limits to Kate Despard. She had worked out her moves, knew each piece on the board—especially Nicholas Chevely. Kate might be a pawn, but he was the king she had to take—and quickly. It was quite some time since she had played this particular game, she realized. It was doubly fortunate that this one had come up. It would serve to keep her hand in . . .

"I think," Rollo said, watching Kate combing through that morning's issue of *The Times* for news of the government's decision on Courtland Park and finding none, "that I would like to go to Hong Kong for this so-called Sale of the Century."

Kate lowered the paper. "You!"

"Why not? I have a hankering to revisit scenes of my youth and get an eyeful of what your sister has been up to."

"You know Hong Kong?"

"I was there during the war."

As far as Kate knew, he had been with ENSA, entertaining the troops during the war. "But Hong Kong was occupied by the Japanese for most of it."

"Not while I was there," Rollo demurred.

"In any case, James Grieve is going in his capacity as head of the Oriental Department."

"And quite right, too. I had in mind a more—unofficial capacity."

Kate searched his face suspiciously. It was wearing that too smooth, newly plastered look that she knew hid a whole heap of ulterior motives. Her eyes narrowed. "What do you know that I don't?"

"Nothing yet," he answered promptly, "but I have a feeling . . ." He laid a long finger to the side of his nose. "If it were your sale she would have spies salted along with the peanuts."

"Why didn't you mention it earlier?"

"I had not received my invitation then."

"Your *what?*"

"Oh, not to the auction. Hardly that. My invitation is from an old friend. He happens to live in Hong Kong."

"How convenient," she marveled acidly.

"Isn't it though," Rollo agreed blandly. "It's not as though I am tied up with anything else. We have done all we can on the Courtland Park thing; preparations are so far advanced that if you don't land it you are going to face a lot of flack from your fellow directors."

"I am aware of that."

"Can't you get Nicholas Chevely to commit himself one way or another?"

"No. He's not the only executor, you know."

"Maybe, but he is the one who counts. He was very thick with old man Courtland." Then maliciously, "If you were to let him thicken things with you . . ."

Kate leveled a look that had him shrugging his shoulders. "Suit yourself. But it is not unknown for such things to happen in the art world."

"It is in mine," Kate said shortly. "My job is to sell Despard's, not myself."

"It never did your stepsister any harm."

"They don't call *me* the Venus Flytrap."

"True . . ." agreed Rollo in a way that made her ask sharply, "But they do call me? What?"

"Well, they do say you place an impossibly high reserve on yourself."

Kate bridled.

"Now come on, dear heart. Everyone knows that Nicholas Chevely is laying siege. I understand that bets are actually being placed . . ." Her eyes flashed. "Our rivals, of course, will unhesitatingly place the blame where it lies—that being bed—should they lose."

"Bastards," muttered Kate from clenched teeth. "If only the government would get off their behinds!"

"Which is precisely why I wish to get off mine. *I* can do no more. And I think you will agree that I have done a great deal."

"Oh, yes," Kate agreed warmly. "Your ideas are right on target. It will more than equal Hong Kong if we can bring it off."

"You are holding the rod and line," Rollo pointed out gently. "It is up to you to play the fish."

"He likes our presentation, I know he does. He really was impressed and I'm sure the other two have not come up with anything like it."

"The heart of the matter is what you can come up with—or should I say across?" Rollo stated silkily.

"I do *not* do business that way. Nor will I ever. Papa always said that if you lose the respect of your market you may as well go out of business."

"Why then, are we steadily losing out to New York? If it

goes on you will be out of business anyway once your stepsister takes control."

"I still have more than half my year left—a lot can happen in that time. I got the Van Halen coin collection, didn't I? And the Picassos made a fortune—thanks to you."

"Small beer. The only way to acquire the champagne is Courtland Park. We have *got* to land it. Otherwise you may as well surrender."

"Never!"

Rollo noted the heightened color and changed tack. "How is the auctioneering coming along?"

"Better and better. David is really pleased with me."

"I'm glad *somebody* is pleased," Rollo sniffed.

Baffled, Kate said with frustration, "You do know something, don't you? Something you want to check out?"

"My curiosity has been aroused. I will tell you this, though. I am now convinced that Hong Kong is where the T'ang horse came from."

Kate's mouth opened. Rollo nodded, held up a hand to forestall more questions. "I have my sources" was all he would say, leaving Kate in a fever of curiosity. "So, why not kill two birds with one stone. See if I can find out if that is where the horse came from and what we can learn from Dominique's style."

The idea had merit, Kate conceded grudgingly. James Grieve would bring back a full report, but it needed a Rollo to do justice to the ambience of the whole thing; he would see and hear a great deal James would miss—would not even think of, come to that. He had not Rollo's devious approach to things, his innate and finely tuned sensitivity to atmosphere, his seemingly worldwide contacts. She would learn so much more from him than from James, down to a detailed description of what Dominique had been wearing, including her perfume.

"You'd never get a hotel room at this late date," she frowned, which told him she had been won over.

"I don't need one," he said smugly. "I shall stay with my friend."

Kate's glance was exasperated. "You've already got it all together, haven't you? Even your plane ticket?"

"I took the precaution of making a reservation."

Kate had to laugh. "Oh, all right. How long will you be away? The sale is spread over three days."

"A week should do it, I think."

"Fine." Kate sighed resignedly. "I'll arrange with accounts to give you an expense account—but for God's sake don't go mad. I'm already in their black books over this damned presentation."

"Worth every penny," Rollo assured her confidently. "Were it anybody but that smoothie Chevely I would say we had it made." An exaggerated sigh. "But it seems it depends on him making you . . ." He retreated in mock alarm.

"Call me when you have news," Kate threw at him.

He shook his head. *"Pas devant les rumeurs,* dear heart. Whatever I find—if anything—I will relate personally."

Again Kate stared. "You *do* know something!"

"Nothing I can say at this time," he intoned immovably.

Because he wouldn't or couldn't, Kate thought. What *has* he come across? There has to be something. Unlike Mr. Micawber, Rollo never wasted time on expectations. But she kissed him goodbye affectionately. He had been a good boy of late; Courtland Park had kept him so occupied he had not had a chance to meddle elsewhere, and his sense of theatre would result in a sale the likes of which had never been seen before—and that included Hong Kong. Surely Nicholas had seen that; surely he was not demanding that she not only give of herself but that very self as well. The cold-bloodedness of it all made Kate's flesh chill. Love would have nothing to do with it. It would merely be the price she had to pay: heartless and soulless sex. The thing was, though, she knew everybody at Despard's was looking to her to land this sale.

The Dominique faction had lost ground; Kate's passionate and wholehearted immersion in the business, as well as her eagerness to learn, had gone a long way toward cementing her position. Her ruthless removal of Piers Lang, not only from the scene but from the picture, had caused a tremor of shock. She had been careful, had taken legal advice, found she was right in thinking she could not fire him without incontrovertible proof of his involvement in the affair of the fake. Without that, he would undoubtedly sue her for wrongful dismissal, bringing the kind of publicity Despard's did not need. But she could transfer him? she had inquired. But of course, they said. An admirable solution . . .

So she had summoned him to her office one morning. He came in with the jaunty air of one who was still confident of his standing. He had professed himself, at the time, to be both shocked and horrified by the Hobart debacle, had sworn he had not dreamed . . . could not for the life of him think who would want to do such a thing . . . he would, in future, be ultra careful. Now, even though it was months later, he still felt a need to repeat his assertions.

"I trust that my efforts of late have gone some way to atoning for my stupidity over the fake horse," he said earnestly. "I think you will agree that I have more than made up for it by the recent acquisitions I have put your way."

It was true he had redoubled his efforts, resulting in a fine Constable, a set of eight Hepplewhite chairs that had the head of that department drooling, and a lovely Jacobean press, circa 1604.

"Since you have seen fit to rely on Mr. Bellamy for personal services," he said, with just a hint of reproach, "I have been able to give all my time to scouting around."

Kate ignored the dig. She was under no illusions. He had done no more than cover his tracks, and her attitude had been that she might as well make use of him while she could. So when he took the chair she indicated, and sat there obediently, like a puppy anxious to prove it would never again soil a priceless carpet, Kate let him have it right between the eyes.

"I sent for you to tell you that I am transferring you to our Australian branch," she said baldly.

His smile congealed. "Australia!" Shock echoes ricocheted.

"The fledgling branch in Sydney. I think it is in need of someone of your considerable . . . talents."

"But—there is no fine art in Australia," he protested. "And I have never been there. I know nothing about that country." And don't want to, remained unsaid.

"Now is your chance to learn. Sydney is, I am told, a very fine city. Think of that amazing opera house, and those fantastic beaches."

"But no fine art," he insisted desperately. "Australians buy, but they have none to sell that I know of."

"Oh, but they have," Kate disagreed, enjoying this. "I am informed that aboriginal art is going to be the next big craze."

"Aboriginal!" he said faintly.

"Yes, indeed. Every bit, they tell me, as powerful as the Benin bronzes that are so fashionable right now. They, too, are primitive art. Isn't Rolf Hobart mad for them?"

That name had the effect of a flick of the whip. "I thought Mr. Hobart was now persona non grata at Despard's London," he said carefully, at last.

"He is." Kate paused, then launched her second missile. "So are you."

His jaw dropped and while he was mentally struggling to get up from the floor Kate kicked him. "In the privacy of this room, Mr. Lang, let me tell you that your explanation of your involvement in the fake piece of T'ang is acceptable for public consumption only. Be in no doubt that I am aware of exactly what you did and who told you to do it."

She saw the convulsive start he gave and the flare of panic in the baby blues, which he quickly quelled.

"Unfortunately, proving it is something I am not able to do—as yet. If I could I would fire you here and now. However . . ." The tone of her voice had his hopes leaping. "Tell me where the horse came from and I will reconsider Australia. Perhaps . . . Los Angeles? I am sure you would be a treat in Beverly Hills."

She saw the hope die. It had been a stab in the dark. Kate had tended to doubt him grabbing the opportunity. Unlike Sir Anthony Blunt, he was more afraid of his "handler" than his hunters. He confirmed her surmise by falling back on injured innocence.

"I repeat, Miss Despard. I know nothing about that fake horse beyond what I told you. We were all taken in . . . why, Julian Pothecary was livid . . ."

"So am I," Kate told him, "to find you are working for my stepsister rather than for me."

"You have no proof of wrongdoing on my part," he said with a confidence Kate proceeded to shatter.

"How about going to see my stepsister on the very day I took over at Despard's?"

She saw him swallow. "I did fly to Geneva that day," he admitted cautiously, "but on my way to Lausanne."

"You went nowhere near Lausanne. You took a taxi from the airport direct to my stepsister's villa. You arrived at one o'clock. At four, that same taxi arrived to take you back to the airport."

Rollo had turned up this information. Kate did not know how and did not want to. All that mattered was that he had done it.

"All right . . . I will admit I did go to see her," Piers Lang said now, with a stricken look, "but only because she summoned me. I would remind you that though circumstances have changed for you, Madame du Vivier is still a power to be reckoned with at Despard's, and as such, must be obeyed by the likes of me. She wanted to ask me about that Constable I brought you; she wanted me to put it her way rather than yours. Naturally, I refused," he said with proud dignity.

"It took you three hours to say no?"

"She offered me lunch," he said haughtily.

"And what else?"

He stiffened. "I resent that remark."

"You can resent it all you like. It is still Australia." Kate paused. "Or resignation. Suit yourself."

"Obviously I do not wish to stay where I am just as obviously not wanted."

"Then I shall expect your resignation on my desk within the hour." Kate was cold, hard, unyielding. She longed to say more but bridled her unruly tongue, ever mindful of the complications that could arise. It was enough that his removal would serve as a warning to any other mole waiting in its carefully concealed tunnel. And just how many of them are there? she thought worriedly. He rose to his feet, stiff with hurt dignity. "You shall have my resignation," he told her disdainfully. "I am as eager to go as you are to get rid of me."

The door slammed behind him.

Adrenaline flowing, Kate next sent for Mrs. Hennessy. Here she again had no proof, only the certainty that her personal secretary was a listening post for information with destination Paris. Besides, she could not stand the woman and had no intention of working with her.

When she informed the Hennessy that she was being transferred to the Kensington branch, the red face deepened to purple.

"Kensington!" she spluttered, likening it to Siberia.

"I need someone of your—caliber—down there to tighten things up. Someone to keep an eye on things, and you always know everything that goes on, don't you?"

The pebble eyes narrowed, but the Hennessy was made of stronger stuff than Piers Lang.

"Wield the lash down at Kensington," Kate told her, again enjoyably. "Things have gotten rather lax down there."

"Nothing ever happens at Kensington except rubbish sales and you know it!" was the venomous reply.

"That rubbish brings in a steady income. Your salary will be maintained because I am placing you in charge administratively. Whatever else you might or might not be, you are a superb administrator."

"Do not think to fob me off with flattery, Miss Despard. Whichever way you look at it, a transfer to Kensington is a demotion."

"*I* do not see it as such, Mrs. Hennessy, and around here, *I* run things. Is that understood?"

The pouter pigeon bosom heaved. "I have done nothing to deserve such cavalier treatment. Twenty-five years I have given to this firm, during which time I have done nothing to merit such a shabby return for all those years of loyalty and devotion."

"I am fully aware of where your loyalty lies, Mrs. Hennessy. I took that into account in making my decision."

The golden eyes clashed with the hard blue ones, which was when Sheelagh Hennessy realized she had backed the wrong horse, while she herself was destined for the horsemeat factory. She would not be in on anything down in the darkness of Kensington. She would hear no gossip, be of no use whatsoever to the woman with whom she had hoped to rise to the heights.

"Very well, Miss Despard," she said as calmly as she could. "I see now why you took on a second secretary. No doubt you will wish me to instruct her as to her further duties . . ."

"Penny knows what to do," Kate replied crisply, "and I trust her to do it."

The purple cheeks deepened alarmingly and the thin mouth worked for a moment, but the Hennessy needed this job, no matter where it was.

"You are expected at Kensington tomorrow morning," Kate told her. "Be there."

Once more the massive bosom heaved with suppressed fury, then the Hennessy turned and marched out. When she slammed the door it rocked on its hinges.

Within a week of disposing of those two, Kate received a flurry of other resignations from people who saw the writing on the wall. To her surprise, they were not as many as she might have expected. Those who are left, she thought, are either for me one hundred percent or dug in too deeply to be worried. Well, time and events will tell.

She had also dealt with Rollo's interfering ways, and his own hard work on the Courtland Park presentation, a major talking point in the building, had served to consolidate her control. She had whipped from under Sotheby's nose the finest Velázquez to come on the market for many a year, and David Holmes had let it be known that Kate was coming along splendidly as an auctioneer. But she knew that everything hung on her ability to acquire the Courtland Park sale for Despard's. Everyone was waiting to see if she would, and how she would accomplish it. Her way, or her stepsister's way. As Rollo had said, people were taking bets.

The trouble was that Kate could not regard sex as a commodity to be traded in the marketplace. To her, sex was an aspect—one of many—of love. To Dominique, and to Nicholas Chevely also, love was an aspect of sex, and one, Kate was convinced, neither attached any importance to, just as they placed expediency way above principle.

Even running her little shop, Kate had never compromised her integrity; the lessons her father had taught her had long been imprinted on her persona; now they were being put to the test. And tonight, she thought now, will see whether they will hold up. Because Nicholas was taking her to the Royal Opera House—Joan Sutherland was singing *La Somnambula*—followed by a late supper. At which Kate was going to tell him that she expected him to judge her by what she could do professionally; that personally she was not on the market, now or ever. If she lost Courtland Park then so be it: but if she went to bed with him, she would never know afterward if it had been she as a woman or she as a businesswoman who had won the prize.

It was blackmail, pure and anything but simple. But in a way, she supposed, she had been using him even as he was prepared to use her. He had been an educator, one she needed.

She talked about it with Charlotte, the first woman with whom she had ever discussed anything sexual.

"Women's bodies have always been a commodity to men— why else prostitutes?" Charlotte said prosaically. "There are those prepared to deal with men on their level and those who are not. You, my dear Kate, belong to the latter group. And I suspect it has a great deal to do with your father."

"In what way?" Kate asked, puzzled.

"You were how old—fourteen?—when he left you, a delicate time when girls are developing sexually. I think his desertion torpedoed that development; sexual feelings became too painful to bear. Your father had given you so much love and admiration and that sense of your own value which is very important to a woman; when he went to another woman who had a daughter only a few years older than you, you saw it as a rejection of your own femaleness. So you turned your back on that and all it meant; you went to the other extreme. Why else the jeans, the lack of any kind of adornment, the stubborn rejection of all that men look for in a woman?"

"I never thought of that," Kate said slowly, stunned.

"You would not allow yourself to think of anything to do with him. But it is different now. Your father has given you much more than Despard's. He has given you back yourself, and that self is strong enough to know that your way is not the road Nicholas Chevely is bent on enticing you down. And you are quite right. It can lead to disaster—look at Marilyn Monroe. Too many men, too much sex for sale did her in in the end. Each time you sell yourself you lose a bit of that self; I think she got to the stage where she had nothing left; no self to esteem at all. It is the fact that you have rediscovered yours that gives you the strength to say no." She smiled. "You perhaps think I am the last woman in the world to be telling you this, three husbands and God knows how many lovers but—and it is a big but—that is what they were . . . lovers. I loved them and they loved me. I never slept with a producer or a director to get *any* part."

Kate had felt an enormous jolt of the confidence she badly needed, beset as she was by doubt as to whether to put herself or Despard's first.

"I never knew your father, but I do not think he would have wanted you to emulate your stepsister, who has lost as many commissions as she has gained through her—methods. There are some men—not many, alas—but some who are actually repelled by such commerce. Her reputation is a byword; her nickname self-explanatory. I do not think your father would have wished you to become so—well-known." An encouraging smile. "There will be other sales."

Kate shook her head. "Not like this one—and not this

year. It would bring me equal with her and the success would bring others."

That she was still deeply troubled was obvious. But she had pondered on what Charlotte said and recognized the truth of it. "Never compromise your integrity," her father had told her many times. "Once it is lost, so much else goes with it. You must be seen to be trustworthy; you must be seen to have honor and probity and a desire to do your very best for the client. Your job is to sell the goods the client has offered you—no more, and for the best price you can reach."

Yes, she thought now, feeling her certainty return. It is. And that's what I'll do. I'll tell him so tonight . . .

Nicholas had a box. "My firm is a sponsor of Covent Garden," he shrugged. "It impresses the clients." He smiled. "As you, my dear Kate, impress me. You look lovely."

Once more Kate blessed Charlotte, who had recommended a bronze paper taffeta gown, one of Bruce Oldfield's best. Kate had winced when she saw its price but ignored the pain.

La Stupenda was in marvelous voice and Kate was enthralled. When the curtains closed after the last of many calls, she turned shining eyes to her companion. "That was glorious . . . thank you, Nicholas."

"Well, you did say you liked opera." He stood up to place her wrap—of mink-lined taffeta the same color as her dress—about her shoulders. "Myself, I don't get as carried away as you so obviously were."

"Music has that power," Kate admitted, with a still dreamy sigh.

"Obviously. I envy it."

Kate opened her mouth, shut it again. Over supper, she decided.

It took an age to make their way down the stairs, and it was as they were making their way through the crowded foyer that a voice, enchantingly accented, purred, "Kate? My dear, I did not recognize you . . ."

Nicholas Chevely saw Kate's face lose its radiance and turned, as she did, to see a breathtakingly beautiful woman, adrift in sapphire silk and swathed in blue chinchilla. Just behind her stood a short, attractively ugly man.

"How are you, my dear Kate? How fortunate to run into

you here. I have not been to London in an age. So much to do elsewhere . . ."

She now looked openly at Nicholas, holding out a hand. "How do you do. I am—"

"I know who you are," he said, raising her hand to his lips.

Dominique's glittering smile matched the sapphires at her throat and in her ears.

"Nicholas Chevely," Kate introduced tonelessly.

"And this is an old friend—Raoul de Chevigny; he is with the French Embassy here."

The short dark man bowed over Kate's hand and in his brown eyes she caught a gleam of either sympathy or complicity, she could not be sure which. Her own smile was merely a movement of the mouth. Her face felt stiff, her body frozen. She had a sudden inexplicable feeling that all was lost, and she shivered.

"Are you cold?" Nicholas asked concernedly. "Let me see if I can find the car . . ."

Kate was so deadened with the sick feeling of sudden and certain failure that she felt nothing; she was not surprised when all four of them got into the big black Rolls. She knew the meeting was contrived, just as she knew what Dominique's purpose in contriving it was: to see that she did not get Courtland Park. Dominique would do what Kate had so far refused to: whatever Nicholas Chevely wanted, in or out of bed. Kate felt her ice begin to thaw as anger began to burn. How could he? she thought. How *could* he? He is the only person who could have told her I was seeing Nicholas. He must have gone straight back to New York and told her everything. How *could* he? She felt sick with betrayal. So much for Blaise Chandler's vaunted policy of noninvolvement. She had been right to suspect he would support his wife in all things, even to destroying Kate's hopes of catching up with her stepsister. That she should come to London now, with her own Sale of the Century only days away, was proof of how important Dominique regarded her task. Even as she thought so, she felt the force of someone's gaze and turned from the window to meet her stepsister's brilliant eyes; they were alight with malice and delighted recognition of Kate's misery. I told you not to take me on, they said. I warned you I had not yet begun to fight . . .

You bitch! Kate's own, unsmiling stare said. You heartless, cold, conniving, cheating bitch!

The rest of the evening was a nightmare; as she had known, all four ended up having supper together, and Dominique bent the force of her sexuality on Nicholas Chevely to such an extent that Kate and the Frenchman might just as well not have been present. As Kate sat in cold misery she caught that same glint in the Frenchman's eyes; it *was* sympathy, she realized. He, too, knew exactly what Dominique was doing. When he asked her to dance she rose at once; it was better than sitting at the table like the Invisible Woman.

He danced superbly; he was a good head shorter than Kate, and she looked over his shoulder sightlessly, drowning in misery.

"You must not, you know," he said quietly.

Kate roused herself. "Not what?"

"Let her win. You withdrew as soon as you set eyes on her. Why?"

Kate's smile was faint. "Have you seen the way his eyes look at her?"

"He is important to you?"

"Not in the way you think," Kate answered, too heavy-hearted to explain. She felt as if the earth's gravity had changed; she seemed to weigh a ton, most of it her heart.

"Ah . . ." nodded the Frenchman softly. "I see. It is to do with your—rivalry in business?"

"Yes."

"I knew there was something." A wry smile. "With Dominique, there always is." They danced in silence for a while before he asked bluntly, "Why do you not fight her?"

"I don't have her weapons or her indiscriminate way of using them."

"Ah . . ." he said again, understanding it all. "Most of all, I think, her assumption that you will not fight her superior strength?"

"I know my own strength," Kate answered, "and it lies in other directions."

"Which is what she is capitalizing on, as always."

"You sound as if you know her well."

"Better, perhaps, than anyone, and for many years . . ."

This time Kate's smile was ironic. "So she does have friends, then."

His answering smile was equally ironic. "She has them

strategically distributed." He must have felt Kate's distaste because he said, with all the realism of a Frenchman, "One takes what one can."

You, too? thought Kate. What is it about her power over men? Even a man like Blaise Chandler. Pain flared again. She felt mortally hurt. After Colorado, after the rapport they seemed to have established, he could still do this. Rollo was right: you could not trust anyone, anywhere, at any time.

"Could we go back to the table?" she asked abruptly.

It was deserted, and when Kate searched the dance floor she saw Nicholas was smiling down at the small, upturned, lovely face, a look on his own that made her turn away blindly. Oh, God, she thought. I've lost, I've lost, I've lost . . . She felt her eyes fill with tears. "I think I'll go," she managed to say, from a thick, painful throat. "I have a busy day tommorrow."

"Please, let me accompany you."

"No." She wanted to be alone. "Please, stay . . ."

"What shall I tell your—friend?"

"That I have a—headache," Kate said, substituting that last word for the truth, which was heartache.

"You are making a mistake," he said quietly.

"No, only having one confirmed."

He rose to his feet with her, took the hand she offered, and raised it to his lips. *"Bonne chance,"* he said sincerely.

Kate forced a smile, then turned and walked quickly away.

In the taxi she leaned back and let her misery sweep over her. Oh, Charlotte, she thought, you were wrong. Around her I have no confidence at all . . .

Who said, when she called Kate next morning to see how it went, "You should not have left the field to her, Kate. You should have fought her."

"How? She's got some—mesmerizing influence on men; one look and they follow blindly. She knew I knew what she was doing and she reveled in it! She was showing me her power."

"Have you heard from Nicholas?"

"No. Nor do I expect to, until he tells me Courtland Park has gone elsewhere."

"You are so sure it will?"

"That's why she came, isn't it? She wouldn't think twice

about sleeping with him, or anything else, to get what she wants. She can do it without thinking. I—I can't, that's all. I just can't."

"But your presentation—I thought you had such confidence in it."

"I do—it's Nicholas in whom I have none."

She heard Charlotte sigh. "No, he is not exactly a rock to lean on. In the city he is regarded as a slippery customer."

"I never did manage to get a good grip on him," Kate said with a half-laugh, half-sob.

"He is also a realist," Charlotte said briskly. "His brief is to make as much as possible for Courtland Park. He is a beneficiary under the old man's will—"

"What!"

"You didn't know?"

"He never said."

"No, he wouldn't. He wanted it all. You and the fattest five percent available. The rest goes to some foundation to give scholarships to young Americans who want to live and learn in Europe—something like the Fulbright. But his aim will be to get the maximum for himself, not some unknown group of Americans."

"That puts an entirely different complexion on things," Kate said, feeling hope, which she had thought had been crushed to death last night, stir feebly.

"Which is why he didn't tell you. If I know Nicholas—and I do, believe me, I do—he will not let your stepsister sway his decision one little bit. His reputation as a womanizer is a smoke-screen for the lifelong affair he's been having with money. He has a very expensive lifestyle to keep up. When it comes down to the bottom line, as our American friends say, it will be in a financial statement. Don't give up, Kate. If your ideas for the sale are the ones which make the prettiest financial picture then he will see to it that you handle it, no matter what your sister offers him."

"Even if he thinks me a shocking emotional coward?"

"He will still not allow himself to make an emotional decision. Like all womanizers, he is, *au fond,* a cold-hearted bastard."

Kate's mercurial spirits had shot from frozen to tropical. "Oh, I hope you are right!" she exclaimed. "And as you usually are, I feel so much better now."

"You are an emotional creature, Kate; you don't stop to

think when your feelings are in full spate, and you don't have your sister's experience either. I wonder," she went on shrewdly, "if it was that quality of innocence which attracted a hardened campaigner like Chevely to you in the first place. Eighty years ago he would have been the kind of man mamas warned their daughters about whilst arranging assignations of their own. Anyway," she ended briskly, "don't regard your flight as your Waterloo. His criteria will be profits, not personalities. I'd take bets on it . . ."

Which would have won. Nicholas Chevely had no intention of changing a mind which had been quickly made up once he saw what Kate Despard had in mind for Courtland Park. It was so audacious as to be breathtaking, an extravaganza rather than a sale. The representatives from the other two houses had been properly appreciative and quietly confident in the reserves they set, but he knew that a good salesman made all the difference and that when it came to salesmanship he had no doubt that Despard's had it all over them.

He had not told Kate because he was intrigued by her; it had been a long time since he had pursued anything so fresh, so untouched, so eminently beddable; he had been amused yet enchanted by her confusion, her blushes, her sweetness. He had sensed she was torn, wanting the sale badly, desperately, even. What he wanted to find out was just how far that desperation would carry her. Like his bed, for instance.

When he had returned to the table to find her gone, he had known at once why. But then, he thought, there were few women who could stand up to Dominique du Vivier in full cry. He showed the proper concern, even while Dominique showed her triumph. And he was the last man to turn away such goodies.

Which were, he thought next morning, soaking himself in the shower of Dominique's sumptuous bathroom, all he had heard them to be. He gingerly soaped his tender groin. He had a voracious sexual appetite of his own, was quite capable of having several women a day, but Dominique du Vivier was incredible. Even when he was exhausted she was still capable of more, much more. It was a long time since he had spent a night of such unbridled eroticism. Now, he thought, smiling to himself, she would present her bill.

Which was shown to him with the same exquisite skill. She never once said the word "don't"; she merely suggested that if he had any sense he would let the acknowledged experts in the field put their talents to work. Subtly, she denigrated her stepsister, pointing out her novice status, her as yet un-proved worth, the chance he would be taking. Nobody in their right minds would back a two hundred-to-one outsider when everyone knew the favorite was unbeatable.

He listened seriously, showed signs of some unease, al-lowed a frown to appear, nodded thankfully. "I am grateful for your undoubtedly expert advice," he told her finally. "You have all the experience and know-how that your sister lacks, but as you know, my hands are tied when it comes to choosing the right house; the late Mr. Courtland was quite phobic in his anti-Americanism." This was said with just the right amount of regret.

Her own matched it perfectly. "I know . . . I could have done so much for you."

"You have already done more than enough."

Her smile bathed him.

"I have asked around," he went on diffidently, "and I must say you are not alone in your opinion. Had the late Charles Despard been alive . . ."

"That," Dominique said with a butterfly sigh, "would indeed have been different." Then, with perfectly judged anxiety, "You understand—it is Despard's reputation which concerns me. Wrongly handled, such a sale could have disas-trous results for its future."

"Indeed," he agreed at once.

Another smile. "I knew you would understand . . ."

"Oh, I do, I do," he assured her, understanding perfectly. Kate Despard had a fight to the death on her hands; she was the Despard this delectable morsel was worried about. As well you might be, he thought. His smile hid his laughter. Oh, but you are in for such a sock to that ego of yours.

"I only wish I could stay in London a while longer," Dominique was saying, "but I return to Hong Kong today."

"Ah, yes, your Sale of the Century. Even I have heard about that."

"I think it is arousing a great deal of interest," Dominique purred modestly.

"I only wish I could be there," he told her truthfully. "I am sure it will be something quite remarkable."

"There has never been anything like it," she allowed confidently.

Nor you, he thought. He would not see her again. She was too dangerous. As it was, once she found out she had failed, he would be on her shit list.

He rose with the perfect amount of regret. Her own shrug was again its match. They were both, he realized, wanting to laugh badly, giving the performance of their lives. Neither of us gives a damn about anyone except ourselves, he thought. Yes, far too dangerous. But a pity, yes, a definite pity . . .

He sent flowers to Kate with a note expressing regret, and saying he hoped that when she was better she would let him see her again. And he did not call her until he saw in the tabloids a picture of Dominique at Heathrow, en route to Hong Kong, radiating the shiny shellac of success.

He then called his friend at the Department of the Environment; there had been no change: the government was still not of a mind to offer for Courtland Park. The economic climate was not right, et cetera, et cetera.

Kate was conducting yet another mock auction when she was told that Nicholas Chevely was asking to see her.

"Will you ask him to wait," she ordered crisply, and to the approving smile of David Holmes, finished the auction.

"Better, Kate," he told her happily. "You are coming on in leaps and bounds. I told you all it took was hard work, and I must say you really have put your shoulder to the wheel."

"Top of the hill?" she asked.

"I think so. It is time you took on your first big auction. There's a sale of Elizabethan miniatures coming up next week. I feel confident enough to let you handle it."

Kate drew a sharp breath. "You are sure?"

"Quite sure. You know what you are doing now."

"Only what you have taught me these past months."

"You have learned a very great deal," he told her seriously. "Your father would be proud of you."

"That," she said, "sets the seal on it. Thank you, David."

When she went into her office, Nicholas Chevely was standing at the window. He turned, and smiled.

"I hope you are feeling better?"

"Much," Kate answered truthfully.

"Good. Now I have news that will make you feel on top of the world. The government is not offering for Courtland Park."

Which was when Kate knew she had won. For a moment she felt her ears ring and her heart expand until it threatened to explode from her chest.

Reading her ever expressive face, "Yes," he smiled. "I am empowered by the executors of the estate of the late John Randolph Courtland to ask you to offer the contents of Courtland Park for sale as soon as may be convenient but not later than December 31st of this year."

Kate flung her arms around him in a bear hug and he found himself sharing her contagious joy. She really was a curious mixture, he thought, feeling oddly tender, not an emotion he normally experienced with women unless in bed—and inside—one of them. So decisively crisp and certain when it came to her work, so unsure and shy when it came to herself. Now, as she collected herself, she colored in that endearing way of hers and said with shy formality, "Thank you. Despard's will do its very best for you."

"I know that."

She seemed to hesitate, eyeing him as though he were Beechers Brook and she on a Shetland pony, before she jumped, "What finally convinced you?"

He knew she needed, even now, to be convinced. "Your presentation, of course. It is quite brilliant, containing ideas that are going to create a whole new attitude toward auctions. I also have every confidence that you will attain the reserves you have fixed. Actually, it was the one you were setting the first time I saw you that impressed me."

"When was that?"

"The day we met. I had been in Despard's for some time, getting the feel of the place. You were talking to an old lady with a coffeepot—"

"Mrs. Swan!"

"Whoever she was; you impressed me by the way you handled her. You identified the pot unhesitatingly and put a price on it which—I later checked out—it reached. I thought, well, it is only a small thing but if it is any indication of the bigger ones . . . Also, you did not attempt to cheat the old lady. Had you told her the pot was worth five hundred pounds she would have been thrilled to death and believed you without question. Her faith and trust in you were evident. I know little about sales at auction, but I am told it is not unusual for a small price to be paid for an object which is later sold for a very great deal; in fact, it is actively looked for."

"We do not have that kind of reputation at Despard's," Kate rebuked. "Nor do any of the great houses; I cannot say the same for some unscrupulous dealers, however . . ."

"No. I have made it my business to—delve into Despard's, as it were, and what I have found out has confirmed my opinion that you are the ones who will do best by Courtland Park."

This was said with the straightest of faces, but they both knew what he meant. Dominique had indeed tried to suborn him, and he had lain back and enjoyed it, but it had not affected his decision. You win some, you lose some, the expression on the handsome face was saying.

Kate repressed her awed amazement. Dominique had failed! But then she recalled Charlotte's shrewd surmise as to the outcome: sex was fine, was Nicholas Chevely's attitude, but even that had to be paid for . . .

"I think a celebratory drink is called for," she said gaily. "Which I just happen to have ready and waiting . . ."

Nicholas Chevely widened his eyes at the bottle of '59 Dom Perignon she handed him to open. "Indeed," he approved.

Kate poured the pale, straw-colored wine into two tall flutes and, as she handed him one and touched it with her own, sent a silent toast to Rollo, now winging his way across the Pacific. When he called her—he had not left her a number so she could not call him—she would give him the good news . . .

14

The news that Despard's had been chosen to handle the sale of Courtland Park made all the columns, the salesroom sections of the dailies and an item on television news—both channels. Kate was interviewed, photographed, and feted. The staff at Despard's was jubilant. Her phone never stopped and telegrams flooded in. Clients, old and new, were highly congratulatory, and a welcome side effect was the increase in offers for sale, including the Cornelia Fentriss Gardner jewel collection. She had been the only daughter of Duke Fentriss, an American multimillionaire, and had married into the English aristocracy before the First World War. Her passion had been jewels; her collection was said to rival that of the queen of England, and her will left instructions that, as her only son had been killed in 1940, the collection was to be sold.

When Kate received a call from the trustees of her estate, she lost no time in consulting Hugh Straker, head of the Precious Stones Department, and knowing little about jewelry herself, wisely left it to him to do the talking. She lent her presence, which since the news about Courtland Park had got out, had acquired a cachet Hugh lost no time in exploiting. She had fed him a few ideas, such as having the jewels worn by models at the auction, as well as *haute-couture* gowns to show them off to best advantage, with the result that agreement was quickly reached and the sale set for four months' time.

"By God, Kate!" Hugh said as they returned by taxi to Despard's. "This will set the cat among the pigeons. We've had some nice pieces to sell from time to time, but nothing like this lot! Your idea of using models was a cracker! Did you see the look on their faces? And yet it makes such sense . . . why hasn't it been done before?"

"I wasn't around," Kate told him with a glint in her eye.

"Thank God you are, then. Did you see those pearls? I've not seen anything like them since the Grand Duchess Natalya's, and that was a few years ago."

"As long as we don't have to buy anything in," Kate said with a twinkle.

"With that lot? Never. Jewels never lose their value, and quite apart from the stones themselves, the settings are fabulous. What with Courtland Park and this little lot you should be riding very high in the betting now, I can tell you."

"Well, the Sale of the Century enters its last day today, and according to James Grieve the net sales total is going to be in orbit. We need all we can get."

"And will get it now," Hugh said confidently. "Nothing succeeds like success . . ."

Which was exactly how Dominique felt. Everything had gone exactly to plan. It was as though fate had become her obedient servant. As it needed to be, once she heard about Nicholas Chevely's double-cross. She had thrown one of her tantrums, hurling things, screaming things, sending her servants scuttling. He would pay for this . . . And so would that conniving, innocent-seeming Kate Despard. At the Hong Kong opening, as Dominique had predicted, her setting caused a sensation; the palatial room, the incense burning headily, her own glorious appearance, and lastly, the pieces themselves, had caused a fever of bidding. At the end of the first day she had exceeded her provisional total by fifteen percent. The second was even better and, like the shrewd general she was, she had kept the best till last.

Now, standing in her pulpit, surveying the crowded room, heated by greed and excitement, she smiled to herself. Already the total sum raised was approaching twenty million U.S. dollars. Let her beat *that*, Dominique thought, as she sold a pair of glazed T'ang pottery Bactrian camels for HK$1,500,000. Really, they were so eager to say they had bought something at the Sale of the Century that prices were ridiculous. Among the T'ang was a sprinkling of treasures from later dynasties: a blue and white ewer of the Ming period that had gone to a Chinese for HK$2,000,000; a blue and white stem cup that had reached HK$650,000. She will need to do very well indeed with Courtland Park to beat me now, Dominique thought, as the last lot, a pair of the famous T'ang horses, was placed on the stand. She heard the collective intake of breath. The horses seemed about to gallop off, so alive were they: manes tossing, tails flying, hooves prancing. She was being entirely truthful when she told her rapt audience that they were the finest examples she had ever had the privilege of selling.

The bidding went mad. Never losing the beat she led her rival bidders up a spiraling ladder of one-hundred-thousand-dollar leaps and bounds, which changed to quarter-of-a-million increments at the end, so intense was the effort to acquire. The room was quivering with tension; the incense wreathed about faces concentrated and breath held as the bid went above HK$2 million, to be greeted with a drawn out hiss of disbelief. When her gavel finally thwacked down on HK$5 million, bid by a Chinese with no more than the barest of nods, the room fragmented into hysteria—on the part of the Europeans, that is. The Chinese sat as still as the carved figures she had sold.

Afterward, a tiny figure in scarlet and gold, she was surrounded by people eager to say they had actually spoken to her, congratulated her, on this night to remember. She should have felt drained, so concentrated had her own effort been—though she had shown nothing but tranquil control of everything and everyone—but she was exhilarated, on a high. She posed for photographs, declined champagne, but accepted a cup of fragrant tea, which she sipped as she listened with a smile to the babble of praise.

Not until much later, in the silk-hung, circular revolving bed in her mirror-lined penthouse bedroom, her explosive feelings having been released in the way she loved best, did she sit up to seize the champagne in its cooler on the bedside cabinet, a sixteenth-century example of Chinese lacquer work at its finest, pour two glasses, and hand one to her Chinese partner and lover. "We did it!" she exulted. "Two hard years of planning and work but we did it, we pulled it off!"

Her Chinese lover looked down at himself. "Not quite . . ."

Dominique laughed. She had never met anybody quite like Chao-Li. He had the sophistication of a five-thousand-year old civilization under the gloss of the very latest in high technology. He was also perfectly made; only a few inches taller than she was, but naked, he reminded her of a small Florentine bronze she had once bought purely because of its sensuality. His sex was commensurate with his size, but what he did with it confounded her, who thought she knew it all.

The Chinese had invented so much the West had not discovered until centuries later, that it was not surprising to find out they had also discovered sex. The names for what he did were as exquisite as the actions that accompanied them. He was capable of withholding until she begged for release, putting her through a whole series of shattering orgasms—the Clouds and the Rain as the Chinese called it. Always after him she felt drained as she never did with any other man, not even her husband. Only Chao-Li could reduce her to a ravening, panting animal and leave her all but dead. She loved it.

Almost as much as she had loved her Sale of the Century.

"The prices!" she gloated, nestling close to him on the high-piled pillows. "The sheer, naked greed."

"I told you," Chao-Li said.

Dominique giggled. "But greedy to buy fakes?"

"But *such* fakes—among a judicious salting of the genuine, for safety's sake . . ."

"True." Dominique glanced at her lover. "They really are something extraordinary." She ran her fingers lightly down his golden brown body. "You still won't tell me who does them?"

"I told you. I cannot. Our being allowed to sell them is on the condition that we ask no questions."

"How you Chinese love your mysteries." It was playful but there was an edge that cut.

"The more people who know the greater the danger of discovery. You have your profit, they have theirs. Why probe what is not your concern?"

Because I don't like to be left out, she thought. Chao-Li could be unshakably close-mouthed, again in characteristic Chinese fashion. When he had approached her she had at first been skeptical; dealing in fakes was dangerous, too many scientific ways of exposing them. But when he showed her one, she knew she was on to something incredible. She had asked how, where, who, had been told she either accepted the figures for sale, no questions asked, or they would find an alternative method of disposal. She accepted at once, biding her time. There are many ways to skin a cat. But over the two years it had taken to produce the necessary number, and all in total secrecy, to prepare the market by carefully placed rumors, to put out a catalogue that in itself was a work of art, she was still no wiser. Only her doubts had gone. Chao-Li had told her with unshakable confidence that there would be no lack of buyers; Hong Kong was the perfect place to dispose of the merchandise and the time was right, too. Red China poised in the wings, people eager to invest their money in appreciable, easily exportable works of art. He had been proved right in every respect. Prices had exceeded even her carefully judged estimate. There was no way Kate Despard would ever catch her now.

She had seen Despard's Chinese expert there, along with those from Sotheby's and Christie's and other top-flight auction houses, but she was disappointed that Kate Despard herself had not attended. Chinese porcelain and pottery was her field, after all. It was probably because she knew it meant the end of her hopes. Dominique laughed.

"Now what?"

"I was just thinking of the horse my stepsister sold to Rolf Hobart . . . the one she unhesitatingly pronounced to be genuine. If it fooled her then it will fool anybody."

"I told you," Chao-Li said again.

"She said it was two thousand years old." Another giggle. "How I would love to have told her it was less than two."

"If you had, you would not be here with me now."

She turned her head to meet his lucid almond eyes. Suddenly she shivered.

"No questions," he repeated.

"No questions," she agreed lightly. For now, she thought. And she had the consolation of knowing she had fooled all of the people all of the time. She liked that. All those self-important experts with their pompous pronouncements. She had fooled them all and made her domination an actual fact rather than a possibility. Not that she had ever doubted. The momentary hiccup in her plans caused by Courtland Park had been passed. From now on it was no more than coasting downhill. And with any luck, she would run right over Kate Despard at the bottom.

She was conscious of Chao-Li becoming amorous again and at once dismissed everything from her mind but him. Not that it was possible to think of anything else once he got started . . .

*   *   *

The shrilling telephone roused Blaise Chandler from dream-haunted sleep. He groped for the receiver and growled an irritable: "Yes?" into it.

"That's what I was hoping you would say, Boy."

"Duchess?" He sat up, switched on the light. "For God's sake, it's four A.M.

"Not here it isn't. I'm sorry if I disturbed your beauty sleep—or whatever else you were doing—but this is an emergency."

The urgency in her voice had him wide awake in seconds, fully alert and anxious.

"To do with what? Are you all right?"

"It's not me, it's Kate Despard."

Blaise swore. *"Now* what?"

"That old fairy she sets such store by got himself mugged in Hong Kong. He was taken to the Queen Elizabeth Hospital but I've been on to Benny Fong and he's had him moved into the Chandler Clinic. That's where Kate is. I want you to get yourself there and see what you can do—as soon as possible."

"What the hell was Rollo Bellamy doing in Hong Kong?"

"Attending your wife's sale, I suppose. Don't tell me you didn't know about that?"

Blaise let the jibe go. "What's it got to do with him being mugged?"

"That's what I want you to find out. I called London just to have a chat with Kate, but they told me she left for Hong Kong day before yesterday."

"Duchess, I've told you before and I'll tell you again. Don't go fixing me up as Kate Despard's guardian angel. She's old enough to take care of herself."

"I am aware of that, but I doubt she's had to cope with anything like this before. Besides," the old lady went on slyly, "didn't Charles ask you to watch out for her?"

"Watch out for, yes—not over."

"Same thing. That fairy is very important to her so she'll be pretty shaken up. I want you to be there for her to lean on."

"For God's sake, he's in the hospital, isn't he?"

"And all but broken, according to Benny. They did him over real good."

"Queer bashers normally do," Blaise said brutally, out of patience and out of temper.

"That's as may be; what worries me is Kate being there all alone with a man who might be dying—and who is also her closest friend. Everybody should have somebody at a time like this. I'd have you, wouldn't I?" Gruffly, "I've come to love that child, Blaise. She's a girl after my own heart—"

"It's what you are after I don't like, Duchess."

"Do it for me," the old lady coaxed. Sounding very tired and old, suddenly, "Do it for me if you won't do it for her."

"Come off it, Duchess," Blaise retorted, unimpressed. "This is me, remember?"

Her voice roaring into top gear, "Then do it because I tell you to, okay? I still run things around here."

"While I am not in the running for the position of Kate Despard's guardian angel," Blaise thundered.

"I still want you to go. Rollo is hurt bad—like to die, they said. That's why Kate's flown out there. If he does die she's going to need somebody." Wheedlingly, "It isn't much to ask, is it?"

Too much, Blaise thought furiously, but said, "All right. I'll get there as soon as I can."

"That's my Boy," the old lady said fondly. "And let me know right off whatever you find out."

She rang off with her customary abruptness.

Blaise replaced the receiver, waited a moment, then lifted it again and dialed. "Benny? Blaise Chandler."

He listened while Benny Fong, who ran ChanCorp in Hong Kong, gave him a concise rundown of the situation. Then he said, "Okay, I've got the outline. Now you color it in. Find out all you can, who and where and what, if the police are concerned, and where Kate Despard is staying. I'm leaving on the first flight I can get; meet me at Kai Tak. Do your usual thorough job, Benny. My grandmother is in on this one . . ."

"Will do, boss," he heard Benny answer cheerfully. Which meant, Blaise thought with a smile, that by the time he got to Hong Kong, he would know everything, down to the name and qualifications of the doctor looking after the injured man.

By the time he got into the car that came to take him to the airport, he was in a thoroughly bad mood. He had arrived in Johannesburg only seven hours before after a long flight from Tokyo. Now he had to go practically the whole way back again. And all because his grandmother was bent on weaving his life into a design of her own making, one that included Kate Despard. No way, Duchess! he thought derisively.

On the plane, when he should have been catching up on lost sleep, he found himself dwelling on his previous visit to Hong Kong just one week before. He had deliberately rearranged his schedule in order to see his wife on the eve of her much touted sale. But she had not had time to spare for him; everything was the sale, the sale, the sale . . . He had found himself hanging around, hoping to catch her in between, recognizing with a feeling of angry frustration that he was neither wanted nor needed at that particular point in time; she had a lot on her mind, and none of it concerned him.

When he had voiced his annoyance she had said at first, "But darling, you could not have chosen a worse time! Tomorrow is the most important night of my life. I must be ready for it."

But she had seen that he was in no mood to be put off and so had, he thought savagely, "squeezed him in." And then, to cap it all, for the first time in his life he had failed with a woman. Dominiqe had been livid. They had gone from that debacle into the worst fight ever. She furious because of wasted time, he manic with humiliation. Never before had he failed to rise to the occasion in the twenty-odd years he had been a practicing—which made perfect, Dominique would tell him—heterosexual. Now, for the first time since he had flung out of her bedroom in a rage, he found himself searching for a reason.

Tiredness was out. He had been in Tokyo, and after a solid eighteen hours of meetings had gone back to his hotel and slept for ten. He had awoken wanting her, known she was as near as dammit and decided to make a quick change in his schedule. Why, then, had it been so humiliatingly futile? Probably because she had kept him hanging about for so long—taken the edge off his desire. And yet always before one touch, one sight, one scent of that delectable, silken body and that exquisite face had been enough to arouse a ravenous hunger. He had once said jokingly that if she wanted to make quite sure he was dead, to come and stand over his coffin . . . Now, she had not only bent she had kneeled—and all to no avail.

The resulting row had been the humdinger of them all.

He'd often deliberately provoked arguments before just for the sheer ecstasy of making up. But not this time. Maybe he should have gone off and got laid elsewhere. Got it out of his system. It would have been the first time. In the two years they had been married he had not so much as looked at another woman. Dominique was more than enough. So why had he not been there? Why had he felt a thousand miles removed? Why had he looked at that perfect body and not ached with the desire to possess it? The feeling had gone, as they said in the songs. Had what started so violently and suddenly ended the same way?

Staring sightlessly out of his window at the heavy clouds, he did not know.

Benny Fong was at Kai Tak and, as usual, the magic words ChanCorp took care of the formalities quickly and easily. A smiling "Nice to see you again, Mr. Chandler," and his baggage was passed through customs. A "How long this time, Mr. Chandler?" and he was through passport control. The big car was waiting and when they were in the back of it, leaving the airport for the twenty-minute drive from Kowloon to Hong Kong, Blaise said, "Okay, Benny. What's the story?"

"He's in a bad way. Multiple fractures, including his pelvis. They had to remove his spleen. But the worst is the injury to his brain stem; that's why he's in a coma. His brain is not dead according to the brain scan they did on him, but it's not working properly—sort of shut down. All the doctors will say is that he has a fifty-fifty chance and that the next forty-eight hours will tell."

"Where did they find him?"

"Lying in a doorway on Tun Chau Street."

Blaise's head came around.

"Yes," Benny said inscrutably. "On the very edge of the Walled City."

"What the hell was he doing there?"

"Dressed and made up as a Chinese," Benny supplied.

"What!"

"True . . . they had no idea he was European till they got him into the emergency room at Queen Elizabeth and started to remove his clothes."

"How the hell was he identified, then?"

"He was reported missing twenty-four hours later by the Chinese he was staying with."

"A Chinese!"

"Man named Ling Po, keeps an antique and curio shop down on Lok Ku Road. Good reputation, nothing known. He says Rollo was an old friend he hadn't seen in years."

"Was that why he was in Hong Kong?"

"He says it was a private visit combined with attendance at Mrs. Chandler's sale—but in a private capacity. Despard's official representative was a Mr. James Grieve, who stayed at the Mandarin Hotel, where the sale was held."

What the hell? Blaise thought. What sort of double-dealing game had Bellamy been playing when they caught him at it? "Good work, Benny," he said out loud. "Keep on with it. Find out everything you can—what he was doing here, where he went." With a frown, "You say they did not know he was European till they got him to the hospital?"

"No, he would have passed for Chinese in the crowds, except for his height. He probably stooped."

Yes, Blaise thought. What I want to know is to what. "And the police?"

"They are expecting you. I told them of your arrival. That's where we are going now."

They were very polite, very respectful to Mr. Blaise Chandler of ChanCorp, one of the city's largest *hongs*.

"Mr. Bellamy was discovered by an old woman very early in the morning some four days ago; he was unconscious and covered in blood; at first she thought he was dead. It was when a passing police car caught sight of her searching the body and stopped to investigate that they found he was alive, but barely. He was taken at once to the Queen Elizabeth."

They confirmed what Benny had already told him: Mr. Ling Po was a respected dealer of antiquities in Hong Kong, and had been these many years. He had reported Mr. Bellamy missing when he did not return after going out dressed as a Chinese. He was an actor, Ling Po told them; he had wanted to see if his skill at makeup and playing a part would pass muster on the streets. He had said he would not be back until dinner time; when he had not returned by the following morning at 6 A.M., Ling Po reported him missing. When the unidentified Chinese was brought in, and turned out, once undressed and the blood and makeup washed away, to be a European, two and two were eventually put together. Ling Po identified his missing friend.

"He is also a friend of yours, Mr. Chandler?" the chief superintendent asked.

"No, a friend of a friend. Miss Kate Despard."

"Ah, yes. She arrived yesterday morning, and has been at the bedside ever since."

"Miss Despard is chairman and managing director of Despard's of London." He paused. "My wife is her stepsister." He said nothing about Rollo working for Despard's. "Mr. Bellamy is a close and old friend of Miss Despard's; she has known him all her life. She would be greatly distressed by what has happened to him."

"And is at a loss to understand it. He came to see his old friend, she says, and perhaps to drop in on the sale." A small cough. "The sale has caused a great deal of talk in the city, quite a sensation I believe. Unheard of prices." His face and voice were bland, but the blue eyes were shrewd. He knew as well as Blaise that something was missing from the picture.

"He was mugged?" Blaise asked.

"Probably. Severely beaten anyway." Another cough. "I believe Mr. Bellamy is a homosexual."

"Yes," Blaise answered shortly.

"That may account for what happened, but what is curious is that he should be found where he was. Europeans do not venture into the Walled City, even disguised as Chinese."

"I understood it was no more than a bit of playacting," Blaise shrugged, playing it down.

"Perhaps. I also understand that Mr. Bellamy was in Hong Kong during the war."

Blaise showed none of his surprise, or his instinctive conviction that there was much more here than the simple rolling of a gay. "I had no idea," he said indifferently. "I do not know him that well."

"We are asking questions, of course, but,"—an expressive shrug—"a European who happens to be a homosexual, masquerading as a Chinese . . . ? He was fortunate not to have been murdered."

"Was he carrying any money, papers, passport?" Blaise asked.

"According to Ling Po, only money."

The chief superintendent accompanied Blaise to his car. As a VIP in Hong Kong he rated such attention.

"Will you be staying in the city long, Mr. Chandler?" he asked.

"That depends. I came at the request of Despard's; I am the executor of Miss Despard's late father's will, and as I was coming to Hong Kong anyway, they asked me to see that she was all right."

"Upset, and worried, naturally, but otherwise she seemed fine," the chief superintendent assured him. "You'll be going to the hospital?"

"Yes, when I leave here."

"We'll do our best to find out what happened, but we may have to wait until Mr. Bellamy recovers consciousness, and the doctors will not commit themselves on that point, I'm afraid."

They shook hands and Blaise and Benny got back in the car.

Well now, thought the chief superintendent, as he went back inside the police headquarters. What has the mighty ChanCorp to do with one Rollo Bellamy? More to the point, who exactly is Rollo Bellamy? Perhaps a few inquiries in certain quarters back in London would tell him.

The Chandler Clinic had been built by Agatha Chandler when, on one of her visits to Hong Kong, she saw the lines at the city's free hospitals. She had a soft spot for the Chinese; Benny Fong's grandfather had worked for her own father, had once saved his life when he was attacked by a disturbed and angry bear. Black Jack had been so grateful that he had paid for the education of the eldest Fong son, a clever boy who later went to work for the Chandler Corporation. Benny, his eldest son, had also been helped along by Agatha, who was his godmother, and had run Hong Kong superbly well for some years now.

As Blaise entered the big white building, built entirely with Chandler money but in accordance with Chinese designs and the proper *feng shui*, and dispensing traditional Chinese medicine as well as the latest European techniques, the doctors—all Chinese—were waiting for him.

Mr. Bellamy, they confirmed gravely, was suffering from multiple injuries, external and internal. There was no intercranial pressure, but he was on a life support machine and a monitor. His other injuries had been treated; two days ago they had operated to remove his ruptured spleen, but there was his pierced lung, his fractures . . . They were not prepared to go higher than a fifty-fifty chance of survival. The next forty-eight hours would tell.

Blaise finally went along to the Intensive Care Unit to see for himself. It was not like the rest of the hospital, where the lighting was soft, kind to the eyes: once through the doors marked ICU the light was white and bright and relentless. He saw Kate at once; no mistaking the bright flame of that hair. He could see through the enormous window of the room quite clearly. Rollo on a high bed, surrounded by and attached to a whole battery of machines, his head bandaged, his face taped, tubes protruding from his nose, his mouth, his arms, and snaking from beneath the bedclothes. Both arms were in splints and there was a cradle over his legs. Jesus! he thought, appalled. What in God's name did he run into?

Kate did not look up as he opened the door in his usual soundless way. Her attention was fixed on Rollo's white and battered face. Not that her own looked much better, Blaise thought, suddenly furious with her. She looked bloody awful, her bones sticking out like those of a Belsen survivor, her cheeks sunken, smudged circles under her eyes. How long had she been sitting there, for God's sake?

When he said her name she looked up, and for a moment, as she saw who it was, her face was illuminated in the most glorious flash of joy and radiant relief; then, as if a hand had wiped it away, it went blank and he felt as if she had shut a door in his face. "What are you doing here?" was her anything-but welcome.

"The Duchess called you for a chat. They told her you were here and why. Naturally, she sent me."

The icy mask melted for another brief moment. "So kind . . ." A gesture at the surroundings. "All this . . . you'll tell her, won't you, how much it means to me, to us both . . ."

"Of course I will." He approached the bed, and again was met by an almost tangible barrier of hostility, like a wounded mother protecting young.

"How is he?" he asked, wanting to hear her version.

"Bad. Very bad." As if you didn't know, her tone accused.

"How long have you been here—with Rollo, I mean?"

"Since I arrived."

"When was that?"

A frown, as though she could not remember, then a dismissive movement of the hand. "Does it matter? I'm here and that's all that counts."

"Have you eaten, slept?"

"I've had coffee, a sandwich . . . I'm not hungry."

"But you must be tired."

"Why? All I do is sit."

"And to what point? The doctors say there is little hope of him coming around for some time. His coma is deep."

"I know that, they told me, too. But there is always the possibility, and I want to be here just in case."

"If it should happen and you weren't here, you could always be brought back."

"No," Kate said. "I came to be with Rollo. He needs me. He was always there when I needed him. Now it's my turn."

Blaise drew up another chair, placed it on the opposite side of the bed. "What was he doing in Hong Kong?"

Again the scathing look, spilling doubt everywhere. "Your wife's Sale of the Century, of course."

"So how come he was way off the beaten track in Kowloon, just outside the Walled City? Tourists never go there; lots of Chinese never go there. It's a dangerous place."

Kate kept her eyes firmly fixed to Rollo's red, white, and blue face. "How should I know?" she asked.

She was lying, he was sure. Why? He was not only shocked, he was angry. They had gotten over their initial antagonism; he had thought they had established a *modus vivendi*. Certainly she had been much more relaxed with him of late, no longer on the defensive, but more confident the deeper she got into her job and the better she became at it. In spite of what he told his grandmother—which was only his own camouflage—he had enjoyed his visits to London, wondering, each time he went, how much more she would have developed, not just the grooming, but also the personality, like a face upturned to the sun after a long hard winter. Now it was back not only to square one but to before the game was even put on the table. She looked at him as she would a stranger, talked to him as if he were an enemy, and lied to him like a traitor.

"Do you know what the Walled City is?" he asked.

She shook her head in a way that said no, and don't care either.

"It's a political anachronism; nobody runs it; it is lawless, dominated by street gangs and dedicated to crime and vice. Why would Rollo go there? There are no gay bars that I know of."

"I don't know," Kate lied.

"Does he know Hong Kong?"

After a moment, and unwillingly, she said, "He was here during the war."

"In what capacity?"

"With ENSA."

Was he now, thought Blaise. ENSA was the British equivalent of the USO, but perhaps Bellamy had only worn the uniform while working undercover. It had been done often enough, yet somehow the thought of Rollo Bellamy—*Rollo Bellamy*—working undercover was positively risible! Bellamy a spy? Jesus, he thought exasperatedly. Your imagination is running away with you. But why, then, was Kate lying? What had been Bellamy's real reason for coming to Hong Kong? And why the Walled City?

That place held the key, he was sure. Not outside, where Rollo had been found, but inside, in the maze of dark alleys that led to the heart of the city, a wholly Chinese part of Kowloon. Rollo Bellamy represented the rich Central District, the Peak, and the Hong Kong Club and the Mandarin Hotel, where he should have been staying, not with some Chinese who kept a curio shop. And just who was he, come to that? Why had Rollo disguised himself as a Chinese?

"Does he speak Chinese?" he asked Kate.

"Not that I know of."

"Does he have friends here apart from the man he was staying wth?"

"Well, if he was here during the war . . ."

She was not telling him the truth. Why? Why was he suddenly in the doghouse? He found his patience—never lengthy at the best of times—shrinking rapidly. This tiresome girl was getting to be a millstone around his neck. "Did you send him here?"

"No, I did not."

"It was his idea?"

"He said he had heard from his old friend and that it would also be a chance to take in the sale."

"But James Grieve was doing that, surely."

"So? I am not Rollo's keeper!" She glared.

"No, but isn't he yours?" Blaise's leash snapped.

Kate's eyes blazed in her white face. "He's been a good friend to me, which is—"

"Go on, finish it," Blaise said unpleasantly. "Which is more than I have?"

Kate's face turned to stone again.

"What the hell is the matter with you?" he exploded. "You would think I'd mugged Rollo myself!"

No answer, but her silence made its own accusation.

Controlling his temper, "Did you hear from him while he was here?" Blaise asked next.

A headshake, but again, from her sudden tension, he knew she was lying. Damn the bitch! Blaise snarled to himself. What the hell is going on here?

Rollo had called Kate, but only briefly, on the evening of the first day's sale to report astronomical prices well justified by the quality of the pieces.

"A match to our own, dear horse," he had said.

Kate had felt her heart do a hop, skip, and a jump. "From the same source?" she asked guardedly but disbelievingly.

"That I cannot confirm as yet, but I'm working on it. All I will say is that I am convinced it is a case of the old three-dollar bill."

"It can't be!" Kate breathed. "She wouldn't have the nerve! Nor would she get away with it! Not *en masse.*"

"The three-dollar bill *and* the Emperor's new clothes."

"It can't be," Kate said again. "You are dramatizing, as always, or you have been at the rice wine."

"As a judge, dear heart, as a judge."

"But how—"

"No questions," Rollo cut in swiftly. "Not until I have the answers."

"And how long will that take?"

"Can't say that either."

"Or won't," Kate rapped sharply. "For God's sake, Rollo, be careful. I still think you are paranoid where a certain party is concerned, but all the same—"

"Softly softly catchee monkee," he interrupted, "except in this case it is a rat."

"If you are right there will be a pack of them."

"Well, I am sure I know one of them—no, I will not say. *Pas devant* the long distance telephone."

"I think you have gone mad," Kate said, suddenly and inexplicably filled with fright. "For God's sake, don't meddle on your own."

"I have never liked crowds, as you know," Rollo said loftily.

"Then come home! You've seen enough to go on with. Come home and we'll discuss it and—"

"What, when I've only just begun to enjoy myself? I'd forgotten the delights of Hong Kong. Now you be a good girl and mind the shop. I'll be in touch." He had rung off before she could say another word.

Now, she shivered. She had been right. There was something dark and deadly here, and nobody she could tell about it. Any word to Blaise Chandler would go straight to his wife. She knew now he could not be trusted, no matter how much he played the injured party. Her upward glance at him was again rancorous and filled with dislike. No, she could not tell anybody anything. All she had were Rollo's suspicions, and anyway, how was she not to know that Blaise Chandler was in on the whole thing? He came to Hong Kong regularly, too, didn't he? If his wife had just perpetrated the most monstrous fraud the art world had ever known—except it was not known—he *had* to be aware of it. And when everybody else was . . . She felt sick. Despard's would be ruined. She would be ruined. All her father's years of work gone for nothing. She had no idea what Rollo had discovered, she only knew that he was all but dead because of it. They had meant to kill him, she was sure. The doctors had told her he was lucky to be alive. Had the old woman not found him and the police seen her searching him, he would have died.

Which led her to another terrifying thought. Rollo alive was in constant danger, because he was meant to be dead. Whoever wanted him dead must be feeling terribly threatened, and when you were threatened you did wild, uncontrollable things. Suddenly, Kate was awash with fear. She understood enough now about her stepsister to know how dangerous she was even when not threatened; she would have to be very, very careful with everything and everyone, because at any moment the enemy could strike, as they had done with Rollo. She would not be able to trust anyone.

Especially Blaise Chandler, in spite of his outward concern, because he was Dominique's husband. Which was why she had lied to him.

Blaise knew it was time to ease up the pressure. "I am going to take you to a hotel; you need sleep. Don't argue," he said, in a tone of voice that made her tighten the lips she had been about to open. "Use your common sense, if you will. What use are you to Rollo if you fall apart through exhaustion? If you are to help he needs your strength and right now that is leaking away badly. Sleep for as long as you can, rest your mind and your body and then come back. It's what he would say, isn't it?"

Kate had to admit it was. Rollo was always scathing of martyrs—"the most selfish people in the world" he called them. "Hooked on self-sacrifice. Give me somebody who knows the score and looks after number one first; that way they are well able to keep an eye on number two." But what if he came around while she was away, said something, something important that she would miss . . .

"Don't go back to being the tiresome girl I first met," Blaise warned. "I didn't care for her much."

It was the wrong thing to say. "I don't give a damn what you think!" Kate flared. "All this is because of you and your—" She clenched her teeth on her unruly tongue and drew a ragged breath.

"Because of me and my what?" Blaise inquired softly.

Careful, Kate warned herself. Bridle that tongue of yours before it gets you thrown and trampled on! He must not even suspect or he'll warn his wife; his loyalty to her must come first; that's the way of things. That it was *her* way of things did not occur to her.

So she said, as penitently as she could, that she had not slept on the plane nor since her arrival thirty-six hours ago. "I'm sorry. You are right, of course. Making myself ill would be stupid. Perhaps there is a room here, or a bed they are not using . . . I don't really want to leave Rollo." She stood up, found she was stiff, and winced.

Blaise was around the bed in a trice, his hands under her elbows. "How long have you been sitting there?" he asked grimly.

"Since I arrived, on and off."

"Bloody fool! Can you walk all right?"

"Of course I can. My legs have gone to sleep, that's all."
But it still helped to lean on him.

"You need food and sleep," Blaise pronounced in a tone
that brooked no argument.

"I couldn't eat anything, but I am tired. If there's a
bed—"

He overrode her forcefully. "I am taking you out of the
hospital. If anything happens they'll let me know."

Kate subsided. She was tired. Her eyes felt gritty and her
head heavy. But she still turned to look at Rollo anxiously.

"He is not likely to come around in the near future,"
Blaise said in more gentle tones. "His coma is deep."

Her eyes were filled with anguish as she turned away from
the bed. She really did have feelings for that old reprobate,
Blaise thought. In the car, she leaned back with a sigh and
closed her eyes. By the time they got to the Peninsula Hotel,
where ChanCorp kept a suite, she was asleep. He had to
wake her, help her up the entrance steps. A sudden gust of
wind sprayed water from the fountain over her face and she
started, asked blearily, "Where are we?"

"The Peninsula Hotel."

"Oh." She seemed to go to sleep again. In the elevator
she leaned against him, and when the doors opened into the
suite he scooped her up in his arms; she was no weight at all.
He carried her into the bedroom, kicking the door shut
behind him, and dropped her onto one side of the big bed.
Going around to the other side, he turned back the covers.
Then he returned to Kate, drew off her shoes, unzipped her
trousers and pushing her back, flopping like a rag doll, he
drew them off. Her legs he noted impersonally, did start at
the armpits: slender, beautifully shaped, the thighs muscled
like those of an athlete. He lifted her up again so that she
slumped forward against him, dead to the world, and he
drew off her sweater, unbuttoned her shirt. He was surprised to find her wearing feminine underwear; evidently her
metamorphosis had been from the skin out. Her bra was
mostly lace, of a pink that matched her nipples, quite clearly
showing through the thin silk and lace. He left it on, and her
French panties. When he pushed her back she made a grumbling noise and curled herself up into a fetal ball. He drew
the covers over her. She sighed once, squirmed some more,
and buried her face in the pillow. He left one lamp burning
but closed the door fully. Then he headed for the telephone.

Kate slept for eighteen hours. When she awoke it was Friday, according to the digital clock, and almost seven o'clock in the evening. She sat up abruptly, stared stupidly down at herself, jerked her head up to see her clothes, folded neatly over the back of a chair by the window. She remembered Blaise Chandler bossily saying he was taking her back to the hotel. Which hotel? She reached for the pack of matches lying in the crystal ashtray. The Peninsula Hotel, it said. He must have brought her here, undressed her, put her to bed. She had a hazy memory of being carried, no more. Oh well, she thought, now he knows the worst. Which word had her reaching for the telephone. She did not know the number but the switchboard would . . . There was no change in Mr. Bellamy's condition. She slumped back against the pillows. Then she reached for the telephone again. It would be twelve noon in London.

She spoke to John Steadman, told him she was staying on in Hong Kong until she knew for sure whether Rollo would recover or not.

"Everything is all right, I trust?" she queried.

"On oiled wheels, my dear. Not to worry. The Courtland Park arrangements are in full swing, all in accordance with your excellent timetable. The firm of cleaners are in the house, Dorothy Bainbridge is also there with her team, the printers have the catalogue in hand, the photographer is in attendance on Dorothy; your sketches are being followed exactly."

"No problems?"

"None that cannot be handled and nothing for you to worry about. Our best wishes for Rollo's recovery. We know how attached you are to him."

"Thank you, John. I'll call you again when I have news."

She replaced the receiver and sat there for a while, thinking. Her emotions felt curiously dead. Probably reaction, she decided. Even the fact that Blaise Chandler had undressed her, put her to bed, had no effect on her. She had slept deeply and dreamlessly yet somehow she still felt heavy, almost listless. It was as though her mind had gone into its own coma. She heaved herself out of the bed. A shower might help.

She was drying herself when the telephone rang. It was the Duchess.

"How did you know I was here?" Kate asked.

"The Boy told me. I sent him to help. Has he?"

"He's been very kind," Kate replied diplomatically.

"And your friend—how is he?"

"Not good, I'm afraid." Kate gave the old lady a brief rundown on Rollo's injuries.

"Well, he's in a good hospital."

"I have to thank you—" began Kate.

"What are friends for?"

"Even so. You are my guardian angel, Duchess."

"No more'n I'd do for any friend of mine," the old lady said gruffly. "Now you take care of yourself; ain't no sense in runnin' yourself into the ground. I've told them you are to have whatever you want and it goes without saying they'll do their best for Mr. Bellamy."

"Oh, Duchess, what can I say . . ." Kate began in a thickened voice.

"That you'll be a good girl and do as you are told."

Not by him, I won't, Kate thought mutinously, but, "Yes, Duchess," she lied.

"You've got me and the Boy, so you are not alone."

Oh, but I am, Kate thought miserably. I never felt so alone in my life.

"The Boy will see to you."

But that's the trouble, Kate wanted to tell her, he doesn't see me at all; even worse, I daren't trust him . . .

"Now you call me whenever you want, if you need somethin' or just to talk."

"I will," promised Kate, wishing that she could talk to the Duchess about it all, knowing that she must never tell anyone, ever.

She donned some fresh clothes—the one bag she had brought had miraculously appeared—and was standing at the window, looking out at the lights of the harbor, when someone knocked on the door.

"Come in."

Blaise Chandler stood in the doorway of her sitting room. "Had a good sleep?" he asked.

"Yes, thank you."

"Hungry?"

Kate realized with surprise that she was. "I could eat something."

"Good. Come on, then."

"Where to?"

"One of Hong Kong's famous floating restaurants. You need a bit of color and excitement."

"But what about the hospital?"

"What about it?"

"Well, I should go there . . ."

"Why? What can you do?"

His ruthless common sense was a bucket of water in the face. He was right, as usual, very much the Superior Shit.

"Call the hospital before we go, if you want to. Satisfy that Scots Calvinist conscience of yours that it will be perfectly all right to enjoy yourself."

"I already called," she mumbled.

"What? I can't hear you."

"I said I already called."

"Then what are we waiting for?" She could have filed her nails on the edge of his sarcasm.

He had a convertible with the top down, as the night was humid, the breeze warm. They drove to the harbor, where a Chinese junk took them out across to Aberdeen, where the floating restaurants were moored. As they neared them, Kate said unthinkingly, "It's like a floating Harrods decorated for Christmas."

Blaise laughed and suddenly her mood changed; her heaviness evaporated as the enticing smell of food, which drifted down the flight of steps they climbed to reach the deck, made her mouth water. Everything was brilliant with color; there were voices, laughter, music. He had been right, she thought. This was what she needed to bring her out of her depression. How had he known she was in one?

The dining room ran the length of the four-decker boat; it was all scarlet and gold, even the tablecloths were red, and the Chinese lanterns were elaborately fringed, the decor over the top. The smiling faces of the waiters, the hum of many conversations, the way the Chinese devoted themselves to their food, all served to lift Kate's spirits.

"Do you come here often?" she asked, as the waiter helped her push in her chair.

"Only when I bring visitors to Hong Kong. Do you like Chinese food?"

"If you mean real Chinese food, I don't know. All I know is Chinese take-out."

"Then you have an experience in front of you. This restaurant serves Cantonese food—the best of the regional cuisines. The Chinese have a proverb, Live in Soochow—that's where all the most beautiful women live; die in Luchow—that's where they make the best teak coffins, but eat in Kwangchow—that's the Chinese for Canton."

Kate was studying the menu wide-eyed. "All I know is chop suey, egg foo yung, and chow mein."

"You won't get them here—they are American inventions anyway."

Kate laid down the menu. "You order for me. I'll trust you."

"Isn't it about time?"

Kate found herself held by those brilliant black eyes, tore hers away and stared blindly out of the window.

What the hell is it with her? Blaise puzzled angrily. One minute relaxed, the next tight as a virgin. Which she probably still is. Best thing was to get some food inside her, and a few glasses of rice wine. Undermine that rock-hard stubbornness of hers, then get it out of her. Blaise had no time for people who nurtured grievances, hugging them close to their chests, which triggered off the memory of Kate Despard's young breasts cupped in their pink silk cradle, the fondant pink of her nipples tantalizingly revealed through the lace—an image he wiped from his mind almost as soon as it appeared. For the life of him he could not think what he was supposed to have done; the last time he saw her in London they had parted on what was, for them, amicable terms. What the hell was she blaming him for now? He determined to find out.

"I would suggest you begin with something barbecued. Cantonese style is unrivaled."

So she had tender slices of pork with a golden and honeyed skin, served on a bed of anise-flavored beans. He had the same. It was delicious and she demolished every morsel. This was followed by Peking duck. Kate watched in utter fascination as the chef, who came to their table, swiftly carved the duck with an enormous, razor-sharp cleaver, first the crispy skin, and then the meat, which was dipped in a mild, sweetish, soya bean paste mixed with spring onions and cucumber, placed on a wafer-thin wheat tortilla not unlike a dry, rolled crepe, and then eaten with the fingers. Blaise said something to the chef who beamed and nodded, and after the duck they had soup made with its carcass. Kate was surprised to find that rice was not served. Blaise explained that you had to request it. They ate noodles instead, also made at the table, and Kate finished off with the most delectable dessert: the Chinese version of toffee apples, all hot and syrupy before being dipped into ice-cold water, which transformed them into a crackling, sesame-coated sensation. Throughout the meal she did justice to several glasses of rice wine. By the time she dabbled her fingers in the bowl set before her and took the hot towel provided, she was both stuffed to the gills—her first real food in almost three days—and slightly drunk. She refused more wine.

"What are you worried about?" Blaise attacked directly. "Apart from Rollo? Something is obviously on your mind and it concerns me. If you have a grievance, state it."

When Kate did not reply, so busy was she hunting for something to excuse the antagonism she had foolishly revealed, he said impatiently, "Obviously I have done something I ought not to have done or not done something I ought to have done. If looks could kill I'd be in the bed next to Bellamy right now."

"I was upset," Kate mumbled. How could she say, "You went tittle-tattling to your wife that I was seeing, on a personal as well as professional level, the man who has the final say in the disposal of Courtland Park, and she at once came over to manipulate him, in her own, inimitable way." No, she could never say that. The very thought made her quake. His present anger would be as nothing to the lava flow that would be released by her more or less telling him his wife was cuckolding him with one Nicholas Chevely.

"I know you were, but you were also mad as hell. Why?" Blaise persisted.

"Well," Kate prevaricated, "I didn't ask you to come, did I? I can manage on my own, you know, even if you don't seem to think so."

"It was my grandmother who was concerned, not me. As far as I am concerned you are on your own, but my grandmother is an old woman with time on her hands and a propensity to take charge of any situation."

"No," protested Kate. "It wasn't like that."

"Then what was it like?"

Just like a lawyer, Kate thought frantically. He would cross-examine her until he was satisfied. "I thought you were the one who was meddling," she lied. "I was tired and I wasn't thinking straight. I'm sorry if I gave the impression that I am not grateful to you and your grandmother; I am, very grateful. But I was tired and I was worried, and I suppose I was somewhat—resentful—at what I thought was your taking everything over—including me."

"I know Hong Kong; I also carry a fair amount of clout. I can go places and do things you can't. However, if you don't want me to . . ."

"No," Kate said quickly. "I want to get to the bottom of this, too." She stopped abruptly, appalled at the thought of what—if Rollo had been right—lay waiting to be discovered. Feeling hunted, she could find no way out.

He saw it in her face; she was still not telling him the truth. And she was frightened. What the hell was going on here? And why wouldn't she tell him? God knows what that bastard Bellamy had been up to. Whatever it was, Kate was obviously afraid to tell him about it. And why Hong Kong? This was Dominique's territory. That name switched on all his lights. Of course . . . It had to be something to do with this damned sale of hers. Why should Bellamy come unofficially if James Grieve was here officially? He was snooping, obviously, and got caught at it. But to find out what? Deliberately, he said, "Very well. I'll do all I can to find out who Bellamy crossed or got in the way of. This city is full of all sorts and kinds, and my wife's Sale of the Century has attracted a great deal of notoriety."

He was watching her face as he spoke and, as he trailed the red herring, saw her sniff it, drop her eyes, and then slide her glance to the window, where she appeared to become engrossed in the view.

Christ! he thought, feeling as if somebody had kicked him in the gut. Now what has she done . . . ?

He had gone to Despard's while Kate was sleeping, found his wife febrile with success.

"So you have heard of my triumph," she teased him laughingly.

"You'd have to be dead not to." He wondered if she had heard about Rollo and seized the opportunity to tell her. "Rollo Bellamy almost is."

For a moment, the blue eyes were puzzled. "Oh, you mean the little Despard's queer friend. Is he ill?"

"He's in the Chandler Clinic, in a coma and suffering from multiple injuries. He got badly beaten a few nights ago."

Her eyes rounded and her mouth formed the same O of

surprise. "He is in Hong Kong! But I did not see him at the sale . . ."

"It was crowded, so I hear," Blaise said ironically.

"Even so, if he had come to make a report for Kate Despard he would have made a point of talking to me."

"I didn't know you knew him."

"Oh, we have met once or twice; he knew Papa, after all."

"And didn't like him."

"Papa couldn't stand him either," she said wrinkling her nose. "Always spying on people . . . Yes, he would have come to spy. He always was the kind who listened at doors."

"What's there to spy on?"

"Who was here, who bought, what they paid, how the sale was conducted—everything. Probably stealing some of my ideas for their forthcoming sale at Courtland Park." Dominique's laugh was not amused. "I wonder what she did to secure that? From what I hear, Nicholas Chevely is the kind of man who expects payment for any favors granted." At Blaise's surprise, "You did not know? But where have you been?"

"In South Africa. I knew London was in the running; I hadn't yet heard they'd won."

"Oh, yes. It is the kind of sale one longs for, of course. I would dearly have loved it myself, but New York was not even under consideration, alas. However"—now her laugh was smug—"she will have to work very hard to beat me. I exceeded every single reserve set. Courtland Park or no Courtland Park, I do not think I have anything to fear. Now then, how long are you staying?"

"I don't know. Depends."

"On what?" And then, sharply, "Do not tell me that you are here because of Kate Despard's Queen Mother and not to congratulate and celebrate with your own wife!"

"I can do both, can't I?" Blaise asked, reaching for her. "You first, of course, as always."

"I should hope so," she said, allowing herself to be kissed and fondled. "But not tonight, I am afraid. I have to wine and dine an important client who spent an absolute fortune at my sale."

"When, then?" Blaise scowled.

"Tomorrow—we shall have all day tomorrow, but I am due in New York for another sale next week—"

"Jesus!" he exploded. "I'm getting tired of these hail and farewell encounters."

"Darling"—she nestled against him—"do you not think I get tired of it also? But this is a very important man." Indeed, she thought luxuriously, it was Chao-Li. "I cannot let him down."

"Like you can me?" Blaise asked unpleasantly. "Where were you anyway? I've called a dozen times."

"Darling," Dominique murmured in gentle remonstration. "Sales like mine are once in a lifetime affairs, ours is forever . . ." She glanced over his shoulder at the clock on the lacquered wall of her office. She had forty minutes to spare before her next appointment. "But for now, let us take advantage of the moment . . ." Leaving him she went to her desk, pressed a button: he heard the door lock click. Still holding his eyes she pressed a button on her intercom. "No calls, no interruptions of any kind for the next half hour," she instructed. Then she came back to him, began to unbutton the jacket of his lightweight suit, all the while drawing him toward the enormous, black leather chesterfield.

Now, thinking back to the conversation, examining it as he would a statement from a witness, he saw flaws that he had, in the heat of the moment, overlooked. He also saw that his heat had been deliberately induced. She had asked no questions, probed no situations. She had expressed surprise about Rollo Bellamy, then apparently dismissed him from her mind. He had had the feeling of being manipulated at the time, but that had been swept away by other, more powerful feelings. He had not failed this time, on the contrary, but it had not been as satisfying as always. He had put it down to being preoccupied with other matters. Now he saw that it was she who had been preoccupied. She had made all the right moves, done all the right things; they had hit the heights but not the peak. She had been on automatic pilot.

He also remembered something she had said that even at the time made him wonder about her choice of words: *Rollo Bellamy had obviously come to spy.* At a public auction? James Grieve would report back officially and he was the expert, not Rollo Bellamy. But suddenly he knew beyond doubt: Rollo Bellamy had come to spy, all right, but not on the auction itself, on something to do with it. Of course, if Kate had landed Courtland Park, Dominique could well be right about her wanting to crib from the unmistakable du Vivier style.

He saw that Kate was still staring out of the window; her expression was tense and she was unconsciously gnawing at her lower lip. Quite deliberately, he said, "I haven't congratulated you on landing Courtland Park. I would have done so earlier but I only heard it from my wife this afternoon."

Kate's head swiveled, astonishment, and something else—was it delight?—plain. "But I thought—" She caught herself. "Thank you," she amended. "I suppose she told you we met in London."

Did you now? Blaise thought with a jolt of surprise. "A flying visit?" he hazarded, feeling his way.

"It could have been no more," Kate agreed in an odd tone, "with her Sale only days away."

Which meant, Blaise knew at once, that it had been of the utmost importance. Nothing else would have dragged Dominique away from Hong Kong.

"Did she call at Despard's?" he asked casually.

"No." Kate's voice was equally casual. "We met at the opera, as a matter of fact."

"The opera!"

"I happen to like it."

Maybe, but Dominique doesn't, he thought. It bored her to death.

"What was it?" he asked, also casually.

"*La Somnambula*—Joan Sutherland was singing."

Which still wouldn't matter to Dominique, Blaise thought. Something—or somebody—else drew her there. And then his memory dredged up a name: Nicholas Chevely. Dominique had mentioned him, and Kate had been on the phone to somebody called Nicholas when he'd called to pick up the Remington.

He took a chance. "Nicholas?" he asked.

She nodded. "Yes, Nicholas."

He ventured further. "Nicholas *Chevely?*"

Kate flicked him a glance before looking away again, confirming his suspicions. "Yes."

He made himself smile. "What's wrong with mixing business with pleasure?"

He could almost feel her relief. "Nothing."

So, he reviewed the picture. Nicholas Chevely was the one with the power to determine who handled Courtland Park;

Despard's of London was under consideration; Nicholas Chevely was—according to Dominique—a man who expected payment for favors granted; Kate Despard was the last woman in the world to grant such favors: she had no experience at the game. She had no experience, period. But Dominique did . . . Yes, that made sense. It also made him flinch. It confronted him head on with his wife's ruthless use of her sexual favors and the price she set on them. But it still hurt. And it also surprised him that this time Dominique had not gotten what she wanted.

He looked at Kate with respect tinged with pity. You may have won Courtland Park, he told her silently, but you've lost any hope of fighting an honest fight. Dominique does not like losing.

Suddenly he felt depression and tiredness hit him like a sandbag. Jet lag, he told himself. It was not as though any of this was news; he knew what his wife was—when he allowed himself to think about it. Most of the time he shut it off, considering it the price he had to pay. Now, he found himself wondering, for the first time, if it was worth it.

Whenever he had considered the whole person his wife was, he had become more and more convinced that some kind of external force was at work, something almost mystical and quite irresistible. She had literally knocked him off balance, and he'd been wandering around in a daze ever since. He knew there were other men; that she was unscrupulous, ruthless in pursuit of her goals. He knew she lied, had confirmed that she cheated. But he had chosen to shut his eyes to everything beyond the beautiful, sensual, sexual being who had him in thrall. When he had tried to rationalize it he had failed. He only knew that the more he had of her the more he wanted. Something like a high voltage current had leaped between them the very first time they met; it had been sizzling ever since, a bright blue arc whose shock he had come to crave. He supposed that what he had was a habit. Some men drank, others used drugs; he needed a regular fix of Dominique du Vivier, and the thought of his supply being cut off was enough to make him deaf, dumb, and blind to what it was doing to him, how dangerous it was, how deadly. He had deliberately denied himself more than once, only to be reduced to a desire that stopped just short of physical pain. He knew his grandmother could not understand it. How could he tell her that he was unable to explain it to himself?

Kate watched his face through the window reflection. It was remote, unreadable. He had gone away inside himself, in that way he had. She wanted to apologize to him, to say she was sorry she had jumped to the wrong conclusion; that she ought to have realized Dominique had more than one informant as to what happened at Despard's London. But how could she apologize for something he did not even know he was supposed to have done? Oh, hell, she thought miserably. Why can't I ever get it *right* with this man?

Obviously she had said something that had not gone down well. She thought it all over, for the life of her could not see anything untoward. But he was a lawyer, wasn't he? He was trained to read between the lines. Oh well, she thought defiantly. If he finds out for himself what his wife has done, that's not my fault. But she knew, all the same, that one of the things that lay between them was her fear of saying or doing anything he might construe as her pointing the finger at his wife. Oh, why did you have to marry Dominique? she raged silently. Couldn't you see what she was? No . . . of course you couldn't. You can't see people's souls, can you?

Her sigh was so gusty that it made the candle flames flicker, and it brought Blaise out of his bottomless thoughts. He checked his watch. "Shall we go?" he asked politely.

"Can we call in at the hospital before we go back to the hotel? Please . . . ?"

It meant doing a double journey—the clinic was on Hong Kong Island, the Peninsula on Kowloon—yet he said courteously, "Of course." In the car he lapsed into silence again, the brooding look back on his face.

Rollo was exactly as she had left him; his condition was stable, the doctors said.

On the ride back, out of nowhere, Blaise asked, "Have you seen my wife since you arrived?"

"No. I don't think she knows I'm here . . ."

"Oh, but she does. I told her."

"Oh," said Kate. They rode the rest of the way in silence. He saw her into the hotel, rode with her in the elevator, opened her door for her

"Thank you," Kate said. "You were right. I did need a little enjoyment."

"We all do," he said in an odd voice, then abruptly, "good night."

15

The next day Kate was sitting by Rollo's bed, talking to him. Blaise had given her a booklet—how he had gotten hold of it she did not know—to do with the work of a body called the Institute of Human Potential, in Philadelphia; they had done lots of studies with people in comas, advised constant stimulation, talking to the patient, making them touch, smell, hear familiar things and sounds. Kate had Rollo's hand in hers; it lay there, protruding from his sling, limp and unresponsive, but she persevered, talking to him about things they had done, places they had been, incidents from her childhood, memories of her mother. She had been sitting for more than two hours and so far the response had been nil; not by so much as a flicker of an eyelash did Rollo show he either heard or knew she was there. But she had been warned not to expect instant results. It could take, the booklet said, weeks, even months.

She did not hear the door open, so absorbed was she. It was when she recognized the perfume that she came upright in her chair and turned to see her stepsister on the other side of the bed, looking breathtaking, her husband behind her. Taken by surprise, Kate's unguarded face betrayed, like a flashing sign, all the hatred and disgust she felt. Like lightning, her feelings leapt across the bed, so forceful that Dominique took a step back, almost stepping on her husband's toes. He, too, saw the look, and the missing piece of the puzzle fell into place.

The only thing that surprised him was his lack of surprise; it had been there all the time; he was the one who had refused to see it, to admit it existed, to acknowledge the disaster it would bring. Now, as the truth leapt from Kate Despard's extraordinary eyes, he felt for a split second his wife's body stiffen against him before she made her usual swift recovery, her voice and body softening as she said, in a tenderly solicitous voice, "I am so sorry, my dear Kate. Had I known before I would have come at once but I had no idea until Blaise told me . . . How is your friend?"

She bent over the unconscious man, very close, her bell of black hair swinging just above his white face. The heady drift of her perfume enveloped Kate, and as she moved her head away she felt Rollo's hand tighten on hers.

"You are disturbing him," she said crossly. "You are too close . . ."

Dominique straightened up, moved back, but then, to Kate's alarm, Rollo began to move his head restlessly, and she saw the sudden sheen of sweat on his forehead.

"He reacted to you!" she blurted incredulously to Dominique. "He knew you were there!" Her voice was incandescent with delight.

"Nonsense!" Dominique said coolly. "I bent a little too close. My hair must have brushed his face."

"But I have been talking to him and holding his hand for the past two hours without any reaction at all!" Kate insisted. "Don't you see—it means his brain *is* functioning! We have to tell the doctors . . ."

Her hand went to the bell before Blaise could stop her. He, too, had seen the reaction of the unconscious man to Dominique, and had thought she had bent too low; that she had, as Kate said, disturbed him. But if Kate had been holding his hand and getting no response, then it could only be the hint of Dominique's presence—her perfume? Which also meant, if he knew anything about comas, that Rollo must have smelled it recently; it was usually the most recent events that provided stimuli. And his reaction—the restlessness, the sweating—showed that the memory association was not a pleasant one. Blaise had seen it in Vietnam many times with battle-fatigued men. The sound of gunfire, of low-flying planes, had produced the same reaction in catatonic cases.

He stood silent, Dominique beside him, while the doctors bent over Rollo, shone lights into his eyes, checked his monitors.

"An encouraging sign," they said at last, but cautiously. "You all saw it—his reaction?"

"Yes," Blaise said, and felt his wife's eyes upon him.

"He knows you?" the doctors asked Dominique.

"We have met several times."

Delicately one of them asked, "Do you always wear the same perfume?"

"It was created for me," Dominique answered. "No one else wears it."

"Then he would know who you were by your fragrance?"

Dominique shrugged. "Everyone does."

"Have you and Mr. Bellamy met recently?"

"The last time was in London, many months ago."

The doctors conferred in low voices. Kate, meanwhile, was hopping from one foot to another. "It is a *good* sign, isn't it?" she pleaded anxiously.

It was encouraging, they said, but if Madame were to bend over him again, perhaps they would be able to see for themselves . . .

With every appearance of an innocent bystander caught up in something that had nothing to do with her but nevertheless willing to assist, Dominique once more bent over the unconscious man, black bell of hair swinging, perfume eddying. Blaise saw one of the doctors sniff appreciatively. Kate had no eyes for anyone but Rollo, and once again he moved his head restlessly, fluttered his eyelids, broke out in a sweat.

"He is responding to external stimuli," the doctor pronounced. "The memory associated with your perfume is obviously a powerful one."

"We have—clashed—more than once," Dominique admitted with a moue.

"Ah . . . then the last meeting was argumentative?"

"You could say that," Dominique agreed.

Once more they conferred, but it was in Chinese so Kate did not understand a word. Finally they announced, 'Mr. Bellamy's brain seems to be responding in certain areas but not in others. He did not hear or feel Miss Despard, yet he recognized Madame du Vivier's perfume. We must now wait and hope that the other areas of the brain will also respond. Only time will tell."

Kate's face was a mixture of delight and dismay, while Dominique's was no more than its usual classic arrangement of features. Blaise was staring at Rollo's white face. Why *her* perfume? he asked the unconscious man. Why not Kate's voice and hand; of all people she is the most familiar. Why

Dominique? And why the obvious distress? The doctors had tactfully not remarked on it, but he understood enough Chinese to know that they had wondered why, decided that Dominique's tact covered a full-scale row that had occurred the last time they met, one on which Mr. Bellamy had perhaps brooded for some time.

Blaise knew Dominique did not like Rollo; he would have taken any odds on the fact that Rollo loathed her, but a row? Months before? Somehow he doubted it. Memories closest to the surface were normally the ones that revealed themselves first, so it had to be a recent meeting. Maybe here, in Hong Kong? Was that why Bellamy had come? Keeping away from the European community and disguising himself as a Chinese in order to enter the Walled City? Blaise could not make head nor tail of it, especially now, with thoughts and conjectures tumbling all over the place. Later, when he could sit alone and write it all down as if preparing a legal submission, perhaps then it would become clear. And only when he knew exactly what he was talking about would he tackle his wife; that was the only way to handle her, now or at any time, and especially now when he knew she was involved in something dangerously volatile.

Dominique was making her good-byes. "You know you only have to call me if there is anything I can do," she told Kate tenderly. "You should have called me the moment you arrived in the city." She sounded hurt; the words, instead of going running to my husband, remained unspoken.

"Thank you, but I have all the help I need," Kate replied woodenly, her own unspoken answer read in turn by her stepsister as: and even if I didn't, you'd be the last one I'd call on.

The Chinese doctors watched impassively, aware of the antagonism that crackled like electricity.

"Are you staying?" Blaise asked Kate.

Again she had the impression of a tightly controlled holocaust of anger. She searched the unreadable eyes and knew better than to tread where she would burn to death. He suspects, she thought. How could he not? Somewhere, somehow, Dominique or whoever she is mixed up with in whatever she is involved in, caught Rollo in whatever he was doing. She did not dare to frame her own suspicions of what that might be. It was too terrible even to contemplate. But he blames me, she thought. It's all because I came on the scene, because Papa involved him, placed him in this invidious position. He didn't want it and he doesn't like it. He doesn't really like me. I have already invaded far too much of his private space, especially where his wife is concerned. He doesn't really want to know what she is, what she has done, what she is doing. He only wants her.

"Yes," she said quietly, "I'm staying."

He nodded, then followed his wife out.

As their car moved off, Dominique asked idly, "I wonder what that *sale pédé* was up to? What do you think?"

Nothing I'm about to tell you, Blaise thought, answering with a shrug, "Probably propositioning where he shouldn't."

"But to disguise himself as a Chinese."

"He was an actor, wasn't he?"

"But," Dominique went on casually, "he would have to speak the language, surely?"

"Perhaps he does. I neither know nor care." He trailed his own lure. "Funny him having such a positive response to your perfume, though."

"Yes, wasn't it," she agreed with unruffled smoothness.

"I didn't know you and he had clashed."

"A mutual antipathy."

"You must have made a strong impression even so."

She dimpled. "Don't I always?"

She was not going to give anything away, and he of all people knew she was a mistress of the art of self-defense. He was just going to have to do it his way. Had to. For his own peace of mind.

Dominique's mind was anything but peaceful when she entered her office at Despard's after Blaise had dropped her off. He could not lunch, he said, a prior appointment, but his evening was hers. This was nothing unusual, but she pondered on his brusqueness as she tossed her fur and gloves onto the leather chesterfield where they had made love the day before. No, she decided finally. He could know nothing. Rollo Bellamy had been found snooping and been dealt with—and she would have something to say about that slipup—before he could report anything to anyone. She had to admit his disguise had been perfect; he had been brought, already unconscious, to where she and Chao-Li were talking in the small room he used as an office in the factory, deep in the Walled City, hanging from the strong-arm grip of two of

Chao-Li's enormous Szechuan guards. His skin, his eyes, his hair, his clothes—he had seemed to them all some Chinese with nothing on him to identify who or what he was. She had been curious, bent over him for one fleeting moment—which was when he must have inhaled her perfume—before Chao-Li had said curtly, "Deal with him," and the guards had dragged him away.

A bad mistake, she saw now. Yet who was to know that Rollo Bellamy was an expert in the art of makeup? But he was an actor, she reminded herself. Even so, there had been nothing familiar about him; the unconscious, blood-covered man hanging limply from the arms of the two guards, had borne no resemblance to the elegant, silver grey *pédé* she knew. He must have had himself totally made over, down to black contact lenses and tape to produce the elliptical fold to the eyes.

Chao-Li had questioned the guards later and they had reported failure to make him talk. And missed their chance when one blow too many and too hard rendered him wholly unreachable. He should have been taken across the bay and dumped in Hong Kong. Leaving him where they did, on the edge of the Walled City, had been a stupid mistake. Obviously the intention had been to give the impression of just another case of Tong warfare. The Walled City was known to be lawless and the Hong Kong police gave it a wide berth. Even so, Dominique thought, Chao-Li would have to be told, in no uncertain terms, that on this occasion he had failed her. But for that she would have to wait another twenty-four hours. He had gone to Macao, and was not due back until tomorrow night, which was unfortunate, because they would need someone in the hospital to report on Bellamy's progress and see to it that his recovery was prevented. It was far too dangerous to let him live, even if, as often happened with such injuries, his memory would be gone. They could not rely on that. No, Chao-Li would have to finish the job, and properly this time.

He would also have to find out how and where the old man had got as far as the Walled City. Was there a leak? Was there a traitor? Few knew of the operation. Dominique had dealt solely with Chao-Li, though she knew there were other Chinese involved. His had been the major contribution to the two-year operation: the siting of the factory, the provision of the unknown genius who had made such incredible fakes. Her own task had been to sell them. Chao-Li took his share, of course, but she had bargained hard. She was of the utmost necessity: her outlet, her expertise, her ability to create the right kind of atmosphere. Hers, too, was the major risk: should anything go wrong she would be ruined. And the only person she could point a finger at was Chao-Li. He had been very clever there, she now thought with a frown. Keeping her on the periphery of things. She should have insisted on knowing everything. As it was, this unexpected development left her exposed while Chao-Li—if that was his real name—was the only link she had to the men behind it all. Something else that would have to be remedied. It was out of the question that what—if anything— Bellamy had discovered should go any further. But Chao-Li would know what to do there, too. She could not be seen to have anything to do with it. There had to be absolutely no whisper of anything crooked.

And, while he got on with things behind the scene, she would have to keep an eye on what Kate Despard got up to. Either in person or through Blaise.

It was turning out really providential that Blaise kept turning up in the path of the little Despard, and she suspected whom she had to thank for that. The old squaw grandmother. Kate Despard would be much more to her taste as a daughter-in-law than the one she had been saddled with willy nilly. Still, it all fitted in with her own plans very nicely. All she had to do was encourage him to do his grandmother's bidding as a good wife would do, then she could abstract all the information he garnered.

Yes, she thought, that would all do very nicely. That problem dealt with, she turned her mind to other things.

At midday, Kate was brought a tray of tea and biscuits by a smiling nurse. She was ready for it; her mouth was dry and her voice was tired. She had been talking for almost three hours, without result. She poured tea into the small bowl, cupped it in both hands, feeling it warm them, inhaling its fragrance. She tried holding the cup under Rollo's nose, but it had no effect. Tea obviously did not have the associations Dominique's perfume possessed. She ate one of the sugary biscuits, then picked up the napkin to wipe the crumbs from her lips. It was when she unfolded it that she saw something was written on it. "Miss Kate Despard," she read. "My name is Ling Po, the friend with whom Rollo was staying. I think it is time we met. I have a shop in Lok Ku Road—Ling Po Oriental—and I would appreciate your coming to see me here. What I sell would be of great interest to you, therefore your visit would not rouse any suspicion. I am entrusting this note to my third niece, who is a nurse at the Chandler Clinic. She will dispose of it. If your answer is yes then fold the napkin in a square; if it is no, a triangle. I have much to tell you."

Kate felt her heart stumble. So Rollo did know something! But suppose it was a plant . . . Suppose Dominique, having picked up Kate's reaction, had decided to draw her out. Suppose when she got there, there was no Ling Po but some strange Chinese who would do to her what they had done to Rollo? Don't be ridiculous, she told herself disgustedly. Dominique would never be so stupid. First Rollo *then* you? That would be tantamount to sending smoke signals. No, it had to be genuine. So, after she had drunk her tea she refolded the napkin in a neat square. When the nurse— pretty, young, slender in the way only young Chinese girls can be—returned, her eyes went at once to the napkin. She said nothing, but it seemed to Kate her smile was broader.

Blaise Chandler came back that afternoon. Kate had eaten a light lunch at Rollo's bedside, but she accepted his suggestion that she stretch her legs.

"It's a nice day outside," he told her, "not that you'd know it in here. I'll stay for a bit while you enjoy it."

Kate hesitated. If Rollo should come to . . . But from the look of him there was no sign of that. Besides, this was the perfect opportunity to visit Ling Po.

"I would like to see Hong Kong," she said hopefully. "I believe there are lots of shops specializing in porcelain."

"Dozens," Blaise agreed dryly.

"Where are the best ones?"

"Depends on whether you want new or old."

"I think I'd prefer old."

"Well, Cat Street is full of curio and art shops, and then there are others in the Central District. But I think Cat Street would be your best bet. They are cheek by jowl there. Hail a taxi and he'll take you—but shop around if you are going to buy; compare prices because they can vary enormously."

"Oh, I don't intend to buy, just look." She tried to joke. "See what the competition is. How long have I got?"

He checked his watch. "It's just about two-thirty. I have a dinner engagement, so shall we say five o'clock?"

"Oh, that will be plenty of time," Kate assured him. "Thank you."

The hospital porter got her a taxi, and Kate had her driver let her out at the top of Lok Ku Road. Then she forced herself into the teeming mass of people, all seemingly dressed in black pajamas, which thronged it. It was colorful to say the least; many of the shops were on the pavement, especially the vendors of food. The smell of hot oil was everywhere, and the sizzle of food being fried in woks. She passed piles of fruit and vegetables, many of them unknown to her, and walked slowly, seemingly engrossed in what she was seeing, but all the time searching for Ling Po Oriental. Then she saw the shop across the road. But she passed it nonchalantly, walked on another fifty yards or so before crossing the road and making her way slowly up the opposite side, stopping now and then to gaze into a shop window, so that she could do the same at Ling Po's. The window was simple, not overcrowded as many of the other shops were; that Ling Po sold superior wares was obvious by the Lokapala placed in its center. Pressing her nose up against the glass, Kate sighed over it. Then she became aware of a pair of eyes and, lifting her own, saw an elderly Chinese, wearing the traditional robe and skull cap, standing just behind the Lokapala. She met his eyes. Almost imperceptibly he nodded. Mentally girding her loins, she opened the door, setting the bell ringing, and entered the shop. There was nobody else there but the Chinese.

"Miss Despard," he said in flawless English. "Rollo's description was, as always, perfect. Please, come in. I think it best you pretend to be a customer and sit in that chair by the counter. I will show you some of my pieces."

"Like the Lokapala in the window?"

He smiled. "With pleasure."

He went behind the counter, reached beneath it to bring out a square of velvet which he placed on the glass top next to a case in which were displayed ivories of a beauty and quality that had Kate's mouth watering. The shop reminded her of her own; everything was displayed with both style and flair. He sold not only porcelain, ivories and jade, but also painted fans—lacquer on chickenskin, pen and ink on silk; gorgeous Chinese robes of the kind she had seen dignitaries wearing in paintings; the paintings themselves, and exquisite embroidered cloths as well as superb lacquerware. He went to the window to remove the Lokapala, which he brought back and placed on the velvet square.

Kate inhaled a breath.

"May I?"

"Please do."

She lifted the magnificent piece.

"I am most regretful about my old friend," said Ling Po, sounding troubled. "I warned him, but he would not listen. I told him too much time had gone by."

"Warned him about what?" Kate asked, turning the Lokapala in her hands.

"The Triads."

Without lifting her head, "The Triads? What are they?"

"You have heard of the Mafia?"

Kate's hands stilled but her voice was steady when she replied, "Of course."

"The Triads are our Chinese Mafia."

Kate very carefully set the Lokapala back on its velvet. "What have they to do with Rollo?"

"They operate the factory that produces the fake antiquities. We believed it was located in the Walled City. That is what Rollo went to find out."

"How do you know all this?" Kate asked, when she could trust her voice.

"I am not at liberty to disclose my sources of information. You must accept that I do know." He paused. "Just as I know that Despard's Hong Kong is very much involved."

Mechanically, keeping up the pretense of being a customer, Kate stared blindly at the Lokapala, not seeing it, not seeing anything but the confirmation she had dreaded.

"That is why I asked Rollo to come to Hong Kong," Ling Po went on.

Walking on eggs, "You are telling me that many of the items sold at the recent sale held by Despard's Hong Kong were fakes?" Kate asked.

"Not some, Miss Despard. Practically all."

Kate set down the Lokapala with a thump, since her suddenly palsied hands were in danger of dropping it. "You must be mistaken," she said when she could. "Nobody could get away with an auction of fakes passed off as genuine. It has never been done. Where would the quantity required come from? Who would authenticate them? Oh, I know even the greatest of experts can be fooled, but usually by a single piece, perhaps two. But a whole salesroom full!" She shook her head as firmly as she could, though it felt like any minute it would fall from her shoulders. "It is impossible to keep such an enormous con trick secret. Somebody, somewhere, would have said something . . . heard something, and had a piece tested . . ." As you did your horse? her inner voice asked sardonically.

"Not fakes such as these," Ling Po said with the flat calm of certainty. "And one must remember that where the Triads are involved, to talk means to die."

"Oh, come now . . ." Kate found herself beginning to bluster. All this talk of death unnerved her.

"You die, Miss Despard, and in the most unpleasant way. You, and your entire family. When you join the Triads you swear a blood oath in the most terrifying of secret ceremonies. Your ensuing silence is ensured by your fear of what they will do to you should you break that oath."

That's why Rollo spoke only of a three-dollar bill, Kate realized with a rill of fear.

"The Triads control Hong Kong, Miss Despard—unofficially, of course. It is well known that the police force is riddled with them. Even the government, it is said . . . which is why it has failed to eliminate them for so long. In this city, Miss Despard, be very careful to whom you speak and even more careful whom you trust."

He saw her eyes flicker as she absorbed his implication and continued, "Rollo is my dear friend. I would do anything to help him."

Kate looked shamefaced. "Of course . . ." she agreed, before going back to what loomed up in front of her, blocking out everything else. "So my stepsister is involved with the Triads?"

"Very much so. They supplied the fakes. She sold them."

"She must be mad," Kate said, half to herself.

Ling Po pursed his lips. "It is quite possible that she has no idea of the true identity of the people with whom she is involved. It is not unusual for the Triads to conceal their identity until they choose to reveal it."

Here he paused and Kate braced herself for the shock of fresh revelations.

"She is involved with a man named Chao-Li, ostensibly a respected dealer of antiques with a shop not far from Despard's in the Mandarin Hotel Arcade." Another pause. "He is, in fact, a high official in the Triad hierarchy, what they call a Red Robe. He, I am informed, is the one behind not only the creation of the forgeries, but their sale through Despard's."

Kate's face was waxy. She felt numb.

"Madame du Vivier may know, but I doubt it. Triad members are known only to other members of their group. But it makes little difference, anyway. She is so deeply involved that . . ." Ling Po spread his hands.

"That there is no escape," Kate finished for him dully. She can't know, she thought. Nobody in their right mind would get themselves involved with the Triads. She is greedy and unscrupulous, but she is not stupid. She probably saw nothing beyond the enormous amount of money she could make and thus defeat me and gain control of Despard's at one fell swoop . . . That is her obsession. To control Despard's. To steamroller over me and be seen to be undisputed champion.

But fakes . . . ! It was not unknown for a fake to be sold as genuine, usually by mistake because the forgery was a very good one and the provenance equally convincing. But to sell hundreds of them, deliberately and with malice aforethought . . . Kate's mind froze at the enormity of it all. The effrontery was breathtaking. Which is why she succeeded, she thought. Nobody in their right mind would so much as think such a thing possible.

Her mind could not seem to take it in. Fakes, like the poor, have always been with us, she thought, but not by the hundreds. It *can't* be, she thought stubbornly. Even she wouldn't have the nerve. Ling Po had gone behind the curtain into the back. Now he came through it again, carrying a small figure, about eight inches high. A man dressed as a groom, hands upraised as though clasping a bridle; that of the horse that would originally have been part of the group. He held it out to Kate. "Please. Examine this if you will."

Kate took it carefully. T'ang, she thought, hefting the figure, turning it in her hands. The balance was right, the feel was right, but taking the loupe he handed her she went over every inch. The modeling was superb, the glaze bore the unmistakable degrading betokening great age. Had her mind not been filled with doubts she would unhesitatingly have pronounced it genuine. As she had the horse.

When her eyes came up to meet his, Ling Po said, "Yes. It was made within the last two years."

"But where? And by whom? And how? I have never before seen fakes which are works of art in their own right. Whoever made this is an unknown genius."

"I agree. I have never seen such a forgery in all my years as a dealer."

"And were they all like this—in quality, I mean?"

"Each and every one. As were their provenances."

"And nobody—absolutely *nobody* suspects?"

"No one. Rollo and I know, and now you know. That is all."

"Thank God," Kate breathed. "If this gets out Despard's is ruined." She hesitated. "But—if the Triads are gangsters, like the Mafia, what are they doing making fine art forgeries? It is not their style."

"Yes, that is true. Obviously, it has become one of their many—outlets. Originally, as with the Mafia, the Triads were an honorable society. Now they are dedicated wholly to terror, extortion, prostitution, and drugs. They recruit mainly from the streets, but at the top are cultured and distinguished men."

Continuing the charade that had Kate as a "customer" Ling Po now placed in front of her a celadon bowl which, in spite of her state of shattered shock, had her exclaiming involuntarily, "Oh, how exquisite . . ." After a moment, "And Rollo knows all about—everything?" she asked.

"Yes. Rollo knows all about the Triads. He learned when he was here during the war."

"With ENSA?" Kate sounded skeptical.

"Entertaining the troops was his cover. In reality, he and I worked for Military Intelligence."

Her second shock of the day had Kate reeling. "Rollo!" her voice soared. "A spy!" Open-mouthed. "You are putting me on," she said feebly.

"No," Ling Po said, sounding puzzled. "It is many years ago now, of course . . . we were both young men then." Regretfully, "The times were different and so were we." He sighed gently. "But we kept in touch, afterward."

"I always knew Rollo had worldwide contacts," Kate said, almost to herself, "but this is ridiculous! Are you saying Rollo was a *real* spy—like the one who came in from the cold?"

"I, too, have read that admirable book. Yes. We were just like that, except our enemy was the Japanese."

"I don't believe this," Kate muttered fearfully. "I shall wake up in a minute, like Alice, and discover it has all been a dream."

"Believe it, Miss Despard," Ling Po said emphatically. "It is all true." Kate shook her head, as if to clear it of the jumble of enormity it could not deal with.

"A spy . . ." she muttered. "He said that was what he was coming to do but I never dreamed he was a real one once." A thought struck, like a gong. "Then he speaks Chinese?"

"Oh, yes. Very well. Mandarin, Cantonese, and Hong Kong's Hakka dialect."

Kate recoiled, her hands covering her face. "I'm going mad," she said from clenched teeth. "I must be. All this is too fantastic to be true." She whirled on Ling Po. "You are the Chinese dealer in antiquities he told me about, right?"

Ling Po bowed. "I have that honor."

"The one who aroused his 'curiosity.' Smell a rat indeed! He had the corpse in his pocket!" She was beginning to sound hysterical. "Rollo was eager to prove that he was still—capable. He said to me, 'Wait until Kate hears what I have pulled off. She will soon change her tune.' " Kate winced. "We had had a difference of opinion. He was angry because he thought I was relegating him to the background of my life."

Ling Po sighed. "Yes. Rollo would not like that."

"God, what an innocent I have been! I knew Rollo was well traveled and knew people all over the world but this is ridiculous."

"I wrote to him," Ling Po said. "We continued to correspond, he and I, and I told him what I had discovered."

"How?" pounced Kate. "How come you are so certain this is a fake?"

"I had it—and others I had friends buy for me at the auction—tested."

Craftily, Kate asked, "By what method?"

"Thermoluminescence. I have old friends from the . . .

past . . . who were in a position to have the tests done. Secretly, of course."

"What else?" Kate said bitterly. "Rollo . . . a spy," she said again. "No wonder he was so good at it." Her laugh rang false. "And to think I believed he came by it naturally."

"No. We both received our training in England," Ling Po said, not understanding the sarcasm.

Kate began to laugh. It got higher and higher until she clapped a hand across her mouth.. When she could, she let out a long, shuddering breath. "Sorry . . . but all this has hit me like a ton of bricks."

"It is understandable. But you had to know."

Kate leveled a look. "Just as you know all about my stepsister and me?"

"Yes. Rollo explained the situation."

"While not telling me a damned thing!"

"He could not—then. I had to write because I did not dare use the telephone—there are Triad members manning the switchboards as there are everywhere else—and I warned him of my discovery. In telling you, I have broken my own vow of silence, but I felt, in the circumstances, that you should know of the danger you are in."

"Me!" Again, Kate ran smack into the reality of a supposition.

"You are Rollo's friend. You have come here to see him. Having failed to eliminate him, they will not hesitate to do the same to you."

Kate shivered. She had thought it, but to have it confirmed . . .

"They will know by now that Rollo was masquerading as a Chinese—if they did not discover it before. They will wonder why," Ling Po continued.

"But if they know about me, what about you?"

Ling Po shrugged. "I must take my chances also."

Kate smiled suddenly, it was wistful. "Rollo used to dress up as a Chinaman for me when I was a child . . . he used to tell me he was Chu Chin Chow. But he never ever said he had been in China."

"He spent some years here as a young man. His father had some connection with one of the big English *hongs* in Canton. Rollo hated the work, but he came to love China. It was then he began masquerading as a Chinese. Always he excelled in theatricals. He became very good at it. His disguise, when he left me, was nigh perfect, but to enter the Walled City was foolhardy. I think that what happened is that he failed to give the correct answer when challenged by someone asking, 'Where do you belong, brother?' That is why you must take him away, and as soon as you can. He represents a danger they cannot allow to continue.'' He paused before asking delicately, "I believe you have powerful friends?''

"You mean the Chandlers? Yes. But they—Mr. Chandler and his grandmother—know nothing of this and must not find out.'' Now she paused before adding, "Mr. Chandler is my stepsister's husband.''

"I know.''

"But—Rollo is a police matter by now. They will protect him, surely.''

"There is no protection from the Triads once they have marked you down, Miss Despard—unless you seek the help of those same, powerful friends.''

"Very well," Kate said soberly. "But—please . . . would you do nothing more as yet. I want to get to the bottom of this myself. You know what is at stake here. Despard's reputation. If there is any way to put this right without the truth coming out, then I must take it.''

"It will be very difficult. The whereabouts of the fake-making factory is not known. If it was in the Walled City, as we suspected, it will already have been moved by now. Rollo's discovery would have ensured that. And to accuse without proof is fool-hardy where the Triads are concerned—sometimes even with proof. Discretion is mandatory. Nor can I be involved. My task is to pass on information—the Chinese are great gossips and I learn a great deal in this little shop. Also, I have contacts who must be protected. Until Rollo is able to tell us what he learned, nothing can be done.''

Kate felt weak with relief. She had had visions of the Hong Kong Police raiding Despard's salesrooms in the arcade at the Mandarin Hotel, and banner headlines in *The Times*.

"In the meantime I urge you, Miss Despard, to take him away from Hong Kong. He is not safe here.''

"But he is in the Chandler Clinic with round-the-clock nursing.''

Ling Po smiled. "I managed to get my message to you, didn't I? Who is to say there is not some Triad member working as a porter or a sweeper? They are everywhere,

Miss Despard." He coughed behind his hand, a Chinese mannerism that meant he was going to be bold. "It is my understanding that Mr. Blaise Chandler is an honorable man, and one to be trusted."

"Maybe, but remember who his wife is. *She* cannot be trusted. Whatever I tell him he could easily tell her. No, he must know nothing. It would be too risky."

"Then perhaps his grandmother? She is regarded with some awe in Hong Kong, such are her riches, her power, and her venerable age."

Kate gnawed a thumbnail. "Yes . . . the Duchess would understand."

"If you use the telephone, do so with extreme caution. I repeat—the Triads have their members everywhere." Without breaking stride, he continued in the same tone, "Yes, it is a most unusual piece . . ." as the bell tinkled and a European couple came in.

"Thank you for showing it to me," Kate said, politely, "but I am afraid it is more than I can afford."

"Perhaps you will honor my shop with your custom on your next visit to Hong Kong," he said with exquisite courtesy.

"Oh, I will be sure to do that," Kate said, aware that the couple, who were admiring a porcelain statue of the goddess Kwan Yin, were English. "Good afternoon."

He bowed her to the door.

Kate began to push her way back through the crowds, not conscious of where she was going, only of the enormity of what she had been told. When finally she returned to her surroundings, she was in a wide, bustling thoroughfare, heavy with traffic: trams, buses, lorries, cars, taxis, vans, and even more people. She saw an enormous modern building and a name that rang a bell. The Connaught Centre. Following the pedestrians she managed to cross the street. A nearby clock told her it was four o'clock. Blaise Chandler was not expecting her back until five. Well, she was supposed to be window shopping, and the Hong Kong guide in her room at the hotel had told her that the Connaught Centre was full of all kinds of shops . . .

The taxi she took back to the clinic delivered her there at five to five. She had wandered aimlessly, looking in shop windows, found a coffee shop and sat over a cup of coffee, so deep in thought that she had had to scramble to get back

in time. But she had got over her first shock. She still felt
stunned, but not quite so much. As she pushed through into
the ICU, she put on a bright smile.

"Here I am," she said cheerfully. "Right on time, I hope."

"So you are. Did you find what you were looking for?"

"Oh, yes," Kate assured him. "It was all quite fascinating
. . . so many lovely things."

She looked at Rollo. He was exactly as she had left him.

"No change." Blaise got to his feet, stretched. "Don't stay
too long," he said. "I'll send a car for you at eight to take
you back to the hotel. Have dinner in your room and an
early night."

"Yes, I will."

"What did you think of Hong Kong, then?"

"It quite took my breath away," Kate told him truthfully.
Then she said diffidently, "I thought I might call the Duchess. Is that all right?"

"Go ahead. She'll be delighted to hear from you."

"I'll do it when I get back to the hotel."

"Just so long as you don't forget the time difference.
Colorado is fifteen hours behind Hong Kong. Do it tomorrow morning; if you call her at nine A.M. Hong Kong time it
will be six o'clock back home."

"Oh, I'd forgotten." Kate was quite crestfallen; she had
wanted to talk to Agatha at once.

She needed to talk to someone, to get another reaction, to
have someone tell her she was not going mad; that it was
perfectly possible for Rollo to have been involved in cloak
and dagger work during the war; that he spoke both Mandarin and Cantonese. She had thought she knew everything
about him, yet she had not known he lived in China as a
young man. How old would he have been—twenty one or
two? He had not met her mother until 1943; yes, it was
perfectly possible for him to have lived a life neither she nor
perhaps anyone else knew about. Charlotte had known him
since before the war—had she known? If so, she had not
said either.

And this Ling Po. Whom did he report to? The police?
MI-5? Had he recruited Rollo in the first place? He looked
to be a contemporary in age. He had been very cagey when
she asked whom he worked for; nor would he tell her where
he got his information from. Gossip, he said. Was his little
shop a clearinghouse for spies?

". . . for them," Blaise was saying.

"What? Oh, sorry, I was miles away."

"I know. Didn't you visit Despard's?" he asked casually.

"No. Nor do I intend to."

"Why not? You've every right."

"It's enemy territory," Kate said crisply.

He met her defiant eyes, his own giving nothing away. How well he controlled *his* emotions.

He tossed her the newspaper he had been reading. "Here, catch up on the rest of the world," he said. "I'll see you tomorrow."

But when he had gone she did not read. She sat on, thinking, thinking, thinking . . .

She called Agatha next morning and the old lady was delighted to hear from her.

"Good news?" she asked hopefully.

Kate gave her a precis of Rollo's situation, then said without preamble, "Duchess, I need to talk to you on a line where we can't be overheard. Is that possible?"

"It is" the old lady assured her promptly, covering her surprise. "All you have to do is get down to the Chandler Building—it's on Connaught Road. Ask for Benny Fong. I'll call him and tell him to set things up. He's trustworthy. How soon can you get there?"

"I'll leave right now; I've had breakfast." Two cups of black coffee.

"Right—you're at the Peninsula so you've got to get across the harbor. You wait right there and I'll have somebody come and collect you. Now don't you worry. It will all be taken care of."

And inside a quarter of an hour her telephone rang to say a car was downstairs. A smiling young Chinese who introduced himself as John Fong—"Benny's my uncle"—kept up a steady stream of chatter as they drove, first to the cross-harbor tunnel, and then through it, eventually arriving on Hong Kong Island at a white, very American skyscraper overlooking the bay. Benny Fong was waiting in the foyer. Kate thanked John Fong, who said cheerfully, "Any time, ma'am." He had told her he'd graduated from UCLA and worked for ChanCorp as a gofer. "You know, go for this, go for that . . ."

Benny Fong, small, roly-poly, shrewd eyes behind thick trifocals, said deferentially, "Mrs. Chandler called me. If you will come with me, Miss Despard."

He led her to an elevator marked PRIVATE, and this took them up to the top—the thirtieth—floor, and let them out into an enormous office with windows on two sides, giving a panoramic view of Hong Kong, the harbor, and Kowloon on the other side. In front of one window was a desk, made of one enormous length of wood cantilevered on a steel X-support. On it were a blotter, a diary, a square crystal clock, a tray of pens and pencils, and three telephones.

"Mr. Chandler's office," Benny said. "He won't be in till later this morning."

He led the way across the vast expanse of sand-colored carpet, and Kate expected him to pick out one of the three telephones on the desk top.

But instead he bent to unlock a desk drawer with a key he took from his waistcoat pocket, and brought out a fourth telephone.

Kate opened her bag to take out her address book.

"You won't need that, ma'am," Benny Fong said. "Mrs. Chandler will call you." Even as he said it the phone pealed. "See?" he smiled, and left her alone in the office.

"That better?" were Agatha's opening words. "This is a private line with some electronic gizmo that prevents eavesdropping, so you can say whatever you want. Nobody but me will hear, and that bein' so, I gather you're in some kind of trouble."

Kate told her everything. ". . . so I have to get Rollo away from Hong Kong as quickly as possible, and the only person I know who can provide that sort of getaway is you and ChanCorp."

"And glad to." For once Agatha did not ask why Kate had not gone to Blaise. Not after what she had just learned. "You leave it all to me. We'll have you both out of danger within twenty-four hours. I may not be able to talk face to face anymore but I can work wonders with a telephone."

Kate was so relieved her voice fell off its perch. "Oh, Duchess . . . I can't tell you what it means to be able to just ask and receive so much."

"It pleasures me to be able to do it at all," Agatha said gruffly, "and I understand why you don't feel you can go to

Blaise, though I don't believe for one minute he'd have anything to do with whatever nastiness his wife has got herself into."

"It's not that," Kate said miserably, "it's—well, how can I ask him for help and then tell him it's because I am afraid of what his wife and her gangster friends will do?"

"I tell you straight, I wouldn't like to have to tell him that myself," Agatha answered, "and I'm the one person can say things to him nobody else can, but he has to know sooner or later, and knowing Blaise it had better be sooner. But you leave that to me. Don't you worry about it. Just get yourself ready to leave. You'll hear from Benny Fong when everything is arranged."

Kate replaced the receiver with a sigh of relief. She had known the Duchess would help. Already she both trusted and respected her as much—if not more—than anyone she had ever known, except perhaps Rollo. She sat back in the big leather chair, feeling as if a heavy burden had just been laid down. She swung around in it, gazed out at the view. The water of the harbor was vividly blue, busy with all sorts and kinds of boats, from the green-and-white ferries that did the eight-minute crossing from Hong Kong to Kowloon, to the big triple-deckers that took commuters to and from the outlying islands. There were speedboats, small yachts, big yachts, sailboats—every kind of sailing craft. Fragrant Harbor, she thought, which was what Hong Kong meant in English, though she was sure the ancient Chinese junk, worn and sea-stained bat-wing sails flapping in the breeze, would smell anything but fragrant. A little further on was a jet foil aquaplaning over the waves at astonishing speed, and in the far distance she could see enormous tankers and container ships carrying their cargoes to the docks. What a place to work in, she thought, as she stared at the giant buildings of the Central District—where she found herself yesterday—a cluster of sky-reaching towers. When she walked across to the other window, she could see Victoria Peak, its top shrouded in cloud, and a tram making its way up the hillside.

She turned back to the desk. Very bare, very—unrevealing. Like the man himself. It brought her problems crowding back in on her. Should she have gone to him? When he found out—and he was bound to because this was his office—he would be mad as hell. But she was still not sure of him, not sure she could trust him. All right, so she had made a mistake about him telling Dominique about Nicholas Chevely. But that did not necessarily mean he would not take steps to protect his wife's reputation—not to mention his own—once he knew what she was mixed up in. No, Kate decided with a heavy sigh. She had to be very careful. Ling Po had warned her. And no matter what Blaise said about strict impartiality, he was still Dominique's husband, and in Kate's book your first loyalty was to your wife, or your husband, as the case may be.

When Benny Fong came back she was still standing in front of the windows, gazing out.

"Fine view, isn't it?" he said proudly.

"That it is. I shouldn't get any work done, though. I'd be staring out of the window all day long."

"Would you like a cup of coffee, tea?"

"Nothing, thank you. But I'd be grateful for a lift to the hospital."

"The car—and John—are at your disposal while you are in Hong Kong. Mrs. Chandler's orders."

Kate laughed. "Does she bully you, too?"

"She only bullies those she cares about," he answered seriously. Then grinned. "I guess we both qualify."

He saw her down to the car, shook her hand and said to call him for whatever she wanted at any time. "Mr. Chandler's orders this time."

"Yes," Kate said, "he can bully, too."

When Blaise arrived at the office at half-past ten, he was in a much better frame of mind. He and Dominique had dined *à deux;* she had been attentive, loving, tenderly passionate afterward. She had, he believed, given the correct answer to every oblique question he put to her, and in a way that was both amused and knowing. "Ask away," it said. "I have absolutely nothing to hide." And this morning she had woken him in an amorous mood, proceeded to lead him up a winding road of sensation until he thought he would die before he reached the top, only to experience, when he got there, an orgasm that went on forever . . . Afterward he had dropped into sleep like a felled steer, woken to find her gone—nothing unusual—and a note that said, in her small, elegant handwriting: *"Now* do you believe me?"

Baby, he thought, when you convince me the way you did this morning I'd believe black was white.

So he was not prepared for the Molotov cocktail Benny threw at him.

"Kate Despard *what?*"

"Miss Despard was here at nine-thirty this morning to speak to your grandmother over the computaphone."

The computaphone was a ChanCorp invention; it rendered telephone conversation into a series of binary numbers so that anybody trying to eavesdrop would get nothing but static. It was used for top-level conversation on an Eyes Only classification.

"How the hell did she know about that?" he demanded.

"Mrs. Chandler called me, told me to get her down here so she could use it." Benny's pause told Blaise there was more.

"Go on," he said grimly.

"I'm to get a suitable ChanCorp plane ready to transport Mr. Rollo Bellamy and Miss Despard back to London soonest, along with all the equipment necessary to keep him alive on the way, including a doctor and a nurse. There's a 737 due in later this morning." Another pause. "Mrs. Chandler has spoken to the clinic."

"Okay, Benny. Thanks."

Blaise's face was a mask. Benny knew he was livid.

Here we go again, he thought, as he headed for the door. That old lady sure liked to dig in her spurs where her grandson was concerned. He was the light of her life but she'd been holding the reins so long they'd grown roots. There'd be another almighty spat. At that, the old lady seemed to thrive on them. Benny was of the opinion that they were her hold on life, and as a Chinese he thoroughly approved of the way her grandson honored her venerable age and wisdom.

"All right, Duchess," Blaise said in deceptively mild tones when his grandmother came on the line. "What the hell is going on around here? You ask me to come all the way to Hong Kong and then, when I get here, do all the work yourself. If I am wasting my time, please don't hesitate to tell me. I do have other things to do."

His grandmother was not deceived by the seemingly calm voice. "There are good reasons why Kate needed to speak without being overheard—"

"Which is why we are now talking on that same unbreachable line. What is so damned secret that it can't so much as be spoken of openly?''

"You ready for this, Boy?"

"Probably not, but I don't expect it'll make any difference, so whatever it is, shoot from the lip, as usual."

But as he listened his face changed, like a slow dissolve in a movie. The hand holding the receiver clenched until the knuckles threatened to burst the skin. He sat rigidly, staring at the view but not seeing anything except the hideous picture his grandmother's words were painting.

When she had done so, he was silent for so long that she was about to say something when he came back on the line. "All this is provable, I suppose."

"I checked out this Ling Po and he's genuine; no record, and he was here during the Japanese occupation. Rollo Bellamy is a different matter. Before the war he was in Canton, where he learned to speak Cantonese and Mandarin— because of his work apparently, some big English trading house in which his daddy, his real daddy on account of he had another one for show, had a large financial stake. He came back to entertain the troops, is the story, and that's all anybody will say. People I put on to it got the old fish eye when they tried to take it further, which in my book means we've caught a shark. Anyway, I think Benny should go see this Ling Po, and you should both see the fake. If any of this gets out, Despard's is down the drain. That's what worries Kate more than anything. Her attitude is if it means Dominique taking over the whole shebang in order to save its reputation, then that's all right with her." Pause. "It would not be right with me."

"I didn't think it would," Blaise said.

"Now look here, Boy. I'm giving it to you the way Kate gave it to me, but only because she couldn't bear to hit you with the truth. 'How do you tell somebody that their wife is not worth a light? I can't bear to have to hurt him that way' was what she said."

"No," Blaise said bleakly. "She doesn't like causing pain."

All he was conscious of was his own, and yet it seemed to him that he stood outside, watching himself suffer, unmoved and unimpressed. Don't give me that broken-hearted routine! part of him said. You've always known your wife had the soul of a pit boss; that she would buy and sell you if there was a profit to be made. And since when was this

Great Love anyway? All you ever shared with Dominique was sensual pleasure. To the rest you either shut your eyes or turned your back. Talk about Pontius Pilate! So suffer. You've always known you would have to pay the piper some day, so don't be surprisd if it's a hell of a lot more than you expected.

I knew it would cost me, he reminded himself. I just took the words at face value. Because that is what this is costing—me . . .

In pride, you mean, his other self sneered. Do you think you are the first man to suffer the insanity of infatuation? You knew she was what she was, but it suited you to disregard it. Serve you damned well right.

We don't always love what is good, he told himself self-pityingly.

Oh, come on . . . love? You had a plain old-fashioned case of the hots. If you loved her you'd accept her—every rotten part of her. Love's shortcomings are part of its nature. You know—the "with all her faults I love her still" routine. If you loved your wife you'd stand by her, even for being involved in fraud on a massive scale, attempted murder, sexual betrayal, and God knows how many other malfeasances. It's an imperfect world, so why so shocked at the exposure of someone you knew from the start was badly flawed character-wise? If you loved her, the minuses would be as nothing against the total sum of her pluses, but all you can see is a disastrous set of figures.

He stared at them. They did not change. They still made him feel sick.

You were thinking with your cock, his other self told him cynically. Around her, what other kind of thought was possible? But you, of all people, should have known better. I mean, your own mother taught you about lies and betrayal very early on. You chose Dominique deliberately because around her you never felt emotionally involved, only physically.

Like I said—a bad case of the hots; all this has done is provide the salutary bucket of water, that's why you're steaming . . . Besides, haven't you forgotten something?

Like what?

Do you remember what she said when you asked her to marry you?

Now you remind me?

She asked if you were willing to take her as she was, for what she was—remember? And you said that whatever she was—or wasn't—she was what you wanted (key word here) more than you had ever wanted anything. Then she warned you—repeat, warned—that if what she was should turn out to be more than you had bargained for, it would be too late to complain, and you said—and here I quote: "No man in his right mind would ever complain about you."

Get to the point, he told himself coldly.

You said a truer thing than you realized. You were not in your right mind. For almost three whole years you have not been in your right mind. That kick in the gut has made you cough up the poisoned apple, that's all.

All, he thought, as in whole, complete . . . As in fool . . .

Benny Fong dealt with all the arrangements for getting Rollo safely away from Hong Kong. Kate neither heard from nor saw Blaise Chandler. He knows what I've done, she thought, and he's furious. She longed to ask Benny where he was, but would not allow herself.

She checked out of the hotel and the car took her to the clinic, where an ambulance transported Rollo, his machinery, his doctor, a nurse, and Kate, to Kai Tak, where the big copper-colored Boeing was waiting. The ambulance was followed by another car containing four large Chinese, and that was followed by a police car.

While Rollo was unloaded, Benny invited Kate to inspect the plane's interior. "We took out some seats, made a space where the trolley could be bolted to the floor and his machines set up—we've put in the necessary electrical connections. There's a bed for you, and another for the medical staff when they are not on watch. The four security guards will also fly with you, though there won't be trouble because it's a nonstop flight. We've fitted extra fuel tanks so you don't need to land anywhere until you get back to London. If there's anything you don't see—name it."

Kate shook her head. "You have done more than enough, Mr. Fong—"

"Everybody calls me Benny."

"—Benny, then. I really am most grateful to you."

"Mrs. Chandler said you were to be given VIP treatment." And Mr. Chandler? Kate longed to ask, but did not.

She stayed in the plane, keeping well out of the way as the

trolley was winched up on a forklift truck, the inert form that was Rollo still attached via various umbilical cords to the machines that helped him breathe, fed him intravenously, drew off waste liquids. She was fastening her seat belt in the comfortable armchair, placed strategically between the bulkhead—so she could look out the window if she wished—and Rollo, when she saw a big black car coming across the airfield toward them. Blaise Chandler got out. As he entered the plane, she saw immediately that he was once more the remote, unreachable, polite stranger, and she knew better than to make mention of her phone call to his grandmother.

He inquired courteously if she was satisfied with the arrangements, and she responded in kind.

She knew that this proud, self-controlled man was aware of her own anguished response to his suffering, yet not by so much as a flicker of the guarded eyes, a dip in the politely empty voice, did he indicate it. He had drawn a line and nobody—*nobody*—had better cross it. He shook hands, his face still an unsmiling mask, said he would call her once she was back home, and left the aircraft.

Kate turned her face to the window, staring out but seeing nothing because of the curtain of tears in her eyes. So she did not know that Blaise Chandler stood on the tarmac until the plane, having taxied slowly away, heading for the runway at the other side of the airport, had taken off, dwindling until it was the size of a mosquito and then vanishing from sight. Only then did he reenter the car and drive away.

The flight home was uneventful. Rollo made neither movement nor sound as the plane droned on. She leafed through magazines, shook her head at food but accepted coffee, tried to doze, all to no avail. It was no use. She had blown it. Done what she had had the nerve to accuse him of: told tales. But I had no choice, she agonized as she paced the bars of her cage. I had to get Rollo out and the only way I could do that with ease and speed was by asking the Duchess. I might have had to wait another twenty-four hours for a chartered plane. Nevertheless, you were a long way from being friends even now, and this has made him your enemy. You have made him look at what his wife really is and he'll never forgive you for it. It was evident in every stiff bone in his body. You have hurt him, and deeply. I had no choice,

she refuted doggedly. Despard's has to be protected. If what
Dominique has done gets out it is finished. She has to be
prevented from doing it again and the only person who can
do that is her husband. If he doesn't like it, then too bad: he
ought to have known better than to get himself sucked dry
by a woman like that.

The doctor and nurse checked Rollo regularly, changed
the various bags connected by tubing, checked pulse, respi-
ration, blood pressure. Both firmly declined Kate's offer of a
spell by the patient. In circumstances like these, expert
knowledge was called for. So she had nothing else to do but
sit and think, think, think, as they flew across half the world,
arguing with herself, trying to find justifications, and in her
struggle, sinking further and further into the bottomless pit
of depression and misery.

By the time the plane finally touched down at Heathrow,
she was both relieved to be home and longing to be back in
Hong Kong where she could confront Blaise Chandler and
unload her feelings. What she did instead was accompany
Rollo in his ambulance to the private hospital in St. John's
Wood—"small enough to keep tabs on" as Benny Fong had
put it—where Rollo would have a private room and round-
the-clock nursing. Kate had groaned at the thought of facing
her Board with medical costs of upwards of three hundred
pounds a day, which was what she had heard these hospitals
cost, and decided she could not possibly expect Despard's to
pay; it would have to be her charge, that was all. But when
she had a word with Social Services, she was told briskly that
on Mr. Blaise Chandler's instructions, all charges were to be
borne by ChanCorp. "Which put up the money to build this
hospital in the first place," she explained, "so he has certain—
privileges. He is also chairman of the Board of Management. Do not concern yourself, Miss Despard, except to
direct your efforts toward Mr. Bellamy's recovery." Another
brisk smile and Kate was left with a positive cement mixture
of emotions. What was she to make of a man who, at their
last meeting, had fended her off with a twenty-foot barge
pole, and yet had gone to the trouble of seeing that a minor
employee of Despard's, even if a major friend of its chairman and managing director, was given the best possible
medical care and all at no cost to himself or her?

She left Rollo in the ICU, and as it was by then only four
o'clock, went straight to Despard's, where she gave her

tight-lipped and disapproving Board an edited rundown of the situation.

"Really, Kate, I cannot think what you were about," Nigel Marsh told her gravely. "There was no need for Bellamy to go to Hong Kong. James Grieve's report is on my desk right now and very comprehensive it is, too. If you had left it all to him, then none of this would have happened." He clicked his tongue. "You look quite dreadful. Worn out and sick with worry."

"I plead guilty to all the charges," Kate replied wearily. "I wanted more than just facts and figures; I wanted ambience and—oh, all the little touches James would not notice, concentrating as he undoubtedly would, on the merchandise. I wanted a whole and rounded picture of what Dominique was up to."

"A military intelligence operation, eh?"

Kate looked down at her desk. If only you knew, she thought, and said, "Yes, that sort of thing. We know she spies on us, so I thought to do a little tit for tat."

"But Bellamy . . ." reproached Nigel. "My dear, he invariably leaves a clearly marked trail behind him."

Only when he wants to be followed, Kate told him silently.

"Well," Nigel sighed, "it is to be hoped that he recovers eventually."

"However long it takes, the responsibility—financially and otherwise," Kate said clearly, "is mine. This was a private visit on behalf of me, not Despard's. I shall not expect the Board to pick up the bill."

Nigel looked uncomfortable. That very possibility had resulted in a heated argument not long before. Now he said diffidently, "I kept this for you . . ." He held out one of the Sunday color supplements. "A four page full-color spread on your sister's Sale of the Century. Free publicity of the very best kind. The report is nothing but a paean of praise." A deprecatory cough. "The sooner your face replaces hers, the better. Powerful pieces of persuasion like this do not sit well with clients wavering in their allegiance." The implied criticism was: Despard's is where your attention should be focused rather than Rollo Bellamy.

"Once Courtland Park starts rolling, our own bandwagon will, too," Kate replied confidently. "Fortunately, before . . . Rollo had already drawn up a detailed publicity schedule."

Nigel sighed. "That will not please the publicity department."

"I know what I am doing," Kate said with all her father's arrogance. "Rollo has a genius for publicity—self or otherwise—and Courtland Park has, as you so rightly pointed out, to be our answer to Hong Kong. Every bit as dramatic; every bit as newsworthy."

There was a brooding determination to her voice that was new, Nigel thought. She had lost weight, she looked drawn, her eyes were shadowed and haunted-looking. But there was the ring of steel about her now. The shy, nervously uncertain girl had gone through the fire and come out annealed. What *had* happened in Hong Kong? he wondered.

"I am tired," she said now.

"You look it," Nigel said, worried and concerned.

"I'm going home to get some sleep. Tomorrow I have to get down to it . . ."

But she had one last stop to make.

"My dear," Charlotte said, obviously distressed. "I have been so worried . . ." She was aghast at Kate's drawn face. Her sparkle was gone. "Oh, my dear . . ." she soothed, and in the face of her kindness, her tender concern, Kate burst into tears.

"If you had seen his face . . ." she sobbed. "He looked awful, as if I'd consigned him to hell, but I had no choice, I had to have help . . . But he hates me, I know he does. I've made him look at something he did not want to see."

And at you in a way you did not want to see, Charlotte thought. Oh, dear. You have not picked an easy man. I thought that the first time I met him. Those tightly contained, overcontrolled men are always like that, because there was a time when they weren't and it cost them dearly.

But she comforted, soothed, made Kate drink hot, sweet tea and then insisted on accompanying her back to the penthouse, where she saw her into bed, the two Valium she had dropped into the tea working their magic. She sat beside her until the agony of tears had subsided into the soft, regular breathing of sleep, then she went to the hospital to see Rollo.

A few days later, Benny Fong sat across from Blaise Chandler in his office. "It isn't easy, Boss. Nobody knows a thing when you ask, but you know damn well that the moment you're gone they are going to be on the telephone to the very people you've asked about. So I went to a friend of mine who got bounced from the police—he actually was an honest cop—because he asked too many questions in the wrong places. He says the Triads grow more powerful every day. They control the 'Hong Kong Connection' which runs all the heroin to Europe. The cops are useless and helpless and most of them are bought anyway. He mentioned some real VIPs who are in hock to the Triads and some others— big noises here in Hong Kong—who actually are members of a Triad."

"Like who?"

Benny told him and Blaise felt a shudder of shock. They were men he did business with, men of reputation and distinction, many of them recipients of honors from the Crown.

"If he says so then it is so. He's got this thing about being given the runaround and he wants to get his own back. If you need a man then he's it." Benny paused and Blaise knew there was more—worse—to come. "There's a man named Chao-Li, a dealer in antiques, runs a shop in the Mandarin Arcade; according to my friend he's a Big Brother in a Triad code named Golden Dragon." Another pause. "He's been doing business with Mrs. Chandler."

After a moment Blaise said, "Go on."

"My friend says he's dangerous. He's the one who reported him when he got too close, put the mark on him as an informer. His Triad is a big one—must be at least five thousand—rumor has it there are at least five hundred thousand Triad members in all Hong Kong but nobody knows for sure; it could be ten times that. Anyway, he says the Triads are like armies; iron discipline, blood oaths and, if you talk, not only you but your entire family dies. Just like the Mafia, they have soldiers—only the Triads call them Fighters, and Paper Scribes, the fixers, what the Mafia call *consiglieri*. Senior members are called Uncles, but the really big boys are the Red Robes, known as Big Brothers. My friend is sure that Chao-Li is a Big Brother." Another pause. "Whether or not Mrs Chandler knows this is open to question, my friend says probably not. They don't tell you anything until they have got you in so deep you'll never get out."

The two men stared at each other, sharing the same thought.

"It is possible," Benny said cautiously. "They use all sorts of covers to ship their heroin. It all comes from the Golden Triangle—the raw opium, I mean—and they have their own factories where it is processed. Then it is shipped from here in the form of the white powder which is the end result."

"How?" asked Blaise.

"Smuggled in with legitimate cargo in the holds of ships and planes. My friend says it's even been found in tubes of toothpaste. Whatever and wherever they can find an ostensibly legal cargo that will hold and conceal the heroin."

"And at the other end?"

"New York has a Chinatown, so does San Francisco. They are both big ports, with a large Chinese population. Also, Chao-Li has a branch on Madison Avenue."

Again they held a long stare, both seeing the same picture. Consignments of antiques from Hong Kong, destined for Despard's in New York and the new branch being set up in San Francisco, concealing plastic bags of pure heroin.

"It may have been done before—the antiques, I mean," Benny went on. "Nobody knows for sure, or it may be that this is a new angle, one they are trying out for the first time."

"You are sure your information is kosher?" Blaise asked.

"My friend knows what he is talking about. He's spent years tracking them down."

"How would it be hidden?"

"Inside statues, figures, that's where the fakes come in. They are made in two halves, or drilled with holes so that the powder can be poured inside, then the holes are sealed and the figures decorated so they can't be spotted. They've probably established a known procedure so that they are familiar to the customs people—and Chao-Li is a legitimate businessman. His shop sells the real thing, so a judicious sprinkling of fakes would not be questioned. Once the consignment gets to the other end they've probably got another setup for extracting the heroin."

"That's what I want you to find out," Blaise said. "I also want a tail put on my wife." Benny pretended to be taking notes; he did not want to look at Blaise's face. "I want her office bugged—you know the sort of thing. I'll do the penthouse myself."

Very carefully Benny said, "I'd be careful, Boss. Triads don't trust anybody; they'll have her covered every which way."

"Even so. She's the only lead we have, and knowing what she is up to is the only means I have of protecting her as well as finding out exactly how deep she is in with them. Use all your contacts, Benny; spend whatever you have to and take whatever backup you need. I want to know everything there is to know."

Benny nodded again. Blaise's voice was even, controlled, yet he still dared not look into the dark eyes. Benny liked and admired his boss, had more than once wondered how he had become so involved with a woman like Dominique du Vivier, wondered now how the hell he was going to extricate her from this mess, and resolved to apply all his efforts to seeing that he did.

"Find out who does Despard's export packing and shipping, how long they've been doing it—I want to see copies of the paperwork—everything."

"No problem," Benny said. He could get his cousin Choy to do that; Blaise had got him his job as a porter at Despard's. And for a shadow, his own brother Eddy was perfect. He could become the invisible man when it came to tailing somebody. Like all Chinese, Benny believed in keeping everything in the family.

"I also want it put out that Rollo Bellamy is on the danger list; that even if he does come out of his coma he will be a vegetable. Let that filter through to those who matter."

"Right," Benny said, smiling broadly. "I've got contacts in London's Chinatown."

"We have to go carefully on this one," Blaise said. "If they are ruthless enough to seek to eliminate Bellamy then I have to protect my wife. She is in great danger, but I can't let her know that we know. She might do something we don't want her to do."

The words "and we know she is capable of anything," remained unspoken.

What a bitch, raged Benny silently, her and this whole damned mess. He knew his friend was suffering; though outwardly he gave no sign, Benny knew him well enough to sense what he was going through. He himself had never liked nor trusted Mrs. Chandler. He did not know when Dominique had been born, but he was willing to bet that in her horoscope, the Snake figured prominently. Snake females were the original *femmes fatales*, the kind who mesmerized men. To the Chinese, the Snake was a supernatural creature with more than a touch of the sinister, and he had seen Dominique wreathe herself around Blaise Chandler like a python. She also thrived on intrigue, had the Snake's lust for power and love of the limelight.

It might be a good idea, he thought suddenly, to let that be known . . . The Chinese were serious believers in the Zodiac; they would be extra careful if they knew they were dealing with a Snake.

"I'll get on to it right away," he promised, rising from his chair, but Blaise did not hear him. He was staring out of the window again, with an expression on his face that made Benny withdraw in silence.

WRONG
FOOTING

September

16

After spending an hour with Rollo, Kate decided to walk home. It was an Indian-summer night, the air clean and fresh after the ether and antiseptic smells of the hospital, though this one was more on the lines of an expensive hotel. Kate was well aware of the prevailing opinion that Rollo Bellamy had received no more than he had deserved and that, no doubt, for sticking his long nose where it was not wanted. But she held on to the hope—all she had— that, one day, he would come out of his deep coma, that he would be well again. And she had exercised her authority, growing now under the frequent doses of success she was taking, in silencing the discontent. She also kept a close eye on Despard's financial position, knew that her efforts to acquire every possible sale, of note or otherwise, was maintaining it in a very healthy state. In that regard, she had, in the weeks since her return, instituted several innovations.

She had not forgotten that on that terrible afternoon in Hong Kong, wandering about the Connaught Centre, she had found a nearby coffee shop with something like profound relief, glad of the chance to sit down, rest her weary body and think. So she had consulted an interior designer, who had produced a plan for remodeling Despard's third floor, so that a coffee shop could be built.

Her idea created a furor.

"We are a reputable auction house!" John Steadman thundered affrontedly, "not some West End department store."

But Kate was bent and determined that browsing customers should have somewhere to sit down, to ponder on a projected buy over a cup of coffee or tea and a delectable pastry or well-filled sandwich. It meant relocating the accounts department to Despard's Downtown, where there was plenty of room, but Kate had overridden wails about distance by expanding Despard's already established computer link; information could be sent and received as well as retrieved.

"But the cost!" her head of Accounts moaned. "We should be consolidating, not expanding."

"Expanding is what I have in mind," Kate told him crisply.

John Steadman threatened to resign, but when Kate had shown no sign of panic he was forced to climb down.

"By God!" he complained to everyone within hearing distance, "she may have come to learn but she is now staying to teach."

But Claudia Jamieson supported Kate, as did one or two of the younger element, who thought it an excellent idea.

"It gives us a more or less captive audience," Claudia sparkled.

"And they can sit and look at paintings up for forthcoming sales," somebody else pointed out.

"It will also be the best coffee in London, and as for the pastries . . ."

"Despard's is not a restaurant," John retorted huffily.

But Kate pushed on; hers was the final say-so, and Charles Despard had always been In Charge, a benevolent autocrat. What nobody had expected was that his daughter, so unsure, so uncertain at first, should suddenly blossom into a woman who not only knew what she wanted, but also saw that she got it.

Her plans for Courtland Park, received at first with shocked disbelief, soon became the main topic of conversation.

"Obviously, she must have learned a thing or two from her sister," some said. Others were of the opinion that Kate Despard would soon be in a position, as John Steadman had said, to teach.

"We've got twenty-eight million pounds to beat," Kate told her Board, "and I intend to see that we do just that."

To this end, she also instituted Despard's Discovery Days, where people who would normally never set foot inside an auction house were encouraged to bring in for valuation and, hopefully, future disposal, any item they thought might be of value. Kate had got the idea while watching the Antiques Road Show on TV. Already, after only four such days, they had acquired an amazing number of items for sale, including one amazing find. A man had brought in a small painting which, he said, his father had brought back from France after the war. During the liberation he had given a Frenchwoman, whose house had been reduced to rubble, food for herself and her children; in return she had insisted he take the painting, which, she had said, was valuable. It had been hanging above the sideboard ever since, but after reading in the papers about the Discovery Days, he wondered if she had been right. She had been. The sharp-eyed junior who had examined it first had spotted what she thought was an early work by an artist whose output had never been vast, and had called down her head of department. He had confirmed her suspicions. The painting was an early work of Henri Rousseau, *Le Douanier,* with a value of between £200,000 and £400,000.

After that, there were no more snotty remarks or snobbish allusions to "Despard's Dustbin Days." They all wanted to be the one to discover another amazing find.

She had also created a furor over the Cornelia Fentriss sale, because the jewels would be worn by professional models instead of being hemmed in by guards.

"Have you thought of the security?" they asked her, horrified.

She had. Agatha Chandler had provided her with the name of a firm ChanCorp used and, after discussing her plans, they had set up a tight security arrangement.

"The auction profession has been languishing in its own, small confines for far too long," Kate told her Board ruthlessly. "There's an enormous public out there. We have to bring them in."

So there was a smiling, very pretty young girl on the reception desk these days; if that did not appeal, waiting in the wings was a whole plethora of Despard's aristocrats. She had also initiated something that had never been done before: offering "advances" to clients planning to sell through Despard's. For the giant Cornelia Fentriss jewel sale, for instance, there was a one-year credit arrangement for potential consignors, after thorough investigation of their background, financial and otherwise, of course.

"There is new wealth out there," she argued. "People with enormous amounts of money who haven't had it long and are in the market for the kudos an expensive piece of art brings. We can't go on relying on our small circle of clients forever. We have to expand." But she eschewed the second rate, and with Dorothy Bainbridge, whose conservatism when it came to reserves was legendary, backing her up, refused to exaggerate the worth of any piece.

Now she felt a contented glow as she once more reviewed the half-year figures: they were up 54 percent—£5,842,793 as against £2,848,671 for the previous year. Of course the Steyning Bequest and Rollo's six Picassos had helped, but the Courtland Park and Fentriss sales would really make the coffers ring.

She began to ponder the flyers Despard's would send out for both sales, in addition to the superb catalogues, glossy in their full-colour splendor. Despard's blue, she thought, with a gold edging. Old Gaston's portrait at the top, with the words, in the elegant copperplate that was associated with the company: *Despard's: On the Premises: Courtland Park, Sussex, the Property of the late John Randolph Courtland. Week commencing Monday, 30 October. View days 23-27 October.* And for the other one—white, with black copperplate. *Despard's, Arlington Street. Jewelry—the property of the late Cornelia Fentriss Gardner. Wednesday, 16 September at 8 p. m. Black Tie.*

So deep in thought was she as she stepped off the pavement to cross over to Devonshire Place that she failed to notice the big black car some way behind her, moving slowly and without lights. There were few people about, it was quiet, but she still did not hear its sudden acceleration as she reached the middle of the road. All she knew was that, suddenly, she was pushed forward forcefully and somebody fell on top of her, rolling her toward the opposite curb. She hit the ground with painful violence, striking her shoulders, her head buried against a broad male chest. I'm being mugged! she thought and then everything went black.

She came to within seconds to find a dark shape looming over her. Instinctively she put her arms over her head.

"It's all right, ma'am. Sorry I had to tackle you like that, but if I hadn't, you'd have been under the wheels of that car."

"Which car?"

"You didn't see it? It missed us by inches."

"No, I didn't see any car or hear one either."

He solicitously helped her up, brushed her down, asking quickly, "You hurt?"

"I'll probably be black and blue tomorrow, but I don't think anything is broken."

"Let's take a look-see."

His hands were brisk, impersonal. "No . . . I think you're okay."

"Thanks to you."

"Lucky I was right behind you. You seemed to be lost in thought."

"I was," Kate admitted guiltily.

She examined him in the light of the nearby street lamp. He was big; six four at least, and built to match. He had a thatch of straw-blond hair and eyes that looked palely blue. All-American, she thought. "You must play football to tackle like that," she said with a wince.

"Used to, in college."

He was about her own age, personable, friendly, like some big, shaggy puppy. His grin revealed flawless American teeth.

"You want me to flag a taxi?" he asked.

"If you can find one." Feelingly, "To think I decided to walk, tonight, for a change."

"I walk myself," he said disarmingly, before putting two fingers in his mouth and blowing a piercing whistle. A taxi some fifty yards away headed in their direction. "Would you like me to see you safely back home?"

"Why not? I owe you a drink at least."

"You live above a shop?" he asked in surprise as the taxi drew up outside Despard's.

"Sort of."

He looked around as they got into the elevator. "Is this some kind of art gallery or something?"

"Or something," Kate answered amusedly. "Have you ever heard of Despard's?"

He shook his head.

"Sotheby-Parke Bernet?"

"Oh, sure."

"Despard's is an auction house like them."

"Oh, I see. You manage it or something?"

"In a way."

The elevator opened directly into her large living room with its view over London. She heard him whistle softly. "Say . . . you've got yourself quite a view." He turned a complete circle. "Inside *and* out."

"What would you like to drink?"

"I could go for a cup of coffee."

He leaned against the door-jamb of the adjoining kitchen to watch her set the coffee to drip.

"What are you doing in England?" Kate asked.

"Working. I'm with the embassy in Grosvenor Square."

"Doing what?"

"Oh, I'm just a guy who issues visas." He stuck out a large hand. "My name's Larry Cole."

"Kate Despard."

He did a double take. "You're the boss!" Turning back to the large room with its comfortable furniture personally chosen by Charles Despard, lit by lamps in warm golden shades, he said in tones that told her he was impressed, "I guess you're pretty knowledgeable about art, then?"

"I have to be, in my job."

"It must be pretty interesting."

"I think so."

"My mother's English," he volunteered. "My father was at the American airbase, Brize Norton, back in the Fifties."

"So you have relatives here?"

"Only my mother's sister."

He was easy to talk to, an amiable, unflappable blond giant, and they sat over the coffee until the little cupid clock struck eleven.

"Hey, will you look at the time!" he exclaimed. "I guess I lost track . . ."

"Where do you live?"

"Maida Vale."

"There's a taxi rank in Piccadilly."

"Yeah, I know."

"How long have you been here?"

"A month, now."

"Then you can't have seen much."

"Not all that I want to." He smiled nicely as he asked, "You wouldn't care to show me the rest?"

"It would have to be a Sunday. It's the only time I have free these days," Kate found herself answering.

"Sunday would be fine. Shall I come for you?"

"Why not?"

"That'll be great" he said enthusiastically.

As Kate rose her shoulders twinged and she winced.

"You hit the ground pretty hard," Larry commiserated. "A hot bath might help."

"I think I'll take your advice."

She took him down in the lift, saw him out.

He stuck out a hand again. "Till Sunday then."

Kate shook it. "And thank you again."

"My pleasure, ma'am."

He gave her another wide grin and she watched him stride off up the street before locking the door after him.

She did follow his advice, filling the tub and liberally sprinkling the water with fragrant oil before climbing in and lying back with a sigh.

Larry Cole, meanwhile, walked rapidly to the taxi rank in Piccadilly, where he was driven to a house overlooking Hampstead Heath. Letting himself in he went straight to a telephone.

"This is Larry Cole." He then gave a terse rundown of his meeting with Kate, describing the car and giving its number and make, and adding that he had made contact as ordered. His manner had changed completely; he was cool, crisp, competent. And when he took off his jacket, he was wearing a shoulder holster.

Kate ached badly next morning, and in the afternoon was forced to call her doctor. He examined her, told her nothing was broken, but she was badly bruised. He advised her to take it easy for a couple of days and gave her some painkillers, shaking his head over hit-and-run drivers.

"It's fortunate that young man acted so quickly," he told her.

"Yes," Kate said, smiling to herself. "Isn't it?"

Dominique paced the floor of the enormous drawing room in her Victoria Peak penthouse. Chao-Li was late. She had bathed herself, anointed her body with fragrant lotion; his favorite champagne—Roederer Cristal—lay cooling; along with a plate of the dim sum he loved. Where was he? He had been due at nine; it was now ten. She checked her reflection in the ornately carved Chinese Chippendale mirror on the wall above the couch, upholstered in what had once been a cardinal's red robes, and adjusted one sapphire solitaire.

Perhaps he had been detained with news from London; perhaps, when he finally turned up, it would be to say that the incomplete matter was now complete; that Rollo Bellamy was dead.

When she had heard he had been flown back to London, and in a ChanCorp jet, her fury had known no bounds, though she had been careful not to let her husband see it. Not that she had seen him much, of late, or that there was much joy to be had from him.

"I do have my own work to do," he had said, when she had remonstrated him for his inattention.

"Like arranging for Rollo Bellamy to be given the VIP treatment."

"Kate wanted him back home. She had work, too, and not in Hong Kong."

"Quite the busy little bee," she had sneered.

"You have your own considerable stocks of honey," had been the short reply.

Dominique went to the fireplace, stared into the arrangement of leaves that filled it. Her long, scarlet nails tapped impatiently on the marble mantelpiece. The little crystal clock now said 10:05. She straightened the twin jade Buddhas that stood at either end, then turned and began to pace again, absentmindedly leaning down to rifle the tray of dim sum as she passed the scarlet and black lacquer table on which it was placed. She went to the windows, curtained in filmy voile, which she pulled aside to stare out at the lights of Hong Kong, glittering below. Her foot tapped impatiently in its high-heeled mule of white satin, matching the clinging robe she was wearing, the wide sleeves trimmed with floating marabou feathers, under which she was naked. She loathed being kept waiting. One hand went to the thick, twisted rope of pearls and sapphires about her throat, and twisted it even more. This was not like him. Always before, he had been either on time or early. Never ever had he been late. She had met him two years before, at a sale at which he had bought a very fine Quianlong white jade jar. He had looked at her boldly, for a Chinese, with a pair of black eyes that seemed to penetrate her mind. She had at once been conscious of a sensuality commensurate with her own. She had invited him into her office upstairs for a drink, and one thing had led to a whole series of others. He was the second man she could not pin down; each time she thought she had him he was gone again, and it was this, as much as his incredible skill and stamina as a lover, that kept her in his orbit.

Now she was beginning to fray at the edges. She, who was so expert at unraveling men, found herself like a bitch in heat.

Then she heard a sound and whirled; he was standing in the archway leading to the lobby. "At last!" she began imperiously, only to stop abruptly as she saw how he was dressed. Not in his usual European suit, but as a Chinese, in a scarlet robe. He looked wholly and disturbingly foreign. Even his bow was Chinese.

"Madame."

"What do you mean, 'Madame'? I've been waiting for you one whole hour and more. Where have you been? Why are you late? And what news have you for me?"

"I have news, certainly."

Again his tone of voice, imperturbable, immovable, made her frown. "Well?" she urged impatiently.

"Please, sit down." It was an order, not a request. "We have things to discuss."

She regarded him with astonishment. "What on earth is the matter with you? Of course we have things to discuss, like why Rollo Bellamy is still alive, and certain other salient facts—"

"The facts which I have come to acquaint you with are ones with which you are not familiar," Chao-Li said.

Again Dominique regarded him with astonishment. "Such as?"

He did not answer at once, merely let his eyes rest on her. She felt as if he had placed a hand against her chest and pushed. Almost without volition she moved toward the big chair, upholstered to match the couch, and dropped into it, the white satin of her robe contrasting sharply with the blood-red background. Her instincts were at full stretch, every one of them shrieking a warning: the wind had changed, and if she knew what was good for her, she had better get on to a new tack.

But she did not let him see her sudden alarm. She reached toward the silver box of cigarettes, extracted one and lit it, blowing smoke at him. "So?" she demanded.

"I have come to discuss your future."

Dominique stared. "*My* future?"

"To tell you that everything has changed—sooner than

anticipated—and that it is essential we proceed with our plans as quickly as possible."

"Plans? You know another auction is out of the question for many months . . ."

"I am not speaking of auctions, Madame."

"Then what *are* you speaking of?"

"If you will conduct yourself as a woman should, I will explain."

Again Dominique felt as though he had shoved her. Conduct herself like a woman! Had she not done so time and time again in her big bed upstairs?

"I have instructions for you," he went on, still in the same, formally polite voice.

"*You* have instructions for *me?*" Dominique allowed herself a small laugh.

"You will memorize them." Chao-Li continued as though she had not spoken. "The first one is that you will change your export packers and shippers. You will engage a firm known as Flowering Cherry Import/Export. They have many years' experience in the handling and transportation of all kinds of art. They collect, pack, crate, ship, and deliver, handling every detail down to the necessary customs forms. In the future, Despard's Hong Kong will use this company."

"I will not! How dare you tell me how to run my own company? I have no reason to be dissatisfied with my present shippers and I do not know this Flowering Cherry whatever."

"It is not necessary that you know them. Your duty is to do as you are told."

Dominique was about to open her mouth and blast him, when again she felt the force emanating from him. Her voice died as her eyes widened and she hung upon his own, unable to move.

"From now on, Madame, you have no say in this matter or any others that concern us. You will do as you are told."

Dominique was pinned to her chair by the force of the brilliant eyes; he was directing something at her, an awesome kind of power against which she was useless. But she had spirit. "You should know better than to dictate terms to me. I know too much."

She had the impression that he smiled though his inscrutable, now so Chinese face showed none. "No, Madame. It is you who know nothing."

Dominique felt a chill; this was not the Chao-Li she knew. This was a cold-voiced, contemptuous superior who looked at her as if she was a servant and talked to her as though she was a prisoner of war.

"You are in this as deeply as I am!" she told him coldly.

"No, Madame. We only dug the pit; you are the one who has fallen into it."

Dominique's skin prickled; she scented danger such as she had never known. A drink, she thought, I need a drink . . . But she would not allow him to see that need. She could not afford to let him see her fear.

"You, Madame," he went on, "have been seen to dispose, at public auction, and for incredible prices, of works of art that are in reality extremely clever fakes. The factory that supplied those fakes no longer exists; the man who made them is also long gone. I have sold nothing; I know nothing. There is no paperwork, no pictures—nothing to link me with the fraud you have perpetrated. The 'anonymous Hong Kong millionaire' was your invention, the auction, from start to finish, your creation. You were the one who authenticated those 'fakes'; yours is the reputation as an expert that has been accepted by your buyers. You are the one who has deliberately duped, deceived, and defrauded. You can prove nothing against me or my associates. We, on the other hand, can prove a great deal against you. We are in a position to expose you. I am a reputable dealer in antiques; I myself 'bought' several items at that sale. All I have to do is have one examined by thermoluminescence . . ."

Too late Dominique saw how she, the arch manipulator, had been manipulated. Unhesitatingly, overconfidently, she had walked right over the edge. She was impaled on the spikes of her own greed. She held herself rigid as rage boiled through her. "Who are you?" she demanded, when she was able to control her voice.

"To you, I am Chao-Li, dealer in antiques. To those who matter I am something else, and as you can do nothing, there is no harm in telling you. I am a brother of the 7K or, as it is more familiarly known, Golden Dragon Triad." For the first time, Chao-Li permitted himself a small, cold smile. "I thought that would strike a chord."

Triad! Dominique's mind screamed the name. Triad!

"Now you must realize that you belong to us, and that from now on you will act according to our instructions."

Dominique's beauty was suddenly haggard as she realized the implications of his words, how far she was entangled in the net he had trawled. She had been set up; the fakes were a come-on, a sprat to catch a very big mackerel. She was only a small cog in an enormous wheel, a small part of a much larger plan. For a moment rage blurred her eyes. That she should have been so completely fooled was a humiliation beyond bearing. This man had made love to her, invaded her body—at her invitation—she had *trusted* him! While he had used her only as a means to an end. Had she had a weapon at hand she would have killed him.

"Now you understand that you are under my orders, Madame." He took one hand from under his wide sleeves, where they had been invisibly folded, and snapped his fingers. Instantly two very large Chinese men appeared, to take up station behind her chair. He said something to them in rapid Cantonese and at once her arms were seized, rendering her an immobile prisoner.

"Do not do anything you might regret." Dominique made her voice coldly arrogant.

"We never do that, Madame." He nodded to a third man, who had appeared from nowhere. He came forward, placed a small black box on the lamp table by Dominique's chair, which he opened. Inside was a hypodermic syringe and a small chunky bottle. Dominique's eyes widened and she drew a sharp breath of shock.

Chao-Li spoke to the man, who lifted the bottle.

"One hundred percent, uncut heroin, Madame. One-tenth of a grain and you are dead. For your own sake, Madame, do not provoke us to give it to you."

Dominique swallowed. Chao-Li spoke again and the man picked up the box and melted away. He spoke to the other two and they released her before also vanishing silently.

"You will now understand, Madame, that we are serious," he said when they were alone. "You are safe so long as you do exactly what we tell you to do. Do you understand me?"

Dominique nodded, dumbly.

"Good. You will receive further instructions from us in due course. He bowed again, distantly formal, a Chinese offering no more than common courtesy to a despised *gweilo* or foreigner, and then he, too, was gone.

It took Dominique a while to realize that it was her own

convulsive trembling that was making her chair shake, in turn rattling the table next to it on which stood the lamp and a heavy green jade ashtray, now clinking together musically. Her arms were wrapped around herself, she was bent forward as though in physical pain or extreme cold. She forced herself to leave the chair, move over to the drinks trolley. Her hands were shaking so much that she spilled whisky all over the place, but when she had enough in the glass she tossed it back neat. It made her eyes water and her breath rasp but it spread warmth through her icy body. She poured herself another, tossed that back, too, and then sank slowly into the nearest chair. She sat there for a long time, her stare fixed, her body rigid, looked up only when she heard an insistent voice saying her name and saw Chang, her major-domo, regarding her with concern.

"What?" she asked irritably.

He repeated his question: would she be in for dinner?

"No, no dinner. No anything, do you hear? I wish to be left alone. Understand? I am not to be disturbed by anyone or anything!" Her tone was violent, her eyes wide.

Chang retreated. He would have plenty to report to Fourth Cousin Benny.

In the main auction gallery at Despard's, the mathematically precise rows of gilt chairs awaited the three hundred people who, in approximately thirty minutes, would bid for the collection amassed by the late Cornelia Fentriss Gardner. The relay systems from the two auxiliary salesrooms crackled and hummed as voices tested them, aiming for an every-word-crystal-clear reception; likewise on the closed-circuit television sets. Security guards bustled, so many that there would be one to a customer, but indistinguishable from them in that they, too, wore dinner jackets and black ties. Assistants and department heads conferred over well-thumbed catalogues; backstage, the biggest and burliest guards kept watch on the locked strongboxes containing the jewelry; in an office that had been commandeered, cleared, and set up as a dressing room, half a dozen models put the finishing touches to their makeup and hair.

Downstairs in the lobby, the doorman went outside to open the door of the first limousine, while two guards, familiar by long study with the faces of those who would attend, scrutinized the engraved invitations and steered the incoming guests past a sensitive, hidden camera that X-rayed for concealed weapons. That done, they were allowed up the stairs and ushered into the gallery, where they were offered a glass of champagne. There was a flurry of handshaking, cheeks being brushed, a chorus of, "Darling, how are you? It's been an age . . ." as the big room began to fill.

Backstage, Kate was standing with Charlotte and David Holmes.

". . . your increments," David was saying. "And be sure to introduce any new bid; where it is in the audience, on the telephone, whatever. People like to know what they are up against."

Kate nodded obediently. She felt sick with nerves. This was her first great auction. It had been her intention not to show off her now polished skills until Courtland Park, but Hugh Straker was down with a bad case of jaundice. It was on his insistence that Kate was taking his place. "This is the big one," he had told her seriously over the telephone. "It has to be seen to be important to Despard's, and as I am *hors de combat* that means you."

"But what about David, or Roger Maitland—"

"Not for this sale, Kate. This is the biggest of the year so far. We must be seen to devote the commensurate amount of attention. That means you."

"But are you *sure?*"

"Yes. You have held dozens of mock auctions, and a dozen real ones."

"Small ones."

"As befits a learner. And you have learned well, Kate. Now you must make your debut with a Big One." He made an encouraging noise. "It will be excellent practice for Courtland Park, and aren't all the revolutionary ideas incorporated into this event from your brain? Yours is the authorship, my dear Kate, therefore yours is also the execution."

"Only if you are *sure,*" she repeated. She had every confidence in Hugh; it was necessary he also had every confidence in her.

"I am quite sure, but I will rehearse you as much as I can."

So Kate had gone to his house, where Angela, his wife, shook her hand and said resignedly, "I am beginning to think his recovery depends on the outcome of this sale." She had studied the catalogue until she knew it by heart; she could recite from all or any part of it. She had handled the jewels, familiarized herself with them, put them on, appreciating their perfection, their dazzle, their fire and color, but she had remained unmoved. They did not kindle in her the warmth that flamed into enthusiasm when she handled porcelain. Jewels were cold. But she had still taken great pains over their presentation, and in that respect Charlotte, with her innate elegance and flair for presentation, had been of enormous help. She had arranged for the loan of the gowns from various London couturiers in exchange for a mention in the work of art that was the catalogue; she had chosen models whose style and coloring would show off the jewels to their best advantage. The stage behind Kate's pulpit was draped in black velvet; thus the colors of the dresses and the brilliance of the jewels would stand out, the more so by being spotlit by another friend of Charlotte's, who was one of the best lighting men in the theatre.

Kate herself was in black—"I'm not for sale," she joked. A simple yet dramatic gown of velvet to match the backdrop, with a tight waist and draped skirt that fanned out into a fishtail, no jewels but a pair of small pearl drops in her ears.

This was her make or break, but the quiet confidence of Hugh and David, as well as Charlotte's warm encouragement, helped steady her. She still wished, though, that Rollo, with his acerbic tongue and trenchant comments, had been there to add his own particular form of confidence. Her clerk went by with a quiet, "Good luck, Miss Despard," and when he was in his place by her rostrum and the signal given that all seats were filled, Kate drew a deep breath and sailed out to face her judges.

"Will she do?" Charlotte asked David bluntly.

"Yes. She is as ready as she will ever be. Training can do no more, nor hard work. Her last hurdle is the all-conquering image of her stepsister. Once she knocks that over there will be no stopping her."

Kate climbed the three steps to her pulpit, a stiff smile on her face. Her audience was a blur of black, white shirt fronts, and jewels, worn by the women as some sort of confidence booster of their own. She drew a deep breath and opened the proceedings.

"Good evening, ladies and gentlemen. Welcome to Despard's, and the sale of the Cornelia Fentriss Gardner Collection of fabulous jewels, and you will have seen from your catalogues that I make no overstatement." The murmur of laughter that came back had the effect of loosening some of her knots. "This is the most important collection of jewels Despard's has ever had the honor to offer at auction; it is also my own most important event in that it is a baptism of fire no less blazing than the jewels you are about to see." This time there was a smattering of applause accompanying the laughter and Kate felt a wave of warmth coming at her.

She pressed the button by her left foot. "The first lot is a brooch in the shape of a bird of paradise; its breast a cabochon sapphire of 63.40 carats, its sail a sweep of diamonds, sapphires, rubies, emeralds, topaz, and turquoises . . ." The first model swept on, in a starkly plain dress of white crepe that bared one shoulder. Pinned to the other one was the brooch. It blazed with color and fire as the perfectly judged spots hit it head on. Kate heard the intake of breath, saw her audience crane forward as the model paraded slowly and dramatically through the aisles, pausing now and then to allow closer inspection. The jewels glittered coldly, the enormous sapphire glowing like some celestial promise. Deliberately, Kate waited, allowing the excitement to build, minds to be made up, loins girded for the coming battle, and then, as the model took up position before her so that the jewels sent forth their silent temptation all the while, Kate opened the bidding with a competent crispness she was far from feeling.

"At 100,000 pounds, then, ladies and gentlemen . . ." They came out of the starting gate like the clappers. "110,000—120,000—130,000—140,000—" Kate's eyes had to be everywhere as the numbered paddles were raised, noting who raised them most often, who was likely to stay the course as the bidding spiraled. "150,000—160,000—170,000 —180,000—" There was no letup, no pauses, only the silent concentration on acquiring the fabulous brooch. "200,000—" There was an indrawn hiss of breath. "210,000—220,000— 230,000—" Kate's voice was calm, helpful, even solicitous, as the paddles rose and fell with monotonous regularity. "At 250,000 pounds, then . . ." For the first time she gave a direction to the bidding. "The bid is on the aisle—250,000 . . ." Her voice was inquiring, giving no hint of the excitement twisting her stomach. "All done?" she asked nicely. "At 250,000 pounds, then . . ." She raised her left hand, gavel tucked into its palm, letting her audience see it. "260,000—270,000—" Once again she waited, letting the momentum pause for breath. "The bid is on the aisle . . ." A well-known dealer, Kate saw, obviously bidding for a client. "At 270,000 then . . ." Her words were solicitous, but also a gentle hint that time was running out. Breath was held, but the already high price could go no higher. Kate's gavel hit its block. "At 270,000 pounds, Mr. de Vries."

With a trembling hand she marked her catalogue in blue: £270,000. The reserve, in red, was £175-£200,000. What a way to begin! she thought exultantly. Let it end the same way . . . Confidence rose in her like the mercury in a thermometer. She was in control; she had her audience—like her gavel—in the palm of her hand.

Lot two was the famous "Tiger" bracelet, a three-inch thick curved band of alternate stripes of rubies and canary-yellow diamonds, with emeralds forming the tiger's eyes. It was very well known, having been created by Cartier of Paris to Cornelia Fentriss Gardner's own design. It was worn on the forearm of a striking brunette in a dress of gold lamé, echoing the gold of the bracelet, and as she paraded through the audience, hand on hip to show off the bracelet to best advantage, people craned to examine it more closely.

"This next piece is, of course, famous enough to need no description from me," Kate began demurely. "Truly one of a kind; a superb example of the jeweler's art. Each ruby is of an exact size, shape, and weight, while the canary diamonds—Mrs. Gardner's favorite gemstone—are among the largest ever used, each stone so set that the bracelet ripples in the true manner of a tiger, surely the most beautiful animal in the world." She spaced her words to give the model time to return and take up position in front of the pulpit, the great band on her arm glittering balefully. By the eager silence Kate knew she was on to a good thing when she opened the bidding at £100,000. Her confidence was confirmed when, within sixty seconds, it had zoomed to half a million, and it continued to climb as two bidders—an elderly woman on the aisle, and a heavy-set man in the front row—fought each other for it.

"At five hundred thousand pounds—" Kate informed them with crisp clarity. "The bid is on the aisle—six hundred thousand . . ." The man in the front row had barely lifted his paddle when the raddled woman irritably hitched her sables and jerked her own paddle upwards. "Seven hundred thousand pounds . . ." The room drew a collective breath. "Seven hundred thousand pounds is the bid, from the aisle . . ." The thickset man sat stolidly, showing no expression as Kate lifted her left hand. "At seven hundred thousand pounds, then . . ."

No response. He would go no further. Nobody else moved a muscle. The atmosphere was palpable as Kate's gavel cracked. "Seven hundred thousand pounds, to Mrs. de Kuyper."

The room broke into excited applause.

"Well done, Miss Despard," Kate heard her clerk murmur. "You've got them—if you will excuse the expression—by the short and curlies."

Filled with exhilaration, Kate flung him a radiant smile, knowing she could not be stopped now; that every single reserve would be exceeded, and the surmised total left far behind. And as the auction continued even the smaller pieces—a lover's knot bow of diamonds; a flame lily brooch of diamonds and rubies; a sapphire and diamond necklace; a necklace of fifty pearls, each one of the same exact weight and size; a pearl and diamond brooch in the shape of an opened fan; a canary diamond brooch shaped like a jonquil, the petals of marquise diamonds, the stem of baguettes—all went for prices never before obtained at such an auction. By the time Kate reached the high spot of the sale, the excitement threatened to ignite, and thunderous applause greeted the last model, a stunning redhead, who swept out from the wings wearing a sculpted masterpiece by Madame Gres. Her narrow waist was belted by a girdle, the sight of which produced a collective gasp of awe. It was some four inches wide and literally paved with emeralds.

Kate waited until she had total silence. "The Ispahan Girdle," she announced reverently. "Once part of the processional trappings of a horse, and formerly belonging to the Nawab of Bhapur. It contains thirty-four flat emeralds, twelve intricately carved emeralds, three hundred and forty-seven lasque diamonds, and two hundred and fifty pearls, the whole being inlaid in pure gold." She gave that stunning description time to sink in, then announced calmly that the bidding would open at half a million pounds. Within thirty seconds it stood at two million pounds. The room shuddered. The battle was between a well-known Swiss jeweler, who was no doubt acting on the instructions of a client, and a Brazilian playboy who had the reputation of bestowing fabulous jewelry on those women who took his fancy and were prepared to put up with him. Kate knew the Brazilian hated to be beaten, but she did not know how far the dealer was prepared to go—or for whom for that matter. She took a chance and pushed. "At two million pounds—the bid is on the left—two million pounds is bid for the Ispahan Girdle . . . the only one of its kind." The Swiss was stony-faced and Kate knew he was done. She closed swiftly. "At two million pounds, then . . ." Her gavel thwacked. "Mr. da Silva."

The room exploded; people were standing, applauding, and cheering, slapping the happy Brazilian on the back and then surging toward Kate, who was as *en tremblant* as one of the diamond necklaces she had just sold. She closed her catalogue with palsied hands, bent down to say, "Well done, John, thank you," to her clerk, and left the rostrum on legs that had been boned, filleted, and rolled.

She was at once surrounded by people wanting to shake her hand, pat her back, tell her "Well done" and "Absolutely marvelous" and "Fantastic." Nigel Marsh fought his way through to her, managed to edge her slowly away to where practically the entire top brass of Despard's waited—for this had been one auction nobody wanted to miss—and Charlotte was able to place in her hands a well-chilled glass of champagne, which Kate drained at a gulp.

"After tonight, champagne all the way," exulted John Steadman, but Kate was looking at her mentor.

"Well done, Kate," David said. "Very well done, indeed. I could not have done better myself."

At the ultimate accolade, she really relaxed.

"I think tonight bears out my contention that the upward trend in jewel prices is here to stay," she heard John announce smugly.

"And did you notice that nearly every piece went to a private collector rather than a dealer?" Nigel pointed out happily. "Eleven lots in excess of half a million . . ."

"The net total"—her head of Accounts cleared his throat as the expected silence fell—"the net total, is £14,800,000— double the previous British record."

"As I was about to point out," Nigel glared, testy at having his thunder stolen.

"More champagne all round I think," Claudia caroled drunkenly.

Kate drained her second glass thirstily. She felt dehydrated.

"And then I think a little judicious circulating," John Steadman urged. "Contact, my dear Kate, that is what it is all about. One thing invariably leads to another, and that other thing we all want to see is more sales like this one. Now come along and show yourself and let me show you off . . ."

Self-importantly he bustled her off to where her public awaited.

"An inspired stroke, to have the jewels shown by models," a woman gushed.

"Your father would have been proud of you," somebody else said.

"Congratulations!"

"Well done!"

"A superb success!"

Kate made her way through the press of people, all wanting to shake her hand, to be able to tell people they had not only been at this incredible auction, but that they had also actually shaken hands with the woman responsible for it.

John Steadman took her arm, ruthlessly bore her away to where the TV cameras and the interviewer were waiting. After congratulating her on the success of the sale, he asked, "Did you expect the prices to go so high tonight, Miss Despard?"

"No," Kate replied truthfully, "but I am naturally pleased that they did."

"Whose idea was it to have the jewels worn by professional models?"

"Mine."

"And have you any other similar innovations for future sales?"

"Yes, but they are not for publication now. Watch for Courtland Park," she said, smiling into the camera.

"That comes up in October, doesn't it?"

"Yes—October thirtieth, at Courtland Park in Sussex."

"And do you hope to repeat tonight's success?"

"It will not be for want of trying," Kate laughed.

She was on a high, and not from two glasses of champagne. Her feet did not touch the ground as she made her way back into the admiring throng. She had done it! She had proved herself; she had shown herself to be her father's daughter. Of all the compliments paid to her that evening, she treasured that one most of all. So she smiled and talked and quipped, said good-bye to those who were going on elsewhere, and gradually the crowd began to thin out, which was when she saw who was standing by himself, back to the wall, at the end of the room. Blaise Chandler. For a moment they held eyes, and then, people making way for her, she walked toward him.

"Congratulations," he said. "You have made your mark."

"Thank you."

He smiled; the remoteness was gone, the door was open. She smiled back. "You saw the auction?"

"Most of it."

"You weren't bidding."

"My grandmother has a collection you could easily sell for as much, I think."

"I thought of her when I first saw the Ispahan Girdle."

Blaise grinned; his face lost years. "Yes, that is her style."

Kate had also thought of Dominique when she saw the sapphire and diamond necklace, but she did not dare say that name—not yet.

"How is the Duchess?"

"Dying to hear how you've done. I came so I would be able to tell her"—a lift of an eyebrow in the old way—"you know me and auctions. But I stayed to see for myself. It was worth it."

Kate felt that light her fire.

"How is Rollo?" he asked next, which had the effect of dousing it.

"The same; off the danger list but still in his coma."

"I saw the half-yearly figures," he said reapplying the match. "Tonight should bring you level with Dominique." There, he had said it, as easily as he would any other name.

"With Courtland Park, I intend to draw ahead," Kate challenged.

"I don't doubt it," he answered, and from the way he said it, she knew he didn't.

Which emboldened her to say gaily, "We are having an après-sale party—I hope you can come."

"Sorry, not this time. Maybe Courtland Park."

Her smile did not falter, though her disappointment felt like a knife. "I'll hold you to that," she warned. She hesitated, and as if he knew what she was going to ask, he said quietly, "No. No news."

Kate nodded, not sure what to say in the circumstances, and he took the wind out of her sails by asking directly, "Was it consideration or commiseration that prevented you from telling me, rather than my grandmother, what you had discovered in Hong Kong?"

For a moment she was nonplussed, then decided only the truth would do. "Both," she answered in the same direct manner. "Plus the fact that I had no proof."

He smiled, and she blinked. "I think Shakespeare had you in mind when he wrote—'They that have the power to hurt and do none . . .' "

Kate just prevented her jaw from dropping. Once again he had confounded her. Blaise Chandler and poetry!

"I do read other things besides legalities," he said, straight-faced.

"Then if you like poetry how is it you don't appreciate art?" she exclaimed.

He raised a hand. "Give me time—I'm learning," he said, adding, very softly, "Yes, indeed, and such a lot."

Their eyes held and he said into the suddenly bottomless silence, "We must talk, you and I, but not now. However . . ." He reached into his jacket pocket, brought out a flat bundle tied with pink legal tape. Kate recognized it with a rush of shock as the letters her father had written to her over the years, every one of which she had returned unread.

"Your father passed them on to me, leaving it to my judgment as to when—and if—you should have them. Now is the time." He held them out to her.

Kate swallowed the lump in her throat. "Thank you," she said constrictedly. Staring down at them, "You've read them?" she asked stiltingly.

"Also part of my brief."

"No wonder you thought me such a spiteful brat."

"You were, then. Time, events—and you yourself—have changed you beyond recognition. That Kate would not have understood. This one will."

Kate blinked, dispersing tears. "Thank you," she said again.

"Now I must go."

"Another plane to catch?"

His answer was a smile.

"You work too hard," she found herself saying, "and travel too much."

"ChanCorp is worldwide, besides, it keeps them on the hop since they never know when I'm coming."

He did look tired, she thought. The remoteness was gone but in its place was strain.

"Good-bye, Kate, and once again congratulations. Your father was right. You are a Despard."

And then, for the first time ever, he leaned forward, brushed her cheek with his lips, and was gone.

17

Dominique did not bother to analyze why she bolted for the only place she considered "home"; that it was to her mother she turned, not her husband. She only knew that she wanted to be somewhere safe. It was in Provence that she would find breathing space, time to think, to ponder, to plan. She needed to distance herself from all that had crowded in on her recently; the shattering news that she had got herself mixed up with the Triads; that she was trapped in a situation she herself had helped create, and for the first time in her life she was unable to find a way out. Her mother would not bother her and the visit would be seen as no more than that; it would give no hint of her terror. Rather the reverse; it would show her as the dutiful daughter concerned for her mother's welfare.

Catherine was even deeper into her fantasy world; she greeted Dominique with bemused indifference, her mind wholly on her husband who, according to Marthe, had now completely taken over.

"Now she will not even leave the grounds; when she goes into the garden to work he works with her; always his chair is set out on the terrace, always the pitcher of *citron pressé*, his copy of *Le Monde*. She has left our world and entered into one of her own creation and gradually the door is closing on her."

"She is happy, is she not? Does she complain—cause you concern?"

"She is no trouble," Marthe allowed grudgingly.

"Is it that you do not feel safe with her?"

Marthe bridled. "There is talk in the village—"

"Let them talk. If you do not feel safe here then by all

420

means take yourself off. I will soon make alternative arrangements."

But Marthe hastily disclaimed any such intention. This was a cushy number; as long as her orders concerning her husband were carried out Madame never interfered, though she still went over the accounts carefully. The rest she left to Marthe, who took all the advantage she could. But that did not mean she approved. Now she inquired how long Dominique would be staying.

"I do not know. I have been working very hard and need peace and quiet for a while. I am not at home to visitors no matter who they are."

"But Monsieur Chandler—"

"Will not be coming. To anyone else I am resting and not available, do you understand?"

"As Madame wishes." Then Marthe said triumphantly, "In any case, Monsieur Chandler was here only a week ago."

"Why did you not tell me?" Dominique asked sharply.

"You did not ask."

"I want to know every visitor who comes here," she said emphatically. "Even if I do not wish to see them." She paused. "How long was my husband here?"

"Only the one night. Madame was happy to see him. She always had a fondness for him."

At lunch, Dominique asked her mother casually, "What did Blaise want?"

"To see me, of course." Catherine was complacently smug. "He wanted to know if I was happy, if there was anything I lacked or might want."

"That was all?"

Catherine's blue gaze was a mixture of surprise and affront. "What else should he want?"

I wonder, Dominique thought. He had always displayed a tolerant affection for her mother, but to come down here . . . Was he snooping? She had felt for some time that he was asking too many questions. He had been in and out of Hong Kong like a yo-yo, but, when she thought back, no more than usual. Maybe it was because she herself was so suspicious of everything and everyone that she was reading too much into his activities. How could he know anything? There was nothing to know. At the first sign of danger— Rollo Bellamy—the factory had been dismantled, moved elsewhere—where she did not know. Bellamy himself, Chao-Li had told her, was not expected to come out of his coma ever, and the prognosis was that even if he did, his mind would be gone.

No, what worried her was that they had wanted her to change shippers. A means of drawing her ever more deeply into their clutches? So that should it become known, people would at once assume she was part and parcel of them and their nefarious activities?

She had received another visit from Chao-Li just before she left—which had increased her resolve to leave Hong Kong. She had told him she had no intention of changing shippers; that he could go to hell. Their association was over and done with; he could go his way and she would go hers. There would be no more sales of fakes, though the original plan had been to work toward a second one in the distant future, should the first one go as planned. Now, she had no intention of having anything more to do with them. She had accomplished her purpose with the first one: made a killing. That brought a smile. Yes, she had thought, killed Kate Despard's hopes of ever having all of Despard's.

Until, in the airmail edition of *The Times*, whose "Salesrooms" column she always perused, she read that, at Despard's London, the largest jewel auction ever held in Britain had realized, in just over three hours, a total of £14,800,000. She read of the "entirely splendid innovation instituted by Miss Catriona Despard of having the jewels worn by models and thus displayed to best advantage—and ensuring the best possible prices." With a foul French oath, she crumpled the paper, twisting it violently, until it tore, but not satisfied, she still ripped and pulled until it was shredded. Then she sat down with pencil, paper, and a pocket calculator and found to her fury that Kate was closing the gap. I am still in the lead, but there is this damned Courtland Park sale to come, and by all accounts it was going to be a monster, she thought. Damn and damn and damn! I've got to stop her, but how, how? Oh, she would not forget that two-faced Nicholas Chevely. That double-crossing Englishman would pay for daring to take without giving.

She began to pace, as she always did when worried. Courtland Park was in five weeks' time, unless something could be done to stop it. She had to find a way to prevent that sale from taking place . . . The two people on whom she had relied for information were now of no use, and since Kate Despard had begun to show her hand, producing all these new ideas, making Despard's a talking point and thus the favored house of people whom she had hitherto regarded as her own, as well as converting many of the anti's into pro's, Dominique had been balked at every turn in her efforts to block Kate's progress. She had badly underestimated her rival, had been convinced that Kate Despard's big feet would never fit into her father's shoes, only to find that, now, here she was in seven-league boots, catching up in leaps and bounds.

I would consign her to the flames of hell if I could, Dominique thought. And then stopped dead. Flames . . . ? Her eyes blazed their own. A little *quid pro quo,* she thought. If they want my help then I have the right to insist they give me theirs. They could do it easily; there is a Chinatown in London . . . Why not? she thought excitedly. It would solve all my problems. If there is nothing to sell she cannot sell it. And there is no way she can come up with another Courtland Park in the time remaining. I shall return to Hong Kong, she decided, and see Chao-Li. I will win him over; the man is not yet born I cannot manipulate to my ends. If they do what I want, then I shall do what they want and change shippers. Which, she now knew, had been their ultimate objective from the start. They had not really been interested in regular sales of fake antiques, which could only be held at intervals of years to keep suspicion to a minimum. No, what they were after were the limitless profits to be made from drug-smuggling, and a legitimate front for that smuggling. Despard's made the perfect cover; it shipped regularly and often. What better than its consignments of antiques—known to customs over many years and entirely above board. Who would suspect that suddenly a chosen selection of those same antiques would contain pure heroin? Oh, it was clever . . . *they* were clever. She would demand a cut, of course. The profits to be made were incalculable. And then, when Despard's was hers . . . oh, but she would leave the other two standing! For the first time in many weeks she slept deeply, dreamlessly, and without drugs.

She was wholly in oblivion when the black shadow easily scaled the wall of the *mas,* dropped like a fallen leaf to the ground and then, hugging the shadows, moved silently toward the dark bulk of the house. Like a spider it climbed the drainpipes, used the sloping roofs as a ladder until it found what it was seeking: a partially open window on the first floor. That of Catherine Despard's bathroom. Dropping soundlessly to the tiled floor, the shadow flowed effortlessly across it to put its ear to the thick olivewood of the door. A faint murmur—the door was old and heavy—penetrated through it. With great care and agonizing slowness it opened the door a crack. The murmur was a woman's voice, in the delirium of approaching orgasm, endlessly repeating a name. "Charles . . . Charles . . . oh, Charles . . ." Through the crack the shadow surveyed the room, lit by the lamp on the draped table next to the bed, revealing the woman, seemingly crouched on all fours, her naked bottom upthrust, her two hands busy at the junction of her thighs. She was lost in her fantasy and approaching orgasm, her voice high and reedy, her body bucking and heaving against the piston of her driving fingers. "Oh, my love . . . yes, oh, yes . . ." She was shuddering, jerking, manic in her desperation for fulfillment, oblivious to everything but the driving demands of her body. She would not have heard a bass drum roll.

Silently the figure reached the bottom of the bed; almost by magic a small glass vial appeared in the black gloved hands, a cork protruding from the narrow neck, which was removed to show the long, thin needle embedded there, dripping a slightly viscous colorless fluid. Swiftly the needle was withdrawn, fitted into a blowpipe as fine as a grass stem, its mouthpiece lifted to the lips that parted to receive it. As Catherine, with a hoarse scream, exploded into orgasm, writhing and gasping, the needle flew from the pipe and, with flawless accuracy, embedded itself in the soft flesh at the base of her skull. Her final hoarse exultant cry was curtailed; her body arched backwards like a bow—straining toward the ultimate in ecstasy that came even as did death, both reaching for and meeting the other. Her eyes glazed sightlessly as her body slumped sideways, one last breath hissing from her like air expelled from a tire.

The figure waited ten seconds before stepping noiselessly forward. First it extracted the needle, replaced it in the bottle, put the bottle back in its pouch. Then it inspected the body, frozen in everlasting orgasm. Seconds later the shadow dropped from the wall and melted into the trees, where it vanished.

Marthe rose at her usual early hour; the habit of a lifetime unbreakable even now, when she could sleep later. She did her usual early morning chores, then prepared her mistress's breakfast tray. One morning-fresh croissant, a small pot of apricot preserve, butter locally made, the small pots of deadly black coffee and hot milk. The morning paper, which she had already read with her own first cup of coffee, was carefully refolded and laid on the tray next to the pretty Limoges china, on the Valenciennes lace tray cloth. Then she laboriously climbed the stairs.

"*Bonjour,* Madame," she called as she entered the bedroom, laying down the tray on the chest by the door before going to draw the flowered print curtains. Normally, a yawned " 'Jour, Marthe" came back. This morning there was no response. Turning, she went back to pick up the tray, took it over to the bed.

"Madame!"

The tray dropped, splashing hot coffee and milk over her legs, but she did not notice. She was screaming too loudly.

"A sudden and massive heart attack, Madame," Dr. Morel told Dominique. "It was over in seconds."

"My mother's heart was perfectly sound."

Dr. Morel coughed discreetly. "May I remind you, Madame, of the circumstances in which your mother was found to have—expired, the strain on the heart at such a time—"

"Surely no greater than it must have been at many times during her marriage."

Another cough. "Madame Despard was getting older . . ." A wholly Gallic shrug. "It is a common death, Madame, and surely, a very pleasant one."

Dominique recalled the expression on her mother's face: agony or ecstasy? Marthe's screams had penetrated even her deep sleep, but the sight of her mother's body, its position, the sightless, staring eyes—bulging slightly—the open mouth, and the fingers buried deep inside herself had shocked her fully awake. Marthe she had slapped—hard—commanding her to help her move the body into a more seemly position. But rigor mortis was just beginning to set in; Dominique had no choice but to allow Dr. Morel to examine the body as she had found it. But he was a wise and experienced man who had in his forty years as a doctor seen everything, and Catherine Despard was not the first human being to have died as the result of a shattering sexual climax. Why, there was the case of old Monsieur Montand, whose fingers had been so highly entwined in the hair of the young woman who was fellating him that they had had to cut her free. And, by all accounts, the marriage of Charles and Catherine Despard had been very much one of the flesh rather than the spirit . . .

"Rest assured, Madame," he told Dominique, "I will proceed with the utmost discretion, and in the circumstances there will be no hesitation on my part in signing the death certificate."

Once the formalities had been completed and Dr. Morel had departed, Dominique went into the kitchen where Marthe was sitting with a glass of cognac in front of her.

"Oh, Madame," she said, tears spurting afresh, "such a shock. To think of Madame your mother dying in such a state . . . unblessed and unconfessed . . ."

"Of which you will say nothing," Dominique commanded. She fixed the blotched and swollen face with eyes as hard as the sapphires they resembled. "Do you understand me? My mother had a heart attack—that is all. The rest—is silence." Trust the English, she thought. Always the last word. "There will be no gossip. Not if you know what is good for you. Do I make myself clear?"

Marthe, deprived of the choicest piece of gossip she would ever have, nodded sullenly, hiding her nervousness. Madame's daughter had never been one to cross, even when she was a child. Well, she consoled herself. It would keep. Like the best wine, the best gossip could only mature with age . . .

As she laid out the body her sharp eyes missed nothing, especially the red patch on the back of the neck, perhaps a sting of some sort, though she could find no sign. And in her curiosity she examined Catherine's body minutely. Not bad for a woman of her age, but then, it should be; Madame had continued with the masseuse, with the creams and the lotions and even the exercise, a penance for one indolent by nature. Yes, Marthe sniffed, the body of a highly sexed woman. Oh, she had heard them both, when Monsieur was alive, the groans and the moans and the occasional screams. Disgraceful, at their age, never being able to leave each other alone. She had known, of course, that Madame was—well, playing with herself, except that from the look on her face earlier it had been no game. She took the big bowl of water into the bathroom and emptied it out, took back into the bedroom Madame's brush and comb. The hair done, she went to the big chest to take out a fresh nightgown; one of the prettiest: pure silk crepe de Chine, heavily trimmed with blond Michelin lace. Then she folded Catherine's hands over her breasts and drew up the pretty, flower-sprigged sheet from Porthault. As a last thought she tucked a sprig of honeysuckle between Catherine's fingers. There, she thought sourly. The picture of innocence . . .

When Dominique went in to see her she thought Catherine looked like a wax doll. But of course, Dominique thought, she is not wearing maquillage.

She went to the dressing table, in the middle drawer of which Catherine kept her makeup, always the same—Lancôme. But as she opened the drawer, her hand was stayed in mid-movement as she caught sight of the object lying beside her mother's hand mirror. Slowly, as if approaching an un-exploded bomb, her hand stole toward it, hovered, and then picked it up. It was a velvet spectacle case, black, embroidered in the shape of a golden dragon. From the drawstring top her mother's reading glasses protruded. Dominique sat down with a thump. She had never seen it before. Her mother's normal spectacle case was done in her favorite petit point; this bugle bead and sequin work was not her style; it was too . . . Oriental. Frantically then, as though released from a spell, she searched the dressing tabletop, the drawers, finally found the other spectacle case in the drawer of the bedside table. Her hands were trembling as she transferred the glasses from one case to another, but her voice, when later she showed the black velvet case to Marthe, was nothing more than surprised. "Do you know who this belongs to, Marthe? I have never seen it before . . . Or had *Maman* changed her style?"

Marthe put on her own spectacles, took the case in her hands. "No, that is not Madame's," she said definitely. "I have not seen it before."

"Perhaps she bought it somewhere or other," Dominique said carelessly. "It was in one of her drawers."

"I expect so," Marthe agreed. "It is not the kind of thing she would use. She often bought things on impulse which afterward never saw the light of day."

Not this one, Dominique thought. *Maman* never bought this. It was given to her—or rather left for me to find.

Once more she went to her mother's room. There she made herself examine, carefully and slowly, her mother's body, looking for any kind of a clue. She found none. How, then? she pondered. How? For she knew—had known as soon as she saw the golden dragon—that it had been left as a signature. Her mother had not died of a massive heart attack brought on naturally; somehow, in some way, it had been induced.

It had not been the food; they had all three eaten what Marthe had prepared. Nor could it have been the drink. Besides, poison left traces—didn't it? Not always, she told herself. Some pill, perhaps? She went through the various bottles and jars in the medicine cabinet in the bathroom— nothing but aspirin and various other popular brands of placebos. Her mother had been robustly healthy; a tranquil mind makes for a healthy body, her grandmother de Villefort had been wont to say. In which case, Dominique thought contemptuously, it is no wonder my mother never ailed in her life. The dates on the bottles were old; her mother never had been a pill taker. What, then? How had they killed her? Some kind of lethal blow? She knew of karate, of judo, of ways in which fingers and hands could kill. But there were no bruises on her mother's body, not a mark except for a faint redness just below the hairline at her nape, as though she had scratched it, and a few scratches on her fingers, brought about by working in the garden without gloves. Which was no doubt where she had also been stung.

Dominique searched everything, even the creams and lotions in the bathroom, as well as the bath oil and talcum. Murder was so sophisticated nowadays; lethal poisons could be added to such innocent day-to-day things, and all it needed was one, tiny drop . . .

She sat for a long time thinking, thinking. They were so clever. They must have monitored her mother's habits, knew what she did to herself every night. And somehow, in a way she could not yet fathom, they had killed her so as to make it appear entirely natural. Had they not taken the trouble to inform Dominique that it was not, she would never have suspected.

It was, of course, a warning. To let her know that she was under their orders and that if she did not do what she was told, her fate would follow the same, deadly end. She shivered. They had not known her mother. They had not cared,

either. She was merely a means to an end. As her understanding of just what she had got herself into permeated
every crevice of her consciousness, her terror grew. She was
their property, their thing to do with what they chose as and
how they chose. And when. For a moment she felt panic
well, almost spill over; she wanted to scream, hide herself,
point an accusing finger . . . Instead, she went back to her
own room where she took another Mogadon, not enough to
send her to sleep but enough to calm her nerves. There were
the arrangements for her mother's burial to be made.

Blaise arrived within hours; she had called the number she
always used when wanting to get in touch. Fortunately, he
had not been far away, in Frankfurt.

She was calm when he arrived, and accepted his condo-
lences with the right degree of wan and disbelieving shock.
When she told him how her mother's body had been found,
he said only, "Yes, I could see she was sinking further and
further into her fantasies. But she was happy, so who is to
blame her?"

"Not I," Dominique assured him.

"It is fortunate you were here."

"Yes, isn't it?"

"And nice of you to take the time to come—you being so
busy, and all."

She examined his face from under her lashes. It told her
nothing. That damned Indian impassiveness of his could be
infuriating. But she let him take over the funeral arrangements; truth to tell she could think of nothing but her own
dire situation. No use in approaching Chao-Li now. If they
would do this, merely to warn her, then there was little
likelihood of their agreeing to anything that would help her
situation.

Blaise knew something was eating away at his wife. She
was honed to a fine edge, seemed shocked far beyond the
mere fact of her mother's sudden death. So he had a word
with the doctor, which did not help either.

"My mother-in-law had no history of heart trouble," he
pointed out.

"That does not necessarily follow, Monsieur Chandler. I
see so many deaths of people who are seemingly vitally
healthy and strong. There may have been some weakness
which had not manifested itself outwardly." Discreetly he
went on, "Madame Despard was a woman of strong appe-

tites. According to Marthe, this was a nightly ritual. The strain on the heart would be considerable. Constant strain would exacerbate the weakness until—" A shrug. "It was quick, painless. Not a bad way to die."

Not in Catherine's case, Blaise thought. Both Catherine and her first husband had strong sexual appetites, though it had taken her second husband to release hers, through love. Was it any wonder, then, that Dominique was such a sexual animal?

The funeral was attended mostly by people who had known Catherine through Charles; she had had few friends of her own because she had not wanted them: all she had ever wanted was him. Now, she had him forever. But there were a few people from her former Faubourg world; the rest were of the village, drawn by curiosity as well as respect. The requiem mass was solemn, the flowers glorious. Marthe snuffled all through the entire thing, from the moment the coffin was brought in until it was lowered into the same grave as Charles, as per the instructions in Catherine's will, which left everything to her daughter unconditionally.

Afterward, back at the *mas,* Dominique gave the performance of her life, almost ethereal in black, drifting wraithlike from group to group, saying just the right thing to the right person. Those old dowagers from the Faubourg, who remembered Catherine from her girlhood, whispered approvingly. Breeding always told, they said. Every inch a du Vivier.

Blaise himself had never seen Dominique look so beautiful; she moved with such subtle grace, and the line of her profile as she listened attentively to some old marquise was the loveliest thing he had seen in any woman.

The old ladies had never seen anything like him, or anyone so unconscious of his attractiveness as a desirable male. They approved of his flawless French, preened under his gaze, gossiped greedily and admiringly about him . . . *"cuisses de fer, magnifique, et tellement excitant . . ."*

He played his part even as Dominique played hers, and occasionally their eyes met in a secret smile. Strange how he felt closer to her, at this moment, than he ever had.

Afterward, when everyone had gone, they sat out on the terrace in the golden glow of late afternoon, still close, still observing some kind of truce. Blaise waited for Dominique to tell him; it was the perfect time. But she did not.

"Will you sell this place?" he asked after a while.

"No . . . I used to think it was the back of beyond, as the English say; now I know it is the end of the rainbow. I will keep it as somewhere to return to when I need to recharge my batteries."

"And are they run down?"

Her sigh was tremulous. "Perhaps, a little . . ."

"You've been working very hard, of late. Can't you relax a little?"

"Not with Kate Despard hot on my heels. You heard about the success of her jewel sale?"

"Yes." He forbore to say he had been there.

"And she conducted it herself."

"Isn't it about time?"

"It was years before I conducted an auction—years! And then it was in Hong Kong."

"She's had to learn fast."

"And has had so many ready and willing to teach her—even you."

"I have not helped Kate Despard in any way where your battle with her is concerned."

"Who got her pansy friend out of Hong Kong? Who invited her back to Colorado? Do not insult my intelligence. Next you will deny that your grandmother is bringing all her considerable weight to bear on her behalf."

"That was your mistake. You never bothered to try and get it on yours."

She lapsed into brittle silence, and he noticed that her hands were fiddling constantly with something that had been within reach all day. A spectacle case of black velvet embroidered with a golden dragon. Not Catherine's usual type of work; she had preferred petit point, and this was done in metallic thread, whereas she had used silks. Also, there were no glasses in it.

That night, he heard a noise in the corridor, and going out to investigate, saw it was Dominique making sure the window was secure. "I thought I heard it banging," was her explanation. But there was no wind. The night was calm. She was afraid of something . . . someone? To reassure her he pretended to examine it, saw that it had probably not been opened for years for the wood was swollen.

And once in bed she moved close, and in a way that told him she was not seeking sex, but safety.

"Thank you for coming," she murmured after a while.

"Why would I not?"

"We both know that things have not been—right—for some time."

"No marriage is right all the time."

"When this year is over it will all be different," she promised.

It had better be, Blais thought.

She sighed. "Two deaths in one little year . . . who would have thought it?"

"If Catherine is with Charles—which is what she believed—then why worry?"

"Do you believe that?"

"No."

"Nor do I. Hell is not when you die. It is being alive and not getting what you want."

"So that is why you are prepared to see everyone else go there but yourself."

She laughed. "Oh, you . . ." she said in the old way, and her sigh, as she made herself comfortable, was one of contented surety. Within minutes she was asleep, but Blaise lay awake for a long time, thinking.

"No!" Wrenching herself violently free, Kate leapt from the sofa.

"Why not?" Larry asked, puzzled.

"Because—" Because you are the wrong man had been the words which sprang to her lips. "Because I'm not in the mood," was what she said.

Larry eyed her sullenly. "Then it changed mighty quick."

"I'm sorry," she said tiredly. "It's not your fault."

"Is there somebody else, is that it? Have I been beaten to the post? This Chevely guy?"

"That'll be the day," Kate snapped.

"Somebody else, then?"

"There is nobody, Larry, nobody at all. I'm sorry if I led you on . . . but it's not as though we were Anthony and Cleopatra now, is it?"

He grinned unwillingly. "More like Mutt and Jeff?"

Kate giggled. That was what she liked about Larry; he was never down for long. Pure sorbo rubber.

"I've got a lot on my mind," she explained truthfully. "Courtland Park gets in the way of everything else these days."

"Can I be of any help? I was an eagle scout, you know."

Kate laughed and turned back to him. "No, but thanks for the offer."

He really was a dear, she thought, comfortable as an old shoe. When he had, of late, come on as the eager lover, she had let him kiss her, handle her body. But tonight, when he had wanted to take that logical step further, she had seen, as if revealed in a flash of lightning, the immovable fact that she couldn't, that she didn't want to, that she liked him as a friend but had no desire for him as a lover, because that role . . . was carved into a likeness of Blaise Chandler. It was hopeless and it was useless but she was stuck with it, however hard she tried to find a way around it. It was five minutes before, in Larry Cole's arms, knowing it was make-or-break time, that she had suddenly realized there was none.

She had been attracted to Blaise Chandler from the word go, put up the safety barriers of dislike and resentment, hoarded every shred of suspicion against him, all in an effort—wasted, she saw now—to keep him at the proper distance. Too late, he had taken up residence in her mind, her heart, and put down roots. He was all her girlhood fantasies come to vibrantly attractive life: Edward Rochester alive and well and living in Blaise Chandler. And she was Jane Eyre only insofar as she, too, was plain.

"It's not because you are still laboring under the delusion that you are a dog?" Larry asked, as if reading her mind.

Kate was astonished at his perception. "Why should you think that?" she evaded.

"Because I get the impression you don't really believe you have what it takes or that anybody—any man that is—might feel inclined to take it."

Kate frowned. "No," she said at last. "I did once," she admitted candidly, "but that was in another country and besides, that wench is dead . . ."

"Is she?" Larry asked.

"Yes," Kate said definitely.

"Okay," he went on lightly. "Then it's me. I don't have what it takes."

"Oh, come on," teased Kate. "You know you don't be-lieve that."

"I don't know what to believe. I thought I'd done and said all the right things—"

"You have. It's just that they are not right for me."

Larry buttoned his shirt, straightened his tie, reached for his jacket. "You can't win 'em all," he agreed.

"And I know you've won more than your fair share."

He stood up in one athletic movement. "I'm not complaining," he shrugged.

But Kate felt she had to satisfy his complaint about her.

"I like you a lot," she said honestly, "but no more than that. Perhaps it's a hangover from the old Kate, but I can't treat this sort of thing"—she gestured toward the rumpled couch—"lightly. For me, it has to be—important."

"And this isn't. Not to you, anyway."

"Or to you," Kate said quietly. "Be honest."

"A guy has to take his chances where he finds them," he admitted sheepishly.

"I have a feeling," Kate said with a smile, "that they come your way pretty often."

He grinned. "Okay, so no broken heart. Only trampled pride."

"I don't believe that either," Kate said crisply.

As the elevator door opened, "Still friends?" he asked.

"I hope so."

"Hospital tomorrow night?"

"No, I've got an auction. Thursday."

"I'll be here."

The door slid across his bright, cheerfully unfazed smile.

Kate straightened the sofa, cleared away the glasses, took them through into the kitchen and washed them. Then, switching off the lights, she went into the bedroom.

She had left the furnishings entirely unchanged; the bed was a big one, the colors wine and grey, masculine colors. They had been her father's choice, as had the highly polished rosewood furniture, from the French bed to the eight-drawer tallboy, and the tailored wine velvet curtains. She settled herself against the big, firm pillows, and reached, once again, for the bundle of her father's letters. She had wept herself to sleep after her first reading, desolately and irreparably ashamed of herself. As she held the letters again, containing so much that was her beloved father, she wondered if perhaps her feelings for Blaise Chandler, stretching and expanding themselves now that they had been released from confinement, were some sort of fateful expiation.

After the first reading she had been full of good resolution; she would fulfill all her father's hopes for her, expressed so poignantly in letter after letter; she would become the girl her father had loved. Too late she realized that after his leaving she had stopped loving herself, had rather hated herself for what she regarded as her own failure. Now, unfolding in the warmth Blaise Chandler had directed at her when they talked so honestly together, she knew that a woman only felt beautiful if she was loved. As a girl she had not thought herself plain, had disregarded what her grandmother had said, even gone so far as to tell her father. He had looked at her gravely and said, "But you are beautiful to me, my little Cat." It was only later, when he had gone, when she had no one to tell her she was lovely, that she had ceased to take an interest in her appearance, had adopted the jeans and denim jacket disguise, and had taken the harsh words of her grandmother to be gospel truth. Since that first, shattering reading of his letters, she had begun to examine the wound inside herself, had realized that with these words of love, of remorse, of sadness, she could complete the healing that had begun when he left her the most precious thing he had to give. The fact that Blaise Chandler had also read them brought him even closer. The letters were intensely private, but somehow she did not mind him knowing their contents, because she knew he had understood: he would not have given them to her otherwise.

Kate found she was glad he knew so much. Now she could confess her feelings about him, did not even mind that nothing could ever come of them because she was so glad just to have the feelings themselves. She had thought herself emotionally dead when she could not respond as both Nicholas Chevely and Larry wanted her to; now she knew it was not that she could not respond to men, but that she had been waiting for the right one. That he should be one she could never have was perhaps the price she had to pay for spurning the one whose love she had never, no matter what she believed, ever lost.

She should have been sad, found she was not; on the contrary, the nagging feeling of emptiness and loss with which she had lived for so long was finally and completely gone. Her father's letters, so full of openly and nakedly expressed love and longing, had given her back to herself.

With a glad heart, she gave herself up to the pleasure of rereading them yet again.

*   *   *

Dominique was in New York, dressing for a dinner engagement, when the flowers were delivered. At first she thought they were from the man who would be calling for her in half an hour, but when she took the lid off the box, saw what it contained, her body froze. A mass of tiny, tightly budded yellow roses in the shape of a fire-breathing dragon. The small white card bore the typed notation: "8 P.M. Monday next." It was a summons. For one wild moment panic had her heading for the telephone. She would call Blaise, tell him everything, fling herself into that sheltering protection, so unaccustomedly yet reassuringly pleasant. He could throw the weight of the mighty ChanCorp around her like some magically impenetrable cloak . . . No, she thought, as her hand hovered above the receiver. Careful. See what they want first. Don't display your hand too soon. Keep Blaise in reserve. Perhaps they want to talk terms. I did not run back to Hong Kong as they expected. I still have not changed my shippers. And they dare not get rid of me . . . Confidence began to seep back. Yes, she thought coolly. Face them down. Call their bluff. So when she lifted the telephone it was to instruct her secretary to get her on a flight that would deliver her at Kai Tak the following Monday afternoon.

In the car that picked her up from the airport, absentmindedly listening to her Chinese secretary's detailed rundown on what had been happening while she was away, she planned her campaign.

When Chao-Li came in, unannounced as before—the servants either being instructed to keep out of the way or doing so by reason of that mysterious osmosis that existed among the Chinese—she was ready and waiting, wearing a black Shantung silk cheongsam, slit on both sides to the thigh, the mandarin collar surrounded by a choker of cabochon sapphires alternating with square-cut diamonds. Talisman sapphires glittered from her ears.

She was fresh from a hot bath and a session at the expert hands of her masseur, who had kneaded the tension from her, leaving her supple, elastic and, most of all, clear-minded. She had taken great care with her face, applied her perfume at judicious pulse points, had her maid polish her hair with a brush wrapped in silk. A last, slow, 360° turn before the wall of mirrors in her dressing room revealed what she sought: perfection, which in turn gave her confidence. Her armor had always been her beauty and there must be no chink in it tonight.

She had chosen the most advantageous position after some thought, so that when Chao-Li came in, she was standing by the big bank of windows, her black dress starkly dramatic against the brilliant white of the filmy curtains, her jewels and her very self presenting a breathtaking aspect. She was rewarded by the sudden hot glow in Chao-Li's sloe-black eyes before it was concealed by his bow. Her own gave no sign of the hate and the fear she was holding tightly in check.

"Madame."

"Chao-Li."

"You are well?" he asked politely.

"Very well, thank you. May I offer you a drink?"

As before, the Roederer Cristal awaited, the dim sum arranged like a picture on its K'ang Hsi plate.

"Please . . ." She indicated his favorite chair, of clear-lacquered bamboo, its plump cushions upholstered in turquoise Thai silk, and as he seated himself, she moved past him with that sinuous grace that was so much part of her, passing close enough for him to breathe in the heady fragrance of her perfume.

She poured the champagne herself, proud of her rock-steady hand, long nails gleaming as though freshly dipped in blood.

"So?" she queried tauntingly, relishing the chill dryness of the champagne. "We have things to discuss, you and I."

"You mistake, Madame. There is nothing which needs to be discussed."

Dominique smiled. The cold, unblinking eyes seemed to give her strength. "Oh, but there is. Things have changed since your last—visit." She paused, letting him think it was because of what had happened in France, and then threw her wrench into the works. "Unless you are prepared to do something for me, I will no longer be in a position to change shippers or even allow you the use of any shipper. My stepsister has been lucky enough to acquire two very important sales; the first has already pulled her level, the second, unless it is stopped, will put her ahead. That, in turn, will mean my losing even that small portion of Despard's I now control. It will be out of my hands and quite out of your plans."

He was silent as he mulled that over, before commanding: "Explain."

"The sale will take place within the next month at a great English country house, Courtland Park in Sussex. Unless it is—prevented—there is no way, in the time remaining, even if I were to hold a dozen large sales, that I could bring enough in commissions to be able to so much as catch up. It is an unlooked-for development, and one which I assure you I tried to prevent, but short of that sale never taking place, Despard's is lost to us both."

After another short silence, "And if this sale should, somehow, not take place . . . ?"

"Then she has no hope of catching me. The lead I established after my own sale here will keep me in front for the time I need; then Despard's will be mine and I will be in a position to—assist you in your own business."

Once more he thought, and then instructed, "You will give me exact details of this house, where it is, what it is, when the auction will be held. As much detailed information as you have. I will then consult with my associates. You will have our answer within twenty-four hours." He paused. "And once the objective has been accomplished, you will then be at our disposal."

Not if I can help it, Dominique thought, as she agreed smoothly, "Of course."

He contemplated her for a moment. "You realize your information will be checked?"

"And found to be correct."

"That being so, I do not think this sale will ever take place."

"How you prevent it is none of my concern; only do it.'

"And then you will do what concerns us?"

"Yes."

"In which case, Madame, you will be hearing from me again." He bowed deeply once more and was gone.

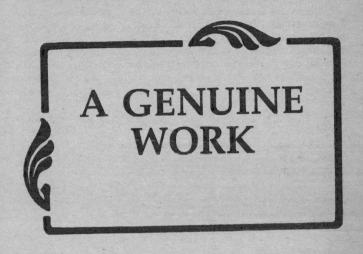

A GENUINE WORK

October

18

Kate went down to Courtland Park at least once a week to see how preparations for the sale were progressing. The contents of the house had been catalogued, Kate giving Dot Bainbridge carte blanche to do the job in as short a time as possible. What was of no great value—and there was a great deal of it—was disposed of to a man who came, looked at it all, and made a cash offer, which was then used to pay the cleaning firm who descended on the house and proceeded to give it a face-lift from top to bottom. The curtains came down and were cleaned, the walls washed where practicable, carpets and rugs shampooed, floors waxed, staircases and furniture polished, chandeliers unwrapped from their cotton bags, china and crystal washed and polished, as was the Georgian silver, badly neglected and left to lie for anybody knew how many years in baize-lined boxes or drawstring velvet bags.

Kate had decided to use the main hall—big enough to hold a hunt ball in—and the two reception rooms opening off it, one a vast echoing dining room and the other a huge two-fireplace salon, for the three days of previewing. The salon she gave over entirely to the glorious French furniture of which the late Mr. Courtland had been so fond: the Louis XVI grey-painted marquise chairs, stamped G. Iacob; the magnificent ormolu-mounted commode of amaranth, tulipwood, marquetry, and parquetry; the Louis XV ormolu-mounted tulipwood and marquetry *regulateur,* signed Herbault à Paris; the giltwood armchair made for Marie Antoinette's *grand cabinet intérieur* in the palace of Versailles; another ormolu-mounted commode in kingwood stamped J.-F. Leleu, circa 1775; a second, earlier commode circa 1740 attributed to Charles Cressent, and a marquetry folio cabinet attrib-

uted to Bernard van Ridenburgh II. The high spot was an
ormolu-mounted *encoignure* stamped I. Dubois, for which
Kate was confident she could get bids of up to one million
pounds. They would all stand on the newly cleaned and
restored Louis XIV Savonnerie carpet of cream, gold, and
blue, which measured forty by thirty feet, and had once lain
on the floor of Madame du Barry's *petit salon*. On the pale
blue silk walls, which had been carefully restored, she would
hang the mirrors she had found swathed in cobwebs in one
of the attics, judiciously interspersed with choice paintings,
all portraits and of the eighteenth century: Gainsborough,
Reynolds, Goya, Fragonard, and Boucher.

On the marble-topped *encoignures* she would set the choicest of the many pieces of French porcelain, such as the Louis
XV ormolu-mounted shell potpourri vase in Arita porcelain
and the Sèvres cachepots, each filled with beautiful flower
arrangements. In the dining room she would set the enormous rosewood table for a grand dinner party, using the
Sèvres *bleu de roi* service and the Georgian silver, along
with the Baccarat glasses and the *famille vert* porcelain deep
dishes—one perfect dozen of them and likely, Kate thought,
to go for a minimum of £100,000. In the hall she would show
the old masters: the two Rembrandts, the Rubens, the volup-
tuous Ingres nude, along with the choicest furniture. The
centerpiece would be the cabinet by Adam Weisweiler, with
its panels of Japanese lacquer. None of these things had
been seen for decades.

Now, Kate thought happily as she drove herself down on
Thursday afternoon ten days before the opening, they would
see the light all right—the light of camera flashes. Publicity
was already running high, and prices were expected to follow. The catalogue, which had been originally priced at £50,
was now said to be changing hands for £100. It had sold out
at once, and she had ordered a quick reprint of a specially
printed utility edition—with no photographs. So many people had notified their intention of attending that she had
recruited additional bid callers; on her own she would never
be able to spot every bid in that vast sea of faces, and she
had insisted on rehearsals so there should be no slipups.
Everything was hanging on this sale: her own future, that of
Despard's, and many of the people who worked there.

Her own reputation was also on the line. She knew that
the museums were keenly interested, had been very careful

to see that those items designated by the government as being of Preeminent Importance were marked with a red asterisk. There would be TV crews from all over the world, the press would be there in force, and the security would be tight, as it was even now, with at least twenty million pounds worth of art on public view.

Despard's commission—ten percent of the gross—would make a handsome addition to her total figure at the end-of-year review and, provided Dominique was not hiding some cataclysmic surprise up her sleeve, would put Kate ahead. But even so she anxiously scanned every salesroom report from Despard's New York and Hong Kong, as well as the other, smaller branches under Dominique's control. So far nothing had given her any cause for alarm, had not even approached her stupendous Sale of the Century in Hong Kong.

All the intense activity had stretched Kate and her staff, but the excitement, the atmosphere steadily building to explosion point, was worth it. Courtland Park would be the high spot of the year; there had been nothing like it since Sotheby's Mentmore.

When Kate arrived at the Park it was its usual hive of activity. Workmen everywhere, cleaners vacuuming and polishing, men on ladders fixing the newly washed and polished chandeliers, superb wedding-cake confections of Waterford crystal, a huge machine buffing up the glaze of the parquet flooring.

She was set on as soon as she set foot inside the hall. "Oh, Miss Despard, thank heavens, what shall I do about . . ." and "Miss Despard, can I have your decision on . . ." or "Miss Despard, I can't seem to find . . ."

She was kept very busy until five o'clock when the workmen and cleaners went home, leaving only her own staff, a contingent of fifteen she had seconded to the Park. At six she packed them off to the hotel where they were staying—she knew they had been hard at it all day—and told the guards they could switch on the alarm system, but that she would be in the house for a while yet. She wanted the place to herself, to wander through it, get the feel of it, try it on for size in a way, to see if what had looked good on paper fulfilled its promise.

"It's beginning to take shape, eh, Miss Despard?" one of the guards said to her.

"You like it?"

"It's a palace . . . The wife and I will be here come sale day—me to guard and her to look. There's nothing here we could afford, I'm afraid."

Kate realigned an Egyptian basalt head. "You should try Despard's Downtown when you come to London; everything there is much more reasonably priced."

"I suppose they'll all be millionaires coming to the sale?"

"They will need to be well-heeled," she joked.

He went through to the huge kitchen, where the guardpost had been established, while Kate wandered around the hall.

Was the Rembrandt self-portrait best on that far wall or should she swap it for the Rubens, a glory of color and composition? Perhaps the Rembrandt was a mite somber . . . She made a note on her pad. The carpet had come up a treat, colors blooming after submergence for decades in layers of dirt, and you could hardly tell where the new silk of the walls began, it merged so well with the old. Her Board thought she had gone mad, spending so much to do up a house that was not hers, but Kate knew the right background, the right ambience, could enhance prices enormously. Also, she had not told them yet that she intended to offer for the house itself, to be used as a permanent base for all Despard's country house sales that were not *in situ*. Her total commission would be the deciding factor. Only if her hopes were well founded would she be able to afford it.

The Flemish tapestry looked nice in that corner of the hall, where a window would shed soft light on it, and at night the lamp—a bronze nymph holding a flaming torch, German, circa 1600—lit it to a glow. Pleasurably, slowly, she wandered through the three great rooms, touching, smoothing, stroking, admiring, making notes every now and again of improvements she thought could be made. The viewing was only days away and she wanted everything to be perfect. Above her head, carefully concealed TV cameras watched her every move, as they would watch the crowds on the view days; four guards sitting at monitors back in the kitchen, on the lookout for the light-fingered, the deliberate, jealous vandal. There were also concealed microphones; every sound was picked up and broadcast in stereo to the watching guards.

Now, she heard a crackle, then a voice said, "Cup of tea, Miss Despard? We are just brewing up."

"Give me five more minutes . . ."

Bad *joss* (luck) and a nasty attack of chicken pox, caught from his youngest daughter, meant that the latest tape from the hidden recorder in Dominique's penthouse, which held the conversation between Dominique and Chao-Li concerning the disposal of Courtland Park, remained unheard by Benny Fong for more than ten days.

The miniature tape recorder, cleverly and wholly unsuspectingly concealed in the portable transistor radio belonging to Chang, the major-domo, who played it all day, was voice activated by the bug concealed in a lamp in the penthouse living room. Chang's instructions were to check the tape every day and change it when it had run out. The recorded reel was then placed in a cigarette packet of the luxury length, filter-tipped brand Dominique smoked, which was thrown, with the rest of the contents of the rubbish bin, down the waste disposal chute. The bin in which it landed was carefully inspected every morning by yet another cousin of Benny's, and if the packet was there it was extracted and passed on to a certain street vendor, from whom it was in turn picked up, eventually to arrive on Benny's desk. But the day after Chao-Li's visit, Dominique went to Macao with some friends to do a little gambling, so the recorder stayed inactive. When Chang checked it, seeing it still had some way to run, he left it intact, and it was not used up until two days after Dominique's return, and then lay on Benny's desk for a week awaiting his return to the office.

Blaise Chandler was in Paris and, as he was so near, decided he would call on Kate on his way home. He had been hearing a great deal about Courtland Park; people kept asking him if he would be attending. "Going to be a big one," they said. "And if the catalogue is anything to go by, they will be at each other's throats. Blood will run . . ."

He had called in at Despard's Paris and been most impressed by their reaction to the sale. "Formidable," the French director had told him. "A pity that the glories of France are not being sold where they should be, but at least it is Despard's who is disposing of them."

He called Despard's from Heathrow and, on being told

that Kate was in Sussex, decided to go down and join her. He dismissed the chauffeur-driven ChanCorp limousine, went to the Hertz desk instead and picked up the keys of a Turbo Porsche. It was a pleasant late afternoon; he should be at the Park by six-thirty. Kate could give him the Grand Tour and then he would take her out to dinner. He felt his spirits lift at the thought of seeing Kate again. She was good company, you could talk to her; something, he reflected wryly, he had not been used to doing much with women. In some odd way he felt proud of her; she had done so well, come to grips with the challenge and, if Dominique's reaction was anything to go by, succeeded in handling it only too well. He knew his wife was leaving no prospect unwined and dined in her efforts to acquire bigger and better sales. He had made a point of dropping in on the branches she controlled, and all told the same tale: Madame du Vivier was a whirlwind these days, cracking the whip and demanding results. Dominique, he thought, was worried. As well she might be. She had got herself in deep; all he could do was monitor her movements, try and prevent, if he could, her getting herself even more tied up with people even she could not handle.

As yet they had been unable to come up with evidence that he could use to pry Dominique loose from the grip of the Triads. Rollo was still in his coma; Benny's only information was that there had been a factory in the Walled City, but that it had been dismantled. Where it was now nobody could—or would—say, and not even Blaise's "fragrant grease" —heavy bribes—had produced any hard information. Fear had put a zipper on all mouths.

Dominique was the only lead and she was playing it safe. When he had last heard from Benny she had not seen Chao-Li, and had not changed shippers, but she was frightened, and it was not until he listened to the tapes again that Blaise realized why. Her mother's sudden death, the spectacle case with its golden dragon—they had come together in a way that had him out of his chair and almost on his way to the police until he realized he had no real proof. Only the absolute certainty that the Triads had murdered his mother-in-law. That was why Dominique was running scared; why she, who took such things for granted, had been examining swollen stiff windows. It was a warning, of course. Of what would happen to her if she did not toe the line. He had told

Benny to step up the surveillance, to have her watched at all times—"even when she goes to the john." It was all he could do, and to ensure that Kate was also safe, he had installed Larry Cole in London and one of his own men as a guard—he had recommended the security firm Kate was using at Courtland Park.

At least she had no idea she was still in danger, but then Kate never did think about herself. She still did not realize that Larry Cole had prevented a deliberate attempt on her life. But Blaise had a nagging sense of unease, that prickle at the back of his neck he had learned to trust in Vietnam. That was one of the reasons why he was on his way there now: to reassure himself. As an added precaution, security at Rollo's hospital was as tight as ever. One of his nurses was an ex-WAC Blaise had worked with in the Special Forces in Vietnam. He thought he had covered all eventualities, but it was this waiting he could not stand.

He rounded a bend and there was the wall: eight feet high and surmounted by ornamental spikes. He reduced speed, followed it for the next mile or so until he came to a stop outside a pair of iron gates, as delicate as lace. About ten yards back was a gatehouse. He got out of the car and, as he did so, a man came out of the gatehouse, wearing the uniform of a guard.

Good, thought Blaise. With what that house is holding, she's got the right idea, and as one thought led to another, he glanced upwards: yes, there atop the carved stone unicorns on the gateposts were small TV cameras, set so as to see all the traffic that came from either direction. He felt even better

"Can I help you, sir?" the guard asked politely. He was big, soft-spoken, but Blaise knew the type. Well trained and deadly.

"My name is Blaise Chandler. I'd like to see Miss Kate Despard."

"Is she expecting you, sir?"

"No. I only just arrived in England earlier today, but she'll see me I'm sure."

"If you'll just wait a moment, sir."

The guard went back into the gatehouse. Blaise approved even more. He had felt uneasy when he had read in the salesrooms columns about the prices expected at the Courtland Park auction; honey to a whole nest of hornets with theft on their minds. This tight security was a good sign that Kate had realized it, too.

The guard came back. His manner had changed. "Miss Despard says to go up to the house, sir. She'll meet you there. Just follow the drive."

Blaise went back to his car as the guard returned to the gatehouse, and in a moment the big gates swung back noiselessly.

He waved a hand as he drove in. "Thanks . . ."

The drive was wide and twisting, leading into the depths of an enormous park. What is it about the English that makes them hide their houses in the middle of estates the size of Central Park? he thought. He passed a grandiose fountain—water turned off—and a scattering of marble statues, and then, as he turned the last bend, the enormous Jacobean house loomed up in front, set behind a vast gravel sweep. Standing on the steps in front of a pair of doors that would have admitted a Sherman tank, was Kate.

"Another nice surprise," she smiled, as she came forward to meet him.

"I called your office but they said you were down here, so I thought I'd come and take a look-see at what all the talk is about."

He tilted his head back to examine the enormous façade, all mullioned windows and ornamental strap work.

"Yes, it's big, isn't it?" Kate said demurely. She turned, gestured toward the wide sweep of lawn on either side of the entrance. "Come sale day, we'll have two large marquees—one for refreshments and one for settlements."

"It's all organized, then?"

"Just about. Come inside and I'll give you a preview."

Blaise was impressed. "Who did all this?" he asked, waving a hand at the exquisitely arranged furniture.

"All my own work," she admitted modestly. "The arrangements, I mean, not the actual shifting of the furniture."

"Well, I don't know about your customers, but it certainly impresses me. Having the pieces arranged to best advantage will make a lot of difference to what they bring, I'll bet."

"I hope so."

"You must have worked very hard," Blaise said.

"It has been a frantic few months," Kate agreed.

"But worth it?"

"Again, I hope so."

"I see you've seen to your security," he said casually.

"Well, there's a lot of valuable stuff lying around. I had those people you told me about come down and give the place a thorough inspection, and then acted on their recommendations. It cost an arm and a leg, but . . ."

"It would cost you a hell of a lot more if somebody was to make off with a few choice items. You did the right thing."

In fact, he had himself talked to the security firm Kate had used, a long-standing employee of ChanCorp, and told them what he would like to see in the way of security, ever mindful of what had happened in Hong Kong and the itch at the back of his neck. Now, seeing how well the place was guarded he felt better, though those enormous grounds, even if scanned by TV cameras, were far too big for his liking; you could hide an army out there. Still, once they got within a fifty-yard radius of the house there was a network of photocell alarms that would give direct warning to the nearest police station as well as alerting the guards inside the house. But the thought of Catherine Despard was a constant reminder of the danger Kate was in. At least she had her own "minder," as the British called them. Nor did she have any idea that the whole set-up had cost considerably more than she realized. Blaise had paid for it. He felt responsible. It was his wife who'd created this situation in the first place.

He picked up a catalogue from the George II rent table. "So how long is it going to take to get through all this?" he asked.

"Five days, starting at ten and finishing at four. Each day a specialty—furniture on the Monday, porcelain and glass the next, then the silver, bronzes, objects of virtu, and so on. The pictures will be the grand finale."

"You are going to be one busy girl." Then, after she had shown him around, he said, "And have been very busy indeed, I see. But the result is well worth it. You've got taste, Kate, and flair, and that eye I remember Charles prized so highly. I'm no collector or appreciator of great art and it takes my breath away. God help the buyers."

Kate flushed with pleasure at the admiration in his voice.

In turn, he watched her pleasurably. She was good to look upon these days, in a grey flannel suit, a cream silk shirt tied under the neck in a pussy-cat bow, her hair springy and shiny and burning like fire, her face a far remove from the unflattering arrangement of bones he had first seen, softer now, filled out, its fine modeling highlighted by delicate shading. She reminded him of a thoroughbred horse: glossy, shining with health and long-legged elegance.

She turned her head to look at him inquiringly, and he cursed himself for staring. "What made you spend so much on a place you don't own?" he asked hastily.

"The hope that I will, one day."

She told him her plans for a country house base for Despard's, to be used solely for single owner collections. "I want a base that reflects the quality of the goods. Fine pieces demand a fine setting, not some large auction room with hard lighting and not particularly comfortable seating. If a buyer can see what a piece of furniture looks like *in situ*, he has an added incentive to possess it because he will then know if it fits what he has in mind. Pictures—the important ones—aren't usually bought to be looked at unless the buyer is a museum; they are kept until such time as they bring a considerable profit."

"Back to great art again?" he inquired silkily.

She put her head back and laughed and, for the thousandth time, he wondered how he had ever thought her plain; she had never been that—never would be that. She had just been in need of refurbishing, like this house. Now, both were objects of beauty on which it was sheer pleasure just to feast the eyes.

"Talking of great 'art,' " Kate said with gentle savagery, "what's new from Hong Kong?"

"Nothing. Information is hard to come by; even my bribes aren't working. This Chao-Li must be a pretty terrible guy because he's got every mouth zippered shut. And Dominique is keeping a very low profile."

Kate said nothing. That name opened up a minefield.

But he was surefooted. "I could have cut out your tongue in Hong Kong, but that was purely a rearguard action. What my wife has done is too big, too terrible to be glossed over with a perfunctory 'Sorry.' And I have come to believe that it was because your father knew something like this would happen that he put me between you."

"Then he must have believed you could handle it. Papa was a shrewd judge of character."

"Maybe . . . I think he liked me and I know he trusted me, but I was also in the perfect position." Blaise paused, staring at the somber Rembrandt, an old man who had painted himself with the compassionate dispassion of genius. "He knew what she was, you see, far better than I. Oh, he liked to show her off—he loved beauty as you know—but he never trusted her. He was telling us that by not giving her everything and setting me to watch. My brief was to see you accepted your legacy; that it was Dominique who did it is one of life's little ironies, but it suited me so I didn't mind. At that time I didn't want her to get Despard's because it meant I would get less of her." He turned back to Kate, a faint self-mocking smile on his mouth but none in his eyes. "You thought I could do no other than be prejudiced in her favor. But I think we know each other better now."

She met his eyes, encountered a look there which had her missing her step, made her turn away in panic. You are letting your imagination run away with you, she told herself roundly. His concern is to extricate Dominique and Despard's—right? And in that order.

"How is Rollo, by the way?" Blaise asked.

"No change. I go and see him as often as I can, which hasn't been much of late." She sounded quietly troubled.

"You can't do everything," he remonstrated gently. "But please do be careful. I've nothing to go on except instinct but . . . I'll be glad when this damned sale is over and done with."

"It will be, soon, and what can they do at this late stage?"

"That's what worries me."

They went down the stairs and into the hall in silence, Kate waiting to hear if he would say any more, but evidently he had already said more than he intended because his next words were an abrupt "You know Catherine Despard died?"

"Yes." Kate had read of it in the trade press, had felt none of the "good riddance" that would once have been her reaction.

"Her heart, wasn't it?"

"That was her doctor's opinion. Whatever it was, I don't think she had really been living since Charles died. Not in the real world, anyway. She opted instead for some fantasy where Charles was all hers and only hers, which was all she ever wanted anyway."

Kate let out a long breath. "I know—now." She sounded sadly regretful.

A quick glance. "The letters?"

"Yes."

"They—helped?"

"They made me bitterly ashamed and yet, as you said—now was the right time. Even had I read them when they were written, I don't think I would have understood. I had to be older and—"

"Wiser?"

"Yes."

"You've learned a lot. I've just watched you."

"I've had to. And unlearn just as much."

"Yes. I didn't appreciate your feelings when we first met." There was that odd bitter note to his voice. "I had no idea just how important an influence in your life your father had been, how much his leaving of it affected you."

"Rollo said I acted like a jealous wife," Kate said honestly.

A short laugh. "He should know . . . I think our reaction to defection by others largely depends on their reaction to us." There was another pause. "There comes a time when you can't handle certain feelings except by shutting them down."

Which is what you did, Kate thought, understanding now the remoteness, the KEEP OUT—THIS MEANS YOU attitude. She wondered if it had worked, or if he had given it up as a bad job, decided he was stuck with them and that if he could not beat them, he'd better join them. Whatever, she would rather have this Blaise than that Blaise any time.

At that moment, they heard a car roar up the drive. "It's Nicholas!" Kate exclaimed with surprise—and pleasure? Blaise thought—as a tall, elegant man came in, and bent to kiss Kate's cheek, putting his hands on her shoulders in a knowing, intimate way.

". . . had to come into Sussex so thought as I was in the neighborhood I'd drop in and take you to a delightful hotel I know for a leisurely dinner."

He eyed Blaise with a scrutiny that was both polite and wary.

"Nicholas Chevely—Blaise Chandler," Kate introduced.

Nicholas' face cleared as if a duster had been used. "Blaise Chandler! I say, this is a pleasant surprise. The very man I've been wanting to meet. I was going to ask Kate to introduce us. She must have read my mind."

That's not difficult, Kate told him silently. It spells MONEY.

"You'll join us for dinner, won't you? Give us an opportunity to talk. I've got a little something I'm sure would be of interest to you."

Which meant that any little something he had intended to say to Kate would naturally give precedence.

Blaise looked at Kate. She looked at him. And bit her lip. "Sounds fine," he said with the studied politeness of the unenthusiastic. His lift of the shoulders in Kate's direction said, "Sorry. Another time." Kate, to whom even this one had come as a surprise, to say the least, was happy to have the next one to look forward to.

"Just give me a minute to have a look-see, chat to the guards, and then we'll go," Nicholas said.

He walked off cheerfully to check that all was well. "No problems?" he inquired briskly. "All systems working?"

He had been quite happy to let Kate pay for the installation of the expensive security system. The house was going to be hers anyway . . .

"Yes, sir."

Nicholas inspected the monitors, the cameras constantly circling the treasures set on display, the quiet shadows of the grounds, brightly lit until the photocell ring took over.

"All your own comforts provided for? Tea and such . . ."

"Yes, sir. Gas stove is working and that old boiler in the basement gives a surprising amount of heat."

"Not too high outside this kitchen," Nicholas warned, checking the thermostat. "The temperature must be controlled in the view rooms—mustn't get too high or too low. Keep an eye on it, won't you?"

"Yes, sir."

He went back to the others with a jaunty step, well pleased with himself. He had made the right choice in Kate Despard. What she had done with this decrepit old barn was incredible, and in such a short time. Those rooms made the mouth water, and from the gossip circulating, come opening day there would be a positive flood. His five percent should be a killing, and what luck Chandler happened to be here . . . If he nibbled at a certain proposition Nicholas had been nurturing ever since he found out that the executor of Charles Despard's will was heir to the mighty ChanCorp, he would qualify as a financial mass murderer.

They had not been gone five minutes when the telephone in the kitchen rang.

"Courtland Park . . . who? Can you speak up, the line's bad . . . Mr. Blaise Chandler? He's just this minute left . . . what? No, I don't know where they've gone, back to London I expect . . . Miss Despard? She left with him . . . No, she won't be back tomorrow. It's Saturday . . . yes, all right, I'll give her a message if she calls . . . how do you spell that? F-O-N-G—Mr. Fong, right. Yes, I'll tell her it's very urgent . . ." As he put the receiver back, "Some bloody Chinaman with his knickers in a twist . . ."

The hotel was called the Pink Thatch, but it was the building, two-story, half-timbered, seventeenth century, that was painted a pretty soft pink. It looked warmly inviting, and the smell of food made Kate's mouth water. As usual, while working she had forgotten to eat. Now she was looking forward to a good dinner, and tomorrow, she resolved, she would visit Rollo. She had not seen him in a week, though she had called the hospital to be told the same, hopeless message. No change.

The dining room was small, so was the menu, but the food, when it arrived, was ambrosial. Kate concentrated on it and let the conversation drift over her head, her own mind still on her sale—the biggest sale not only she but also Despard's had ever handled. Her make-or-break time. The high spot of her year. Oh, the calendar was filled with sale dates, but none likely to bring the enormous prices she expected to achieve in ten days' time. So as she ate her salmon trout poached in white wine sauce, and drank a crisp Chardonnay, her mind turned to ways and means of acquiring sale items that would give her commission of the kind needed to consolidate the lead she was sure she would take.

She surfaced again as coffee was brought, to hear Nicholas saying confidently, "It's a sure thing, old boy. They are in big financial trouble. Sloppy management and a real cash-flow problem. Child's play to take over, honestly, and if properly run, a real asset to ChanCorp . . ."

Kate turned off again. Nicholas was on his favorite hobbyhorse: money. But she glanced at Blaise. His face was polite, but Kate sensed he was bored, and as he caught her eye she made a face as if to say, "Sorry, I know he's a bore," but his own reaction made her glance hastily away again. With the eye that Nicholas could not see—they were sitting side by side on a corner banquette—he winked. Why do I bother? Kate thought. He is always one step ahead of me . . .

Checking her watch, she decided to make a move and left the table to go to the ladies. As she went through the small lobby she heard the loud braying of a Klaxon and the roar of a heavy engine. They were burning the stubble and some farmer must have got careless.

She went to the loo, washed her hands, tidied her hair, hoped Nicholas was not going to linger in the hope of landing his fish. As she went back through the lobby some of the hotel guests were talking.

" . . . must be a big one," she heard a man say. "That's the third engine."

"I never saw anything," a woman complained.

"You wouldn't; the house is well off the road in a great big park, but the gates were wide open and they are usually shut. It's an old house and probably tinder dry—great big barn of a place actually."

Kate felt her heart stop. "Excuse me," she asked, "but which house are you talking about?"

"Courtland Park," the man said. "There's nothing else down that road . . ."

Kate ran. Blaise saw her coming and was on his feet by the time she reached him. "What is it?" he asked tersely.

"The house . . . a man says there's a big fire and there's nothing else down that road . . ." Her face was chalk, her eyes enormous.

Blaise had her by the wrist and halfway out of the restaurant before Nicholas had laid down his napkin.

"I heard the Klaxon as the fire engine went by and the man said it was the third so it must be Courtland Park—"

"Then let's find out." The Porsche roared out of the car park and accelerated up the road.

As the man had said, the gates were wide open, the gatehouse deserted, and as they reached the first bend in the drive they saw the black smoke beyond the trees.

"Oh, my God . . . moaned Kate.

Blaise pressed his foot down, and Kate half rose in her seat as they rounded the last bend and the full scale of the disaster hit them. The back of the house was a mass of flame, smoke billowing. There were three big red fire engines, and the hoses were already playing. But what Kate stared at wild-eyed was the men staggering out of the house carrying whatever they could lay their hands on. In a flash she was out of the car and running to join them.

"Don't be a fool!" rapped Blaise. "That's no place for you."

"Of course it is! This is my sale—I've got to save what I can." He had caught hold of her arm and she was trying to wrench it free.

"So check what comes out—there's nobody else who can."

"I can check once it's out and I'm not standing by and watching it burn."

She yanked her arm free of his restraining grip and sprinted for the house.

"What happened?" she demanded of a guard who was staggering past under the weight of a Louis XV *fauteuil.*

"Explosion . . . probably boiler in cellar . . . not sure . . ."

She ran on, into the dining room, where she yanked a drawer from a commode and then proceeded to fill it with china and glass from the elegantly set table. "Here!" she cried to a man who looked in. "Take this outside and come back for the next one." She got a second drawer and filled it, then a third and fourth, clearing the table of everything. Then she began to stack chairs, working quickly, frantically but methodically. As she did so she heard the wail of police sirens and in moments two policemen appeared in the doorway.

"Oh, thank God . . . will you help me get these pictures down?"

"You shouldn't be in here, Miss," one of them said authoritatively.

"This is all part of a sale I'm holding—or was going to hold—here in ten days' time. Now come and help or there won't be anything to sell!"

They got the paintings—Boucher, Fragonard, and Watteau—down from the red damask walls, and then Kate began to dismantle the table. It was made of three parts fitted together as it was too big to get through a door in one piece, and she quickly found the key, kept in its own slot underneath the overhang, and began to unwind the long spiral bolt. When the policemen came back they carried the three pieces out one at a time. When they came back again she was rolling up the carpet.

"The two of you will never carry it," Kate fretted. It will take four at least . . . here, you—" The figure passing the door, cradling a silver gilt epergne, turned. It was Blaise Chandler. "We need help with the carpet," she pleaded. "Is there a pair of spare hands?"

"Hold on," he said, disappeared and came back rapidly. "Right," he ordered, after a fast assessment of the carpet—an eighteenth-century Aubusson—and its size. "One at the end, me in the middle, and you—other end. When I say lift—hoist, okay?" They bent down. "Right—lift!" The carpet was raised, levered onto shoulders, and carried out.

Kate ran back to the fireplace, where she picked up a clock—ormolu with Sèvres plaques—and two Chelsea figures. As she ran out with them she met Blaise coming back in.

"I think your people are arriving—at least a dozen of them."

"Oh, thank God . . . we need as many as possible."

"The fire's out of control, I'm afraid. The back is done for and it will soon be eating at those walls . . ." He nodded at the far end of the hall.

"Then we've got to work fast." She darted away, this time into one of the drawing rooms, which she saw with relief was already half cleared.

"Keep an eye on the walls," Blaise said, appearing beside her. "Once the smoke begins to thicken, get out—you hear me?"

"Yes, of course," Kate answered mechanically, busy taking down a beautiful arrangement of miniatures.

"I mean it!" Blaise said in a voice that had her turning to him open-mouthed. "I know your sale is important, but if you are not here to conduct it, it will all have been a waste of time—so keep your eyes and ears open. Fire makes a noise—you won't fail to hear it. When you do—get out at once."

"All right, I hear you," Kate retorted crossly. Bossy boots, she thought, as she ran for the second lot of miniatures on the other wall, at the far end of the room. It was hot to the touch.

This time, as she ran outside to place her rescued items on one of the rapidly growing piles, she took a moment to look at the house. The roof was well ablaze, flames licking greedily from windows now without glass, and, as Blaise had said, it made a noise. It roared. The air was full of soot flakes, and the rising wind blew smoke into everyone's eyes. It was like some surrealistic nightmare: the flames lit the night sky in patterns that were straight out of hell. Time, she thought, as she frantically ran back into the house. Please, God, give us enough time . . .

Running back into the drawing room Kate met a wall of heat, and the smoke was suddenly thicker. It stung her eyes and made her cough as she went down the long room toward the fireplace. The Gainsborough that she had hung above it was safely gone, but on the carved marble of the mantel itself were the Meissen monkeys—twelve of them, dressed as eighteenth-century court musicians and playing musical instruments. As she lifted them down she noticed that the pale blue silk of the wall had darkened. Stripping off her jacket, she laid the figures in it before carefully wrapping them in a bundle, using the sleeves to tie it. Then, gingerly, because the figures were in perfect condition, she picked up her bundle. Even as she got to her knees the wall above her exploded into flame with a giant whoosh. Bending low, she ran, but as she did so she heard, above the noise of the fire, a clear, musical chime. It stopped her in her tracks, turned her gaze upwards.

"Oh, no . . ." She could have wept. The exquisite Waterford chandeliers. They were doomed. No time to go upstairs and unscrew their heavy mountings; it was a skilled job requiring slow and painstaking care. Anguished, impotent, she could only stare at their glittering beauty shining in the glare through the swirling smoke.

"What the hell do you think you are doing?"

It was Blaise again, soot-smudged, water-stained, and snarling at her like a tiger. "The fire is through to the front, you stupid little fool. Did nothing I say penetrate that thick skull of yours?" He stopped dead as he saw the glitter of her tears. "What is it?" he demanded aghast. "Are you hurt?"

Kate shook her head. "Nothing you would understand," she said bitterly, and stumbled past him to the door.

Outside, after untying her bundle and carefully bestowing the precious porcelain, she donned her jacket again—the wind was cold as she stared, still with tear-blurred eyes, at the burning house.

The smoke was now a pillar, the interior hideously lit by a red glare. Courtland Park was an inferno. The back was gone, and now the fire, still ravenous for sustenance, had broken through and across the central hall to consume the front half. Too late now, to save the du Barry bed with its original hangings, the painted panels that had graced her bedroom, the chandelier in that and every other state room; too late to save the Cristofle dressing table and the silver mirror and toilet set—"Oh, no!" gasped Kate. "I am damned if I'll let that go . . ."

Without a second thought she was off and running back to the house, but this time she made a slight detour. She went via the powerful jets of water being sprayed from the fire engines, ignoring whatever it was the firemen shouted at her, but receiving what she had intended to receive: a soaking. Dripping water, she sprinted up the enormous staircase, not yet alight. The bedroom she sought was on the right side of the house, at the far end of the landing. It was large, but the dressing table was placed in front of the wide bank of windows. On it, stood the glorious, twenty-four inches square mirror, framed in solid silver, its matching toilet set distributed around it. Again Kate stripped off her jacket, now sodden with water, and made of it a carrier for the various jars, pots, bottles, and boxes.

Fortunately, the glass was of the thick, pebble kind of the seventeenth century, not easily broken unless struck, besides which, she thought as she worked swiftly, it only has to drop thirty feet. Carefully she placed the small objects in a roll, before wrapping them around in the material of her jacket and then inserting another roll, finally tying the sleeves securely so that none should fall free. She worked with frantic fierceness, conscious all the while that time was being consumed, even as the oxygen was. Finally, hefting her bundle, she staggered to the window with it, where she opened one of the leaded casements, out of which she leaned as far as she safely could, before screaming at the top of her voice, "Please . . . will somebody catch this?"

Somebody quickly produced one of the smaller rugs—seventeenth-century Chinese—and Kate dropped the bundle into it. They shouted something at her, but she could not hear for the roar of the fire, and shouted back, "I'll just get the mirror. Hang on . . ."

She went back for the mirror. It was heavy; it took all her strength to lift it and stagger again to the window, but once there she found there was no way she could raise it high enough to get it over the sill. So she reached for a nearby stool and stood on it. Lifting the mirror and cradling it in her

arms, she shouted again to those below, "Please, somebody
. . . will you catch the mirror . . ."

Again they looked up, but this time one of them was
Blaise Chandler. Kate did not see him; she was too busy
concentrating on keeping her balance and a tight hold of the
heavy mirror, but he saw her, leaning perilously out of a
window in an upstairs room which was lit by a red glow, and
trying to drop what looked like a heavy mirror into a rug
that was being held below it. Jesus Christ! He had heard of
blood running cold but his froze. He also thought his heart
had stopped. The firemen had told everybody to get well
away because there was danger of the roof collapsing. Now,
visions of Kate Despard falling backwards, along with that
same roof, into a maelstrom of fire, evoked in him a sensation of the most helpless, hopeless, anguished despair he had
ever known. He thought he heard himself scream, a long,
gonized cry of disbelieving supplication that came from inside him. After which he ran, his only thought to get to Kate
before the roof went. I have to get her out. I have to.
Please, God, let me get her out. He took the stairs three at a
time. He skidded around the balustrade at the top and
sprinted down the long corridor. The smoke was heavy,
much heavier than before, and the heat was fiercer. "Kate!"
he bellowed. "Kate!" Smoke got into his lungs and he began
to cough. His eyes began to sting and blur. As he burst into
the bedroom he saw her, kneeling on a small squabbed
stool, half in, half out of the window and looking as if she
and the mirror were about to go together. He did a flying
tackle and even as her feet left the stool he grabbed her
ankles. As she dropped the mirror at the same time, she
came up like snapped elastic, and they both fell backwards
on the floor.

"Jesus Christ," Blaise snarled, releasing his feelings in
anger, "but you are a stubborn bitch!"

Then, as she stared at him affrontedly, face all smudged,
hair atangle, soaked shirt unexpectedly and disturbingly erotic
as it clung to her small firm breasts, he began to laugh. His
eyes smarted, his lungs felt seared, but he seized her in his
arms and laughed like a madman. "God, but you are a sight
for sore eyes," he grinned maniacally.

"You don't look so good yourself," Kate gasped, held in a
grip that threatened to crack her ribs. He was filthy, smoke-
and water-stained, smelling of it, too, but as he put her

slightly away from him, still holding her by the elbows, she caught his soaring delight and also began to laugh.

"I thought you were going to die," he said laughing madly. "When I saw you almost out of that window I thought any moment the roof was going to go and you'd be gone forever . . ."

Kate was staring at him wonderingly. This wild-eyed, almost hysterical man was not the Blaise Chandler she knew. But even as she stared at him, not a little mystified, his laugh died, his wide grin straightened until it was gone and his face, that had been threatening to split, suddenly became taut and strained. "And I couldn't bear that," he said. "I couldn't bear that at all . . ."

Kate felt as if she had run full tilt into a brick wall and had the breath slammed out of her. She saw by the way his eyes seemed to get even darker that he felt it, too; that he was also holding his breath. Amid the smoke and the heat and the crackle of the approaching fire they stared at each other, wide-eyed, and once again Blaise felt everything shift and slide inside. "Kate . . ." he said in a voice that made her shiver and look wonderingly at her arm covered in gooseflesh. Slowly she raised her face again, felt herself falling toward him. As their mouths met each felt the other flinch as if from an electric shock; then he engulfed her in an embrace that at once terrified and glorified, and was kissing her in a way that was the summit of her wildest dreams.

It lasted only seconds, but it seemed to last forever, until a sound from above jerked them apart. The cracking of some gigantic whip. Raising their gaze to the ceiling they saw the cracks that zigzagged along the carved and gilded stucco like deadly snakes.

"Christ, the roof!" Even as Blaise said the words the wall at the far end of the room exploded. He pulled her toward him again. "Hold tight to my hand and whatever you do *don't let go*—do you hear me?"

He was shouting above the roar of the fire. Kate nodded. For the first time she realized the awful situation her impulsive foolhardiness had got her into. And that Blaise Chandler had come to rescue her. She felt him take her hand firmly and strongly, lacing his fingers with hers. His hand was warm, firm, immensely secure. Still caught up in the sticky web of what she was sure must be a dream, she ran her thumb over his. He glanced at her quickly, and as their eyes met she again felt that swift kick in the stomach, knew by the way his flickered that he had felt it, too. What is happening here? she thought dazedly, as he led her quickly from the room.

The hall was now thick with smoke, the fire having taken hold of the front of the house, eating away silk damask, ancient varnish, newly cleaned and exposed gilding, intricately carved stucco, handlaid satinwood floors.

Kate felt Blaise tugging her to her knees, and then to the floor, where he put his mouth to her ear to be heard above the fire roaring like an express train. "I'm going to hug the balustrade till we get to the stairs—don't let go of my hand; I'll never find you in this smoke."

Slowly, inch by inch, they crawled along the upper landing, Blaise feeling his way because it was not possible to see for the smoke. Kate's lungs were burning and she labored for oxygen, which the fire was taking in great gulps. She could not see Blaise; his hold on her hand was their only contact. Grimly, tenaciously, she clung. If they were going to die then let it be together . . . Having found him so miraculously she was not going to let him go now.

The rear of the hall was well alight; the heat scorched and the smoke choked, and the noise . . . Kate had not known that a fire made so much noise. Her chest felt as if it was being seared by a red hot poker, and she could not see for tears and smoke. But Blaise was feeling his way by hand, baluster by baluster, and when his outstretched, groping fingers hit air, he knew they had reached the staircase. Thank God! They would have to go down the stairs slowly because there were at least thirty of them, but as he drew Kate to him, to tell her to go down them on her bottom, like a toddler, there was another series of ear-popping cracks. Oh, my God! he thought. It's too late. The roof is going . . . Damn, damn, and fucking damn! Why now? Why when it is too late do you show me what I might have had? What I have been too blind and stiff-necked to see under my very nose . . . Is this what they mean by hell? He pulled Kate toward him, enfolded her in his arms, pressing her head against him, and put his mouth to her ear. "The roof is going," he shouted, and his anguish and rage was every bit as searing as the fire. Kate heard it, felt it, understood it. The fire had burned away so much more than a house. She put her arms around his body, pressing herself against him, breast to chest, thigh to thigh, cheek to cheek as they knelt on the top landing. Kate thought she heard him say her name again in that plangent, aching voice, and then the roof collapsed.

But it was that that saved them, because instead of ancient roof beams, ceiling joists, and the charred remains of what the fire had left, like gnawed bones, raining down on them, it was water. The enormous lead tank on the flat roof had split in the heat, and thousands of gallons of water cascaded out, smashing through the already weakened leads and gushing down into the house like some gargantuan waterfall. The force of it knocked Blaise and Kate off their knees and down the stairs like dead leaves. Kate screamed Blaise's name once, then water choked her and she felt herself rolling over and over, colliding with him, hitting the stairs, the balustrade, being hit—some glancing blows, some painful smacks—by debris that was being swept along with them. Blaise had instinctively threaded his fingers through Kate's hair, which as it became soaked, clung tenaciously and, for Kate, painfully, to them, but she did not mind because it meant he was all right.

In a torrent of water they were swept down the stairs, tumbling like the washing in a dryer, the breath knocked out of them and the heat knocked out of the fire, which steamed and hissed like a furious snake. Blaise still held on to Kate's hair with almost insane determination, but as he fell down the long flight of stairs, something hit his head a glancing blow and knocked him unconscious. So entangled were his fingers that they were swept on together, down the last few steps and across the tessellated marble floor of the hall, where with a last, contemptuous sweep, the water tossed them against the enormous iron-strapped front doors with such force that Blaise's shin, which struck the iron edge, snapped like a twig. Kate in her turn was flung against him, so that he broke the force of her fall, and they came to rest in a jumble of arms and legs, he bleeding from a deep cut above his left ear and his left leg dangling oddly from the knee, she with her face jammed in his groin.

Kate was out only for seconds; she came to dazed and hurting all over, groggily realized where she was and lay for a moment longer getting her breath back, coughing from the water in her lungs. Then she became conscious of how she was lying. Oh my God . . . she thought, almost giggling hysterically, talk about taken at the flood . . . Then, as she heaved herself up, she realized that Blaise was out cold, blood flowing from his head, and that his left leg was splayed at an unnatural angle. She could hear hissing, and painfully getting to her hands and knees, felt Blaise's hand rise with her. Hurting everywhere she struggled to pry his fingers loose, but her hair was so entwined and his grip so strong that she could not free herself. She raised her voice in a shout. "Somebody, please . . . help!" As she began to lose consciousness again she heard footsteps, felt hands on her, a voice exclaim disbelievingly, "My God, they are both still alive! Quick—get the stretchers . . ."

"Blaise . . ." mumbled Kate, fighting the engulfing darkness.

"He's all right . . . in good hands and being taken care of . . ."

"See him . . ."

"You will, Miss, you will . . ."

She smiled beatifically before she passed out.

19

She came to lying in a narrow bed under the bright lights of a room instantly recognizable by its smell. A hospital. She sat up, winced as every muscle in her body screamed its protest. The nurse sitting at a small table looked up and then came over.

"How do you feel?" she asked, automatically taking Kate's wrist and checking her pulse before raising an eyelid to inspect the pupil.

"Like I've just done fifteen rounds with Muhammad Ali."

"Not surprising. You are badly bruised. I gather you were tossed down a long flight of stairs by a great deal of water."

Kate looked down at herself. "Just bruising?" she asked hopefully.

"Yes, fortunately. You will feel stiff for a while, but you've only superficial cuts and grazes and best of all, no concussion."

"And Blaise—Mr. Chandler?"

"He is concussed, I am afraid, and suffered a nasty gash above his left ear. He also broke his left leg—a clean break, no complications—and he is as battered and bruised as you are."

"Can I see him?"

"I'm afraid not. He is still unconscious. He had to have twelve stitches."

At Kate's suddenly haggard look, she smiled understandingly. "Not to worry. He's a big, strong man who obviously takes care of himself," she said, and added dryly, "We had every nurse in the hospital making an excuse to visit the casualty room while they were attending to him. Do I break the news—and their hearts—that he is spoken for?"

"Yes," Kate found herself answering. "He is."

The nurse sighed. "The best ones always are."

"Where am I? I mean—which hospital?"

"Foresham Cottage Hospital—about eight miles from Courtland Park and by far the nearest hospital with a casualty department—and that not for long. They are closing us down next year, so it will be Chichester General from then on. Now, is there anything I can get you?"

"Could I have a cup of tea? I would love a cup of hot, strong tea—milk, no sugar."

"I think we might run to that. Oh, and a Mr. Chevely has been waiting since you were brought in. He seems anxious to see you.

"Nicholas!" Kate had totally forgotten him since leaving the restaurant. "Yes, please, send him in."

He was no longer immaculate; his elegant suit was smoke-and smut-stained, but he had obviously had a wash and brush up because his face and hands were nursery clean, his hair brushed into perfect order.

"My dear Kate!" he exclaimed, with both pride and consternation. "You look like those battered wives they are always going on about. Does it hurt?"

"I feel somewhat wrung out," she admitted. "But the fire—what happened when the roof went? Is the house gone? How much was saved? Has anybody told London? I must see Anthony Howard—"

Nicholas held up a traffic-stopping hand. "Steady on, there. The fire is out—the tank going did it. It split like a melon and thousands of gallons of water quenched and drenched everything. The house is done for, I'm afraid. What is left will have to be demolished. Yes, I believe your deputy—that same Anthony Howard—has already been on to Nigel Marsh. Mr. Howard himself is still at Courtland Park checking on what was saved and hopes to be able to present his report later on today."

"What day is it?" Kate asked, suddenly struck.

"The morning after the night before. To be precise, 2:35 A.M.

"Is that all?"

"You were out for the count for some three hours. The fire began by an explosion, so I am reliably informed, at exactly 8:54 last evening. The tank went at 11:16—you and Chandler went with it. By 11:30 the fire was out. So, I am also reliably informed, were most of the contents. The feeling is that a miracle was worked last night."

"Most of the contents?" Kate repeated, giving off more light than the sun.

"Most. I cannot say for sure what was lost; this is no doubt what Mr. Howard is finding out for you."

"Most of the contents," Kate repeated, as if chanting a magic invocation.

"But at what cost?" Nicholas asked severely. "Going back into a house whose roof was about to collapse was foolhardy, to say the least."

"I didn't hear what they shouted at me," she defended herself guiltily.

"Would you have changed your mind if you had? Thank God Chandler had you in his sights most of the time. He shot back into that house like a bullet, so I'm told—I didn't see it myself, but I'm told the look on his face boded ill . . ." Nicholas lifted his patrician eyebrows. "Except he was the one who got the worst of it."

His pointed look made Kate shift uneasily and wince when she did.

"Ah, I see you have your own pains to bear," he went on, with more satisfaction than sympathy. "Now then, I am about to go back to town. I shall return with the insurance assessor. When I do, is there anything I may bring you? Clothes, for instance."

"Oh, please . . . just tell my housekeeper what happened; she will know what I need. When will you be back?"

"Early afternoon, I should think. I need a bath and a shave and a few hours' sleep at least. But I also don't want to waste time. The sooner the insurance johnnies get to work the better."

"I gather you were well insured?" Kate inquired sweetly.

"But of course." Nicholas was unruffled. "Would you expect less of me?"

Not you, she thought with a giggle. More is your favorite word.

Nicholas got up to go, then turned back as an afterthought struck him. "Oh, by the way . . . you might tell Chandler that some man named Benny Fong has been telephoning everywhere trying to get hold of him. Evidently he called the Park not five minutes after we left for dinner, and was most upset to find he had just missed him. He had—and I quote the guard who spoke to him, 'his knickers in a twist.' " One last smile and he was gone.

Benny Fong! Kate felt the old fear evaporate her happiness. Not more skulduggery! Oh God, she thought fearfully. Now what? Why was Benny so frantic? And Blaise still concussed . . .

When the nurse came back she said severely, "Now look at you. What you need is sleep and lots of it. Here . . ." She thrust a paper cup and a tiny white tablet at Kate. "It will ease your aches and pains." She did not say it was also a sedative.

Kate swallowed it obediently, though with what she had on her mind how could she sleep? So much to think about, go over, dwell on. Her stomach dived to the basement as she thought of what had so magically, so incredibly taken place only hours before. What *had* happened? She was at a loss to understand the lightning that seemed to have struck them both. The fierce look in his eyes, the slam in the gut, the unimaginable pleasure of his kiss . . . Never in her life had she felt anything like it. Her two abortive ventures into the world of "romance" had, she now knew, left her unstirred; Larry Cole had also failed to touch her. But Blaise had created an earthquake . . . Every time she thought of it her stomach turned over. She wanted to curl into a ball, though it hurt every time she moved, and hug the knowledge even as she hugged herself. He came back for me—for me! He was afraid for me. He wanted me—me! It's all a dream. she told herself. I will wake up and find it is raining and I am late opening up the shop . . . Why now? Why here? Why . . . She yawned drowsily. Blaise, she thought. One last replete sigh. "Blaise . . ." she murmured and sank gently into sleep.

When she woke again it was light, and the clock above the door, which she had not noticed before, said ten minutes to twelve. She sat bolt upright and winced again. She felt stiff as paint, and when she looked at her arms, discovered that they were livid with bruising. She threw the bedclothes back; her legs, her thighs when she pulled up the short hospital gown, were the same. Pulling open the loose neck she peered at her body. The same yellow, purple, and blue splotches. Talk about body paint, she thought. It hurt, but she managed to get out of bed. As her feet touched the floor even they hurt. Just then, a nurse, a different one, came in.

"Well," she said brightly. "And how are we this morning?"

"Like I've been trampled by a herd of elephants."

"A nice hot bath will help. Shall I run it for you?"

"Oh, would you?"

"Then some breakfast. The doctor will want to give you a last look over but I don't think they will keep you in."

"I hope not," Kate frowned." Too much to do." Then she asked, "How is Mr. Chandler?"

"He had a restless night, but he's sleeping peacefully now."

"Oh . . ." Disappointment crashed like the roof of Courtland Park. Well, later, she thought. As long as he is all right.

She soaked in the bath for as long as she could and felt better when she got out. There was no sign of the clothes she had asked for, so she had no choice but to don her hospital gown again, though she did not get back into bed. Breakfast was fruit juice, bacon, egg, fried tomato and mushrooms, and with toast and marmalade to follow. She demolished the lot.

"That's better," the nurse said approvingly when she came back. "Now then, there's a Mr. Marsh and a Mr. Steadman outside waiting to see you. Are you up to it?"

"Am I! Send them in, please."

Both were full of eager curiosity, high praise and consternation when they saw the state of her.

"Oh, my poor Kate," Nigel clicked his tongue, while John patted her hand in a fatherly manner.

"There's my clever girl. Eighty percent saved . . . who would have thought it?"

"Eighty percent!'

They beamed at Kate's joy.

"Anthony did a rough estimate. We were both on the spot by nine this morning—poor fellow worked all night. We've packed him off to sleep the rest of the day."

"He was marvelous," Kate said proudly. "They all were . . ."

"The results confirm it."

"What did we lose?" she asked, prepared for the worst. "I know the chandeliers went, and the du Barry bed and furniture, and the lacquer screen—"

"Everything from the ground floor was carried to safety," Nigel told her happily. "All the major paintings, the furniture, the crystal, the porcelain. A marvelous effort, marvelous. To have rescued so much from such a disastrous fire . . ."

"The house is a goner," John said, financially practical as ever. "But we weren't selling that. Chevely tells me it was properly covered, however. He is full of praise, by the way, for your organization down here. I had thought you just a mite extravagant in your preparation but you were proved right. Had you not had so many guards and staff the result could have been catastrophe."

"And the police, thank God, and the firemen . . ."

"A magnificent effort," John said. "Nigel and I think some token of our appreciation should be made."

Kate nodded. "And a bonus for the staff."

"Of course," John agreed, readily for once.

"And Mr. Chandler? How is he?" asked Nigel compassionately. "Quite the hero of the hour, so they tell me."

"He saved my life," Kate said simply.

"Then we must thank him, too."

"He's asleep right now. I haven't seen him myself."

"And you? A few days' rest and you will be back to work and as good as ever."

"Not on your life! I don't have time to lie in bed and do nothing. I've got to start organizing the sale."

They stared at her. "But—there is the question of another site, the proper preparations, people to be informed . . ."

"There will be no other site. I shall hold the sale at Courtland Park as planned, only it will be outside not in. I shall need at least two more marquees—can you organize that, John? I can't show the furniture and paintings in their proper setting, but I am going to do my damnedest to show it off to advantage. We can lay the carpets, put up some hangings, and arrange the furniture as it was in the house. There must be some way we can hang the paintings. And everything will have to be cleaned, I expect. Will you get on to Jorgenson's, Nigel? Ask them to send a team down soonest. Was there much damage?"

The two men looked at each other. "Obviously," Nigel said with relief, "there is not much wrong with you."

"And a press announcement—all the major salesroom columns and I think some display advertisements. Perhaps television, too . . ." Kate thought for a moment. "We have nine days. That should give us time to circulate everyone who expected to attend; tell them to come as planned."

"I think you can forget the publicity," Nigel smiled. "It is stop the press in all the papers this morning. I expect this evening's *Standard* to have it on the front page. The Park is already crawling with reporters and photographers."

"And the BBC are sending a camera crew—and ITV," John added smugly.

"Good. I'll talk to anyone who will get it across that the sale goes ahead as planned." She gave vent to an exasperated sigh. "Where are my clothes?"

"Oh, we brought your case. Nicholas said we might as well, seeing as we were coming down before him—"

"Then let me have it. Time's a-wasting."

Her face was the only part of her she could not hide. She had a scrape covering practically the whole of the left side, and what would eventually be a fine black eye on the right. Oh dear, she thought dismayed. Not even Blaise could love this . . . She had to hang on to the basin as her stomach somersaulted again, but when she rejoined the others she was briskly competent again.

"Right—I'll just go and see if I can have a word with Blaise and I suppose the doctors will have to officially discharge me. I won't be long."

But Blaise was still asleep. The most they would do was let her see him. He lay against a bank of pillows, a big clump of bandage over his left ear, his face also bruised and scratched, and his leg in a temporary splint under a cradle. The bandage had displaced his hair, and it fell over his forehead in a way that made him the Boy his grandmother always called him. She wanted to kiss the relaxed mouth, but the presence of the nurse proscribed that.

The doctor gave her a quick but thorough going-over, told her not to do too much, and to report to her own doctor if she got any headaches. He also gave her some ointment to apply to her bruises and a small bottle of pills to ease her stiffness. Then he said she was discharged.

"Right," Kate said to her waiting supporters. "Let's get down to work."

The full extent of the disaster was apparent by daylight. The house was a façade at the front, a ruined shell at the back, and waterlogged. What had been rescued lay in piles under tarpaulins, already being sorted, examined, and placed to be either cleaned or marked for slight repair. Most of the damage was from smoke and smut; one of the priceless cabinets had a weak leg and one of the clocks had stopped. Apart from that, there was no damage that would prevent so much as a single piece being offered for sale. All the great pictures were intact, carefully wrapped in sheets of plastic; a few tears in the backing where they had hastily been wrenched away, but the canvasses themselves were unharmed. And the porcelain was still perfection. No cracks, no chips. All it needed was careful washing. Kate was overwhelmed with relief and gratitude, insisted on shaking hands with everyone, speaking her personal thanks. The bonus she kept to herself as a surprise.

That afternoon she was interviewed by both networks for the evening news. She made full use of her chance to publicize the fact that the sale would go ahead as planned.

"But was it not supposed to take place inside the house?" she was asked.

"Yes, it was. But that, as you can see, is not the proper frame any more—though frame, alas, is what it now is . . ."

The cameraman did a sweep of the house, rafters stark to the sky, empty windows gaping, blackened stonework still waterstained.

"Then where will it be held?"

"In marquees on the lawns. I already have two earmarked for use as an office and a refreshment tent; now I shall erect another two—the largest available—and arrange everything in them. It will not be exactly as I had planned, but it will be held. I want to say to everyone who had intended coming, be assured, the sale will begin on October thirtieth as originally planned. Please, if you intended to come, then do so. We will be here and so will all these glorious works of art we worked so hard to save. They will be on view from the twenty-third. It is only a matter of rearrangement. See for yourself—almost everything is miraculously preserved."

By now, many of the smaller pieces had been arranged on trestle tables, and Kate took the opportunity of displaying to the camera several of the better pieces: porcelain, silver, crystal, ivory, bronze. She took the plastic sheeting off a Rembrandt and a glorious Poussin; their colors glowed in the afternoon sunlight. She had the camera close in on one of the superb pieces of French furniture (already cleaned and polished specially) to show its superb condition. She milked the interview for every last piece of publicity, confi-

dent that it would be seen countrywide—even worldwide—
and bring the customers in droves. Who knew, those who
came out of curiosity might well stay to buy.

"And Mr. Blaise Chandler," the interviewer asked. "Is It
true he risked his life to save yours?"

"Yes," Kate said. "I was not aware that the roof was
about to go. I am afraid all I could think of was rescuing
some superb silver. This . . ." She walked to where the
mirror had been arranged, its accompanying pieces around it.

"Well worth saving," the interviewer commented.

"Yes, but not at the risk of lives. Fortunately, the water
tank gave."

"And are these the marks of your valor?" the interviewer
asked with a smile, indicating her bruises.

"Water is no respecter of persons," Kate admitted ruefully. "I got off lightly. Mr. Chandler has a gash on his head
and a broken leg. It could have been much worse."

"And your stepsister—Mrs. Chandler? Is she at the hospital with him?"

"She is on her way," Kate said. Nigel Marsh had told her
he had contacted New York, asked them to find Dominique
wherever she was, and give her the news.

"Will she be at your sale?"

Kate smiled, hiding her annoyance at the probing. "I have
no idea."

"You don't normally attend each other's sales, do you?"

"We are too busy holding our own."

"She's holding hers, all right," John Steadman murmured
appreciatively to Nigel Marsh, as they stood watching on the
sidelines. "By God, she's come a long way."

"Her father would have been proud of her," Nigel praised.

"I don't know about her father, but I am!"

The interview over, Kate checked her watch. Three o'clock.
Eight A.M. back in Colorado. Agatha would be up by now.
She went to one of the Portakabins that had been brought in
for use as offices.

Agatha was delighted to hear from her. "Well now, what
a nice surprise."

"How are you?" she asked, wanting to be sure the old
lady was up to the shock.

"They tell me I'm good for a few more years yet, but I
could have told them. I'm as good as ever I was. Now then,
tell me all your news. Have you seen the Boy?"

That gave Kate her opening and she took it. Agatha stood it like the monumental piece of the Rockies she was.

"A broken leg, you say? Well, it ain't the first one. By the time he was twelve he'd broken all four limbs in one place or another so he knows what to expect. How bad is his head?"

"A deep gash but a clean one. They stitched it—twelve of them."

"And that's it?"

"Isn't that enough?"

"I only wanted to know for sure."

"He is not in any danger," Kate emphasized. "More inconvenience, I think. He'll have to be on crutches for a while."

"Do him good to rest," was the Duchess's practical response. "All the same, I'll get myself on the first plane. Should be there tonight—your time. Don't tell the Boy. I want to surprise him."

When Kate went back outside, she sought out Nigel. "You did get a message to Dominique, didn't you?"

"I didn't speak to her myself, but I was told my message would be passed on."

Blaise had woken up with Kate's name on his lips, her face in his mind's eye, had asked at once how and where she was, only to be told she had left the hospital some three hours before.

"They would have preferred to keep her in for another twenty-four hours just in case there was any sort of delayed reaction, but she insisted on leaving because she said she had far too much to do to be able to lie in bed doing nothing." Blaise smiled. "She wanted to see you but you were sound asleep, and orders were not to disturb you, so all she got was a look. But she said to tell you she would be back. She was most insistent that I tell you that in exactly those words."

Blaise felt a relief bordering on euphoria. It had not been a fantasy brought about by the bang on the head, which felt sore and ached abominably. His leg also throbbed, but thinking of Kate brought a glow that both warmed and soothed. Who would have thought it? Who in God's name would have thought it. Kate Despard! He said her name out loud. "Kate Despard." I didn't even *like* her, he thought bemusedly. Not my type by a million miles. He had always, he saw now with brightly lit hindsight, gone for the lookers, the ones who knew their way around and what the score was. Kate had never even played the game. Yet with her he was as comfortable as he was with only one other woman: his grandmother. Kate was no strain; you could talk to her, but talk had not been what he wanted, from Dominique or any of the other women he had—what? Taken up with? You could not say involved, because all he had wanted from them was their bodies. Emotionally he had been frozen, he now saw. And the frost had set in with his mother's rejection. After that he had been careful not to let any woman get close enough to damage him emotionally. Kate had melted the ice; without him realizing it, over the months, being around her had caused some kind of chain reaction that reached the explosion point when he saw her half in and half out of that window. That was another thing: Kate had guts. Nothing could quench that valiant spirit of hers. His grandmother had spotted it at once, of course, while he had still been frozen in his prejudices. Charles had known it, too.

"You were a wily old fox, Charles," he said out loud. Had he and his grandmother planned it, she wanting the best for him, Charles for Despard's and his beloved daughter? Why not? Charles knew that Dominique would never have stood for the total humiliation of being passed over, would have made it her life's work to be revenged. So he had protected Kate by giving her as much as he could, and Dominique what was left, and counted on me—not to mention my grandmother—to keep her in line. No wonder the Duchess was so interested in Kate. She knew from the start what was going to happen. That's why she asked me, only minutes after I had told her Charles was dead, about his will. You crafty old Indian, he thought lovingly. How the hell did you *know?* Because you know me, he answered himself.

He sat back and examined his preposterous thesis. Fact was a hell of a lot stranger than fiction. Oh, come on, he thought. You'll be writing to *Dear Abby* next. But it fit . . . This last year, for instance. Time for so much to happen: for his eyes to be opened, for those eyes to see Kate as she really was; for Dominique to overreach herself, as Charles had expected her to. They must have sat and plotted, those two. The two people in the world who knew both of us best; they must have compared notes, defined characters, examined motivations. And hoped for the best. Well, he thought, it took a fire to fulfill those hopes, but by God, it was worth it.

The nearness of it all still made him break out in a sweat. It also bore out his dragging sense of unease; that itch that would not be scratched away. But whatever he had expected, it had not been this terrible destruction of Kate's hopes. Anger filled him at the thought of the house—ruined, like her months of preparation. It would take too long to set up another situation such as this had been. How? he thought. Who? When?

And then his answer walked in the door. He didn't know how—but he knew. One look at that bewitching beauty and the gleam in those sapphire eyes and he *knew*.

"Darling—don't be so unflattering. Why should you be surprised? I came as soon as I heard . . . You look as though I was the last person you expected to see."

She was enchantingly framed in a mass of dark red roses, through which her face glowed at him. She was swathed in mink, though the day was mild, and her kiss was warm, lingering.

"My poor darling . . ." Her voice was concerned, but there was about her the ineffable richness of satisfaction, the sheen of appetite satisfied. He could have killed her. But years of controlling his feelings produced a mild voice which asked in surprise, "Who told you?"

"Nigel Marsh rang the New York office. He sounded terribly upset apparently. What is all this about a fire? All I was told was that the most dreadful disaster had occurred . . . that you had been injured and I was to come at once." She produced the right twitterings at his bandaged head, the cradle over his splint. "What on earth happened?"

"Courtland Park went up like a torch."

Her perfect mouth shaped an O to match her eyes, and her catch of breath was perfect. "Oh, no . . . how awful! But—what on earth were you doing there?"

"Taking a look-see. It was well worth seeing." *As if you didn't know,* he raged.

"But—is it all gone? Was nothing saved?"

"The house is a ruin." He let that spread a glow which he then quenched by adding, "But I think we managed to save most of the contents."

There was no change to the rapt interest but his newly released sensitivity caught the change in its quality. "Saved?"

"Kate had a lot of people on site. Guards, her own staff—and the police turned up in short order. Fortunately the fire began at the back which gave us time to evacuate the front . . ."

"Is that how you got these?" She gestured tenderly at his injuries.

"I happened to be in the house when the roof gave—fortunately the water tank also went. It swamped everythng and took me with it."

"Oh, my poor darling . . . And Kate? She is no doubt in a terrible state."

"I don't know. I haven't seen her. I was unconscious when they brought us both here last night and she was discharged this morning."

"Both?"

"She was in the house, too."

She looked around for a chair, brought it up to the bed, the roses lying forgotten at its foot. "I am agog. Tell me everything . . ."

He gave her an edited version, from going to dinner to the water sweeping them down the stairs.

"So you rescued her! But how brave . . ." A sigh. "Poor Kate . . . this sale was very important to her."

And to you, he thought, careful not to say so in case he put her on guard. If she thought she had won she might let her confidence end in carelessness.

"So how long will you be here?" she asked concernedly.

"I don't know. The break is a clean one but evidently it is in an awkward place just beneath the knee—the splint is only temporary. They'll keep an eye on it and X-ray again in a day or two. If there are no complications they'll put me in plaster."

"And your head?"

"Just a cut." But it had given him a headache that was getting progressively worse.

She looked around the small room, wrinkled her nose. "Do they know what they are doing here? It is no more than a clinic, surely?"

"It's what the British call a cottage hospital—and not for much longer. It's being closed next year because they've built a big new hospital in Chichester to serve the entire district. Which is a pity because they do indeed know what they are doing. I can't fault the care they have given me."

A shrug. "Well, if you are happy . . ."

"As my injuries will allow."

"And Kate was not injured, you say?"

"We both went over Niagara Falls but I was the one who fell out of the barrel. Cuts and bruises were her portion."

She made a moue. "Darling, it is not *my* fault you are stuck down here miles from civilization. But I suppose you must be bored to death. Here—I have brought you something to read . . ."

From under the roses she produced a sheaf of magazines: *Time, Life, Fortune, Forbes,* and the *International Herald Tribune.*

"I picked them up in Rome . . ." She did not add from the coffee table of the Roman prince in whose bed she was when Despard's called, blowing more than his mind in an effort to make him give her the sale of his particularly fine Andrea del Sarto.

Blaise frowned. "If they called you I suppose they called the Duchess."

"Of course they would—they would not dare do otherwise, would they?"

Blaise ignored the dig.

"Would you like me to call her?"

"No." Nor would the Duchess, he thought.

Dominique was looking around. "But you don't have a telephone?"

"There is one, on some sort of a trolley. They bring it if you ask."

Dominique's shrug said: Well, if you will take up residence in Hicksville . . . Exasperated by his unresponsive curtness, and dying to go and find out exactly how things stood at Courtland Park, she asked, "Is there anything I can get you?"

"Yes, out of here."

"Darling, what is the matter with you? You are like a bear with a sore head."

His smile was grim. "What do you think this is?" he asked pointing to it.

She decided to humor him, as well as take advantage of the lack of his own. "I think I shall go and do some shopping," she announced. "There are shops, I suppose?"

"Try Chichester. It has a theatre, so it should have shops."

"Is it far?"

"About twenty miles."

"Oh, that's all right then. I came away in such a rush I had no time for anything. Let me see if I can find some tempting things to eat. Hospital food is always so inedible."

"I had a good breakfast," Blaise disagreed. "There's nothing like a traditional English breakfast."

"The only meal they can cook," Dominique retorted. "I shall only be an hour or two. Is there anything I can get you?"

"I'm sure you'll think of something."

But Dominique went to the Park first. She had to know how things stood, just how successful her attempt at sabotage had been. From what Blaise had said not one hundred percent, but when she saw the ruin of the house she heaved a satisfied sigh. Surely they had not been able to rescue much from that . . . Until she saw the long rows of trestle tables, where the rescued pieces were being placed. The place was crawling with people, most of them Despard's employees she recognized, but none of them belonging to her party. Kate was nowhere to be seen.

Anthony Howard saw her coming, all smiles and sharp eyes, and before she could see him, made a beeline for one of the Portakabins. "Miss Despard, your sister has just arrived."

What for? was Kate's first thought.

"My dear Kate, I had to come as soon as I had seen Blaise . . . oh, but your poor face!"

It was bruised, scraped, and discolored, but Dominique made it sound as if it presented the aspect of a gargoyle.

"And the house . . . how dreadful! But I see you have managed to save a few things."

"About eighty percent," Kate replied proudly.

"So much?" Far too much, Dominique seethed. Chao-Li had let her down again. What was the use of destroying the house if its contents were still intact? She could have done better herself. Still, there was one saving grace. The sale would have to be postponed, which would give her time to fashion another spoke for this unnaturally lucky bitch.

"Well, it could have been worse," she soothed. "From what Blaise has told me you could have lost your life. How fortuitous he should have been on the scene." And why was he? her eyes wanted to know.

"Yes. I owe him my life."

By the time I've finished with you, you will wish you didn't, Dominique vowed. "So what will you do now?" she commiserated.

"Hold the sale outside instead of inside."

"You will go ahead as planned? But how? Where?"

"Marquees on the lawns."

"But—the viewing? It was due to begin on Monday, wasn't it?"

"And will. We are working through the weekend to have everything ready."

"Such dedication."

"Yes, I am very lucky in my staff," Kate returned smoothly.

"Lucky! My dear, you are incredibly fortunate. You obviously have a guardian angel."

"Blessed are the pure in heart," Kate murmured, meeting Dominique's suddenly suspicious eyes with a dulcet stare of her own. If you've come to gloat I won't give you the satisfaction, she thought. "Would you like to see how well we are doing?" she suggested ingenuously.

"Time, alas, prevents me. I am on my way to Chichester to do some shopping. Poor Blaise, cooped up in that tiny hospital, he is bored to death. I thought some books, perhaps one of crosswords—he loves doing crosswords . . ." Her laugh said it was odd, but at this particular moment he was to be indulged.

"Then don't let me keep you," Kate said, asking as if on an afterthought, "How is he, by the way?"

"Oh, very grumpy. Literally a bear with a sore head. He hates being confined, poor darling . . . but he will be, I am afraid, for a while yet. Why don't you pay him a visit? Cheer him up."

"If I have time," Kate said, doing her best to sound unconcerned.

"Of course. First things first, as always."

Tell him what you like, you harpy, Kate thought. He will know different. "Give him my best wishes," she called, as Dominique walked away, and got a casual wave of a hand in reply.

Kate went back to work. By six, she was struggling against exhaustion. Her body ached, her head throbbed.

"My dear girl, you look positively whacked," Nicholas remonstrated when he found her, white-faced and wan, doggedly making a note of the erratum slips which would have to be printed very fast for insertion into the catalogue, as well as a list—fortunately not very long—of what would not be on view because it had been destroyed. "Enough is enough," he said firmly, "and you have had more than that. Now come along. I am going to drive you back to town. There are plenty of people here to do what has to be done."

Kate sat back, moved her aching shoulders. "Yes, I want to go home. I have to have a master copy of this list for photocopying. I know Penny won't mind coming in tomorrow—"

"Then let her do it," Nicholas said sharply. "Unless you get some rest you will be spending tomorrow in bed."

"Oh, don't fuss . . ." Kate said tiredly. "Besides, I want to stop off at the hospital and see Blaise."

"Well, I suppose you should, seeing as it is due to him that you are able to in the first place, but not for long."

Just as Kate was locking the door of the Portakabin, she heard its phone start to ring.

"Let it ring," Nicholas said irritably.

"No, I can't. It might be important."

"So is your health!" On it depended his five percent, because with the publicity this little lot was getting, Kate Despard would be a Household Name, and being able to buy something from that Name would bring the sheep in droves. Any other one would just not have the same cachet.

"Wait for me in the car," Kate requested. "I'll be as quick as I can."

He went, but grumbling.

"Miss Despard?" a familiar voice asked in relief when she answered.

"Benny! I suppose you've heard about Mr. Chandler?"

"Only just now, through a contact in London. He saw it on your television news. I feel awful about this, Miss Despard; it's all my fault. If I hadn't caught the chicken pox I'd have known earlier what they planned and been able to warn the boss—"

"Warned?" Kate shivered. "Warned of what?"

"That Mrs. Chandler did a deal with the Triads; if they torched Courtland Park she'd provide the front they need."

Kate felt as if a mule had kicked her in the stomach, and it left her speechless.

"Miss Despard—you still there?"

She swallowed the nausea that threatened to choke her. "Yes, I'm here . . ." She shifted the phone from one hand to the other, wiped her clammy hand on her jacket. "I think you had better start at the beginning," she said as calmly as she could.

He did, forgetting in his anguish that Kate knew nothing of the bugging, the surveillance, how far gone was Blaise Chandler's distrust and disbelief in his wife.

Nothing had shocked Kate so much in her life; not even what had been done to Rollo. For anyone involved in the art world to connive at the destruction of works of genius for personal gain was heinous in the extreme. She is mad, she thought. She has to be stark, staring mad!

". . . all right?" she came back to hear Benny asking anxiously.

"What? Sorry, Benny, bad line . . ."

"I said, is Mr. Chandler all right? My contact said he was in hospital . . ."

"A broken leg and a cut on the head, nothing he won't recover from in time."

A gusty sigh came down the phone. "Thank all gods for that. You'll tell him then, Miss Despard, what I've just told you? I need instructions on what to do next—not that there is anything I can do now," he added bitterly.

"It is not your fault, Benny. Only one person is responsible for all this . . ." Kate's face set. "As for that tape—can you see that it reaches me as soon as possible?"

"So you can give it to the boss? Sure. I'll have it couriered within the next thirty minutes. You should have it inside twenty-four hours."

"It's Saturday tomorrow . . . could you arrange for me to get it by the evening?"

"Sure. Delivered to Despard's?"

"Yes—but to me in person, nobody else."

"Will do. I've got a good man in London I can trust."

"Thank you, Benny."

"Thank *you*, Miss Despard." Benny hesitated. "My contact said Mrs. Chandler had arrived to be with her husband, is that right?"

"Yes. She came to do a little gloating this afternoon but she should not have counted her chickens—" Kate's voice turned savage.

"And the old lady—I mean Mrs. Agatha Chandler?"

"Is on her way. Don't worry, Benny. Your boss is in good hands and I know he will understand and not blame you. It was bad—what do you call it?"

"Joss, bad joss."

"Yes. Very bad *joss.*"

"Give the boss my best, won't you?"

"Of course I will." But nothing else, she thought. This is my fight. I'm the one she is after and I'm the one she'll meet. Later, when it's over, then I'll tell him . . .

When she rejoined Nicholas, impatiently drumming his fingers on the steering wheel, he said, "Good God, girl, you look worse than ever. Not bad news, I hope?"

"I've had all the bad news I can take for one day," Kate said, sinking into the comfortable passenger seat of his Jaguar XJS. "And I've changed my mind. I'm too tired to visit the hospital. Just take me home, Nicholas, take me home . . ."

Dominique and Blaise were watching the six o'clock news and the interview with Kate. When the newsreader went on to other topics, she switched off the set.

"Such publicity," she marveled. "One could not buy it. Oh, they will come in droves, all right. She is a clever one, that seemingly naïve innocent. That was a masterstroke, showing the pieces 'saved from the flames' and with all those bruises on her cute little face. But then, the English always did admire Joan of Arc." She turned to her husband. "What are you? Her knight in shining armor?"

"Too heavy on a horse," Blaise replied, wondering who had crossed her now.

"How convenient, this fire. One would almost think it had been arranged."

"I was with Kate all evening and until we heard of the fire."

"Oh, come now. There are such things as delayed action explosives."

"You would know about them. I doubt if she would. Don't endow Kate Despard with your own deviousness."

Dominique considered her husband. "Yes, you have always had a soft spot for her, haven't you? I thought only the English favored the underdog."

"I was always fond of dogs, myself." He fixed her with his eyes. "Whatever started that fire, it will be discovered. They have experts these days who can give you even the brand of matches used."

They held an inimical stare. What had happened to the sweetness and light? Blaise wondered. "You're spitting mad because you know she's going to pull ahead. I've seen the latest figures. You have the lead now—just—but this sale is going to pulverize it. And you've only got five months left."

"A lot can happen in five months. Was not the world created in seven days?"

"Jesus, I've always known you had delusions of grandeur, but isn't that going a bit too far?"

Dominique broke the hostility with a laugh. "You never could stand being teased could you?" She ruffled his hair, which he hated, and he jerked his head away. Nor was he fooled. There had been a change in the wind this afternoon; it was now blowing a gale.

Someone knocked at the door and a nurse poked her head in. "Miss Despard called," she said. "She's sorry but she can't manage to come to the hospital tonight. She'll do her best to call in tomorrow."

Dominique laughed. "I knew it! She told me she had a lot to do—"

"You've seen her?"

"I called in at the Park. It would have seemed churlish not to do so when I was so near."

Blaise felt a vast relief. That was why she had not come. Oh, wise and clever Kate, he thought. You know you can't hide things like I can . . .

"You don't seem to mind," Dominique observed maliciously.

"I don't. You spoke the truth. After what has happened she does have a hell of a lot to do . . ."

But she still thought of me. He felt content, now. She would come when she could, and no doubt at a time when Dominique was out of the way. Casually, "I hope she is up to it. She looked pretty beat up to me."

"Yes," Dominique said with relish. "That is exactly how she looks."

Oh, you callous bitch, Blaise thought, eyeing the exquisitely delicate flower face of his wife. I wish to God it had been you in that fire. I'd have let you burn . . . That's the only thing to do with witches.

She was now giving instructions to the nurse who had

come in to see what he would like for supper. "I have brought Mr. Chandler some food I should like you to prepare . . . and I shall dine with him. Here is smoked salmon, and there are two *poussins*—to be plainly roasted in butter, I think—and some *mange tout* and some—"

Blaise switched off.

The Duchess arrived just after nine, in presidential style, in a black Lincoln Continental along with a proliferation of bags and boxes as well as a huge wicker basket, lifted from the car by a chauffeur with shoulders as wide as a buffalo, who also lifted Agatha into her wheelchair with ease, but left it to Minnie to push, while he carried in the basket.

When she saw Dominique, the old lady's black eyes snapped. "Well now," she said in a voice that had Blaise's hackles rising, "if it ain't Old Home Week."

"How are you, Madame?" Dominique asked, with such sincere solicitousness that Blaise felt queasy.

"Same as I was last time we met." The old lady turned to her grandson. "What's all this Superman stuff you've been pullin'? The papers are full of it."

"Oh, he is full of himself," Dominique said mockingly.

The old lady ignored her. "You don't look too bad," she decided.

"I don't feel it either."

"Well that's a mercy." Agatha heaved herself from her wheelchair and reached across to hug him.

"Who told you?"

"You didn't, that's for sure. It was Kate who took it upon herself to put me in the picture."

Dominique smiled but the look Blaise shot her stilled her tongue.

"Where is she, anyway?"

"Gone back to London."

"She ain't hurt none?"

"No."

"That's all right, then. No doubt she'll be comin' back."

"I'm sure she will," Blaise said.

"Right. Now, I brought you a few things from home . . . Hospital vittles ain't what I call food and you need feedin' up when you are off color. I got some prime steaks, and a couple of Louella's pecan pies and one of her chocolate cakes; there's some ham and a basket of fruit I picked myself from the hothouse. Grapes and peaches and such."

"Duchess, the British haven't had rationing for more than twenty-five years," Blaise said long-sufferingly.

"A hospital this size ain't goin' to be able to do much in the way of fine food," the Duchess scoffed. "Such an itty-bitty place. No more'n a dispensary."

"Walter Reed it isn't," he agreed mildly, "but they seem to know what they are doing."

"Well, as long as you are satisfied."

"I hope you had a good journey," Dominique offered.

"Slept most of the way. Right handy havin' that airport nearby. Ain't never used it before. Real pleasant and helpful folks. Had my car all ready and waitin'. And this hotel Kate's got me into—is that nearby, too?"

"What's its name?"

"The Pink Thatch or some such thing."

"Yes. It's not far. Small, but first class. You should be all right there. How long are you planning on staying?"

"Depends. Havin' come all this way I have a mind to take in Kate's sale. After all the fuss it might be worth a visit."

"We can go together," said Blaise.

Dominique looked at him sharply.

"I feel personally involved," he added modestly.

"And why not?" demanded the old lady. "You helped save a good deal of what she'll be sellin', didn't you?" Her look became sly. "Savin' females from burnin' buildin's is not exactly your line, is it?"

"Don't worry. I don't intend to make a habit of it."

"Fine, but before you swear off it, tell me how you happened to save this one?"

Dominique rose, and as she gathered her furs she said casually, "Perhaps, when Blaise is able to travel it would be a good idea for him to convalesce back home in Colorado. It would also be a nice break for me."

The old lady leaned back in her chair. "I thought you didn't care for the wide open spaces."

"I don't—but for Blaise . . . And it has been an exhausting year so far."

"I'll bet it has," Agatha said enjoyably. "You bit off a sight more than you can chew."

"I have very good teeth," Dominique replied, showing them.

The Duchess laughed. "You've still got more front than Macy's," she rumbled. Then, attacking directly, "You still think you are goin' to come out ahead?"

"It is the only place for me."

"Just like Colorado is for me." The old lady turned to her grandson. "By the way, I tied up that museum business. All signed, sealed, and delivered. I've set up what they call an irrevocable trust. When I die, the ranch and everythin' in it goes to the state of Colorado. And a trust foundation—the Chandler Foundation—to see to its upkeep. That was a fine idea of Kate's. The Governor was right pleased."

Blaise was watching his wife's face. It did not flicker as she shrugged herself into her coat. "I will leave you to discuss it," she said smoothly. She bent to kiss her husband. "I shall not be down tomorrow. But I will call, and I shall return on Sunday."

She knew better than to kiss the old lady. *"Au revoir,* Madame."

"And the same to you," returned the Duchess affably. When Dominique had gone she guffawed with laughter. "That fixed her. 'How are you, Madame?' indeed. She makes me sound like the chief whore in a cathouse." Then, with a sniff, "And she should know."

Agatha fixed an expectant eye on her grandson, but he did not take her up. She frowned. "What's up, Boy? Or is it that what should be, ain't?"

Still no response. Normally remarks like that led to five rounds.

The old lady turned to Minnie who had, as usual, made herself almost invisible in a corner. "Minnie, go see if you can find us a nice cup of good English tea."

When she'd gone, "Out with it, Boy," the old lady said sharply. "You don't fool me none, not now, not ever. Somethin's on your mind."

"How about a five-pound cast?"

The old lady glanced at his splinted leg. "That contraption don't weigh five pounds."

"No, but the plaster one will."

"You've had broken legs before—and arms, come to that. I know that look. Somethin' is chewin' at you. I can see the teethmarks."

"Duchess, a couple of hundred years ago they'd have burned you at the stake."

"It's what's burnin' you I'm askin' about."

"I'm covered in bruises, my head aches, and I've got a broken leg. Will that do?"

Her expression softened, and for the first time she opened her Russian sable coat. Underneath, her caftan was scarlet and gold and she was hung with rubies from here to breakfast. "You want I should move you? Take you up to London?"

"No." It came out sharply and his grandmother's eyes were suddenly equally sharp, but, "Please yourself," she said mildly. "Want to watch some television?"

"No—yes." He glanced at the clock, picked up the remote control, switched it to ITV. The news had just started, and they were giving the headlines. Geneva arms talks. Mrs. Thatcher. Another atomic test in Russia. Mysterious blaze at country mansion; millions of pounds worth of art saved. The old lady glanced at her grandson's face. It was intent. She held her peace. As Blaise had known, the interview shown at six o'clock was repeated.

"Why, if it isn't Kate!" exclaimed the Duchess.

"Shh," he commanded.

She subsided, but while he watched Kate, she watched him. And found her answer.

Kate dropped into a chair and sat there, staring at nothing. Since talking to Benny Fong, her mind seemed to have shut down. She could not take in the monstrous implications, try as she might, and she had wrestled with them all the way up from Sussex. She felt numb, exhausted with trying to sort out all that had happened to her. She did not realize she was undergoing a delayed reaction; that she had done too much too soon. She only knew that she felt disoriented, muzzy, mentally disabled. As a car is put out of action by the removal of its rotor arm, so had Kate been immobilized by shock. She sat on in her chair, staring at nothing. When the phone rang, she did not hear it. It stopped, rang again shortly afterward, and still it did not penetrate her immobility. It kept ringing on and off for the next hour or so and she never heard any of it.

Nor did she hear the key in the door, or Charlotte Vale come in.

Kate had given her a key back at the beginning, when she was being refurbished, so that she could come in and out with things she thought Kate might need. It was she who had been ringing. She had called Courtland Park only to find the number constantly busy. So she had called the flat, and her uneasiness increased as time went on—it was by now almost eleven o'clock. Perhaps Kate had stayed on in Sussex . . . She then called the local hotel and they mentioned that Kate had been at dinner when the fire started—but she was not staying there. Something must be wrong . . . Without another thought she put on a coat and went down to her car.

Kate was sitting in the big Georgian wing chair by the telephone, her hands in her lap, unnaturally still. When Charlotte bent to peer at her face it was stiff. Shock, she thought, recognizing the signs, having driven an ambulance during the war. She lifted Kate from the chair; she moved like an automaton. She walked her into the bedroom, undressed her like a child, got her into bed. Then she called her own doctor.

He confirmed her diagnosis. "Shock and delayed reaction. In too much of a hurry to leave the hospital. She underwent quite an ordeal, so I understand. Keep her quiet, give her one of these. It will put her out, give her mind time to unwind. I'll call back tomorrow. Stay with her just in case."

When he'd gone, Charlotte undressed, borrowed a nightgown, and slipped into the other side of the big double bed. She was both surprised and amused to find that her feelings were maternal. She had not wanted children. Her career had been more important. Now she reflected that had she had a child with one of her husbands, it would have been around Kate's age . . . She raised herself to look at the slack, colorless face. Poor child, she thought. Everything gone up in smoke . . .

Kate was still asleep twelve hours later when the phone rang.

Charlotte gave the number and a man's voice asked sharply, "Who is this? I want to speak to Kate Despard."

"That is not possible right now."

"Why not?" She could feel his anxiety like a blade. "Isn't she there? If not, where is she?"

"She is sleeping."

"Oh . . ." Anxiety gave way to relief.

"May I ask who is calling?" Charlotte asked, already having a good idea because of the American accent.

"Blaise Chandler."

"I thought so. I'm Charlotte Vale."

"Oh, Miss Vale. Is Kate all right?"

"She had a delayed reaction last night. I found her in a state of shock. The doctor has prescribed rest."

'I thought something was wrong because I was expecting her down here today."

"I'm afraid Kate won't be going anywhere for the next couple of days or so."

"Are you looking after her?"

"I am."

"Thank you."

And in those two simple words, Charlotte's intuitive and astute mind read the most passionate of love letters. Ah, she thought, so that is the way of it.

"Do you want me to keep you informed?" she asked.

"Would you? I'm afraid I have no phone of my own here—but could you call my grandmother—Mrs. Agatha Chandler? She's staying at the Pink Thatch Hotel in a village called Thatcham—I haven't the number right now but I'm sure you can find it easily enough."

"Of course I'll do that. It is the least I can do, seeing as it is thanks to you Kate is still alive."

His voice was savage when he said, "If I hadn't been penned up because of this damned leg I would have seen her and perhaps stopped her from leaving. She took a nasty fall on top of seeing a dream go up in smoke. Take care of her, Miss Vale."

"I will," Charlotte promised.

Then she went in to look at Kate, still deeply asleep, but it seemed to Charlotte that there was more color to her face. No wonder it hit you hard, Charlotte thought. Of all men, Blaise Chandler . . . You've picked a tough one, Kate.

Agatha was all for taking off for London at once when Blaise told her flatly, "No way, Duchess. Charlotte Vale is a good friend to Kate, helped her a lot. She's older, knows her way around. She'll do what's necessary. Besides, there's an invalid here who needs pampering."

Kate, sleeping the sleep of exhaustion, would have thought she was experiencing a nightmare had she seen who it was her stepsister warmly greeted as she was shown to her table at *Tante Claire*.

"Venetia, my dear . . ." Dominique raised the small veil that entrancingly shadowed her eyes under the chic scarlet cloche of her Paulette hat, to press her fragrant cheek against the unusually flushed-with-excitement parchment one of Venetia Townsend. "It has been an age . . . How good to see you again. I trust you are well?"

"And still Poor Venetia," was the dusty answer, accompanied by a chuckle that would have given Kate the shivers.

Dominique gurgled. "If only they knew . . ."

"It would never occur to them. You are the last person in the world they would expect me to have for a friend." Venetia's smile was one nobody at Despard's had ever seen. "Serves them right."

Just so long as you continue to serve me, Dominique thought, taking the chair the obsequious waiter drew out for her. She had cast her spell on the barren-with-deprivation spinster from her arrival at Despard's, when her killer's instinct had sensed the thwarted passions smoldering away beneath the drab exterior, and she made it her business to liberate them in her own cause. Venetia Townsend, she had discovered, was not what she seemed. Underneath the dessicated scholar was a woman who passionately longed to be all that Dominique du Vivier was, but knew she never could. True dog in the manger, she loathed men for ignoring her, but still longed to be able to deal in them as Dominique did: taking them, using them, discarding them. Through Dominique she obtained a vicarious kind of revenge against them for availing themselves of her scholarship but callously denigrating her femininity.

Through Dominique, Venetia was able to live her dreams, to enter the glittering world her idol inhabited, to partake, if secondhand, of the glamour and excitement her starved soul craved. She listened gloatingly when Dominique described, with cruel dispassion, how she treated the men who pursued her. When Dominique came to London, she usually took Venetia out to lunch, to the kind of restaurant the repressed spinster would never visit, always far enough away from Despard's to be safe, but chic and fashionable enough to serve up Venetia mental as well as gustatorial pleasure. And while Venetia ate Sole Veronique, or *coq au vin*, Dominique would skillfully mine her retentive mind of every nugget of information it contained.

She knew exactly what it was Venetia craved. Not the real, of which she was afraid, but the imagined—so much safer than reality. What she wanted—needed—was to experience through Dominique's eyes the first nights, the gala receptions, the gallery openings, the cruises on enormous white yachts, the feel of couture clothes, the taste of vintage champagne. She was happy to sit, wide-eyed and gleeful, listening to Dominique recount how she used her lovers: taking, using, then discarding, as Venetia longed to do, glorying in their abject slavery and their inevitable disposal, applying their humiliation as balm to her own lacerated pride.

Dominique knew all about Venetia's arid existence. She worked all day, went home to her aged mother at night. She went nowhere, had no friends. She sat, eyes glittering, while Dominique regaled her with how she had disposed of her latest lover—a rich Brazilian who was utterly besotted.

". . . and then what did you do?" Venetia asked greedily.

"What else? He groveled, begged, pleaded, bribed . . ."

"But you did not weaken?"

"I? Weaken? He was on his knees, so I put my foot in the center of his chest and shoved . . ."

Venetia giggled, her eyes glistening, her tongue licking her lips.

"Oh, how satisfying . . . Was he humiliated?"

"Devastated."

Venetia heaved the huge sigh of one replete with satisfaction. Then they both laughed.

"But you, my dear Venetia. We must not chatter about me all the time. How are things with you, these days?

Venetia leaned forward. "Well, you know about Piers Lang, of course . . ." she began.

Old news! Dominique thought impatiently behind an attentive face. He had come whining to her at once. She had shown him the bitter disappointment of one who had trusted, giving no indication of the fact that she had regarded him from the start as expendable; that she had expected him to be found out; that the affair of the fake horse had been, on her part, a warning to Kate Despard of what she might expect once things really got rough. What had surprised her was that it was Kate herself who had followed the clues Dominique had so carefully laid, and not that sharp-nosed old *pédé*. Well, she would have to have been an imbecile not

to have followed them, Dominique had reasoned, so this
had at least proved that she was not . . .

To Piers Lang she made it clear that he had failed her,
and she had no use for failures. But as a sop (and because
she was always careful not to create enemies of people who
knew too much) she had given him an introduction to a
dealer she knew in Rome, where talents such as Piers Lang
possessed could be used to good advantage on elderly, rich
ladies interested in acquiring, at great expense, pieces that
had hardly any real value whatsoever.

Sheelagh Hennessy's transfer, though, had been an unpleasant shock. Stupid woman! Dominique had been aware of,
and played on, her jealousy of Kate Despard; what she had
not known—and Sheelagh Hennessy had not told her—was
that Kate Despard reciprocated the dislike in full measure.
That blunder had resulted in a prime channel of information
being closed. And when several other people on whom she
had relied to feed her information also suddenly resigned,
Dominique was left with only Poor Venetia. Poor Venetia
my foot, Dominique thought, as she listened to her now,
recounting every bit of information she had squirreled away
since their last meeting. Poor Venetia is worth her weight in
gold to me . . .

". . . and then there is all this publicity," her treasure was
saying now in discontented tones. "Honestly, you can't pick
up a paper or a magazine without finding something about
Kate Despard. Now they want her to go on television to
show the glories of Courtland Park." Here she bent a re-
proachful gaze on her idol. "I had expected you would deal
with Nicholas Chevely."

Dominique sighed. "I would have, had I been able to
spare the time," she lied. "But Hong Kong preempted every
minute of it."

Venetia's eyes brightened. "Tell me," she begged greedily. Having successfully deflected that dangerous arrow, Dominique gave a full description, Venetia hanging on every
word, her imagination working overtime. Dominique gave
no hint of the true situation. As always, Venetia blindly
believed that Dominique was totally in control.

"Oh, how I would liked to have seen it. It sounds absolutely magical . . ."

"But there is Courtland Park."

"Courtland Park, Courtland Park—I am sick of Courtland

Park. That fire did her the world of good. All that free publicity . . . She's lucky, that one, like her father before her."

Venetia had hated Charles Despard more than anyone because he had been the one to tag her Poor Venetia, and when he had left his wife and daughter she had thought, "I always knew he was no good." What she had not expected was that his stepdaughter would be of the very stuff her dreams were made of and, once under her spell, any sympathy she may have had for Charles Despard's poor deserted daughter had evaporated under the hot arc-lights of Dominique's fascination. Her hatred had intensified when she heard what he had done in his will, because in her opinion, Dominique should have had everything. She was the only one who deserved it. Over the months, she had watched Kate Despard usurping her goddess's place and burned with frustrated fury. Now, her voice spat venom as she castigated the woman she regarded as Dominique's sworn enemy.

"Inquiries are flooding in from all over the place . . . the sales calendar is filled for months—years, even—ahead."

"Really?" Dominique asked, sounding bored. "Like where?"

The names Venetia intoned had Dominique's hand gripping the stem of her wineglass until it threatened to break. Instead she picked it up and drained her Chablis, motioning the waiter for a refill for her and for Venetia. People would have been surprised to see Venetia drinking alcohol. Any Despard's function she attended—and they were few and far between—always laid on pure orange juice for her specially. But lunching with Dominique she was always good for several glasses, and held them well, the only effect being to make her more garrulous, which was why Dominique plied her in the first place.

Now, shrewdly assessing the slight flush on Venetia's colorless cheeks, she judged the time right to plant her seed.

"I quite agree with you," she soothed. "That fire made her much vaunted sale into even more of an event. One could not buy such publicity. In fact, it makes one wonder if she did not arrange the whole affair . . ." This last was said with a gay "I'm only joking" note of laughter, but she saw Venetia's eyes flare as the seed took root. "I mean . . ." Dominique went on, with just the slightest of frowns, "it is not like Blaise to take such an interest. Poor darling, he has been so scrupulous to avoid the taint of partiality. And yet—to *be* there on such a disastrous occasion—even saving her life; I mean, would *you* go into an inferno knowing you might never come out? Oh, I know she *says* she never heard the warning that the roof was about to go, but one can *say* anything . . ." The little frown deepened. "It was almost as if she wanted an absolutely unimpeachable witness."

Dominique sat back, sipped at her Chablis, and let that bit of fertilizer germinate the seed. "But of course," she ended, spreading a final layer, "myself, I never thought her *that* clever."

"Don't make that mistake," snapped Venetia on cue. "She's as crafty as they come, added to which she's got that warlock Rollo Bellamy on her side. Don't be fooled by that Little Miss Guileless act of hers. It never fooled me, I can tell you."

Dominique smiled to herself. Already Venetia was watering the seed with that imagination of hers. By the time she got back to Despard's it would have taken root and the sprouts would be judiciously harvested and offered—in that diffident, apologetic way of hers—to anyone who would listen, thus would the rumors start: "I say . . . you'll never guess what Poor Venetia has heard . . ." What she had sown would spread like weeds. But to make sure, Dominique added one final dollop of manure.

"One thing did strike me as rather . . . odd." She frowned. "The number of people on site. I mean—*eight* guards? Or so Blaise told me. I know they were guarding millions, but she had half Despard's there, too."

"Fifteen members of staff," Venetia supplied readily.

"Plus a contingent of police! Blaise commented to me that her precautions were extraordinary." Dominique's smile was all shared complicity. "Men . . ." she gurgled. "So gullible, so easily—seduced . . ."

Venetia's mouth opened as she drew in a shocked breath. "You don't mean . . ."

Dominique threw her head back as her laugh trilled. "Oh, no, my dear Venetia. *Me* fear the little Despard?"

But she knew that little seed would produce a whole crop of mutant blooms, those that stank of an unscrupulous woman poaching on another woman's preserves.

"Now then . . ." Dominique adroitly changed tack as their rack of lamb was served. "Tell me, what did you think of that Titian which came up at Sotheby's last week? Was it overpriced as they are saying . . . ?"

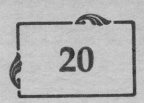

20

Kate slept for eighteen hours, was surprised to find herself in bed when she awoke. She had no memory of anything after sitting down for a moment to think . . . She was just lifting aside the covers when her bedroom door opened and Charlotte came in.

"Hello," she smiled. "Feeling better?"

"What are you doing here?"

"That's a long story. Let me get you a nice cup of tea and then I'll tell you."

Later, sitting by the bed sipping her own tea, she said, "I just had this feeling. I do get them from time to time and I have learned to act on them, so I came round and there you were, looking like a zombie."

She noticed that Kate's golden eyes had darkened to amber, that her gaze was turned inward.

"By the way, Blaise Chandler rang."

Her head snapped up and suddenly the eyes were golden again, glowing like topaz.

"He was worried because you had not turned up as expected."

The pale skin rosied. "I did leave a message for him saying I would be down today . . ." Her color deepened before Charlotte's clear-eyed gaze.

"So that's why he risked his life to save yours . . ."

Kate buried her nose in her cup.

"You realize you have taken on a world champion?"

"I know."

"That's a stunningly attractive man, Kate, and, frankly, not one I would have thought—"

"—would go for me?" She sighed, shook her head. "Nor

496

did I." In a faraway voice, "It was the strangest thing, Charlotte . . ."

It was a relief to tell someone; it helped her get it straight in her own mind, and once into her tale she went on to read the whole chapter.

It was Charlotte's turn to shake her head. "Mad . . ." she said. "She has to be mad. It is possible, you know. The world is full of people, ostensibly ultra-sane on the surface, who are barking lunatics underneath."

"Mad with hate, perhaps."

"Once she finds out you have opened a second front—watch out!"

"I know. That's what worries me."

"Well, one thing is certain. Blaise Chandler is not going to call a press conference about it. He must know his wife better than anyone and he is well aware of her—capabilities. If he feels anything for you then his instinct will be to protect. But you will have to be careful, *very* careful."

"Funnily enough, it's not in that area that I feel most shocked," Kate said slowly. "It's that she was cold-bloodedly prepared to destroy great works of art for personal gain . . . I am not talking about their salesroom value, I mean great works of creative genius. And yet she wants Despard's? Why? I just don't understand her. What is she after? What does she *want?*"

"Power . . . position? Although she is already Mrs. Blaise Chandler."

"She would regard that as secondhand—so would I, come to that. I, too, would hate to be known only as some man's wife. I am worth much more than that. Besides, Blaise did not object that she was known to the world as Dominique du Vivier. The only person I know who calls her Mrs. Chandler is Benny Fong. Mrs. Chandler is the Duchess."

"I see. A case of Mrs. Astor all over again . . . Let's not go into that story right now," she added hastily, seeing Kate's puzzled look. "It has to be money, then, which she equates with power. Many people do."

"But to be willing to sacrifice works of genius . . . priceless heritage . . ." It was beyond Kate's comprehension.

"That's the difference between you. You do what you do because you love it; she does it because of what it can bring her."

"I have to stop her," Kate said.

"How?"

"The tape."

"But that belongs to Blaise."

"It concerns me more than him. I am the one she is out to destroy."

"Which is why he had her flat bugged in the first place. He was already protecting you."

"Oh, he will know—but not until it is all over."

"Is that wise?"

"It is expedient." Kate was intent, decisive now. "I have to beat her first, and not by default. I have to prove beyond doubt that I am better than she is, and Courtland Park should do it. Nigel told me Despard's has been flooded with calls. More people than ever want to attend. They saw on television what I have to sell. That's what I can never forgive her for—her rotten selfishness and willingness to sacrifice greatness for gain. So I am going to achieve prices that will choke her. Then, when I've shown the world that I have won, I'll hold the tape over her head. If she so much as puts a foot wrong I'll expose her."

"She'll turn on you, bring everything down," Charlotte warned doubtfully.

"Not her. She'd really lose all hope of winning then. No, she'll look for a way out. She is so overwhelmingly vain she won't think for a moment that she can't beat me, even if it has to be honestly. Besides, I'll offer her a deal. If she plays fair and still beats me, then the tape is hers. If I beat her, I'll keep it—and use it if she continues to do me down."

"It sounds easy. But aren't you forgetting she cannot be trusted?"

"I'll have the tape."

"But you know her way of acquiring sales—"

"I'll take that chance and continue to acquire mine honestly."

"And Blaise?"

"Will know nothing until it is over. I only need until after the sale."

"But what if Benny Fong gets to him as he wanted to in the first place?"

"He's in hospital, remember?"

"They won't keep him there forever."

"No, but he will want to stay down in Sussex because of me . . ."

Charlotte regarded her protégée with something like admiration. *"Now* I see what he sees in you."

Kate was silent then. "To be quite honest," she said awkwardly, "I can't—see what he sees in me, I mean. After Dominique—"

"A long way after. That was no marriage, Kate. From what I know of it—and that is only what 'they' say—they lived separate lives. She may be breathtaking on the surface, but underneath . . ." She shuddered. "They should have called her Messalina. Besides, it was you he risked his life for."

"I know . . ." Charlotte caught her breath at the radiance that suffused Kate's whole being. "He came back for me . . . for *me*. It was so strange. He looked at me in such a way . . . And when he kissed me—" Her eyes closed and Charlotte saw her swallow convulsively. Oh, yes indeed, she thought. I know what you mean. I have been there myself.

Kate's face was rapt, dreamy, and Charlotte brought her back to reality gently. "You'll need to be fighting fit for your coming battle, so I think an early dinner and then more sleep. The doctor will be here shortly—you were asleep when he came before—and we'll see what he says about you."

Kate's eyes opened abruptly. "The tape!" she said in a strangled voice. "It was going to be delivered today. Oh, my God! I wasn't there like I said I'd be . . ."

"Well, you don't have far to go to find out if it was or not . . . It's just six-thirty. Ring down and see what happened. Penny won't have left yet, I'm sure."

Kate had an internal telephone from which she could contact any of Despard's departments, and she at once buzzed her secretary's office.

"Miss Despard!" Penny sounded relieved. "How are you? People have been asking me all day . . ."

Earlier, Charlotte had gone down to say that Kate had been ordered to rest and would not be in her office that day.

"Much better, thank you, Penny. All I needed was a bit of peace and quiet."

"Everybody is talking about it. We are all thrilled that so much was saved. What could have been a disaster turned into a triumph, thanks to you."

"Not just me," Kate said. "Now, Penny, I was expecting a

package to be delivered today—a rather important package. Did it come—by hand?"

"Oh, yes. A Mr. Benjamin called—on behalf of a Mr. Fong. I told him you were resting and he said he understood and if it was convenient he would call in on Monday morning at eleven o'clock."

"Well done, Penny," Kate said, warm with relief. "I'll be at my desk as usual."

"You are sure you are up to it?" her secretary asked concernedly.

"Quite sure. See you on Monday. 'Bye." Kate fell back against her pillows with a heartfelt sigh. "He's coming back on Monday. Mind you, I might have known Benny would play safe."

"Right, that's settled. What would you say to one of my mushroom omelettes?" Charlotte asked.

"Yes, please," Kate replied promptly.

And when the doctor came, after a quick check he pronounced her fit.

"So I can go back to work?"

"If you promise not to do too much. You suffered a physical battering and severe mental shock. Take it easy for the next few days and there should be no relapses."

"Oh, I promise that," Kate vowed. "I've got my biggest auction coming up and I must be fighting fit by then."

"In that case . . ."

Her mind relieved, Kate slept dreamlessly and deeply for another ten hours. On Monday morning, at nine-thirty, she was back at her desk.

For the first hour, people kept coming in to see how she was, congratulate her, ask with eager curiosity about the fire. Kate could see that her day was going to be useless unless she did something, so she called a meeting at which she thanked her assembled staff for their good wishes and told them the auction would go ahead as planned. This was greeted with applause and cheers. "Despard's rules, okay?" somebody shouted, and there was general laughter and more applause.

She got back to her office just before eleven o'clock and, precisely on the hour, Penny announced that Mr. Benjamin was here.

He was English, looked like a prosperous solicitor and talked like a politician. He shook hands, inquired solicitously after her health, made a few complimentary remarks about recent events, and then without further ado, spun the combination locks on his expensive hide suitcase, from which he extracted a small flat package.

"With the compliments of Mr. Benson Fong."

"Thank you." Kate closed her hand around it. "And thank Mr. Fong, won't you, and tell him all will be handled as arranged."

He bowed. "I will indeed."

Another bow, and she saw him out of her office. Going back to her desk she buzzed to Penny. "No calls, no more visitors until I tell you, please."

"Very well, Miss Despard."

The tape turned out to be of the same kind and size as the ones used by the Grundig on which she dictated letters. She inserted it in the machine and pressed the PLAY button.

Dominique's voice was unmistakable. That smoky, filled-with-sexual-promise huskiness was hers, all right, so was the enchanting hint of accent. The second voice was soft, unreadable, somehow dangerous. But the purport of the conversation was clear. Kate sat and listened to her stepsister coolly offering the support of Despard's in the smuggling of drugs in exchange for the destruction of Courtland Park and its contents. Even listening to it made her feel sick. When she had switched off the machine, she sat with her chin on her hands, thinking, thinking . . .

What *is* it with her? she wondered with fresh puzzlement. I want to win; I want Despard's International, but not at *any* price. Nothing in this world is worth any price. Not even Blaise? her mind asked slyly. Think—the width and depth of your want for him is the way she feels about Despard's, only by now it has become an obsession. Blaise, she thought again. She looked at the telephone. But she did not trust her self-control around him. Besides, he was sharp. No, she thought, not yet. Not until you have digested this and you can look at him and listen to him and feel him and still carry it off.

She took the tape from the machine, locked it in her private safe. That evening, when the building was empty but for the night guards, she would make a copy. It would not do to confront Dominique with the original. She was quite capable of bonking Kate over the head and seizing it. That done, she turned her attention firmly to other things.

*   *   *

Blaise's cast was fitted on Tuesday and he was able, with the help of metal elbow crutches, to hop around. He was to return in two days to have his stitches out, but as he intended to stay in Sussex for the sale anyway, there was no problem. His grandmother picked him up in the big black Lincoln and he left the hospital in a welter of good wishes from an assembled crowd of wistful nurses, sad to see him and his grandmother, who had brought such excitement to the quiet little hospital, soon to be closed, take it away with them.

At least, he thought, once he was safely installed in his room at the Pink Thatch, I've got my own phone. His grandmother had said there were no messages, which on the one hand meant that everything was all right, but on the other tempted him to call Kate just to talk to her.

He settled himself in the comfortable armchair by the window, a small table with the telephone at hand, his briefcase ready and waiting and a whole slew of calls to be made. Perhaps, he thought hopefully, Kate would come down today. Charlotte had called him the day before to say she had gone back to work, but that the doctor had told her to take things slowly. "As far as I know, she intends to be in Sussex on Wednesday."

"She is all right?"

"Yes, but I think tranquillity is called for. A lot has happened . . ."

There was a pause. "She told you?" Blaise asked intuitively.

"She felt a need to tell someone . . . It was not only the fire which knocked her all of a heap, Mr. Chandler. Kate is an emotional creature, as you know, and highly strung. I think everything combined to snap her wires for a while. I don't want her around anything that would tighten them again."

It was an oblique reference to Dominique and the awkwardness, even guilt that Kate, with her transparent honesty, would feel about a woman who wished her nothing but ill and who would, if she knew what had happened, take an even more dangerous turn for the worse.

"There is no way I would allow Kate to be hurt," he said, in a voice that made even Charlotte back off, and say quickly, "It is not herself she worries about, Mr. Chandler."

"No. It never is." He was silent a moment, then said,

"Okay, I'll let Kate take it at her own pace. That she takes it is all that matters to me in the long run."

Oh, wise and patient man, Charlotte thought admiringly. Kate will be all right with you.

Now, gazing out of the window at the pretty garden at the back of the hotel, with a large pond at the end of it on which swans and ducks swam, Blaise thought, If patience is a virtue then I'm St. Blaise the Long-Suffering . . . He turned to his briefcase with a sigh. Work, he thought. Still the best antidote there is. But someone knocked at his door. "It's open," he called, and Kate came in. The briefcase went flying, scattering papers, even the small table and the telephone as he grabbed for his crutches and heaved himself to his feet. "Kate!"

His smile, his eyes, made her knees buckle but she went forward and straight into the arms he held wide open.

"Surprise, surprise," she said shakily.

"Miss Vale said you weren't coming down till tomorrow. Ah, I see . . . I suppose the Duchess was in on the plot?"

"I wanted to be sure it was all right."

"She was here just now, won't be back again until later."

"I know," Kate said demurely.

He laughed exultantly, held her a little away so he could look at her. "Still a sight for sore eyes," he said in a voice that made her tremble.

Her fingers lightly touched the small dressing above his ear. "And is this sore?"

"Not when you touch it."

His mouth was warm, tender, infinitely loving. He cupped her face in his hands and stared deeply into her golden eyes. "I'm serious about this, Kate."

"I know."

"I didn't expect it, but I know it is the last thing I am about to turn away."

"I know," she said again in a tender voice, as though soothing a worried child. She kissed his cheeks, his nose, his mouth again.

She had been flutteringly nervous about seeing him again, but her previous resolution had given way under the pressure of a longing that grew worse when, the night before, having slept herself out, she had lain wakeful, unable to stop thinking about him. It was not fair on him, she reasoned. Charlotte had told her of his call, and of hers to him, and what he had said. No, he would never hurt her but wasn't she hurting him by staying away? Wouldn't he, too, be wondering, waiting, hoping? Oh, the hell with it, she thought. If the coast is clear I am going and that's that. She had called Agatha before she could change her mind, and when she found Dominique was not expected, had said she would be down straightaway and not to say a word.

"I'm right glad not to," the old lady had answered happily. "The Boy's been mopin' like a lovesick steer. I knew somethin' was up and I suspicioned what it was. He ain't never been able to fool me."

"I couldn't stay away any longer," Kate said to Blaise now.

"Thank God for that."

He scooped her up, carefully lowered himself into the big chair again, cradling her on his lap.

"But your leg . . ."

"I've still got two good thighs."

"I know," Kate said unthinkingly.

Eyebrows raised, "Do you now?"

That flush he had come to love colored her still bruised face, while the endearing shyness that was so much a part of her touched him deeply.

"In Colorado," she said, staring fixedly at the V of his cashmere sweater, "I came down to swim one night and you were already there."

"I didn't see you—or hear you, come to that."

"I—hid . . ."

"Well, at least you know what you are getting," Blaise pointed out straight-faced.

"That's the unholy marvel of it all, because I never thought I would."

When the Duchess returned, she could hear the murmur of voices, punctuated by long silences, and proceeded to make as much noise as she could, bumping the door with her wheelchair and berating Minnie for not looking where she was going. When she finally got through the door, Kate was standing by the window, smoothing her hair, her face flushed and her eyes bright. Blaise was in his chair, looking like a man who had not only been given the world but kept his soul in the bargain. Thank the Lord, Agatha Chandler said to herself prayerfully. Her grandson was her whole world, and it had grieved her to see him looking as if his had just been handed a demolition notice.

Kate at once came forward to be embraced.

"Now let me look at you," Agatha said, examining her with loving eyes. She clicked her tongue at the bruising, patted her hand anxiously. "Between the pair of you I reckon you've cornered the market in black and blue," she exclaimed. Then she turned to Minnie. "Go see if that champagne I ordered is ready. And that special lunch I asked to be sent up."

"Don't count your chickens," Blaise teased.

"Seein' as how I can hardly see for feathers you ain't got no cause to talk."

She beamed at them, her smile dimming the diamonds interspersed with emeralds that she was wearing today.

"Oh, Duchess, it is so good to see you again," Kate said emotionally.

"Likewise," was the cordial return. "Now then, I want to hear all about this sale of yours. Seems it's all folks hereabouts can talk about these days."

"But Blaise says you are both coming."

"That we are. I want to see you rub her nose in it—you are goin' to, aren't you?"

"I am going to trounce her from here to breakfast," Kate said with a kindling eye. But she told the Duchess all she wanted to know, conscious of Blaise's gaze, turning to smile at him every now and again, while he held her hand, raising it now and again to run his mouth over her knuckles. The Duchess could have warmed herself at the glow between them. This time it's right, she told herself. This time it ain't because he can't help himself, it's because he wants to.

Kate, basking in the love of the two people who, along with Rollo, meant most to her, found herself opening up like a flower to the sun. Her only moment of dimmed brightness was when the Duchess asked after Rollo.

"I haven't seen him in over a week," she confessed guiltily.

"Well, there ain't much you can do 'cept look at him and he don't know if you're there or not."

"Even so," she said, troubled. "I must go and see him. I'll call in on my way home tomorrow."

"When he does come to you'll have a lot to tell him."

Kate's laugh bubbled. "And no doubt he in turn will have a lot to say to me!"

"Let's hope so," Blaise said, in a way that had Kate look at him quickly.

"He will be—difficult."

"So can the Boy, if he's a mind," said the Duchess, brushing Rollo aside like a gnat. "There ain't nobody can handle trouble the way he can."

Which was when Kate, again acting on impulse, went flatly against her previous resolution. "We do have trouble," she said.

Blaise at once caught the inflection in her voice. "Out with it then," he said.

Taking a deep breath, Kate told them about Benny's call, the delivery of the tape, what it contained. When she had finished, Blaise's face was again the mask she now knew indicated ruthlessly controlled feelings, while the Duchess was shocked to silence and reduced to shaking her head like a metronome.

It had seemed to Blaise, as Kate told her sickening story, that he could feel his wife's presence: chilling and evil. The revelation had only confirmed his own strong instinct. In the past few days, he had felt himself emerging, newborn, from the imprisoning chrysalis of Dominique's spinning; breathing fresh air instead of the narcotic of her presence, feeling almost painfully sensitized to stimuli other than her own, and all because of the powerful impact of Kate. But the confirmation of what he had sensed in Dominique still hit him right between the eyes, because in spite of his gut feeling that she was involved with what had happened at Courtland Park, having it proved was still something he recoiled from.

He was so deep in his thoughts that the touch of Kate's hand made him start. She was gazing at him with guilt-ridden eyes. "I shouldn't have told you. Me and my uncontrollable impulses . . ."

"No, you did right. As a matter of fact, I had been thinking along the same lines myself." He hesitated, looking for the right words. "It was a feeling; she looked—indecently pleased with herself, all creamy with a satisfaction that could only be there because she had got what she wanted. Oh, she said all the right things, made all the right noises, but—"

"Just like my daddy," Agatha interrupted with quiet satisfaction. "You couldn't fool him none, either. It's the Indian in us," she said to Kate simply, as if that explained everything.

"Oh," Kate said, feeling relieved even if she did not wholly understand. "Anyway, I have *got* to beat her now, and out in the open, where everyone can see. Then, once I've proved not only to her but to everyone that I'm the best, I'll blackmail her into good behavior for the rest of the year."

The Duchess pursed her lips and Blaise said gently, "She would never believe you, my love. Think, Kate. You are not known in nor do you know Hong Kong. What resources have you to place the most sophisticated state-of-the-art listening devices in her apartment? And why would you, in the first place? Again, how would you retrieve them without her knowing?" He shook his head. "She would know at once you'd had help and where that help came from—me." His eyes were loving, but his voice was firm, even with regret, when he said, "She knows you don't think like that, just as she knows I do . . ."

"I never thought of that," Kate admitted.

"Why should you?" asked the Duchess stoutly. "It ain't your style."

"She's right about beating Dominique in the salesroom though," Blaise said thoughtfully. "There is nothing she can do about that except work like hell to catch up. And if *I* held the tape—"

"Or I did," said the Duchess. She slapped the arm of her wheelchair. "That's the way of it. She knows I can't stand the sight of her and would do anything to pry her loose." Her eyes kindled. "And she'd think twice about takin' me on."

"But that was just what I didn't want," Kate protested. "To drag you into this. It is me she is after."

"We are in it," Agatha snapped. "The Boy because of you and me because of the Boy. She wouldn't think twice about believin' I would have her place bugged because she knows I have never trusted her as far as I could throw the Eiffel Tower. She'd know I meant what I said if I threatened to expose her. I've got resources and backup and more money than even she could count. That's what she respects—power. 'Sides, she knows I'm on your team. I followed your advice about the museum, didn't I? And it was ChanCorp who helped you in Hong Kong, she'll know all about that. She also knows I've got a suspicious mind. No," she finished resolutely. "You do what you are best at, girl. Hold your sale and make enough to get yourself way out in front. I'll do the rest. That way, she'll leave you and the Boy alone."

"Will she?" Blaise asked ironically.

His grandmother scowled. "Well, maybe not you . . . that one always has to get her own back, but she knows what you are capable of, too, so she'll be a sight more careful."

"I like it," he said. "As you say, the only thing she respects—admires—is power and she'd think twice about taking you on."

"I'll have her on eggshells." The Duchess guffawed maliciously. "Right," she turned to Kate. "I know this sale of yours is going to put you ahead—I want to know by how much."

"I can let you see the latest figures," Blaise said.

"And we could leak them," Kate suggested. "The news would spread like butter once dropped in the right ears."

"And appeared in print, Agatha added slyly. 'I own more'n one newspaper and not a few magazines. And there's a columnist as owes me a favor or two . . ." Her grin was pure spite. "We'll play her at her own game."

But Dominique's latest throw of the dice threatened to stop Kate in her tracks.

She returned to London feeling that her impulsiveness had, for once, paid off. She and Blaise and the Duchess had discussed tactics; she had taken them both to Courtland Park to see how preparations were progressing; Blaise had produced the latest figures, which showed them neck and neck, but Kate's own provisional reserves for the Park, if reached—"And they will be," she had said confidently—would put her ahead by ten million pounds. "Which means she's got to come up with something very big in the remaining five months."

She felt jubilant and eager, therefore, until, three days before the sale, Nigel Marsh came to see her, grave-faced, and said, "I think you ought to know, Kate, that there is a most scurrilous rumor circulating not only here at Despard's, but all over the art world."

"About what?"

"The fire at Courtland Park. That you arranged it, that you took so many precautions and had so many people down there to enable you to save so many treasures, that the fire was conveniently started at the back to allow the necessary time to stage the 'miraculous' rescue."

Kate's mouth dropped as her face whitened. *"What?"*

"I am afraid so. Such a rumor could have a disastrous effect on the sale."

"Then it must be stopped."

"I have spoken to Jane Bowman"—she was an influential arts correspondent—"and told her that the rumor is totally without foundation; that if it persists we shall sue for slander. She is going to print the item in her column tomorrow. But that is not enough. We have got to get it across as forcefully as possible that you had nothing whatsoever to do with the fire, and, if possible, publicize the real cause."

Kate reached for the telephone.

"You've heard," were Nicholas Chevely's first words.

"Only just."

"It's all nonsense, of course, as I've told everyone who has told me."

"What I want is for the insurance investigators to reveal their findings and prove it. I want a public announcement— I'll make it if you can get me that information."

"I tried, old girl; first thing I thought of, but all they say is that their investigations are not complete. It takes time and careful expertise to sift through all that wreckage. They are down there now—"

"They've been there for days!"

At the desperate urgency in Kate's voice, Nicholas said quickly, "I'll have another go at them."

"This is a matter of life or death, Nicholas. Unless it is stopped here and now it will be my funeral—and yours, come to that, because you insured the house."

"I'll get on to them straightaway."

"Right." Kate put the phone down and turned back to Nigel. "I want a press conference—now! What the hell have we got a public relations department for? Why haven't they done anything by now?"

"It was thought the rumor would die down . . . but instead, it is gathering force."

"And we know why, don't we? Just like we know who. Oh, that bitch! That bloody bitch!"

"I'll have a word with Bill Saunders at once," Nigel said hastily. He had never seen Kate so angry. Her temper was as fiery as her hair.

Kate's denial appeared in the *Standard* that same night: FIRE HEROINE DENIES RUMORS. "I'LL SUE," SAYS DESPARD HEIRESS. Her statement was to the effect that there was absolutely no truth in the unfounded rumor circulating that the fire that had destroyed Courtland Park, while enabling the rescue of millions of pounds' worth of fine art, had been deliberately set in order to ensure the maximum publicity. There was also an item on the six o'clock television news. Sitting at her desk, Kate spoke directly into the camera, vehemently and indignantly. Her anger was apparent, her hurt plain.

"I have an auction house to run and a reputation to maintain. Courtland Park is one sale. Would I be so stupid as to jeopardize all the sales I hope to hold for the sake of that one? Worse, would I deliberately put at risk the life of another human being for publicity's sake?" She then revealed that she had hoped to buy Courtland Park. "I had made an offer to the trustees of the late Mr. Courtland. I wanted Despard's to have a fitting setting for future sales; I had already spent a great deal of money refurbishing it. Nobody in their right mind does that and then sets fire to it!"

Watching the interview, Agatha Chandler nodded vigorously. "You tell 'em, girl," she encouraged.

Blaise was on the telephone.

"Was it convincing, do you think?" Kate asked him anxiously.

"I think so. You came across very well. And you were wise not to lay blame. Leave that to me."

Next morning, she opened her papers to see the statement issued by Mr. Blaise Chandler. It made no bones about attributing the gossip to "certain people who stand to gain should this sale not go ahead" and denied flatly any involvement on the part of Miss Despard or himself.

As he expected, it brought Dominique down in full fury.

"How dare you do this to me!" she raged.

"I mentioned no names."

"You did not need to. Everybody knows who you meant."

"Then you shouldn't have started the rumors in the first place."

"You have no proof of that."

"I don't need it. It's got your claw marks all over it."

"Ah, I see . . . allegiances have been declared, is that it?"

"Let's say that any I had to you have gone down the drain."

Dominique released a breath that hissed. "So . . . the much vaunted impartiality is now revealed as a sham."

"You, of all people, should know about shams and about fakes and about double-dealing and duplicity."

Dominique felt the full force of the tar-black eyes and a contempt that was a wall she could not breach. And a terrifying knowledge.

"You've had it in for Kate Despard from the first. So now hear this—you have had it with me. You couldn't fight fair, could you? If you are so God-almighty good, why not? Because you don't get your kicks that way. Well be warned, one more in Kate Despard's direction and I'll kick you black and blue."

"You would not dare."

"Try me!"

Dominique felt a flicker of fear. Not only had she lost his infatuation, she had found his hatred. There was a looming menace about him that was almost palpable.

Once he would have sold his soul for a smile; now she knew he would never glance in her direction again. Her thoughts darted here and there with feverish panic. She had counted too much on his enslavement, relied on her ability to charm away any suspicion, seduce any wavering doubts. She had gambled—and lost.

But she did not lack for courage. "Do not interfere in my affairs," she spat.

"I never have, have I?"

Now, as well as contempt for her there was the even worse rejection of Blaise's self-contempt. It broke the camel's back. She released a spate of gutter French in his direction, calling him every foul name she could think of.

Blaise watched from behind the mask of impassivity he erected when controlling his feelings. What he wanted to do was put his hands around that slender white neck and squeeze. To fling in her face every foul deed, every vicious act; he wanted to accuse her, revile her, but what he did was stand and look at her in a way that made her seize the nearest thing—a now cold pot of coffee—and hurl it at him. He ducked, and it smashed against the wall behind the dressing table. The door was the next thing to slam. Then she was gone.

Twenty-four hours later the insurance investigators released their findings: a fractured gas pipe leading from the main to the boiler. A slow but lethal buildup had resulted in an explosion. The pipe was old—prewar at least—and much corroded. Once the old boiler had been lit, it was only a matter of time.

"Thank you, Nicholas," Kate told him gratefully.

"Not me. Chandler did it. I gather ChanCorp is a major shareholder in the insurance company. He made it known that time was of the essence and that if they didn't pull their fingers out he would personally poke his own in somebody's eye. These Americans don't waste any time. He also sent down an investigator of his own, some Raymond Chandler type whose specialty is arson frauds. Tough as old boots and up to all the tricks. I gather he left our own dear Gas Board in something less than perfect order, but they came up with the goods, and your name, my dear Kate, is shining clean."

Kate smiled at the acid that etched Nicholas's urbane tones. She had suspected he was jealous of Blaise. Now she knew he was.

"You have friends in high places," he went on thinly. "Talk about absolute power. I always knew money talked but his speaks every language known to man."

All I care about is that he speaks mine, Kate thought.

"So . . ." Nicholas ended, "come Monday you can show them all the way home."

"You'll be there, won't you?"

"Wild horses could not keep me away, though I have no doubt they will need police to handle the crowds."

He was right. Kate stayed at the Pink Thatch overnight, and when she arrived at the Park at nine o'clock, she found thousands of people hoping to get in, and the carpark already full.

Precisely at ten o'clock she mounted her rostrum to tumultuous applause. There, in the front row among the big spenders, sat Blaise and his grandmother, she on the aisle because of her wheelchair. As Kate smiled down at them Blaise threw her a look that blurred her eyes while Agatha raised her clasped hands in a boxer's salute.

Then the sale began.

They said afterward that there had never been anything like it. The numbers and opulence of the items were mind-boggling. The catalogues had created intense excitement; the viewing days had brought this to fever pitch, and the fast—the average time for a lot was thirty seconds—and furious bidding, including those from bidders all over the world, left people gasping.

Instead of a marquee, Kate had used a circus tent huge enough to seat a thousand people, and every seat was taken. She had draped it in thousands of yards of pale pink silk that she had bought, ironically, at a fire sale, and her rostrum was in the center of the ring. At intervals, closed circuit television screens allowed those people at the back a close-up view of the sale items, and she had sited bid-spotters at intervals on every aisle to make sure none were missed. It meant she had to be in tip-top form, her eyes everywhere, her attention concentrated at all times. She had a microphone so that her voice reached the topmost tier. The atmosphere was one of intense, even feverish excitement, and as the prices scaled heights unheard of, the very air seemed to crackle.

The first day was furniture, all the glorious examples of French genius, and every item exceeded its reserve, several of them fetching over one million pounds, beating the previous record of £822,500 that the Getty Museum had paid for a marquetry corner cabinet by Dubois.

When they broke for lunch—there was so much to dispose of it could not be done in a morning—there were refreshments provided in the other marquee; a superb buffet, laid on long trestle tables, which you could then take out on to the lawns. The sun shone, the ruin of the house made a dramatic background, and as a final touch, the local band played Gilbert & Sullivan while guests strolled about or ate their lunch. It was not, as one old gentleman said bewilderedly, in the least like Arlington Street.

As Agatha said that night, it was more like a garden party than an auction.

The next day it was porcelain and glass; the third, silver and bronzes; the fourth, carpets and tapestries in the morning, bijouterie and gold in the afternoon. The last and final day was the pictures and drawings.

By then, Kate was very tired. It was hot in the tent; the lights, the television cameras—the sale was shown each night as a special item on the news and was being filmed by crews from international networks—the concentration needed, all were taking their toll.

Blaise was worried about her. She, who could not afford to lose weight, had dropped several pounds, and as usual when emotionally keyed up, was not eating. He thanked God it was the last day. Any more and she would crack up. What she needed was peace and quiet and rest, and he turned his mind as to where the best place for that would be.

But Kate had hidden reserves; she was spurred on by burning determination to beat her stepsister hollow, and when the first drawing, a Dürer of an ancient crone, shot from the opening bid of 50,000 to 700,000 pounds in thirty seconds, she knew she had done it.

Each night, after the sale, she had gone over the figures for the day; each night they confirmed her growing lead. Now, with the pictures, she had no doubt that she was home free.

The Rembrandt went for 2.5 million pounds; the Rubens for 2.25 million; the French paintings achieved a gross total of 3.6 million, including a Monet that went for 520,000, and a Cézanne for 1.75 million. Before Kate had sold half the pictures she knew she had achieved her ambition. In front of a thousand people, fair and square, she had beaten her cheating rival. In spite of the fire—and probably because of it, she thought vengefully—she had done it. In spite of the foul rumor, the implied slur on her character, she had done it. She had won.

The applause that greeted each stunning item, the keen and vigorous bidding, the beautifully organized *whole* of the thing, were establishing standards that would become a new norm. Likewise the prices: she had written her reserves in ordinary figures, not in the code normally used, so confident had she been; now, as again and again she crossed them out and wrote on the other side the actual figure achieved, her hand became progressively more unsteady.

People had started to stand with excitement, and the ground swell of voices had begun to overtake the temperature. When Kate, having intoned "At one million pounds, then," for a particularly fine Renaissance masterpiece by Dosso Dossi, was met by silence on the part of the two men fighting for it—a New York dealer who looked like Franklin D. Roosevelt and sounded like Groucho Marx, and an elegant Frenchman who was known to be bidding on behalf of a Greek shipping tycoon—she looked astonished. "What? Is that it, then, gentlemen?" she asked, sounding genuinely taken aback that two such experts would let a painting of this exceptional quality go for so paltry a sum. A roar of laughter and applause shook the tent.

And when it was finally knocked down to the Frenchman for 1.2 million pounds, the whole audience rose to its feet to clap and cheer, giving not only Kate but the whole, splendid, attention-riveting five days their unqualified approval in a five-minute standing ovation.

Kate was overwhelmed when she left her rostrum, but Blaise was there to provide a bulwark, shouldering aside those who would have pressed too close, in their excitement not seeing the paleness, the tired smile, the drained quality of her nods: she was too exhausted even to talk. Slowly but steadily he got her through the press of people, his arm about her shoulders, holding her when she stumbled. He took her to the Portakabin she had been using as an office, and when she shook her head at the brandy he poured her, helped her up and led her out to the waiting car, leaving Nigel Marsh and John Steadman and the rest of the Despard's contingent to handle the congratulations, the praise, the adulation. By the time he got her back to the hotel she was all but out on her feet. As they went up the stairs, he remarked, "We did this once before, remember?"

Her only reply was a drowsy smile. As he had done in Hong Kong, he undressed her, tucked her under the covers, but this time he kissed her good night.

"Well done, my love," he said. "Very well done."

Her heavy eyelids fluttered. "Am I?" she asked drowsily.

"Are you what?"

"Your love?"

"My one and only. I mean that."

She sighed contentedly. "So do I . . ." were her last words before she drifted into sleep.

The press coverage was worldwide. Not only did the British press give the sale lavish praise, with two-page center spreads in the dailies and page-long features in the Sunday editions, as well as whole sections in the color supplements. There were also reports in *Time, Newsweek, Apollo, Harpers & Queen, Connoisseur, Country Life,* the trade press, of course, plus the *Economist* and the *Spectator.* Even *Private Eye* got in on the act. *Art News* commented, "The prices set during these five tumultuous days will undoubtedly be the market index for some time to come."

The total sum raised was 23,490,000 pounds, a world record for a house sale, but it was the style that was talked of for weeks afterward, and not to have been there was a social disaster. "But of course," people said, "one has to remember that Kate Despard is half-French."

"What about her sister? That poor bitch is wholly French and not much good it has done her."

There had been neither sight nor sound of her since she had stormed out on Blaise. It was as though the publicity and acclaim had obliterated her. The day after the sale, Kate, Blaise, the Duchess, and her entourage moved back to town, and that night Kate threw a party at Claridge's. Champagne flowed, and Kate, in a gorgeous dress of gold tissue, her red hair flowing, was its dazzling centerpiece. Charlotte was there, in pale blue chiffon, and Larry Cole, everybody who worked at Despard's, down to the boy who took the post every evening. Kate invited the guards, the firemen, and the police, as well as the representatives of the insurance company who had made Nicholas Chevely a very happy man. He, counting his five percent, was voluble in his praise of Kate, "the saleswoman of the century." The Duchess, a barbaric glitter of jewels and gold-embroidered Indian silk, beat time to the music as she contentedly watched her grandson with her dear Kate. "I knew it would take if I grafted 'em together often enough," she observed smugly to Minnie, an object of intense curiosity in her pale cream doeskin dress embroidered with intricate beadwork and fringing. "Now all we got to do is get that other one out of the way. Things ain't watertight until then."

Helping herself to another glass of champagne, she brooded as she sipped, and thus missed the entrance "that other one" made. It was not until Minnie touched her arm that she looked up to see her nod in the direction of the double glass doors. There, wearing a dress of scarlet paillettes and sequins that gleamed like fish scales, her lucky sapphires flashing like lasers in her ears, stood Dominique.

As an entrance it stopped the party in its tracks. The buzz of talk faded, the dancing stopped, the orchestra fumbled and came to an untidy halt. Kate, who had been on the floor with

Nicholas Chevely, disengaged herself and, head up, golden dress flowing, walked composedly toward her stepsister.

"Dominique," she said politely, meeting the beauty, the presence, the glamour, head on and for the first—but not the last—time, retaining her own in full measure.

"Kate," Dominique returned, with equally grave politeness.

They did not brush cheeks, shake hands, or touch each other in any way.

"What's that whore up to?" Agatha muttered, searching for her grandson, finding him at the far end of the room, standing very still, his gaze fixed on the two women.

"Congratulations," Dominique offered coolly.

"Thank you." Kate was equally composed, withstanding the battery of those incredible sapphire eyes as they went over her in a deadly scrutiny.

"Success suits you," her stepsister went on.

"I intend to wear it from now on," Kate returned with a smile.

For the first time, Dominique was conscious that Kate was armored in self-confidence. The gauche, sullen, defensive girl imprisoned in a bitter past was now a poised, lovely young woman sweet with the honey of success. It was as though her fire had at last been lit, and Dominique knew from her own experience that once that began to burn, it would be very difficult to put out. But no situation was entirely hopeless, was her belief. There was always an angle somewhere, which was why she had made this raid tonight: to gain the element of surprise and find one.

"Would you offer an adversary a glass of champagne?" she asked mockingly.

"I wouldn't offer you the time of day," Kate returned conversationally, "but do help yourself."

Head up, a faint smile on her lips, entirely conscious and wholly uncaring that every eye on her was inimical, Dominique flowed toward the long table, and that end of it where her husband stood watching her. Going right up to him she laid a hand on his arm, stood on tiptoe to graze his chin with her lips. "Darling . . ." she murmured, the sapphire eyes alight with challenge. She felt a surge of triumph when she saw the well-cut mouth twitch, saw a flicker of amusement in the dark eyes. But the arm she touched gave no response. It might have been wood. However, it was he who handed her a glass of champagne. Turning, Dominique raised it toward

Kate. "To the victor the spoils," she said, before draining it. "Shall we talk, now?"

"Let's," answered Kate, before turning to lead the way through the aisle that had unconsciously been formed by the party guests, toward the mirrored doors at the end of the long room. Opening one of them she stood back to allow Dominique to precede her, before following through and shutting the door behind her.

"By God!" somebody said. "Talk about *chutzpah!*"

That released bedlam.

"Did you ever see such gall?"

"Kate handled her beautifully."

"Whatever she lacks it is not courage."

"Now what's she after?"

"Did anybody search her for concealed weapons?"

People turned to look at Blaise, who gave no sign of what he was feeling, standing tall and dark and faultlessly elegant in his dinner jacket and whiter than white shirt. Then they turned to Agatha, who said imperiously, "The party ain't over yet, folks."

The orchestra started up again, couples took the floor, others gathered into groups. After a moment, Blaise put down his glass and made his way over to his grandmother.

"What the hell is she playin' at?" she wanted to know.

"For Dominique, the game is never over until she has won."

"Ain't no way she can win now."

"That's what she has come to find out."

"You think Kate can handle her?"

Blaise smiled. "Now she can, and has to. She was right. This is her fight; she has not only to win, but has to be seen to win and to tell Dominique why."

"I hope you know what you are doin' all the same."

"I usually do, but everyone is allowed one mistake. Relax," he told her calmly. "Here, have some more champagne . . ."

Inside the small room, all gold and white and crystal, the two women faced each other, mirrored in the glass of the doors and the far wall, so that their two figures seemed to dwindle into infinity.

"I underestimated you," Dominique opened.

"I cannot return the compliment."

"It is too late for it anyway."

"It is too late for you, also."

Dominique opened her clutch bag, which matched her dress, took from it a flat gold cigarette case and lit a leisurely cigarette. "Tell me," she said conversationally, "how you did it."

"Hard work and total honesty."

"Oh, I am not referring to your Little Miss Integrity act; I am referring to Blaise."

"I did nothing. I just was."

"And always there, everywhere he turned, shoved into place by that interfering grandmother of his. She never liked me, you know. I never bothered to take her into account. You, on the other hand, began with her . . . That was very shrewd. She is the one person in the world with any influence over him."

"She loves him."

"Yes . . . and yet he is not, strictly speaking, a lovable man. Attractive, certainly, very—masculine. I wanted him from the start."

"But never loved him."

"That was not what he was looking for."

"Then."

"How easily you dismiss the past," Dominique murmured.

"It is the future that matters. I found that out the hard way."

"Yes . . . Charles knew, of course. He knew much, much more than I gave him credit for; most important, he knew you."

"He was my father." And, Kate thought, you no longer call him so. That, more than anything, was indicative of her victory. While he had been of use Dominique had been prepared to grant him status in her life; now that he no longer had it he was merely the man who had married her mother.

"You are very clever at getting the right people on your side."

"I was never so overwhelmingly confident as to suppose I would not need their help."

"And still will. Our year is not yet over, you know."

"It is for you."

The silken eyebrows lifted at such presumption.

"I—*we*," Kate emphasized, "know too much to allow you

to throw every wrench you can find into the works. That fake T'ang horse you planted, from the same hand as those pieces you cold-bloodedly sold at your Sale of the Century; Rollo"—here Kate felt anger undermine her voice, caused by grief and her own dragging sense of guilt because she had so neglected him of late—"almost killed on your instructions. The fire your gangster friends set for you, and lastly, that scurrilous rumor you planted."

"You seem well supplied with information." Dominique gave no sign of the tightening of every nerve, the cold fingers that stole stealthily over her body.

"You supplied it. We had you watched and listened to."

The perfect body was rigid, the exquisite face a mask. "Blaise . . ." The word escaped as if under pressure.

"Yes." Who was so right, Kate thought gratefully. She would never have believed it of me. How well he knows her, she thought, feeling jealousy lift an inquiring head.

"It was Rollo's visit to Hong Kong that started it off. He was of the opinion, you see, that there was something not quite 'right' about your sale, and he had received information which confirmed it. You picked the wrong city for a conspiracy, even the walls have ears."

"Only when put there deliberately," Dominique said lividly. "I presume you have proof?"

Kate met the head-on derision so imperturbably that Dominique answered herself. "Of course you do . . . Blaise never acts on less."

"What matters here and now is that in the last analysis, *I* acted right," Kate said. "I have beaten you; I am 10.4 million pounds sterling ahead in the profit stakes, and without your usual suborning and seducing methods you haven't a hope in hell of catching up by April first. I have beaten you—not at your own game because I don't play that way— but at the original one, the one called fair play." Her chin was up, her head back, her hair a glowing aureole about her face.

Dominique laughed. "You will be telling me next you are a virgin . . .

As she had intended, that rocked Kate on her pedestal, but she righted herself swiftly. "No. But I could never muster your tally."

"Why, you little bitch!"

"If you want to play dirty, I should so much love to watch, because nobody plays dirtier than you."

"Be careful," Dominique warned softly.

"No—you are the one who must take care. One wrong word, one wrong look, one toe across the line, and I'll ruin you!"

"And Despard's? I do not think so."

"I have just put Despard's far beyond your reach. Right now, I am what's called 'flavor of the month' and by the time I'm finished with you, there will be a nasty taste in everyone's mouth. I've got you on tape, loud and clear and flagrantly foul-mouthed. You are mixed inextricably with Chinese gangsters and the Hong Kong police would dearly love to nail them—and you—to a crooked cross. If you want a public confrontation then you shall have one. I have nothing to hide, but I won't hesitate to dig up every stinking corpse you've buried these past months." Kate took a step forward. "As it is, I want you out of Despard's. It was winner takes all, remember—and I am giving you notice that I intend to take it and keep it. I'll give you your remaining months—but you'll use them honestly or not at all, preferably not at all. I've had enough of you. Anybody who would willingly destroy great works of art for their own ends has reached that end."

"The investigation concluded that the fire began by accident."

"Until I produce the tape proving that you arranged for it to be set!" She paused to catch her breath. "I'll make you a deal. Use what is left of your year honestly, and if you can come up with something that will beat me, then the tape, along with everything else, is yours. But don't even *think*, as they say in New York, of cheating here."

Five short months! Dominique's mind screamed the words at her.

"You can hold as many sales as you like—but there must be no double-crossing or double-dealing."

"Done!" Dominique did not hesitate. She would come up with something; she would lean on people who owed her favors; work on men who wanted her in exchange for what she wanted; use every contact she had; beg, borrow, or steal as long as she managed to *sell!* One big sale should do it . . . she'd have to work at the speed of light, but if she could get together enough high-priced merchandise . . . God knew there was plenty of it around. And didn't she have the best scouts of any auction house? Had she not been one herself for the long years of her own apprenticeship? Oh, the debts she would call in, the IOUs she would collect! How fortunate that she had been so careful to provide such—insurance . . .

Kate could see the wheels whirring behind the lovely face, the ice-cold computer calculating where and what and when and how much. "Well?" she demanded.

Dominique looked up at the no longer plain face, the deep-set eyes glowing like those of a predator tiger, the filmy stuff of her dress flowing about her. "You have changed," she observed finally.

"I hope so."

"And learned a lot."

"Not least from you." Kate walked past her to the door. "Now let us see if you are capable of changing—and under scrutiny."

"There is nothing *I* cannot do if I put my mind to it," Dominique said softly.

Kate smiled. "I am here to prove that wrong, for a start."

Dominique came toward the door, which Kate held open. "You have not heard the last of me yet." She swept through, head up, her dress making a soft susurration as she walked across the carpet, in the direction of the exit, and with a last flash of glittering scarlet, was gone.

Kate let out a long breath.

"Well?" She turned with a start to find Blaise beside her.

"I hit her with everything I could."

"The tape?"

"She knows we've got it—and how we got it."

"And the deal?"

"She accepted it."

"Which means the fight is still on."

"But a straight one—or else."

"You told her she would continue to be watched?"

"Yes."

"Which means she will be extra careful."

"I know that—so will I."

But Blaise was not smiling. "Dominique will cease to be dangerous only when she is dead."

"I wasn't planning on going that far!" Kate protested.

That produced from Blaise the smile she sought. "I was

. . . thinking of going far—with you, I mean." He saw Kate's glow deepen. "That, too . . . but I was actually referring to distance."

"Oh? Where?"

"You won't know until you get there."

"As long as it is with you, I don't mind where it is."

They held eyes and once again things inside shifted and slid.

"This goddamn cast," Blaise said in a voice that weakened her knees. "I can't do any of the things I want to do with you—even dance—"

"I can."

They turned to see Larry Cole. "Can I offer myself as a substitute once more?"

Kate laughed. She now knew the role he had played at Blaise's behest.

"Go on," Blaise said resignedly. "At least I can watch."

"I don't suppose I will be seeing as much of you in the future," Kate teased as they took the floor.

"Oh, but you will. Mr. Chandler's orders. I'm to go on keeping an eye—both eyes," he said admiringly, "on you."

Kate glanced across to where he was sitting, his plastered leg stuck stiffly out in front of him, his eyes never leaving her.

Larry sighed regretfully. "If it was me, I wouldn't take any chances either. He's the reason I couldn't get to first base, isn't he?"

"Yes."

"Just my luck."

"Oh, I don't know," Kate said demurely. "We will be keeping company, after all."

Sitting down beside Blaise, Charlotte said, "How lovely she looks."

"You must be proud of your pupil."

"I am, and deeply fond of her, too. Kate has a way of growing on you.

"Don't I know it," he agreed with a smile.

"I only wish Rollo could be here to see it, she said wistfully.

"How is he?"

"The same. We are going to see him tomorrow—I'm afraid Kate has a bad case of the guilts, but I have told her there is no need. He never knows she is there anyway."

"They are close," Blaise said neutrally.

"Were . . . It sounds awful, but having to do without Rollo has been good for Kate. She was already beginning to detach herself from him when, through no fault of his or hers, he was forcibly removed from his dominant position in her life." She turned her fine eyes on Blaise. "You have replaced him."

"I want to be first, with her," he said quietly. "She is of prime importance to me."

"That she has forgotten him—even if only for days—is proof that you are," she mocked him gently. "And have been for some time."

"She hid it well for a girl whose emotions run close to the surface."

"She learned the hard way, alas, from her father."

"Perhaps it is the best way to learn," Blaise said slowly. "The lesson sticks."

"Is that your way of saying you learned yours the same way?"

He laughed. "You are a shrewd cookie, Charlotte Vale. You and my grandmother should get along well."

"Oh, but we do, we do."

"I'm glad to hear it," Blaise said truthfully, for he liked Charlotte. Apart from what he now knew she had done for Kate, which alone would have earned his gratitude, she also had his respect. She would be invaluable when it came—if it ever came—to dealing with the fury of Rollo Bellamy scorned, because Kate had told him she would know exactly how. Well, he thought, that is God knows when in the future, gave him time to deepen and tighten his hold on Kate. For he was a man in love for the first time, and like all lovers, greedy for total possession.

Kate and Charlotte went to see Rollo on Sunday afternoon. He was very thin now: cheeks sunken, eyes deep-set. He was out of splints and bandages—it was four months since he had been injured—but his coma showed no signs of releasing him.

"Do you think he will ever come back to us?" Kate asked sadly, holding one wasted hand.

"The doctors say there is no reason why not."

"But it has been so long!"

"Months only. I have known people to be in comas for years."

"Oh, God, I pray not . . . I would rather he died than this living death."

"You miss him, don't you?"

"Well . . . that's just it. I did at first, terribly, but these latter months . . ." Kate sighed.

"You have grown up and no longer need a nanny, that's all."

"Yes, I suppose he did stand in that light." She smiled. "When my mother died he definitely treated me like a stubborn child—you know, 'Rollo spank' . . . not that he ever lifted a hand to me."

"Only a tongue."

Kate shuddered. "Oh, yes . . ." Another sigh. "I would not mind one of even his most painful tongue lashings if he would only come round to give it to me."

But Rollo, as always, made his entrance when *he* chose.

They had left him and gone to the Connaught, where they were to dine with Blaise and Agatha, and it was as they were sitting down to their first course that Blaise went to answer the telephone, came back slowly with a smile on his face that Kate read as good news.

"ChanCorp just made another billion dollars," she teased.

"No, but I am about to make your day. Rollo has recovered consciousness."

Kate's chair went flying.

"Put dinner on hold, we'll be back," Blaise said quickly, as she flew past him.

"Shoot, they can give us a fresh one," Agatha exploded. "I'm not missin' this. Come on, Charlotte . . ."

He was no longer lying but sitting, reclining against a bank of pillows, and his eyes were closed. Kate, who had irrationally expected him to be sitting up and barking orders, stopped dead in her tracks. "Rollo?" she faltered. His eyes opened. They were cloudy, like an overcast sky, not the darting silver fish of old, but when he saw her they scowled in a way that had her catching her breath in delighted recognition.

"Rollo?" she said again, "it's Kate."

"I'm not blind." The voice was weaker, thinner, its nail-file rasp muted.

"What are you doing here? Why aren't you at school?"

He had returned to a point in the past, the doctors said.

Leave him to cover the distance to the present in his own time. Talk to him, answer his questions, but do not pose any of your own. Just be there when he needs you. He recognized Charlotte, but asked her how her play—a revival of *Private Lives* (that was in 1962, Charlotte told them)—was doing. He did not recognize Blaise but tried to proposition him, while Agatha evoked a lift of the eyebrows and a pained, "Not a drag act, dear heart. I never work with drag acts." Kate bit her lip, but Agatha laughed hugely. Rollo Bellamy was living up to his reputation, and afterward it was she who visited him more than anyone. Kate took to dropping in of an evening, with Blaise, which had Rollo remarking with a sniff, "Got yourself a boyfriend at last, I see."

"Yes, Rollo."

"Well, I'm not having you staying out all hours of the night, swinging London or no swinging London . . ."

"Well, I suppose 1960-odd is better than 1930 something," Kate said later, as they drove home. "That he is back at all is something to shout about."

But Blaise was not shouting. He was suddenly in the grip of the most virulent of jealousies. Rollo Bellamy had been a formative influence in Kate's life; he had been tenaciously possessive of her, was not likely, when he finally arrived at the present, to regard Blaise with either grace or favor, and would do his best to shove him out.

When he did not reply, Kate glanced at him, saw the way his face was set, and with the finely honed perception of a woman in love, squeezed the hand she was holding and said, "No, my love, it won't be the same, not ever again. It can't be. I've changed. I don't need Rollo anymore, but I do need you."

She saw his look lighten. "But will he recognize that?" he asked.

"He will have to. It is the way things are, the way I want them."

The dark eyes searched hers. Her heart ached for him. This big, strong, self-contained man was painfully, insecurely jealous, yet it brought him even closer to her, made him more fallible, more human, eradicated forever the remaining traces of the Superior Shit. He was just a man, she realized, like any other, but he happened to be the one she loved.

"I can handle Rollo," she said simply, but with terrifying power.

His sigh of release was shaky. "It's me I can't handle," he admitted ruefully. "Not since you . . . It's like I've lost my shell and am prey to every shade and shadow of feeling. No other human being ever meant as much to me as you do. You are the last thing on my mind when I go to sleep at night and the first thing I think of come morning. I can't work, I can't concentrate—and I can't make love to you properly because of this goddamn cast . . ."

"You don't do badly for a one-legged man," Kate said demurely.

With a shout of laughter he pulled her into his arms. "Sassy wench," he grinned. "Always the fast tongue . . . that and so much else has me held fast, Kate. I never knew it was possible to be so tied to another person, but I think I suspected it, which was why I took good care never to be, before. Yet all those months you were tying me to you, I never saw the bonds, certainly never felt them until the fire—but then I knew. Kate, I love you so much it scares me . . ."

Her hand pressed his, her golden eyes suffused, her face luminous.

"That's why I was jealous of Rollo, because you were so close, the two of you—and I thought—what if he wants it that way again? What if what they had was so strong even I can't break it . . . ?"

"It didn't break, it fell away when I realized I didn't need it," Kate said lovingly. "It fed on my need; when that stopped it withered and died. I love Rollo dearly and always will, but not as I love you. He was important in my life. You *are* my life . . ."

This time, Blaise's sigh was one of contentment. He pulled her into his arms and they rode the rest of the way back in pleasurable and utterly communicative silence.

There was only one more thing Kate wanted. Her father's portrait to hang in the entrance hall at Despard's.

"It belongs to Dominique," Blaise pointed out. "Your father had it painted for her mother."

"But Despard portraits always end up where they belong —at Despard's."

"Then so shall this one. I'll buy it for you."

"She should give it," Kate muttered mutinously.

"But she won't. Not to me, not to you, certainly not to Despard's."

"But she'll sell it?" Kate asked wonderingly.

"For the right price, yes." He shook her gently. "Money is the least of my worries," he said.

But it was the most of Dominique's. After Kate's startling revelation, she had embarked on a frenzied campaign of selling herself, only to discover, shatteringly, that nobody was interested anymore. Time and time again, when she thought she had a prospect nailed, she would find that Kate Despard had already got there with a pair of pliers. She found that several clients withdrew articles previously sent for sale; that men who had sweated for her calls were now never available. She had suddenly become the badly burned Toast of New York.

When her name appeared in a gossip column it was usually in an unfavorable or derogatory light. Used to queening it, she discovered she was not even in the running as a courtier. She found too late that being Mrs. Blaise Chandler had been of more help than she realized. With time running out, she knew she had no hope of winning. She was, she realized with a painful shock, out of fashion . . .

Now it was Kate Despard who was on everyone's lips; she was the one they courted, fawned over, hung on, and when she paid a visit to New York it was like a Royal Tour. Even her own staff at Despard's, sniffing the wind, set their sails to catch it. And when, at a dinner held at the Lucky Dollar to celebrate the handing over of the Chandler Collection of Western Art to the state of Colorado, Agatha Chandler publicly proclaimed Kate as the instigator of the whole enterprise before invited guests who included the President of the United States, Dominique found nothing in her cup but bitterness. And it overflowed when she saw, on the front pages, in the glossies and the gossip magazines, picture after picture of the woman who had beaten her and the man she had lost, smiling at each other in a way that, she discovered painfully, actually hurt.

And all the while Kate went on selling. The lists of future sales made Dominique physically ill. They were lining up to use her services; all those people who had wanted to know

Dominique du Vivier when she was winning now turned their backs as she lost and went on losing.

Only Poor Venetia had not turned her back. But she was of no use now.

Dominique retreated to Provence. From there, she wrote formally to Blaise as executor, relinquishing any claim to Despard's, and informing him that she was suing him for divorce on the grounds of desertion. Shrewdly she realized that if she sued him for adultery, they would probably stone her.

"You were a devious man," she toasted her stepfather's portrait which hung above the mantel in the drawing room. "I think you planned all this. I thought I had you exactly where I wanted, but all the time you were maneuvering me . . . Well, so Despard's is lost to me. I still have all that money I made in Hong Kong, and all those profitable little deals I did on the side have made me popular with a certain Swiss bank. They have not heard the last of me yet. I will return. Time will do it. People have short memories. And I shall take as much as I can get of the Chandler billions. I can play the deserted wife—I can play anything if it suits me. He can have his freedom, but he will pay for it, because I have uses for all the money I can get. Dominique du Vivier will emerge from the ashes. And such a phoenix will never have been seen before . . .

Yes, she thought. Plans. Schemes. Watertight ones, this time. And no holds barred.

She went to get the small Fabergé casket normally kept locked in her private safe. She turned the small silver key, lifted the chased and jewel-encrusted lid to reveal a tightly packed mass of papers: letters, notes, photographs, receipted bills, copies of certain provenances. What foresight I possessed when I decided to keep these. She smiled as she lifted them out, one by one. Yes, Lucca di Czenza, he of the forged Tiepolos, all four of them, and Eduardo Santa Anna of the dubious Goya; so many men, so many doubtful transactions . . . and so many photographed encounters, in none of which her face appeared, only her body. Ah yes, that party at the Caraccio villa in Venice, the one that had turned into an orgy . . . a whole group of well-known faces, men and women, all well able to pay for the negatives—and continued silence. My insurance, she thought happily, as she dealt them on the desk like a spread at solitaire. Now then, she pondered with delicious perversity, which one first . . . ?

Blaise turned up at the *mas* unannounced, and for one wild, incredible moment Dominique thought that she had won after all; that her hold on him had been too strong; that he was back because he could not help himself. When she heard what he had come for, she said viciously, "It will cost you."

"I had expected no less."

"Oh, not less . . . more, much more."

"Name your price."

She was as exquisite as ever; her devotion to herself had not lessened, even if that of others had. She was wearing loose silk pajamas, with wide sleeves and bottoms the color of wild poppies, and her hair was its usual immaculate helmet of black Chinese lacquer. She smelled, as ever, of her unique fragrance, but now Blaise found it cloying. Nor did her beauty move him. He only wanted to get the portrait and get away. It would suit him, he thought, if he never set eyes on her again. Well, he thought, nobody likes to be reminded of their mistakes . . .

"So," Dominique invited with a lazy smile, "what am I bid for this fine portrait of the late Charles Gaston Despard . . . ?" She was confident enough to play cat and mouse with him, sure of her claws, her incredibly swift action. "It is not a masterpiece, but it is a rarity."

She looked up at it: Charles sitting at his desk in his office, a pen in his hand, a smile on his face, the white wings of his hair distinguishing the dark, sensual face and warm brown eyes. Behind him hung the portrait of old Gaston, the founder.

"It is not great art," she judged, "but it is an excellent likeness. Who are you thinking of to paint your Kate? Not Annigoni, please—so much like wax models—what a pity Boldini is no longer alive; now he could transform even the plainest woman—"

"How much?" Blaise asked, unmoved.

Because she no longer had the power to control him, she found she needed to punish him for it.

"It was you who had me spied on, wasn't it? You who had my every word overheard, who put the little Despard on to blackmailing me?"

"I had you watched, yes, and listened to—but it was Kate who knew what to do with the results."

"She will never have the nerve to use them."

"Kate does not like to hurt. But I'm part Indian," Blaise said with a small smile. "We never let sentiment stand in our way."

They held a long, measuring stare and Dominique repressed a shiver. Yes, she thought. It was that underlying savagery that called out to me. She had always known he could be pushed only so far, but she had never been able to resist extending the boundaries . . . "What put you on to me?"

"Kate. Her emotions run close to the surface and you produced a hatred in her I could feel. She is not the type to hate unless given good cause, so I looked for one and found it in Rollo Bellamy. He recognized you, all right. And not just by your perfume. As the Duchess would say, he 'suspicioned' you from the start. That's why he went to Hong Kong. And that's why you had him beaten—to death, you hoped, but he's a tenacious man, and he has a strong hold on life. It was after that I had your apartment bugged and everything you did watched. I know the people you saw, and how often; I know how much time Chao-Li spent with you, in your bed and out of it."

Dominique was scornful. "I do not believe you; Chao-Li would have known."

Blaise smiled. "You forget, I was in Vietnam. I learned a lot about the Oriental mind in my two years there. You see, your trouble was vanity. You never for one moment thought that anybody could be on to you. Your sale was such a success it went to your head—and it was an incredible piece of effrontery. You got so completely carried away that you thought you could get away with anything, even murder." And you still don't give a damn, he thought. Only one person means anything to you and that is yourself.

"You also failed to give credit to Kate for knowing what she was doing. Did you really think that she would leave a huge house stuffed to the gills with priceless antiques unguarded and unprotected? Would you?" He got no answer, just a blank stare.

"You'd have taken exactly the same precautions as she did; where you went wrong was in not granting her that much common sense. You also overlooked me. You'd have seen us both burn and done nothing more than send overelaborate flowers to the funeral. Too bad," he finished laconically, "that the funeral is yours, after all . . ."

"Do not be too sure," Dominique hissed at him, eyes ablaze, teeth bared. "Do not assume that because I am down I am out. Bide your time, because be assured, I will bide mine and when the time is right and I am ready you will have to reckon with me again! And as for the picture, I want ten million dollars for it."

It was not worth ten thousand as a work of art, but she knew it was priceless to Kate Despard, who was priceless to Blaise.

"I'll arrange to have that sum placed in your New York account."

"Not New York—Geneva. I shall be living there for the foreseeable future."

"As you wish."

He went to the fireplace, carefully unhooked the picture.

Dominique watched as he lifted the painting down; after so many years it left its mark on the whitewashed wall. She instantly resolved to replace it with something else—the fake Matisse still life that she had, in her first years, unhesitatingly accepted as genuine, along with everyone else, until the man who had painted it, a failed artist but a master forger, blew his cover. She had kept the painting as a reminder ever since *not* to make the same mistake twice. But she had gone and done so just the same. Why else was Blaise Chandler leaving her life like water rushing down a drain? A desire to hurt overcame her. "She is worth that much, then, the little Despard?"

He paused to look down at her. "All the money in the world could not buy my Kate," he said in a way that lacerated.

"Enfin!" she exclaimed, savage with spite. "You are in love!"

Again he paused and she saw a slow smile appear. He had never smiled at her like that. "Yes, I am," he said.

She was unable to stop the orgasm of self-destruction now. "Then what was it we had?"

ON THE HAMMER

February

21

Blaise and Kate lay naked and entwined at the edge of the water, letting the languorous ocean cool their love-heated bodies, and watching the enormous blood-red orb of the sun drop into the horizon like a coin in a slot.

It was quiet; only the wind soughed the palms, ruffled the water, which pulled and dragged at the pebbles, clicking like castanets, and the cicadas began to tune up for their evening concert.

Kate was in a state of almost catatonic bliss. Never in her life had she felt like this, never had she believed it possible to be so bottomlessly content, so fulfilled, so brimming with happiness.

All because of the man in her arms, and still, because she liked to have him there, inside her body. She had arrived at this point in her life one month ago as Kate Despard, girl; she would leave it tomorrow as Kate Despard, woman, who swam naked, no longer ashamed of a body now rounded, golden from long days in the sun, supple and limber; capable of receiving—and giving, now—incredible sensations; whose appetite for love, once awoken, had come to clamorous, demanding life, generating a passion that in turn satisfied him to heights and depths he had never expected but received with an almost humble gratitude. She was the woman who was up at dawn to swim, who ate food in quantities that astonished, who played tennis, rode, made long, slow, lingering love in the heat of the afternoons, before sleeping until another swim before dinner; after which they would dance to the erotic pulse of Herb Alpert's muted trumpet, bodies welded together, eyes closed, riding the beat, until, minds blurred with desire, they would drift into the bedroom for yet another exploration of the outer limits of pleasure.

He had brought her here to this remote tip of the Yucatán peninsula one month ago by seaplane, to a white-walled villa that seemed to stand at the end of the world. On three sides was the sea, at their backs the jungle. There was a swimming pool, a turquoise lozenge that was cool even in the heat of midday, and at night they descended by means of the elevator cut into the living rock to the empty beach some 150 feet below, where they swam naked, there being nobody else in the vicinity but the house servants.

How had he known? she marveled on arrival, to be further stunned when he went on to reveal a knowledge of her that both exhilarated and excited. Not only her body, which at last (freed of his cast and any other impediment) he had explored with a slow-motion, mind-bending, exquisitely unhurried thoroughness, until she cried out for him to take her—but her mind. She was astonished at how well he had studied her, during what he now called "his celibate confinement."

She had told him of a film she had once seen, of a villa—she could not remember where now, it was so long ago—only that it had been white, had stood high above the seas, all arches and black and white marble flooring, cool drifts of white, filmy curtains, tall white candles flickering in a warm breeze, and a table laid for two, champagne cooling, magnolias floating in finger bowls and, somewhere, a piano playing Chopin, a particular nocturne that had caught her spellbound mind. It had been a young dream of hers to be taken to such a place, by a man who then had no face or identity.

Arriving at Yucatán by night, they had walked onto a tessellated, balustraded, marble terrace, with great white arches behind, cool drifts of white curtains, champagne cooling, and magnolias floating in a pool where a fountain played, as well as a certain Chopin nocturne . . .

She had told him how she adored the color green—and found that their bedroom was of the palest, silvery green and whitest white; she had told him her idea of luxury was a sunken bath and found that her bathroom—he had one for himself—had an enormous one at the bottom of six marble steps. She had told him how she loved music, and the kinds that moved her, and found the latest stereo music center with every single disk she had ever mentioned, including the particular recordings she preferred. It seemed everything she had said had been memorized, and was now created here.

Like the white azaleas in the bedroom that scented the night air, and the silk crepe de Chine sheets, and the enormous bottle of her now favorite perfume, Vent Vert.

She had darted through every room like some bright humming bird, searching in each for its particular kind of nectar.

"But who does it belong to?" she asked breathlessly.

"Me, now," Blaise answered.

"Now?"

"I bought it only six weeks ago, the moment I knew it was up for sale . . . I came here once, as a guest, and never forgot it."

They were far from everything, so far that Kate had the sensation of being on the very edge of the world, yet according to Blaise there were two small inland towns nearby: Puerto Juárez and El Díaz. They were where the servants came from. Everything else was flown in from Miami: the food, the wines, the water. Crates and crates had been unloaded from the seaplane to stock the enormous freezer, the closet-sized fridge, the kitchen cupboards. None of the servants spoke English, but Kate discovered that Blaise spoke Spanish.

"What else do you do that I don't know about?" she asked, fascinated, as she prowled around the villa, opening louvered doors to find closets full of clothes—all her size, picking up carved Aztec and Maya figures, examining beaten gold masks, jeweled headdresses, feathered capes. "Was all this here, when you bought it?"

"Yes. That was the stipulation I made when I offered for the place, that it came as I remembered it, down to the last teaspoon—"

"Of chased silver with a handle of inlaid turquoise," Kate finished, laying the one she held back in its green baize compartment. "You were so right about the surprise . . ."

"It's heaven . . ." Kate sighed dreamily later, as they stood with their pre-dinner drinks, watching the sunset.

"No . . . that comes later," Blaise corrected, with a look in his eyes that had her bones dissolving.

But also, later, had come fear, almost akin to panic. She had sat at her dressing table, wearing a fluid, white crepe robe-cum-dress that looked intricate but actually came apart at the unfastening of one single stud, fastening the topaz ear drops he had given her earlier—"because they match your eyes"—and knew she looked beautiful, but felt ugly inside because she was terrified of disappointing the man she knew was expecting so much.

When he had been wearing his cast, heavy, cumbersome, impeding, he had done no more than kiss and caress her. "No point," he said wryly, "in starting something that might be awkward to finish. Besides, I want it to be perfect, so by God I will be, too . . ."

It had been in his eyes all evening, and had not she herself dreamed of it, even prayed for it? But now that the time had come she wanted to say, "Thank you, but I've changed my mind. I don't think I had better after all . . ."

She was so damned inexperienced. Only two men had used her: one as a stepping stone and the other as a practice model. It had hurt both times and left her disastrously disappointed. Now, what terrified her was that she might disappoint the one man in the world she could not bear to disappoint; that her ignorance and inexperience would begin by boring and end in distaste.

Oh, God, she thought. Help me get through this, that's all I ask. But to help Him along she drank copiously of every glass of wine set before her, from the champagne before dinner to the brandy afterward—and remained despairingly sober. She stared at the magnolias floating in their crystal bowl, at the flickering flames of the white candles, and thought: Is this what dreams are made of? It was fine in the films . . . it was flat and on celluloid and you sat in the front row eating licorice and weeping sentimental tears because it was all so romantic and beautiful, but the reality was not; it was nerves and great expectations and not being able to fulfill them and—

"Kate?"

She lifted her eyes to meet his and at the look in his at once looked away.

"Kate . . ." He was standing beside her, and his voice was so gentle, so understanding that she felt her eyes fill with tears.

"Are you trying to tell me something—like you have to get drunk to stand me?"

"I'm not drunk," she told him miserably.

"Not for want of trying. Why?"

She made herself meet the dark eyes. "Because I'm afraid . . . It's all so perfect and I am so afraid of not matching up to everything else . . ."

"Don't you know by now that nothing you do could ever disappoint me?"

"I disappointed the others . . . they said I was a cold fish . . ."

"There are no cold women, only inept men."

"Oh." She shook her head, fervent with worship. "You couldn't be one of them. Dominique would not have wasted her time on you otherwise . . ." The wine was getting to her now.

"Then you do want me to make love to you?"

"Oh, yes . . . yes, yes! It's just—I'm not—I haven't—there haven't—" Her disjointed sentences all reached the post at the same time. "I'm not very experienced."

"That's all right. I am."

"But—after Dominique . . ."

"Ah, I see. You think I want another Dominique?"

He smiled into her troubled eyes. "One is more than enough, thank you. I want Kate. I bought this house for Kate. I have waited and hoped for Kate. I don't give a damn about Dominique, and the last thing I want is for you to feel I am making comparisons. You are you, and there is nobody else like you, and it is you I want. Don't worry about what to do or when or how. All I want from you is complete cooperation . . ."

He picked her up in his arms and carried her over to one of the wicker loungers, where he stretched out, cradling her against his body. "There is absolutely no hurry . . . no hurry at all . . ."

And bit by bit he gentled her, bringing her along as he would a nervous filly to the rein, murmuring sweet words, bestowing even sweeter kisses that at first nibbled and nuzzled and then grew deeper and more impassioned as she relaxed and her shyness evaporated in the heat they were generating, so that she unfolded like a flower, beginning to ache for him, to clamor for him, her nervousness replaced by a desire and a finally awakened sensuality that, like a slow fuse, burned its way along his nerve endings until they were both trembling.

"Love me, love me, oh, please love me . . ." she breathed against his mouth, her tongue flickering and increasing his arousal. He picked her up again, carried her into the house, to the silvery-green bedroom, whose shutters were wide open so that broad bars of moonlight lay across the cool tiles of the floor, and the big, king-size bed.

And in that bed he loved her as she had never been loved, making her arch and gasp and shudder until, when she felt him fill her, expand her until she thought she would take wing, she cried out in astonishment: "Oh . . . !" And again, on a higher keening note: "Oh . . . oh . . . oh!" and she locked her long legs around his waist and met his thrusts with an instinct that emerged from its long confinement with a ferocity that blew his mind. For him, it was like the shock of being inside a woman for the first time: the sweet delirium of her warm tightness, her ravenous yet innocent greed, her unstinted giving of everything she had, even her soul. It was so intense, so deeply felt that he thought he would die of pleasure and when he felt Kate peak, stiffen, arch like a bow, head thrown back, mouth wide, he let himself go and they left reality and were swallowed up in a vortex that robbed them both of consciousness. When they came back, he still deeply embedded in her body, Kate was fused to him, as though the sweat of their bodies had merged to make them one. She opened dazed eyes to see his own, wide pools of darkness, regarding her with an expression that matched his voice when he said thickly, "You see . . ."

"Oh, I do . . . I had no idea . . . except now I know what they mean when they say I was blind but now I see."

"No," he said, in that same odd voice, "that was me . . ."

She stretched like a cat, rubbing her instep up and down his now unplastered leg, and her body against his, all but purring with sensual delight.

"You were well named," he smiled down at her. "You are just like a cat . . . that is what I shall call you from now on."

"Yes, I should like that . . . only my father ever called me that."

"Yours was the last name he spoke, did you know that? His wife thought it was her he meant, but I never heard him call her anything but Catherine or *ma belle*. She told me he said, "Cat . . . my little Cat." When I read the letters, I knew he had meant you." He smoothed away the heavy, damp hair from her face. "Now I know why he loved you so much . . ."

Kate buried her face in his throat. "Oh, thank you for telling me now. It makes everything—perfect . . ." She raised her face and it was proud. "I didn't disappoint you, did I?"

"You astonished me . . ."

Blaise drew the silk sheets over their cooling bodies and they lay in contented silence. Kate looked around the beautiful room: the fingers of moonlight through the half-open shutters, the broader bars through the archways, the massed white of the azaleas, the shine of the cool tiled floor, the slow drift in the lazy breeze of the filmy white curtains.

"Perhaps I am dead," she murmured dreamily, "and this is what heaven is like."

"No, not dead, but aware, now, of what it means to be alive."

She rubbed herself against him again. "Oh, yes, oh, very yes . . ."

Now, lying on the beach, lazily somnolent, Kate stirred. "This has been the most perfect month of my life . . . I feel I've been reborn, all new and clean and—and pure, if that word can be used to describe an adulterous relationship. But there is nothing impure about this, is there? I feel that all the impurities have been burned away . . ."

"Like your white skin?"

"Not bad for a redhead. Even next to yours it is still a tan."

She was deeply golden; he was mahogany.

"How quickly it has gone . . ." Kate sighed, sitting up to hug her knees.

"Like your inhibitions," grinned Blaise. "And to think you had a bad case of nerves—"

She flung herself on him and for a while they wrestled like children until, as always, Blaise won, pinning Kate beneath him, his hands imprisoning the wrists of her outstretched arms, but the sight of her laughing, glowing face was too much for him. As he bent down to kiss her, releasing her wrists, Kate rolled swiftly away, to run down the shore and plunge into the water.

"One last swim . . ." she called.

That night, after they had made slow, sweet, lingering love, Kate said, "I wonder if I am pregnant?"

Blaise smothered a laugh. "It won't be for want of trying."

"Would you mind if I was?"

"I should be delighted and the Duchess would cease to nag about me providing the Chandler heir."

"And the Despard heir."

"In that case you had better make it twins."

"In which case," Kate said innocently, "hadn't we better try again?"